Sheri Stewart Tepper was born, reared, and educated in Colorado, U.S.A. She worked for many years for various non-profit organizations including the international relief organization, CARE, and Planned Parenthood, the American family planning organization. As executive director of Rocky Mountain Planned Parenthood, she was responsible for the administration of some thirty medical clinics in Colorado, Wyoming, and New Mexico.

A longtime writer of children's stories, she sold her first book for adults in 1982. Other sales encouraged her to leave her job and retire to the family ranch in Larkspur, Colorado to write full time. She lives there with her husband, Gene, and an assortment of wild and domesticated animals including a small pack of Norwegian Elkhounds to keep the coyotes at bay, a herd of Belted Galloway cattle, and a family of shorthaired silver tabbies.

She is the mother of two children, one son, a scientist with the National Laboratories at Los Alamos, and one daughter, who is also a writer. She has one grandchild.

Also by Sheri S. Tepper

THE ENIGMA SCORE
THE TRUE GAME
THE CHRONICLES OF MAVIN MANYSHAPED
JINIAN FOOTSEER
DERVISH DAUGHTER
JINIAN STAR-EYE
THE REVENANTS
BLOOD HERITAGE
THE BONES

and published by Corgi Books

THE GATE TO WOMEN'S COUNTRY

published by Bantam Press

SHERI S. TEPPER

THE AWAKENERS

CORGI BOOKS

THE AWAKENERS

A CORGI BOOK 0 552 13295 0

Originally published in Great Britain by Bantam Press, a division of Transworld Publishers Ltd.

PRINTING HISTORY

Bantam Press edition published 1988
Corgi edition published 1989

This book is set in 10/11 pt Baskerville
by Colset Private Limited, Singapore.

Corgi Books are published by Transworld Publishers Ltd., 61–63 Uxbridge Road, Ealing, London W5 5SA, in Australia by Transworld Publishers (Australia) Pty. Ltd., 15–23 Helles Avenue, Moorebank, NSW 2170, and in New Zealand by Transworld Publishers (N.Z.) Ltd., Cnr. Moselle and Waipareira Avenues, Henderson, Auckland.

Reproduced, printed and bound in Great Britain by
Hazell Watson & Viney Limited
Member of BPCC Limited
Aylesbury, Bucks, England

For my children,
Alden, Cheryl, Mark and Regan
a password

NORTHSHORE

1

There was no need for watchmen on the boats that plied the World River. Since everything moved at the same speed, pulled by the same invincible tides, there was little chance of collision; this no less on the barge *Gift of Potipur* than on any other boat. Thrasne, third assistant owner's-man, had appointed himself watchman nonetheless, borrowing the title from those who manned the gates between townships on Northshore.

Northshore.

Northshore with its Awakeners and frag powder merchants, its oracular Jarb Mendicants and blue-faced priests of Potipur, glittering with sacred mirrors. Northshore, with its processions of black Melancholics, flailing away at the citizens with their fishskin whips and given good metal coin to do it. Northshore, with its puncon orchards and frag groves and wide fields of white-podded pamet and blue-tasseled grain.

And Northshore's River edge, where lean forms of stalking Laughers, tight-helmed in black, announce their approach with cries of scornful laughter, ha-ha, ha-ha, making the heretics run for cover. Echoing the Laughers, stilt-lizards hoot through their horny lips, scattering the song-fish from around their reedlike legs only to snatch them up one by one to gulp them down headfirst. Ha-ha ha-ha.

Once in a while Thrasne would see the up-pointed finger of a Tower, scratching at the sky, fliers gathered around it like flies around dead fish. Once in a greater while he would see the lonely knuckle of a Jarb House. And the River itself, some places smooth as a rain pond, other places full of rocks as a worker pit, everywhere dotted with blight-buoys and striped with jetties, as wide as half the world.

Township after township, town after town, with fences between to keep people from moving east and gates between to let people move west, the World River tugging the ships along on the endless tides, and all the panoply of life laid out for Thrasne's watching.

He knew watchmen were necessary on land to keep fool-hardy youths from sneaking between townships in the forbidden direction or greedy caravaners from rushing too quickly westward, clogging the orderly flow of commerce. He knew that on a boat a watchman could only watch, but that was what Thrasne did best. He wasn't bad at handling sails or sculling oars. He could make the fragwood deck gleam as well as any boatman. He could give orders and see they were carried out, which is what gained him the third assistant's post. And he could stow a cargo so that what was wanted next was always on top. These were necessary and useful talents, but he felt his talent for watching was better than these. Certainly it was more developed.

He had created a little cubby in the forewall of the owner-house, up top deck, where the ventilation shaft opened from the forward hold. Across this shaft he rigged a high grating of poles with a sack of loose pamet on top. When his round was done for the day he could sly up to top deck, wait until no one was looking, then hang himself by his fingertips from the owner-house roof with his toes on a handwide railing and shinny around into the cubby. No windows there; no owner's wife looking for anyone not occupied so she could find something unnecessary for them to do; only the sun-warmed boards of the owner-house wall vibrating to the ceaseless flow of the tides. Sometimes he'd stay until dark, and sometimes past that if there were things to see.

It was from the cubby he had first seen a flame-bird set fire to its nest, from the cubby he'd first seen a strangey, rising from the depths like some great green balloon, looking at him out of huge, wondering eyes from its fingers as it spit its bones at him.

It was from the cubby he had first seen a whole ship and its crew caught by blight, drifting ever farther into the unknown

10

southern currents with wooden men standing at the rail as though they'd been carved there.

It was from the cubby he had watched the golden ship of the Progression gliding by on its seven-year journey, the doll-like figure of the Protector of Man held high on the arms of the personal guards.

It was from the cubby he had watched the crowds on shore, thousands of shouting townspeople and file on file of mirror-staffed Awakeners and gem-decked priests all shouting the Protector's name, 'Obol, Obol, Obol.'

It was from the cubby he had seen all there was to see for the four years he had been Blint's man, and it was from the cubby he now noticed the hard lines of jetties wavering over the River surface not far ahead, where no jetty was supposed to be.

According to the section chart-of-towns, there were no piers closer than Darkel-don, a good ten-days' tide yet, and just yesterday owner Blint had told them they could fish as they liked till then with no worries at all. Now, having seen what he'd seen, there was nothing to do but slither below and tell Blint of this, though it might put him to wondering how Thrasne had seen the piers. They wouldn't be visible from deck level for some time yet, and it wasn't Thrasne's shift to work the rudder deck at the high stern of the boat.

He reported the sighting in a quiet voice, hoping his very mildness and lack of excitement would throw Blint off the scent. Which it might well have done had not Blint-wife been standing near, overhearing him, going at once to peer over the rail.

'Jetties? There aren't any jetties! I can't see any jetties!'

'Well, boy?' demanded Blint.

'Yessir. Piers.'

Blint's eyes crinkled at the corners. 'He saw them from above, wife. I told him to be sure to check the owner-house roof was tight.'

'Tight? Of course it's tight, Blint. It was rebuilt only a Conjunction ago. What do you mean, tight?'

Blint, who answered few of her questions, did not answer this one. 'How close?' he murmured.

11

'Close enough, sir. We'd better get our nets out of the water or the fisherman caste of the place – assuming there is one, for why else have piers – they'll be heaving stones at us.'

'We could move into deeper water.'

'There was that bunch in Zebulee with the catapult.'

'Ah. So there was. Well then, go tell the boys. Haul in and hide the evidence, tell them. No fishskins drying on the deck. No strangey bones lying about. I'll leave it in your good hands.'

'Any chance of trade, you think?'

'Well, we'll have to see, won't we?' Owner Blint strolled away, no whit disturbed, leaving it in Thrasne's good hands. If Thrasne hadn't been available, he'd have left it in first-man Birk's good hands, or secondman Thon's. Thrasne scrambled into action. At least the boatmen wouldn't argue with him. The memory of that catapult was too recent.

When they were hard at work getting the nets in – they'd have to be stowed wet, which would stink up the net locker – Thrasne went to the chart room to take another look at the Northshore section chart. They were passing Wilforn now. Nothing of interest listed on the section chart for Wilforn. Next place was Baris, and the section chart didn't say a word about Baris having jetties. Baris had pamet, art work, confections, puncon fruit – when the weather was right – and toys. The Baris Tower was listed as middling active, not fanatical, which meant the Awakeners weren't likely to search the *Gift* for any kind of contraband, books or such. And that's all Blint had written down six, seven years ago when he'd been by last. Thrasne made a mental note to hide his own books – if there were changes in one thing, there might be changes in others – and to add a description of the piers as soon as he'd had a good look at them. Probably some fisherman moving west had come to Baris and decided piers would be a good idea. Probably sold the local Tower on the idea and got a worker crew to build them. In which case, Thrasne snorted, spitting in habitual disgust, it was sheer luck they were still standing.

He returned to the deck in time to help empty the nets. Not

much in the way of fish and two or three hard, clattering things bumping on the deck with an unmistakable wooden sound.

'Blight-fish!' one of the boatmen cursed. 'I swear by the carrion birds of Abricor, it's too much. All we get lately's the blight.'

'Come on, Swin, it's not that bad. We haven't really seen any of it since Vouye. Be careful!' Thrasne pulled him back. 'You almost touched that one.'

'It's hard. Probably blight's gone out of it. Almost.'

' "Almost" gave the boatman a wooden leg.'

The men snorted. An old jest, but a true one. What the blight touched, it turned to wood, slowly or quickly, and if it touched the boatman's hand he would have the choice of cutting the hand off – if he moved without hesitation – or becoming a life-size carving of himself.

Some said once the blight hardened completely it lost its power of contagion, but Thrasne had seen a man lose a foot kicking something that seemed very hard indeed. 'Just push it over the side, Swin. Don't stand there looking at it, or you'll forget what you're looking at and pick it up.'

Swin grunted and pushed the fish overboard with a boathook. The few remaining fish were free of blight, thrashing around on the deck making high-pitched squeals from their air bladders. The men began clubbing and cleaning them, tossing the gutted fish down where other crewmen waited with the salt kegs. Thrasne turned to stowing the nets. Blight meant extra care there, too. They would have to be lowered into the net locker without touching them and sprayed with a mixture of sulphur and powdered frag leaf. Only when they had steeped in this mixture for a day or two could the men safely handle them again. Now they were plying the long hooks in gingerly fashion, pushing the nets below, and Obers-rom was already mixing frag powder. A good man, Obers-rom. Never needed to be told anything twice.

Thrasne leaned over the rail to watch the blighted fish moving alongside, sinking very slowly as they went, still

13

visible after long minutes had gone by. They floated right side up; they looked almost alive, only the lack of movement betraying that they were fish no more. Or perhaps fish of a different kind. Thrasne had seen a man touched by blight once. In fact, Thrasne had been the one to use the axe, and he still woke in the night sometimes sweating from the memory of it. The boatman had kept his chopped-off leg in a netting sack, sprayed down with blight powder. He carried it about with him to taverns, where he sold topers a look at it in exchange for drinks, daring the foolhardy to touch it and see whether the blight had left it or not.

'Dangers in every caste and trade,' said owner Blint from time to time. 'None free of peril.'

Thrasne supposed that was true. He went below to change his shirt and hide his books. Not that he had many, but those he had he wanted to keep. His book of fables about the South-shore. His *History of Northshore* in three volumes, nine-tenths of it nonsense, Blint said, and all of it forbidden. Thrasne didn't care. It made a nice thing to do some evenings when the winds were warm, sit on the deck in the light of the owner-house windows and read about how humans first landed on Northshore, down from the stars, and about their great wars with the Thraish, whoever they may have been. Winged creatures, by the sound of it in the stories, who could talk just like men. And all the men using metal tools and weapons, which was enough right there to show you why it was false and unapproved. But who wanted to read approved books? Lives of the Great Awakeners. The biography of Thoulia. Poof. One might as well read the chart-of-towns; it was more interesting.

They'd be in Baris by noon, and owner Blint would likely seek trade. Most of the towns along this stretch were short of spices and salt. They'd want to give pamet in exchange, and the *Gift* couldn't take it. No room left in the holds. It would have to be something less bulky. Dried fruit, jam, jelly. Candies, maybe. The confectioners were supposed to be something special along here. Something about candies in one of their Festival myths. And toys. Little things for

14

children. Mechanical ones that could be wound up. The toymakers on this stretch were notable. Not that Thrasne had been along this stretch before; he'd been only four years on the *Gift of Potipur*, starting when he was twelve as go-get-boy.

As he struggled with the buttons of his shirt, he examined the row of carvings set on his storage chest. There was a long, slender piece of clear fragwood he'd been saving, and he thought he'd make a fish of it. A surprised fish, with blight halfway up its tail. The carvings stared back at him from the chest top: merchants, children, the tall robed figure of an Awakener, even a worker, shapeless and hopeless in its canvas wrappings. The little figures seemed almost to breathe. One at the near end of the row looked at him in eternal supplication, and Thrasne took it into his hands with a little groan, warmth pouring into his belly.

'Suspirra,' he whispered. It was his name for her, the otherwise nameless ideal, loveliest of all women, created out of his head and his aching loins. She lay on his pillow when he sought his solitary comforts. She watched him when he dressed and washed himself, always with the same expressions of supplication and entreaty. 'Love me,' she begged silently. 'Love me.' And he did love her, in a lonely fever, almost forgetting sometimes that she was no longer than his forearm. He had carved her in one day-long frenzy of creation, the wood curling away from his blade as though it sought to reveal what lay within it, the pale soft grain of the face, the darker grain of the long, smooth hair, the gown, clinging to her as though wet so he could see every line of her sweet breasts and belly, the curve of her thighs and the soft mound where they joined. Even her feet had sprung out of the wood magically, every toe perfect, the lines of the nails as clean as the line of her lips.

'Suspirra,' and he set her down, turning her slightly away from him.

'You should be artist caste,' Blint had said when he first saw Thrasne's carvings. 'Some of these towns give high status to artists.'

Thrasne had shaken his head. 'I'd rather see everything.

15

Not just stick in one town. Maybe, someday, when I'm tired of the River.'

Though he could not imagine being tired of the River. There was always something to see on the River. As there was right now – the new piers fringing the edge of Baristown.

When he reached the deck he gave it a careful look over. No signs of nets or hooks. The net poles were put away. He could still smell the sulphur and frag, but the River breeze would carry it outriver this time of day. He checked the hatch over the net locker to see it was tight. Funny the way shorebound fishermen resented any fishing done by the Riverboats. Even though the Riverboats caught different kinds of fish, to say nothing of the deep River strangeys, which probably weren't fish at all. Glizzee spice, now. Everyone wanted that, even fishermen. And Glizzee spice was nothing but ground strangey bone, though the boatmen didn't tell everyone that.

When he'd completed the round, he went back and climbed up to the rudderman. 'What did Blint say?'

'Told me to pick the longest piers and see could I come around it.'

'No side wharfs, hmm?'

'None we can see from here.' Some of the towns had at the end of their piers sideways extensions that ran along the River flow rather than across it. A Riverboat could steer close, toss a line to be made fast, then let the tide turn the boat on the line to lay alongside. Coming around a long pier was harder work than that.

'Is Blint getting the sweeps set?'

'He got Birk out of his hammock. Said for you to stand by here where you could see everything.' The man sniggered, not maliciously, and Thrasne grinned at him. Taken all in all, the boatmen rather liked having a carver aboard. There wasn't one of them he hadn't carved something for, as a pretty for themselves or a gift for someone they treasured. When a man only came to his home place every six to eight years, he wanted to have something special for his children, at least. Though it wasn't uncommon to find more children than reason suggested was appropriate. Many a man gone

16

six years came back to find two- and three-year-olds, but such was the life of a boatman and accepted as such. The women couldn't be blamed, not with the procreation laws the way they were. And after all, if things like that mattered to a man, he wouldn't be River.

The pier was coming up on the right, a long one, not completed yet. The oarsmen had the sweeps set in the rope locks to turn the ship as soon as the pier was past. The tide wasn't strong just now, not with the moons all strung out like this, not like Conjunction, when no one in his right mind would try to tie up except at the Riverside itself.

'Hold fast,' breathed Thrasne, locking the sculling oars out of the way of the rudder. 'Hold fast.'

'I see it,' grumbled the steersman. 'Been doing this for twenty years.'

Thrasne ignored him. If Blint wanted him on the steerhouse, it was to take charge of things.

'Hold fast,' he muttered again. 'Now! Hard over!' He bent his back to the rudder as the bite of the oars took hold, taking up the slack on the tackle until it was tied hard over and they could watch the sweating men at the sweeps. Blint himself was at the line cannon. In a moment it went off with a dull *thwump* of its huge wooden springs, and the line arched out over the pier, where half a dozen standabouts made it fast.

'Sweeps up,' cried Blint. 'Stand by the winch!' The ship shuddered as it began to draw toward the pier, moving against the surging tide. Thrasne shook his head, remembering the time they had taken on a boatman from a place called Thou-ne. 'Born in Potipur,' he said he was. Sanctimonious half-wit. Insisted that no ship had the right to oppose the tide, and the only way to moor was at the end of a line along the bank. Fool had said winching was evil, antilife, and against the will of Potipur. He lasted until the time he took an axe to the rope during a winching operation. Assuming he had been a good swimmer and hadn't encountered the blight, he might still be alive. Since Blint had dropped him over the side in the far mid-River after dark, however, his survival was only conjectural.

There were no other boats at the Baristown piers. Despite this, there was a considerable gathering at the end of the jetty, engaged in some noisy set-to.

'What're they doing?' Thrasne asked.

'Couldn't say,' offered Blint. 'Have a look if you like. I'll need the walkway down anyhow for those fatbellies coming.' He nodded toward the town. Several members of the merchant caste were bustling toward them, each trying to be first without being ostentatious about it. None of them quite broke into a run. Thrasne set the walkway, then strolled over it, hands in pockets, down to the end of the pier.

Most of the crowd were simple standabouts, though there were a few fishermen and merchant apprentices who should have been elsewhere. There was one Laugher in his polished black helm, fiddling with the flasks at his belt, staring at each member of the crowd in turn, as though he would see through to the bones. Those at the end of the jetty, however, were Awakeners directing a worker crew in dragging the River.

Thrasne got a whiff of the workers and moved back a few steps. Using workers to labor in Potipur's behalf was a religious requirement in every town they traveled by, but Thrasne thought it a stinking one, literally and philosophically. The shambling figures were so damned inefficient. Everything had to be done six times over. It took a crew of Awakened workers four times over a field to plow it, and Thrasne had never seen a ditch dug by workers fit to run water through until some competent irrigation manager cleaned it out and trued the sides. Now they were heaving hooks at the ends of long lines, tossing them about a fourth of the distance Thrasne could have thrown them, dragging them back with slow tugs against the tide.

'What're they looking for?' he asked one of the standabouts.

'Some woman went in the River. Drowned herself.'

'So? Why the dragging?'

'She did it to get out of bein' Sorted. So they say. I don't know. All I know is the Awakener's mad as a fisherman with a blight-fish on a new line.'

18

The Awakener was indeed very angry. He could hear her clearly as she spat at a long-faced, miserable-looking man before her. 'Fulder Don! It was your duty to come to us if you thought she would do this!'

'I didn't think she would,' the long-faced man said plaintively, his voice flat, almost without expression. 'I thought it was just her talk. She talked about a lot of things she never did. I didn't think she'd ever leave the baby. She cared so for the baby.' The little girl in his arms was crying. About three or four years old, Thrasne thought. Old enough to remember what was going on, without being old enough to understand it.

An old woman with a tight, lipless mouth stood beside the depressed-looking man. 'Fulder Don,' she said, 'I've known since you married that silly fool she'd do something like this. I wouldn't have thought heresy, but who could put it past her? She hadn't an ounce of loyalty in her.'

'Mama,' begged the man placatingly. 'Now, Mama . . .'

'Don't "Mama" me. You married beneath you and beneath artist's caste, and that's all there is to it. Take that idiot child and give her to Delia, will you. I can't stand the sight of her. It wasn't enough her mother had to do this dreadful thing, now you're saddled with the child for her whole life.'

'Well, Mama, she's my child, too.'

'I'm not even certain sure of that.' The old woman stomped off down the pier, the cane in her hand slamming down in a furious *whap, whap, whap*, which sent angry echoes booming under the pier over the lick and slap of the water.

The Awakener threw up her hands, twirled her staff, and began a slow, mind-curling chant. Thrasne shut it out, humming to himself. He couldn't stand Awakener chants. If it was to escape this, this chant-driven pretense of life, this shambling excuse for existence, he did not blame the nameless woman who had drowned herself. The band of workers turned from the River to shamble back up the pier, following the glittering staff, eyeless, faceless, only their feet and hands indicating what lay beneath the loosely woven canvas sacks and hoods they wore.

'Papa,' the little girl was pleading. 'Papa.'

The man paid her no attention, merely stood staring at the River as though he wanted nothing more than to be deep inside it himself. The passivity of that face moved Thrasne. His hands twitched, wanting to capture that face. This was a man who had given up. He would not do anything, not ever again. He would only float, pushed by the tide of others' lives, waiting his end under the canvas hood, deserving it. The child turned, caught by the watchfulness in Thrasne's face, stared at him, eyes wide and accepting with something of that same passivity. 'Papa,' she said again, hopelessly.

A woman came out of the crowd to take the child, a nothing much of a woman, small and plump, older than middle-aged. 'There, there, my Pammy,' she said. 'There, there.' The child sobbed once and laid her head on the woman's shoulder. That, too, Thrasne coveted, that line of child against the woman's body, limp and exhausted, giving up everything in the acceptance of this comfort.

Thrasne moved toward the man. What had the old woman called him? Fulder Don. 'Fulder Don,' he asked casually, as though he were only another standabout, 'why did your wife go in the River? How do you know that she did?'

The man looked at his feet, mumbling, 'A fisherman saw her. She was sick. She was afraid to die. Afraid to risk Sorting Out. My mother . . . was always at her. Telling her how bad she was. How incapable. I guess she thought . . .' His voice trailed away into nothing as he stared into the water, his long, mournful face intent upon another time. 'She was so beautiful,' he whispered at last. 'So very beautiful.'

Something in the intonation made Thrasne look at him again. Yes. Under the shabby cloak the man wore the smock of the artist caste. An artist. Not a successful one, from the looks of it. For which Fulder Don's mama probably blamed the dead woman. Thrasne turned quickly to return to the *Gift of Potipur*, his hands itching for his carving knife. The man, the woman and child; if he was lucky, he could get both the carvings started before Blint found something else for him to do.

They spent three days in Baris. The merchants wanted

spice, but they insisted on trading bulk pamet for it. Blint would take no more pamet. 'Silly blight-heads,' he complained as still another delegation left the boat unsatisfied. 'Can't seem to understand every town in this section has more pamet than they can use. We'll have to go all the way to Vobil-dil-go before anyone will want pamet. I told them we'd take toys, or those dried puncon candies, or woven pamet cloth, provided it was something out of the ordinary. They'll come to it eventually. Just takes them two or three days to make up their minds.'

On the third day they did make up their minds, and Blint did a brisk business. By dusk all the trading was done, and the crew of the *Gift* went into Baristown for some jollifications. Thrasne offered to guard the ship. He wanted to finish the carvings and brought them on deck to do so, working in the lantern light from the owner-house windows. He had caught Fulder Don to his own satisfaction, the sorrow, the loss. Now he was finishing the carving of the woman, Delia, and the child.

There were no sounds except the soft push of the water along the sides, an occasional burst of laughter or song from the taverns. The soft bumping had gone on for some time before he even heard it.

Once alerted to the sound, it still took him a while to find it. It seemed to come from everywhere and nowhere. At last he leaned over the side and heard it clearly. Something in the River, knocking against the side of the boat.

He lowered a lantern on a line to see only the oily shifting of the water. Then she came from under the wavelets to look up at him for an instant, turning in the ripples to glance sideways at him from half-closed eyes.

'Suspirra!' He set the lantern down, shaking, rubbing his eyes with his hands. The face was Suspirra's face. The bumping went on. He lowered the light again, and again she shifted to look upward at him, the water flowing across her face, the line in which she was tangled making a silver streak across her breast.

Sick cold in his belly, he could no more have left her there

21

than he could have burned his own Suspirra for firewood. It took long moments to realize the bumping made a wooden clattering rather than the soft sound of flesh. He thought of a carving, first, and only then of the blight. This was the woman they had been dragging for. The woman who had been so beautiful, who was so beautiful. Blighted now. Wooden. And deadly. Still, he could not leave her there.

He brought up one of the small nets, safe enough after its frag powder soak. He rigged a line to the boom. Working silently, cursing the amount of time it took, he pushed the net under her with poles, then heaved the boom all alone against her weight, heavier than he'd thought, to lift her dripping body to the deck.

She turned in the lantern light, toward him and away in a silent dance, eyes half-open in invitation, lips curved as though about to speak. 'So beautiful,' he murmured, wanting to touch her, holding himself from doing so only with difficulty. 'So beautiful.'

A burst of laughter as some Riverfront tavern opened a door and spat revelers into the street. Blint would be bringing the crew back shortly. If Blint saw her, he would sell her to the family, or to the Awakeners, though what good she would be to either, Thrasne could not imagine. No. He wouldn't do that. She had fled from them, family and Awakeners both. The woman who had fled was gone. This was his own Suspirra now. He plotted furiously, discarding one notion after another.

Then he thought of the ventilation shaft beneath his own watching post. Up went the net once more as he guided it from the owner-house roof, down into the shaft, suspended there in its netting bag from the pole grating upon which he so often sat, where none could see it, wonder at it, touch it – save Thrasne himself.

When Blint and crew returned, he was crouched beneath the owner-house window, finishing the carving of Delia and the child. That night, for the first time since he had made her, he did not even look at the small carving of Suspirra.

2

Night on the River in the township of Thou-ne. Lanterns gleaming along the River walk, on the quays and jetties, where the oily water throws back slippery reflections, fish-belly lights, momentary glimmers. Rain misting the cobbles into fishscale paths, River sucking at the piers with fish-mouth kisses, all watery and dim, silver and gray, evasive as dark bodies turning beneath dark water. Lantern man strolling along beside his wagon, wagon boy tugging, head down, sliding a little on the slick stones. Fish-oil cans in the wagon; fill the lanterns; trim the wicks; light the lanterns; then move on. Behind these two the lantern light lies in liquid puddles on the stones, pools of light, wetter than water as the crier follows after, 'Dusk falls, night comes, let all abroad take themselves to home and hearth.' The call so well known over lifetimes it comes out in drawn vowels, 'Uhhhs aaaahs, aiiit uhmmms, aaaad ohhhhm arrrrh.'

Peasimy Flot trots along the River path, behind the crier, stepping carefully into each puddle of light to splash it onto the path. Slap, slap, slap with the soft soles of his boots, slap, slap. Light has to be distributed. Nobody sees to it but Peasimy. What good are these puddles with all the dark in between? Have to splash the light around. He does not look behind him to see the pools of light still separate and rimmed with black. He has splashed them; now the walk is lighted. Never mind what the eyes see. Never mind. It is what the soul sees that's important.

'Uhhhs aaaahs,' the crier calls. 'Aiiit uhmmms.'

Night is already here. Potipur glares in the eastern sky,

full and ominous, his face half-veiled in River mist. Viranel is half herself at the zenith, skittish behind clouds, as she becomes at these slender times; Abricor has whetted his scythe on the western horizon and goes now to harvest the crops of night. Peasimy stops in midsplash to contemplate the scythe-moon. 'Harvest,' he calls in a whispery fishvoice, full of bubbles and liquid gurgling. 'Cut down the lies, Moon of Abricor. Foul weeds of untruth. Cut them down, down, down.' Then back to the splashing once more. Pitty-pat, pitty-pat, slap slap slap.

Twelve years old, Peasimy is a neat one in his high-collared coat with the shiny buttons, his tight dark trousers fitting down into the soft boots, his perky little hat perched high on his tight, shiny hair. Daytimes he sleeps, like a strangey, lost in the depths of his sleep as in a cavern. Night-times he comes up for air and to look at the moon and splash lantern light. Peasimy knows Thou-ne would wither away if he didn't splash the light around. It doesn't matter no one else knows it. All night long he will continue this per-ambulation, spreading the light. Dawn will mean a bite of breakfast, then pulling the shades down, hiding in the dark. No one knows why, but he's been that way since childhood. No trouble to anyone. Just see him decent dressed and let him go. So says Peasimy's mama, the widow Flot. So says her kin and kith. Let him alone. He doesn't hurt any-thing. Poor little fellow. Lucky when he can remember his name.

Peasimy . . . well, Peasimy remembers a lot of things. Peasimy remembers catching his mama putting Candy Seeds on his bed when it was supposed to be the Candy Tree growing there that did it. Peasimy remembers things Haranjus Pandel said in Temple. Peasimy remembers every lie ever told and some he only suspects. Peasimy can recognize true things when he sees them.

Lanterns, now, they are true things. Water is true, and the widow Flot. The lantern man is true, and the crier. Daylight is so true he needn't even stay awake to watch it. All light is true. Dark is a false thing, full of lies, making you think a thing is one way when it's actually another. That's why Peasimy splashes the light. Have to fight the dark. Can't just let it overcome.

There's an image Peasimy sees sometimes in the dusk, maybe only in the dusk, maybe only in his head, he's not sure always where things are. But the image is there, somewhere, shining. A glowing thing. Looking at him. Looking at him and shining with its own light. Truth. Shining. He doesn't know what it is, but he expects to find it. Somewhere. Along this alley, perhaps, between splashes of his boots. Along that street.

And until then, he goes along.

'Aiiiih uhmmmms,' calls the crier.

'Night comes,' whispers Peasimy. 'Light comes.'

3

It was six days before Thrasne was left alone and could look at the drowned woman again. Under a grove of enormous frag trees, tied up at the Riverside past Shabber, he was able to lift the net once more. He stood on the owner-house roof, staring at her in lantern light where she swayed in the net. She was dry now. Her hair had fluffed out like fine pamet fiber, a warm, lovely brown. Though he had thought her eyes open when he brought her aboard, they were closed now, the lashes lying softly upon her cheeks as she seemed to sleep. His eyes marked her, measured her, trembled over every part of her, fascinated and aroused. He had to hold his hands behind him to keep from touching her. At last he could stand it no longer. He went below and took a live fish from the cook's cage where it hung over the side. Carrying this squirming burden, he went back to her to thrust the wriggling thing against her, careful not to touch the part of it that touched her. He laid it on the roof, watching closely, and within moments the front part of it stopped thrashing and began to bump against the roof, moved by the tail, which was still alive. The blight lived in her still. He brought the sprayer up and covered her with a powdery, golden shower before lowering her into the shaft once more. The fish was still bumping, and he shoved it overside with a pole.

'Suspirra,' he whispered down to her. 'It's all right, Suspirra. A few more days' drying, the good powder will do its work, then you can come out of there . . .' Except, he told himself, she could not. Where would he put her? How would he explain?

26

'Blint, sir, would you mind making me a small payment on my wages?'

'How small, Thrasne? And what do you suddenly find yourself so needy of? Isn't wife Blint seeing well enough to your food and clothing?'

'It isn't that, sir. I have a mind to make a large carving, and I'd like to purchase a block of wood from a frag merchant . . .'

Which block of wood was not easily come by. Some were too crooked and others too straight. Some had harsh graining that would spoil the features, others were too dark. Thrasne found one eventually, at the bottom of the pile, and paid for it with good coin. He put it in one corner of his little room aboard the *Gift*, knives and chisels ostentatiously by. When he began to carve it, the wood opened up to reveal the Suspirra within. Still, it was a largish thing, life size, and it was longer than he liked before it resembled her, longer yet before it was her, line for line. Then was a long time between towns, during which he was never left alone, so that when he finally came to take the drowned woman from the net, replacing her with the carving – in case he might ever need to hide the real woman again – it seemed a season had gone by.

The drowned woman came gladly to his place, standing in one corner of it as though invited there for dalliance. She looked at him through barely opened eyes, lips not quite curved, as though she were thinking of smiling but had not yet accomplished it.

'Well,' said Blint when he saw her first. 'I still say you should be artist caste, Thrasne. Not that I'd like doing without you. Still, that's a beauty, that is. Pure fragwood, is it? Surely not the hair? That doesn't look carved.'

'Well, no sir,' he lied without a change of expression. 'That's a wig I bought in Tsillis. Somehow the carved hair didn't look . . . well, it didn't look soft.' Her hair had not looked soft, either, when he had raised her that last time, matted and filthy as it was from the frag leaf and sulphur. He had rinsed her time and again with buckets of clean water, brushed her hair, and run soap through it. Now it lay gleaming on her shoulders, not unlike the color of frag, yet more silken. The rest of her gleamed in nut-brown colors, also, with a hint of rose at nipples and lips.

'What do you call her?' asked Blint.

'Her name is Suspirra. It was the name of a girl I knew once back in Xoxxy-Do, where you found me.'

'And where you'll be again in a year or so. What will she think of this, your having a life-size doll of her to keep you company?' Blint was roguish, twinkling.

'She wouldn't mind.' Since Thrasne had invented such a girl on the spot, he was not concerned about what she might think. What Blint would think had concerned him, but evidently Blint thought nothing untoward. If a boatman wished to have a life-sized carving of a beautiful woman in his cabin, well, so be it. It took all kinds, as Blint would say, to do all the things needing doing.

At first Thrasne merely looked at her in the lantern light before he slept or in the early morning before he rose. He touched her face sometimes, almost reverently. He did not presume to touch her breasts, though once he laid his cheek against them, almost sobbing as the promise of softness was betrayed. After a time he stopped touching her at all and began talking to her instead. At a short distance he could forget the blight, forget her petrification, believe that she was living flesh. He still called her Suspirra. He told her all the things he had never been able to tell anyone, not even Blint.

'Blint saved my life,' Thrasne told her.

'I lived in Xoxxy-Do. Halfway round Northshore from anywhere. A mountainous place, where the falls come over the cliffs into World River, and the ships have to tie up behind great shattered rocks along the sheer walls and the boatmen climb steep, twisty stairs to reach the towns above. My father was a builder there, a builder in stone. My mother was an artist – though there was not so much of the caste system there in Xoxxy-Do as I have seen elsewhere. It was she who taught me to carve – or let me learn it, I suppose. She gave me a knife when I was only five. She was a wonderful carver. When Father finished a place, it was she who orna-mented it. They had a great success together. They were very happy. So was I.'

He was silent then, waiting for Suspirra to say something, to comment. He heard her saying, 'I was not happy. I envy your happy family, Thrasne. My own was not like that.'

'I saw your husband's mother,' he replied. 'My father's sister was like that. All pinch-lipped and hating. She could not bear it that they were happy. Could not bear it that they were in love. She had predicted doom on them, and the doom did not come. Not the kind she threatened.' He fell silent again, this time out of pain. The memory still had this power to undo him, to turn his muscles to water, his bowels to aching void.

'Ah,' said Suspirra. 'Then we have much in common.'

'They died. They had gone to the quarry together, and there was a great storm. The worker-built road was inade-quate even in calm weather. In the storm it dissolved like sugar. They were found at the bottom of the gorge, crushed beneath the stone. My father's sister took me in.'

'I know that kind of taking-in,' said Suspirra.

'The first thing she said to me was that my father and mother were in the worker pits of Ghasttown to the east, being raised up by the Awakeners. I could not stop crying, but she went on saying it. She took my knife away, saying I might hurt myself. It was the knife Mother had given me. I stayed with her for almost a season, but then I lay awake one night planning to kill her.'

'You had to get away,' prompted Suspirra.

'I had to get away. Blint found me along the Riverside, half-starved, talking to a little carving of Mother I had made.' It had been his first attempt at carving Suspirra, but he did not remember that.

'A kindly man, Blint.'

'Blint is kindness itself.' He stopped talking, appalled. She could not have spoken, and yet he had heard her speak. He left the little room to go out on deck and stride about, back and forth, hour on hour.

'What's troubling you, boy?'

29

'Do you ever find yourself talking to yourself, Blint?'

'All us boatpeople do, Thrasne. Never known one that didn't. Married Blint-wife just to have someone to talk to and found out it didn't work. Have to talk to yourself. How would you find out what you think about things otherwise?'

'Did you ever – did you ever pretend it was someone else answering you?'

'Always. Makes it more interesting that way.'

So he came to accept it. Boatpeople came to the River because on that everflowing current they could talk to themselves about Northshore without that world forcing its own opinions on them. On the River one could repudiate the Awakeners, hate the workers – both for their hideous existence and for the shoddiness of the work they did – cogitate upon Potipur and Abricor and Viranel, question their very existence, perhaps, without being accused of heresy.

'Do you think Potipur is loving?' whispered Suspirra.

'I don't think Potipur is anything,' he answered. 'Except a moon which pulls the tide around. And a moon-faced god in the Temples with the priests all bowing and waving incense and sparking their staffs at the congregation every tenth day and twice at the end of the month.' Ten days make a week, and when five weeks are gone, then you've a month with a holy day tacked on. Or so Thrasne's mother had always said.

'Then why?' Suspirra murmured. 'Why, why, why? . . .'

They had been on the River some forty days from Shabber when Blint complained that the pamet stacked in the forward hold smelled of mildew. 'Must be something blocking the ventilation duct,' he said with a sigh. 'We'll see to it next mooring.'

Thrasne was annoyed with himself. The wooden likeness of Suspirra was undoubtedly blocking the duct, and he should have seen to it long since. 'Let me do it, Blint. I've a cubby up top where I sit and watch things. Perhaps I've let something fall into the duct.'

'Have you now? Well then, you see to it. I'll leave it in your good hands.'

He did it at night, with all the crew ashore, the fitful light of torches from the pier throwing orange stripes across the netted burden as it came out of the shaft. Once lowered on the roof, he stripped the net away to have a long look at it before giving it to the tide.

There was something wrong.

He had carved it to be like the blighted woman. Like her line for line, eye for eye, lip for lip. And this was not like. These eyes were half-shut, these lips not quite curved, as though about to smile, but the Suspirra in his cabin had wide-open eyes, her lips were compressed. Leaving the statue where it was, he went below to make sure. Her eyes met his as he entered the room, her lips set tight as though humming, as though admonishing, as though about to say something.

'I'm going mad,' he whispered to himself, knowing he was not. 'Suspirra, am I going mad?'

'The world is mad,' she said. 'You see what you see.'

He put the carving into the tide, watching it until it vanished on the wavelets, casting a glance at the moons. Slack water would not come until early morning. It would travel far by then. He would never catch up with it again. Perhaps someone would fish it out along a pier and wonder at it.

Below in his room he began a small carving like the one just thrown away, line for line. When it was done, he did another of Suspirra as she was now. If the drowned woman was changing, he would make a record of those changes.

Over the next five years he carved forty little Suspirras. They were stowed under his bunk, numbered on their bases, and once in a very great while he would take them out and stand them in a long file before him, from first to last, the position of each slightly changed, the eyes and lips slightly opened or closed. Something about this silent throng oppressed him and bothered him at once, as though he should infer some meaning that evaded him. He still spoke to the drowned woman, and she still answered him, but this throng of small Suspirras seemed to shout at him in silence, a mute demand: 'Pay attention.' He looked and looked, not understanding.

'Are you alive?' he asked her.

'What is alive? Perhaps you stopped the blight before it was finished with me.'

'Do you want me to put you back in the River?'

'It is cold in the River, and lonely. Perhaps you will let me stay a while.'

So for five years he let her stay, carving each new expression as it showed itself, recording this strange slow life, if it was life, in every minuscule manifestation. Day succeeded day, river, pier, town, boatmen leaving and new ones coming aboard. Blint grew grayer and Blint-wife more loquacious. They had made almost a round since the drowned woman had come aboard. They had come to Xoxxy-Do to find Thrasne's aunt long dead, had passed it by, and were almost at Baristown once more.

'I wish you'd carve a baby for that woman,' said Blint-wife in an unaccustomed tone. There was worry in it, and sorrow, and a kind of aching that Thrasne had never heard her use before. He was surprised.

'What woman?' he asked. 'What do you mean?'

'That woman, those women, the little ones. All in a row, saying "My baby." '

He went below to look, she behind him, peering over his shoulder at the array. 'I came down to change your bed. I hadn't seen them all standing that way before. You see, look from the front to the back, that's what she's saying.'

He was only puzzled. His artist's eye had missed it. Blint-wife left him, returning after a time with a box of children's toys from the hold.

'See here,' she said, handing him one of the little books they had traded all along the River. On each page a festival clown was drawn, each drawing slightly different. When one flipped it rapidly, between thumb and fingers, the picture of the clown seemed to cavort and jump. Seeing his puzzlement, she went away.

That night he drew Suspirra's faces and arms on small squares of paper, binding them into a similar book. When he flipped the pages the hands and eyes moved, the mouth said, 'My baby.'

Blint-wife, of course, had talked to Blint of the matter.

'Murga – that is, Blint-wife – she lost the only baby we ever had,' said Blint. 'She used to sit before the mirror down there crying, saying it over and over, "My baby, my baby." It's no wonder she thought your carvings were saying the same.'

The carvings weren't, but the drowned woman was. 'My baby.' The little girl at the end of the pier, the one saying so hopelessly over and over, 'Papa. Papa.'

'I'd like some time ashore in Baristown, sir,' he said. 'There's some private business I'd like to attend to.'

He had no real idea how to find her. He had left Xoxxy-Do when he was twelve years old, not old enough to have perceived or understood the intricacies of town life. He had had no substantial contact with a town or village since. Still, intuition told him that there would be someone who made it his business to know things, all kinds of things. It did not take long to find him.

'Fulder Don?' the barber asked, waving his scissors in a vague gesture toward the center of town. 'Oh, surely, I know Fulder Don. Him and the old lady, and isn't she a termagant. Makes his life a misery, she does. Oldest girl got married young just to get out of the house, and the story is that Prender – that's the middle one – can hardly wait for the same chance.'

'There's a baby, isn't there?'

'Baby? There's been no wife there for six, seven years now. No. There was a baby when the wife killed herself, little girl, about four. But she's tennish, now. Half-grown. Lives with old Saint Delia the gardener on Outskirt Row.'

'Saint Delia?'

The barber laughed, amused at himself, 'Well, that's what they call her. Anybody needs something, anybody hungry or sick, they can go to old Delia and get taken care of. More of a saint than I ever thought Thoulia was, that's for sure.' He laughed, somewhat uncomfortably, making the ware-eyes gesture to keep Laughers away.

Thrasne went to Outskirt Row to find Delia's house. It was the one with the greatest profusion of flowers, the most sweetly scented with herbs. He stood in a redolence of fragrance and color, peering over the low wall. The little girl was there, crouched over a book as though to protect it from thieves, twiddling one long lock of hair with her fingers, winding and unwinding. The book was licit from the looks of it. It had the Tower seal on the cover.

'Pamra,' came a voice from inside. 'Come have your supper.'

The girl arose, half sighing, closing the book unwillingly. As she turned, she caught sight of Thrasne standing there and hesitated for a moment, puzzled, almost as though she might have remembered seeing him before. Then she shook her head and went into the house, leaving him as shaken as he had been by the first sight of the drowned woman. For it was she again, line for line, in a smaller frame and compass, a younger face. There was the same passion, the same willful disbelief, the same stubborn intensity turned within. He knew, having seen her face, that she lived inside herself, seeing her own visions, making her own world, not seeing half of what went on around her.

Seriously shaken, he made his way back to the *Gift*. What message could he give the drowned woman? How could he pierce the isolation of her blight to tell her her child was well? The child who was like her, line for line.

At last he printed a message large and put it upon the wall before the drowned woman's eyes. 'PAMRA IS WELL. DELIA CARES FOR HER.' He could think of nothing briefer, nothing more reassuring. He did not really know whether she would see it or not. Perhaps time was slower for her. Perhaps it would take her a year to see it. He was careful not to move her so that her view of it would be undisturbed.

They still talked.

'Blint is getting older,' he confided to her. 'He talks to me all the time about not being as young as he once was and needing someone to be a son to him.'

'If he says that, he hopes you will be such a son.'

'That's what I thought. Almost as though he needs reassuring about something. When he talks so, Blint-wife makes a kind of face, as though she had tasted something bitter.'

'It is bitter for women not to have the fruit of their bodies when they are denied the world's fruits. Bitter to have her man seek for a son in his old age. Men, who harvest the world's fruits, care less for their own.'

'It's true she gets little of the world's fruit,' Thrasne agreed. 'The River is a man's world.'

The thought stayed with him as he moved among the boatmen in the following years, proving its truth to himself again and again. Those who had little enough of the world's fruits were most needy of their own. He thought often of the old woman, Fulder Don's mother. What had she had, after all, but Fulder Don himself? Had him, and had been disinclined to share him. Had she driven his first wife to her death, too? As she had his Suspirra? If she were dead, which he was not at all certain of.

Blint came to him one day with a bulky document, wrapped about with tape and sealed with wax. 'My boy, I want you to keep this. I want you to swear oath to me you'll see I go into the River when my time comes and not into any town workers' pit.' He looked deep into Thrasne's face, gray lines around his eyes, loose jowls betraying a loss of flesh. His hands trembled, too, and Thrasne was moved to such a sympathy of feeling, it was a time before he could bring himself to speak.

'You know I would do that without any oath, Blint. You have been a father to me. You may rely on me.'

'Tie ballast to my bones, boy. Don't let the Awakeners get me into those damn pits. Put me deep as the strangeys swim.'

'I'll do it, owner Blint. And where no blight is, either.'

The man looked at him oddly then, and for a bit Thrasne thought he had given something away, but nothing more was said. Time went on. Blint seemed to recover some of his jovial ways. He put on a little weight. Thrasne sighed in relief. He was to open the document if anything happened, and he knew Blint-wife would be furious that Blint had not given it to her. Still, he owed much to Blint.

'Why didn't he give it to her?' he asked Suspirra.

'Because he knew he could rely on you to do what he wanted. He knew she might not. Often she does the opposite of what he says, you know, only to remind herself she is still a person. Otherwise, she forgets.'

Thrasne knew it. He made a carving of it. A man, climbing, carrying a woman on his back, not looking at her. She, gazing at him, tripping him as he went. The faces were not anyone's faces. Still, Blint blinked when he saw it and looked at Thrasne with widened eyes.

Suspirra went on changing. Now that Thrasne had the hang of it, he simply drew a picture of her every twenty days or so, binding them together as he had previously. He thought she was beginning to say the same thing again. More than that, however, her body was changing shape. She who had been slender as a frag sapling, yielding as a reed, seemed thicker, more stolid, as though she fattened upon the air of the little room, gained substance from their conversation.

They came one warm second summer to the Straits of Shfor. All the boatmen were on deck with the fending poles. They had lashed great bundles of rope and sacks of pamet to the side of the boat to protect it against the fanglike stones of Shfor. One could not go through at slack water on the oars, for the way was too narrow. One wanted a low, easy tide and a slight wind to get through the straits, or one wanted a long voyage out into World River to go around. As they moved into the canyon, Thrasne looked up to see great birds gathered in hundreds along the rimstones.

'Owner Blint,' he called, pointing up.

'Ah? Oh, this is a Talon, boy, full of fliers as a strangey is of bones. There's many of 'em up there, isn't there. Servants of Abricor. Takes a clear day to see 'em. Last time we were through was wrapped up in a fog like a blanket, remember? Those peaks up there are all full of holes and caverns, so I've heard. And you never see any young ones at the Talons, so they say. Certain the big ones gather up there, though. Other things, too, from what I hear tell.'

'What other things?' Thrasne drew nearer, drawn by something mysterious in his tone.

'There's Talkers and Writers up there.'

'Now, owner Blint! Are you joshing me?'

'Well now . . .' The old man squinted against the sun, moving along the side to assist a boatman who was thrusting against a toothy rock. When he came back panting, holding his chest, he sighed. 'I'm trying to remember what it was I heard about that. My old owner told me. He was a flier watcher, he was, and he said there was two kinds of fliers.'

'Sure.' Thrasne laughed. 'Big ones and little ones.'

'No, no. Two kinds of big ones. He said the kind that nested up there on the Talons could talk. And write.'

Thrasne could not help himself. He sniggered. 'Like in the stories about when men came to Northshore, owner Blint? Talking fliers?'

Blint shook his head reproachfully. 'I didn't say I believed it, Thrasne. I just said that's what he told me. According to him, there's some people up there, too. They live there, to talk to the fliers.'

'Where did he hear that?'

'I don't know. He didn't say.' Blint seemed vague, clutching his arm as though it hurt him, disinclined to discuss it further.

They came through the straits without incident and tied up at Shfortown. Blint started to move a bale of pamet, gave a startled exclamation, and fell down. He breathed hard for a moment, cast a frightened look at Thrasne, and lost consciousness.

'Plank aboard,' called Thrasne in a calm voice.

'We just got here,' grumbled a boatman.

Thrasne whispered to him imperatively, nodding at the pier where several Awakeners walked, and the man moved to pull the plank aboard. Two other boatmen carried Blint below as Blint-wife lamented. They moved quickly out onto the tide.

37

'Sorry, Thrasne,' mumbled the boatman. 'Wasn't thinking. You think he's too bad?'

'I don't know,' Thrasne murmured. 'Just I've been watching him. He keeps clutching his heart as though it hurts him . . .'

Blint regained consciousness only for a few moments, learned they were well out in the River, gripped Thrasne's hand gratefully, and died. They put him into a small net with ballast stones and dropped him in the deepest part of the current while Blint-wife sobbed.

When she had had time to steady down, Thrasne went to the owner-house with Blint's document.

'Blint asked me to look after you,' he said, seeing the fear leave her face a little as he said this. He and Suspirra had thought it out, this approach, after Suspirra told him Blint-wife was afraid.

'I agreed to do it, Blint-wife. He wanted me to take over as owner.'

'You!' she screamed. 'You, boy! You nothing boy we picked up from the rocks! Why not me, who was his wife these thirty years? Hah? Tell me that?'

He let her rage, saying nothing, until his silence weighted her down and she quieted, lips trembling.

'Because the men won't obey you, Blint-wife, and you'll not be able to find others who will. If you take the *Gift*, soon she'll be against a rock in quick-River with none to fend her off. And if you sell her, you'll not get enough to keep you for your life. But if I'm owner, I promised Blint I'd set you safe ashore and bring payment to you each time the *Gift* comes round. Enough to live on and be well cared for. So, that's what Blint planned, and I promised. Unless you have some better plan.'

Which she didn't. The only thing she cried about then was the possibility of falling into the hands of the Awakeners, but Blint had thought even of that.

He had written: 'There's secret groups in most towns call themselves Rivermen – not boatmen, they've had nothing to do with the boats – who see that their people end in the

River and not with the Awakeners. See Blint-wife is set near some such group, and give them what gifts they require to see to her.' So Blint had written. Boatmen wrote a good deal more than other folk, it being the kind of business it was. Thrasne wasn't the only one aboard with hidden books, either. Blint had some secreted in the owner-house, Awakeners or no Awakeners.

Thrasne, when he went looking, was surprised to find many groups such as Blint had described. They were secretive and careful, but open enough once they knew who he was and what his life had been. Boatmen in general were known to be rebels against the laws of the Awakeners, Thrasne no less than others. He set Blint-wife down in a pretty town called Zephyr, about midway between Shfortown and Baris, full of ponds where lily flowers grew, in a stout little house all her own near a quiet cluster of Rivermen and -women.

'You'll need to hold your tongue, Blint-wife,' he said to her, carrying the last of her goods into the new place to the accompaniment of her incessant clacking. 'Else you'll betray those who would want to help you.'

She quieted, turning a weeping face on him at the last. 'I know, Thrasne. Believe me, I hear myself and I know. It's only I was so lonely there on the River among all those men and not a woman, not a child to talk to. So lonely. I'd have come ashore long since had I not loved him so. Blint. Don't judge so harsh, Thrasne. There's more pain in us clacking old women than you'll ever know, most likely.'

He went shamefaced to Suspirra with this.

'She talked just to hear a voice. A woman's voice,' confirmed Suspirra.

Which didn't make Thrasne feel any better about it. Blint-wife had given him all of Blint's books, and he was feeling he'd been ungrateful for all her care over the years. He wrote her a letter, saying so, which he had no means to deliver. Anyway it was not to his liking, so he wrote another. And as the days passed, he wrote still other letters, to Blint-wife, to Blint, to himself. In time, he began to keep them in a book, which he called, to himself and very secretly, 'Thrasne's book.' He was sure the things he wrote there would mean nothing to anyone but him.

From Shfor to Baris was only a few days' float, if one did it without stopping. Suspirra had asked once more, 'My baby?' and it had been seven years since Thrasne had seen Pamra. So they came to Baris, and owner Thrasne went ashore, leaving the boat in the good hands of firstman Birk. In the same shop he found a new barber, who might well have been the old barber for all the difference between them.

'Fulder Don's youngest daughter? Why, boatman, she surprised all her kin and became an Awakener. Been at the Tower four or five years now. Seems someone told me just the other day they'd seen her with an older one herding a bunch of workers out on the piers.'

Sick at heart, Thrasne took himself off to the house he remembered from before.

'Pamra?' Delia asked, surprised. 'Why, boatman, why would you come looking for Pamra?'

Thrasne mumbled something about having known her mother.

'Oh, sad, sad. Pamra's mama was the loveliest thing I've ever seen. Like a flower. Like a flame-bird, bright and graceful, and like a flame-bird gone too soon. Ah. Well, Pamra's an Awakener now. Did it out of rebellion, I think. To get even with her grandma and her half sisters. They were always at her. It was because she looked like her mother, don't you know?' She wiped the nose of the infant she was juggling and called a quick set of instructions to two toddlers who were picking herbs, explaining, 'Their mama died, too, and they needed a place for a few days until their papa could make arrangements. Well. You didn't come to talk about my kiddies.'

Which he hadn't. He left her with words of thanks, taking himself off to the vicinity of the Tower, far enough away not to be questioned by the Awakeners but close enough to see her if she came. When she did, he knew her at once.

'Pamra,' he called, not certain it was allowed to speak to

her, but needing to do something more than merely look and go away.

She turned to him, that expression he so well remembered intensified, if anything, into a stubborn, blind naiveté, a face that said, 'I will do what I will do!'

'Do I know you?' she asked, a little haughtily, as all the Awakeners were.

'I knew your mother,' he said.

'She went in the River.' Her voice was forbidding. Cold. 'She was a coward, a heretic.'

'That's very harsh,' he said, shocked at her tone.

'No more than she deserves. Did you have something to say to me?'

'Nothing,' he said. What could he say to her? 'Nothing.' He turned away, confused, not liking her and yet not wanting to leave. 'You look like her,' he called over his shoulder. 'Exactly like her. And she loved you.' There, he thought. Let her make what she will of that.

He went back to the boat downcast and miserable to write a new sign for Suspirra. 'PAMRA IS WELL.' She was well. So beautiful it put his heart into his throat, half longing and half anger at her, at what she'd done. About sixteen or seventeen now, and the perfect copy of the drowned woman except that Pamra was slim where this woman had a rounded figure, gently swelling.

'How could she?' he whispered.

'She believes,' Suspirra said. 'Truly believes. Not in my love, for I abandoned her. Not in her father's love, for he left her, too, in his way. But in the love of Potipur, for she *must* believe in love – of some kind.'

Sickened, Thrasne could not believe in the love of Potipur. It was with a kind of guilty relief he put Baristown behind him.

41

4

Haranjus Pandel, Superior of the Tower of Thou-ne, saw fit
to visit the home of the widow Flot.

'There's this law, Widow Flot. You know it, and I know
it.' He said this in his usual manner, as one might who is
dreadfully bored with the necessity but feels it wise to go
through the motions.

Widow Flot, unawed, shook her head at him. 'If you're
talking of Peasimy, have a little sense, Superior.'

'He's thirty years old.'

'He's thirty in years. He's four or five in his head, and as
far as his wee private parts go, he's not got enough to bring a
blush to a maiden's cheek. I'll swear that part of him hasn't
grown since he was born.' She flushed a little saying it, but it
had to be said. Gods, hadn't she said it to her friends, many
a time, and hadn't they breathed it around? Sure Haranjus
knew it, just as he knew every other blessed thing that went
on in Thou-ne.

'Still, there's the law.' It didn't come out with the force
Pandel would have wished. He had suddenly remembered
several other things about Peasimy that he had known at
one time but had conveniently forgotten until that moment.

The widow Flot was no more awed by the law than she
was by his presence. 'The law says no celibacy, no boy-
boying, that's what the law say, Haranjus Pandel. The law
says there must be wedding and bedding and enough children born to keep our numbers strong. That's what the law
says. And Superior or no, don't come all over haughty with
me, Haranjus. I knew your ma, and I've known about you

since you were no bigger than Peasimy's cock. Peasimy's not celibate, no more than any infant is. And Peasimy's no boy lover, neither. Peasimy's an infant, a neuter, no more sex to him than to a blade of grass. So what's this about the law? You got some ugly, godforsaken maiden you've got to get matched up, is that it?'

Haranjus had the grace to blush. He had, as a matter of fact, the daughter of the Merchants' Guild Hetman to get mated, somehow. She with the face like a song-fish and the body like a tub. No matter, face nor figure, so long as she was able to produce. With the constant drain on their numbers, producing was important. And rumor was that human numbers needed to be slightly increased for a . . . well, for a reason. No way it could be done unless the birth rate went up.

Seeing him redden, she went on relentlessly, 'You'd be laughed out of Thou-ne. And if word got back to the Chancery you was wasting your time on such silliness – and I'd see it got there, one way or another – they'd put an end to any hopes you might have. Give it up, Haranjus. Find your ugly girl some other housemate, but give it up so far as Peasimy's concerned.'

He argued some, but it was only halfhearted, a kind of face saving before he went away with scant courtesies. It had been a silly idea. Everyone in Thou-ne knew Peasimy, and the idea of Peasimy with a wife would strike them all as a mighty funny thing. Compromising to the dignity of the Tower. Meeting the letter of the law, but contrary to its spirit. Besides, it wouldn't gain the favor of the Merchants' Hetman, either, if he got no grandkids as part of the deal. Widow Flot was right. Leave it alone.

Behind him in the little house, Widow Flot wiped one or two tears away. Hadn't she suffered enough? No hope for grandbabes. No hope for someone to care for her in her old age. Just Peasimy, sweet as any toddler, and with no more sense. 'There, there,' she told herself, cheering a little. 'Still, he's good as a pet anyday.'

In the bedroom, Peasimy sprawled in moist, infant sleep

as he always did daytimes, unaware of the catastrophe that had narrowly missed him, dreaming of a time when all the darkness should be driven away and the light made whole. There were no words in these dreams, only visions in which winged figures moved through radiant space. Dreams, not unlike those dreamed by many, except that Peasimy remembered them when he woke. When he rose, walked, prowled through the dark, splashing light where he could, he always remembered them and longed to be deep in that dream again.

Days and nights go by. Moons swing up from the east in round, ripe glory and fade to mere slivers of rind on the western sky as time passes. Conjunctions come and go.

Comes a night. Dusk in Thou-ne, a misty dusk in which all is veiled, mystery made manifest, ghost faces in the wisps of fog that waft in from the River, ghost voices, too, which become, on long listening, the sounds of song-fish, wooden bells, the tinkle of glass chimes, the crier's call. Only the Tower has a brazen bell, metal being too scarce to waste on anything except coin and holy purposes, but it is silent tonight, its voice withheld. Tower bell only rings when something is wrong. There is seldom anything wrong in Thou-ne, edged as it is on the east with the scarps and valleys of the Talons. No workers come to Thou-ne from the east. Potipur knows what the Awakeners beyond the Talons do with their dead, though Peasimy supposes a workers' pit somewhere. Peasimy has it all figured out. Lies, all lies what they say. It was lies what they said about his father being Sorted Out. It was lies what the body fixer said about his arm, that time it broke. There hadn't been any Sorters, and the arm had hurt, terribly. Peasimy no longer listens to what they say. Only what they do is true, so he watches but does not hear. He has turned his ears off, long and long ago, to most words. Sounds, now, those he will condescend to hear, and tonight he listens from his post beside the warehouse wall. Chimes and woodbells and the crier's call.

Night along the River in Thou-ne. Mist, tonight,

blowing in from the slupping surface, softly suffused globes of it gathered around each of the lanterns, holding the light in glowing spheres that hang along the jetties like a string of ghostly balloons. Song-fish making a chorus under the shore reeds, harummm, rumm, lummm, rumm. Three of them. One soprano-fish and two deep-voiced droners. Harumm, sloo, harumm.

Light cannot get far enough from the lanterns to make puddles on the cobbles. Lanterns are scarcely bright enough to see by. Jetties lying in shadow. He stands, Peasimy, head cocked, listening to the song-fish. Something there, disturbing them. Most nights they've finished up by now, danced on their tails, done all their calling and telling, but tonight there's something keeping them awake. So Peasimy listens, almost understanding what it is the song-fish sing, as much in tune with them as with the dark and the fog.

'Oh,' he whispers to himself, 'don't I hear you, don't I? Somethin' comin'. Somethin' wonderful comin'. Don't I know that? Haven't I been told? No need to keep sayin' it, over and over. No matter was it tomorrow or forever, I'd still be here, waitin' for it.' He rocks to and fro on his heels, thinking they may stop now, now that he's told them, but the song-fish go on, harummm, harummm. No, whatever they're telling him, it's something different from the ordinary.

Peasimy tiptoes along to the Riverbank, out onto the jetty, down to the place the reed bed thins out and the fish sing, flings himself down with his head snaking out over the slosh and slurp of the black water.

Harumm, lumm, sloon, rumm. Fish playing with something, pushing it back and forth. They do that. Push an old barrel back and forth. Push a log, a stump. Chunk, chunk on the jetty, far down. Chunk, chunk, coming closer. And he can see it! Even in the dark, down there under the water, glowing, shining, a greeny glow, like new leaves in the sun, like moon on grass, light!

He stares and stares as the fish bring her up, up to the surface, she glowing ever more brightly, until at last he

45

looks directly into her face. All around her the fishes, singing, the glowing fishes spread either side of her like wings. Bump, bumping her against the stones, looking up at Peasimy as though to say, 'Here she is!' He knows her at once, one of the creatures from his dreams, one of those who bring the light.

Oh, but she has changed since Thrasne carved her and put her into the River. All the features are the same, and the hard fragwood has not softened, but the little creatures of the depths have been at her, smoothing her all over with their phosphorescent slime so she gleams, shines, beams up from the waves like a beacon of greeny light, smiling, one hand held out as though for Peasimy to take it and welcome her ashore.

And Peasimy reaches down, stronger than he could possibly be, tugging and lifting, pulling like a boatman at the capstan, hauling with an excess of power he has never had and will never have again, until she stands there, dripping on the jetty, peering at the town of Thou-ne. Only then does he go screaming off after the crier and the watch, hallooing for the lantern man, for the people to come see, and such is his fervor and volume of voice it is not long before there is a crowd gathered, full of muttering as the reed beds, staring at the woman from the River, who smiles back at them, shining, shining, shining in the dark.

'There,' Peasimy cries, over and over, in a voice totally unlike his own. 'There in the River. The Truth Bearer. The Light Bearer. She shines, oh, she shines!'

'What's he saying?'

'Says she's the Truth Bearer.'

'What's that?'

'Somebody who brings the truth, I guess. Look at her. Ain't she lovely.'

'What'd they say?'

'Said the lovely Truth Carrier was come, I think. That's her. Up there.'

'What's a Truth Carrier?'

'Oh, that's religion, that is. Foretold to happen.' This

from one of the standabouts, a know-it-all who makes up half of what he says and switches the other half around to suit himself. No one believes a thing he says in daylight, but the dark and mist make him an anonymous voice, speaking with the authority of conviction. 'Foretold to happen,' he says again, pleased with the way this is received.

And the circumstances of it all, the mist, the dark, the voice saying things that seem authoritative, Peasimy's transfigured face, the beauty of the carved woman, all that reaches them so they go away from the place nodding their heads, believing she is whatever Peasimy calls her. Believing they had heard of the Truth Bearer all their lives, pleased and delighted, though mystified, that she has come.

The day after goes on with saying and saying until what is said by one is said by everyone and believed by everyone. Someone – years later the distinction is claimed by half the families in Thou-ne – someone says the glowing image belongs in the Temple. By evening she is there, in the Temple of the Moons, there at the top of the sanctuary steps in front of the carved visages of the gods, looking down at the people in kindness and wonder. By evening the ritual surrounding her has begun. From the balcony high above, a novice ladles water from buckets, an endless line of buckets carried from the River itself, and in this dank sprinkle the image of Suspirra stands, shining wetly and smiling, as though forever. Peasimy kneels at the altar rail, his face glowing like the moon.

Behind him in the sanctuary, Widow Flot stares at his back, not knowing whether she is thankful for this or not. Peasimy hasn't been up in the daytime for a dozen years or more, and this could mean he will start sleeping at night, like most people. Which means he'll be underfoot, during the day, most likely.

'Flot-wife,' says a voice behind her in gloomy tones, and she turns to confront Haranjus Pandel.

'Superior,' she says formally in her most discouraging tone. What is he going to make of this, now? Some new thing to bother honest people with?

47

Instead he asks in gloomy tones, 'What is all this? You can tell me, Widow Flot. Haven't I the right to know? All the responsibility, and no one tells me? Did he carve the thing? Did he?'

She stares, laughs, stares again. He doesn't expect an answer. He doesn't even believe it himself. He sits there on the hard, uncomfortable bench, head propped on one hand, his long, lugubrious face attentive to the glowing woman behind the rail. Is he thinking, too, that it may really be a miracle? Behind the shining woman are the faces of Potipur, Abricor, and Viranel, so familiar the worshipers do not even see them. Now, for the first time, Widow Flot sees these carved faces of the gods contrasted with a human face, the shining woman's face, and knows them for what they are.

'Haranjus,' she breathes in the grip of discovery. 'Potipur's face! That's a flier's face!'

And he, casting his eyes upward, sees the faces of the gods for the first time. Really seeing. Peering down at him with a hooded-eyed cynicism, beaks gaped a little as though hungry. Fliers' faces. He has never questioned them before, never before even noticed the expressions they wear. How long, he wondered in sudden panic, how long had he been worshiping the fliers without even knowing it?

5

In the Awakeners' Tower in Baris, Pamra Don lay sleeping.

The Candy Tree filled all the space above her, glitter and shimmer of leaf behind leaf, blossoms squirming open in a sensuous dance of hue and scent, explosions of amber and gold, bursts of gemmy reds, all rustling, flushing, burgeoning into every empty space, thrusting its light and color upon her, drawing her up into itself, weightlessly . . . toward glory . . .

Something rasped, scraped. A hard sound. Nothing alive in it. Metal on stone. The Candy Tree shivered. Pamra ignored the sound, hating it, clinging to the tree . . .

'The new drainage ditches along the Tower wall,' a voice in her mind said clearly. 'A worker crew digging drainage ditches.'

With that recognition the Candy Tree dream slipped away like smoke, and she woke thinking of Delia.

Tangled warmth of bedcovers; a ghostly reflection staring back at her from the glass across the cubicle. Last evening, the bleeding. This morning, heavy sleep and slow waking. A longing for comforting arms. That was why she was thinking of Delia today, when she had not thought of her for a season.

Groaning, Pamra rolled herself half upright, huddled at the edge of the bed, hugging herself as the weak tears runneled her face. Oh, it was hard enough to waken oneself after bleeding without thinking of Awakening the workers. She should have known better than to have angered Betchery with her comment about the woman's appetite. Betchery was well known as a glutton, but she hated being reminded of it. Bleeders had ways to retaliate; unconscionable, but predictable.

She mouthed the furred, foggy taste of sick depression; only the result of weakness, true, but enough to make one doubt one's strength. For a moment, predictably, she regretted being an Awakener. Why keep on when it meant submitting to Betchery and all the other necessary unpleasantness?

She responded to both regret and question as she always had. 'Because of what my mother did.' Muttering, the words coming out in a single connected string, as though they were all one word, an incantation uttered from habit.

It was years since she had actually heard herself saying those words. At one time they had stirred her anger, renewed her resolution. Now they were only part of the morning litany, the childhood humiliation buried beneath ten years of ritual and acceptance. She slumped away from the bed, aching, sagging, knowing her face must be pale as ice. What a lot to go through. And yet she was so close to senior grade.

Senior grade. Senior retreat first, learning the mysteries that juniors were not privy to. Danger there, carefully avoided in thought. Not all those who went on senior retreat returned afterward. Skip over that. Senior retreat, then senior vows, then a luxurious room of her own on the upper floors. Meals cooked to order, not ladled out of the common pot. Respected by everyone, without exception. Even Papa wouldn't be able to think of her as a failure when she was senior grade.

She leaned against the window, letting the glass cool her skin, remembering Grandma Don's sarcastic voice: 'Pamra's mother was a coward and a heretic. Pamra herself shows no sign of expiating that sin. She will never make an artist.'

And her own words in response, unplanned, unintended, raggedly defiant in the subdued gathering. 'I can be an Awakener. That's better than artist anytime.'

Silence had opened to receive that statement, an embarrassed silence that grew into coolness, into distaste, into disaffection. There had been no way to back down, no way to change her mind. They had rejected her when the words were said; she could only go on after that.

Once in the Tower, she had not seen Prender or Musley or Papa or Grandma again. Someday she would see her half sisters and Papa, perhaps. After she was senior, not before. And not Grandma Don, of course. Grandma would have been taken to the Holy Sorters long ago, though Pamra doubted she had been Sorted Out.

Disgusted at the memory, she pushed herself away from the window. Nothing was real this morning. Propelling her weakness through the day would be like swimming through mirage. Stripping off her gown, she began the morning ritual which got her dressed, her hair braided in the distinctive Awakeners pattern. Robed and sandaled at last, she left the cubicle to pause at the top of the women's stairs for the Utterance.

'Rejoice! I go to Awaken those whose labors sustain us. Thanks be to the Tears of Viranel, to the Servants of Abricor, to the Promise of Potipur, and amen.' Though her shaking hand upon the banister belied her voice, the statement was made firmly aloud, requiring response.

'Rejoice and amen!' chanted a voice from down the corridor, echoing and anonymous.

So released, she stumbled down to the women's refectory and a deserted table. The smell of the morning grain ration sickened her, but she held her breath and forced the porridge down. Her body would not make new blood if she didn't eat, and no amount of religious posturing would get her through the day unless she felt stronger.

Ilze's voice came from behind her, formally cool, yet with a slight tone of anger. 'Pamra, you're white as pamet. Have you just been bled? Who did it?'

Pamra kept her face forward. While talking at morning meal was not forbidden, it was considered indicative of a lack of seriousness. Still, he was a senior and her mentor. He had a perfect right to come into women's quarters, a perfect

51

right to question her. She whispered, 'It was Betchery.'

'Betchery indeed. I should have known without asking.' He was lean and brown with a bony, handsome face and hungry eyes. Despite his evident concern, Pamra felt a sense of danger whenever he was near, as though she might burn if he focused on her more closely. She shifted uncomfortably beneath his unsmiling regard, keeping her eyes down where they belonged, uneasy under his stare.

'You're in no condition to be on labor roster. Take it easy today, and I'll see what I can do.' He touched her, almost a caress, lingering longer than necessary. Beneath his hand, her skin quivered, not welcoming the touch, not daring to reject it. He turned, saying, 'Well, enough of this rejoicing. I have yesterday's plowed fields to inspect.'

'*Rejoice!*' Pamra responded formally. '*The Awakening is at hand.*'

He left her with an amused smile, shaking his head very slightly. Ilze frequently seemed to find her amusing, and this slight, half-concealed mockery often puzzled her. This morning, however, she was too weary to be puzzled by anything.

In the open corridor between men's and women's quarters, she waited at the bleeders' hatch for someone to bring whatever supplements the Superior had ordered. Betchery brought them out, fat Betchery, sneering and popping candies into her mouth as Pamra tried to choke the pills down dry. It was Betchery's habit of gluttony that Pamra had commented on to Jelane. Unfortunately, Betchery had overheard the conversation.

'Rejoice, Awakener,' said Betchery, handing over the two daily flasks of blood and Tears. 'Lookin' a trifle pale, there.'

'Rejoice and amen.' Pamra would not give her the satisfaction of anything but ritual. Rejoice and amen, and amen to you, Betchery, bitch. If you come dead under my hands, you'll not be Sorted. She went out into the morning, no longer trembling, merely angry-sad as bleeding usually made her. It brought a brooding melancholy that made the world seem colorless – a painting done in shades of brown and tan with none of the usual life and vitality.

The water in the trough on the high steps riffled in the light wind of the year's second summer, warmer and less rainy than the autumn that had just passed. Thin, early-morning clouds streamed north in the onshore winds; later they would puff like pamet pods to hang their heavy veils over the fields. A flight of young flame-birds fled across the sky, their orangey feathers spark bright in the sun. Down in the Baristown plaza, a line of swaying Melancholics moved across the pave, chanting to awaken the people. Only they or the Awakeners would be up this early. The parkland that separated the Tower from Outskirt Road at the edge of Baristown lay green in this early light, quiet, silvered with dew.

Beyond the park and the plaza, the avenue stretched south to the bank of the World River. There the tidal bulge pulsed westward as it followed the god-moons Viranel and Abricor, hanging like pale, round lanterns in the western sky. Potipur brooded beneath the horizon. Conjunction would come at midwinter this year, more than a season from now. Conjunction, when all the Servants of Abricor disappeared for a time and the workers were allowed to lie quiet.

Along the pulsing waters of the Riverside a worker crew was dumping loads of rock to extend one of the fishing jetties, the workers crawling like gray maggots on the clumsy structure. Beyond them on the brown-dun flow a boat passed, pushed onward by the tide, and the striding form of a Laugher moved on the River path at the same speed, as though boat and man were tied together. Pamra made the sign of Aversion, turning her eyes from the Laugher. Always better not to see them. Against a hillside to the west another worker crew was plowing, the shapeless forms oozing among the occasional copses of broad-leafed puncon trees left standing both for their shade and their fruit. Beside each crew an Awakener leaned on a tall mirrored staff, blood flasks hanging from the shoulder. Pamra was usually first to the day's labors. Seeing these others before her reaffirmed her weakness, her tardiness. She must move, get the day's work under way.

But first she could receive her own Payment, that moment of her day blessed by Potipur. No matter what else happened, the early-morning rapture made it all worthwhile.

She took a deep breath, and raised both arms in the ritual gesture toward the west, the direction of the World River, of the moons, of the sun, toward which all things moved. Her breathing slowed, her skin began to tingle. Eastward then, holding her hands before her face in the gesture of negation, the unworld direction, the way no one could go, from which all things came but into which nothing could return. She bowed north, to the forests that carpeted all the lands to the edge of the Great Steppes and beyond the steppes to the Chancery, where the Protector lived, mighty and omniscient, behind the Teeth of the North; bowed south to the River, World-Girdler.

Then she held her breath, waiting for it.

A welling joy that had no focus in this world, a transcendent glory in her flesh, a dizzying beat of her blood, a rush of pure pleasure throughout her body, a bath of ecstatic fire.

'It's the pills they give you,' Jelane had said to her. 'It's the pills that give you that feeling.' Jelane was a junior who had come into the Tower shortly after Pamra.

'No,' Pamra had told her. 'It couldn't be just pills. That wouldn't be fair.'

'Well, it is, Pamra. By all the three gods but you're dumb. Why do you think you get that rush every day right after they give you your supplements! It's kind of a little Payment, for being a good girl when they bleed you.'

'No,' Pamra had said, choking down her resentment and anger. Why should anyone listen to Jelane – Jelane, who spent every third day being restricted or getting two lashes for infractions? Jelane was a selfish, heretical little fool. If it was the pills, then how explain that the rapture came at other times, too? She said this, defiantly, not expecting Jelane to believe it and not caring whether she did or not.

54

'Well, maybe you get other times,' Jelane had sniffed. 'None of the rest of us do.'

How could one live in the Tower without the rapture? How could one do recruitment without the rapture? How could one get through the day? The rapture came from Potipur as Payment to His servants; nothing else made sense.

When the glory faded, she went to Awaken the workers.

Of the twenty or so fresh bodies brought every week from Wilforn, the next town to the east, several still lay in the Baristown pit, their canvas wraps virtually unstained, the masking hoods whole and untattered. Only the swollen blue feet emerging from the wrap showed the first signs of corruption. These were the Wilforn dead who had not been Sorted Out, who had instead been left in the workers' pit to fulfill their obligation.

Pamra bowed her head and gave the invocation in a calm, beckoning voice, then raised the first hood just above the purple-lipped mouth to pour the mixed Tears and blood from her flask between the dead lips.

'Drink and rise,' she intoned. 'For work awaits you.'

One never raised the hood high enough to see the faces – though every Awakener had probably done it once. Having done it once, no one would do it again. A few years before, she might have waited to verify that each worker did indeed rise up. Now she merely dropped the hood and moved on. Other Awakeners would arrive soon, and she wanted as many of these fresh workers in her own crew as she could get. Too many times lately she had had to take shambling forms directly from the worker pits to the bone pits because some other Awakener hadn't bothered to put them where they belonged the night before. Of course it was unpleasant to get something barely able to hold itself together to walk the extra few hundred yards, and of course they had to be moved in a barrow sometimes, but that was part of the job. Though, thank Potipur, not a part she would need to do today.

'Thanks be to Viranel,' she intoned, meditating upon the Tears that were mixed with the blood.

Long ago, said Scripture, Viranel had revealed the power of Her Tears, shed for the sins of mankind, to the Holy Sorter Thoulia, and in furtherance of that revelation all the Towers and Awakeners had come to be. In class, Pamra had been told that the fungus, brought into a spate of growth by fresh blood and sunlight, grew rapidly throughout the dead bodies, duplicating nerve and muscle cells with tissues of its own, copying and revivifying the structures that were there. Pamra thought there were other things the Tears did as well, but it was better not to ask questions. Undoubtedly, she would be told whatever was important for her to know, in time.

'Anything you do badly reflects on me,' Ilze had said to her that first day.

Pamra, half-terrified, had trembled. 'Yes, Mentor,' she had murmured.

'Anything you do badly, I have to answer to the Superior. You understand?'

She had bowed, hands folded, eyes down, only to start at the lash of something around her ankles, a stinging on her bare feet. She was staring down at a whip, coiled serpentlike around her feet, and the shock brought her eyes up to confront the snakelike stare in Ilze's eyes, covetous and cold.

'And if I have to answer,' he had whispered, 'so will you.'

Pamra had never forgotten. Ilze had never had to answer for anything she had done. She had kept the rules, not asked questions, done what she was told. As she was doing now.

'Drink and rise,' she said again and again until she had the full hand of workers on their feet. Five was about all one could manage while plowing, though up to ten could be used in carrying stone. She twirled her staff as she led them northwest to the pamet fields, the mirrored facets throwing sparks of light before them. The harnesses and plow lay where the last crew had left them. Driven by the mirrored lights and her murmured chants of command, the workers shambled into the harness and began to plow, slowly, soundlessly, the

56

blind hoods faced in the direction Pamra faced, seeing, if at all, through her eyes.

When evening came, she led them back, judging the distance carefully so that the power of the last blood she gave them would just last until the workers reached the pits. None of them were ready to be dropped into the bone pits, thank Potipur. A good fresh crew. She would rise early the next few days and attempt to keep them for herself. The thought frayed away, lost in weariness at the thought of any next few days, fatigue wrapping her with an aching sigh. She could not consider tomorrow. She could not even consider the night. Though she felt stronger than in the morning, the mindless evening hours in the Tower seemed more than she could bear.

She'd been neglecting Delia lately. It was a good time to visit her.

The gardens of Outskirt Row spilled over their walls, shedding perfume into the evening, fragrant with herbs and warm from the day's sun, as welcoming a place as it had always been. Delia's house was at the end of the row.

Despite the welcoming appearance of the place, Pamra delayed as she went down through the parklands, heavy with nostalgia, last night's dream and the morning's resentments all mixed together. Skittering sparks of light fled from her mirrored staff to scramble across the path and the stones. The lights attracted Delia's attention, and she came to the gate of her garden, waving her cane as though it were a wand held by some good witch to make a welcoming enchantment.

'Pamra! Something told me you would come, so I baked spice cakes . . .' No reproach for all the days she had been forgotten. Reproach was not Delia's way, and Pamra warmed to Delia's way, as she always had.

'I haven't had a spice cake in . . . oh, a thousand years.' She could not help smiling. This was good Saint Delia, who always remembered things, all of them warm and happy, even when there were few enough of those to choose among. 'Not since I was a child. A long time ago, Delia.'

'Not all that long. No. Scarcely yesterday. Only a

conjunction of the moons or two, nothing to mention.' Delia laughed, but the cough turned into a hacking convulsion that left her weak, wiping her eyes and shaking her head. 'Oh, me, me. My days are surely few before I am carried to the west and put into the Sorters' hands. Tsk.'

Pamra made a gesture, her revulsion scarcely concealed. 'You mustn't say things like that.'

'Oh, Pamra, child! All us ordinary people talk like that. You know it. Only you Awakeners never talk of going into the west. Do you worry so that we have no faith? That we will not be taken into Potipur's arms?'

'It isn't . . . it isn't that, Delia. I have no doubt about your being Sorted Out and received by Potipur. Among us it's just accounted bad manners to talk of it with . . . people close to us.'

'But, child, we're not among you Awakeners. There's just you and me, and haven't we always said honest things to one another?'

'Of course we have,' Pamra took the old woman's hand in her own, feeling the fragile flesh give way between the slender bones. Delia's wrists were like a flame-bird's legs, like a reed stem. 'And when all the family turned away from me because I decided to be an Awakener, only Delia stayed my friend.'

She smiled into the old face, reaching out to touch the tiny, leaf-shaped blue birthmark on Delia's chin as she had when she was a little one. 'Wiggle the leaf, Deely. Make it move!' She had been only two or three, but she could remember saying that.

'Well, I hope more than any friend, child. You were more like my own child, and you stayed my child, stubborn though you were. And *angry*, sometimes. I remember how excited you were about the Candy Tree. And how furious you got when Prender told you it didn't really exist. You were seven. Lots older than the others were when they found out. Ah, you flew at her with your little fists, hitting and screaming at her that she lied, she lied. You cried for hours.'

Pamra protested. 'But it was *you* told me about the Candy

Tree, Delia. Of course I believed you. You made such a story of it. And sure enough, in the morning the seeds were always there. So good. I can taste them yet. And how hard it was to save even one as "seed" for the next year's tree! I tried so hard to stay awake and see the tree grow, even though you said it wouldn't grow at all if I did. And then Prender . . . well, I didn't like her much anyhow, and she was calling you a liar.'

'Oh, child. Now, you know that isn't true. It wasn't a lie. It was just a kind of story. A pious myth. To make children behave well. And they get such fun out of it.'

'Well, I got more fun out of the myth than I ever did eating the candy after I knew you had put it there. Especially since it was Prender who told me.'

'Prender wasn't supposed to tell you. She was supposed to let you believe as long as you could. We always let the little ones believe as long as they can; they get such pleasure out of it. She probably wouldn't have told you if it hadn't been for jealousy in the family. You two didn't get along then and most likely never will. I've told Prender a hundred times, "We eat the crops the workers grow! Why should we turn our backs on the Awakeners?" Ah, well, but you know your oldest sister.'

'I know her well enough.' Pamra was grimly certain about this. 'The whole family. Rejecting me because of what I chose to do.'

'Oh, child. They just doubt sometimes, that's all. Don't you ever doubt? Are you always sure Awakening is for the best?'

'Delia! What do you expect me to say? That's the kind of question Mother would have asked! And you know how everyone felt about that! Of course Awakening is for the best.'

'I know you believe so, child. But lots of people don't, truly. It doesn't make them bad. Perhaps you know something they don't. It's better when all the people know, Pamra. It's better not to be alone.' She sighed. 'I wish you'd forgive your mama, Pammy. What she did wasn't so bad.'

'It was bad enough! Deserting me and Papa that way!'

'She had her reasons, Pammy. She was pregnant, sick, frightened.'

'That's no excuse! How could she give up an eternity of blessedness in Potipur's arms for no more reason than that!'

'Perhaps . . . perhaps because she doubted she'd be Sorted Out, child. We all have our little sins.'

'And Potipur is merciful,' Pamra grated, teeth tight together. 'Delia, stop this. I didn't come here to argue with you!' Remembering, suddenly, why it was she had not come more often. Delia always pressed her for forgiveness. And it always evoked this old guilt. This old pain.

'All right, all right, child. We won't fight over it. I wish you'd forgive her because you'd be happier so. But you won't. And that's that. It doesn't change I-love-you.'

'No,' she said, softening enough to put her arm around the old woman. 'No, Delia. It doesn't change I-love-you.'

They sat beneath the flowering puncon tree, the sky beginning to flush with sunset. 'I'm glad you've come, Pamra. I prayed you would, because your old Delia wants your help to break a rule. Just a little bit.'

Pamra's mouth twitched. Because she could not imagine Delia breaking any rule at all, it took a moment for the enormity of the woman's request to sink in. 'You want to *what*?'

'I want to go back east, to the village I was born in, to see my sister. She's old. I want to see her.'

For a moment she did not believe she had heard. Then she believed and was appalled at the fury of anger that took her. Anger. At Delia. She choked on it. 'By the three, Delia! You want to get us both whipped? Or used? That's no small rule breaking. That's a major infraction – *the* major infraction. No one crosses town lines eastward. No one!'

'Oh, well, child, sometimes people do, you know. They just lie about it a lot. I heard that someone on the other side of Baristown went to Wilforn and stayed for the Conjunction festival and then came back, all in one piece and in his right mind.'

'Don't tell me!' she demanded, feeling her face grow

white and stiff. 'Honestly, Delia. Of all the things I'm sworn to uphold, the direction of life is one of – is *the* most important.'

'Why?'

'What do you mean, why? Because it's Potipur's commandment, that's why. The World River moves west, the moons move west, the sun moves west, we move – all west, in the direction of life. To go east is antilife, against the Three. It's evil, in and of itself! Blasphemous! It's like those foul same-sex lovers who refuse to propagate in accordance with Potipur's will, like those rotten celibates the Laughers keep rooting out. If you want to visit your sister, you'll have to go west to Shabber, and keep on going until you come to it.'

'But it's only to Wilforn,' Delia whispered forlornly. 'Not more than a day or so walk east from here, even for an old woman like me. If I go west, love, I won't live to get there. How long do they figure it takes to come all the way around? Twelve years if you walk, isn't it? Six or seven years on a Riverboat. Something like that? I don't have twelve years, Pammy. Not even six.'

Pamra shook her head angrily. This wasn't fair. Not when she was so tired. Oh, Delia. What could she do? Travelers did go all the way around the world, traveling west, some on boats on the River tide. Some afoot. Pilgrims did it afoot, making Potipur's Round. They carried messages and told kin of kin, and walking it did take about twelve years, more or less, and Delia was right. She couldn't survive such a trip. She fought to be calm, forced herself into quiet.

'Now, let's talk it over. If it's so important you go back, how come you ever left there? You never told me you had a sister there.'

'I came from there when I was about your age, following my curiosity. Oh, Pamra, truth to tell I was following a man. He wanted to see somewhere else. So we came here, and he wanted just to go on and on, but I didn't. I'd had enough of him by then, and your grandma gave me a job doing the garden in this place, and time went by. Your papa was only a child then, and he needed me.

61

'When he was grown, I could have gone on around west until I had come home again, but I delayed and dillied, and by the time I thought of it again, there was you. You, with your mama gone and that family of yours gnawing at you because you looked like her . . .' She fell silent, stroking the little blue birthmark at her jawline. Then she shook herself and went on. 'It's just that lately I've been thinking of my sister. Wanting to see her. Wanting to say, "Well, Miri, how has it been with you?" ' She stood up, clapped her hands as she tried to smile.

'It's not important. Not at all. Not important enough to worry my girl. Now, have another cake. After all, I baked them for my own Pammy.'

She did not speak of it again while Pamra sat in the garden in the glow of evening, smelling the kindly smells of the growing things, hearing the cries of the fishermen on their way home from the long jetties, sitting quiet as the sun fell lower to touch the horizon in blazes of crimson and orange and streaks of crushed berry color, bright and bruised at once. It should have been a time of contentment, of quiet, but too many memories had been jostled awake in Pamra. She kept the calm smile on her face, kept her voice low and peaceful not to distress old Delia, but it was a quiet surface over a turmoil of remembering.

Mama. Lovely as a dream and as fragile. Pretty as a soap bubble, and as useless. What did one remember about her? Softness and singing, sadness and tears, and at last – at last the unforgivable thing.

And Papa. Winning that second mention when he was young, very young, enough to set Grandma talking of his great future as though it were real. But there was no future. No other awards. No other mentions at all for Fulder Don. Not a second, not a fifth. And even that fact was blamed on Mama, somehow made out to be Mama's fault – in turn to become Pamra's fault, who so resembled lovely Mama.

And saintly Delia had been there through it all, the substitute mother, the kindly one, the only one who did not turn away when Pamra made her choice and went to the

Awakeners' Tower. She squeezed Delia's hand now in remembrance of that. If it hadn't been for Delia . . . Well, there must be a way to repay her now, a way to solve this problem.

'Delia, I'm not promising anything, but I'll ask around. Honestly I will. I'll have to sound out a few people, find out who to ask, but maybe there'll be a way we can send a message or something.' She surprised in the old woman's face an expression of longing – no, more passionate than mere longing, a fanatic desire, an impassioned pleading with fear in it. 'Delia, why does it matter so?'

The old woman sighed. 'I wronged her, Pamra. My own sister. I wronged her with him, the one I followed away. He was hers, my sister's man, and he turned from her to me. He told me if he couldn't have me, he would not have her, he'd go to the west without either. And oh, I followed him, foolish as it was, and then did not care enough to follow him farther when he went on. I must ask her to forgive me. *It must be done, Pamra child. It must be done.* Otherwise . . . I may die unforgiven, and it may be Potipur will not take me up. I'm so old, child. There isn't time to do anything but just go to her and ask . . .'

The old woman sat there, head bowed, grieving over a wrong done forty or fifty years ago. Pamra shook her head. Even though it was dangerous for ordinary mortals to die unforgiven, it was silly for Delia to be upset like this.

'If you did a little wrong when you were young, you've made up for it a hundred times since. If there is any person within twelve days' travel who will be Sorted Out to receive Potipur's kiss, it will be you, Delia, so stop this grieving. I'll figure something out for you.'

She felt better for having said it. It was all true. Delia was one of Potipur's own. If reaching Delia's sister was important to the old woman, Pamra would do what she could, and she told Delia so again, and yet again as she left after taking a last breath of the clean garden air.

The water in the ritual cleaning trough was chilled by evening, holding little of the day's warmth as she dipped her hands, sprinkled her face and feet. She leapt away from the trough as black wings swept by, buffeting onto the step where a great flier fixed her with a calculating eye, clacking its huge serrated beak softly together. She leaned against the wall to let her heart stop pounding. It was only one of the Servants of Abricor. They seldom landed on the Tower steps, though they clustered thickly around their aerie on the Tower top and in the bone pits, always silent, never making a sound. She dried her hands on the towel by the door, aware suddenly that the door was open.

'Pamra.' It was Ilze in the doorway. She realized he had been there, watching her. 'Pamra? Come on, you'll miss your meal. Where've you been?'

'I'm sorry, Senior. I've been down in town. Visiting my old Delia. She's half-stuffed me on spice cakes. I'm not really hungry.'

'Spice cakes don't build blood.' He sounded irritated. 'Come on. I've arranged something for you.'

The hall was busy, echoing with feet and the clatter of plates. From the men's refectory there was a bass rumble of voices, a harsh shout of laughter, quickly repressed. The women's tables were half-empty, only a few tardy diners plying their spoons, breaking their bread. Ilze waited with her at the service hatch, then drew her away to an empty table. 'I've got you on recruitment tomorrow.'

'Senior! That's kind of you. I thought my turn on the roster wouldn't come up again for ages.'

'It wouldn't have. But I told the Superior that no one was better at recruiting than you are, that you have a sincerity which is very effective.' There was a moment's odd hesitation in his voice, but then he went on, 'And I told her you'd been bled dry.'

'You told the Superior!' Pamra was momentarily aghast. While some said the lady Kesseret was only human, and a kindly human at that, Pamra could only think of her as a moving presence beneath the shining crown and floating veils, a mystery and a glory. Despite her reputed more than hundred years, her unlined face and clear eyes implied she had already received the Payment. 'Mentor, I heard some-one say once that she's a Holy Sorter. I'm still petrified to go near her.'

Ilze looked at her in that coldly amused way of his, head tilted to one side. 'One needn't go that far,' he said. 'It's enough that she's Superior of this Tower. I told her, also, that if someone didn't do something about Betchery, she'd end up killing someone. The Superior agrees you need light duty, so you do your usual sincere job of recruitment for the next two days, and by then you'll be feeling better.' Actually, it had been the Superior who'd suggested this, but Ilze did not say so. He preferred to let Pamra think he was responsible for the favor.

Pamra chewed thoughtfully, lulled by his informality into an almost social feeling. 'I sort of like recruiting. It's a pain dealing with all the crazy stories they have about us, of course, but I guess I heard the same ones when I was that age.'

'Better you than me, young one. I hate mixing with the damn other-castes. You'd think they'd been touched by Potipur not five minutes before, the way they look and act.' His face was hostile, nostrils pinched.

Pamra shrugged. 'Nobody could be any worse than my father's family was. I just ignore them.'

'Well, you can't ignore them on recruitment duty. You're expected to be reasonably diplomatic, and that's what pisses me off most about it.' He flushed, abruptly aware of his manner, not the appropriate one for a mentor to a junior, certainly. 'Why were you so late?' Now he was her mentor once more, demanding an accounting.

'I shouldn't have been. Except Delia was after me – Senior Ilze. May I not be judged harshly if I ask a question which may be . . . not in accord with doctrine?'

He gave a dramatically astonished look, lifting one eye-brow. 'A question, Pamra? From you? Are the final days upon us?'

She flushed. 'I know I don't ask many. I wouldn't ask this one, either, except for old Delia. She came from the next town east, Wilforn, many years ago. She has a sister there, or thinks she does. She'd be a very old woman . . .'

'And Delia wants to go east to see her sister?'

Pamra nodded, relieved not to have had to say it. 'She says some do.'

Ilze nodded. 'It's quite true. If you asked an occasional question, you'd have known it. It's common talk.'

'Where? How? There are guards! There's a fence!'

'Through the workers' pit at night. They go in there and sneak up the other side of the pit where there's no fence.'

Pamra's face wrinkled in concentration. At the other side of the pit, marked by a burning lantern, was the Sorting place. Surely . . . 'But they might encounter the Sorters on the Sorting ground! That's sacrilege!'

He paused, eyebrows drawn together almost as though she had angered him. He seemed about to say something, then changed his mind. 'I've answered your question, Pamra.'

'That's the only way?' She was disappointed. 'Isn't there some way to send a message?'

'That's much easier. You go to the east gate and pay one of the gate guards on the Wilforn side of the fence to take the message into his town, and you tell him you'll pay him that much again to bring you an answer. That's not really licit, but it's not heretical, either. It's quite common. Even if it's reported, it would only count a day's duty against you. The gate guards might abuse an old woman, but they will not trouble an Awakener. You can tell your old nursemaid that after recruitment tomorrow.'

But she could not wait until then. She went early in the morning, moved by an urgency she did not try to identify, to explain how a message could be sent.

To which Delia nodded, frowning a little vacant frown, as though this was not what she had wanted at all, as though this new suggestion had come between her and the comfort of some long decided action with which she had reassured herself in time of pain.

'Just get the message written, Delia. Exactly what you

want to say, just as you'd like to say it to your sister – Miri, wasn't it? – and I'll take it to the border either tonight or tomorrow. Tonight, if I can. Much better to do that than go sneaking off through the worker pits in the dead of night. That's not something I want you to do. I'll be back as soon as I can, and you have it ready.' And she went off, late already, looking over her shoulder to catch that same expression of stubborn puzzlement, which she saw with a catch in her throat, wondering if she could not somehow have been more convincing and more hopeful.

But then it was all driven from her mind by the day's work, so different a day from the one before. As she went toward the plaza, she passed the merchants' hall and the gardeners' mart and the guildhalls and artists' council houses, and from each of them representatives were coming out in the customary garb of their professions and guilds, all wandering in the same direction. They took no notice of her, or she of them, but each one of them had to give way when she came by, and she knew it ate into them like acid. 'Scoff and sneer,' she murmured to herself, 'but stand aside when I come by, other-caste.'

At the plaza each representative went off to his own booth, there to spend the day in earnest conversation with the casteless youths who were not yet fastened into any way of life. For her there would be the usual curiosity seekers and those who came on a dare. And among them might be the one or two she would recruit, though they had often not intended it when they came. It was true that Pamra could recruit better than any of the senior grade. Perhaps because she was not much older than the young people she talked to. Perhaps because she cared more about it. Though Ilze was a stickler for duty, sometimes he seemed almost to mock the Tower and the law. Almost as though it were no better than law mongering, or body fixing, or garbage shifting, some low-caste activity that no one would bother with if they could do something better. Occasionally Pamra wondered if any of the high-grade Awakeners took it seriously, though of course they must! The religious glory, the ecstasy, would only come if one were serious. How could they remain in the work otherwise?

And it was the ecstasy she talked about with the recruits. By midmorning she had collected a small group – two gigglers and one swaggering boy with a perpetual sneer. There was also a narrow-chested, fire-eyed youth who glared at her as though she guarded the gate to a treasure he sought. She could almost feel the spear of his glance skewering her, as though he feared she might oppose him rather than help him!

'Do you remember when you were children,' she began, 'at the time of Conjunction, at festival time, when the Candy Tree grew in your bedrooms at night?' She smiled at them, and they back, unable not to smile, even the gigglers and the swaggering one, though he covered the smile with a sneer pretending mockery. 'When you awakened in the morning, the evidence of the tree was there, on your bedcovers, sweet and marvelous.

'Later, of course, you learned that it was your kin who put the candy there, and you believed the story of the Candy Tree must be false, a simple myth for little children. You did not realize that there was a greater truth – that the Candy Tree did indeed grow on the night of festival, not in your bedroom alone, but over all the land of Baris, to drop its festival spirit into the hearts of everyone. If you looked into their faces, your mothers and fathers, you would have seen that festival spirit blooming.' Her voice began to sing, she herself began to sway. Her exhilaration in what she said began to catch them, and herself. She felt the blood rising into her face and knew she was beautiful to them.

'There is indeed a Candy Tree, though it is a more complicated concept than children know. And just as the sweetness spread upon your bedcovers is the physical evidence of the spiritual tree, so the existence of the Awakeners is the Northshorely evidence of a greater mystery, the love of Potipur. It is true that we Awakeners raise up those who come to us from the east to provide a service they failed to provide in life. It is equally true that we carry the dead of

Baristown to the place of Sorting, west of here. There the good and righteous, their faces shining with the radiance of a life well spent, are Sorted Out by the Holy Sorters to be dressed in silk and placed in the arms of Potipur. We know this. We can testify to it. We are the evidence of it, the evidence of the love of Potipur, and Abricor, and Viranel.

'Because we know this wonderful thing of our own experience, we believe we are more likely to live in accordance with Potipur's will, more likely to be Sorted Out at the end.' Pamra swept over this point quickly. She was sure. She wouldn't lie, not to recruits. It wouldn't be fair. But she didn't really know whether all Awakeners had the radiance in their faces. All Baris's dead were collected at the Tower for transport to the place of Sorting, and though Pamra had been on duty in the death room several times, there had never been the body of an Awakener there.

She took a deep breath and went on, 'Other castes denigrate us, it is true, calling us names and making jokes about our caste. When I was a child I thought this was because of something atrocious or dirty about Awakeners. I came to know that it is simple fear. The other castes know they will come into our hands, and they are afraid. That is all.' She looked firmly into the eyes of the gigglers, of the sneerer, and found there the fear she sought. 'Just as you are fearful now. Perhaps you worry that the Awakeners somehow can decide whether one is Sorted Out or not. I tell you we cannot control it, but without us it would not happen. Your fear, however, is a key which may open the door of our Tower. If you fear us, join us and conquer your fear. Learn the truth of what we say.' The rapture was seething within her now, as it did on the steps of the Tower at morning dedication, or sometimes during prayer, or when she had gone long without food, or during these sessions of preaching to the youth of Baris.

She felt herself smiling, felt the radiance of it, knew that her face was glowing as she did it. This was her heritage from pretty Mama, this smile, and her gift from Potipur. The gigglers had stopped their fidgeting, the sneerer his facial contortions. She might not have them as applicants, but they would not mock for a time. The other one, the pale-faced youth who had fastened himself upon her words as a baby upon the breast – him she had.

'Will you show me?' he begged. 'Show me the Tower?'

She took his hand, letting the others go with an expression of tender regret. They would remember what she had said. 'Remember the Tower with your gifts,' she whispered to them as she turned away. They would make gifts in the future, certainly they would when they were old. None of her effort was wasted. She sighed, feeling the rapture fade. Until next time.

She took the youth to the Tower, as she had taken others. So precious they were. Young, full of idealism and wonder. She could not resist them, or they her. From a great distance, the lookout had seen her coming, and when the door opened the Superior stood there in all her robes with the entourage around her. 'Come,' said Pamra, giving the youth her hand once more. 'Come into the Tower.' Then he was welcomed with wine and praise and flattery and a very late night, as she had been in her time.

She hadn't known what it really meant then, no more than he did now: the bloodletting, the endless hours in chapel without sleep during those first years, the constant repetition of litany. She had only seen the robes and the glittering staffs, the solemn figures at the forefront of any procession, only heard the whispers concerning the Payment of Life. The rest – the rest hadn't been mentioned. She had been only twelve when she'd said, 'I can be an Awakener . . .' Said it out of bravado and hurt and in ignorance, only to have the rapture become her reason for living.

She woke late. An officious senior caught her lingering at her ceremony upon the steps and sent her with two or three others onto the wastelands north of the Tower to gather Tears of Viranel. So, she had lost the second day's recruiting by her own inattention to duty. 'My own sin,' she'd told the Three in a whisper. 'My own sin. Forgive.'

The Tears were so small as to be almost invisible against

the stones, transparent, drop-shaped, attached to the soil from which they grew by a glassy, hairlike root. They grew thickly but in widely scattered patches, each patch marked by a tall, skull-topped pole. Impossible to transplant, fruiting only during second summer. Tears grew throughout the lands of Northshore, when and where they would, and the skull poles warned away the unwary. Of late, the patches of fungus had been even more scattered, more difficult to find, almost as though something had been rooting them out. This was an unholy thought, and Pamra made a religious gesture, ashamed of herself.

Gathering was hard, back-bending work that made bones and muscles ache. The Tears had to be scooped into baskets without touching them. The sun was hot, the dust sticky, provoking an unending damp itch that distracted and annoyed. Attention could not be allowed to waver. There were many cautionary stories about those who had touched the Tears accidentally, only to feel the tiny fungi passing through the skin in an instant of fatal error for which there was no cure. Those who touched the Tears were possessed at once by Viranel. Those possessed by Viranel were living workers. Unlike the dead, they were able to speak, for a time. Like the newly dead, they knew what they were and felt the agony of possession.

It was only as she returned to the Tower, her basket full, that she remembered what she had promised Delia. The sun bulged upon the horizon like a single oozing drop before she came to the garden and the little house to find both empty.

The note was there on the table, half-written, scratched and erased, tried again and again. The words fumbled, crawled like crippled fliers on the page. 'Miri, forgive . . .' 'I did not know . . .' 'Only now, in my age, Miri . . .'

Pamra heard her own words in the silent room as though someone had spoken. 'Much better than to go sneaking off through the worker pits in the dead of night,' she had said. 'Sneaking off through the worker pits . . .' Cursing herself that she had not kept her word, that she had not even guarded her tongue.

So. Delia had gone. There was not even a chance to say good-bye. The house did not feel of parting. It welcomed, even now, even empty. In the kitchen the pots shone in the level rays of the sun. Pamra ran her hand over them, smooth and cool, as she had used to do when drying them for the old woman. Spice cakes filled a covered jar. Dried fruit rested upon the sill. High in the rafters bunches of herbs hung like autumn brought home, smelling of the fields. In a cupboard her own child's apron was folded away where she had left it the day they took her to the Tower. She felt it now, shaking out the sweet-smelling buds that lay in its folds. 'Delia, ah, Delia. Why didn't you wait?' knowing as she whined into the silence that it was her own fault, her own. And at the end, as the sun darkened in startled ambers and bruised purple and the kitchen room settled into a quiet she remembered from childhood, all she could say was what Delia had said to her then, time after time: *'Rejoice. May the Sorters protect you and bring you to Potipur's arms.'*

She skulked out late that night, a shadow in her robe, striding to the hill overlooking the pit where the little light burned to guide the Sorters, where all were forbidden to be after nightfall. She sat there, invisible. It was no good. Delia, if she had gone this way, had gone long since. It was too late to do anything about it. Against the stars, she could see the wings of the great fliers, moving in and out of the bone pits, seeming to peer down into the worker pits. What was the sound she heard? A croaking murmur? As though someone had spoken? A chill went through her. If she sat here until the Holy Sorters came to bring those who had not been Sorted Out, they would turn her to stone for her presumption, and it would still be too late to do anything for Delia. Suddenly fearful for herself, she turned back, sneaking into the Tower as silently as she had left it.

Each evening thereafter she took herself to the Tower by way of Delia's house, hoping that the old woman had returned. On the third day she found her half sister, Prender, sitting in the silent room, dusty now and beginning to smell of disuse and damp, weeping over the scribbled note. Pamra had not seen her for years. The face raised to her was familiar and strange at once, familiar in its outline, in the well-known quirk of the lips, the expression she had so often interpreted as a sneer, but strange in its softness, in the lines above the eyes, around the mouth, lines of pain. 'Gone,' her sister said. 'Pammy. She's gone.'

'I know. She went east. Crossed the line. I was going to help her, but I was late . . .' The words came out without planning, naturally, even kindly. They might have been children again, before any terrible things had been said or done to be forever remembered.

'Delia. Oh.' Prender's weeping went on. 'She was always there. When Grandma was having those rages of hers, when Papa shut himself up and wouldn't talk to anyone – I'd come here to Delia. It was Grandma's house, you know. She didn't like it, here so near the edge of town. She put Delia in it, just to keep it. It was all bare then. No garden. But Delia . . . Delia . . .'

Without knowing how she had come there, Pamra found herself at her sister's side, stroking her hand as she had not done since they were children. 'I know.'

'Delia said we treated you badly. We did, you know. It was Grandma. You looked too much like your mother, and she said we were Papa's girls, but you – you were your mama's girl. And then when your mama . . . when she did it, Grandma was just hateful about it. I know you became an Awakener just to make it up. Just to prove you had faith, even if your mama . . . I used to hate you, Pammy, for that. I don't anymore. You need to know that. Papa's gone. They're all gone but me. I don't want to be like Delia, unforgiven by my own kin. Forgive me, please. Please.'

Musley gone? Papa gone? Not to see her reach senior grade? Not to know what she had become. She choked with surprised tears. 'I forgive you. Really. I do.' Saying it, astonished to find that it was true.

She was even more astonished afterward to find that nothing had changed. There had been an hour or so when they had been friends, a transient solidarity of grief that gave way almost at once to old habits. For a few days Pamra went to the house in the evenings to hear if there were any news of Delia, but other people began to frequent the place now that Prender was there, and the stiff discomfort of these encounters drove Pamra away. Even Prender could not keep herself from suggesting that Pamra leave the Tower, give up her life, return to them in some more acceptable form and manner.

'There's no reason anymore, Pammy! You could come live with me!'

As though Pamra's oath were nothing!

Pamra could preach the rapture to strangers, but she could not bring herself to discuss it with Prender, to defile it by letting Prender mock at it as she would, setting it to nothing. She nodded, said nothing, went away as soon as she could, and did not return.

Nothing had changed except that for a time the rapture failed her. It seemed to fail others, also, and there was much use of the whipping post in the courtyard. More than once she looked down to see Ilze plying the long whip on some crouched, tortured junior and gave thanks through dry lips that she found compliance easy. He had never whipped her, though she had never doubted he would if she did not keep her oath. If it were not for that, perhaps she could have heard Prender's words, but it was too late for such words now.

The weather grew windy and harsh. Summer robes were laid away and the winter ones taken from the chests. The moons were moving toward a winter Conjunction – there had not been a winter Conjunction for twenty-two years, not since the year she was born – and the festival season began to fizz on the horizon of her time like something boiling in an adjacent room, a small excitement, a new possibility, the end of another holy year.

'You've been selected,' Jelane announced at evening meal, grinning as the bearer of bad news. 'Tomorrow you get to fetch the first load of wood for winter!'

'Oh, Jelane! No. Why me? I hate that trip. The forest is

all dim and murky. It takes forever to get there with the wagon. The workers are no good with axes, half the time they cut themselves to pieces and the wagon comes back full of worker parts instead of wood . . .'

Jelane made a moue. 'Politics, junior Awakener. Some of us play and get out of things. Some of you don't play and so you get to go for wood.'

It wasn't fair. Pamra conducted herself strictly by the rules, and the favors went to those who broke them. She shut her mouth in a grim line and said nothing. When Pamra became senior, she told herself, Jelane could expect an accounting.

The forest trip required an early start. It was scarce dawn yet, half-dark still, and the first worker lay under her hand, blood trickling between its lax lips before she saw the blue, leaf-shaped mark upon its jaw.

Her hand moved to raise the hood before she could stop herself.

In the instant she had known what would be there. Delia's eyes, full of knowledge and terrible awareness, staring into her own.

She dropped the hood to stand frozen in position, one hand still holding the dripping flask. A voice that she could not hear, could only feel, screamed inside her, '*Strangers. You're supposed to be a stranger! Always strangers. No one we know. Not our family, our friends, our people. Others. Sinners. People from the east. People who are being punished for the sins and omissions of their lives . . . Oh, shame! Shame Potipur that he did not take you. Shame Sorters that . . . that . . . that . . .*' But as her voice screamed mindlessly, her eyes saw the little lantern at the eastern lip of the pit and knew it for what it was, knew it for what it had always been – the light to guide the Awakeners from the town to the east to the place they might leave their dead.

There was no Holy Ground.

There were no Holy Sorters.

If either of those things had existed, then Delia would

not be here. Delia was here, therefore they did not exist.

'Delia!' Her throat bled at the rasping agony of her own cry. A great cloud of black wings rose from the bone pits to circle above her, looking down, aware of her.

'Delia,' sobbing, knowing finally why it was the people scorned the Awakeners, lived by them and hated them. Before her the canvas-covered shape rose up to confront her. Despite the heavy veil, she knew that it saw her still. 'A lie,' she whispered, wanting that shape to know that she, Pamra, had been lied to no less than any; used and betrayed no less than they; knowing as she whispered that all the truth had been there for her to read, all the lies open, all her life long, as they had been open and easy to read for children when they woke to find candy on the bed. 'A lie,' she said once more, hopelessly, disbelieving it. Not even a pious myth. Merely a blasphemy.

She could not bear the blank canvas of the hood. She could not bear what lay behind it. She turned to flee, only to turn again. If she left, another Awakener would come to begin the long punishment, the seasons of unending labor while the flesh reawakened by the Tears of Viranel diminished slowly through an eternity of time and the rotting brain within the corrupted flesh counted each hour, each day, until time could be laid down forever in the bone pits to be eaten by the fliers.

And then a calm came, a calm more terrible in its cold quiet than the frantic horror that had gone before. She went down into the pit and raised up all the workers who were there, a small pitful. Thirty-five or forty, perhaps. She led them away, chanting them along the road, her mirrored staff casting a glittering warning before her in the rays of cold sun. 'Rejoice,' she gargled. 'Work awaits you.' Her voice was a mockery. 'Work awaits you.'

It was very early. No one saw her go. She led the workers away from the city, away from the Tower, north into the forested lands where they could not be seen, then farther still, farther than she had ever gone before among the endless trees of the roadless wilderness, using the blood and Tears for distance only, not for labor. She went in wild ways, guided only by the pale sun, leading a tangled, shambling line that stumbled in its witless wandering through the day, into the evening, into violet dusk. She found a chasm at last, a rocky place, deep and solidly ranked about with high-piled edges of balanced stone. The workers had begun to stumble, but she had driven them on with the last few drops in her flask and then by her voice alone, a harsh cawing, like one of the carrion fliers. She led them onto the sparse brush and hard stone of the chasm, and there she let them drop. There she let Delia fall as well.

When she raised the hood, Delia's eyelids lifted to give her one look of terrible intelligence before they closed once more. Pamra told herself it had been the final look, the last awareness.

'It's over,' she whispered. 'Over. Done. Soon the dark. Soon the silence. The forgiving silence. Soon the true peace, Delia. Delia. Forgive me.'

Then dark surrounded them, the sound of night fliers, the rustle of small living things, the dim ghostlight of Abricor, the silver radiance of Viranel, the red looming power of Potipur, gathered together to stare down at her as she stared up, daring them to strike at her. In their light she raised the hoods, leaving them up to see whether any still looked at her or whether they were only dead. She could not tell, for the moonlight shifted and threw strange shadows on the faces. From the top of the chasm wall she levered the loose rimrock until it tumbled in a thundering avalanche across them, a growl of stone that piled above the pathetic bodies and shook the silent fabric of the wilderness.

It ended in a shivering cascade of gravel, a roil of dust that hung for long moments in the still evening, moving as though it were sentient. She dropped onto the rimrock, choking on the dirty air.

Where had the stubborn naiveté come from that had kept her enthralled with myth long after those around her knew the truth? Where had her blindness come from? Had it been willful? A way of getting even with them all?

Slowly, so slowly that she did not know if she truly saw it

or only imagined it, a line of fliers moved across the face of Potipur toward her, bent and moved as though a lip had moved upon that face, mouthing a word. Was it 'Go'? Or perhaps 'Good'? Or 'God'? Fliers. Investigating the sound of the falling stone.

'A lie,' she said defiantly. It made no difference what the Servants of Abricor said. It was all a lie.

She broke her mirrored staff and threw the shattered pieces into the pit. Her hands went to her hair to remove the identifying braids. When it hung loose as any market-woman's locks, she remembered she had never seen an Awakener die. Had never seen one dead. Perhaps there had been many come beneath her hands, their hair unbraided hidden behind the canvas hoods.

After a time she climbed down from the high rimwall and began to walk through the dark trees into the west. She would pass through the workers' pit on the westward boundary and come to Shabber.

What would she do then? Tend garden, as Delia had done? Go westward farther still?

Or stay in one careful place, close to the River, so that in good time she could seek her own end in deep water as gentle, fearful Mother had done. Seek the long pier's end deep in the lonely night as Mother had done. As Mother had done, so that no amount of fishing could bring her forth again. No amount of dragging bring her to answer to Potipur for her sin in not trusting to the Holy Sorters to Sort it all out.

Wise in her weakness; better able to face the truth than Pamra herself.

Behind her the dust settled. Hands moved feebly beneath the rocks. Through chinks in the stones, eyes stared upward at the red light of Potipur.

Out of the night the black wings settled upon the stones. Great fliers walked here and there, thrusting the rocks aside with monstrous beaks and talons.

'Rejoice,' a croaking voice chuckled softly, almost inaudibly. 'The Sorters are here.'

6

Ilze had spent the day inspecting the plowing of pamet fields northwest of Baristown, a vast stretch of fertile soil that lay between two slightly raised banks, as though at some time a side channel of the World River had run there, depositing its sediment over centuries. The inspection was perfunctory, more a matter of ritual than actuality. Pamet did very well when scattered on unplowed ground. The uneven scoring of the soil by a crew of stumbling workers neither helped nor hindered the crop. Nonetheless, the workers had to be kept moving if the Tears were to permeate all the flesh, growing throughout it, reducing it in volume by at least half and making it suitable for the Servants of Abricor to eat. Worker flesh was all that they ate. Presumably Abricor had destined the fliers for the purpose of eating workers, or workers for the purpose of feeding fliers – though Ilze regarded this idea cynically. In his opinion, fliers were outrageously ugly, and they stank.

Also, junior Awakeners had to be kept busy. All juniors – like the populace at large – were supposed to believe that the labor provided by worker crews was necessary. They were supposed to believe it until officially told otherwise during senior retreat. Most of them did believe it, or pretended to. Therefore he stalked across the field, a solemn junior trailing behind as he commented aloud on rows that were uneven or corners that were scamped, twitching his whip suggestively from time to time to enjoy her shudder.

He lunched in Baris in a small cafe where he went from time to time and was a familiar-enough figure that the tables did not automatically empty as soon as he entered. Townsmen had a way of sniffing the air when Awakeners entered a shop or tavern, sniffing ostentatiously, then moving away, perhaps leaving the place. Ilze had known since childhood that Awakeners didn't smell. Still, the rudeness rankled, and he went to the town tavern from time to time to exercise his fury. They did not dare press too far, and Ilze was readier than most to make them pay for each jot of license. The Superior of the Tower occasionally ordered a conscription of townspeople. One or two, usually, for some mysterious purpose of her own. Each time Ilze was sent on that errand, he had certain individuals in mind.

A singer enlivened the hour at the cafe. Perched in a shadowy corner, the boy's voice crept over the conversation, into the pauses, into the hesitations.

'Devious as fire,
Ubiquitous as care,
Cruel as the flame-bird's byre
And the waiting air,
Your love encompassed me
And left me dying there.'

Ilze smiled. It was a kind of love he recognized, his own particular kind. He knew the singer's voice very well but had no intention of recognizing him. That was over. Superficially enjoyable, slightly dangerous, and over.

'High as the flier soars,
To Abricor's breast,
From such height I fell
Onto my nest,
To burn, to burn, to die,
Like all the rest.'

Ilze snorted. Why was it they all thought reproaches gained anything? He fingered in his purse for the smallest coin possible, summoning a servitor. 'Give this to the singer.' He smiled. 'Tell him his song is pretty, but boring.'

He stayed to see the message delivered, delighting in the

80

bonelike pallor that suffused the boy's face and the tears swimming in his eyes. Stupid. He would end as a living worker, a felonious boy-lover brought to justice. Ilze considered turning him in. No. Not yet. Perhaps later, when he needed amusement.

The boy picked at his instrument, sang again, sadly:

'When we are sunk so deep
in madness' sleep
Who, who shall be our Awakeners? . . .'

After lunch there was pretty little Seesa, the fish merchant's wife. The fish merchant had been one of those who moved away in a tavern while making some ostentatious statement about the odor in the place. He and his wife had since learned how dangerous such an impudence could be. Now they took no license with Ilze whatsoever, though the lesson had taken them some time to learn – an interesting time for Ilze. Seesa's submissiveness bored him now. Soon he would find another woman or another boy. What he needed he could not find among colleagues in the Tower – that is, not yet. When Pamra came to senior status, perhaps then. With her naiveté she would not know she was allowed to refuse him. Until she learned that, perhaps he could enjoy her. In anticipation of that day, he had never whipped her, though the thought of her body tied to the stake made him grunt explosively at odd times, his penis twitching in spasms almost like orgasm.

He returned to the Tower very late. There were no juniors at the trough, none who had been with the workers enough to need the cold ritual bath, and it was not required of seniors. He passed it by, humming, not dissatisfied with the day, a little puzzled at the unusual buzz of conversation in the junior dining hall, the air of mystery. The puzzlement gave way to amazement and then to baffled anger as he learned that Pamra seemed to be involved in some strange occurrence. Pamra! Obedient as any dog from the first day, with only that dazzling beauty to make him hold his hand! Never even whipped, and now this?

81

No one seemed to know what had happened. She had not returned from the forest, and the worker pit was empty. No one had known about the workers until late in the day. Each Awakener had assumed that other juniors, rising earlier, had taken what workers there were. There were shortages from time to time when the people of Wilforn obstinately refused to die. Or, as Pamra would have said, 'when most of those who died were good ones who were Sorted Out.' Ilze snorted, remembering, a slow, hot anger beginning to build in him. It was very late, unexplainably late, and she had not returned. No one had seen her.

By morning it was assumed Pamra and the missing workers were connected. There were only half a dozen new workers in the pit, scarcely enough to keep one Awakener busy. The work at the Tower would be disrupted for weeks. There was a feeling of unease in the place, a whispered buzz of conjecture and secretive hissing of words like heresy and conspiracy. The day wore slowly on, and the Superior did not put in an appearance.

Ilze received the message at the evening meal. It was delivered by the Superior's own servant, veiled, silent Threnot, she who spoke no word except what she was told to say by the Superior. 'Now?' asked Ilze. Threnot gestured toward the stairs. He laid his napkin down and followed her, feeling a twitch of fear, an uncustomary emotion, one he did not like.

They stood outside the heavy door at the head of the stairs, waiting for a response to Threnot's tapping. Though he had spoken often with the Superior in her office on the ground floor of the Tower, Ilze had been summoned to the Superior's personal rooms only three times before. Once to receive senior status from her hands. Once to be commended for zeal in recruitment. Once to be assigned the supervision of a clutch of juniors, Pamra among them. He knew this summoning had to do with Pamra. It had to be. He wet dry lips and entered behind Threnot, eyes downcast in appropriate humility before the throne. The Superior wasn't alone, but he would not risk looking up to see who else was there.

'Ilze.'

He bowed deeply, waiting.

'One of your juniors has disappeared.'

'So I heard this evening, Your Patience.'

'The one in which you found such amusement.'

'Amusement, Superior? I'm sorry, I—'

'At her naiveté. So I am told. You were most amused at Pamra, a true believer. Such is the gossip among the seniors. Never mind, I have been amused at naiveté in my time. I am told the old woman who reared her went east.'

'I was not told so, Superior.' The other figure in the room shifted impatiently from foot to foot. Ilze wished he could look up. There was a strong musty smell in the room, like a wet pillow. And something in the Superior's voice that rubbed upon his ears, knifelike.

'I was told so. Pamra had been unlike herself recently. She was seen making frequent trips to the house where the old woman had lived. I sent Threnot to find out why. Threnot found a sister living there. Prender, her name was. She told my servant that the old woman had gone east. Pamra, it seems, was deeply grieved.'

'I didn't know.' Ilze was puzzled. It would not have been his job to follow Pamra or inquire about her, unless the girl's work had suffered. Why this note of accusation in the Superior's voice?

'Since Pamra was naive enough to cause you amusement, Ilze, would it not have been prudent to watch her? Just in the event the old woman showed up in the pits?' There was a tone in the Superior's voice he did not recognize, one he had never heard before.

'It would have been, certainly, Superior. Had I known the old woman was gone . . .'

'Perhaps if you had paid less attention to Pamra's body and more to her emotions, you would have known?' The Superior sighed, and Ilze dared look up, just for a moment. The other figure was a flier. A Servant of Abricor. He

83

dropped his eyes, gulping. Here. In the Superior's own rooms. A Servant. Nausea roiled in him. He had not known this was possible.

'Have you heard of Rivermen, Ilze?'

For a moment he could not hear her voice, could not understand her words. Rivermen. What was she talking about? 'Yes, of course, Superior. Those who bring cargoes on the boats . . .' Suddenly he knew what it was in her voice that so cut at him. Fear. Nothing but fear.

'No. Rivermen have nothing to do with boats. Rivermen are members of an heretical sect who place their dead in the River. They do not trust in the Holy Sorters. A cult of apostates, Ilze. Had you heard that Pamra's mother was a Riverman?'

'I knew she was a madwoman, Your Patience. A sick woman. A heretic, if you like. I had never heard she was a member of any cult.' He gulped, heard only the silence, went on. 'The initiation master told me Pamra was deeply shamed by her mother's behavior. It was probably her mother's heresy which brought Pamra to the Tower in the first place. Her dedication had some redemptive quality to it. So he said.'

'So I thought. So you thought . . . perhaps. But now she is gone, with a pitful of workers. And the . . . Talkers have sent for you, Ilze. And me. They have questions about our orthodoxy.'

Talkers? In this context the word didn't make sense. He opened his mouth to ask – to ask anything that would help him out of this confusion . . .

'I think you had best let me speak with him for a moment alone,' she said to the Servant of Abricor, her voice wheedling and groveling. 'He is totally ignorant of your existence. As naive, in his way, as Pamra was in hers.'

'And did you find this amusing?' croaked a strange voice, not a human voice, though using human words. 'Was he amusing to you?'

'No. He knew as much as any senior. Seniors are not privy to the decisions of the Chancery, Uplifted One. May I appeal in the name of the Protector?'

'The Talons do not recognize the Protector.'

'Surely you jest, Winged One.' There was a note of desperation in her voice. 'Your treaty is with the Protector, and through him with the Chancery and with the Towers. How can you have a treaty with an office you do not recognize?'

Ilze had heard the Superior's voice for years, leading the observances, reciting the litany, directing, assigning. He had never heard it as it sounded now, tight as a harp string, aching with strain, almost with panic.

'We do not recognize the Protector in this instance, human. Still, we do not desire further disruption of your duties. I will give you not long,' the inhuman voice croaked again. 'Other Talkers await you on the aerie. You will not attempt escape.' There were sounds, wings, clacking of beak, a harsh scrape of talons upon the floor.

'Ilze?'

He breathed deeply, trying not to vomit. 'Superior.'

'You must help me in this, Ilze. I am depending upon your strong sense of self-preservation.'

'What was it?' he grated, furious at himself for this loss of control.

'A Talker. A leader among the Servants of Abricor. One of their Superiors, I suppose you could say. Though this one seems rather higher in rank among its people than I consider myself among mine.'

'Talking?'

'They talk, yes. Though not to us. Never to us. This is the first time I have heard one talk. I have been told that only a few of the Servants can talk. The ordinary fliers do not. Only these, these others. Or perhaps only these are allowed to talk. That also is possible.'

'What does it want?'

'It expects to take us to one of the Talons. The closest one is east of here in a tall mountain range near the Straits of Shfor. The Talons are where their leaders live, as the Chancery is where our leaders live. They want to take us for questioning.' Where I cannot go, she thought. Where I must not be taken. For they will certainly learn what I know, in time, and I know too much. 'They want to take you, Ilze. And me, me as well. This is not the way it should happen, Ilze. Listen now. In the northlands, the Protector of Man dwells with his people, his retinue, the officers of the Chancery. You know of the Protector. You have seen him.'

'During the Progressions. Of course. I saw the golden ship. Everyone does. The last Progression was years ago.'

'So long ago that the next Progression is almost due. Once each eighteen years the Protector makes the trip, taking six or seven years to visit Northshore, allowing himself to be seen at every township. You have seen him!'

'I've seen him.' He was sharply attentive. Why was she telling him this? 'All citizens are required to observe the Progression.'

'I remind you of that so you will remember it. The Protector exists. He lives in the northland. He heads the Chancery. He is my Superior, as I am yours. I work at his command.' She reached for the man before her, reached into him. By all the gods, this unworthy tool must bend to her purpose – for all their sakes.

'I understand.' He did not understand, though his hard, clever mind was beginning to chill, beginning to listen attentively. He had accepted that his life might depend upon that. She smiled at him approvingly.

'There is a treaty between the Protector and the Servants of Abricor. It is the treaty which prohibits the Servants from . . . from troubling us. It prohibits our troubling them as well. If the Servants are troubled by men, the treaty requires them to report to the Chancery. This Rivermen business, this heresy . . . if there is something like that going on, *if they think we have something to do with it, we should be summoned by the Chancery, not by the Servants themselves. Do you understand that?*' She was begging him, and for the first time he came out of his own bewilderment to hear her. He thought she was frightened for herself, and this focused his attention.

'I . . . yes. Yes. If this Servant is disturbed by something we've done, something it thinks we've done, it should have gone to the Chancery about it. And they would have questioned us.'

'Yes. Exactly. And our one chance of coming out of this alive is to get to the Chancery. Not go with this one to the Talons. We go to the Talons and we're dead.'

He did not ask her how she knew. It did not seem to matter. His heart was drumming, and he felt the blood rush to his fingers, making them tingle. 'Can we escape from the Tower?'

'They will see us. They see well at night, and there are dozens of them.'

There were dozens, of course. All around the Tower top, the bone pits, here and there in the forests. Ilze himself had counted up to twenty of them in the air over Baris at one time, as many over the neighboring towns. 'Stay inside where they can't get at us? Send a messenger? Ask for help?'

'We could not live locked inside the Tower that long. The Chancery is half a year away, through the Teeth of the North by way of the Split River Pass. It is how the Protector comes down to make the Progression. By the Split River. We could walk there in a year or two if we stopped for nothing.'

'And the Talons?'

'Not so far. East instead of north.'

'How do they plan to get us there?'

'In a basket, the leader said. In a basket, carried by two or three of them. Through the air. For four or five days. He spoke of flying without stopping. He spoke of a "tailwind." I can guess what that is.'

He had looked at the Talker only briefly, but it had not looked unlike the usual Servants. The long, almost human-looking legs with their feathered, two-taloned feet. The folded wings, tips almost dragging the floor, three-fingered hands of the wrist joined. The face, not long-beaked like the small fliers but flat-beaked, so that in profile it did not look unlike his own except for the absence of a nose. Ear tufts. Wide-set, round-orbed eyes surrounded by plumed

87

circles. The chest, protruding at the center like the keel of a boat. And the neck. Not really long, but it would be stretched out in flight. He thought on that, anger moving him now, a well-known kind of anger. So, they would misuse and mock him, would they? They would break the rules of respect. Well then.

'When you were senior, lady, did you use the whip?' he asked, whispering. 'And have you whips here still?'

When she nodded, he whispered again, and she sped to find the things he suggested. She knew then she had guessed aright in choosing the tool to save her life and in saving that to save more than that. She took a moment to speak to Threnot, dictating a message to be sent to Tharius Don, Propagator of the Faith, at the Chancery, in case they did not arrive there themselves.

'Enough,' croaked a voice from behind her. 'Enough time spent enlightening your lackeys. We will go now.'

'Of course,' said Lady Kesseret of the Tower of Baris, as though she were going for an afternoon walk into the parklands. 'We will go now.'

7

In a monstrous fanged circle halfway between the River and the pole, the Teeth of the North gaped at the swollen sun, their peaks thrust eight miles or more into the glittering sky. Here, driven deep into the frozen stone, were the only mines on this metal-poor planet, icy tunnels plunging into the heart of the towering range, warmed only by the feeble lamps of the slaves who dug the ore, the mines incessant in their demand for new flesh, for few men lived long in these frigid, airless holes.

The wall of the Teeth was riven in only one place. High against the southern light the jagged jaw of Split River Pass snarled at either side of the sky-filled notch, bared now and briefly, before the snows came again. There black rock tumbled from black rock down an ogre's stair to the loess of the slopes and taiga of the plain with the river lunging over it in frantic starts and sorties, like a drunken man-at-arms waked suddenly from dreams of battle.

Within the lofty circle of the mountains stretched an enormous basin, taiga and grassy plains, dotted here and there with a few tens of migratory weehar and thrassil. When the Teeth leaned toward the sun, the lands of the northern basin bloomed and burgeoned toward a hasty harvest. While the people along the River shivered in the chill rains that separated their first and second summers, above the Teeth the sun rolled up from the north around the circle of the sky like a swollen fruit upon the sides of a bowl, never setting, and the Chancery folk walked out of doors in their shirt-sleeves to smell the flowers while the woodsmen piled thick fortresses of firewood along the walls. Axes, axes on the height! Oh, yes, the summer sound in Chancery lands was the crack of the axe and the creak of wagon wheels behind the plodding feet of weehar oxen.

In the winter, when the Teeth turned from the sun after months of lengthening autumn dusk, the long night came down to drown Highstone Lees under a cold cataract of stars. Then the weehar and thrassil dug deep into ice caverns to sleep the three-month night away, and the residents of the Chancery retired to their tunnels and rooms burrowed into the rock below while they made other tunnels into the mighty walls-stacks of wood, carrying it inside load by load, leaving snow-covered, canvas-roofed tunnels behind, widening as the winter went on until the outside walls could be taken in to be burned in the half sun of early summer.

And it was summer yet, though there were few flowers left and evenings brought chill winds to curl at the corners of buildings and rattle the fastenings of windows. The broad leaves of the mime trees in the ceremonial plaza were beginning to roll into tight cylinders, fronds of papery green sheets becoming brushes of fine needles, black as jet. The fountain in the plaza still played, but plaintively, and North Split River rattled a shallow complaint upon its black stones beneath a hundred high-backed bridges. There would be little more melt from the heights to feed it and then no more at all until spring came again.

It was the time some people of the Chancery liked best, after summer's labor and before the cozy hibernation of the snow time. The High Lodge of the Jarb Mendicants preferred the season, the fading sun of autumn, the needling of leaves, the plaint of water. The Mendicants moved abroad to draw into their pores each scant ray of the slowing sun, drug pipes hanging cold in their lax hands, for a time unpossessed by oracular visions. And the Mendicants were not alone in their enjoyment.

To the palace garden, tippy-toe with tiny mandarin steps, sweet as a leaping lamb upon the grass, came the Protector of Man, Lees Obol, in his padded robes, one Jondarite at either arm, half carried, half escorted in his gentle perambulation of the cloisters. Such an old, old man, Lees Obol, beneficiary of the fliers' Payment for almost five hundred years, all the youthful passion spilled away over the centuries to leave this vague contentment in its stead. Not that all that youthful urgency leaked away unremembered and unremarked. At the center of him was an ache sometimes, a feeling of vacancy, as though an essential vessel had been drained, an important room left untenanted. This hollowness echoed occasionally, a dim seashell sound, the susurrus of his blood, perhaps; or a thudding like the boots of armed men come to rob a temple of all its valuables, only to find it empty and the worshippers gone.

So he quivered once in a while, shaking with a memory of passion, knowing he had cared once and unable to think of any reason he should not care now, but too frail to hold the notion for long. So he moved on the strong arms of his guards in the pale sun of polar summer, stopping to sniff at the brilliant northern blooms in the carefully tended gardens, easing through the muslin veils that clouded the doors, flung open now to the sweet airs and the sound of water, when it could be heard over the sound of chopping.

Still, at this noon hour the axes had fallen silent and the fountains could be enjoyed by the Protector of Man, held aloft and protected from harm like a little doll, by the strong arms of his keepers. So he was held up during the last Progression; so he would be held during the next one if the Payment proved efficacious and he lived still longer. Though, said those who performed the functions of the Chancery, there was little enough left now to work with. An occasional spark was all, like the last glow of a fire banked against the morning and left too long without fuel. A fugitive gleam, without heat, consuming itself in the instant.

He stood on the gently curved span that crossed Split River, his old eyes seeking a gleam of golden fishes in the complaining flow. There was no peace in Split River. From the cold white heights it ran north into the Chancery lands, and from those same heights it ran south across the steppes of the Noor, and from there through Ovil-po township to the World River. Once each eighteen years a caravan carried the Protector through the pass and down the other side as far as Ovil-po, where the Progression ship was docked, its gold and gems wrapped against the harsh winds of early first summer. Six or seven years later, the Progression done, he returned to be met by the caravan and taken home to the Chancery, home to the warm familiarity of near five hundred years.

'Looky,' said the Protector, staring up at the distant mountains in senescent surprise. 'The pass is all melted black.'

The uniformed Jondarites shared a conspiratorial glance and suggested it was time for his tea. His acquiescence was no less charming and inconsequential than his participation in the walk. One item of ritual more or less gracefully done. Let us move on, he seemed to say, to the next and then the next.

The next being tea before the soft warmth of a porcelain stove. Cuddled deep in his curtained bed, Lees Obol nodded over his cup. His alcove was just off the main audience hall, its thick, squat walls dwarfed by the lofty barrel vaults above, its rock floor warmed and softened by carpets. Though it was too early for fires, the Protector of Man had a fire. The Jondarites were careful for his comfort, solicitous for his welfare. They would die for him without a moment's question, just as they cared for him day by day, hands busy in his service, knives ready at their belts, eyes watchful. Two of them stood guard outside the alcove now. Two more stoked the tiny stove and closed the curtains. The stove burned only a few pieces of charcoal at a time, but with the alcove curtains closed, it developed a cozy warmth. Stretching in the heat like an old, pained cat, Lees Obol puffed a little sigh and sipped, remembering a sense of sharp discomfort without being able to identify the memory at all. Outside the alcove the Jondarites heard the sigh and remembered it. General Jondrigar would demand an accounting of them. Each sigh, each word, each breath, had to be remembered.

High on a parapet of the household wing, Maintainer of the Household Shavian Bossit peered through a glass into the southern sky. Sun glow filled the wedge of sky that marked Split River Pass, and a flying speck showed black against this fruity shine; a Servant, maybe even a Talker, here inside the Teeth, where no flier of any kind had any business being. Shavian frowned, his mouth making a point-up triangle of concentration. Not merely *a* flier. More than one of them, he told himself as the speck wobbled toward the Chancery lands. Several. Two or three at least. Trouble of some kind coming, and Lees Obol vacant as ever while his people plotted, some against one another, some against the Protector himself. Bossit did not pretend to himself that he was not one of them, even while breathing a quick prayer that Gendra Mitiar and Tharius Don could set their growing enmity aside for a few hours or days, if real danger portended.

'Do you think it's Servants?' he asked the guard, one with younger eyes than his own.

'It looks like it through the glasses, Your Grace. Carrying something. It's a new one on me. I've never seen those fliers carry anything.'

'If you're in attendance when they land, Captain Velt – that is, assuming it does land – remember not to say "flier." The correct title, if there's a Talker, is "Uplifted One." If there's no Talker with them order the bowmen to kill them as soon as they land.'

'I'll remember, sir.' The captain flushed.

'In the meantime, perhaps you'll be good enough to find the Deputy Enforcer and suggest he join me here . . .' He took the glasses back from the guardsman and peered into the wedge of sky once more. At least two Servants of Abricor, flying north of the Teeth in defiance of the treaty, carrying something. 'Hurry, Captain,' he suggested through clenched teeth.

Shavin Bossit was not the only one to have spotted the flier. From a window of his suite high in the library wing, Propagator of the Faith Tharius Don stared through a glass both newer and more powerful than the one used by the Maintainer. After much searching and many trials, he had had it secretly procured from the lens makers in Zebulee, an acquisition not to be displayed but to be kept wrapped in an old sheet in the bottom of his clothes chest. He had had his own watches posted here and there throughout the Chancery. More than one rooftop at Highstone Lees carried his men, one of whom had called his attention to the approaching blot on the sky. When he identified the winged speck as probable Servants of Abricor, he buried the glass beneath his clothes once more and stood gnawing his lip, cold beads of sweat starting out on his forehead and in the edges of his beard. Servants. Possibly one or more Talkers. If a Talker, then certainly one concerned about heresy. It had been all the fliers had wanted to talk about at the recent convocation. Heresy. By the waters of surcease, he was not yet ready for this. Not ready at all. It was too soon. But if he avoided being part of whatever confrontation was about to take place, the others would interpret his absence not to his credit, though they might assign him varying motives depending on who was doing the assigning.

'So long as they do not know my true motives, it should not matter,' he told himself. It was a kind of litany. There had been a time when Tharius Don had cared much for the opinions of others – even of others here in the Chancery. That time was long gone. Now he played the moralist, sometimes the fool, and told himself it did not matter. Wiping the sweat from his forehead, he slipped out onto the stairs. Like it or not, he would have to be obtrusively present – a need with which the Maintainer of the Household might not be entirely sympathetic.

Gendra Mitiar was told about the approaching Talker by a servant sent by Shavian. 'His Grace says to come to the small council room as soon as you can.' The servant bowed.

94

Thin and dried, a woman of great age, her face long since settled into a vertical assemblage like eroded gully walls, her skin the same dun color as the winter fields, Gendra Mitiar stared at the messenger. When she spoke, it was to reveal vast yellow teeth jutting like monuments from her pale gums; flat, inexorable teeth that ground together from time to time, making the sound of millstones. Her voice was like herself, colorless and strong, betraying an unostentatious but terrible will.

'Tell His Grace I will be with him shortly,' she said.

'And may Potipur help us,' she added to herself, grinning in vicious humor. 'For it is certain old Obol won't.'

Shavian Bossit was irritated beyond measure. 'I can understand your annoyance at being . . . ah . . . flown here against your will, Uplifted One. I can appreciate the discomfort of having a whip lashed about your throat in midair and being threatened with strangulation. However, I can also understand the panic felt by our Superior of Baris. Your action was in defiance of the treaty. You admit as much.' He tapped his fingers impatiently, glaring at the Talker standing against the wall. The damn flier would not take tea, would not act like a rational creature, would not sit, though they could and often did. Shavian hated looking up at people, much less fliers, though his diminutive size let him do little else. He ran his fingers through jet-black hair, dyed each ten-day by his mute body servant, and frowned in exasperation. Where in the hell was Gendra!

'I have explained already,' the Talker croaked from a throat not only unaccustomed to human talk but largely unfitted for it by the recent and lengthy half choking he had experienced at Ilze's hands. The flight had taken some days, and the whip had been around his throat for most of that time. 'The treaty does not apply in this instance.'

'You have said so.' Shavian kept his voice carefully without emotion. 'You have not said why.'

'I am not required to do so. I demand you accept my word that such is the case.'

Shavian pondered the possibility of simply sending this creature away. He would never have thought of insulting a Talker, any Talker, when he was younger and the promise of life offered by the Payment had seemed irresistible. Now he toyed with the idea. It was sad to think the wisdom and resolution of age might be only weariness and pain. Effort avoided became pain avoided, and ennui masqueraded as good sense. So he told himself, not speaking any of it aloud. When he spoke again, with every appearance of courtesy, it was to remark in an uninterested voice, 'The treaty does not permit you to demand anything of the kind. I will listen to reasonable talk, flier. I will not listen to bombast, which is what you have given me thus far.' To call a Talker 'flier' was no less an insult than to turn one's back, which Shavian also contemplated doing.

The Talker's beak flushed red, a deep, winey color betokening fury. Shavian regarded this without apology or change of expression. The damn thing had very nearly forced his way into the Protector's bedroom. Potipur knows what old Obol would have made of that! Or what the Jondarites would have done! Killed the Talker, probably. Then they would have had to kill the others to keep the word from getting back to the Talons. Which might not have worked, for other Talkers or mere fliers might have seen these during their long flight toward the Chancery.

Well, it had been a disaster narrowly averted. Shavian had called on a hand of Jondarites to bring the Talker here, to the small council room. So far as the Lord Maintainer was concerned, Talker of the Sixth Degree Sliffisunda of the Talons had received as much courtesy as was due him.

This thought, or some similar sentiment, must have occurred to the angry Talker as well, for in a few moments the furious color faded. When the flier spoke again it was with grudging courtesy.

'We believe these two may be implicated in the Riverman heresy.'

'Indeed? I find that hard to credit. In any case, this suspicion should have been reported at once to the Propagator of the Faith, and he would have sent for them to accuse and ascertain the truth.'

'We did not wish you to send for them. We wanted to question them at the Talons.' The words were clear enough, though it was hard to tell what the intonation was meant to convey.

'So you have said. Still, you have not said why.'

'I will not say,' Sliffisunda's beak flushed again, only slightly this time.

Oh, these Talkers didn't like subordination. High mucky-mucks, all of them, and proud! By Potipur, they're proud. A servant came forward with tea. Shavian took a cup, offering none to the flier. It had refused before; let the refusal stand. When the silence was broken by a rap on the door, he called, 'Enter,' knowing already who was there. The woman and the man who came in wore faces as carefully blank as his own; their bows toward Sliffisunda were sketchy, a bare politeness. The Talker stood against the wall, unmoving, looking them over with unblinking eyes.

'Uplifted One, these are staff members of the Chancery. At the most recent convocation you met the Dame Marshal of the Towers, Gendra Mitiar. The gentleman with the large knife is Bormas Tyle, Deputy Enforcer to Lord Don. Put the knife away, Bormas. The Talker is not threatening us. Yet.'

He beckoned them to the table, offering cups only to them, interrupted in this calculated insult by another tap at the door and the entry of someone he had not sent for.

'Lord Maintainer,' said Tharius Don with an ironic bow. 'I saw my Deputy Enforcer waiting upon you and came to inquire if I might be of assistance.'

Shavian Bossit poured another cup, seething inside. He had not wanted Tharius Don this morning. Lately he had not wanted Tharius Don at all. The man had a chilling way with him. Like the knife cut of cold conscience. 'The Lord Propagator of the Faith, Tharius Don,' he said, making introductions. 'The Uplifted One, Talker of Sixth Degree Sliffisunda of the Talons. I have apologized to the Uplifted

One for the absence of other members of the council.' Of the seven, four were present. A quorum, he thought. Though he would have traded Tharius Don's presence in a moment for that of the Ambassador to the Thraish, Ezasper Jorn.

He turned back to the table, making a wry mouth at the Dame Marshal and commenting, sotto voce, 'Ezasper Jorn should be conducting this little exercise as Ambassador to the Thraish, but both he and Koma Nepor are off somewhere. The Protector, of course, would be of no help.' He shrugged, taking more tea for himself. 'I know I am discourteous. This Uplifted One has set my teeth on edge.'

'I assume you have reason for discourtesy?' She turned toward the Talker, millstone jaws loud in the quiet room. Only the Talker heard it. The others were too long accustomed to the sound to be aware of it.

'Indeed,' he murmured, loud enough for the other humans to hear. 'This Talker and two of his subordinates, also Talkers, went to the Tower at Baris and abducted the Superior and one of her senior Awakeners. They went with him under threat of great harm to all those within the Tower. His reason for doing so is that he believes them to be part of the Riverman heresy.'

'He need not have troubled,' said Tharius Don, his gray brows pulling together over black, suddenly angry eyes, in a face become as suddenly and unnaturally pale. The pallor had struck him at the mention of the Superior of Baris, and it did not leave him now. The bones of his striking face stood out in relief as he sucked in his cheeks, biting back a set of too revealing words to replace them with, 'We would have fetched them here had he but sent word.'

'Ah, but it was not his intention to fetch them here at all. He sought to take them to the Talons.'

'The Talons! Human prisoners?' Bormas Tyle slid the knife in and out of its sheath, cutting his words as he cut his hair, short and soft as velvet. The hair grew upon his forehead and down his neck onto the bulging muscles of shoulder and back, joining the velvet beard that half hid his mouth, making his head appear upholstered except for his

98

cold serpent's eyes. 'By what right? The treaty forbids this.'

'Indeed,' Shavian smiled his three-cornered smile at them all and then at the Talker once more. 'So I have said. To which the Talker replies that the treaty does not apply in this case, though he will not say why.'

There was a silence that began as mere hesitation, becoming tumescent with something more ominous than that, a brooding expectancy broken only by the hiss of the Deputy Enforcer's knife and the grinding of the Dame Marshal's teeth. These hostile sounds pervaded the room, sliding in it like serpents.

The silence was broken by Tharius Don. Such tension could breed nothing good, and in the absence of the Ambassador to the Thraish, someone had to take the responsibility of ending it. He moved with practiced ease, crossing the room and bowing the Talker to precede him into the corridor. 'I am sure the Uplifted One would like to sit down. Perhaps he would honor us by joining his subordinates and having a cup of tea. I will prepare for him below, and we will beg his return when we have finished our discussion.'

The Lord Maintainer sighed. For a moment there, he had felt something almost wonderful within, like lust, or youth, or rage. The possibility of hot conflict, maybe some blood spilled? His hands trembled. Whose blood? Most likely his own. 'By all means, Tharius.' He sighed. 'By all means. Uplifted One? Will you go with the Lord Propagator? We will meet again a little later, when we have considered this matter.'

It was quiet in the room after Tharius left. Gendra Mitiar cast questioning glances at Shavian Bossit from time to time, which he affected not to see. Gendra Mitiar had been uncollegial latterly. No, not only latterly, but for some time. Irascible. Given to ineffectual quarrels about trifles. She would not be content until her enmity for Tharius was out in the open, where she could gnaw on it publicly, something Bossit wasn't sure he wanted to see. At least, not yet. He sighed, and then sighed again, drifting toward the window, his inconspicuous form gliding like a shadow.

Suppose Lees Obol died. Shavian considered this, not for the first time. Suppose Lees Obol died of ostentatiously natural causes, and suppose, therefore, that General Jondrigar did not turn Highstone Lees into an abattoir through seeking the cause of Obol's death. Suppose this not totally unlikely state of affairs. Who would be the next Protector?

Gendra was in line, but she was not popular among the members of the Chancery council who would elect the next Protector. There were factions there. The Mendicants had a faction for themselves. Meaning what? Potipur knows. Shavian had his own supporters, of course. And Ezasper Jorn would be supported by the Thraish, who had their own way of bringing influence to bear. Research Chief Koma Nepor had been in Jorn's pocket since Jorn got him his first dose of elixir, so those two council members could be said to make up a faction. And there was a faction for Tharius Don among the lower ranks of the Towers. Perhaps a stronger one than was generally known. Which would explain Gendra's antagonism toward him, if an explanation were needed.

Shavian ticked the connection into memory. He did not doubt Bormas Tyle had also a claque, ready to come forward. Bormas Tyle, however, could be managed, though he sometimes needed simple reasons to do what more complex motivations required, able to accept the former but being only confused by the latter.

So, of the six surviving council members, there would be at least four contenders. Only Jondrigar and Nepor would not seek the office of Protector for themselves. Four would, including Shavian himself. Enough, he thought, to make rampant confusion.

The door opened, closing behind Tharius Don with a final snick, like a scissors.

'Guarded?' Bormas Tyle asked, his knife sliding with creepy persistence in the sheath. 'You have them well guarded?'

100

'Relax, Deputy. I've put them in the reception room at the end of the corridor over the garden, the one with barred windows. You'll recall there's a grilled gate at the end of the corridor, and I've stationed six Jondarites there, all growling at the insult almost offered to Lees Obol. Sufficient?'

'The damn things fly, is all,' snarled Bormas. 'You have to remember they fly.'

'As we do remember,' Shavian commented. 'Well, you've all heard everything I've heard. If you'd care to offer advice.' As when haven't you? he asked himself. All of you. Endlessly.

'How did the captives end up here?' Gendra asked, shaking her head and running one fingertip up and down a long wrinkle on her cheek. She did this sometimes for hours at a time, engraving her fingertip into her face as though to deepen the crevasses already there. Up, down, up, down.

'The senior Awakener – Ilze, his name is – brought a couple of whips with him, wrapped around his body under his clothes. Once in the air, he snapped them around two of the fliers' necks – evidently he has had considerable practice with the whips – and Lady Kesseret told the Talkers they had the choice of flying to the Chancery or of being strangled to death. Luckily, she knew the way up the Split River Pass, or they'd have died on the heights. Damn fliers can't get high enough to come over the Teeth. We may regret they came through.' Bossit already regretted it, but it was not time to talk of that.

'And where is the Lady Kesseret now?' asked Tharius in a carefully neutral voice. 'And the Awakener?'

'I've got them both in the Accusers' House. It seemed prudent.'

'Prudent!' He covered his terror with a pretended scorn. Kessie! In the Accusers' House!

'Until we know a bit more?'

'Such as why they are suspected?'

'Among other things, yes,' sighed the Maintainer. 'I was much tempted to send this Talker packing. Something told me it would be a mistake to do it or not do it, either way.'

101

Shavian pondered this. Prudence had come with age and was as tasteless in his mouth as food had become. Lacking the spice of feeling.

'And the Talker won't say why the treaty does not apply.'

'I think we can figure it out,' Shavian murmured, moving across the room to the tea service, taking a cup with him to a comfortable chair, where he sat, face wreathed in fragrant steam, making owl eyes at them through the mists. 'At the recent convocation with the Talkers, we learned they are barely reasonable upon the subject of the Riverman heresy.'

'That's true,' said Tharius Don carefully. 'It was all they wanted to talk about. We traveled a great, uncomfortable distance to cross the pass to the place of meeting. There were matters of true import to discuss. This demand of theirs for a higher food quota in order to increase their numbers, for example. Gods, but that needed talking of. But no! All they wanted to do was huddle in dusty groups, ruffling their feathers – full of dander as they are to make me sneeze endlessly – and fulminate about the heresy.' He fished a handkerchief out of his sleeve and erupted into it with a great play of gloomy recollection. Let them think him a fool. It was safer than the truth. Besides, the kerchief helped to hide his face.

'True.' Gendra considered this. 'It was the same with all of them. They spoke of nothing else, always watching out of the corners of their eyes, as though to catch us in some cover-up. The Riverman heresy, and was it connected to the homosexuals or the celibates? As though they had anything in common!'

'And we?' Shavian smiled a tiny, three-cornered smile, a mouse smile, wicked on that small face. 'What did we do?'

'I told them it was all nonsense,' said Tharius. 'No more to it than the usual few Awakeners who can't get past their junior vows and a coven or two of recalcitrants who put their dead in the River out of misplaced sentimentalism. I told them in my opinion it was not a widespread heresy, and not a conspiracy of any magnitude. Probably not more than a dozen or two Rivermen per town, mostly individual families. I doubt there's a Riverman anywhere in the towns who even knows that Talkers exist, so it would be hard to imagine a conspiracy against them. And I told them the boy-lovers were only aberrants! Genetic, if anything. Not a matter of politics or belief at all. And the same with the celibates. They want to believe all humans think of nothing but endless breeding, and it's hard to disabuse them of the notion. Though the gods know, Talkers ought to understand that if any creature can. They don't breed. They can't.'

'And I told them the same thing,' sneered Gendra, as though having agreed with him for any reason was of questionable taste.

Bossit bowed. 'Your Graces were no doubt right to do so. However, if I were one given to paranoia, deeply suspicious that some human group was plotting my downfall, and if the Propagator of the Faith told me it was all nonsense and then the Dame Marshal of the Towers told me it was all nonsense – both of them telling me this as a mere aside, mind you, not with any appearance of grave consideration – might I not feel even more suspicious? Why would the leader of the humans be so offhand unless he wished to mislead me?'

'You mean the Talkers thought we were lying? That there is indeed some vast Riverman plot which we know about?' Tharius kept his voice calm, unmoved, feeling the sweat crawling on his forehead but trusting the shadows of the corner where he sat to hide him.

Trust Shavian, thought Bormas Tyle, drawing no attention to himself whatsoever. If there is one conspiratorial breath inhaled within ten thousand paces, trust Shavian to hear it and smell upon it what rotten fish the speaker ate for dinner. He sat quiet, watching the others think about this.

'It would fit,' Gendra continued. 'It would explain this particular action. They wanted to do some independent questioning.' She raked both sides of her face simultaneously, fingers up and down the gullies, up and down.

'And, of course, they could claim the treaty wouldn't apply if they really thought we were breaking it.'

'There's something more here . . .' Bormas Tyle turned to stare out the window. 'Something going on.'

'It may be wise to give them the Awakeners,' Gendra said. 'A quick way to show them we aren't lying.'

Tharius turned pale, miming another sneeze to hide his pallor and his tight lips. Behind the linen veil he composed himself. 'It would show them nothing of the kind. They will find whatever they believe is true. The Talkers are experts at torture. What do you think the Lady Kesseret of the Tower at Baris will tell them under torture? That she knows nothing? Perhaps, for a time. At last, however, she will say whatever they most want to hear. "Yes, there is a conspiracy. Yes, they are heretical. Yes, all the homosexuals and the celibates and the Mendicants are part of it. Yes, I was in on it, and so was my senior Awakener; in fact, so was the whole Tower and all the Chancery, including the Dame Marshal of the Towers and the Protector himself!" '

Gendra blanched, compressing her lips. Obviously she had not thought deeply enough, but she resented Tharius Don's immediate apprehension in the matter. He was too often right. She longed for his pride to be riven, longed for his downfall.

He, seemingly unaware, went on. 'No, Dame Marshal. Allowing our people to be questioned at the Talons is the last thing we should allow, if for nothing but humanitarian concerns, much less for the sake of our own skins.'

Gendra hated admitting he was right, but she was forced to agree. 'Still, if we keep them here, the Talkers will believe their suspicions about us were true.'

'It would be better not to upset them . . .' Bormas frowned. The mutual benefits conveyed by the Treaty of Thoulia included provision of elixir for all high-ranking Chancery officials. His next scheduled Payment was to occur very soon. Not a good time to have the Talkers upset, angry, or suspicious.

'Then we must do something to make them believe their

104

suspicions about us are false.' Gendra moved to the table, stroking the polished wood as though it were some cowering animal she sought to tame. 'Let us give them the Awakeners, but don't let them be taken away. Let the Talkers question them here. Under the eyes of my own Accusers.'

Shavian agreed, turning his wicked three-cornered smile upon them. 'Yes. Let the Dame Marshal supervise the questioning. The lady Kesseret will no doubt be willing to bear some discomfort for her faith.' His glance at Tharius might have been only casual, though there were needles in it.

'Allow her to be questioned by Talkers? When we know she is innocent of any wrongdoing?' Tharius Don turned on them, hands knotted, lips tight. They moved away, annoyed at his challenge of conscience. Expedience often dictated, but Tharius Don would seldom let it dictate in comfort. 'Let her be questioned under "discomfort," as you put it, Bossit, when we all know she is a faithful Superior, guilty of absolutely nothing? Shameful!'

'Come, come, Tharius. She may not be entirely innocent,' Gendra challenged him, grinding her teeth like stones in an avalanche. 'We are all guilty of something. Some minor thing. Sufficient to warrant some suffering, no doubt. It will not compromise her receiving further Payment, as she has been promised. In fact, we might make that day come sooner, as a reward.' The younger one was when the elixir was first provided, the more powerful its effect, and to provide it earlier than promised could be a powerful inducement to many things. Enduring torture included.

There was another brooding silence. Tharius Don seemed about to object once more, but he contented himself with an internal monologue and an angry glare before subsiding into his chair, one foot tapping at the carpet, a muffled heartbeat of annoyance. At last Bossit asked, 'Are we agreed? The Accusers and Ascertainers are your people, Dame Marshal. I trust you will not allow more harm than necessary to come to these Awakeners. They are, after all, *our* people.' He used the royal possessive with heavy irony.

Tharius gave him a hard, intent look, as though to see whether this was to be interpreted as a sensible instruction or as something with double meaning.

Gendra, who wanted no interference from Tharius Don, returned her agreement in like form. 'No. Our people shall receive no more harm than is necessary, Lord Propagator. No more than is necessary.'

Later that day, Tharius Don leaned in a window of his rooms. The Library Tower overlooked the Accusers' House. Somewhere behind one of those windows in that cold pile was the Superior of Baris Tower.

Tharius Don put his head in his hands, for the moment unconscious of those on distant Towers or roofs who might be watching.

'Kessie,' he moaned in an agony of empathetic pain. 'Oh, by the gods, Kessie. Kessie.'

Thrasne had not wanted to think of Pamra again. He had put her out of his mind; he had refused to speak of her to Suspirra; he believed he could forget her in the years that followed his last departure from Baristown.

But during these six years, the drowned woman had moved her lips once more to say, 'My baby!' This time Thrasne had not needed to draw the sequence of facial expressions. He knew them as well as he knew his own. What should he have done? he asked himself in irritation. Should he have abducted Pamra there on the steps of the Tower? Should he have dragged her away like some impetuous lover? What could he have done? After a time he stopped thinking about what he might have done and began thinking what he would have to do next time.

When he came to Baris for the fourth time, Thrasne was thirty-six, a stocky, thatch-haired man with a boatman's crinkles around his eyes from looking into the sun half of every day. He had stopped to give Blint-wife her first promised moneys, surprised to find her stout and healthy, happier looking than she had ever been aboard the *Gift*, eager to come aboard and hear all the news, bearing gifts of cakes and a keg of ale. She asked Thrasne, somewhat shyly, and with careful attention to who might be by to overhear what she said, if he had time to carve some gifts for her. 'I'm being married again,' she said. 'To an old Riverman [this in a whisper] who lost his wife long ago. He has grandchildren. His daughter has gone to the River [whisper], and the children spend much time with me.'

So he carved a jump-up-jakes and a dancing doll and a set of fancy building blocks, knowing as he did so that Blint would be glad of this marriage. Blint had loved her once, likely more as she was now than as she had become aboard the *Gift*.

And he left her to come to Baris at the beginning of the cold season, well before festival, with the tides pulsing ever higher. By this time there were many cross piers to tie to in Baris. There was a procession of Melancholics, dark faces fierce and demanding, waving their fishskin lashes in invitation to the watchers. Thrasne saw more than a few citizens taking a lash or ten in return for Sorter coin. When he found the barber's place he remembered from before, Thrasne sat in the chair, commenting on the scene.

'I don't know why they do it, barber. Let themselves be whipped in return for a worthless bit of glass!'

'Ah, well,' the barber remarked, snipping around Thrasne's ear with close attention, the obsidian shears making a repeated *snick*, like the teeth of a stilt lizard, unpleasantly voracious. 'It's harmless, I suppose. Who knows, maybe the Holy Sorters would Sort you Out if there were enough Sorter coins in your purse.'

'Superstition,' muttered Thrasne. 'Even the Awakeners don't allow as how that's true.' Then, seeing argument about to fall from the barber's lips, he changed the subject. 'I wanted to ask you about the family of Fulder Don. Would you remember them?'

'All that family's gone, boatman. Fulder Don died a year or so after his mama. One of the older daughters died, too. The youngest girl, she that became an Awakener, she up and vanished not long ago. Quite a scandal!'

Thrasne was silent, shocked. Vanished? Pamra? 'The old woman who cared for them? Oh, sure now, I heard something about that. Went east, I think. Bad business, that was.'

'Wasn't there another daughter?'

'Oh. Sure there was. Prender. She's staying at the house the old woman had. Now how did I forget Prender?'

Prender was stiff and cold, angry at being questioned.

'She's gone, that's all I know. A servant came from the Tower. I couldn't see her face for the veils, but her voice was hard. Then a Laugher to question me about it, sent from somewhere else. He was stone in his face, and mean. His words were like threats. He said they'd find her no matter where she's gone. They don't know where she went, except she went early one morning. She was supposed to take workers to the forest for wood. Very early. All the workers were gone.'

She started to shut the door against him, her face creased deep with all the bitterness of the years, opening it just far enough to spit a few more words at him through the crack. 'He wanted to know what she had said to me about Delia. About Delia going east. As though she would have said anything to me. This is all her fault, Pamra's. She and her mother both. Neither of them could ever be sensible about anything.'

'When did she disappear?'

'I said. Early in the morning.'

'No. I mean *when*? How long ago?'

'Not long. Twenty, thirty days, perhaps.'

As he turned to leave, she called after him, 'She only did it to get even with us, you know. That's what I told him, that Laugher. She only did it to hurt us.'

Thrasne didn't turn. He was too busy feeling ashamed of himself. He had blamed Pamra, blamed her, when all she had really done was flee from voices like the one behind him.

What would he tell Suspirra now?

He told her nothing. When he entered the owner-house, she was turned toward him. He saw her lips, her teeth, the lower teeth touching her upper lip. He copied it with his own, breathing out. 'Ffff.' He did not need to wait to know what she would say.

'*Find her!*'

'How can I find her, Suspirra? No one knows where she went.'

'*Find her!*'

'She will have gone west, probably. Why? Why did she go at all?' And even as he asked the question, he knew the

109

answer. He could see it as clearly as the pictures he had drawn of Suspirra. The barber had said Delia went east. He saw Delia leaving. She was old, too old. She died there, east of Baristown. He visualized her returning in the pit. Pamra's arrival there, early in the morning. He assumed the Awakeners looked at faces. So, she would have seen the face, seen, known, all at once known everything she had not wanted to know. That stubborn rebellion, that rigid naïveté, breached, overcome. Suspirra had said, 'She had to believe in love – of some kind.'

And having seen, having known, where would she go? Not to the River, not at once. No. West. For a time.

He took the *Gift* west, stopping at every town, no matter how small. He searched everywhere, talking to Rivermen, patronizing barbers.

And he found her, as much because she had not had time to go far nor strength to go fast as for any other reason. She was serving drinks in a tavern, hair loose as any marketwoman's, silent as a wraith with haunted eyes, and yet more beautiful in her fear than she had been in her complacency at the Tower. There were men drinking in the place only to look at her, but she was blind to all their looks.

'Do you want drink?' she asked, her haughtiness gone and only a haunted, terrible conviction of danger remaining.

'Pamra, I've been looking for you.'

She started with fear, thinking he might be someone the Awakeners had sent after her, but he put a hand upon her arm as she trembled.

'It's all right. Your mother wants to see you.'

'My mother is dead,' she said, eyes wide with horror. 'She's dead.'

'Yes. But no. Will you come with me?'

'She went in the River. You're mad!'

'Say I am mad. But I will not harm you in my madness. I swear by all that is good and holy . . .'

'Then you swear by nothing!' Her face was wild. She would have run from him if she had had anywhere to go. She would have screamed, except to do so was to attract attention, and only in being quiet and unnoticed did she have any chance of life at all.

'I swear by the River, then, the River you have planned to go into, the River where your mother went. Come with me.'

He coaxed her as he might have coaxed a frightened animal, until at last, terrified of him but more afraid of the looks being cast their way by those in the place, she consented to come with him to the place the *Gift* was moored. He led her along to the owner-house, letting her stand there in the door while he fumbled with the lantern, she ready to run, but too weary and beaten to do it.

The light shone down on Suspirra, facing the door, lips slightly open, though they had been closed when he'd left. And it was Suspirra's twin who stood in the doorway, eyes wide and lips open in surprise. They were alike, line for line. From the drowned woman came a sound, the only sound ever heard from her, almost a sigh, or perhaps a sigh of dissolution.

'Mother?' Pamra cried. 'Mother!' She went to touch the still face, drawing back her hand in horror. 'You lied. A carving.'

'No,' said Thrasne, heartbroken. 'She is as I brought her from the River.'

Pamra sobbed, laying her hand on the hard breast. Above that head the lips curved upward, moving visibly. The lips moved, seemed to utter a word, 'Remember?' A question, perhaps. In that instant the smile vanished, smoothing like windswept sand, becoming a hinted curve, coherent only for the moment, cloud-edged, shining with light, as Pamra reached out to hold it.

'Mother?' she said.

The word released the last ties that held the figure whole. Suspirra went, all at once, the golden cloud falling in the instant into a hillock of powdery dust, leaving behind a transparent golden pillar in the beam of light as though something incredibly tenuous maintained its structure still, after all that was dross had fallen away. Something solid fell as well, resting upon the dust like a little moon, softly glowing. Pamra

111

knelt to pick it up; Thrasne was too late to stop her as he muttered, 'Blight!'

Undeterred, she knelt there, stroking the thing, round and heavy as a melon. 'Was that what made her like that, the blight?'

He nodded, watching her hands. The globe seemed to breathe between them. 'Out of her womb,' Pamra whispered. 'She was pregnant when she died. I was too young to know at the time, but Grandma saw that I heard the story often as I grew up. Mother almost died when she had me, and the midwives told her she would die next time. She was afraid. Afraid of the Awakeners. Of us . . .'

'You are not an Awakener now.'

She turned her haunted eyes upon him. 'Once past the junior vows, an Awakener is an Awakener forever. They will remind me of that when they send a Laugher with the flask of Tears for me. I have been lucky to escape them this far.'

'What would they do to you?'

'They will feed me Tears of Viranel. I will remember who I am, but I will have no will of my own. I will exist for long years until I truly die and can be eaten by the Servants of Abricor. Perhaps, since I will not be dead and stinking, the senior Awakeners may use me for a while. Jelane says they do that. I saw a woman like that in the Tower once. They have almost caught me twice already. I cannot sleep, cannot live, for fear of them. They will find me. I have nowhere to go.'

'You have somewhere to go.' He took the strange roundness from her hands, turning it in his own. It shifted as though something within it moved, turning in slow sleep. 'What shall we do with this?'

'It lives,' she breathed. 'See, that place on the side seems to swell, like a pamet pod opening.'

A thin, light-colored line upon the roundness widened, stretching as they watched. He set it upon his bed, and they leaned over it, not daring to breathe too loudly. The line strained, shifted, strained, opening wider over a lighter lining, which began to tear with a thin ripping sound like rotted canvas.

From inside came the sound of shallow breathing, slow as the tide.

Pamra reached out to tear the shell open gently with her hands.

A child lay within. Tiny. Perfect. Brown as Suspirra had been, yet moving. Breathing. Opening its night-black eyes to look up at them as though it saw them entirely and comprehended them utterly, moving its lips as though to speak.

They said nothing. It was a wonder too great for speech. They could have made exclamations of disbelief, but in the quiet of the room it would have seemed blasphemy to speak at all. When those eyes closed at last and the baby half turned as though into sleep, they took the shell away. It was connected to the child by an umbilicus, a dried, brittle cord that shivered to fragments when they moved her. A girl child. Pamra reached a tentative, fearful finger to touch that flesh, warm and soft as her own. Silently, she wrapped the child in one of Thrasne's towels and laid her in the basket he used for his mending while Thrasne stared and stared, lost in the wonder of it.

'Now you must come with me,' he said. 'To care for her.'

'Who . . . what is she? How can I care for something like that? Surely this is no human child.'

Thrasne took her by the shoulders, shook her gently. Though the child was a wonder and a miracle, had not Suspirra been both a wonder and a miracle? 'A strange child, yes, but I believe she is your sister. Born of the same parents.' He did not say what other strange parents might have been involved in that birth. The strangeys of the depths? The blight?

'Where will we go?'

'For a time, we will simply go on,' he said firmly. 'They will not look for you on the River.' He would make this so if it were not so already. Perhaps it would not be safe enough forever; perhaps some other provision would have to be made. For the time being, it was enough that Suspirra – who had been in turn a dream, a small carving, a drowned woman, an almost carving once more – was with him now, alive.

9

The Accusatory of the Chancery at Highstone Lees was a cold stone building, built high along one side of the ceremonial courtyard, where dark-needled trees made a solemn shade around a jetting fountain. The room in which Ilze found himself confined was no less chill. He could walk around in it to warm himself. He could stare out the high, shuttered windows at the mountains along the horizon, which seemed to nibble at the sun as it moved along them. After a very long time of alternate walking and staring, Ilze realized that the sun would get no higher than the low northern sky where it swung in a long arc from east to west barely above the peaks. When darkness came, he huddled on the narrow bed, beneath the two blankets.

There was nothing else to do: walk, stare, or huddle on the bed, staying as warm as possible. There was food in the room and two buckets, one of water, one for his waste. The sun went once around the mountains before anyone came near him. Then it was only a silent guard with more food and a lackey to deliver two clean buckets, one full and one empty, and take away two dirty buckets, one full and one empty. Ilze had a vision of himself spending years in this cold room, moving water from one bucket to the other by way of his guts, moving solids from the plate to the bucket, consuming, being consumed. Somewhere nearby was another such room, he imagined, with the lady Kesseret in it. He had been separated from her almost immediately, but he thought he would be released as soon as she had had time to tell their story.

He slept for a time, woke again, looked out the window to see the sun rolling upon the mountains, the day not quite half-gone. He stared, walked, huddled, began inventing pictures from the crevices and holes in the walls. There were a line of rounded depressions that looked like fish. He half slept, the fish emerging from the wall to swim about him, slowly, like blight-fish. He woke. The shadows had moved. Now the same depressions were eyes, watching him.

Another day passed before the door opened again to admit two tall Servants of Abricor. Talkers. They had come, they said, to accuse him. They were accompanied by a silent human in a dark robe and half veil. Ilze was angered by this, horrified by them.

'What am I accused of?' he demanded. 'Tell me! What do you think I've done? I knew nothing about Pamra's disappearance until after it happened. I know nothing about it now.'

'Tell us about Rivermen,' they demanded. They were taller than other Servants he had seen, cleaner, their feathers gleaming with blue highlights. One of them might have been the one who had been in the Superior's room. Perhaps not. He could not tell. The fingers at the last joint of their wings were hard and clever. When he didn't answer quickly, they pinched him. Their beaks were soft, almost like lips, and though the words they spoke were more croaked than enunciated, he learned to understand them very quickly. 'Tell of Rivermen,' they repeated.

'I know what the Superior told me. They are a heretical cult who put their dead in the River.'

'Tell us something more.'

'I don't know anything more.'

'Do you think they infiltrate the Towers? Put their own people in as Awakeners?'

'I have no idea. It seems unlikely.'

'Do you think Pamra was a spy? For the Rivermen?'

'She was only twelve when she came to us. Would a spy be that young?'

'For a person, she was very pretty, wasn't she? Did you like her a great deal? Did you lust for her?'

'Seniors are not allowed that sort of contact with juniors. Yes, she was remarkable looking. Everyone thought so.'

'Did you lust for her?'

'Not really, no. There are always plenty of women in the town.'

'Did she confide in you?'

'No. She did ask me about sending a message east for her old nursemaid.'

'Did you tell her to do that?'

'I told her it wasn't particularly in accord with doctrine, but it wasn't actually heretical. I told her how to do it.'

'When did she tell you her old nursemaid had gone east?'

'She never did,' he said in a fury.

They went on asking these same questions for hours. From behind the veil a grinding sound emanated from time to time, as though the veiled person were chewing stones. That person said nothing. Tomorrow they returned to ask the same questions again. These returned, or others who looked exactly like these. Until his anger got the better of him.

'Where is my Superior? Ask the lady Kesseret!' It was obvious, even to him, that they had already asked the lady much. Where else would they have gotten the information they needed to question him? 'She knows I'm telling the truth. What do you want from me?'

When they left him alone at the end of the day, he was too tired to move, too angry to care. He lay on the bed, the blankets drawn carelessly over him, letting the night come. There were bruises all over his body where they had mishandled him. He had stopped eating. The food tasted foul. The water tasted foul, too, but he was always thirsty.

'Why did you choose Pamra to be your junior?'

'It doesn't work that way. I didn't choose her. She was assigned to me.'

'Who assigned her?'

'My Superior. But even she didn't pick Pamra. Pamra

116

was just one of the handful who came in about the same time. As soon as the initiation master was through with them, I was in line to get that clutch. And the next senior got the next clutch. A clutch is five. It didn't mean anything. Whichever of us was next senior got the next bunch that came in.'

'Did she confide in you?'

'No. She didn't confide in me.'

'Did you lust after her?'

He hadn't, really, not in any way that was culpable. 'No,' he said. 'I didn't lust after her.'

'Tell us about discipline. It is said you never whipped Pamra.'

'I never whipped any of them unless they deserved it. Of the five of them assigned to me, I only whipped three.'

'Why did you whip them?'

'Because they were lazy.'

'Was Pamra never lazy?'

'No. Pamra was a zealot. She was never lazy. She believed. She believed everything.'

'Didn't such excess of belief seem at all suspicious to you?'

'Why would it? That's how I believed when I was seven or eight years old. It seemed childlike. Endearing. I thought it was funny.'

They went away again. He pushed a shutter aside and leaned in a window, exhausted. His room was on a corner, with two windows. On this side the flat, bleak moorlands stretched to the foot of the jagged mountains, the sun rolling like a red ball on their tips. He could not see the moons.

For a moment the world whirled, shook, and there was a great darkness behind his eyes. He could not see the moons. After a time he figured it out. The moons circled this globe at its center line, above the World River. He could have seen them, low on the horizon, except for the mountains. The Teeth had bitten off the moons. Not seeing them was like an accusation. But an accusation of what? 'I really haven't done anything,' he snarled furiously into the dark.

117

A dark anger welled up from within him, and he tried to wrap himself in it. Sleep would not come. He rose to run around and around the small room until he was panting, gasping, his heart thundering away inside him as though it would burst. His hands knotted, unknotted. He would kill the fliers. Strangle them. If he ever got out of this place, he would kill them. One at a time, lingeringly. Wherever he found them. At last, worn out, he fell once again into that sleep from which they always woke him.

'Where did Pamra take the workers?'

'I don't know that she took them anywhere. If she took them anywhere, some of you must have seen her. How could she take a whole pitful anywhere without the Servants seeing it? I didn't see her. I don't know.'

One of the Talkers looked at the other, almost disconcerted, he thought. Had he told them something they didn't know? Suggested something? They gave him no time to think about it. 'Did you ever discuss the workers with her?'

'Discuss? No. Except in class. I had her for a class in hermeneutics. Scripture. The Scripture talks about workers.'

'Did she doubt the Scripture?'

'Pamra? I told you Pamra never doubted anything.'

'Did you lust after her?'

Perhaps he had. Perhaps he had. 'Yes,' he said. 'Sometimes. But I didn't do anything about it.'

They went away, leaving him, returned again, went away. After an endless time they seemed to tire of it.

'Tomorrow,' they said to him. 'Tomorrow you will go to the Ascertainers.'

He didn't know what that meant; he didn't care. It would be different from this, something to look forward to. Perhaps they would give him an opportunity to kill some of them. He went to sleep, dreaming of them tied to the stake and himself with the whip in his hand.

10

Pamra, at first fearful and hostile in equal measure, became gradually accustomed to being aboard the *Gift*. Thrasne had given her a room in the owner-house with a comfortable bunk, a basket for the child, Lila, and a chest full of simple clothing such as the boatmen wore. He taught her to braid her hair in River fashion, high in the back, with bead-decorated locks around the face. He named her Suspirra as he had named her mother before her and his lady of dreams before that. Relieved of the constant bleeding of the Tower, which kept the juniors both slender as saplings and free of any trace of sexual feeling, she put on a little flesh. Though she looked unlike the woman he had found in the tavern and much unlike the Awakener he had seen outside the Tower, she looked more like Suspirra than ever, and with this Thrasne was content.

Had to be content. Though he wooed her with his eyes and his gifts and his constant, calm solicitude, she showed no sign of perceiving what was in his mind. He kissed her cheek, and she accepted it as a child might a kiss from an uncle, not unwillingly, but as though it did not matter. Nothing moved her. Nothing stirred her. At certain times, when she was drowsy, perhaps, she would answer his questions about life in the Tower, though never at length or in any great detail. From these infrequent comments he formed a picture of her existence there and on the basis of that troublesome image forgave her much. She could not feel attraction toward him, he told himself. She did not know what it was. She was like a child, innocent of sexual

119

feeling. She was sometimes angry, but it seemed an anger unformed and unfocused, and if she had any feelings toward Thrasne at all, she did not recognize what they were.

Still, she began to keep house for him, at first absent-mindedly, and then with a small show of concern for his comfort. She learned to cook in the same way, at first from hunger, and then with a kind of dim pleasure, remembering the aromas of comfort found in Delia's house without having to remember Delia herself. She could not remember Delia. Would not. The fall of rock in the lonely place was shut away inside her. The faceless regard of the canvas hood was shut away. Herself as Awakener with the flasks at her belt was shut away. There, inside, where love might have lived, was a stone house into which all such things were put. There was no room for love. The house was so large it took up most of the room there was. It had to hold too much.

Thrasne, looking deep into her eyes, knew it was there, for he could see the shape and shadow of it and the feral glow of eyes that peered out of its windows now and again. A ghost house. Tenanted by her mother and Delia and who knew how many more. He hoped the hard prison space inside her might grow smaller in time. He had time.

She never went ashore. He showed her his watching place in the high cubby by the owner-house, and she sat there for hours watching the Riverbanks flow by. Long months went by. He brought the shore to her, little gifts, bits of foliage and flower, fruit and confections. And toys. And carvings he made for her, which said all the things his mouth left unsaid. And she did not much notice.

Meantime the child of the drowned woman grew like a little tree, slowly yet observably, and moved like a reed blown gently by the wind. They had tried feeding her everything, softly stewed grain, vegetables, bits of fish. She took only the brackish River water and sunlight. On days of cloud, she lay quiet in her basket, scarcely moving. On sunny days she learned gradually to crawl about the deck with the deliberation of a tortoise and the curiosity of any infant confronted with a new world to experience.

She seemed to love best to be held on Suspirra's – Pamra's – lap facing the sun, being shown things – a fish, a bit of rope, a frond of flowers from a tree they floated under when early first summer came. The boatmen stopped to talk with her, never touching her, regarding her half with affection, half with superstitious awe. So far as they knew, Suspirra had brought the child with her when she came, her arrival as mysterious as anything else about the matter. The carved woman in the owner-house was gone. A live woman who looked like the carved woman was there, except that the live woman had a child that could have been carved. Except that it lived, of course. A wonder. A living wonder.

Thrasne and Suspirra had agreed to name the child Lila. It had been Thrasne's mother's name. He liked the sound of it. The crewmen accepted this as well but did not use the name. Instead, they were inclined to hint to Thrasne that they suspected a story that might be told, at which he shrugged and smiled, unresentful. Suspirra made the matter no less complicated when she referred to Lila as her sister.

'They'll talk ashore, you know, Thrasne,' said Obersrom. 'Seems to me you aren't sayin' much about this and would rather the matter was kept quiet. But they will talk, Thrasne. You know that. Best you give them something to say, or they'll say something you won't like.'

Thrasne thought on this. It was true. The men would talk ashore, and the more mystery they made, the more likelihood of curiosity seekers trying to sneak aboard to catch a glimpse.

Something close to the truth would be best. 'Tell them the baby's mother was pregnant. She drowned in the River and was blighted. So the baby was born different from you and me. She has a different sense of time, that's all. Perhaps all creatures which are blighted have that sense of time. Maybe blighted fishes live their whole lives out but do it a bit slower than we do. Now, my old friend Suspirra – her I had the statue of until she herself came aboard – Suspirra calls the baby her sister because the drowned woman was her . . . her friend, and she cares for her friend's child as she would for a baby sister. It wouldn't be fitting for her to call Lila her own child, her being an unmarried woman. And Suspirra came to stay with us because the Awakeners wouldn't leave the child alone, not if they knew. You know that. She had to come to the River to be safe. That's all there is to it.'

This won their sympathy and went a way to shutting their mouths. Boatmen were accustomed to avoiding Awakener attention and keeping shut about River business. It began to seem to all of them that Lila and Suspirra were River business right enough.

Obers-rom gave it considerable thought. Next time he stopped to speak to Lila he stroked her face, at which she made an indeterminate sound of pleasure, almost a word. 'She's not different, really,' he said to Pamra. 'She just moves real slow, that's all. Real slow. I'll call her slow-baby.' He turned away, smiling, the smile vanishing as he thought of the watchful, perceptive expression in the child's eyes. 'Not so different,' he repeated to himself, 'except for that.' He still determined to call her slow-baby.

Which, thereafter, Lila heard more often than she heard her name.

11

Where the great log came from, Thrasne could not say. It had the look of something prehistoric about it, like some ancient monster heaving up from the depths to wreak havoc upon the works of man. As it did. The *Gift of Potipur* ran upon the log – or the log came up beneath her – with such force as to stave a man-sized hole in her bow planks, through which the water alternately poured and gurgled as the *Gift* rocked from the shock. There were several hours of panicky struggle, after which the *Gift* gurgled rather less, though still dangerously, and the most threatening part of the damage had been controlled for the moment.

'What will you do now?' asked Pamra. She had stayed out of the way during the worst of it, trying not to show how frightened she was, clinging to Lila as though to some raft on which she might have expected to float to safety. Later, when they had patched the hole, she had gone below to see the black oozing around the patch and had realized it could be only temporary. 'You'll have to fix it ashore, won't you?'

Thrasne nodded, still numb. It was the first real injury the *Gift* had received, and he felt it himself, looking at his ribs from time to time as though expecting to see great bruises and rents there, surprised to find himself whole. 'It'll take a while. That third rib back is sprung all out of line. All the planks are loose along there. They're not leaking now, but they will be. Next town's hopeless, no piers, no shipwrights. Next one on down's some better, but I'll have to do most of it myself, most likely.'

'How long?'

'A long time. Thirty, forty days, at least. Probably more. They won't have the planking we need. It's almost impossible they'd have seasoned wood available. Chances are if they have any, it'll be green. Or, more likely, still standing. Over a month.' A month was fifty-one days. 'Sixty days, maybe. Seventy.' Still in shock, he wasn't thinking of her at all. Then he turned to see her look of fear and apprehension, understanding it in the instant. 'That'd be too long for you to be in one place, wouldn't it? Dangerous for you. Those hunting you would likely find you. I should have thought of that right off.'

'I can stay here in the owner-house.' She tried to smile. 'If the men won't talk about it.'

They would talk, of course. No way he could prevent it. 'You can't stay cooped up that long. You'd turn all pale, like a mushroom.' He tried a not-very-successful smile. 'No. We'll think of something else.'

When he came back to the owner-house some hours later, he brought the local chart-of-towns with him, laying it on the table under the lantern where she could see it. 'I've found something,' a tired smile telling her it was the only thing he'd been able to find. 'I'd forgotten all about it. Strinder's Isle.'

He pointed to the chart, the ragged edge of the River at one side, with its endless list of places, products, local idiosyncrasies, religious taboos. There to the south, a good day's sail out into the World River, lay a long, wide, inky interruption among the careful notes and the River flow. The eastern end of it was behind them, two towns back. The western end was three towns yet ahead. 'The only people there are the Strinders,' he said. 'And only a few of them left. No guards. No gates. They have a pier here, a little east of Chantry. Chantry's where we'll have to get the boat fixed.'

'An island? I never heard of an island in the River.'

'There's many of them. Most of the ones close to shore are so small they're only rocks on the charts, dots, places to steer clear of. But Strinder's Isle, well, it's a good way out.

Out of sight of the shore. Blint used to call there every time he came around. Used to bring in flour and cloth and sweetening. Take out dye shells. The thing is, we can run down along the island, drop you off, then pick you up again at the western end after the ship is fixed. All we'll need is some kind of signal so you can come down to the west end of the island when it's time. That way we'll be with the current, taking you in and getting you off.'

He misinterpreted her doubtful look. 'It's safe enough, Pamra. We've got time to drop you off. The *Gift* isn't going to sink under us.'

'No, no, no,' she said, hating herself for seeming to question his provision for her when that very provision might delay and endanger him. 'It just seemed – is it an empty island? I mean, *are* there still any people there?'

Now he was doubtful himself. 'There used to be. Right along here. A bunch of little houses, some of them scattered back in the trees. Of course, the island mostly belongs to the Treeci. They're a little like the fliers.'

'Servants of Abricor!'

'Not carrion eaters. No. Not the Servants of Abricor. A different kind of creature. I've never seen them anywhere but there, on the island. Bigger legs than the Servants. They have beautiful plumage, but they don't fly. Flat kind of beaks on them, almost like lips only harder, not those hard, hooked beaks the Servants have. From a distance, they look almost human. I've only seen them at a distance, of course, but the Strinders got on well with them.' He ran a hand across his face, as though trying to wipe away the tiredness. 'If there's any way to let you stay there, Pam, it's best. Truly. Even if you had to stay alone in one of the old houses. The people looking for you won't find you there. I can guarantee. And we can make it safe and reasonably comfortable for you, even if you have to stay alone.'

It sounded like abandonment, and he knew it. She could not help but know it, and it made a slow, burning anger in her that there could not be some other way. There was no other way. The alternatives were worse. The Awakeners

125

would send Laughers after her, they weren't going to stop looking for her, and even death alone on an island would be far preferable to their finding her. She shook herself, made herself sound cheerful about it.

'I'll go there, Thrasne. Even if there's no one there. I'll take Lila, she'll be company for me. However long it takes, I'll wait for your signal.'

When they came to the island, however, she was less sure.

There were little houses along the shore, most tumbled into piles of gray fragments, log and plank silvered by the sun and the River wind. At last they saw a vague line of smoke ascending, and this led them to a rickety pier and a ramshackle dwelling showing light among the trees.

The woman who answered their calls had aged like the house. She was rust and dust held together by a net of wrinkles with gray hair wisping around her like smoke. 'Strinder? Me? Well, of course I'm Strinder, and damn near the last. Did you say you were old Blint's boy? I seem to remember he had a boy. Think of that, and come in.'

There were two others on the island, as old as she; an old curmudgeon named Stodder and her own cousin, Bethne. 'Joy,' she said to Pamra with a keen glance from under bushy brows. 'That's my name. You wouldn't think it, would you? Not exactly a joyful object, am I? Often wished I'd had a name that aged better. Sophronia. Eugenia. Something with some dignity to it.'

She looked them over, Pamra and the slow baby. She did not remark then or ever upon the baby's strangeness, and Pamra came to believe for a time it was because human babies were so far in her past she had forgotten what the usual ones were like. Lila might have fitted her memories of babyness as well as any other.

When Thrasne left her, it was with a goodly supply of food and with a large supply of wood cut for the old woman's fires. Though it was warmer on the island than on the shore, the evenings would still be cold for the next three months. Thirty days was the minimum time the repairs would take, but it could be three times that. After thirty days she was to watch the northern shore each evening, a little before dusk, to see three pillars of smoke. When she saw them, she was to make the two- or three-day hike along the flat shore to the western end of the island and camp there until he came for her. 'If it takes us longer than that, we may be delayed by the Conjunction tides,' he told her. 'So don't be impatient. You can get down to the west end all right?'

'Oh, yes, yes,' said the old woman. 'She can get there easy enough. There's no more wilderness on Strinder's Island. No more wildness at all. Except for . . . well, except for what there is, of course.' If this had been meant to convey something, it failed. Pamra was too agitated at being left behind to pay much attention.

The *Gift* pulled away from the isle, Thrasne turning from the high rudder deck to wave to her. When sight of him had faded into the River haze, down and cross stream toward the distant shore, she turned back to the house, the old woman meeting her halfway there.

'Oh, girl, I saw he left you puncon jam. Couldn't help but see it. I haven't had puncon jam since my youngest daughter was born, she that's gone now and left only the memory. Would it be ugly of me to beg puncon jam on our fry cakes tonight? I do have a light hand with fry cakes.' For a time it was as though Joy had returned, so young she sounded, and Pamra was ashamed not to greet this enthusiasm with more spirit of her own. Though she kept counseling herself to be calm, not to consider herself injured, still she felt bereft, grieved, and abandoned, senseless though that was. She found herself blaming Thrasne, senseless though that was as well, ashamed of it and yet unable to stop. Still, faced with the old woman's delight in having company, she assented to the scheme of puncon jam, assented to having Stodder and Bethne as guests.

These three were the entire remnant of the Strinders. There had been some younger who had gone away on the River, there had been many younger and older who had died. And now these three remained, not one among them who had ever seen the northern shore or an Awakener or a

127

Servant of Abricor. They knew only the island and the waters around it and the Treeci, who shared both with them.

It was some time before she met the Treeci. First there were days of walking here and there, weeding a bit of garden, checking the nets to see if anything worth eating had been caught, raking shellfish from the River to dry upon the shore, carrying the dried shells to the pier, where great, wobbly baskets bulged with this reeking harvest awaiting the next Riverboat.

'Not many stop here,' creaked old Stodder. 'Let's see, there's *River Queen*, and *Moormap's Fish* (Moormap died, but his daughter's husband kept the *Fish*) and the *Gift*, o' course, and the *Startled Wind* . . .' He went on with his enumeration, Riverboats afloat, Riverboats long gone.

After their supper they sat on the rickety porch beneath the trees to watch the moons assemble before the old man and the other old woman stumped off to their own falling-down houses in the woods. Pamra stood looking after them, wondering why they did not live together. It would mean only one house to heat, less wood to cut. Far off in the trees came a plangent, bell-tolling sound, and she remembered the creatures Thrasne had mentioned.

'Treeci?' she asked old Joy.

'Treeci,' whispered Joy, face in the lamplight alive with old memories, eyes gentle as doves. 'Treeci. Honoring the moons.'

They went next day to rake shells. Pamra, Lila, and Joy. Three Treeci came through the trees, calling in bell-like voices, then in human sounds. 'Joy! We greet!'

The old woman waved. 'Binna! Werf! Come meet a visitor from over the River. Her name is Pamra. And the baby, Lila.' The Treeci bowed, acknowledging the introduction, while Pamra stared.

They were as tall as she, standing upright on legs not unlike her own, with feathered buttocks that curved as hers did into a narrow waist. The long, two-toed feet might have been human feet stuffed into feathery socks except for the knifelike talons. Above the waist the likeness to humans was less. The arms, ending in three-fingered hands, were fully feathered with long, winglike primaries; their breasts were keeled; their large-eyed faces were full of candid intelligence. 'Pamra,' they said, bowing again.

She bowed in return to Binna, to Werf, then turned to bow to the third member of the group, feeling Joy's hand tugging at her as she did so. She looked down to see the old woman shaking her head, embarrassed, whispering, 'No, don't bow. That's a male. You don't bow to them.'

'Why?' It was startled out of her, not really a question.

'Shhh. Later.'

'Are you having a pleasant visit?' Binna asked her, taking no notice of this gaffe. The words were clearly articulated, slightly accented but in a pleasant way. Though the lower part of each Treeci face was visored by their shallow beaks, those beaks were soft and flexible, protruding little, moving almost as lips did.

'Yes, thank you.' They talked of the weather for a few moments, of the tides. The third, unnamed Treeci wandered to the shore and stood there, watching the water.

'I came to tell you, Joy,' said Werf, 'there's a new bed of inedible shellies just below the big rocks, beyond the frag grove. Good dye shells! They're small now, but by Conjunction after this one, they should be good size for your gathering.'

'That's kind of you,' she responded warmly. 'Will you return with us and take tea?'

They demurred, demurred again, then accepted. It had the pace and quiet predetermination of a ritual. At the house they were joined on the porch by Bethne to drink tea out of fragile old cups as they recited memories of former times, so many memories it was obvious they were more than acquaintances. Joy had brought six cups. Without saying anything to anyone, Werf filled the extra cup and carried it to the rock, where the third Treeci perched in lonely silence. The two conversed in low tones. Werf returned. No one seemed to notice. Before leaving, Werf retrieved the cup and set it upon the table with the others.

'We rejoice in your friendship,' they called as they were leaving. 'May your lives extend.'

Joy gathered up the cups. 'If you could get me a pail of water, child, I'd get these washed.'

'In a minute. First, tell me about the – the male. Why don't we talk to him? . . .'

'It isn't done.' The old woman laid a trembling hand on Pamra's own. 'Werf is Neff's mother. She talks to him, you see. And his own sisters do, of course. But no one else. It just isn't done.'

'Cruel,' Pamra said, remembering herself as a child. 'It's cruel to treat people like that.'

'Ah, but child, they aren't people, don't you see.'

'They're people, Joy. You wouldn't sit here drinking tea with them unless they were.' She said this as she would have done to Delia, mistaking Joy for Delia, perhaps, without realizing it.

'In that sense, yes, they're people and my dearest friends, but you know what I meant.' She turned away toward her wash basin, holding out the empty pail. 'They aren't human people.'

Pamra forced her feelings off her face. She was living in the old woman's house, a good old woman, not unlike – not unlike another good old woman whom she had failed in a time of trouble. Let her not trouble this one more. As a guest, she had no right.

But she felt a sympathetic rebellion for the lonely Treeci, even as she admitted to herself the loneliness might be more in her than in Neff. The rebellion in her was the same it had been when she was eleven or twelve, the same that had led her to say, 'I can be a Awakener.' She did not think of this, but only of the sad Treeci. His separation spoke to her.

Among the Treeci, it seemed, hospitality must be returned. Two days later Joy dressed herself with unaccustomed attention, digging through dusty boxes in search of old finery. She found a glittery scarf for Pamra, a shiny bit of ribbon for Lila's blanket, and they set out along the shore.

'I suppose eventually you'll tell me where we're going?'

'Well, Werf and Binna will expect us. Among the Treeci it's considered nice to drop by in a couple of days so's they can show hospitality. They call it returning the opportunity. Very set on it, they are.'

'Why all this sparkle?'

'Do them honor. You wouldn't have noticed, not being island reared, but they were got up fine for us t'other day. Talons painted; feathers around the eyes dyed. They were making an opportunity to honor us – so they call it. Curious, I expect. About you and the baby. Not been a human baby on Strinder's for thirty years.'

Pamra found herself lost in wonder at this, not so much at the fact of it – another race of creatures upon the world with its own habits and customs, speaking not only its own language but a human language as well, curious about human babies – no, not so much at the fact as at her ignorance of it. How could she have grown to be adult without having heard of them? Why had no one spoken of them? And if no one had spoken of the Treeci, how many other wonders in the world might there be, unspoken of?

Joy had something to say upon that subject. 'My brother used to say all the Northshore people were so stuffed full of Awakener shit they hadn't room for anything else. Is it true they forbid books there?'

It was true. Or true enough. There had been books in the Tower. Homiletics. Hermeneutics. Scripture. Difficult books breathing an atmosphere of dusty mystery, unenlightening. There had been no others. Without books, without travel, Pamra could explain her own ignorance. She could not really forgive it.

The Treeci lived in houses, better kept and better made than those of the human occupants of the island, and there was a teahouse set in a grove where water burbled tranquil music into a stone basin. Young Treeci, half the size of the adults, gathered on the meadow in murmuring groups. Tea was served in ceremonial fashion. Pamra watched the others to see what was proper, getting through the formal

131

bits with some degree of grace. When everyone had a cup, when every cup had been tasted and approved, when the nuts and cakes had been passed around and those had been complimented, then the group could sit back and indulge themselves in conversation. Joy had been right. It was curiosity. All the questions they had been too polite to ask on Strinder territory they felt empowered to ask on their own.

'Is the child yours?'

'Is it a customary child?'

'We thought it was not a customary child. We believe she is *t'lick tlassca*.' After some discussion, this term was translated as 'wonder.'

'Yes,' Pamra agreed with a rare smile. 'She is a wonder.'

'Would Pamra stay long?'

By this time Lila lay on Werf's lap, patting her feathery bosom with long, stretched gestures, murmuring her own legato music. Werf dripped tea into her mouth, and the baby smiled, an endless smile, like dawn.

'Why had she come?'

Without thinking to censor what she said, Pamra told them why she had come. Not all, merely some. Awakeners were part of the reason, and the Servants of Abricor. There was a sad murmuring, a shaking of feathered heads.

'They were kin to us one time, those fliers of the Northshore. Those you call Servants of Abricor. We remember that time in our histories. There was a time when honor could have been retained. Our tribe, the Treeci, chose the way of honor. They, those who remained, chose otherwise. There are certain words in our language which go back to that time which those on the Northshore no longer know. Words like "decency." And "dignity." It makes us sad what they have become.' Werf shook her feathered head in sadness, widening the plumy circles around her eyes.

Binna changed the subject, and Pamra kept quiet, abashed at the sadness she had caused.

'We thought you might like to see some of our dancing,' said Binna, nodding at a young Treeci, who went racing away with this message. In moments there were sounds of a drum and a rhythmic tinkling.

From the teahouse the Treeci watched indulgently, even proudly. On the lawn the young Treeci sat, whispering, a few going so far as to point with wingtips, as though accidentally. Looking at these youths, Pamra could not tell whether they were male or female; they had no distinguishing colors, they were merely young. Perhaps there was a stage in development in which it did not matter, for all the young ones murmured together, moved about in giggling groups, walked with entwined fingers and heads tilted toward one another.

The dancers, however, were all male. Pamra could feel it. They twirled and postured, stamped, wings wide with each feather displayed, chest feathers fluffed, those around the eyes widened into flashing circles. Their flat beaks had been rouged, their talons painted. Beside her Werf sat smiling, wing fingers tapping in time to the drums, eyes moist. Pamra followed the direction of her eyes. Werf's son, Neff, among the dancers, magnificent in his grace and strength, the dance itself stimulating, breathtaking. Without thinking, Pamra started to say something about this, some small, complimentary remark, only to feel Joy's fingers biting into her arm. Confused, she confronted the old woman's forbidding eyes with wide, excited eyes of her own. This, too, was not to be spoken of. Pamra pulled her arm away. She wanted to say something, do something. Her face was flushed, red; she could feel the heat in it, in her arms trembling with the music.

Binna had been watching her. Now she said something loudly, a cutting metal sound, and the dance ended in a ragged cacophony of drum and bell. There was conversation then, apologies, a rapid murmur of polite talk covering the sudden end of the entertainment. Pamra did not understand it.

Then they were on their way home. 'Binna apologized,' said Joy. There was sorrow in her voice, as though she had been given news of a grave illness or death.

'For what? I don't understand.'

'For the dancing. They had not realized you would be – moved by it.'

133

'It was exciting! That's wrong?' Pamra wanted to laugh. 'Isn't that the object of it all?'

'No. Never. That would be unseemly.' This, too, was forbidden ground. Joy would not talk of it further.

Her reticence broke the fragile confidence that had been building between them. Now Pamra could not feel comfortable. Each remark had to be weighed for acceptability. There were too many areas of taboo. She began to take long walks, carrying the slow baby in her shawl, far down the shore toward the west, far into the forest toward the south, roaming the rolling island woods to pass the time and leave the old woman alone. Joy did not object. She seemed to have withdrawn from Pamra as though Pamra had been culpable of some social error that only time would dilute. Her feelings did not seem to convey disapproval so much as sorrow. It was easier for them both when they were apart.

Once or twice she encountered Binna or Werf on her solitary walks. She transgressed politeness to ask them a few things about old times and the Servants of Abricor. They were not reluctant to talk, merely distressed by it, their pain so palpable that she gave it up. What she had learned from them was already a lumpish knot in her throat, confirming her knowledge that in the Tower she had been used and lied to.

Pamra found a favorite place along the shore, high among a cluster of lichened stones. It was almost a little room, sheltered from the sky, with a tiny moss yard and minuscule pool of rain-water. Here Lila could lie for long hours on the moss, singing her drawn-out notes of gladness. Pamra merely sat, hypnotized by the sound and the River flow.

It was there that Neff came.

She arrived at her sitting place one afternoon to find a spray of flowers laid upon the moss, a delicate crimson bouquet tied with a knot of violet grass, the whole displayed as in a picture. Someone.

From the top of the rock she searched the area. He was sitting on the Rivershore, face turned from her as though to make it easy for her not to see him. She did see him, and the frustration that had simmered in her for days brought a flush to her cheeks. She would not take part in this silly custom of silence when he had been so thoughtful. She waved, beckoned, called, 'Come up!'

He came leaping up the rocks in one flowing motion of power, posed upon the ridge in a posture so unconsciously graceful that she drew breath, belly clenching and loosing like a knot untied. 'Artist's blood,' they might have called such a feeling on the Northshore. 'Artist's eyes,' Thrasne would have said. She was not thinking of Thrasne; she was breathing deeply, almost unaware of her own body.

She motioned to the rock across from her, a flat place with a convenient arm and back for leaning, her own favorite seat. He sat there, looking at her from enormous eyes. 'You're Neff,' she said. 'Aren't you?' He would not speak, she thought, unless she spoke to him first.

'Yes,' he said in his bell voice. 'Neff!'

'Your mother has been very kind to me. Won't you tell me something about that dance you did the other day? It was very beautiful.'

'Just the dance.' He turned away in shyness, looking at her from one eye only. 'The dance we do.'

'I see.' She was at a loss. 'We have no dances like that on the Northshore. At least none I have seen.'

'Tell me of the Northshore,' he begged, the words tumbling over one another in their eagerness. 'Tell me of the Northshore. There! Over there!'

Poor thing, she thought with immediate sympathy. He's an explorer at heart. She told him about the Northshore. Wary of those subjects that caused discomfort, she did not speak of the Awakeners or the Servants of Abricor, but of more usual things. Festivals. The Candy Tree. Planting pamet and gathering the ripe pods. Fruit harvest in the puncon groves. As she spoke, she realized how little she actually knew of the life of the people. All her memories were of childhood, before entering the Tower. She could not share with him any memories after that.

'The one who brought you, will he come back for you?'

'Yes. He'll be back. When the boat is fixed.'

'Would you – would he let me see the boat?'

'Haven't you seen boats before? Haven't you seen them when they come to pick up the dye shells?'

'I mean, would he let me go on it? See it? See the inside of it?'

'I'm sure he would.' If those biddies will let you, she thought. 'Would that be all right with the . . . others?'

He shook his head, the edges of his beak flushing as though rouged. 'Mother wouldn't let me.'

'We'll have to arrange it without her knowing, then.' There it was, out in the open. Rebellion.

He seemed frightened by this; frightened and stimulated at the same time. He stood, posing, stamped, extended his wings, looked at her flirtatiously out of one eye. Then she blushed, and he turned away, as suddenly shy. 'That would be wonderful. Please. Do that.' He jittered from foot to foot, finally murmuring, 'I have to go now.' He sped away down the rocks.

'Neff,' she called, unable to let him go. 'Thank you for the flowers.'

'We give them like that,' he called. 'We Treeci. To our sisters.'

So then, she thought, half in amusement. I'm one of his family. So much for the old woman's distinctions. If he thought of Pamra as a sister, then it would be all right to talk to him. They did talk to their sisters.

That night she got out the puncon jam. Jam seemed to loosen Joy's old tongue. Forbidden subject or not, Pamra wanted to learn about the Treeci.

'The young ones,' she said casually, 'all appear to be about the same age. I didn't see any babies.'

'No, there won't be any babies for almost a year. They only breed one year in ten. My brother used to say it had something to do with keeping the population in balance. They don't have any more than the island can keep. Sensible of them, he used to say.'

136

'I didn't see any males among the children.'

'You probably did. Far as the Treeci are concerned, children are just children. Can't tell male from female till they get to be about fifteen.'

'So the one that came here, with his mother, he was over fifteen?'

'Nineteen,' said Joy, burrowing into the jam pot. 'Nineteen last Conjunction.'

'You know that? So exactly?'

'Well, of course. I know all Werf's children, have for years. She used to bring Neff and his sisters here from the time they were just hatchlings. I used to feed them nut cookies and play hide and go find with them in the woods.'

'But now you don't talk to Neff? After being his friend when he was a child?' She could not keep the outrage from her voice.

The old woman pushed her chair back from the table, stood to confront her accusing look. 'Girl, you're my guest and I'll give you guest rights, but don't lay your voice on me for things you don't understand. I never said I couldn't talk to Neff, being almost his mother and him as dear to me as my own ever were, I said *you* couldn't. I said to you before, they're not people. Not human people. You've got to give them their own way!'

There were tears in the old woman's eyes, and it was that which softened Pamra. If she was already grieved over whatever it was, there was no point in adding to her grief. So Pamra bowed her head in submission, making her apologies, promising not to bring up the matter again. It did not change her mind. Cruelty was cruelty. If Neff got pleasure out of making her an honorary sister, why, then she would be his honorary sister.

At the end of thirty days, she began to make regular trips at dusk each day, looking for Thrasne's signal fires. More and more often during these excursions, Neff appeared, though he never did when one of the old people accompanied her. At other times during the day she would find flowers strewn in her path, a necklace of bright petals strung on grass, bouquets of herbs smelling of damp woods or sunny meadows. She began to look forward to the evening walks, began to slip away early without inviting Joy or Bethne or Stodder to come along.

'Your man, he'll be back for you,' said Joy.

'I know he will. He said it might take a long time.'

'Thought you might be worried. You're spending so much time alone.' This with a sidelong, questioning look.

For several nights thereafter she invited the oldsters to come with her, paying particular attention to being chatty with them. Thereafter she included one or more of them every few days, merely to allay their concern, she told herself. No point in distressing them.

'Tell me about the baby,' said Neff. He would hold Lila for hours, fascinated by her leisurely, graceful movements. Pamra saw him trying to mimic them in dance, long, stretched extensions of wing and leg as though he would reach himself through into Lila's timeless world and make himself a place there. Often he danced for Pamra, without music, humming to himself in a strangely moving, unmelodic way.

'What is that music?' she asked at last.

'Just . . . just music. The music,' he said, flushing. He had done that more in recent days, the red moving in from the edges of his beak toward the center. The feathers on his chest were turning crimson as well, and the wide, plumy ones around his eyes. When he looked at her like that, she wanted to hold him, tell him everything was fine. It made her ache for him.

'Tell me of this man who hunts you!' he asked.

'How did you know about that?'

'I heard Mother talking. They think the Awakeners are very cruel to raise up the dead, who should lie asleep. Also our kin, the Servants. They think them stupid, vicious, and cruel, also.'

Not more cruel than they, she thought, stroking the line of his jaw, the feathers of his chest. She could tell he liked having her do that, liked having her near him.

'I suppose every group of people has its own cruelties,' she said, wondering if he would say anything about his own treatment at the hands of his people. Remembering her own rebellion as a child, she could not accept his passivity. Perhaps it lay in the fact that all males were treated much alike; perhaps that made it seem less cruel. 'Don't your friends miss you when you're off here with me?'

'They are mostly alone. Besides' – he flushed – 'I am a Talker. They aren't Talkers. Males aren't much. Only one in each thousand males is a Talker, they say.'

'You mean other males don't talk? Never did?'

'They talk like everyone when they are children. When they grow up, though, talking goes. Except once in a while, one like me. It makes it harder.'

She could not bear the thought. The safest one to ask seemed to be old Stodder.

'Is it true the male Treeci can't talk?'

'Oh, they can talk. They just don't much.'

'What do you mean, they don't much?'

'They just lose interest, that's all. I suppose they figure why talk if you don't have to?' This seemed to her to be Stodder's own philosophy. She seldom heard him speak unless asked a direct question.

Upon examination, his comment made some sense. During visits to the Treeci village, Pamra noticed how cosseted the males really were. Why would they talk when every need was met before they had a chance to utter it? Each one had a circle of children seeing to his grooming, his food, his drink. Every male had a mother, sisters.

Though she went to the watching place each evening, there were still no signal fires. Stodder counted the days until Conjunction and remarked that the *Gift of Potipur* would likely not come until after the flood tides. 'Thrasne's a good boatman. He won't risk the *Gift*.'

'Do you really think he won't come until after the flood tides, Stodder?'

'Ah, girl, he could still get here. Don't leave off looking for the fires. Just don't be disappointed.'

139

Was she disappointed? Did she care if Thrasne came soon or late? What were they to one another, after all? She frowned at this new consideration. It was an uncomfortable thought because she should have been able to answer it and could not. She didn't know. 'Does he love me?' She whispered the question, looking for the answer in Lila's eyes, which lightened almost imperceptibly into a smile. 'Does Thrasne love me?' Suddenly she thought of things he had done, gifts he had given. Was that why?

What did the question mean? If he did or not, what difference did it make?

She wrapped herself warmly in a heavy shawl and went to the rocks with Bethne, seeing nothing on the Northshore, hearing nothing but the usual *shush* of wind and River sounds. They turned to walk back along the ridge in the dusk, the light of Potipur casting a ruddy glow along the slopes, making black pits of shadow. In a clearing at the foot of the hill, there were two Treeci dancing, male and female. 'Beautiful,' whispered Pamra. 'Look, Bethne. Look how beautiful.'

The male Treeci called plaintively into the dusk; the female responded, the two voices like a duet, sweeter than one could bear.

'What are they saying?' Pamra stopped, straining to hear, until Bethne tugged her along.

'Come along. It isn't polite to listen in. What he's singing is "Tell me of my children . . ." ' It's a song the young males sing. So she sings to him of his children, how strong and graceful they will be.'

'Tell me of my children,' Pamra mused. Sentimental, that. Unlike Neff. He was all 'tell me,' but about a hundred other things.

'Tell me about the Southshore.'

'Neff, no one knows anything about the Southshore. Maybe people went there once, but no one does now. Thrasne says the World River is twenty-four hundred miles wide, and no one goes farther out than Strinder's Isle. All the measurements are in the old chart-of-towns. That amazes me, but it's true.'

'Are there Treeci there?'

'For all I know there could be.'

'I could get there, in a boat. With a sail.'

'Why would you want to do that?'

'I just thought of it, that's all.' He rose, jittering, unable to keep still, pulled her up to dance with him. This was new, their dancing together. When they were exhausted by it, they lay curled in the moss bed side-by-side, she stroking his feathered chest, dreamy and quiet.

'You are my sister,' he said. 'Aren't you. It's all right for me to be here. You really are my sister.'

'Of course,' she choked. 'Of course I am.'

The next evening Pamra and Joy found the approach to her lookout place ankle deep in water. 'Conjunction,' said Joy, measuring the water with her eyes. 'Moons are pulling that water right up here, aren't they. Well, if Thrasne doesn't get back for you in the next few days, he won't come until low-water-after-the-moons. There's no place to tie up for long at the west end. He'll have better sense than to try.'

Pamra tried to feel disappointment. The feeling would not come. She was not concerned. Not upset. All it meant was she would have more time with Neff. More time to dance, to sing, to lie together in the dusk watching the moons move among the stars. He had become so beautiful in recent days. Because of their friendship, she told herself. Because he had someone to talk to.

'Only ten days or so to Conjunction,' said Joy, saddened by some recollection, some nostalgic connection that Pamra could not follow. 'Think I'll go over to the village tomorrow to visit . . . Werf. Few days she'll be too busy.'

'I'll go with you.'

'No. No, just a friendly visit between Werf and me, I think. Two old friends. You can visit later. After Conjunction. There'll be plenty of time. Thrasne's not going to get here before.'

The drums began to sound nightly, throbbing like hearts,

like bruises, like the pulse in wounds, painfully immediate. Joy stood at the window, listening, tears standing in her eyes. 'Memories,' she said abashedly, wiping the tears away. 'So many memories.'

Of her childhood, Pamra thought. Of her young womanhood, of her children. Sad to be old and almost alone with only these other-people for company; sad to think of their children as one's own because one has none of one's own.

Still the drums. Pamra put Lila in a shawl and started to go visiting.

'No,' said Joy. 'You wouldn't be welcome.'

'I thought I'd just watch the dancing.'

Joy didn't speak.

'It's their religious time,' said Bethne. 'Their farewell time.'

'The old year?' Pamra asked, unwillingly taking off her shawl, remembering the celebrations of her childhood when they said farewell to the old year and welcome to the new.

'Something like that,' said Bethne.

Neff came earlier each day. He was thinner, fined down to pure muscle and bone, light as reeds in the wind. 'All the dancing,' he explained. 'I haven't been hungry.'

She tested this, bringing cakes, bringing tea in a bottle. He drank the tea thirstily but gagged at the cakes. 'Too much dancing.'

She worried about him as he lay in her arms, eyes shut in sleep. And yet he didn't look at all unhealthy but vital and alive, his beak bright red along the edges, the feathers on his neck and chest turning a brilliant crimson. He had never asked so many questions, had so many things he wanted her to tell him. He seemed to want to be with her so much it was an agony to leave him and return to the house.

'We must have festival,' exclaimed Joy. 'We must have a celebration of our own! I haven't made a festival dinner for twenty years. With Pamra and Lila here, we must! With wine! We'll open up the big front room we used to use!'

Pamra found herself drawn in, involved, sent scurrying here and there for everything imaginable, pulled in to help with long, detailed recipes. There was something a little frantic in the way Joy set herself to this task, as though she wanted terribly to remember, or to forget. Or perhaps it was only a festival for Lila. Festivals were for children, after all. The Candy Tree. That was for children.

On conjugation evening, Pamra went to the lookout rocks, watching for Neff, seeing no sign of him. Well, she told herself, he couldn't come. Not until after Conjunction. With the water this high, it was sure that Thrasne wasn't going to be signaling, either. Still, she climbed the rocks one more time.

There were flowers on the stone. She went on to the mossy place, holding her breath, to find him there, already there, moving like a windblown cloud in a tiny circle. 'Pam-ra,' he sang to her in a voice unlike his own. His eyes were so bright she thought he might be drugged. 'Pamra, tell me about the River.'

He wouldn't wait for her to tell him anything, wouldn't let her sit down. 'Tell me about the Towers. Tell me about fishing.' He wanted to know everything, couldn't sit still to listen to anything. 'I have to go back.'

'Come again tomorrow, Neff. I'll wait for you tomorrow.'

'Come again tomorrow,' he cried. 'Oh, Pamra, tell me of my children . . .'

Her mouth fell open in surprise, but he did not wait to be told. He fled, leaving the smell of himself behind, a rich fragrance that made her breathe as though she had been running. When she returned to the house, her trousers were wet between her legs. She washed herself at the spring, hanging the clothes out to dry, drying herself in the wind. Her nipples were hard, like little stones. She had never felt them like that, so painful. She put her hands over them, trying to soften them, but it only made them worse. She should have been cold in the wintery wind, but she was warm, fiery, alive with the dance. It was the drums, she knew, the hectic batter of the drums, like her own heartbeat gone mad.

The oldsters made their festival dinner, scattered the seeds of the Candy Tree upon Lila's cot, sang festival songs in quavering old voices, unsure of the words. There was wine, more of it than was good for any of them, Pamra felt, repeatedly emptying her own glass out the window, only to have it refilled solicitously by Joy. Then it was over. They had exhausted themselves as if purposely, worn themselves fine and dry so they could only fall into their beds.

'You'll sleep, won't you?' asked Joy, nodding with weariness, half-drunk. 'You will sleep.'

Pamra yawned. Of course. Even without the wine, she would sleep.

In the deep dark she woke, sitting straight up in the bed, hearing Lila stir beside her, where she, too, had heard the sound. Pamra had not heard it before but knew in the instant what it was. Neff's voice calling in the night, bell-like, insistent, reverberating with an inexpressible vitality. 'Come. Come. I'm waiting for you.' Farther off were other such sounds, other such calls. Come, come. She heard only Neff, disregarding the others as so much noise.

She threw a cape over her nightdress, sandals on her feet, went out into the night, three moons from the top of the sky casting diffused shadows under every tree. 'Come,' he called. 'Come.' The voice came from the woods, from the meadows deep in the woods. She began to run, wondering what wonderful thing he had found to be calling so, her breath eager in her throat and her skin burning. She had never run so before, never so long and tirelessly, never run before without pain or effort.

Trunks of trees going by, dark and light, masses of moon and shade, splashing of stream shallows, silver fountains beneath her feet, meadow grass dotted with pale faces of winter-blooming flowers. 'Come.' A hillside of moss velvet. 'Come.'

Far to her left another voice called, and across the valley before her a figure ran toward that voice, wings extended as though to fly, feet seemingly scarcely to move as they skimmed the grass. Two met; two danced. There were angels alive in the night. Treeci.

'Come!' He danced upon the hilltop, posed in glory, silver and black on the light of the moons, head back, caroling, bell sound on the hill, voice of joy. 'Come!'

She ran toward him, panting now a little, wondering what marvelous festival this was, what occasion called the Treeci out into the night, remembering only then that it was Conjunction. Of course. A second celebration.

He turned, seeing her, eyes wide in their circles of feathers, wider yet as he realized who it was ascending the hill. 'No,' he cried, a wounded sound. 'No. No.'

What did he mean? She paused, puzzled at this denial, stopping short when he threatened her with widespread wings. She could see him clearly now, feathers on his abdomen spread wide to disclose a pulsing, swollen organ on the bare skin, black in the night, oozing silver. 'No,' he begged.

She went toward him, her thighs sliding slickly, wetly on one another. 'Neff? It's Pamra. Neff?'

An agonized cry from him as he clasped her, his body beating against her, one thrust, two and three, breaking away only to close again, then away, this time really away to flee down the hillside faster than she could pursue him, no longer calling, now only crying, more like a child than an adult. She stared after him stupidly, brushing at the front of her cape, where the copious jet of sticky fluid clung, slowly, very slowly flushing as she realized what had happened, what she had been too preoccupied with her own feelings to see.

'Mating,' she whispered to herself, aghast. 'It's their mating time. Oh, by Potipur, but I've shamed him and myself.' Sudden tears burned hotter than her skin, and all at once she felt cold.

She trudged homeward, a longer way than she could have imagined, trying various apologies in her head, how she would say it, how she would rectify the situation. Her cape stank of his juices, a smell as wild as the woods themselves. She would have to wash it. When she returned to the house, however, she could only fall into bed, leaving the cape where she dropped it beside the door.

She was wakened by Joy shaking her, shaking her, screaming at her. 'What have you done, damn you, Pamra, what have you done?'

She sat up stupidly, drawing the blanket over her breasts as though against attack. 'What . . . what do you mean?'

'Did you go out ? Last night? You didn't go out. Not with all the wine I gave you. You couldn't have. No. You couldn't have done that to him. He was my son, like my own son.'

'I woke up.' Pamra cowered, trying to explain, still half-asleep. 'I intruded. But I didn't hurt him. I'm sorry. How in hell did you find out, anyhow?'

'I smelled it. Smelled it. On your cape. That smell. Oh, stupid, stupid, selfish, unhearing, unheeding stupid girl.' She was weeping too hard to talk, weeping herself away, out of the room, leaving Pamra to stare foolishly at the door. In the cot beside the bed, Lila made a sound of pain, a creaking agony. Pamra pressed her hands over her ears, willing not to hear it.

It was Bethne who came to her about noon. 'Joy asked me to have you pack up your things. Food in the cart. Stodder'll help you take it downshore to the west end. Joy'd rather you weren't here. Makes it too hard for her.'

'Bethne, I told her I was sorry. I didn't mean to intrude. Where is Joy? Why doesn't she tell me herself?'

'Look, girl, I'd have just thrown you out. I might have killed you. Didn't she tell you not to talk to Neff? I know she did. I heard her say so.'

'He thought of me as his sister. He said so. They can talk to their sisters.'

'Sure they talk to their sisters. That's so their sisters recognize their voices and have the common decency to stay away from them on the night. You didn't have the decency to listen to Joy, and you didn't have the decency to stay away from him, either. Now he's gone, wasted, all for nothing.'

'Gone? Away?'

'Gone. Dead. Lying on the funeral woodpile down there in

146

the village, all dressed in his pretty feathers, all spent. All the pretty males. Dancing, dancing, all danced out, mated out. I've thought about it sometimes, how it would be. Knowing it would all go so fast, all in a few years, a few days. Losing friends, losing words, becoming what they are at the end. No wonder they comfort themselves by asking their sisters to tell them of their children. Remember! I told you about that. "Tell me of my children!" Did Neff ever say that to you? Probably not. He was a Talker, poor little tyke. Talkers shouldn't have to go through it. They want to know so bad. He wanted to know so much . . .

'No one to tell him of his children, now no children. Him gone. His seed gone. His line gone.'

The old woman was crying. 'He was like a son to Joy. Like her own son.'

'I'll go there. I'll explain.'

'Oh, stupid girl, stay away from them. They're singing now. They'll sing each name, and some young Treeci girl will stand up and sing that she carries the children of that one. They'll sing Neff's name, and there'll be no one, no one at all, but that's better than having it be you, you stupid human, trying to explain!'

Bethne cried herself away. Pamra crouched on the floor, unable to move, to think. Dead. Unable to move. Dead. The smell of him was still in her nostrils, the sight of him dancing.

Tell him of his children.

147

12

Apprentice Melancholic Medoor Babji accepted a fat copper coin from her weeping victim, gave the paunchy shopkeeper a dozen halfhearted strokes of her fishskin whip, then put a glass Sorter coin into the sweating merchant's palm.

'May the Sorters accept the pain you have already borne as payment for your sins,' she singsonged in formula, slipping the merchant's warm metal into her own jingling purse. Medoor's purse was almost as stout as the merchant, full of the coin paid for whipping Northshoremen across a hundred towns this season before ending here in Chantry.

'Amen,' said the merchant, wiping his eyes. Though why he should weep, Medoor could not say. Medoor had not struck him hard enough to get through the lard to anything essential, a fact brought forcibly to Medoor's attention by her Leader, Taj Noteen, who came up behind her and cuffed her across the back of her head.

'The man paid you, Babji! Put some muscle into it! What's all this patty-pat, as if you were playing with a babby.'

'He was such an *old* fart,' Medoor responded, knowing it was the wrong thing to say.

'So much more in need of Sorter compassion!' The leader leered at her, daring her to say anything more, an invitation Medoor sensibly refused. She knew as well as Noteen did that Sorters, Sorter compassion, and Sorter coin were all equally mythological, but it was Melancholic policy to appear to believe in the myth, at least when moving among the shore-fish – so-called because the townees schooled at the edge of the River, waiting to be caught, just as song-fish did in the waters along the shore.

'The shore-fish believe, they pay because they believe,' Noteen was fond of saying. 'Who are you to question their belief?'

Which was another way of telling Medoor not to bite the hand that offered her hard metal coin. Coin that would buy food, wine, woven pamet cloth. Coin to send to the Noor kindred on the steppes – some for the near-kin of each Melancholic; some for the coffers of the Queen. Thinking of Queen Fibji, Medoor made a reverent gesture and saw the leader's glance change to one of understanding approval. He thought he understood how she felt, but he did not, not at all. Medoor Babji had more reason than most to care about Queen Fibji. It was Queen Fibji's need for coin that made any of them willing to serve a term as Melancholics, despite the precarious life of the Noor steppe dwellers and the relative luxury the Melancholics knew. But Medoor's feelings for the Queen were of different kind and intensity. And private, she reminded herself. Very private.

'I don't know why the Queen needs all that coin,' Riv Lymeen had said once during a fireside argument with Medoor. 'I've been at Queen Fibji's encampment, and even her big audience tent isn't that wonderful. My uncle Jiraz has one almost that big.'

The leader had intervened in that argument, too, saving Lymeen from a pounding. 'None of your business why she needs it, Lymeen. It's for some great plan of her own, for all us Noor; for us here on Northshore getting coin out of shore-fish pockets and for them on the steppes, fighting off the Jondarites. She's planning for all of us, woman, so we don't question what she needs it for. She needs it, and that's enough.'

These reflections fled as the leader raised his signal bells and struck them with a flexible hammer, blindingly fast, the shrill tunes cutting through all the babble of the marketplace. 'Assembly,' succeeded rapidly by 'Stores,' 'Wagoneers,' and then 'Return to camp.'

149

Medoor had been on stores detail for one Viranel, with some days of the duty yet to run. She coiled her fishskin whip into its case, slinging it over her shoulder as she looked around for the others. Riv Lymeen, very white teeth in an almost black face and a voice like a whip stroke; Fez Dooraz, plump and wobbly with sad brown eyes; and old white-headed Zyneem Porabji, who could add up in his head faster than the merchants could on their beads. The three of them were already together at the head of Market Street, waiting for her.

'Come on, Babji,' Lymeen called, her fuzzy head wagging disapproval and her lips curled to show her fangs. 'Step it up, Medoor. All the camp will go hungry waiting on you.'

Which was unfair, for Lymeen often scamped her whips late in the afternoon. 'Match coin!' Medoor growled at her, pleased to see the other turn away without accepting the challenge. Whatever Riv might say about Medoor being distractible and absentminded, she couldn't say Medoor was lazy – something Riv Lymeen had often heard said of herself. The amount of coin each Melancholic gained was an accurate measure of the amount of effort each Melancholic expended. 'Match coin' was a way of ending argument on the matter.

'Leader says to see can we get song-fish,' remarked old Porabji. 'Fillets or whole. Some to eat tonight and some to dry and smoke for the trip. I'll see to that. You, Babji, go along to the wine merchants. Lymeen, you to Grain Alley, and Dooraz will see to the greens. If there's fresh puncon fruit, call me. They'll want the price of a copper bracelet for it, but maybe I can talk them down. Remember, we're buying for tonight plus two days. We're westering tomorrow. Three or four more towns, Taj Noteen says, and then back to the steppes.

Three or four more towns. Then the long walk north-ward, through the dry, white-podded pamet fields on the arid heights and the wet grainfields along the little streams, blue with tasseled bloom. Many days with no markets, no one allowed to sell them food, and fliers hanging high, black dots on the pale sky, to see they ate nothing from the fields. Many days living on what they pulled in the carts. Then the line of watchtowers, marking the edge of Northshore, and beyond that the steppes. There would be roasted jarb root. Medoor would never understand why anyone would dry jarb root skins and smoke them as the Mendicants did – visions or no visions – when one could bury them in the coals in their skins and eat them, sweet and satisfying as nothing else edible could ever be. And there would be stewed grains from the traveler fields, small grain patches that were harvested, weeded, fertilized, and replanted by any Noor who traveled by. Every Noor carried seed grain in a pouch, and every Noor learned to control his or her bladder, too, so as not to waste fertilizer on empty sand.

Medoor longed for the steppes, that great sea of grass dotted with the gray-green rosettes of jarb plants and interrupted by occasional thorn trees with their tart, crimson fruit. The rivers of the steppes were full of silvery cheevle – tiny toothsome fish, perfectly safe to eat – and equally full of shiggles – plump, ground-running birds that could not be eaten at all unless one cooked them with grain but when cooked with grain tasted of heaven. Medoor told herself she would trade all the wines and sweetmeats of Northshore for the food of the steppes.

She hurried toward the wine merchants' stalls, as though by speeding this part of their necessary preparation she could speed their departure. She was heartily sick of Northshore; tired of the babble and bellow of its people, the muddy taste of its food, and the stink of its workers, glad as she had never been glad before of her dark skin, which prevented the Tears of Viranel from invading her body, dead or alive. Tears wouldn't work on black folk. Something about the light not getting through. It didn't matter why they wouldn't work. The fact was enough to be thankful for.

'Thanks be to the Jabr dur Noor,' she murmured to herself in the ritual prayer of the Noors. 'Thanks be that I

151

am black.' Thus assured of the attention of the All-Seeing, she lifted a merchant's purse as he pressed through the market throng, slipping it into her trouser leg. At the wine merchant's she bargained well. Between what she bought out of the merchant's purse and what she slipped into her wide pockets without paying for, the price would be acceptable, even to Porabji. There was fresh puncon for sale, but Medoor did not bother running to the old man with word of it. When they returned to camp, she simply emptied her capacious trouser legs, placing russet fruit after russet fruit onto the meal wagon tailgate, grinning as she did so until Porabji, who had begun by scowling at her, had to grin in return.

'You'll be caught one of these days, girl,' he said, shaking his head. 'You'll be caught and brought up before the Tower charged with theft.'

'What'll they do, let the fliers eat me?' She grinned. Criminals were dosed with Tears and given to the fliers for food, at least white ones were, or so it was rumored.

Porabji shook his head. 'They'll burn you, girl. That's what they do to us Noors. If the fliers can't eat someone, they'll burn him and scatter his ashes on the River.'

Medoor sobered somewhat, if only for a time. She had witnessed a burning once. It was not an end that appealed to her. She promised herself for the hundredth time to be more careful. Still, stealing was the one thing she did really well, and it was hard to give up one's only talent. She went toward the campfire in a mood of mixed self-congratulation and caution. One more night among the stinking heathen of this town, then three towns more, then home, to the tents of . . . well. Home. That was enough.

When the Noor had been fed, Medoor was free to amuse herself until roll call. There was never any question where she would go or what she would do with her free time. She had had only one passion since she had first seen the River. Boats. Boats spoke to Medoor. Their planks oozed with mysterious travel, far destinations. Their crews had been all-the-way-around. They had seen everything, been everywhere. Sometimes the owners would let her come aboard. More than once she'd gone aboard at some lecher's invitation and had to show her knife and whip to get off again, but no owner was going to bring the curse of the Melancholics down on himself. He might hint a little, or make an outright proposition, but he wouldn't try rape. At least, Medoor thought with some satisfaction, none had yet. It had been the danger her mother had most feared for a Noor daughter, here among the heathen. Medoor had had to promise utmost prudence before she had obtained permission to join the Melancholics.

For some days now, there had been one particular boat at the Chantry docks that interested Medoor, and it was certain the troubled man who was owner of the *Gift of Potipur* wouldn't bother her. Though he seemed to like to talk to her, he hadn't once looked at her with that particular expression men sometimes got. It was almost as though he didn't know she was a woman at all, and this was part of the fascination. Most boatmen were garrulous sorts, full of tales and exaggerations, but the crew of the *Gift* was of a different kind. Quiet. Almost secretive. Not fearful, she thought, but with a kind of separation about them, as though they knew something the rest of the world didn't. Thrasne himelf had a habit of standing on the deck, staring southward over the River at one particular spot, as though there should be something there he could see.

'Thrasne owner,' she called, making her way up the plank.

'Medoor Babji,' came the call in return. He was below, where she often found him, supervising the repair of the ship's planks stove in by some great floating tree on the wide River. She poked her head down, attracted by the strange smell from below. Most of the crew was there, caulking the new planks with frag sap. The hot pungency of the caulk took her breath away, and she wondered how they could bear to work in the close heat of the hold. She went back to the deck, pausing for a time to admire the great winged figure that poised at the bow of the vessel, a giant flame-bird, perhaps, or a winged angel. Tired of this, she leaned against the rail, watching the water. There, after a time, Thrasne joined her.

'Another day or two,' he said, wiping his hands on a scrap of waste. 'We'll be done with it.'

'How can you breathe down there?'

'Oh, after an hour or two, you get drunk with it. When everyone starts giggling and stumbling, then's time to call a halt for the day. They'll be coming up soon.' He nodded at her, a friendly expression. 'Medoor Babji,' he mused. 'What does your name mean? It must mean something.'

'It does mean something,' she retorted. 'As much as yours does.'

'Thrasne?' He thought about this for a moment. 'It was my grandfather's name. It was the name of the place he came from, inland, where they had a farm. So, what does your name mean?'

'The Noor have a secret language of naming. We usually don't share our secret names with Northshoremen.'

'Oh.'

He said it flatly, accepting rejection, and she immediately sought to make amends.

'I just meant it wasn't customary. All our names are two words, and the two words put together have another meaning. Like in our home tribe, there's a man named Jikool Pesit. Jikool means ''stones,'', and Pesit means ''nighttime,'' ''dark.'' Stones in the dark are something you fall over, so that name would mean ''Stumbler'' in the Northshore language.'

He turned an interested face, so she went on. 'I have a good friend whose name is Temin Suteed. Temin means ''a key,'' and Suteed is ''golden'' – ah, like sunlight. If you lock up gold with a key, that means ''treasure,'' so that's her name. Treasure . . .

'My grandfather's name was M'noor Jeroomly. M'noor is from the same word as our tribal name. Noor. Noor means ''a speaking people.'' And m'noor means ''spoken.'' Jeroomly means ''promising,'' so the two together mean ''oath,'' and that was his name.'

154

'How about Taj Noteen?' asked Thrasne, who had met the troupe leader.

She laughed. 'In Northshore he would be called Strutter.' Thrasne shook his head, not understanding.

'It comes from the words for cock and feather, that is, plume, and the plumed birds always strut, you know.'

'But you won't tell me what your name means.'

She flushed. 'Perhaps someday.' Actually, Medoor Babji still had her baby name, and it meant something like 'dearest little one.' She did not want Thrasne to know that. Yet.

He let it go, staring out across the River, upon his face that expression of concern and yearning that had so interested Medoor.

'What's out there?' she asked, taking the plunge. 'You're always looking out there.'

'There!' He was startled, stuttered a reply. 'Oh, someone – someone from the crew, is all. Someone we had to leave on an island when we came in for repairs. We're to pick . . . her up when we're solid again, and it's been longer than we planned. We thought it would be before festival.'

'Oh.' She didn't comment further. With some men she might have teased, but not with Thrasne. Whatever bothered him, it was no light thing. And whoever he had left behind, it had been no common crew member. 'Well, we may see you down River, then. Our leader says we'll visit three more towns before turning north.'

'Possibly.' He wasn't interested. She could tell. His lack of interest was irritating enough to gamble on. 'Thrasne?'

'Hmm?'

'Who is she, really?'

His silence made her think she had overstepped, but after a time he turned toward her, not looking at her, heaving one hip onto the rail so he could sit half facing her.

'Did you ever dream of anyone, Medoor Babji?'

She had climbed onto the rail and teetered there now, trying to make sense of his question. 'Of anyone? I guess so. Mostly people I know, I suppose.'

155

'Did you ever dream of someone you didn't know? Over and over again?'

She shook her head. This conversation was not going as she had thought it might. Nonetheless, it was interesting. 'No, Thrasne owner. I never have.'

'I used to. When I was only a boy. A woman. Always the same woman. I called her Suspirra. A dream woman. The most beautiful woman in the world. I made a little carving of her. I still have it.' He was silent again, then, and she thought he had talked all he would. Just as she was about to get down from the rail and bid him a polite farewell, he began again.

'When I was near grown, I found a woman's body in the River. It had been blighted. You know what that is?'

She nodded. She had never seen it, but she had a general idea.

'It was the woman I'd dreamed of. Line for line. Every feature. Face. Eyes. Feet. Everything. I brought her out of the River and kept her, Medoor Babji. Kept her for many years. And then one day I met the daughter of that woman. Found her, I guess you'd say. Truly, her daughter. The daughter she had borne long ago, before she had drowned. And the daughter was alive and the same, line for line. And she came onto the *Gift of Potipur*. It was before Conjunction, winter, when I found her. And that was more than a year, now.'

'And it was that woman you had to leave on the island?'

'That woman, yes.'

'Why? Is someone after her?'

He looked her in the eyes for the first time. 'Can I trust you not to go talking about this business, Babji? It could be my life. And hers.'

'Laughers?' She held her breath. This was the stuff of nightmare and romance. Laughers and dream woman.

Seeing his discomfort, she changed the subject. 'It's nice you found your dream woman, Thrasne. Things like that don't often happen.'

'I don't know what's happened,' he said in a kind of quiet

156

sadness. 'Her body lives on the *Gift*. But her spirit – it isn't here yet, Babji. So, I'm patient about it.'

He went on then, for some time, talking. He told her everything he knew of Pamra Don, everything he had ever thought, even some of the things he had hoped, though he did not realize that. Far off along the shore she heard the sound of 'Noor count' shrilling over the water.

'I must go, Thrasne owner,' she whispered, interrupting him. 'My leader will whip me with my own whip if I am not in place very soon.' Though he would not if he knew who she was, she thought. Still, it was important he not know.

'Ah,' he said, his unfocused gaze coming to rest on her and gradually clearing to reveal the girl perched there before him, dark smooth skin gleaming like the surface of the River. Her hair fell in a heavy fringe all the way to her knees, twisty strands of fifty or so hairs, each of which hung together, never tangling, like lengths of shiny black twine beneath a beaded headband, all gold and blue in the evening light. The scales of her fishskin vest gleamed also, laced tight over the long, full-sleeved shirt she wore tucked into pamet trousers died blue with mulluk shell. Her dark hand rested upon the rail, inches from his own, and he took it, turned it over to examine the pink brown of her palm, scarred and calloused from the whip. Her eyes were dark, and her pink lips parted in complaint.

'Come now, owner. I must go.'

'Go, Babji. I didn't mean to keep you. It's just – I had not really seen you until now.'

She ran down the plank and along the shore, wondering at the expression on his face. A kindly, surprised alertness, like a child finding something interesting and unexpected. Well. What to make of that? Nothing. Nothing at all.

Still, she was not sorry to hear him calling after her.

'Return again, Babji. Talk has done me good. Perhaps your people would like a ride to the next towns west?'

157

13

When the *Gift of Potipur* left the Chantry docks, Babji's troop of Melancholics was aboard, paying nothing for the transport and living on their own provisions. Thrasne had come to trust them, and, wisely, had seen their presence as a kind of camouflage. The *Gift* put on sail and headed out into the River, cutting across the tidal current toward the west end of Strinder's Isle, hidden in the southern mists.

Two days later, decks crowded with the curious Noor, Thrasne lowered a boat with two men to row ashore at the west end of the island, shot them a line, and tied fast to a great tree that leaned above the flood. It was twenty-two days after Conjunction.

Pamra had camped on the tiny beach for most of that time. She came aboard with Lila, hardly noticing the dark faces of the crowded passengers, not seeing at all the concern on Thrasne's face. Her eyes were deep set in a haggard face, and her hair was tangled as though she had not combed it in days. She was no less beautiful than ever, but it was a terrible, anguished beauty.

'Are you all right?' he begged, appalled. 'You look as though you've been ill.'

'I should have seen there were no older males,' she told him earnestly. 'I should have seen how worn away he was.'

'Pamra?'

'I was so sure it was cruel. So sure. Sometimes things are cruel and can be changed. Sometimes we only make them worse. Sentimentalizing. Pretending. So tied up in my own ideas. I couldn't see what was in front of me.'

158

'Pamra! Who are you talking about?'

She shook her head, handed Lila to him, made her way on board to her old refuge in the owner-house, glancing over her shoulder as she went, scarcely noticing the curious group of Melancholics at the rail, the young girl who was pressing close to her with open curiosity on her face. Passengers. Well, sometimes the Riverboats did carry deck passengers.

She did not really need to look behind her to know that Neff still followed her, as he had since the night after the fires. The smoke had risen in the village, and he had come. Stodder hadn't seen him. Pamra had. He had been with her since, face alight with curiosity and wonder, flowers in his hand, a recusant ghost.

And he was not alone. The pillar of golden dust beside him was her mother. And the accusative formless shadow was Delia. Three.

'Pamra, love. Are you all right?' Thrasne asked, following her into the house.

She let him hold her, even held him in return, aware at some subconscious level of the need in him, perceiving feeling in him she had never recognized, not even in herself until it was over, depending upon his kindness not to bother her with whatever it was.

'I'll be all right, Thrasne. I'll be all right.' She stepped away from him, shutting him out. She had to be all right. There was something Neff wanted to do, something she owed him. Him and her mother, and Delia.

When she was very quiet, she could hear their voices.

14

The Ascertainers maintained a domiciliary compound with dining hall, exercise yard, and dormitory, some above the ground, some below for winter occupancy. All was gray, splintery, very old. They kept it neat but could not keep it clean. The dust was too ancient, too deep in the cracks. When Ilze was given a broom to sweep it away, he knew he swept only the top layer of something that had been there for longer than he could imagine. Lifetimes. Some of the boards in the walls were newer than others. Some of the beams a lighter color. He saw it being replaced, piece by piece, over the centuries, never changing, always renewed. Why had they needed a place like this that long ago? Why did they need it now?

His Superior was in the compound, as well as some dozens of others, all with the same dazed look of incomprehension that Ilze knew he wore. There was no prohibition against talking together, but they seemed reluctant to do it, as though someone might be listening. As though anything said by anyone might lead to more questions. Even conjecture seemed dangerous. Only with his own Superior did he whisper his questions, await her answers.

'I don't understand,' he said, gritting his teeth, trying to reach her with his voice as he had been unable to reach the fliers. 'I thought if we got to the Chancery, we were safe! I haven't seen any humans at all except the guards and someone in a veil and some half-wit carrying buckets. Why were those foul poultry allowed to misuse me so? I don't understand any of this. Help me understand it.'

160

'Shh, shh. Ilze. Be thankful you are alive. I am thankful I am alive. You were not the only one mistreated, so hush. Think. You will need to think.'

'Think of what? I've done nothing but think since I've been here, and I've been here forever. I need some answers.'

'I meant for you to think strategically. Listen to me. We came here, to the Chancery. We demanded to see the Protector. Instead, we were sent to the Accusatory and sometime later were there questioned by the Servants of Abricor. But there were human Accusers watching, Ilze. Behind the veil you may be sure was a human Accuser.' Her mouth twisted bitterly at these words, as though she needed to spit. 'And the Servants of Abricor didn't take us away. We stayed here.'

Her hand on his arm stopped his quick, angry words.

'We stayed here, Ilze. And we're alive.'

He was forced to consider the implications of this. 'You think . . . you think it was some kind of agreement?'

'I listen to my mind, Ilze, for hints of conspiracy or ignorance or trouble. What words were said here? I can imagine what the Talker said, the one who came for us, the one you forced to bring us here. He demanded that you and I be bound securely and given to them. And then Lees Obol, the Protector of Man, would have said, "No, no, my friends, my treaty mates, but these are humans. Humans are not sent to the Talons. Humans must be examined here. By us." And then the Talkers would have blustered and demanded. What would they have said?'

Ilze thought about this, frowning, realizing he knew quite well what the Talkers would have said. 'They would have said they did not trust the humans. They must question us, they would have said, because they did not trust the humans. Perhaps that is not what they said, but that is what they meant.'

'Such was my own thought. A certain lack of trust. So, the Protector, for some reason – which I will learn if Potipur grants me time – allows us to be questioned by the

Talkers. But not taken away. And not seriously injured. I will not even have scars.' Think about that, she urged him silently, wanting him to realize that both of them had been equally mistreated. Both of us, Ilze. When you leave here, you must remember they tortured both of us.

Ilze, who believed he carried scars he would never lose, did not reply to this. 'And now?'

'And now something else. Some further part of the game. These fliers . . . oh, but they are concerned with Rivermen. Endlessly they asked me about the Rivermen. They asked you as well, I suppose. Always about the Rivermen.' About which we know nothing, she urged him silently. Nothing at all. Either of us.

'They did. But I know nothing about the Rivermen! I'm not one!'

'But they must find out, Ilze. If they cannot find one who knows, then they must ask those who do not. They must find out.'

He ignored the illogic of this, still trying to comprehend. 'I didn't know the Servants could talk. I didn't know they had . . . had a society of their own.'

She became very dignified, almost prim. 'Just as there are secrets seniors do not share with juniors or novices, so there are secrets Superiors do not share with seniors. You would have learned all about the Talkers in time, if you had earned advancement. As you would have done.' Oh yes, she told herself. He would have done. And pity the Tower he would have headed in his time.

'These others, the Talkers . . .?'

'There are not many of them. They come from the flier caste, from the Servants of Abricor. They do not seem to run in particular lines of descent, so I am told. They are hatched infrequently, once in a thousand hatchings. It is what our scholars call a sex-linked characteristic. All Talkers are males. When the ordinary flier males breed, they die. The Talkers are identified while still young; they are fed a special diet to prevent both breeding and death.'

'A special diet?' He thought about this before answering.

162

'When we're through with the workers, we drop them in the bone pits and the Servants of Abricor eat them. We all know that. No one cares. Who do the Talkers eat?'

'Our flesh is poisonous to the flier people, Ilze. In time you would have studied our history, how we came to this world to find the Servants already here; how they grew monstrously in number until the world could not feed them, until the herds of thrassil and weehar were gone; how they hunted us, only to find us poisonous. You would have read of Thoulia, one of their Talkers. Thoulia the Marvelous. It was Thoulia who showed them how to soften our flesh with the Tears of Viranel, and it was then the wars began in earnest between our two races. We killed them by the hundreds, Ilze, and they killed us, until there were few of them left and not many more of us. Until the treaty was made at last which allowed them to take our dead . . .

'Our dead are what they eat. Do you see why they fear the Rivermen so?'

He did not see. He could not see because of his anger. He did not realize she had not answered his question.

She went on, voice calm, willing him to listen and understand. 'If the cult of the Rivermen were to prevail, the fliers would die. All the Talkers. All the Servants. They would starve. There would be nothing for them to eat.'

Gradually he perceived the implications of this, implications so enormous he could not face them. All the philosophy, the theology, all his studies – oh, one knew there were evasions, one knew there were euphemisms employed, but still. Basically, one believed. Every senior Awakener knew that all the dead go into the worker pits except the Awakeners themselves. Even knowing this, still, still one believed. One understood the need for a pious mythology to keep the ordinary people quiet, but that did not nullify the essential truth. Senior Awakeners knew that truth. They had been accepted as the elect of Potipur. Common people – common people had to be led, instructed, used, then purified through that final agony. It was not Holy Sorters who put the sainted dead in Potipur's arms, it was the Servants of Abricor who carried their souls to Potipur. The common folk could not expect a fleshy resurrection, but that did not affect the spiritual one. But for Awakeners – for Awakeners it was a real immortality. In the body. It was the Servants of Abricor who carried the bodies of dead Awakeners directly to . . .

The thought stopped, blocked, destroyed by what she had been saying. Obviously this was not true. Obviously.

'What happens to us, to the Awakeners?' he snarled at her, his fingers digging deeply into her arm. 'If the Servants don't carry our bodies directly to Potipur, what really happens to us?' He hated himself for asking the question, sure she was laughing at him as he had always laughed at Pamra.

'If we are not clever and if our colleagues detest us sufficiently to take vengeance, we go into the pits with common folk,' she said haughtily, ignoring his grasp. 'With our hair rebraided to make us look like merchants or carpenters. In this way the myth is kept alive that no dead Awakener is ever seen in a worker pit.

'If we are more clever, or less disliked, we are burned to ashes at one of the crematories of the order. There is one here, at Highstone Lees. And if we are very clever, if we do our jobs well and cause no trouble to the Chancery or the Talkers, we are given the Sacred Payment. We are given what the treaty requires we be given, the elixir. If we receive that gift, we live a long, long time. Hundreds and hundreds of years. So be clever, Ilze. Let go of me.'

He let go of her, let go of her entirely, left her, did not try to speak with her after that. He had seen angry laughter in her face, bitter amusement. It was not unlike the amusement he had hidden so often from Pamra. The lady Kesseret thought him funny. Because he had believed. He burned with savage, humiliated shame at this. Because he had believed!

When the day came, he went before the Ascertainers, a kind of court with several humans sitting on high chairs to hear what was said. These, he was told, were members of the

164

Court of Appeals of the Towers. Judges, he thought. His Superior, the lady Kesseret, was there. She appeared little worse for her experience, though Ilze knew he looked like shit. Bruised, uncombed. They had not let him put his hair in braids, and it hung about his face like tangled rope. The Talkers were there, both the ones who questioned him and others he had not seen before. Old ones. With silvered feathers.

It was one of these who asked for the Accusation.

'Ilze, senior of the Tower of Baristown, is accused of heresy; of conspiracy to aid and comfort the Rivermen; of sheltering a Riverman spy in the Tower. He is accused of erroneous beliefs. He was led astray by lust. It may be he is essentially orthodox.' The humans on the bench accused him. He did not believe it.

He was given no chance to answer these charges. The silver-feathered ones merely nodded as they turned to the human people on the high chairs, and one of these said clearly, not looking at either Ilze or the lady Kesseret as he spoke, 'We will allow the Uplifted Ones to be present as Ilze is examined by the Ascertainers.'

The Talkers left. Ilze stood in the room alone with Lady Kesseret, he in the cage they had put him in, she behind the railing that separated him from the others.

'Poor Ilze,' she said. 'If you can withstand it, they will let you atone.' There was a strangeness in her voice that he could not identify. Only her words were sympathetic.

She went away then, saying nothing more. In the days of pain that followed, he remembered her words.

They threatened him repeatedly with the Tears of Viranel. He defied them. 'Give them to me. I don't care anymore. I might as well be dead.' They did things to him, things he had in the past done to others to shame and humiliate them. Ilze, however, felt no shame, only a slow, burning fury. He knew too well their purposes, but he learned his resolution and understanding could be weakened by pain. When they hurt his body, it insisted upon healing itself so they could hurt again. When he tried to

starve himself out of fury at them and to deprive them of
their obvious pleasure in his pain, they fed him by force.
They would not let him kill himself. And through it all the
veiled watcher stood, listening, peering, silent except for the
sound of millstones.

And yet, even throughout it all, he knew they were not
hurting him as much as they could. It was as though they did
not really want to break him. As though they were playing
with him. Waiting.

Finally he demanded they give him the Tears of Viranel
in order to prove he was telling the truth.

The Talker was amused.

'Accused, if these Ascertainers gave you the Tears, all you
would tell them would be the truth. Then we would eat you.
A temporary pleasure which would not advance our cause.'

'Oh, by the lost love of Potipur, isn't the truth what you
want! Isn't that what you've been putting me through this
pain for, to get the truth!'

'Oh, no, accused. If we wanted only the truth, we would
have given you the Tears long since.'

The winter wore on. He was moved to a cell below.
Gradually, through the pain and his own anger, he realized
what they wanted. Something to confirm their suspicion.
Something to save them embarrassment before the Chancery officials. Something to justify their opinions. Not
merely whatever it was Ilze did or did not know, but something more. Not the truth that he had, but some future
verity, something they could build upon to make themselves
secure. It came to him slowly, through the agony of their
knives and pinchers. It came to him slowly, and clever as he
was in the ways of submission, he did not realize they had
led him there.

'If you will let me find Pamra,' he said at last, believing
he had thought of it himself. 'I will find what it is you need to
know. Just let me find her.'

'Well,' mused the Ascertainer who twisted the iron, 'it
would serve her right. To have repaid your concern in this
fashion was an abomination. To have treated you so when

166

you had been so kind to her. This accusation came about through her, Ilze. Your pain is due to her, Ilze. If it weren't for Pamra . . .' Against the wall the veiled watcher made the sound of grinding.

'Let me find her,' he begged.

After that there was a long quiet time when the pain passed and was more or less forgotten. 'Your heresy came about through her,' they told him, both the human Ascertainers and the Talkers who watched. 'We're sorry for your suffering, but it was all her doing.' It was a revelation that he knew to be absolutely true. He had almost compromised his own future. Because of her. Because of Pamra. If they had not been so understanding, he would have been condemned, because of Pamra.

'Are you feeling well, Ilze?' It was the lady Kesseret once more, rather gaunt and wan looking, as though she had been many nights without sleep. She wore a robe he had never seen before, one that covered her hands and feet. When she moved, she winced. 'Are you recovered?'

'Quite recovered, thank you.' It was early spring. He had recovered. Obviously, the lady Kesseret had not.

'The Ascertainers met this morning. I was in attendance. They have ascertained that you were not entirely guiltless, but misled. Tricked. You have been offered an opportunity to atone through special duty. As a Laugher, I understand, for Gendra Mitiar, Dame Marshal of the Towers.'

'I know,' he said, his anger hot at her tone. It would be more than atonement.

'I am told they plan a reward for you when your mission is done. A Tower of your own. An initial offer of the Payment.' Her voice was without emotion or encouragement, uninvolved in this, as though it had happened quite separate from her life and without any connection to it.

He bowed, silent. Hatred moved him, not ambition. When he felt his wounds, hatred moved him.

'The Payment comes from the Talkers, and they must

167

approve its recipients. That they have done so speaks well of your future expectations, Ilze.'

Hot curiosity still burned in him. 'Tell me again about the Talkers. Who are they?'

'They are the leaders of those who lived here before we came.'

'What was it they ate before we came?'

'Beasts, so they say. I've told you.'

'Tell me again.'

'They ate hoovar and thrassil and weehar, animals with hot juicy bodies. They ate them all. All but a very few who survived here behind the Teeth of the North. The Protector has small herds of thrassil and weehar here in the Chancery lands. A few hundred animals. The hoovar are extinct.' She rose, moved about the room, stiffly, uncomfortably. Again, Ilze wondered what they had done to her. 'When all the beasts were gone, they had no choice but to eat us – us or fish.'

'Why not fish, then?'

'Because, as they say, fish eaters lose the power of flight and thereby blaspheme the will of Potipur, who made them fliers. Some essential ingredient is missing in fish. Eating fish changes them in other ways, too – makes their females more intelligent, for example. The female fliers are as you have seen them. Dirty, quarrelsome. I am told they, too, can talk but do so very little. Eating fish makes them less aggressive, as well. There is a tribe of fish eaters some-where, so they say, a tribe called the Treeci. In their lan-guage, "treeci" means "offal." Talkers speak of fish eaters as we do of heretics.' She winced, sat down, cradled her hands as though they pained her.

'No, given a chance of eating fish or dying, they might well eat fish. However, they prefer to eat us. And the Talkers eat us alive, Ilze. Not dead. There are not many Talkers. Two or three living humans taken from each town each month are enough to feed them. You will learn how to do it when you are Superior of a Tower. It will be your task to *recruit* citizens for this purpose. The Talkers do not eat the dead. The fliers would not eat the dead if they had anything else to eat.'

'So they might feast on me, or on you!'

'The Servants have nothing else to eat,' she said simply, as though his statement were irrelevant. 'They are the Servants of Abricor. We worship Abricor. We worship Potipur, and Potipur promised them plenty.' These are truths, her voice said. Truths beyond question. 'Do you think you will be able to find her? Pamra?'

Was this another test? He stared through her, not seeing her. Who was she, really? Another like himself or one of them? A betrayer? Or a betrayed? Had she, too, really been tortured? If she had, he knew with sudden certainty, they would have told her the suffering was Ilze's fault, and she would have had no choice but to use him as he would use Pamra in turn. What was she up to now? 'I will find her,' he said.

'Find her. That's good. Bring her back to the Tower.'

'I will give her Tears.'

'No, Ilze. You will not. That is an order. Not at first. She can only tell us the truth if you give her Tears. We must have more than truth. The Talkers need more than that.'

He knew that already. The Talkers needed far more than truth. He had learned there were occasions the truth did not serve, when only the presumptive lie would serve at all. He had not yet learned what they needed to know, but he would. He was resolved upon that.

They set him down in the glowing springtime upon the Rivershore far west of Baris. His scalp had been shaved clean and covered with a curious dark helmet, close as a second skull. None of the scars they had put upon him showed. He turned his face to the west and began the hunt. Pamra. Rivermen. Along the river in both directions others like him moved; others with similar scars. Everyone called them Laughers because of their scornful cries, ha-ha, ha-ha. Even the Rivermen they sought called them that. And they never really laughed.

15

On an evening not long after the *Gift* had been repaired, Pamra stood on the quiet deck watching Thrasne lay out the boom lines while the ship rocked gently along a pier at Sabin-bar. The Melancholics had gone ashore, even Medoor Babji, who these days seemed reluctant to leave the *Gift*. The sun lay low along the River, making a dazzle that beat against their eyes. Neff stood in the dazzle, and her mother stood there as well, bathing in that effulgence as though to draw nourishment from it. Delia was lost in it, a black shadow obscured by brilliance, so that she, Pamra, could not distinguish one from the other but merely stood at the edge of a glowingly inhabited cloud. All was very still. Sometimes at this hour an expectant hush would fall upon the Riverside, upon the waters themselves, calming and stilling them, making the song-fish hum in voices one could scarcely hear, so soft they were. So it was tonight.

And so it was that Ilze appeared at the edge of her vision like a striding monster, all in black, the black soaking up the glow as though to empty it, to absorb it all, and it flowing toward him as water flows toward a drain, whirling down into blackness.

'Ilze!' she breathed, quiet, her stomach telling her the truth of this more than her eyes. There was a striding figure there on the River path, but she did not truly perceive it. Her belly saw it before her brain knew who it was. Then it shivered her, all at once, like a tree cut but not yet fallen, and she collapsed across the rail. 'Ilze,' she breathed in a tone of mixed relief and horror. 'He is a Laugher. Come for

170

me.' It was relief he had not seen her yet, horror to know he was seeking her, a verification of everything she had known all along. He bore a flask at his waist, and she knew what it contained. Tears, and a little water to keep them fresh. They would last like that for years, remaining potent to the end, her destiny there swinging at his hip, a threat more monstrous in that she had almost escaped it.

'Lie down,' Thrasne whispered to her, pushing her below the line of the rail. She seemed hypnotized by that distant figure, leaning out across the rail as though asking to be noticed. He thrust her down into the piled nets with one hand, then set his foot upon her, holding her there as he tied off the lines to the boom, his stance betraying nothing except attention to the task at hand.

Across the stretch of water the striding figure stopped as though it had heard its name. Sound carried over the River. Perhaps her voice had been loud enough for the Laugher to hear, for he stared out over the long pier to the place the *Gift* rocked slowly on the tide, holding his right hand to shield his eyes from the brilliant glow in which the *Gift* was bathed. Thrasne watched him covertly, memorizing the face, the form, the strange helmet he wore. Thrasne had seen such helmets before. This hunter was not a new thing but an old one, at least as old as Blint's youth, for Blint had told him of these men – always men, the Laughers. Beneath the contorted helmet the face was narrow, full of an unconscious ferocity, a violence barely withheld. It was a cruel face in repose, one that could lighten into sudden, dangerous charm when it was expedient to do so. Thrasne looked at his own hands, square upon the ropes, thinking of men he had known with faces like that. Often they died of violence. One time his own hands had pushed the knife home. Sometimes the knives were held by women. Such men were always feared. And hated. Had they not been Laughers, still they would have been hated.

When he looked up again, the Laugher was gone, perhaps into the town.

'You can get up now,' he told her. 'The hunter has gone.'

'It was Ilze. Come after me.'

Thrasne decided upon calm acceptance of this. There would be no point in lies between them. 'Pamra, you knew that someone would come after you. It is time to talk of that now. Make plans. Decide how we will avoid them.'

The moment stretched between them. For a moment he thought she would answer him, for she was looking at him as though she actually saw him. Ilze had made her aware of her surroundings, of him no less than of all other things. He waited, breathless, hoping she would speak.

She, however, turned toward the sun glow again. From that glow came a voice, Neff's voice, speaking for her ears only, soft as the feathers of his breast had been. 'Cruel, Pamra. Cruel to so raise up the dead, who should lie at peace.'

'Remember,' instructed her mother, also silently. 'Remember.'

And from the wrapped darkness that was Delia came a sigh.

'Cruel,' Pamra said. 'Cruel!' A flame-bird called as though in answer to this.

'Yes,' said Thrasne, thinking she meant the man she had just seen. 'Very cruel. But we can deal with that.'

'It has to be stopped.'

He nodded. He had already decided to stop Ilze himself, in the only way possible, but Pamra took his agreement for more than he had intended. Her eyes clouded with mystery once more; her spirit disappeared along some road he could not follow.

'We must go to the Protector of Man. He must be told. He must be told to stop it.'

Her face was utterly calm. Behind her in the golden light Neff's voice seemed to breathe an assent.

And her mother's voice. 'Remember!'

And for the first and only time, Delia's voice, breathing from the effulgent silence. 'It is better when all the people know, Pamra. It is better not to be alone.'

Pamra turned to Thrasne, smiling. He had not seen her

172

like this before, though the novices of Baris Tower would have recognized her radiant face, her eyes lighted as though from within by rapture. Her arms went out, out, as though she would encompass the world. 'We will go, yes,' she breathed to him. 'But we must take the people with us, all of them, to the Protector of Man.'

And he, lost in her eyes from which the dark shadows had suddenly gone, stared at her in terror, seeing her flee away from him down a long corridor toward a blinding glow into which he could not see and would not dare to go.

From the shore, Medoor Babji saw them there, saw their faces, both, seemed to see an effulgency of wings hovering at Pamra's side, put her hands to her eyes and drew them away again to see only the sun glow and two people silhouetted against it.

Soon the Melancholics would be leaving the *Gift* to begin the trip to the steppes. It had been disturbing to travel aboard the *Gift*, disturbing and strange. Now she found herself glad that they would be leaving in a short time. She could not bear the expression on Thrasne's face.

173

16

The lady Kesseret, Superior of the Baris Tower, former prisoner in the Accusatory of Highland Lees, now convalescent, her injuries received under the question slowly healing, leaned in the window of the library wing looking out upon an evening of early summer. Beneath the window on a narrow ledge was a flame-bird's nest, a tidily woven basket of straw and wild-pamet fiber, holding three spherical golden eggs. An additional pile of pamet fiber lay to one side, weighted down by several small stones. In a flash of orange and gold, the flame-bird itself came swooping down the wall to perch on the ledge and move restively between this pile of tinder and the nest, fluttering its wings as though in indecision whether to stay or go.

The window was in the lady's bedroom, hers at least by guest right. She had occupied this room since the laggard sun had broken winter's hold upon Highland Lees and let them all come up from the caverns. Cozy though the caverns had been, she preferred this room, windowed to the air. Through the open door she could hear Tharius Don's flat-harp virtuoso, Martien, as he flicked his hammers over throbbing strings. Behind her on the porcelain stove a kettle sang an antiphon to itself. She was warm, well wrapped in a thick robe and in Tharius Don's arms, for the moment forgetful of her pain.

'You comfort me,' she said drowsily. 'I am wondering why.'

'Because we remember really comforting each other,' he said. 'When it was more than this.' For a moment there was

174

something virile and intemperate in his voice, as though for that instant his passion had been more than merely memory. His arms tightened about her, strong arms still, capable of stirring her own recollection so that her mind lusted briefly over old visions while her body lay aside, like some discarded garment.

'It isn't fair,' she complained. 'Why can we still feel pain so very well when all the other feelings are gone?'

'All the other feelings aren't gone,' he said patiently, knowing she knew, knowing she needed to hear him say it. 'Only lust. And lust is gone because the Payment is a Talker gift.' He did not need to explain that. They both understood it. The Talkers died if they bred. Therefore they did not breed or value breeding. They did not lust. They had no experience of passion. Though they perceived it intellectually, their bodies rejected it, and the elixir made of their blood rejected it as well. 'We could have refused the elixir, Kessie.'

Refused it. She thought of having refused it, of having grown old with Tharius Don. There were old lovers in Baristown whom she had watched over the years. She had seen them, too, aged past passion, walking hand in hand in the market square. She imagined them snuggled side by side in their beds, complaining to one another like old barnyard fowl, full of clucks and chirrs, grinding the day's events in their leathery gizzards to make each one reasonable and useful to them. 'My, my,' they would say. 'Did you see? Did you ever? What's the world coming to?'

How was it different for them, those old people? Remembering the loves and lusts of youth? Little different, perhaps, except that their twilight was brief, the memories strong enough to last that little time between age and the end, their flavor and fragrance scarcely dimmed by the years, death coming at last while the perfume lingered, making their old lives redolent of youth. They breathed the scents of childhood, a potpourri of their green years.

But for Kesseret? And Tharius? What remained?

'Dust,' she whimpered. 'All our love, dust.'

'Not while I hold you,' he told her urgently. 'Not while I grieve for your pain.'

The memory of pain made her fleetingly angry. 'Pain and anger,' she said. 'Those we keep.'

'And curiosity. And laughter. And determination. So you see, it isn't all hopeless.'

'It seems so sometimes,' she said, remembering the pincers at her fingers, the wedges driven beneath her toenails. 'Ah, gods, Tharius, but it seems so.'

He buried his face in her hair so she would not see his tears, thinking to himself, 'Pity. We haven't lost pity. Which is why we go on plotting, always plotting. Oh, gods, when will the plots be thick enough to clot into action!'

She moved in his arms, as though aware of her pain. 'You shouldn't be here,' she said.

'Because of Martien? He wouldn't say a word to anyone.'

'No, not because of your musician friend, love. Because you shouldn't be here. You shouldn't be showing any interest in me at all. Someone may be watching the corridor to this suite, to see if you come and go – or come and stay.'

'You are thinking in township terms, Kessie. Those of us here at the Chancery no longer have the habit of thinking in terms of sexual misconduct. We are beyond scandal.'

She hid her face in his shoulder, very white at his words. 'I know. Stupid of me.'

'Yes, my dear. Stupid of you.'

'Do you ever . . . are you ever sorry?'

'Sorry to have outlived my passions? Yes. Sorry to have time, still, to do what we are trying to do? No.'

She shuddered, trembling at his words, fearful of what they were trying to do. In the past, the cause had seemed the only righteous way to live, and it had not brought her pain. Now it had brought her more than she was ready to bear. 'Still, love, they may wonder at your interest in me. What am I, after all? Superior of a Tower. There are thousands of those.'

'I made my interest very clear,' he said, folding her more closely in the robe. 'I said before the questioning started that it was shameful treatment of a loyal member of the service. I've said it in the interim, several times, and I've capped it by demanding they recognize your courage by providing you with care and attention until you can be restored to duty.'

'Which I could have been yesterday, or last week.'

'Not true, Kessie. You may have come here the direct route, by flying. The road back is not so easy.'

'Easy! By the true God, Tharius, I hope you didn't think that was easy!'

'You lived through it,' he said, caressing her. 'That's the important thing. You lived.'

'I lived because I dragged the most ambitious and viciously self-serving Awakener in my Tower into my problem and linked his future to mine. He's one I should have rid the Tower of early on. I didn't. I saved him, for just such a need. As a stratagem it worked, but I'm not proud of it, Tharius.' She trembled again, and the slow tears gathered at the curve of her eyes. She blinked, driving them back, willing that he would not see her so weakened. 'Now he is loose out there, a Laugher. And I am among those who sent him.'

'You lived,' he said again. 'That's all that matters.'

She had begun to feel real pain again, but it was too soon to take more of the waters of surcease that Tharius had provided. 'Tell me,' she whispered in an attempt to distract herself from her pain. 'Tell me how far we have come?'

He looked around carefully, being sure they were not watched or overheard, a movement made habitual through a hundred years of conspiratorial conversations. 'The cause has members in over five thousand Towers,' he murmured at last, like a litany, well learned, often rehearsed. 'One-fifth of all Towers. Over half of them include the Superiors of those Towers. We have strong lay groups in ninety percent of all the towns. Over half the signal routes are ours, at least on some shifts. I am now informed within a day or two of things happening anywhere on Northshore.'

She concentrated, remembering conversations held long ago. 'The cause is about where we planned it would be, then. Somehow I had thought it lagged.'

'No. It has not lagged. The suspicions of Mitiar and Bossit were planned for. The only thing we had not foreseen was this untimely suspicion on the part of the fliers. Now there must be some kind of diversion, something to draw them away. At the moment, they are too much focused upon the Chancery.'

'What are you planning?'

'I've sent an actor friend to the tents of the Noor, to visit Queen Fibji.'

'Oh, Tharius, haven't those poor devils suffered enough?' Her own pain was forgotten for the moment in the pain she felt for the Noor, constant victims of the Jondarites. 'Can't we leave them out of it?'

He shook his head sadly. 'It will mean nothing worse for them than they already suffer, Kessie. I've sent someone to talk of Southshore, that's all. I've had him say nothing which wasn't in the palace library. There's every possibility Southshore really exists, just as I've had it described to her. If I know Queen Fibji, she'll send an expedition within the year. General Jondrigar would try to stop them, of course, if he heard of it. He would not let all those possible slaves go. He enjoys his expeditions among the Noor too much to let them escape. We must make sure he does not hear of it. The fliers will be much confused if *they* hear of it. So, we must make sure they do.'

'And it will turn eyes away from us. When do you think, Tharius? Soon?'

'I think soon. If nothing else happens to upset our plans. If no other junior Awakener goes off with a pitful of workers. If no eager Riverman starts the uprising ahead of time. If there is no spontaneous religious uprising of one kind or another.' He brooded over this while Kessie moved restlessly in his arms.

So much to keep track of; so much to control.

Many years ago there had been two factions within their movement. One for immediate war; one for the hope of peace. The war faction had plotted to kill the fliers, all of them. They had planned to pick a time when the Talkers would be out of the Talons and simply murder them all.

Tharius had been a leader of the peace party. He recalled impassioned speeches he had made, phrases he had used. 'We would be forever guilty of the murder of an intelligent species.' He believed it. Much though he detested the fliers, including the Talkers, still he believed it. Moral men did not do such things. Not to another species with intelligence, with speech, with a culture of its own.

Some years of covert exploration into the actual attitudes of Talkers had followed. He laughed bitterly sometimes when he recalled that time. His thesis had been so simple. What the fliers were doing was immoral, unethical. They were eating intelligent beings. They were raising the dead, who were possibly aware of that fact. If they ate fish, they could continue to live, but in a moral way. Wouldn't that be preferable? Wouldn't it be a better arrangement? He had asked this of Talker after Talker during convocations. 'Wouldn't it be better?'

To which they had cawed hideous laughter or turned to deposit blobs of shit at his toes, showing what they thought of the idea. Eventually he had been forced to understand. Morality was not an absolute. Theirs was not his. His was not shared even by all humans, much less by this nonhuman species.

He had quit trying to sell the idea after a time. He had been warned it wouldn't work, and it was becoming difficult to disguise his stubborn efforts as anything but what they were. He had called it research, but research was not Tharius's affair, after all. Council member Koma Nepor was Chief of Research. Questioning the fliers was not Tharius's responsibility, either. Ezasper Jorn was Ambassador to the Thraish. When it became evident Tharius's efforts were drawing unpleasant attention from both the Talons and the Chancery, what had been confidential attempts at negotiation became deeply covert. There were to be no more attempts at persuasive conversion of fliers.

Which left, he was convinced at last, only conversion by

179

necessity. If there were no bodies to eat, then the fliers would eat fish or nothing.

And in that belief, the cause had been born. From that statement all else had followed. Agents moving among the towns, increasing the fisheries against the day when fliers would need fish to eat. Superiors of Towers sending worker crews to build more jetties. Rivermen holding themselves ready for the day when every worker pit would be emptied in the deep of the night. Even now agents moved across Northshore seeking patches of Tears to spray with fungicide, reducing the number of locations where they were found. When the day came, there would be no human bodies available, at least none treated with Tears. And when the morning of the revolution came, fliers would eat fish or die.

His arms tightened around his burden once more. The fliers would eat fish or die. And the humans in the Chancery? Those in the Towers? Well, they would eat fish or whatever else they liked, but in a little time they would die as well. When the cause struck, there would be no more elixir to keep their superannuated bodies alive. On some days, Tharius actually looked forward to that time. It was not so much that he tired of life as that he tired of the lives of others. His mouth quirked, thinking of this. Oh, to see the end of Gendra Mitiar!

'Why are you smiling?' asked the lady Kesseret, amused at his expression despite herself.

'Because what we are doing is right,' he said. 'Because it is right.'

The flame-bird left its nest to swing out across the courtyard, the vivid circle of its flight seeming to linger on the air. Then it returned to the ledge and began to dance, wings out, legs lifted alternately as it hopped to and fro on the narrow stone, bowing, stretching, stopping occasionally to shift the little stones, sharp-edged with red in the ruddy evening light, as though bloodstained.

'Do you think it will light the nest soon?' She could ask this without crying, distracting herself.

'Probably.'

'I always feel so sorry for them.'

180

'Shh. Kessie. Don't waste your time feeling sorry for them. If you must feel sorry, feel sorry for yourself, or for me, come to that.'

The flame-bird danced gravely to a music and song it alone could hear, forward on one leg, then back, on the other leg forward, then back, bowing with wings wide, pointing its beak upward as though invoking some far-off presence. In the adjoining room, Martien seemed to sense the rhythm of its lonely ballet, for the music began to accompany the performance.

'I wonder what the bird thinks.'

'I'm afraid we'll never know.'

Whirling rapidly, the feathered dancer picked up a stone and held it firmly in its beak to strike it against the ledge with a tiny battering sound. Sparks flew, dwindled, died. It struck again, and again.

'Oh, Tharius. Can't you stop it?'

'I could. But then the young ones wouldn't hatch, Kessie. The eggs won't break without it.'

'I know.' She turned her face into the hollow of his throat, not wanting to see.

A spark caught the tinder. The flame-bird picked up a beakful of burning tinder and laid it upon the nest, fanning it with her wings. Smoke rose in a white coil. The sticks and straw of the nest began to burn with tiny, almost invisible flames.

'Did it catch?' A muffled question from her hidden mouth.

'Yes. It caught.'

The flame-bird began to roll one of the golden eggs about on the burning nest, charring the surface of the shell, seeming not to notice its own feathers were on fire, the flesh of its legs crisping, its bill beginning to blister.

The first egg cracked wide in the heat, the tiny nestling within it pushing out a questing beak, then thrusting the shell fragment aside with strong, infant wings as it flew upward in a wild flutter of damp feathers amid the smoke. The mother turned to the second egg, then the third. Only when this last nestling flew did the flame-bird raise itself into

181

the air, singing, alive amidst its flaming plumage, spiraling as though in a frantic attempt to escape its own immolation.

'Oh,' cried Kessie. 'I hate hearing them sing like that.'

'Shh. They say it sings in ecstasy, Kessie.'

Above them in the sky, the singing faded into a whisper of sound, the wings stopped beating. A black speck planed away, trailing a line of misty smoke beyond the walls of the palace.

'I don't believe that,' she wept, raising her stained face to look at the fading trail of smoke. 'I think it sings in agony. It would scream if it could.' She trembled, suddenly aware of her own pain, wanting not to think of that, wanting to forget, to think of anything else instead.

'Pamra used to use the flame-bird as a parable in recruitment homilies,' she chattered, letting the first thing that came to mind flow from her mouth like water. 'She tried to liken the Awakeners to the mother flame-bird, sacrificing itself for its children. It wasn't a successful parable at all. Too painful. The last year or so she'd been using one about the Candy Tree which worked better. She was a marvelous recruiter.'

His mouth turned down, reminded now of the cause of all their recent pain. 'Where is she, do you think?'

'Oh, Tharius, I hope she got away. I hope she's safe somewhere, if anywhere can be called safe. Perhaps there was enough time before Ilze got onto her trail for her to find safety.'

'Or the River.'

'I think not, somehow. There was a toughness about her. A kind of impenetrable naiveté, but tough, nonetheless.'

'The last of the Dons,' said Tharius. 'My great-great-grandchild. I had such hopes for her, somehow. I thought she might be another you, another Kesseret . . .'

'I know. I know you wondered about her, cared for her. That's why I kept close track of her. Though not close enough, it seems. She came very close to ruining everything.'

'How could you keep track of her at all without attracting

182

notice? Superiors don't normally interest themselves in novices or junior Awakeners. Not as I remember.'

'Oh, my dear. You of all people to ask such a question, when you taught me every subterfuge I know. I kept track of her through my servant, Threnot. Threnot always goes veiled, and she goes everywhere. And sometimes it was Threnot herself, and sometimes it was me, listening to a recruitment parable or watching someone at the worker pits. I spent a lot of time watching Pamra.'

He shook his head, drawing her closer. 'Risky, love. But kind of you in this case. Great-great-granddaughter Pamra. Well. I hate her causing you this agony, but it wasn't the child's fault. Perhaps we can locate her, provide some kind of assistance. It would be sensible to do that. I don't want the Laugher to get her. I don't want the fliers to get her. Not alone that she's kin; more important, it would set them off again. When I heard it was she who had started all this, I thought how ironic it was – my own great-great-grandchild, without knowing it, coming close to betraying us. I'd like to help her, since she's the last. Not that the intervening generations were much to brag about.'

She ticked them off on her bandaged fingers. 'Your son, Birald. Your granddaughter, Nathile – bit of a fishwife, that one, so I've heard. Pamra talked to Jelane about her unpleasant grandma. And then your great-grandson, Fulder Don . . .'

'Useless. Like a piece of fungus. All sweaty and damp. Not much of an artist, either, I'm afraid.'

'And finally your great-great-granddaughter, Pamra Don. Something about that one, Tharius, love. Something more to her than to the others. A kind of shining, sometimes.'

'Awakener, heretic, and now fugitive,' he said bleakly. 'The best of the lot, and what an end to come to.'

She squeezed his hand. 'Old Birald wasn't that bad, actually.'

'You knew him?' He was astonished at this.

'I knew everyone in Baristown. I knew Birald before I

came to the Tower. I was twenty then. He was a couple of years younger than I, a stiff, fussy youth, always looking over his shoulder. He ended as a crotchety old man who carved leaves and flowers on door lintels, holding on to the artist's caste by his fingernails. Oh, God, Tharius, but speaking of fingernails, my hands hurt . . .'

He reached for the carafe on the table and poured a glass of its waters for her. 'Kessie. Oh, Kessie, you did get the drugs I sent? You did get them in time?'

'You know I did.' She drank what he had given her, thankfully. 'I've told you over and over. It was all that kept me going. Knowing I wouldn't actually feel the pain, not in my body, at least. Knowing you were here, doing whatever you could to get me out of that . . . that nightmare.'

'I couldn't do anything! I saw Shavian Bossit throwing suspicious glances my way when Gendra spoke of putting you and the Awakener to the question. He knows I came from Baristown, and he knows I've spoken out against this inquisition atmosphere the fliers want to force us into. Trust Shavian to put egg and fire together and hatch a plot.'

'You think he suspects?'

'Suspects? Of course he suspects. Everyone! Of everything! Suspicion is his standard mode of operation. He maintains the household by suspicion.' Tharius gritted his teeth.

'I mean, do you think he suspects us? Do you think he is convinced there really is . . . a heresy? From his point of view, I suppose that's what it would be.'

'No. Not yet. The thing that's occupying his mind just now is another matter. There's supposed to have been a miracle in Thou-ne. Some idiot fished an image out of the World River, and the people demanded it be taken into the Temple. They're almost worshiping it, calling it the "Bearer of Truth." It shines, so they say. There are people traveling from six towns east just to visit the Temple, even though they know they can't come home again.'

'The Bearer of Truth?' Kesseret frowned. 'An image? I hadn't heard about that. Do you think it's connected in any way?'

'Shavian may. He has a habit of connecting everything. And it may be more than habit. During the last convocation, he spent an unwarranted amount of time with the Talkers. It was almost as though he were trying to usurp Ezasper Jorn's prerogative as Ambassador. He's ambitious, is Bossit.'

There was a sound from the next room, a hesitation in the music, then the dissonant fall of a hammer. In the silence they could hear a monotonous thrumming. Martien thrust one hand into the room, knocking on the open door.

'Tharius. Someone's coming down the private corridor. It sounds like the old weehar. Mitiar.'

'Damn,' Tharius said, unwinding himself from the lady Kesseret. 'That's Gendra's majordomo with that damn drone. Quick, Kessie. Get yourself into bed.'

'I really should sit up—'

'Quickly. Don't argue. Back to your hammers, Martien.' Quickly he closed the window, pulled the chair into the center of the room, and seated himself in it, reaching a long arm toward the bookshelves. 'Something dull, Kessie? An eschatological essay, perhaps?' He leafed through the volume and began to read, his voice dry and instructional.

The thrumming came closer, a low moaning, 'Whoom, whoom.' The sound ceased outside the door to the suite. In the outer room Martien's music was interrupted once again, this time by a crash as the door opened and a loud voice cried, 'Dame Marshal of the Towers, Gendra Mitiar.'

'She didn't even knock,' Kesseret hissed between her teeth. 'Your private corridor, and she didn't knock!'

'Shh, Kessie. Remember who she is.' He smiled quickly as he leaned back in his chair and called through the open door, 'Ah, Gendra! I see you do not need to be invited to come in. Have you come to tender apologies to the lady Kesseret?'

There was a bark of humorless laughter from the outer room. 'I'm sure all my subordinates understand necessity.' She came into the doorway, showing a voracious arc of yellow teeth. 'We must all make sacrifices. And it is not necessary to apologize for necessity. Isn't that so, lady?'

185

'I'm sure it is, Your Reverence.' Kessie lay pale upon the pillows, not needing to play a part. At the sound of Mitiar's voice her hands and feet burned agonizingly, and she found herself remembering the flame-bird as unexpected tears flowed unheeded down her face, sudden and unstoppable as the spring spate.

'Gendra, if you will?' Tharius was on his feet, escorting the woman out, pulling the door almost shut behind them. Kesseret heard him in the outer room. 'Have you no sensitivity at all? By Potipur's teeth, woman. At least let her recover!'

'I was told she was little injured,' the Dame Marshal snarled, aggrieved. 'The Ascertainers said she seemed to feel little pain. Had it not been for the infections, she would have been long since healed.'

'Let them do to your hands and feet what they did to hers, Gendra, then tell me if you consider yourself little injured. Let your hands and feet swell to twice their size in the winter caverns, let you burn with fever! Would you have been happier if your blasted Ascertainers had broken her? Made her whimper for mercy? Made her confess to something she hadn't done in front of a roomful of fliers? Would that have satisfied you, made you sympathetic?'

'Why should I be sympathetic? It was she who housed the conspirator.'

'Oh, pfah, Gendra. Conspirator! Don't talk nonsense. Only the Talkers profess to believe that, and even they doubt it. You owe the lady Kesseret your thanks. Don't you understand she protected us all by her demeanor? If it weren't for the lady Kesseret's courage, the entire Chancery might be under siege by some thousands of paranoid Talkers. By all three gods and their perverted offspring, Dame Marshal, but you've more gall than good sense.' He heard himself raging and didn't care. Let her make what she would of it.

Stiffly, she answered. 'I would not have come if I had thought she would not welcome—'

'She may understand the necessity of what you did to her,

but for the love of Potipur, don't expect her to welcome your visits now.'

This was a word too much. Gendra snarled, 'She'd better welcome them if she intends to go back to the Baris Tower as Superior under my orders.'

He did not relent. 'Of course she goes back to the Baris Tower. And you'll let her alone until then and not harass her after she's returned. I swear to you, Gendra, you've laid an obligation for vengeance on me already. Don't make it worse.'

'Why you, Tharius? Hnnn? What is she to you?' It was both a sneer and a threat.

'An old friend and my cousin – oh, yes, Gendra, my cousin. Though we must perforce set aside family relationships when we receive the Payment, those of us who have family members also receiving the Payment are blessed with kin who remember us as we were. My cousin, I say it again. Also a loyal member of the service. That's what she is to me, and should have been to you, if you'd forget your damned Tower discipline for a moment and think of people . . .'

Their voices dwindled away down the corridor. Into the silence behind them the sound of the flat-harp flowed; water music, a few tones repeated over and over in differing orders. Rippling. Lulling. Martien was covering the anger with calm, washing the pain away.

Tharius shouldn't have spoken so. He shouldn't have angered Gendra. He shouldn't even do anything to make her angrier or more suspicious. And yet Kesseret warmed at his words, at his defense of her. For a little time she forgot the conspiracy to which her life had been given and let the waters of surcease wash around her.

After a time, the lady slept.

17

Six stone courtyards separated the library wing from the Bureau of the Towers, each succeeding each through long, echoing corridors lit by occasional oculars that split dim puddles of watery light onto the clattering stone. Jorum Byne, majordomo to the Dame Marshal, led the procession, the long neck of the single-stringed viol held against one shoulder as he plied the bow with his right hand, *whoom*, *whoom*, *whoom*. Two functionaries followed after, laden with documents and dispatch boxes. Then came Gendra herself, her teeth grinding endlessly in time with the viol, and last her personal servant, Jhilt, in a shankle, shankle of chains and rustle of stiff fabrics. Jhilt was a Noor slave from the lands north of Vobil-dil-go. There was no reason for her to wear chains. Though her personal duties in providing various kinds of pleasure for the Dame Marshal were not pleasant for her – were, indeed, often quite painful – escape from behind the Teeth was impossible. Still, she wore chains. Gendra Mitiar liked the sound of them, finding them even more pleasing in that there was no reason for them at all.

Except for the palace itself, the Bureau of the Towers loomed higher than any building in the Chancery, its vast hexagonal bulk heaving skyward in stark, unornamented walls of black brick, windowless as cliffs. Behind those walls in serried ranks were four divisions, each with six departments; each department with ten sections, each section with a Supervisor; each Supervisor responsible for ten Towers and thus ten townships. Each Supervisor had a deputy and an assistant. Each of these had a clerk, perhaps more than one. Some Towers, after all, were much larger than others, and the supervision of them was therefore more complex.

Deep in the bowels of the bureau lay the labyrinthine vaults of Central Files, their complexities guarded and their secrets plumbed only through the let and allowance of the Librarian, Glamdrul Feynt, who did not, as might be naively supposed, have any responsibilities at all for the library wing of the palace. There had not been any books or records worthy of attention in the library wing for generations. What was there could be cared for, if at all, by Tharius Don, cared for by Tharius Don simply because it did not matter. Such was Feynt's opinion. He had not seen the books in the library wing. He did not need to do so. He had seen what was in the files, and everything of importance was there.

So now, Gendra Mitiar, passing by the great corridor that led to her offices and reception rooms, her dining halls and solaria, elected to descend the curving stone staircase that led to the vaults below. The railing of this stair was carved in the likeness of fliers slaughtering weehar, thrassil, and an unlikely animal that was the artist's dutiful though uninspired conception of the legendary hoovar. None of the party except Jhilt – who shuddered to see the ravenous talons so bloodily employed, reminded thereby of certain habits of the Dame Marshal's – paid any attention to the railing. Gendra did not see it. She had stopped seeing it several hundred years before.

The *whoom, whoom, whoom* of the viol announced her coming. Far down an empty corridor that dwindled to tininess at the limit of its seemingly endless perspective came a faint echo – a door slamming, perhaps, or a heavy book dropping onto stone. At this, Gendra halted, snarling at Jorum Byne to stop the noise. Jhilt, too, was silenced with a gesture, and the five waited, heads cocked, listening for any defect in the dusty silence.

''Roo, 'roo, 'roo,' came the call, softened by distance into a whisper. 'Haroo. Your Reverence. Dame Marshal. Haroo?'

'Tosh,' growled the Dame Marshal. 'Jorum, go find him. Bring him here. And don't lose sound of him. He's half-deaf and likely to go limping off in six other directions.'

Pleased with her own wit, she chuckled, grinding her teeth together as she found a bench along the wall to sit upon, not bothering to dust it, though it was deep with the even gray coating that covered every surface in the files. The bench was in a niche carved with commemorative bas reliefs, fliers and humans locked in combat, fliers and humans solemnly making treaty. Dust softened the carving, obscuring the details. No one had looked at it for generations.

'Glamdrul Feynt is too old for this job,' Gendra assured her clerks and bearers, going so far as to glance at Jhilt as though the information were so general it might be shared even with so insignificant a person as she. 'Too old, and too deaf, and too crippled. Trouble is, hah, what you might suppose, eh? Trouble is, no one else can find anything! We give him apprentices, one after the other, boys and boys, and what happens? They vanish. Lost. So he says. Lost in the files, he says. Can you imagine. Hah!'

'It is said,' ventured Jhilt in a whisper, 'that a monster dwells below the tunnels here, coming out at night to feed upon those in the Chancery.'

Gendra found this amusing. 'A monster, hah? Some toothy critter left over from ages past, no doubt? A hoovar bull, mebee? Got frozen in a glacier until we built Chancery atop him, hah?' She roared with laughter, stopping suddenly to listen to the clatter of approaching footsteps, one firm, one halting.

Glamdrul Feynt was a young man by Chancery standards, only slightly half past a hundred, but he seemed to hover on the edge of dissolution, his aging unstemmed by the Payment. It had been given him tardily and with deep frustration by certain underlings of the Dame Marshal who devoutly wished him dead but were unable to replace him. It amused Glamdrul Feynt, therefore, to act even older and feebler than he was while still conveying omniscience on any matter relating to the files. Bent and gray, shedding scraps of paper from every pocket as he came, he approached the Dame Marshal with dragging footsteps and failing breath, leaning heavily upon his cane, meantime whispering his compliments in a gasp that bid fair to presage extinction at any moment.

'Oh, sit down, sit down,' she snarled at him. 'Jorum, make him sit down. Now get off down the corridor, all of you. I've private business to discuss.' She watched them malevolently as they retreated out of earshot, then leaned close to Feynt's side and said in a low voice, 'I need you to do some research for me, Glamdrul Feynt. And if you do it well, I'll see you get a dose of the Payment that'll do you some good.'

'Ah, Your Reverence. But I'm too old, I'm afraid. Too late. Much too late, so they say. On my last legs, I'm afraid.' He fished in a pocket for a wad of paper fragments, drew them forth, and peered at them with ostentatious near-sightedness.

'Nonsense. Play those games with those who believe them, Feynt. Now listen to me.

'There's a thing going on. The Talkers call it the River-man heresy. What it is, it's people putting their dead in the River instead of giving them to the Awakeners. Now, it's no new thing. Seems to me I've heard of it off and on in passing for a few hundred years. There's been a flare-up of it in Baris. Maybe other places, too. There's a new thing in Thou-ne. Some fisherman pulled a statue out of the River. Now it's set up in the Temple, right under Potipur himself. Rumblings. That's what I hear. What I want to know is, where did this heresy start? And when. *When* is important, too. And could the two things be connected?'

'I can look, Your Reverence. I don't recall the heresy, offhand. Don't recall anything about Rivermen. But I can look . . .'

'Go back two or three hundred years and look in the records of Baris. Find out who was Superior of the Tower then. Find out what was going on. Hah? You understand?'

He did not answer, merely wheezed asthmatically and bowed, as though in despair.

For her part, she took no notice of his pose but shouted for her entourage and went back the way she had come. Something within her quickened, hard on the trail of a connection she merely suspected. Tharius Don. The lady Kesseret. Hah. Both from Baris. And she seemed to recall something about Baris as a center of rebellion, long ago.

Behind her on the bench the old man peered after her with rheumy eyes, his hands busy with the scraps of paper he had drawn from a pocket, sorting them, smoothing them, folding them twice and thrusting them into the pocket once more. 'Oh, yes,' he muttered to her retreating back. 'I'll bet you would like to know where it started, old bird.' He sat there, perfectly still, until he was alone in the files once more. Then he rose and moved swiftly down the corridor, shedding scraps from every pocket as he went.

A door halfway down the long corridor opened as he approached, and a figure came halfway into the hall, beckoning imperiously.

'Well, what did the old fish want?' The question came from a mouth thin-lipped as a trap and was punctuated by the snap of fingers as long and twisted as tree roots. Ezasper Jorn was a man of immense strength and enormous patience, though this latter characteristic was not now in evidence. 'Come up with it. Feynt! What did old Mitiar want?'

Behind the Ambassador the shadowy figure of Research Chief Koma Nepor stared at the file master. 'Yes, yes, Feynt. What did she want?'

Glamdrul Feynt entered the room, casting a curious glance at the boyish figures that lay here and there in its corners and along its walls. These were his apprentices. They were also the materials Nepor had used in his research on the effects of Tears and blight and half a dozen other substances found here and there on Northshore. 'Any luck?' he asked, purposely not responding to their questions. 'Did you have any luck with that last one?'

'It talked,' whispered Nepor, his pallid little face with its pink rosebud mouth peering nearsightedly at one of the forms. 'It talked for quite a while, didn't it, Ezasper? I was quite hopeful there for a time.'

Ezasper Jorn refused to be sidetracked by these considerations. He gripped the file master in one huge hand and shook him gently to and fro, as a song-fish might shake a tasty mulluk. 'Out with it, Feynt. What did the old fish want?'

And Glamdrul Feynt, chuckling from time to time, explained what it was that much concerned the Dame Marshal of the Towers. After which came a long and thoughtful silence.

Mumros Shenaz rolled out of his blankets well before dawn,
awakened by the peeping of the ground birds, a repetitive,
percipient cry that seemed as full of meaning as it was without purpose. There was no mating, no nest building, no
food searching going on. No defense of territories. Only this
high, continuous complaint of bird voice, as though only by
this sound could the dawn be guided to the eastern horizon
and only by these cries driven to mount the sky.

Such thoughts amused Mumros. He sat often by himself,
thinking such things, and was called the Lonely Man
because of the habit. He did not mind. Since all who were
his had died, he was indeed a lonely man, spending his life
seeing the joys of others and remembering his own that were
past. One such was to be remembered this dawn time. He
stretched, bent from side to side, working the kinks out of
his back and legs. All around him lay the lightweight pamet
tents of the Noor. Last night's campfires were hidden
beneath lumps of half-dried bog-bottom. Smoke leaked
upward in thin, coiling bands. He stretched again and bent
to pick up the pottery flask of sammath wine laid by for his
father's ghost. His father's mud grave was nearby, only
over the hill, and Mumros walked away from the camp
toward it, the walk turning into the distance-eating trot of
the Noor as his sleep-tightened muscles loosened with the
exercise.

At the top of the hill he looked back, hearing someone in
the camp call, a long-drawn cry to the new day. There was
movement there. Flames. Someone had risen as early as he

and built up the fire with dried chunks of bog-bottom cut by some other traveling Noors, days or even months ago. Such was the life of wanderers. Planting grain to be eaten by others, harvesting grain others had planted. Cutting bog-bottom for another's fire, burning bog-bottom some other Noor had cut. 'Of such small duties is the solidarity of the Noor built,' he remarked to himself, remembering something similar his father had once said. 'Of our concern for those who travel after us comes our unity as a people.'

He trotted down the hill, head swinging to and fro in its search for the mud grave. His tribe had not been this way in several years. He could have forgotten where it was – no. No. He had not forgotten. It stood in a slight declivity, the sculptured face looking toward him. Rain, though infrequent, did come upon the steppes from time to time. It had washed the mud face, leaving it bland, almost featureless. In a way that was a good sign, for when the mud grave fell to dust, the spirit would move on. Some were ready to go on in only a year or two. Others so longed for their lives and kin that they stayed in the mud graves for many years, even a lifetime. This grave was neither very old nor very young.

'Father . . .' He bowed, pouring the sammath wine onto the thirsty clay that covered the bones. 'I have brought you drink. And news. The tribe has been chosen by Queen Fibji to take part in her great plan. We go now to her tents, all of us. Your friend Mejordu is still well, though he tires sometimes after a long day, and he asks to be remembered to you.' He had several anecdotes about Mejordu to share, for the man had always been clownish and amusing. After this he was still for a moment, trying to recall the last bit of news. Oh, yes. 'Your grandson Taj Noteen has led a group of Melancholics south to net shore-fish for the Queen.'

He fell silent then, thinking he had heard cries from the camp. Well. Whether or not, it was time to be getting back.

'I take my leave, Father. I will visit you when we next come by this way.' He bowed again and turned back toward the camp, not trotting now but running, for he did hear cries, screams.

Before reaching the crest of the hill, he dropped to his belly and writhed upward to peer over it.

Glittering figures moved among the tents of the Noor. Jondarites! Shiny fishskin helms plumed with flame-bird feathers sparkled over the huddled people of Mumros's tribe. He wriggled forward, serpentlike in the sparse grass, down the hill into a slanting gully. Over the cries of his people he heard the voice of the Jondarite captain.

'Women and children here. Men over there. All boys over ten with the men. Boys under ten with the women. Speed it up there, move! Move!'

Mumros risked raising his head. The men were herded together at one side of the camp. The women were all in the center, near the fires, surrounded by the Jondarite soldiers. Suddenly, without a word of command, the soldiers began slaughtering the women and children. All at once. Quickly. Like fishermen clubbing fish, they struck them down. Like stilt-lizard beaks, swords dipped in and out, emerged dripping, plunged in again.

The men of the tribe tried to break loose, but they had been tied. Over his own howling blood, Mumros heard their voices, crying names: 'Onji, beloved!' 'Creedi, Bowro, children – ah!' 'Girir, oh, Girir!'

Then the voice of the captain once more.

'You men are to be taken as slaves to the mines. You will be roped together and marched there. Before we go, you are to look at the bodies, closely. Make sure all are dead. We have had men try to escape in the past to get back to their families. We want you to be very sure you have no families to come back to.'

Mumros dropped his head into the grass. He could not move. There was bile in his mouth, an agony in his head. He wanted to kill but had nothing to kill with. He was one and they were many. He could go to them, but what good would it do? They would only take him with the others.

So he lay, not moving, while the chain of roped captives was led away into the distance. When they had gone, he went into the camp. The captain had been right. None of those who had been taken away had anyone left to return to.

He lit three fires, spread them with damp bog-bottom, tended them while the smoke rose in pillars in the still air. By noon the first helper arrived. By nightfall there were several more. After several days there were many, and where the camp had been now stood the mud graves of the women, those of the children clustered at their knees.

'Come,' said one of the helpers to Mumros. 'There is nothing more you can do here. Join us.'

'I know I can do nothing here,' said Mumros. 'But I will not come with you. I must go and tell of this thing to Queen Fibji.' And he turned his face from the cluster of graves to begin the long march.

19

In Thou-ne, Haranjus Pandel had been expecting a visitor for over two years, since the day he had sent a signal to the Chancery announcing the finding of an image in the River and the elevation of that image in the Temple. As a matter of policy, the existence of the signal towers – or, rather, of their purpose, since the existence could not be concealed – was kept from the general populace. No one except Haranjus Pandel knew of the message he had sent or that it was possible to send a message at all. Thus, no one knew the eventual visitor had come in response to that message. The whole township saw the boat, of course, and the Chancery man getting off it, but it was all very casual.

Bostle Kerf was his full name, a Section Chief in the Bureau of Towers, sent south in all haste through the pass, thence quickly west, and then south again to arrive after a year's travel in Thou-ne after a short detour to Zendigt, two towns east. His arrival from the east would evoke less concern, he had been told, than if he had appeared suddenly, coming down from the north like a migrating Noor. It was necessary to come to Thou-ne. It was not necessary to cause more talk than had already occurred. Gendra Mitiar had been clear about that. Once safely ensconced in the Tower, Kerf had a long, troubled conversation with Haranjus Pandel.

'How did you allow this to happen, Pandel? Her Reverence is in a fury over it, I'll tell you. Bad enough to have no workers in Thou-ne, without having a miracle here as well.'

The Superior nodded, sweating a little. He had never

198

aspired to the Payment. Indeed, he had never aspired to be Supervisor of a Tower, but then, no one with aspirations would have taken the job in Thou-ne. The mountains to the east prevented any traffic from the next township that way. This meant there was little enough need for Awakeners in Thou-ne, and little enough to do for the few there were. The Tower was small, cramped, and needed only one recruit every decade or so. Since there were no workers, there was no fieldwork, road or jetty building. All the Tower really had to see to was the transport of Thou-ne's dead to the worker pit in Atter, next town west, and since Thou-ne itself was small, there was little work in that. Haranjus had been content to be what he was, letting happen what happened, and in general the people of Thou-ne had approved his stewardship. Now he sweated more than a little, wondering if he was to be blamed for what had happened despite his innocence.

'I wouldn't call it a miracle,' he said now, not wanting to contradict the Section Chief but unwilling to be blamed for more than was just. 'It's only some image from old times, floated up on the River, that's all.'

'It shines, man. I went to the Temple. I saw it for myself. It's all wet, and it shines.'

'Well, there's that, yes. But dead fish often do that, and mulluk shells.'

'She shines and smiles,' Kerf went on, not listening. 'And holds out her hand. More attractive than the moon faces, I'll tell you.'

'Oh, well, now, Your Honor, but nobody's suggested the thing's a god! No. I wouldn't have tolerated that for a minute. No. No heresy here. All they've said is the thing is an image of . . . well, of the Bearer of Truth.'

'And what's that? Not a goddess? You're sure?'

'Well, nobody's said it's a goddess. I shouldn't think anyone believes so unless they've said . . .'

'If they haven't so far, depend on it they will soon.'

'Well, if they do, I'll just have to pick up a few, that's all. Pass around a few Tears. Settle things down.'

'Why haven't you settled things down already?'

Haranjus shrugged, a bit uncomfortably. Why hadn't he? 'Well, because if I did, you know, they'd think there was something in it. Something important. Something the Tower needed to defend against. If I let it be, it's a wonder for a few years, and it brings some curious travelers to spend their money here in Thou-ne – which won't hurt, Your Honor. Potipur knows we're poor enough. And it will blow over. When it does, let enough time pass for them all to forget it, then take the thing and burn it, shine or no shine.'

Bostle Kerf was no fool. He liked having his own way but wouldn't push it to the point of causing trouble. Here, he felt, the local man had the right of it. Don't fuss it. Don't make a racket. Let it die, as it would, of its own accord, without drawing more attention to it.

'How long since it was found?'

'Two and a half years. Maybe closer to three. I signaled the Chancery the very night of the day it happened.'

As he had, sweating away at the handles of the signal light, clickety-clacking the coded message across all those miles to the nearest signal tower, first time he'd ever done it; first time he'd ever had anything to report. And it had taken over a year for the Chancery to decide it wanted to investigate, so why all this uproar now? Well, thought Kerf, Haranjus was probably right. Let it alone. For now.

He snarled a little, letting the local man know he was being watched. No harm in that. Keep him on his toes. When it was dark, they went to the signal room, polished the mirror and lighted the lantern while Kerf worked the shutters. He did it a good deal faster than Haranjus had done, but then, he'd had more practice. 'Reported image of local interest only,' he signaled. 'Thou-ne Tower recommends allowing interest to die of its own accord. Kerf in agreement. Returning to the Chancery.'

All that travel for nothing, Kerf thought. Not even any good food in Thou-ne. And certainly none in the lands of the steppe people, going back. Noor bread always tasted of ashes, and no one but a steppey could pretend to enjoy roasted roots. Besides, Noor hated Chancery men. Only his escort of heavily armed Jondarites guaranteed passage and food at all. Though they hadn't seen many steppeys, come to that. Fewer than he'd thought they would. Perhaps they were traveling, east or west of the route Kerf had taken.

He shrugged, setting those thoughts aside as he bullied Haranjus a bit more before leaving. It had taken him a year and a half to get to Thou-ne. It would take that long at least going back. In his eagerness to leave, he did not ask the local man if devotion to the image had increased or decreased since shortly after it was found. Haranjus had very carefully not mentioned that subject. Bostle Kerf was able, therefore, to leave Thou-ne in good conscience.

Three days after Bostle Kerf left Thou-ne, the *Gift of Potipur* arrived there with a boatload of Melancholics who intended to disembark in Thou-ne and begin the trek north to their home country. Pamra was also on the ship. She came ashore in Thou-ne. By that time, however, it was too late to summon the Chancery man back again.

20

The Queen of the Noor sat upon her carved throne, legs
neatly aligned in their tall fishskin boots, eyes forward,
feathered scepter in hand, dying a little more as each delegation from an outlying tribe made its appeals, thankful for
the protocol that insisted upon an expressionless face. As a
young Queen she had rebelled against the requirement; as
an old one she realized its necessity. Had it not been for
protocol she would have wept, screamed, howled in frustration, anger, and pity.

Now the last of the delegations was on his knees before
her. One lonely man.

'They came on us before dawn, Highness,' said the
lonely man in an emotionless voice. 'Most of the camp was
still asleep when I left. When I heard the cries, I came back.
They rounded up the women and children, even the babies,
and killed them while the men were forced to watch. After
the killing, they let the men see the bodies just to be sure all
the women and children were dead.' He went on in that
same dead voice, describing the scene, the cries. 'The
Jondarite captain told them they had no families to return
to,' the man said at last, falling silent. He knelt before her,
eyes on the floor, as though he expected nothing from her at
all, as though he expected nothing from anyone.

Fibji had bitten her tongue in the need not to speak.
Strenge had spoken for her, as he usually did, knowing what
was in her heart.

'How did you escape?'

'I had gone out before dawn to visit the mud grave of my

202

father, to leave offerings to his spirit. I was returning when the Jondarites came. I hid, watching from the hill. I should have been taken with the others, but I could have changed nothing, and someone needed to tell you, Highness.'

Fibji had recently spent some time at the Chancery, going there under a banner of truce, appealing to the Protector of Man, attempting to get something from the Council of Seven, a treaty, an understanding, anything that would stop the taking of slaves and the mindless killing. She had not even seen the Protector. The council had refused to consider her request. She had failed in every effort, all the time afire to get home. Now she regretted being here. At the Chancery there might be something more she could do; there was nothing here. She could do nothing here except listen to the endless tales of slaughter and rapine, endless pleas for action against the Jondarite tax collectors and slavers and murderers, pleas that received a sympathetic hearing and no action at all. 'Because they have me,' she told herself. 'That damned general has us all, like birds caught in a net.' General Jondrigar would not mind if all the Noor were dead. He welcomed those times when the young men of the Noor rebelled against their queen to wage war against him, for then he could kill them more quickly. He welcomed uprisings, for then he could mount a major assault. The only hope for the Noor lay in not provoking him to a major effort, not until the plan could be put into effect. Then . . . well, then they would either live or die, but they would not go on as victims.

If the young men would hold their peace. If they could move onward with the plan. If she could have seen the Protector.

Oh, surely, surely Lees Obol would have listened. Surely the Protector of Man would not consider the Noor unworthy of his protection. Were Noor not men? But she had not seen the Protector. Only Maintainer of the Household Shavian Bossit, who had put her through half a dozen inconclusive and frustrating sessions.

'Have you seen Jondarites take your people slaves?'

he had asked half a hundred times. 'Have you seen it?'

No, she had not seen it. Had not seen the slavers come, had not seen the tax collectors come, had not seen the murderers come, had only heard about it afterward, from the survivors, when there were any. 'Take me to your metal mines, Lord Maintainer. Let me identify the slaves there. They are my people.'

'Tsk. Your Highness is misinformed. We have no slaves in our mines. Only bondsmen from Northshore. And as for those who took your people, how do you know they were Jondarites? Rebel townsmen, perhaps, in Jondarite dress? I'm sure that's who it was. Apply to the Supervisor of the Tower of whatever town they are from, Queen Fibji.'

As well apply to the moons, she thought viciously. There were no rebel townsmen, only Jondarites, Jondarites who kept the depredations remote from the Queen's tents and thus could not be directly accused by the Queen.

'We will accept without question anything Your Highness has seen personally,' said Bossit, smiling, always smiling, dripping politeness and courtesy as a rotten fruit drips juice. 'In accordance with the treaty the Chancery has always had with the Noor,' he said, showing his tiny teeth, a curve of threatening ivory, like a knife.

In accordance with the treaty! A treaty, made generations before, in an untrusting age when the Noor King had feared anyone speaking in his name and would speak only for himself. Used against them now to prevent her speaking. If she camped north of Thou-ne, the Jondarites struck above Vobil-dil-go. If she went to the lands above Vobil-dil-go, the Jondarites would take captives above Shfor. Wherever the Noor moved upon the open steppes, the Jondarites could find them. There was no stone, no tree, to hide behind. There were no chasms, no caves. There was only the steppe, open to the sky, and the tethered balloons of the Jondarite spies, who would see their quarry from miles away. And she, Fibji, would see the pain of the wounded and the mud graves of the dead – assuming there had been anyone left to bury the dead – but she would not see

Jondarites. She knew that someone reported on her movements. Perhaps those winged demons, seeing where she went and being sure the Jondarites knew it.

So, now, she heard the man from the slaughtered tribe. He was alone. Without near-kin. Well, that, at least, she could pretend to remedy. She gestured, a tiny movement, at once interpreted, as she called out a few words in the secret naming language of the Noor.

'Mumros, Her Highness takes you into her tribe, into her family. She calls you *Kalja Benoor*. Adopted Near-kin.'

The man who had brought the news leaned upon his hands and wept. It was not for joy. He knew as well as she the adoption was only a gesture. Near-kin could not be so easily replaced, nor grief so easily stayed. Still, when he left the tent it was with a steadier gait than that with which he had entered.

'Your Highness?' A murmured voice at her ear.

'Yes, Strenge, what is it?' Of all her men he was her favorite: strong, not at all servile, yet attentive to her dignity, virile, father of two of her children.

'The delegation from the boatmen.'

'Haven't there been enough delegations for one day?' There was despair in her whispered voice. He heard it. Among all her people he was the only one she let hear it.

'They have Glizzee spice, Your Highness.' His eyes were down, his posture dignified. If they were alone, he would call her Fibby. They had been children together. And lovers later. And lovers still.

'And we have no spice, is that it? And our people have few enough pleasures, they should not have to do without this one. And the boatmen won't deal without seeing me?'

'Your Highness sees the invisible and hears the inaudible.' He gave her a secret glance, one she knew as well as she knew the feel of her own skin.

'My Highness is dying of the agony of my people, Strenge. Of inanition and frustration. Of the duplicity of the Chancery and an unapproachable creature that calls itself the Protector of Man. Put them off.'

'Ma'am, one of them is the man called Fatterday. He claims to have seen Southshore.'

Fatterday! Was Fatterday a real person, then? Not a mere story hero, favorite protagonist of the Jarb Mendicants' tales? Was he here, now? Bringing word of a larger world out there than this circumscribed one, squeezed between the Teeth of the North and all the little, biddable towns of Northshore, and chewed to death by Jondarites? Fatterday, who had perhaps seen what Fibji had only dared hope for, a homeland beyond the reach of the general's troops? She gasped, holding Strenge with the fire of her eyes. 'Do you think he tells the truth?'

'Who could know, ma'am? However, I knew you would want to see him.'

'In the small tent, then. I've a cramp in my butt from sitting on this damn thing, and I must be able to question him.'

Strenge affected not to have heard her, his face impassive as he turned to bellow at the courtiers and warriors hanging about. 'You have Her Highness's leave to go. The boatmen may await her pleasure outside.'

They left quickly. Protocol prevented her rising until they were gone, and they knew her displeasure at being kept waiting. When the heavy tent flaps dropped behind them, she stood up, rubbing her rump, kicking off the jeweled boots and harness, handing over the holy scepter to be put in its case. Strenge was ready with a soft robe and shoes of quilted pamet embroidered with flowers. Against the white fiber her skin glowed dark, like oiled fragwood, and when she pulled off the high, feathered crown, her hair tumbled across the fabric like a thousand twining little vines, twisty and moving as though each lock had its own life. Her hawk-nosed face relaxed somewhat from its audience expression, the lines around her mouth and eyes smoothing out, dropping decades from her appearance. I'm an old woman, she thought to herself, knowing she wasn't, yet, but needing to get used to the idea. Too old for all this sitting.

The small tent adjacent was her own living space, the

piled carpets dotted with soft pillows and small tables. 'Let them come in here,' she said, taking one of the huge pillows for her own. 'Have someone bring us some wine. I ache all over.'

They came in, three of them, one lean, two stocky, brown men all, though none so dark as she. Their darkness was merely of the sun, while hers was of an ancient race, so it was said among the Northlings.

'Your Highness.' Three voices, all of them muffled from being spoken into the carpet, three backs bent impossibly to prevent their eyes meeting hers.

'Oh, stand up,' she said impatiently. 'I have to have all that out there where people are watching, but I haven't time for it here. Which one of you is Fatterday?'

He stood forward, the leanest one of the bunch, burned almost as dark as she by the sun and with deep white lines radiating from his eyes where the sun had not reached down into squint lines, smiling irrepressibly. 'Your Highness. I'm Fatterday.'

'And you've truly seen Southshore?'

He bowed again, nodding assent, not speaking.

'Well, tell me! What is it like? Are there people there? Are there fliers?'

'Your Highness, we were cast ashore on a rocky coast among high mountains. From the top of a mountain I saw an endless plain under the sun.' His eyes were alight, his fingers twitching as they described the outlines and dimensions of the lands, the rivers. 'I saw no fliers, no people. After many days, we managed to repair the boat enough to sail northward once more. Only we three survived to bring you the tale.'

'A great land.' She regarded him thoughtfully, wondering if he told the truth. 'For the taking, boatman?'

'From all I could see, free for the taking, Your Highness. If one could come to it. I saw no fliers.'

And that was it, of course. No fliers. No Jondarites. She lusted for it. The dream required lands. Lands for the people of the north, free from fliers, free from attacks by the

207

Jondarite tax collectors, free from the constant pressures of the Chancery. Lands to hold without taxation. And lands with beasts. In her mind she saw wagons pulled as they were in the Chancery lands, by beasts instead of by her people. Oh, with beasts one could move, move, out of reach of pursuing armies. Oh, why not have lands, Northlings? Why not have beasts?

'How did you come there?'

'We were prospecting among the islands for Glizzee, Your Highness. We followed a great school of strangeys. Came a strong, wild current in World River, and we were driven south. Came storm and great wind driving us, days and days, until we lost track of them. Many died. Most. Only seven of us came to that shore, and only we three returned.' He did not say how they had lived or what they had eaten. They could not have eaten the local animals and survived, not without human grains to go with them. They could have eaten fish. It was better, perhaps, not to know how they had survived.

'So, how would we come there, if we chose to go?'

'If you chose to go, Highness, you should go well provisioned. It is a long voyage. Still, I would not hesitate to make it again. There are wonders there.'

She waved him away. That was the question, wasn't it? How could one get better provisioned with the Chancery taking all but a bare sufficiency. They were lucky if the scavengers from the Chancery left them grain enough for the cold season and a spare bit more should the warm come late. When that was all they were allowed to assemble, how could they put together a store for a long voyage? And how put together the boats, come to that? Fibji's people numbered some hundreds of thousands, not many compared to the population of Northshore, but a great horde when one considered the size of most boats. Fifty at a time, perhaps. Hundreds of thousands of Noor, and only fifty at a time. If they took one boat from every town . . .

She shook herself, shedding the vision of lands beyond the River. Fatterday was still standing there, as though he had not seen her excuse him. The man was still to be dealt with.

'You came north across the World River to Thou-ne?'

'We did, ma'am. With Glizzee spice as the whole of our property, all that was left us after the storm save the shell of our boat.'

'And you brought it here because the price is better so far from the World River?'

'As Your Highness says.' He grinned knowingly.

'And it would help you, now, if we bought your spice from you?'

He bowed, unspeaking. It was probably the only thing that would help him, she thought. He had likely been impoverished by his adventure. He must have had everything he owned lost on the voyage. She beckoned to Strenge, signaling him to send for the coffer keeper. They had little enough in stores of food or obvious possessions, the Noor, but the Melancholics did keep the Queen's coffers filled. So let Fatterday be paid, and let him think it was for the spice. Actually, the payment was for the news he brought her. News she could use.

When the boatmen were gone, she summoned her near-kin, not forgetting the lonely survivor most recently adopted. They drank sammath wine as they talked of Southshore, of the goddess, of themselves and the Jondarites.

'But what of the plan?' they asked, uncomfortable at the thought of giving up the thing they had been working on for so very long.

'We are not yet changing the plan,' she replied. 'It was too long in the making to change it unless for something far better. So far, we have only the word of an explorer. He could be lying. He could be mistaken. No, we are not yet talking of changing the plan. But let us investigate the dream. If Southshore is within reach . . .'

She did not need to complete the thought. The old plan had been fifty years in the making, thirty in implementation. Here and there across the steppes were great complexes of tunnels dug secretly by the Noor. There beneath the steppes were towns, cities. There beneath the scattered grainfields were dormitories and meeting halls and storehouses now beginning to hold some grain and roots hidden from the tax collectors. Timbers supported the corridors beneath the earth, timbers bought from the Queen's coffers, moved at night, hidden by day. Clever mechanisms brought air into the depths, mechanisms paid for from the Queen's funds. Melancholics went south into the cities and returned with goods and coin, and both went into the underground cities Queen Fibji was building. Fifty thousand of the Queen's people dwelt beneath the moors already, and more were descending every day. In twenty years more, or thirty, all would have made themselves a redoubt within the earth. Then, the scouts would watch for Jondarite balloons, would signal the approach of armies, but those armies would find no one on the open steppes, no one to enslave, no one to tax. Or if they did, they would fight tunnel by tunnel, room by room, against strong defenses.

And across the breadth of the steppes hundreds of thousands of mud graves stood mute evidence of the soil dug out in the dark hours. If any had had sense to see it. How could so sparse a people have had so many dead? But the Jondarites had not asked that question.

'And yet,' she whispered to herself, 'and yet, in that thirty years or fifty years, how many more will really die?' The young men grew belligerent in the underground places. If they could not fight the Jondarites, they fought one another. Queen Fibji had made a rule that boys could dwell below only until they had fathered two children; then they must return to the nomad tribes above. Which made it more peaceful below but left the children without fathers to learn from. She sighed. Thinking again of Fatterday, she wondered how many of her people might be saved if there were truly a Southshore and she could find some way to come to it.

Now her near-kin were saying the same things over and over, worrying the subject to rags. Her mind wandered, remembering.

On one particular day long ago she had walked with her father across a stretch of the arid lands, away from the tribe, free for the moment from servitors or petitioners. He had taken her on these walks sometimes, talking and talking, as though to gift her with the essence of his thought to store for some future time. She was his only child.

'The young always want to go to war,' he had said. 'And the old are too often eager to send them. The young revel in thoughts of battle. They think blood is wine, that it can be spilt without consequence and a new vintage bought for tomorrow's feast. And the old are sometimes willing to have young men gone, to have their exasperating numbers thinned to a biddable fraction, for they, the young men, are the source of dissent and confusion. It is among them that revolution breeds, often to no point. But what good are dead warriors, Fibji?'

He stopped, as though taken by a sudden memory. 'Long ago, when I was only a youth and my father was yet King, I came upon a Jarb Mendicant sitting on a stone here on the steppe, wreathed in the smoke of his pipe. I was joyful and sanguine then. I said to him, "Mendicant, give me a prognostication for our people." He looked at me through the smoke, as they do, and said at last, "I see peace and prosperity for the Noor, Prince, but only when the ruler of the Noor can answer the question, 'Of what good are dead warriors?' " '

He brooded again. 'I have never answered the question, Fibji. See the mud graves of the dead as we pass. Is our way not marked with the bones of our people? And what good do the dead do themselves or us?'

He had intended it as a rhetorical question, but it had caught Fibji's attention. What good indeed? The mud tombs were scattered everywhere on the endless plains, thinly in most places, thickly around much used campsites. Inside them the bones of the dead, rolled in their robes, sat inside thick mud shells sculptured into the shapes of them as they had been in life. Children played among the clayed-over bones, thinking nothing of it. Death had no reality to

211

children. Fibji herself had played among the tombs, knowing what they were well enough. They had no more reality for her than for other children.

Until that moment. Her father stood at her left hand, staring off across the steppe where the sparse grass moved in a small wind, the half-dried blades making a gentle susurrus, barely audible. To her right was a cluster of mud graves, three almost alike, as though of one family, two men and a woman, their faces staring toward her from the clay. She fancied they would speak in a moment, greeting the King, and in that instant her mind saw into the clay to the place the bones rested and beyond the bones to the people who had once lived. It happened all at once, like a vision. Almost she could have called the names of those who rested in the shells, gone now. They stared out at her with eager eyes, those young men, eyes anxious for battle, hungry for death. And in that instant she knew mortality, all at once, entirely. Even she, Fibji, would stop! She, Fibji, would cease to be!

'Of what good are dead warriors?' her father had repeated, and she had screamed, cowering against him in a sudden spasm of fear so palpable it was like a presence, as though death itself had touched her.

'Fibji?' he had said, looking her full in the face with total understanding. 'Daughter?' And then he had held her tightly, waiting for the fear to pass. 'I know,' he said. 'I know.'

She had been about seven when she'd realized death. When she had taken up the scepter, she had tried to explain why they must not wage war. And yet there were always the young men who rebelled against her. Young bloods, always, in love with their concept of justice, eager to prove themselves, making it easier for the Jondarites, plunging into battle with a scream of defiance and naked chests.

Now she was fifty-five with perhaps a decade or two left before understanding became reality. For the Chancery there was the elixir and an almost immortality. For the people of Northshore, the Promise of Potipur. For the steppe dwellers, the Noor, nothing. Seven tens of years and then the mud grave and the cold wind. Now, though she was closer to that end she had perceived when she was seven, she did not fear it as much for herself as she had feared it then. She feared it more, however, for her people and knew what her father had tried to tell her.

'Think well,' she said now, speaking earnestly to the near-kin, an interruption of their wrangles. 'I remember the words of my father. We walked upon the steppe, and he told me the Noor would not have peace until they could answer the question, "Of what good are dead warriors?" Think well, kinfolk. Let us consider the possibility of South-shore. But whatever we do, let us save every Noor we can in the doing of it.'

Then she turned away from them, went into the small tent where she slept, where Strenge waited for her now. 'Old friend,' she said, 'when Medoor Babji, our daughter, begged to be allowed to accompany a troop of Melancholics to the cities of the River, we thought it well she should see the world in which the Noor must live.'

He nodded. 'Those she is with do not know who she is or what she is to be.'

'True, but she carries sufficient proof to command them to her service. Here, in her tent, is a cage of seeker birds kept by her servants. Send the birds south. Tell our daughter what we have heard of Southshore.'

It was a daughter, not a son, selected to be Queen Fibji's heir. Her sons were too brave, too puissant, too eager for war. They disbelieved in death. 'Tell our daughter,' she said once again, 'what we have heard of Southshore.'

21

Shavian Bossit drank wine with General of the Armed Might of the Chancery Jondrigar and described the futile embassy of Queen Fibji.

'Honest as the day,' he sneered, reaching down with his toe to tap the floor in emphasis. All the general's chairs were too large for Bossit, but he forced himself to sit in them, forced himself to fill whatever chair he sat in, whatever room he occupied, whatever role he chose for himself. 'The Queen will not lie, General. She has not seen Jondarites herself, and she will not say she has.'

'The woman's a fool.'

Shavian twitched his shoulders in a quick shrug. 'Perhaps. A very tortured fool, General. I would not take her honesty as her only foolishness. She may be foolish enough to attack you.'

The general snorted. 'Don't be stupid, Bossit. So long as she does not see what we do, she remains comfortable. She will not disrupt herself over deaths she does not see.' He considered death in the abstract. To him the victims of his raids were not men, not women or children, not babes as he had once been a babe. They were simply steppe dwellers, Noor, tribesmen, proper targets for a military exercise. How else should troops be sharpened against the inevitable time of need, against the time when someone or something might threaten the Protector of Man? He used the steppe dwellers in various ways, sometimes working parties of young males up into a killing rage, then quelling them in a well-planned exercise; sometimes surprising whole tribes and taking the males captive – for the iron mines or the copper mines or to be given to the woodcutters as slaves – sometimes merely slaughtering them because Jondarites must become accustomed to killing.

'You may underestimate her,' nagged Bossit, staring at the other man with frank curiosity. The general wore his helm liner, its flaps covering his head and neck. Beneath it his face was gray as lava and pitted as dust after a spring shower. No disease had caused this skin coloration or texture. Jondrigar had been born with it, born with the gray, pitted skin and the wild, iron-gray hair – now kept shaved – the massive shoulders, the long arms that let his standing figure touch his knees without stooping. He was a hideous man. He had been as hideous a child. His mother, so Bossit had been told, had screamed at the sight of him and shortly thereafter had died. Bossit, though more or less accustomed to Jondrigar's appearance, sometimes amused himself imagining what had gone through her head, that faceless woman who had given him birth. Had she thought, perhaps, of Jondrigar's father? Whoever that might have been? Had she thought of her sins, wondering whether this monstrous baby was some old sin made manifest? What had she thought? Or had she thought at all?

Bossit had had Jondrigar's antecedents looked into, insofar as that was possible. Jondrigar had been reared by his mother's sister, Firrabel. Firrabel was as resolute and dutiful as her sister had been flighty and hysterical. It was Firrabel who had taken the ugly infant, reared him, fed him, and schooled him, teaching him more of letters than ninetenths of Northshore thought necessary; it was Firrabel at last who had sent him to the Chancery to be of service, claiming the Chancery had picked him for that service when he was still a baby, as, in a sense, perhaps it had.

If that is what had happened, it had occurred during a royal Progression. The shore had been lined with people, the golden ship of the Protector moving slowly along the Riverbank with the Protector held high above the crowd in the arms of his servitors, leaning down now and then to

215

toss a glittering token to one of the common people.

And Firrabel, taken up with the drama of it all, had held Jondrigar high above her head, waving him like a banner, him ugly as a mud grave, all wide-eyed, reaching out with his little gray paws, grab, grab at anything. The hands caught the robes of the Protector, and the Protector had laughed and turned to someone else with a remark.

Someone had given the baby a token. 'By the moons, look at the face on him,' someone had said. 'Send him to the Chancery when he grows, mother,' someone else had said to Firrabel. 'We have need of those who can frighten demons just looking at them.' Had it been the Protector who had called out, saying these things? Or someone in his entourage? Who knew? Firrabel didn't remember, then.

He was a child who had had to fight for his life, many times. He learned to fight very well and to despise weakness, in himself, in others. Then, when he was a strapping youth of such horrible mien and reputation that people hastily hid when they saw him coming, Firrabel had given him the token and sent him north. 'Go to the Chancery,' she had said. 'Ask for the Protector and remind him that he chose you out of thousands to serve him.'

By this time, she had convinced herself the Protector had said it all. Actually, it had been Bossit himself who had said most of it, and it was Bossit who remembered the whole thing when Jondrigar came to the Chancery at last. The guards had laughed in his face when he'd passed into Chancery lands. They had laughed, but they had passed the word. Bossit had seen monstrousness in the child, he saw the promise of that monstrousness fulfilled in the man. Bossit had given him a spear to see what he could do with it, and he could do a good deal. Jondrigar had become a guardsman, and then the leader of a company, and then head of a battalion. And by the time the old general had died, all the guards in the Chancery were Jondarites, and no one suggested any other candidate to lead the Chancery army.

Jondrigar the gray, the scaly, the pitted, wild-haired, long-armed monster. Jondrigar the untouchable. Jondrigar,

216

who cared for only two people in all the world: Firrabel, who had raised him and cared for him; and Lees Obol, Protector of Man, who had picked him – so he thought – out of all the world. He had never loved a woman, never cared for a child. To Firrabel he sent money and gifts and infrequent letters. To Lees Obol he gave all his devotion and his life. And to Bossit, who furnished the general with tempting morsels from time to time, the monster served as a constant amusement, a source of daily wonder.

As for the general's own feelings, he did not think he had underestimated Queen Fibji. The northlands might rise under one of the male advisers to the scepter, perhaps, but not under the Queen. She was a pacifist. She would not fight. Her young men would fight, but she would not. From what he knew of women – that is, of his dutiful aunt and some even more dutiful whores – Jondrigar believed that women put comfort above all other considerations. Fibji was a woman, and she was comfortable as she was. He, Jondrigar, would allow her just enough comfort to keep her quiescent by exercising his troops at some distance from the Queen's tents. When Noor were to be murdered, maimed, or otherwise brutalized, he would do it out of Fibji's sight or hearing. Though she might learn of it later, it would be after the blood had dried and most of the grieving done. None knew better than Jondrigar how difficult it was to work up an outrage over something that had happened a long time before. So wherever Fibji went, the balloon scouts came to tell him, and he sent the troops elsewhere. A kind of game, really, but effective. The ceaseless depredations of the Jondarites kept the steppe dwellers' population in check and prevented them from assembling the stores they needed to wage outright war: the confiscated grains and roots filled vast storehouses behind the Teeth, enough to keep the Chancery for a generation if it were ever needful.

General Jondrigar was well satisfied with Queen Fibji. If General Jondrigar was grateful for anything, he was grateful for comfortable, dutiful, compliant women.

22

In a hidden room off a remote corridor of the palace, Ezasper Jorn, Ambassador to the Thraish, built up the small fire in his porcelain stove and invited his guest to bring a chair closer to the warmth.

'Glad the winter's well over,' he said, holding his hands to the stove. 'One can find out absolutely nothing in the winter.' His mighty form was close-wrapped in a heavy cloak, his pendulous ears half-covered by a floppy cap. Still he shivered, holding his huge hands almost upon the surface of the stove. Ezasper Jorn was never warm. Even at the height of polar summer, he shivered. In winter, he was almost immobile. He had fulfilled the duties of his office for many years, mostly by virtue of saying almost nothing to the Thraish and agreeing with everything they said to him. Since no action was ever taken on any recommendation made by Ezasper Jorn – indeed, he seldom made any at all – it did not matter. The position of Ambassador was filled harmlessly, and all at the Chancery were satisfied by that.

'We have to find out somehow,' said Koma Nepor, purse-lipped. Chief of Research was a position lacking clear duties but implying vast and often unnameable expectations. Koma brought to the role an instinctive appreciation of mystery coupled with an inquisitive, persistent mind. The mystery over which he now troubled himself was the reported disappearance of animals from the Chancery herds of weehar and thrassil. It could have happened late last fall, perhaps. Not during the winter, when the creatures were dug deep into the ice. Perhaps early this spring, when the first thaws came and the grass turned green on Chancery lands.

The surviving herds had been kept small at the command of Shavian Bossit, Lord Maintainer of the Household. Generations ago he had perceived the dangerous temptation large herds of weehar and thrassil might present to wandering fliers, assuming any such abrogated the treaty and flew north of the Teeth. It would have been wise, he had felt then as now, to kill the remaining beasts, leaving no cause for temptation at all.

However, the Protector of Man enjoyed red meat from time to time, and General Jondrigar, who regarded each least notion of the Protector as though it were an order given under penalty of death, had seen to it that the herds remained. The Protector received his roasts and chops at intervals, carefully augmented by certain grains and herbs. Men who ate the native animals had learned to serve them thus or risk a bewildering loss of intelligence. On Northshore the relationship between what eats and what is eaten was closer than on many worlds – or so the histories implied. There were those foods, for example, that allowed the fliers to retain their wings while others would have confined them to a life on the ground. There were foods that allowed those in the Chancery to live long, long lives, and others that would have condemned them to an early and brief idiocy. So it was that the fliers ate what they ate in order to maintain their wings, and the Chancery officials, when dining upon roast thrassil, consumed it with leguminous garnish. Which they would not do soon again if too many animals were missing.

'Bormas Tyle has investigated the report and is sure some of the animals are gone,' said Ezasper. 'He's told Tharius Don about it, you may be sure of that. Bormas may go his own way most of the time, but he is not derelict in his deputized duties. And Bossit won't drop the matter, you may be sure.' His flaccid arms were held toward the welcome warmth of the stove, his pouchy face reddened by the heat. 'Just *gone*.'

'How would he know? We don't keep them on inventory,

for the gods' sake. They wander. They get killed. Some of them die.'

'Bormas says the two herds were small, almost household herds, kept close to the Chancery. The herdsmen had counted the young last fall, marking some to be set aside for the table of the Protector. When they went to do the butchering last week, there were only a few of the younger animals left. Up to a dozen of them gone, says Bormas.'

Ezasper frowned. 'Almost enough to make one remember those old legends about the monster in the main files. The one who eats all the apprentices.'

Nepor giggled, appreciating this reference to the legend of the monster. 'Most likely fliers,' he said. 'That's really what everyone is worried about. That Talker was here before winter set in. First time ever, him and his friends. And he wasn't blind. He saw the thrassil, the weehar.'

'Bormas wanted those herds killed off, long since.'

'Bormas was right to urge it.' Koma Nepor mused, 'The general should have listened to him. Well, if the fliers have taken the animals, they haven't taken them to a Talons. Nothing for grass eaters in those rocky places. No. They'll have them on pasture somewhere. Most likely on the steppes, or in the badlands. Whichever, they'll have to be found.' He scratched himself reflectively, thinking. 'Bormas says we must send Jondarites. I told him no, it would be better to get the Noor to find them. Bormas asked why the Noor would bother, considering what use had been made of them in the past. To which question, of course, one cannot give convincing answer. Still, I think no Jondarites. Too much room there for conflict of an undesirable kind. Perhaps we had better consult with Tharius Don?' He left it as a question. Both of them knew what such consultation would mean – an hour's lecture on the morality of the situation. Still, better Tharius Don than Mitiar, who disliked unpleasant news and retaliated against those who brought it. Better than Bossit, who would definitely seek a scapegoat to take responsibility for the disappearance.

They postponed the decision in desultory chat. 'And

what of your researches?' Ezasper asked. 'What new and remarkable things have you found?'

Nepor giggled again. 'I've been experimenting with blight, Jorn my boy. There are, ah . . . interesting applications. Applications I do not intend to reveal to General Jondrigar. Oh, by the moons, none of us would be safe if he knew them.'

Ezasper turned his wide face toward the other, held up a cautioning fist. 'Careful, Koma. If you have found something like that, be very careful speaking of it. To anyone at all.'

The other shifted uncomfortably. He never knew exactly what Ezasper meant. Perhaps he meant not to speak of it at all; perhaps he meant to speak to no one except Ezasper himself. Sometimes Nepor felt he did not understand what was going on. Experimental situations were very different from people. In experiment, one could control what happened – or, if not what happened, the conditions under which it happened. Results could be duplicated time after time. With people, very little was controllable. They acted quite unpredictably. It seemed wisest to let the subject go, for now. Still, it was quite remarkable what a sprayer full of blight could do to a living person.

23

The lady Kesseret prepared to depart from Highstone Lees.
On the morning she would go to the top of Split River Pass
and down the other side, carried in a palanquin by Noor
slaves while she meditated upon the evil of their slavery.
Slavery, like Awakening, would vanish on the day. Until
then, she could not appear to disapprove of it without
coming under suspicion. *More* suspicion, she told herself,
sure that she was already suspected of much.

'Have you any word?' she asked Tharius Don.

'The man who played the role of Fatterday did his
job well. Queen Fibji will send an expedition to the
Southshore.'

'When? How soon?'

'Probably not until late summer. Still, that is only a little
time. When she does so, we will see that the fliers hear of it.
It will give them something to think about besides Rivermen. Also, I've sent an envoy to ask her to search for the
missing beasts. The envoy will plant the idea that such
beasts should be taken on any voyage, in case there are none
beyond the River. They will steal the beasts – if they find
them. And this, too, will draw the fliers' attention.'

She was not sure this feint would have its desired purpose.
The fliers were subtle, more subtle, she thought, than
Tharius realized. 'When the time comes, Tharius, do you
really think the fliers will capitulate? Do you really think
they will give up their wings? Become like the Treeci?
Legendary Treeci, I should say. We don't even know if they
really exist.'

'There are books in the palace library that say they do, Kessie. Old books, which have stood on those shelves for hundreds of years, talk about the Treeci islands. Books no one looks at but me. Luckily, Glamdrul Feynt cares for nothing but his files. Strictly speaking, the books should be his responsibility, yet I thank whatever gods may be that they are where I can read them. And yes, to answer your question, I think the Thraish will capitulate. Rather than see us die or themselves. Once they have experienced the other kind of life, I think they will prefer it.'

'You're so sure.' She shook her head at him, smiling wanly. He had always been sure, very sure. Perhaps it had been that quality in him that she had loved. So nice to be sure, without doubts.

'They've seen us, Kessie. We don't fly. And yet we have a civilization better than the one the Thraish have. They borrow our craftsmen, they borrow our writing. They take from us constantly. They can't be unaware of the difference. It's only custom that keeps them to the treaty. A hard custom, and one tightly held, but when it comes right down to it, I think they'll be relieved. By all accounts, humans and the Treeci live very well together.'

'So you've said, Tharius. I wish I were as sure as you are.' She choked, oppressed by this act of leaving him. In a moment her voice came back and she went on, 'Sometimes I lie awake in Baris Tower at night. Everything is very quiet. Far off in the town the crier sings out, and his voice comes gently. There is wind, perhaps. I lie there, almost at peace, my mind drifting quietly.

'Oh, Tharius, there is a peaceful place inside the head where one may wander. Like fields, new mown, green and moist and fragrant. One wanders inside oneself, at peace, unconscious of being oneself. Then, suddenly, out of nothing, a hard, hurtful thing intrudes and one cries out.'

'I know.' He smoothed her hair from her forehead. 'I forget, too, sometimes. I drift, dream. But I always remember again.'

'There is such peace in that forgetting! But yes, one

223

remembers again, and the future looms up like a rocky cliff, creased with bruising edges and sharp corners, a thing which cannot be drifted over but must be climbed, hard stone by hard stone.' She fell silent for a time, lines starring from her eyes and lips, her face for that moment incredibly ancient.

'When I remember, I start to think of the morning of the rebellion, of the day itself. Our people will have been to the pits in the night and every worker pit will be empty. All the bodies will be in the River. Weighted down. We will have killed every patch of Tears we have been able to find. The fliers will have nothing to eat . . .'

Tharius Don took up the account. 'In every town the crier will call watch against fliers who may come seeking living meat. There will be Tears in the Towers, and these must be sought out and destroyed by fire, by our friends within the Towers. By those outside the Towers, if necessary.'

'I think of Towers burning,' she said.

'But not Baris Tower,' he said. 'In Baris Tower the Superior will tell her Awakeners of a new revelation.'

'Yes,' she agreed sadly. 'A new revelation, to be preached by the Awakeners to the fliers. A revelation from Potipur which demands that they give up their wings . . . When I look at someone like Sliffisunda, though, I'm not sure he will ever accept it. There's a kind of hatred in him. For us. For all our kind.'

'Tradition. Custom. That's all. The attitude they've adopted. It doesn't mean that's the only attitude they can adopt.'

'Does the Ambassador to the Thraish agree with you on that point?'

'I don't discuss anything with Jorn. He returned from his journey some time ago, but all I've said to him thus far is ''Good evening.'' Ezasper cares for nothing except that the stove be well alight and he not expected to go out on cold days. Don't seek confirmation from those like Jorn, Kessie. Don't doubt our cause. Have faith. When the time comes to

224

choose between wings or life, the Thraish will choose life and life with us as . . . well, if not as brothers, at least as kin.'

'And we, Tharius? When will the day come?'

'Soon. There are only a few more pieces to be set into place. A few more patches of Tears to kill. A few more Towers to recruit. A few more groups to get organized for the night of the strike. Not many. Have patience.'

She, who had had patience for some hundred years, snorted at this, and he joined her in wry laughter.

'Have you any word of Pamra?'

'No signals. If Ilze had found her, we would know.'

'Let us hope we hear nothing.' She stretched, moved her fingers and toes to be sure they had healed. 'Let us pray we hear nothing.'

He nodded. Time pressed, now. Secrecy had to be maintained. They needed some minor distractions to keep the Talkers busy. They needed absolute quiet from those involved in the conspiracy. They needed no more upsets such as the one provided by Pamra Don. Not too much to keep track of, really. He kissed her on the forehead, a valedictory. They might never see one another again.

'If I am killed while you still live, Kessie, find Pamra then. Tell her I cared about her.'

She shook her head; a tear gathered that hung, unshed, like a gem upon her lashes. 'Better I don't see her again, love. Better for all of us. Let us pray she has gone to ground and is well hidden. Pray we do not hear of her again.'

24

High in the Talons above the Straits of Shfor in his aerie, Sliffisunda – the Uplifted One, by the grace of Potipur articulate, a Talker of the Sixth Degree – met with his students, newly located Talkers, still awed by their selection. The aerie, once a graceless, chilly cave, full of wind and the stench of guano, had been reshaped by the hands of human slaves. There was a privy slot in the outer wall, set in a niche covered with a heavy curtain. There was a low, broad perch, on which Sliffisunda stood to receive visitors. There were carvings on the walls, and a meat trough with an ornamental post and chains to hold the meat down until it died. Though heavily dosed with Tears, the living human bodies tended to thrash about unpleasantly while they were being eaten. Sliffisunda sometimes believed that despite the stench of carrion, he might have preferred to eat as the ordinary fliers did, in the bone pits.

The students before him, three of them, were egglings who hardly knew the meaning of the Covenant. They did not understand humiliation. It was Sliffisunda's job to teach them, to let them know how far the Thraish had fallen from their onetime communion with the gods, and by imparting that knowledge to cleave these youngsters to the doctrine of rage that governed the Talons.

'Perch,' he directed them, waiting impatiently while they settled before him, wings outspread, heads carried well back on their flexible necks, foot talons stretching beyond their knees as they crouched, knees on feet, in the posture of subordination.

226

'I want you to imagine you are a flier,' he said at last, when they were well settled. 'Just a flier, a female. Not a Talker at all. I want you to imagine it is long ago, more than a thousand years.' There was a snigger at this. There was always a snigger at this, but Sliffisunda waited without outward show of impatience for his own heavy regard to make their eggishness manifest. Soon they felt his disapproval and became uncomfortable, shifting from foot to foot, staring at him from lowered eyes.

Sliffisunda's voice became a monotone, a rhythmic chant. 'It is spring. You have slept the winter away in the caves low in the mountains of the north. Now the time of warmth has come, and you emerge from your cave to the time of rejoicing. Your name is Shishus, flier of the Thraish . . .'

His voice was hypnotic. They would imagine, combining what they knew in their blood with what they had learned and what he would tell them in his chanting. They would fall into a trance, and in the trance they would dream that last awakening of ancient times.

In the trance it seemed that the season of warmth had come upon the northern plains. The cold rains were over. On the endless prairies the tall grass moved like water, silver blue like the River the grass moved, breaking around the herd of weehar as the River broke on the rocks of Shfor, near the Talons. The herd whuffled nervously as Shishus's shadow fell across them, she crying, 'Rejoice! Warmth is come!'

The weehar rejoiced in their own way, heads down, legs trembling. Each thing rejoiced in its own way. Even trees, doubtless. With warmth came the end of hibernation, the season of rejoicing, the season of Potipur's Promise to the Thraish.

Shishus whispered the name of her people. 'Thraish.' The word was a rejoicing in itself. After the lonely time of cold, she longed for Thraish, for huntmates. First the rejoicing. Then the obligatory trip to the Talons for the dancing as the moons gathered. Then mating. Then

227

nesting, the joy of nestlings. 'Thraish,' she whispered, turning on her strong wings above the prairie.

Though perhaps the Talkers would suggest again that the dancing not take place. As they had at the last Conjunction. Last warm season there had been rebellious muttering against the Talkers, and Shishus had been a leader in that rebellion. In old times Talkers had been wise, settling disputes over nesting sites or huntmates. Last season – no, the season before that and before that as well – they had not been helpful. Not orthodox. Of late the Talkers seemed to doubt Potipur's Promise, the promise of ten thousand years. 'Do my will and ye shall have plenty.'

Thinking of it made Shishus angry. Among the free fliers there was talk of overthrowing the Talkers. Shishus had told them it was foolish talk. It was not necessary to overthrow the Talkers. They could simply be ignored!

Potipur's Promise was holy. Long, long ago the Thraish had been hungry. All the hoovar had been eaten and were gone. Then came the Talker Shinnisush, bringing Potipur's Promise to the people. 'Follow me and ye shall have plenty!' And after the promise there had been great explosions in the northlands, mountains jutting fire, and endless herds of thrassil came, driven out of the north by the fire, driven from behind the great mountains. The Thraish had rejoiced in plenty once more.

But in time the thrassil also were gone, eaten. Then the world had shaken again, and the weehar had come, down in great herds to the silver-blue plains that lay between the Riverlands and the northern mountains.

Great herds.

Shishus planed in a wide gyre, peering down. One herd only. Small. Perhaps she should wait to find a larger herd. No. Cold season had been long, and soon huntmates would arrive. She threw back her head and cried loud into the sky, 'Invitation! Join! Rejoice! Summer beasts are here.'

Below, Shishus's shadow fell across beasts, and they began to gallop, a frenzied flight, knowing time to rejoice was near. Far on the western horizon two winged specks moved toward Shishus, crying as they came, 'Rejoice, rejoice.' Her huntmates: Slililan, Shusisanda.

They met in midair, wingtips caressing, beaks touching the tender sweet places behind ears, glorying in touch, in flight. Then they cried together, fell together, talons extended, crying the great invitation to the weehar. 'Rejoice! Rejoice!'

The weehar rejoiced, galloping, snorting, leaping in a wild dance upon the grass, evading, skipping, falling at last beneath the clutching talons, beneath the spearing beaks. Blood ran hot into Shishus's beak.

In Sliffisunda's aerie the young shifted uncomfortably from foot to foot, beaks agape. They tasted the hot blood of the weehar, heard the cries of the huntmates. Sliffisunda chanted to them, telling them what to feel, what to experience. In the trance they heard Sliffisunda's voice:

'Rejoice! Rejoice!'

Away upon the prairie the few remaining weehar stopped running, stood trembling, the few young in the center of the group. This was how weehar prayed to Potipur. This is how the herd beasts rejoiced. Shishus stood upon one of the beasts she had killed, gorged now, beak dripping, and called to her huntmates to see the beasts rejoicing.

'Not rejoicing,' snapped Slililan. Slililan did not always sound like free flier. Sometimes she sounded almost like Talker. 'No rejoicing, Shishus, silly flier. Weehar scared. Only scared. Herd too small.'

'Rejoice in own way,' Shishus screamed. Slililan was spoiling their first feast. 'Slililan makes unorthodox talk. Doubts Potipur.'

Slililan flew at Shishus then, battle ready. Only Shusisanda's bulk thrust between had stopped them as they stood with wings cocked high in threat, spear-beaked and blood-eyed. 'Huntmates,' Shusisanda whispered. 'Time to rejoice.'

What had made them grow so angry? There had never been anger among free fliers before. They had fought only the mock battles of conjugation, vying for the dancing males. They had not fought one another. Was it something in the look of the plains? In the trembling silence of the few weehar?

'Find bigger herd,' Shishus demanded, lifting away from the many bodies that littered the ground. Perhaps they should not have killed so many. They could have killed only three, one for each of them, though they could have eaten only a tiny fraction even of that. Already grouped in a wide circle around the corpses were the silly fliers, those with no speech, waiting for their own time to rejoice. Shishus and her huntmates winged toward the Talons, uneasy as distances drifted by, uneasier yet when they came within sight of the peaks.

There the hunters of Thraish, free fliers, gathered in their hundreds of thousands, thick as grass, their clattering so loud it reached the huntmates when they were still far away.

They had flown half around the world, to arrive at the Talons, but there had been no bigger herd of weehar.

There had been no herds at all.

They arrived to sounds of the summoning rattle, propelled to and fro on its flexible sapling base by young fliers, telling Talkers to come out of their rocky towers. Speaker's rock was empty. No Talkers sat upon it. Rattle went on as sound of Thraish grew louder, more agitated.

Then silence, for Talker came out, old Talker, blue with age, eyes deep-pouched, beak silver and ragged-edged. He came from a dark hole in rock, perched on doorstep, peered nearsightedly at great throng there, said in a dry, uninterested voice, 'Rejoice, people of Thraish.'

There was only muttering from free fliers. Shishus, alone among throng, called response. 'Rejoice!'

All eyes came to Shishus, fastening upon her. Muttering grew louder. Talker fixed his old eyes upon her, called to her.

'You found weehar then, flight leader?'

Shishus could not reply. This was not the way ceremony went. Talker asked again, and yet again, before Shishus could think to say, 'Huntmates have rejoiced.'

'How many weehar did you find?'

Shishus conferred with Shusisanda. How many had there been? Five claws? About that. Fifty.

'And when you had rejoiced, how many left?'

Three claws, perhaps. Or less.

Silence then upon Talons. A long, uneasy silence, unbroken except by rustling of thousands shifting from foot to foot in an agony of apprehension. 'Promise of Potipur,' one called from midst of free fliers, whining. 'Promise of Potipur.'

'Ah, well,' cried old Talker. 'If Potipur has promised, then free fliers of Thraish have nothing to worry about.'

Muttering began again, angrily this time. Potipur had promised plenty, but there was no plenty. So. So. There must be fault somewhere. Evil. Sin. Talkers, most likely. Their fault. Their sin. Doubting.

The old Talker might have read their minds. 'Who told you free fliers last warm season not to eat weehar?'

Muttering. It was true. Talkers had told them that. Talkers had said weehar were too few. Free fliers had told Talkers something different instead. Free fliers had told Talkers to keep quiet. Had told them, 'Promise of Potipur.'

'Last warm season, who told males not to dance? Who told free fliers not to breed last Conjunction? Who told the fliers to break their eggs?'

The Talkers had told them. Talkers said to eat fish. Foul fish that softened beaks, made feathers fall, which made free fliers unable to fly at all. Talkers said not to nest. Not do Conjunction. But flight leaders had cawed laughter. Promise of Potipur. Shishus had cawed laughter with all free fliers. Do will of Potipur! Breed. Grow more numerous. Have plenty!

'Who told fliers to eat, breed?' Old Talker had a voice like rocks rubbing together in flood. 'Flight leaders said eat, breed. Flight leaders, like Shishus there. She called shame on Talkers. Told you Potipur would provide plenty. So. Ask flight leaders where is rejoicing Potipur will provide.'

The Talker had gone then, quickly, down inside the stone, where it would be safe against Thraish, for Thraish were very angry at Talkers.

231

At first.

Anger was there. But Talkers were not there. Free fliers could not attack them. Could not spear beak, wing buffet. Talkers were different. Males who would not dance. Males who changed, instead. Knew more. Used more words. Had different thoughts. Lived down in stone, somewhere deep where Thraish could not get to them.

So, wrath turned against others.

Against flight leaders.

Against Shishus, flying, flying, hiding among stones, in grass, walking along streams to hide, not flying, huntmates lost, pecked to death, only Shishus living, eating stilt lizards, eating worms, living, while all around Thraish died by thousands, thousands. Starving.

In the towns along the River lived the two-legged out-landers, humans. Despicable nonfliers. Good smelling. Full of hot blood. Weak. Slow. Some fliers hunted this meat. Some fliers ate this meat, died. Screaming, insides burning, they died. Human meat was poison to the Thraish.

Some ate fish. Feathers dropped out for a time. Bones changed. Couldn't fly. Treeci, meaning 'crawler.' Fish eaters. Filth. Betrayers of Potipur.

Some, like Shishus, ate lizards, worms, bodies of dead fliers. Only those few like Shishus lived, eating dead fliers, smaller birds, not eating the poisonous humans, not eating fish as the foul Treeci did, who forsook Potipur's Promise, giving up their power of flight. It was a test, a test. Potipur testing. Soon would come Potipur's Promise.

Of the Talkers, only a few lived. Of the fliers, only a few, like Shishus, survived.

In the aerie, the egglings woke from their trance, gagging, no longer full of giggles.

'Attend,' said Sliffisunda. 'Some survived. Shishus, whose story you have heard, survived. And many of us, the Talkers, survived. It was one of our number, Thoulia, who learned that the flesh of the humans could be softened by Tears of Viranel and then safely eaten by us. We took them, the soft, weak humans, took them to eat.

232

'We chose not to eat fish, not to become flightless, not to betray the Promise of Potipur.

'But the humans fought us. Many of them died. Many of us died. Thoulia said to us, "They will never let you take them without fighting. And if you kill them all as you did the weehar, what will you eat? And if they kill us all, who will keep Potipur's name alive?"

'We chose rather to arrange matters in order to assure ourselves a sufficiency of human flesh.

'We made treaty with humans. We offered some few of them the elixir of the Talkers in return for the flesh of other humans. Dead flesh for the fliers, who are many. Live flesh for us Talkers, who are few. We gave some few of them the elixir if they would worship our gods. We offered some of them long, long life if they would become Awakeners, build the Towers, let the Thraish feast in their bone pits and live upon those Towers. One Tower at first, then two. Then four. Then many. Few free fliers at first, then more. Not many, about eighty thousand. Living on Towers of life. Towers.'

The young ones shifted on the floor. They had not yet had time to take in what they had learned. They looked at him with baffled eyes, one, bolder than the rest, whispering, 'But we despise the Towers?'

Sliffisunda nodded his approval. This one would go far.

'Yes, egglings,' he said in a grating whisper, lifting his tail to deposit a symbolic dropping on the subject under discussion. 'Never forget it. We despise the Treeci, our own kind, who betrayed the Promise of Potipur and gave up their wings. We despise those who are consumed by us, made into shit by us. We despise those among them who will sell their kindred for a few years of stinking human life.

'Yes, egglings. We despise the Towers, and the Chancery. We despise all humans in the world of the Thraish. We allow mankind to live only that we may live winged as Potipur commands. If we could not live as our god commands, we would die. And every human would die with us, for we despise them all.'

When the egglings had gone, he left the wide perch to go to one of the openings in the stone. The humans called them windows and put glass or oiled paper over them. The Thraish called them spy holes and hid them behind hangings or piers of rock. This one looked toward the north.

The north! Behind the great mountains. Sliffisunda had seen thrassil there, and weehar. Though he had not yet been hatched when the great beasts were last seen, he knew them when he saw them, as he knew his own wing feathers. He already knew the taste and smell of them. And he knew filthy humans had them and would never give them to the Thraish voluntarily.

Which did not matter. Now that the Thraish knew they were there, it would not take long to get them. A few strong fliers had already been instructed to go through the pass in the deep night, find young ones, carry them out. Indeed, the task might already have been accomplished.

A dozen young ones would grow up, become a herd. A herd would become a great, great number in time. And when there were enough of them . . .

'Now, egglings,' he imagined himself saying at some not-too-distant time. 'Now, egglings, every human shall die, because Potipur our god commands that we kill them all.'

25

Once Pamra had heard the voices clearly, her doubts and fears left her. Rapture and joy had returned. The rapture that had abandoned her at the worker pit when she had found Delia; the rapture that she had thought forever gone; the joy she had felt in Neff's company; the joy she had thought eternally lost; now they had returned, both, so that she walked encircled by peace and sureness, unable to remember a time when she might have doubted.

Thrasne watched her and hated what he saw.

Before Strinder's Isle she had begun to talk with him, begun to care about the *Gift*, begun to take part in the daily life of the River. He had begun to plan for their future together. He knew of a carpenter in Darkel-don who would rebuild the owner-house into a fit place for Pamra, Pamra and their children. He thought of a weaver he had met in one of the little towns past Shfor. From her he would buy covers for the beds and hangings, for the colors she used were the colors of sunset and dawn, warm as light itself. He would buy gowns for Pamra herself, gowns of that long fiber pamet grown only in the bottom lands near Zephyr, soft as down. She would respond to these gifts with affection and approval. They would plan together for their future. It was all there, in his mind, how each thing would happen in its time.

Now she had left him, gone elsewhere, become as remote as the girl he remembered outside the Tower in Baris, tolerating his presence, perhaps. Perhaps not noticing he was there. She spoke to him of voices, gently, as though to a

235

child, as though he should be able to hear what she heard. She nodded, smiled, as though in conversation. Sometimes she sat upon the deck of the *Gift* with Lila on her lap, pointing to something Thrasne could not see, but which he suspected Lila did see. At least the child's eyes followed Pamra's eyes, followed and fixed in a kind of concentration that was not childlike.

Seeing Pamra like this, he began to be afraid she would leave him, though for the time being she seemed willing to stay on the River. He saw her sometimes murmuring to herself, as though rehearsing words she would say, but when they stopped at Trens and Villian-gar, or any of a dozen other small townships, she made no move to go ashore.

Once, she had shared in his life, at least a little. She had chatted with him of the sights along the shore, sometimes gone to the market with him in the towns where they stopped. She had cooked for him, appearing to enjoy it. He had told himself it was only a matter of time, of patience – both of which he had in seemingly unlimited quantity.

Now, since Strinder's Isle, all his plans seemed moved into some future so remote he was not sure there was enough time after all. For the first time he thought of himself growing old, still without her. Old, still alone. No children to roll about the owner-house floor and learn to be boatmen in their turn. No woman to share the everlasting voyage, no Suspirra. What right had she to destroy his hopes? When he had watched over her, sought her out, saved her?

He found himself growing angry at her. What right had she to change in this way! And for what? Some Treeci who had died. Some dream she had had. When compared with his hopes, what was that? Nothing!

Nothing, he assured himself, going to the room he had given her and entering it without asking her leave. He took hold of her before she quite knew he was there, his arms tight around her, his lips on hers, forcing her lips apart, tasting her mouth, pressing her beneath him onto the bed.

236

And she did not move, did not seem to breathe. When he drew back to look into her face, it was like looking into the face of an image he might have carved from pale wood, then smoothed until its reality was blurred into mere shape. So she was, mere shape, eyes wide and unseeing, not Suspirra, not Pamra even, not anything.

'Pamra!' He shook her, slapped her. She fell against the bed, slumped, limp.

Slowly her eyes focused, saw him. 'But you must help me, Thrasne. Don't you see? You were meant to help me. That's why you came for me. Mother sent you, don't you see? To help me.' Her eyes filled with hurt tears, and his heart churned within him, creating a vertigo, a sick dizziness. 'Help me, Thrasne.'

Her face cleared then. The tears dried. The rapture came into her eyes once more, and she nodded, hearing something he could not hear.

He stood up unsteadily and left her, feeling a deeper loneliness than he had felt since long, long ago in Xoxxy-Do.

Medoor Babji saw him leave the cabin, saw the unsteady walk, the drunken demeanor. He leaned over the rail as though he might be sick or readying himself to leap into the water, and she moved up beside him to lay a hard, small hand upon his back.

'Thrasne owner,' she said, risking everything for his pain. 'It doesn't take a Jarb Mendicant to tell us the woman is mad.' Jarb Mendicants had a reputation, not often undeserved, for treating mental troubles of one kind or another, and it was in the Jarb Houses that the truly mad found refuge.

For a time he seemed not to have heard her. 'Mad?' he asked at last, as though he did not know the meaning of the word.

'Mad, Thrasne. Though she had not tasted jarb to see visions, still she has visions of her own. She is not your Suspirra because the Suspirra you dreamed of was not mad and this woman is. Your Suspirra is an ideal, Thrasne

237

owner. Not a real creature of this world. This woman, Pamra, she is only a semblance of your ideal, and she is real. Of this world. Therefore, imperfect.'

'No, not of this world,' he disagreed simply. 'But I love her with all my heart.'

She shook her head, tears forming at the corners of her eyes. She, Babji, hardened by the marketplaces of a half hundred towns, to cry so for this man. She shook her head angrily, letting the tears fly away. 'Then love her if you must, Thrasne. But you must look somewhere else for the things you dream of.' She left him and went to her bedding where it lay upon the deck. Long into the night she lay there, alternately angry and sorrowful, picturing herself and Thrasne, together, without realizing she was doing it. He was not Noor. Given only that, he was not her equal, for the Noor were what they were only to others of their kind. To mate with one outside the Noor was to diminish oneself. She had no right to consider him at all, but consider him she did. Finally, just before dawn, she said to herself in an ironic voice, 'Well, love him if you must, Babji; but look elsewhere for the things you dream of.'

The morning brought them to a mountainous region, a place of towering peaks and precipitous cliffs; a Talons. Upon the stony peaks they could see the clustered forms of fliers, and high above were their spread wings, floating in great circles. Thrasne kept the *Gift* well offshore, away from the cliffs and the treacherous currents that swirled around the tumbled stone at their feet. Pamra stood at the rail, peering forward, shifting from foot to foot, speaking aloud, as though to a company of friends, pointing to the fliers far above in increasing agitation. Thrasne watched her, telling himself he did not care what she was doing. He had not spoken to her since the night before except in passing, as he might speak to any member of the crew. Now she acted as though she had been told to go or do something she was uncertain of, for she asked something again and again, almost plaintively. Whatever answer she received was eventually enough, for when night came she went to her bed with

238

a calm face. They would come into Thou-ne on the morning tide.

When they tied up at the jetty and edged out the plank, he was not really surprised to see her leaving the boat. He wrestled with himself for a moment, deciding not to follow her, then deciding that he must. He had promised to keep her safe. He had made no conditions then; it would not be fair or proper to set conditions now. Still, he was hard put to it to follow her as she went through the town, one foot in front of the other, as sure as the wind. She had a cloak drawn over her head, but when she reached the public square she drew it back, hair floating wildly free as the drowned Suspirra's had used to do. She mounted to the steps of the public fountain and turned, arm outstretched, face glowing like a little moon. 'People,' she cried in a voice like a flute, softly insinuating. 'Is it not better when the people know?' Those in the marketplace turned to see her, astonished, drawing close and staring as she stood there, gathering them in with her hands.

And from some little fellow at the edge of the square came a scream, almost hysterical, a treble cry as from a child but with the force of a trumpet blown, announcing war. 'She has come, in flesh, the Bearer of Truth!' It was Peasimy Flot, alert to the coming of light as he had always been, always remembering the dark, the lies.

(Peasimy, remembering following the Awakeners when they took his father to the next town east and then just threw him in the worker pits in the dark, as though they didn't care; Peasimy remembering when the body fixer told him it wouldn't hurt, what they were going to do to him that time he broke his arm, and it did hurt, a lot; Peasimy remembering the shining face from beneath the water, and it was this face.)

'She has come,' he cried again, like a call to battle.

A shout went up then. It was half surprise, half recognition, from a hundred throats. Thrasne had lingered at the edge of the square and was suddenly at the back of a crowd, all watching her. Pamra's eyes opened very wide, as though

239

to take this in. Then she nodded, answering their shout as a sigh went through those gathered by.

'I have come,' she agreed, beckoning to the thin, hectic-looking young fellow who had called out. 'I have come bringing the truth. You have been expecting me, and I have come.'

Thrasne turned back to the docks, sick at heart.

He went to a tavern, where he drank among a crowd of doubters and nay sayers, then returned to the *Gift*. Medoor Babji stood on the deck, reading something while stroking the feathers of a large, dun-colored bird. When she saw him coming, she tossed the bird into the air, then put the missive in her pocket as she came toward him. She was the only one there. She had stayed behind when her fellows had left the boat to buy stores for their journey. Perhaps she had known he would return.

'Medoor Babji,' he croaked. 'You were right. She is mad. Mad or possessed. Or something else I have never heard of. What shall I do?'

His agony was manifest. She held out her arms, and he fell into them as into a well. She held him, kissing his sun-browned face where the hair grew back, tasting the sweat of his forehead along with his tears. What could he do?

'I have kept her hidden, but she is in the square now, where anyone can see her. The Laughers will find her! Or the fliers. I think she will preach revolt against the fliers.' So much he had inferred from her soliloquies over the past days.

'If she is surrounded by people?' Medoor asked abstractedly. She was still thinking of the message the bird had brought, a letter from her mother, Queen Fibji. A letter commanding her to a great exploration, a voyage. How could she think of something else just now? Yet she did, seeing in the agonized face before her all agonized faces, Noor and shore-fish alike. 'How can the Laughers take her if she is surrounded by a multitude?'

'If the Laughers cannot take her, they will send Jondarites. Jondarites to put down a rebellion.' Thrasne had seen this happen once or twice in the past. He was sure of it, hopelessly sure.

Jondarites.

Holding him in her arms, close against her girl's breasts, Medoor felt the chill of the word. Jondarites. Now, now she began to realize what was really happening here. It was not a matter merely of a madwoman and a man. There was more to it than that.

Jondarites.

Jondarites and the Noor.

Queen Fibji, far to the north, bearing greater burdens than anyone should have to bear. The endless depredations of the Jondarites. The great plan. And now this word of an even greater possibility, which the seeker bird had brought. If the Jondarites were sent in great numbers to Northshore, to put down a rebellion, there would be fewer to prey upon the Noor. And if there were fewer depredations among the Noor, then the Noor might better do what was best for them.

'Come,' she whispered at last. 'Let us go see what Pamra is really doing.'

Pamra had gone to the Temple, together with half the town. Thrasne and Medoor Babji pushed their way into a corner of the crowded sanctuary, where they could kneel with the others before the image of the glowing woman. At first Thrasne did not recognize his carving of Suspirra, for it shone with a light he had never seen. Only when Pamra stood before it and claimed it as a precursor, divinely meant, sent to announce her coming, did he become truly aware of what it was. He wanted to laugh. He would have laughed except for the ominous stillness in the place. Precursor? Yes, but from his knife and a lump of fragwood, nothing more than that.

Afterward he scarcely remembered what she had said. There had been something in it of love and something of righteousness. She had spoken of being misled. Of a conspiracy to keep the Protector of Man unmindful of the evil that flew upon the winds of the world. She spoke of the worker pits and of the great lie of Sorting Out. She told them truth, that the true Sorting took place in another realm, beyond the world, and what happened in this world was a blasphemy. She called the fliers Servants, not of Abricor, but of their own pride. She said all that, over and over, in different words, making them laugh and weep and cry out. Someone called to her, asking how she knew these things, and she said her voices had told her to stand before them and tell the truth, at which many had shouted out they would follow her in the telling.

'Crusade,' she cried. 'Let all who can, join me in crusade. We will carry the word of this injustice around the world. And when we go to free the Protector of Man from those who hold him in ignorance, we will be many, a multitude, a great tide to sweep away the evil of the world.' Lila lay in her arms as she said this, looking out at the crowd with great, wide eyes, reaching out her baby arms toward them all.

The strange little man who had first hailed her called out again, 'The Mother of Truth,' and others echoed these words. His face and theirs were shining with devotion.

Thrasne thrilled to her voice, as did everyone within sound of it. He could not stop himself. His flesh responded even when he told himself it was all foolishness. There were others there, Awakeners among them. They, too, looking at her with an expression of alert surprise and wonderment, nodding their heads as though she had been Viranel herself.

Not Viranel. No. Viranel's face carved on the wall behind Pamra was only an image, crude and somehow horribly inhuman. One could not worship a god that was a stranger. Not Viranel. Something finer than that. Holier than that.

And even then, he wanted her still. The impossibility of that wanting struck him like a blow, and he leaned forward on his knees and wept as Medoor Babji regarded him thoughtfully, fingering in her deep pocket the message she had received.

And Peasimy crouched at Pamra's feet as she went on

teaching, lit from within as though by flame. He crouched there, cheeks red with the fire of her talk, eyes burning also, all of him lit up as if from within by that hot, plasmic vapor, as though he were liquid, without form except as her words gave him form and meaning, shaped by her with that shape crystallizing in every instant to something more refined, simpler, with keener edges and corners to it. 'Light comes,' he murmured to himself, a litany, an obligatto to her speech. 'Light comes, light comes.'

But then, his eyes lighting upon the tall, dark-cloaked Jondarites, who made a shadowy enclosure about the sanctuary, unable in their uncommanded state either to attend to what Pamra was saying or prevent her from speaking, held in abeyance as the dammed River holds itself, full of force and power that is for the moment unused, not out of conviction but out of simple inability to act – seeing these, their high-plumed helmets nodding as they craned their necks to observe all who came into that throng, Peasimy spoke again.

'But first, night comes. Night comes.'

SOUTHSHORE

1

When Pamra left Thou-ne, moving westward along the River road, some thousand of the residents of Thou-ne went after her. Most of them were provisioned to some extent, though there were some who went with no thought for food or blankets, trusting in a providence that Pamra had not promised and had evidently not even considered. Peasimy Flot, for all his seeming inanity, was well provided for. He had a little cart with things in it, things he had been putting by for some time. The widow Flot would have been surprised to find in it items that had disappeared from her home over the last fifteen years or so. There were others in Thou-ne who would have been equally surprised to find their long-lost belongings assisting Peasimy in his journey.

The procession came to Atter, and though some of the Thou-neites dropped out of the procession, many of Atter joined it. Pamra preached in the Temple there, to general acclaim. Then came Bylme and Twarn-the-little, then Twarn-the-big – where the townspeople made Pamra a gift of a light wagon in which she might ride, pulled by her followers – then a dozen more towns, and in each of them the following grew more numerous, the welcome more tumultuous. Peasimy himself began to appoint 'messengers' to send ahead with word of their coming. It was something that came to him, all at once. 'Light comes,' he told them. 'That is what you must say.' As time went on, the messages grew more detailed and ramified, but it was always Peasimy who sent them.

It was on a morning of threatening cloud that they left Bycebarrens for the town of Chirubel.

The storm did not precisely take them by surprise; the day had brought increasing wind and spatters of rain from very near dawn until midafternoon. Still, when in late afternoon the full fury of the wind broke over them and the skies opened, the multitude were in nowise prepared for it. Some stopped where they were, crawling under their carts or pitching their tents as best they might, to cower under them out of the worst of the downpour. Others fled into the woods, where they sought large trees or overhanging ridges. Pamra, high on her wagon, simply pointed ahead with one imperious finger, and the men who dragged the wagon, half-drowned by the water flowing over their faces, staggered on into the deluge. It was not until they stumbled into the outer wall of the Jarb House that they realized she had pointed toward it all along. Pamra came down from the wagon, and the dozen or so of them, including Peasimy Flot, struggled around the perimeter of the place looking for a door.

It opened when they pounded, warmth drifting out into the chill together with a puff of warm, dry air laden with strange smells and a haze of smoke. Peasimy coughed. Pamra pressed forward against the warding arm of the doorkeeper, the others following, gasping, wetter than fish.

They passed down a lengthy corridor into the main hall to stand there stunned at the scale of the place. It was like standing in a chimney. At one side stairs curved up to a balcony that spiraled around the open area, twisted up, and up, kept on going around and around, smaller and smaller, to the seeming limit of their eyes, where it ended in a dark glassy blot, a tented skylight black with rain. It was, Pamra thought, like being inside the trunk of a hollow tree with an opening at the top and all the tree's denizens peering down at you. Heads lined the balconies, went away to be replaced by others, and throughout the whole great stack of living creatures came a constant rustle and mumble of talk, a bubbling pulse of communication that seemed to be one seamless fabric of uninterrupted sound.

From some of the balconies nets hung, littered with a

flotsam of clothing and blankets. From other balconies long, polished poles plunged to lower levels. A brazier was alight at the center of the floor, its wraiths rising in dim veils in this towering, smokestack space.

'Come in,' said the Mendicant ironically. 'So nice to have you.'

'It is raining out there,' announced Pamra evenly, no whit aware of the sarcasm. She drew back the cloak that had covered Lila to disclose the child, not at all discomfited by the soaking she had received.

'Wet,' affirmed Peasimy. 'Dreadful wet. A great flood out of the skies. Mustn't let *her* drown. Too important.'

'Ah,' assented the Mendicant. 'And you are?'

'The crusade,' said Peasimy. 'We are the crusade. Light comes! She is the Bearer of Truth, the very Mother of Truth.'

'Ah,' said the Mendicant again, frowning slightly. He had heard of this. All this segment of Northshore had heard of this, one way or the other. As one of the Order's more trusted messengers, he had more interest in it than most. A message had come through Chiles Medman, Governor General of the Order, from Tharius Don asking the Order to assist in procuring information.

'Trale,' he introduced himself. 'Mendicant brother of the Jarb. What can I offer you by way of assistance?'

'Towels,' said Pamra simply. 'And a fire to dry ourselves. Something hot to drink if you have it conveniently by.' She stared around her, up at the endless balconies where people came and went, staring down at her, leaving the railings to others who stared in their turn. Pale blots. Mouths open. Hands moving in beckoning gestures. Something distressed her, but she could not identify it. Something was wrong, missing, as though she had forgotten to put on her skirt or her tunic. She looked down at herself, puzzled. She was damp but fully dressed. Why, then, this feeling of nakedness?

Trale led them across the hall, through an arch beneath the balcony and into a wide, low room that curved away just

249

inside the outer wall. A refectory. Pamra shivered. It was not unlike the refectory at the Tower of Baris. The smells were not unlike those smells. Cereals and soap, steam and grease, cleanliness at war with succulence. Trale beckoned to them from an angled corner, a smaller room opening off the large one, where a fire blazed brightly upon the hearth.

'I'll return in a moment,' he murmured, leaving them there. Those who had drawn the cart stood back, waiting for Pamra to approach the fire. She gestured them forward. The room was warm enough without baking herself. She took off her outer clothing and spread it on a table. Her knee-length undertunic was only damp, clinging to her body like a second skin. The men turned their eyes away under Peasimy's peremptory gaze, one of them flushing.

Trale was back in a moment with towels and a pile of loosely woven robes over one arm. He did not seem to notice Pamra's body under the clinging fabric but merely handed her one of the robes, as impersonally as a servant. Behind him came a man and a woman, one bearing a tea service, the other a covered platter at which Peasimy looked with suspicion.

'Jarb,' said Trale. 'It is our custom.'

'We won't—' Pamra began.

'No. It is *our* custom. With any visitor. Call it – oh, a method of diagnosis.'

'We are not ill.'

'The diagnosis is not always of illness. Do take tea. This is a very comforting brew. It has no medicinal qualities aside from that.'

They sat steaming before the fire, moisture rising from them and from their discarded clothing in clouds. Rain fell down the chimney, making small spitting noises in the fire. The wall at their side reverberated to the thunder outside, hummed to the bow-stroke of the wind. In the great hall the voice murmur went on and on. Beside the fire Trale knelt to scrape coals into a tiny brazier. Beside the brazier lay three oval roots, warty and blue, each the size of a fist. Jarb roots, Pamra thought. Trale peeled the roots carefully, dropping

250

the peels into a shallow pan. When all three were peeled, he laid the roots into the ashes and began to dry the peels over the brazier, stirring them with a slender metal spoon. The woman who had brought in the tea buried the peeled roots in the ashes and turned to smile at Pamra.

'It is only the peel which has the power of visions. Jarb root itself is delicious. The Noor eat it all the time. Have you ever tasted it?'

Pamra shook her head, oppressed once more by the sense of something missing. 'No.' She ate less and less as the crusade wore on. Hunger seemed scarcely to touch her. Now, for some reason, however, she felt ravenous. Perhaps it was the smoke. Perhaps the smell of food. 'I am hungry, though.'

'They only take a few moments to steam. Some scrape the ashes off, but I like the taste.' She drew a pipe from her pocket and handed it to Trale, who filled it with the powdery scraps from the pan. All three had pipes, and in a moment all three were alight, seated before the fire, the smoke from the pipes floating out into the room, into the refectory, away into the chimney of the great hall. The fragrance was the same one that already permeated everything. Sweet, spicy. Pamra folded her arms on the table and laid her head upon them, suddenly both hungry and tired. She had not felt this hungry, this tired, in months. Why was she here? She thought briefly of the *Gift of Potipur*, wishing she were aboard, translating the murmur of Tower talk into the murmur of tidal current, the thunder outside into the creak of boat timbers. She could be there. With Thrasne. Instead of here. Beside her Lila chortled and said, clearly, 'Over the River. Thrasne went over the River.'

Peasimy turned, his little ruby mouth open, cheeks fiery red with the drying he had given them. 'She talked!'

Pamra nodded sleepily. 'She does, sometimes.'

'I hadn't heard her before.'

'She talks about the River a lot. Mostly that.' She rubbed her forehead fretfully. The sweet smell of the Jarb had soaked into the top of her nose and was filling it, like syrup.

251

She turned to find the three smokers knocking the dottle from their pipes onto the hearth. The immediacy of the smell was dissipating.

The woman raked the baked Jarb root from the fire, brushing it off and placing it upon a little plate. This she placed before Pamra with a spoon. 'Try a little.'

Pamra spooned off a bite, blowing on it to cool it. The root was sweet, too, but delicious. The slightly ashy taste only complemented it. She took another spoonful, then hesitated.

'Go ahead, eat it all,' the woman said. 'There are people bringing plenty of food for you and for the others.'

By the fire, Trale sat, rocking back and forth.

'Did you have a vision?' asked Peasimy curiously, studying the man's face.

'Oh, yes.'

'What was it of?'

'Of you, Peasimy Flot. And of Pamra Don. And of what is to come.'

'Oh!' Peasimy clapped his hands, delighted. 'Tell us!'

Trale shook his head. 'I'm afraid it can't be told. There are only colors and patterns.'

'Red and orange and yellow of flame,' said the woman. 'Black of smoke.'

'Red and orange and yellow of flowers,' said the man. 'Black of stony mountains.'

'Red and orange and yellow of metal,' said Trale. 'Black of deep mines.'

'That doesn't sound like much of a vision,' pouted Peasimy.

'Or too much of one,' said Pamra, one side of her mouth lifted in a half smile. The Jarb root had settled into her, making some of the same kind of happiness Glizzee spice often made. Not rapture. More a contentment. Warmth. It had been a sizable root, and her sudden hunger was appeased. She smiled again, head nodding with weariness. 'I'm so sleepy.'

'Come with me,' the woman said. 'We'll find a place for you to rest.'

They went out into the great hall again and up the spiraling balcony. A twist and a half up the huge trunk, the woman pointed into a room where a wide bed was spread with gaily worked quilts. The door was fastened back with a strap, and the woman loosened it now, letting the door sag toward its latch.

'Sleep. When you've slept enough, come back down to the place we were. I'll be there, or Trale. Will the baby be all right, here with you?'

Pamra nodded, so weary she could hardly hold her head up. She heard the latch click as she crawled into the bed, felt Lila curl beside her with a satisfied murmur, then was gone into darkness.

Outside the room people moved to and fro, some of them pausing to stare curiously at the door before moving away to be replaced by someone else. Inside the room, Lila squirmed out of Pamra's grasp, turned to let her feet drop off the edge of the bed, then stagger-crawled to the door to sit there with her own hands pressed to its surface, smiling, nodding, sometimes saying something to herself in a chuckling baby voice, as though she watched with her fingers what transpired outside the wooden barrier.

Below in the firelit room, the three Mendicants crouched before the fire, staring into the flames. Peasimy had fallen asleep where he sat, as had the men with him.

'Mad,' said Trale at last. 'There's no doubt.'

'None,' agreed the woman. 'She hasn't eaten for weeks or months. She's all skin and eyes. She's an ecstatic. A visionary. The fasting only makes it worse. The minute the smoke hit her, she felt hungry. She's half starved herself.'

'How long do you think we can get her to stay?' the man asked.

'No time at all. Tomorrow morning, perhaps. If the storm goes on, perhaps until the rain stops.'

'Not long enough to do any good.'

'No.'

'It's too bad, isn't it?'

Trale nodded, poking at the fire. 'Well, a time of changes

is often unpleasant. I don't see the Jarb Houses seriously threatened. Or the Mendicants.'

'There will be a need for more houses.' The woman made a spiraling gesture that conveyed the wholeness of the edifice with all its murmurous inhabitants.

'Perhaps some of the people in residence will be able to leave,' the man said. He sounded doubtful of this.

'Some are ready to leave as Mendicants.' Trale sighed. 'Taking their pipes with them, as we do. The others – if they go, they go into madness once more. More houses will be needed, but it's unlikely we'll be able to build them.'

'We could keep her here.'

'By force?' It was a question only, without emotion. But the woman flushed deep crimson. 'I thought, persuade her, perhaps.'

'Try,' Trale urged her. 'By all means, Elina, try. It has not a hope of success, but you will not be content unless you try.'

Late in the day a bell rang and people began filing down from the chimney top toward the refectory. Children leapt from the railings into nets and from these into other nets below. Some whirled down tall poles. A train of whooping boys came spinning down the spiraling banister, loud with laughter. The tables filled, and there was a clatter of bowls and spoons. Out in the chimney hall, Elina pared Jarb-root peels onto the brazier, renewing the pale wraiths of smoke which filled all the space to its high, blind skylight. Pamra opened the door of her room and came out onto the balcony to look down, Lila held high against her shoulder. Elina beckoned to them, and Lila squirmed out of Pamra's arms, over the railing, plunging downward, arms spread as though to fly. Elina caught her, without thinking, only then turning pale with shock while the child chortled in her arms and Pamra, above, put hands to her throat as though to choke off a scream.

'All right,' said Lila. 'You caught me.'

'Did you know I would?' the woman asked in an astonished whisper.

'Oh, yes,' said Lila. 'The smoke is nice.'

Pamra was coming slowly down the twisting ramp, her eyes never leaving the child below. Lila squirmed to be put down and staggered toward the foot of the ramp, face contorted in the enormous concentration necessary to walking. She did not fall until the ramp was reached, and Pamra scooped her up.

'Lila, don't ever do that again.' In her voice was all the anguish of every mother, every elder sister, all imperiousness gone. She smiled at Elina, shaking her head, and they shared the moment. Children! The things they did! It lasted only a moment.

'I should be getting back to my people,' Pamra said. 'They will be wondering what has happened to me.'

'They know you are here,' the woman responded. 'It is still raining. They will be more comfortable if they believe you are comfortable. Do not add your discomfort to their own by going back into the wet.'

'You're right, of course. And it will not hurt to have a warm meal.' Pamra was amazed at herself, but she was hungry again. She looked around her curiously. 'I got only the general impression before. Are all Jarb Houses built this way?'

'Yes. So the smoke can permeate the whole structure.'

'The smoke? I see it does. But why?'

Elina took her by the arm, drawing her close, as though they had been sisters, used to sharing confidences. 'The Jarb smoke is said to give visions, you know? But in reality, Jarb smoke erases visions and restores reality. For those disturbed by visions of madness, the Jarb smoke brings actuality. You see that woman going into the refectory? The tall one with the wild red hair? On the outside, she is a beast who roams the forests, killing all who pursue her, sure of their ill will and obsessed by the terrors of the world. Here she is Kindle Kindness, a loving friend to half the house.'

Pamra peered at the woman, not seeming to understand what was being said.

'Outside, she has visions of herself as a beast, of herself

hunted. In the house, the smoke wipes those visions away. In here, she is only herself.'

Pamra stared at her, awareness coming to her suddenly, her face paling. 'Neff,' she cried. 'Neff!'

'Shhh,' said Elina. 'Shhh. There is no need to cry out.'

'Neff! Where is he?'

Trale came from the refectory, joining them, taking Pamra's other arm. Wearily, pointedly, with a resigned look at Elina, he said, 'Your visions wait for you outside. They cannot come into a Jarb House.'

Pamra drew herself up, regally tall, becoming someone else. 'Truth cannot exist in this place, can it, Mendicant? Light cannot come here? Only darkness and smoke?'

He shook his head. 'All your – all your friends are waiting for you. Come now. There is food waiting, also.'

She shook her head at them, pityingly, but allowed them to take her to the place where Peasimy stook impatiently with the others, all standing beside their chairs, waiting for her to be seated; then all waiting until she began eating. She nodded at the others, saying, 'Eat quickly, my friends. We must leave this place.'

'Dark comes?' asked Peasimy, glaring at the Mendicants. 'Pamra?'

She shook her head. 'They are not evil, Peasimy. They are only misled.' She had been hungry, but now she began to toy with the food before her, obviously impatient to be gone. Elina laid a hand upon her shoulder, tears in the corners of her eyes. 'Pamra! Courtesy! ''Neff'' is not impatient.' Pamra took a bite, chewed it slowly, watching them with that same pitying gaze. Now she knew what had been missing since she had entered the house. Neff, and Delia, and her mother. Them and their voices. Gone. As though they had never been except in her memory. Did these poor smoke-blinded fools think she would let them go? Though she could not see them in this smoky haze, the center of her being clung to what she knew to be true. They – they were true. Neff was true. She took another bite, smiled at Peasimy and encouraged him to eat.

From the side of the room, Trale watched, eyes narrowed in concentration. Elina came toward him. 'She did not make the connection with her own condition at all.'

'Oh, yes. She knows what we tried to do. But she has rejected it.'

'Why, Trale?'

'Because her madness is all she has. Whatever else there might have been once has been taken away. Whatever else there might be in the future seems shoddy in comparison. Who would wed a man when one might wed an angel? Who would live as a woman when one might rule as a goddess?'

'We could keep her here by force.'

'Setting aside that we would break all our vows, yes. We could.'

'In time, she would forget.'

'Ah.'

'She would grow accustomed.'

'Elina.'

'Yes, Trale.'

'Clip the flame-bird's wings if you must, Elina. Set it among your barnyard fowl. Tell yourself you do it to save the flame-bird's life. But do not expect it to nest, or to sing.'

She bowed her head, very pale. At the table behind her, Pamra rose, her hand shaking as she wiped her mouth with the napkin. 'Where are my clothes?' she asked.

Peasimy found them for her, beside the fire, and she put them on. They were warm and dry.

'Won't you stay until it stops raining?' Elina asked her. 'Only until morning.'

'No,' Pamra said, her eyes darting from place to place in the high dwelling, marking it in her memory. Another time – there might be converts to be had in places like this. 'No. Neff is waiting. Mother and Delia. They're waiting. We have set our feet upon the road and must not leave it. This is a bad place, Elina. You should come with us. You can't see the road from in here, Elina. Come with us . . .'

Her face lit from within, glowed, only for a moment, but for that moment Elina felt herself torn, wrenched, dragged to the gate of herself. Fear struck at her and she drew back.

'No, Pamra. It is safe here. The people here find much joy and comfort.'

'Joy,' said Pamra. 'Comfort!' The scorn in her voice was palpable, an acid dripping upon those words. 'Safety. Yes. That is what you have here.'

Peasimy was suddenly beside her, swallowing the last bite of his supper. Then they were moving toward the entrance, out across the open chimney, through the hallway, pulling at the great doors. They went into the night, a night miraculously cleared of storm, with the moons lighting the sky. Potipur, half-swollen and sullen above them to the west; Viranel a mere sickle dipping beyond the western horizon; Abricor a round melon, high in the east.

'You see,' said Pamra. 'Neff has arranged it. Here he comes now.' And she turned her radiant face to the woods, from which some invisible presence moved to join her. Elina, in the doorway, gasped, for she saw it, for that moment saw it, a towering figure of white light, golden wings outstretched, its breast stained with red.

Trale was behind her. 'Come in, Elina.'

'Trale, I saw . . .'

'Saw what she sees. As do all those who follow her. Come in to the fire, Elina.'

Behind Pamra and the others, the doors of the Jarb House shut with a solemn clang. From the forests came the multitude, and Pamra's heart sang. 'Crusade,' she called. 'Let us go on.'

2

Thrasne thought of what he was about to do somewhat as he might have regarded taking the axe to himself if he had been touched by blight. He would have rejected the intention to lop off his own leg with horror, yet he would have done it because the alternative was more terrible still.

So without enthusiasm, with a kind of deadly reluctance, he fell in with the plan to go with a group of Medoor Babji's Melancholics on a voyage of exploration to find Southshore. He resolved upon it because staying anywhere near Pamra was more horrifying than leaving the world in which she moved. If he stayed, he would have to follow her. And it would be terrible to watch Pamra, to hear of her, to be told of the crusade. Any of these were more repugnant to him than risking his own life. He told himself he would welcome death if it meant he need not realize the danger Pamra ran and go in apprehension of that terror.

'I love her,' he said to Medoor Babji. 'Whether she is mad or not. I love her.' And he did. His loins quivered at the thought of her. He knew every curve of her body, and he dreamed of that body, waking in a shaking sweat from agonies of unfulfilled passion.

And Babji, having observed his obsession over the days that had just passed, was wise enough to hold her tongue, though she thought, Stupid man, at him, not entirely with affection. How could she blame him for this unfulfillable desire when she had a similar one of her own?

Here, in the city of Thou-ne, on the same day Pamra cried crusade in the Temple of the Moons, Medoor Babji came to Taj Noteen and gave him the tokens she carried with few words of explanation about the seeker birds, watching his face as it turned from brown to red to pallid gray, then to brown once more.

'*Deleen p'Noz,*' he said, sinking to one knee. 'Your Gracious Highness.' The secret Noor language was used these days only for names and titles, little else.

'We need none of that,' she told him firmly. 'This is not the courts of the Noor. I do not need to hear ''*Deleen p'Noz*'' to be recalled to my duty. We are not in the audience tent of the Queen. Though I am the Queen's chosen heir, we are here, Noteen, in Thou-ne, as we were this morning when you whacked me with your whip stock. I've told you what we are to do. I want you to pick me a crew to go. Thrasne will need his own boatmen, and we cannot expect to live on the deck if there is storm or rough weather. We must limit our numbers, therefore, to the space available. Thrasne kindly offers us the owner-house. There are three rooms for sleeping, with two bunks in each room. There is an office and a salon. Not large. We can have none among us who will cause dissension.'

'Not Riv Lymeen, then,' he mused. 'How about old Porabji?'

'He has a good mind,' she assented. 'Which we may need far more than a young man's strength. Yes.'

Noteen thought about it. 'Do we need a recorder? Someone to keep an account? A journal of the voyage?'

She thought a moment, then nodded. Queen Fibji had not commanded it, yet it was something that should be done.

'Then Fez Dooraz. He was clerk at the courts for ten years as a younger man. He looks as though a breath would blow him over, but he's the most literate of all of us.'

She suggested, 'Lomoz Borab is sound. And what about Eenzie?'

'Eenzie the Clown?'

'I'd like one more woman along, Noteen. And Eenzie makes us all laugh. We may need laughter.'

He assented. 'Six, then. Porabji, Dooraz, Borab, and Eenzie. You, Highness. And me.'

'You, Noteen?'

'I will send the troupe back to the steppes. Nunoz can take them.'

'I had not thought of you, Noteen.'

'You object?' He asked it humbly enough.

She thought of this. He had not bullied her more than he had bullied anyone else. She could detect no animosity against him in herself. 'Why not. And I have a thought about it, Noteen. You will command our group. So far as they are concerned, Queen Fibji's message came to you.'

He thought on this, overcoming his immediate rejection of the idea as he confronted her thoughtful face. It might be better, he thought to himself, if no one knew who Medoor Babji was. 'It might be safer for you,' he murmured.

'I was not thinking of that,' she said, 'so much as the comfort of the voyage. We have done well enough with me as a novice. Why complicate things?'

'Thrasne owner doesn't know?'

'I told him we were ordered to go. I didn't tell him the seeker birds came to me, or what words they carried.'

'Do you have enough coin to pay him?'

'Strange though it may seem, Taj Noteen, he isn't doing it for coin, or at least not primarily for coin, but yes. I have enough.' Among the tokens she carried was one that would open the coffers of money lenders in Thou-ne. The Noor had accounts in many parts of Northshore.

'We'll need more yet for stores. How long a voyage do we plan?'

'Queen Fibji commands us to provision for a year. A full year. We will need most of the hold space for stores. Thrasne knows that.'

'Well then, I'll get Dooraz and Porabji ready. They're good storesmen, both of them.'

And it began.

Thrasne talked to the crew. He didn't give them his reasons, just told them they'd be well paid. Several of the men told him they'd go ashore, thanks for everything but they were not really interested in a voyage that long. Thrasne nodded and let them go. The others chewed it over for a time.

'You'll want me to replace the ones that left,' Obers-rom said at last. 'We'll need full crew, Thrasne owner. I don't suppose those blackfaces will be up to much in the way of helping on a boat.'

'I don't suppose so. And we'd better get in the habit of callin' 'em by their names, Obers-rom. Or just say "Noor." They count that as polite.'

Obers-rom agreed. He hadn't meant anything by it. Boatmen weren't bigoted. They couldn't be. They'd never make a copper if they couldn't deal with all kinds.

And it was Obers-rom who worked with Zyneem Porabji and Fez Dooraz – they were Obbie and Zynie and Fez within the day – to fill the *Gift of Potipur*'s holds. From the purveyors and suppliers they ordered dried fish and pickled fish and salted fish, grain in bulk, grain in dry cakes, and grain in flour, dried fruit, jam, hard melons, half barrels of slib roots – ready to sprout salad whenever they were wet down, even with the brackish River water. They ordered smoked shiggles, procured by Fez from some unspecified source along with kegs of Jarb roots. They bought sweetening and spices and kegs of oil, both oil for cooking and for the lanterns and stove. They paid for bolts of pamet cloth and coils of rope, extra lines for fishing, and bags of frag powder. They bought a pen of fowl for the rear deck with snug, watertight nesting boxes, and the cooper began making an endless series of kegs for fresh drinking water.

They ordered spices and medicines, a set of new pans for the cook, and supplementary tools for the carpenter's locker.

Not all of this was available in Thou-ne. Some of it was mustered mysteriously by the Noor and arrived as mysteriously on other boats coming from the east. This meant delay, and more delay, but the Noor were patient, more patient than Thrasne owner, who wanted only to put some great challenge like an impenetrable wall between himself and the way Pamra had gone. The harder he worked, the less he thought of her, yet he could not give up thinking of her entirely and went each day to the marketplace, asking for news of her, unable to tell truth from rumor when news was given.

And in between times he sat in his cubby or alone in his watching place and distracted himself by writing in his book. Though, as it happened, sometimes the things he wrote were not a distraction at all but led him deep within himself to the very things he would rather not have thought of.

3

Talker of the Sixth Degree, by the grace of Potipur articulate, Sliffisunda of the Gray Talons perched in the entryway of his aerie waiting for the approach of the delegation. He had asked for a report on the herd beasts, and the keepers had told him they would send a delegation. From the northlands somewhere, wherever it was they kept the young animals they had taken. So, let them send their delegation and be quick about it. Sliffisunda was hungry. They had brought him a new meat human just that afternoon, and he could hear it moving about in his feeding trough. It made him salivate disgustingly, and the drool leaked from his beak onto his feet, making them itch.

Rustling on the rampway. Wings at far aperture. So, they were assembling. Now they approached. Stillisas, Talker of the Fifth Degree. Two fours, Shimmipas and Slooshasill. He knew them, but then . . . he knew all Talkers. There were only some fifteen hundred of them in the whole world, divided among the Gray, Black, Blue, and Red Talons, the only four that had not been allowed to fall into ruin at time of hunger. Well.

'Uplifted One.' Stillisas bowed, tail tucked tight to show honor. The others, one on either side, bowed as deeply.

'So,' Stillisunda croaked. 'Stillisas. You have something to report to me.'

'About young thrassil and weehar, Uplifted One. We have six of each animal. One male, five females of each. They are carefully hidden. I have just come from place. By next summer they will be of age to breed. Slave humans say we must capture other males, next year or year after, if

264

herds are to grow strong. No more females are needed.'

'And how long, Stillisas, before we may dispense with shore-fish?' Many of the Thraish had adopted the Noor word for the human inhabitants of Northshore. It conveyed better than any other word his feelings for humans. Shore-fish. Offal. To be eaten only when one must.

'Realistically, Uplifted One, about fifteen years. And then only under most rigid controls. There is already some trouble with fliers assigned to me as help. Fliers must be prepared for restraint. Fliers must be sensible!'

Sliffisunda twitched in irritation, depositing shit to show the extent of his offendedness. 'You may leave that to Sixth Degree, Stillisas. To those of us who no longer share meat.'

Stillisas flushed red around his beak. It was true. Stillisas did share meat with others, one wriggling body for four or five Fifth Degree Talkers instead of having one for each of them. Only the Sixth Degree could eat in dignified privacy, without the stink of others' saliva on their food. He should not have spoken so. He abased himself now, crouching in the female mating position while Sliffisunda flapped twice, accepting the subordination.

'If all goes well, there will be herd of some sixty to eighty thousand in thirteen years, Uplifted One. Weehar females often throw twins, according to *sloosil*, captured humans. At Thraish present numbers, fifty thousand animals will be needed annually to feed Thraish people. In fourteenth or fifteenth year, that many may be slaughtered.'

'Enough if *horgha sloos*, sharing meat,' sneered Sliffisunda. He shat again. 'And if Thraish do not share?'

'Many years longer, Uplifted One. One and one-half million animals each year would be needed if all are to have fresh meat, without sharing.'

'At Thraish present numbers.'

'Yes, Uplifted One.'

Sliffisunda hissed. There were only seventy some-odd thousand of the Thraish. Only fifteen hundred of them were Talkers. At one time there had been almost a million fliers. But it would take two hundred million weehar and thrassil slaughtered a year to support that many. Dared he dream of that?

Power. Power over many. What power was it to be Talker over this pitiful few? He dreamed of the ancient days when wings had filled the skies of Northshore, when wings had flown over the River, perhaps to the fabled lands of the south, in the days before the fear came to prevent their flying over the River at all. But why not? There had been that many once. If the fliers had stopped breeding when the Talkers suggested it, all would have been well. So, somehow the fliers must be brought under control. It would require some new laws, some new legends. The opaque film slid across his eyes as he connived. *An elite order of fliers to carry out will of Talkers. Breeding rights given as awards for service. Eggs destroyed if flier did not obey. Number carefully controlled. And yet, that number could be larger than at present. Much larger.*

He came to himself with a shudder. Those crouched before him pretended not to notice his abstraction, though he glared at them for a long moment, daring them to speak.

'Tell me of disturbance among the *sloosil*,' he asked at last. 'I hear there is disorder among humans, near Black Talons, in places called Thou-ne and Atter.'

'It is same person as before,' murmured Slooshasill. 'Uplifted One sought same person in year past. Human called Pamra Don.'

So. Human called Pamra Don. Human who emptied pits in Baris. 'Rivermen!' Sliffisunda hissed. It took him a time to recognize that the three before him had not replied. Contradiction? 'Talkers do not agree?'

'Pits are full,' ventured Shimmipas. 'Full. Fliers gorge.'

'Not Rivermen.' Sliffisunda almost crouched in amazement, catching himself only just in time. 'Tell!'

'Procession.' The Talker shrugged. 'Many humans walking. At sunset Pamra Don speaks to them.'

'Words?'

'Tells of Holy Sorters in sky. Tells of Protector of Man. Says humans must know truth. Says will tell Protector of Man.'

'*Shimness,*' snorted Sliffisunda. It was the name of a legendary Thraish flier, one who had always accomplished the opposite of what he tried. In common parlance it meant 'crazy' or 'inept,' and it was in this sense Sliffisunda used it now.

'Pits are full,' Shimmipas repeated stubbornly. 'If procession goes on, more pits will be full.'

Sliffisunda looked narrowly at the others. They dropped their eyes, appropriately wary.

'See with eyes,' Sliffisunda said at last. It was all he could do. In the room behind him the chains in the meat trough rattled, reminding him of hunger. He drooled, dismissing the delegation, and returned to his own place. They had brought him a young one this time. Soft little breasts, tasty. Tasty rump. The Tears had softened it nicely, and the mindless eyes rolled wildly as he tore at the flesh. It screamed, and he shut his eyes, imagining a weehar in his claws. It, too, would scream. Why, then, did these human cries always annoy him? He tore the throat out, cutting off the sound, irritated beyond measure, no longer enjoying the taste.

He went to his spy hole and looked out upon the sky. The delegation was just leaving, three Talkers and three ordinary fliers, flying east along the River against a sky of lowering storm. *Foolish to fly in this weather. They could be blown out over water.* Sliffisunda postulated, not for the first time, where the fear had come from that prevented the Thraish from flying over water at all. *Survival*, he told himself. *During Thraish-human wars, many Thraish ate fish. Other Thraish killed them. Only Thraish who did not eat fish survived. Perhaps reason some Thraish did not eat fish then was fear of water.*

It was possible. Anything was possible. Even this thing in Thou-ne and Atter was possible.

He would go to Black Talons. He would see for himself.

4

The Council of Seven was gathered in the audience hall of the Chancery, the round council table set just outside the curtained niche where Lees Obol lay. By an exercise of willful delusion, one could imagine the Protector of Man as part of the gathering. The chair nearest the niche was empty. Perhaps the Protector occupied it spiritually. Or so, at least, Shavian Bossit amused himself by thinking.

As for the other six, they were present in reality. Tharius Don, fidgeting in his chair as though bitten by fleas. Gendra Mitiar, driving invisible creatures from the crevasses of her face with raking fingers. General Jondrigar, his pitted gray skin twitching in the jellied light. Koma Nepor, Ezasper Jorn. And, of course, Shavian himself. A second ring of chairs enclosed the first, occupied by functionaries and supporting members of the Chancery staff. So, Tharius had invited Bormas Tyle to attend, though Bormas was a supporter of Bossit's and Tharius knew it. Gendra had her majordomo, three district supervisors, and her Noor slave to lend her importance, though Jhilt squatted on the floor behind the second ring of chairs, conscious of her inferiority in this exalted gathering.

Koma Nepor and Ezasper Jorn supported one another. And Chiles Medman, the governor general of the Jarb Mendicants, was there – supporting whom? Shavian wondered. The Jarb Mendicants were tolerated by the Chancery, even used by the Chancery from time to time, but they could not be considered a part of the hierarchy. So what was Medman here for? Supporting some faction? There were three factions, at least. Tharius, the enigma, who would do the gods knew what if he were in power. Gendra, advocate of increasing the elixir supply and the power of the Chancery with it, and of increased repression. She enjoyed that. And Bossit himself, practical politician, who plotted enslavement of the Thraish and no more of their bloody presumption. And old Obol, of course, behind the curtains, lying in his bed like a bolster, barely breathing.

The general had no faction. His Jondarites stood around the hall as though carved of black stone. The scales of their fishskin jerkins gleamed in the torchlight; their high plumes nodded ebon and scarlet. Their axes were of fragwood, toothed with obsidian. Only their spear points were of metal. From time to time the general pivoted, surveying each of them as though to find some evidence of slackness. He found none. The soldiers in the audience hall were a picked troop. If any among them had been capable of slackness, that tendency was long since conquered.

'Let's get to it,' Shavian muttered at last, tapping his gavel on the hollow block provided for it. It made a clucking, minatory sound, and they all looked up, startled. 'We are met today to consider the matter of this "crusade" – preached and led by one Pamra Don. I might say, this person is the same Pamra Don who caused us some difficulty a year or so ago.' He stared at Gendra, letting his silence accuse her.

She bridled. 'You know we've set Laughers after her, Bossit. Including that Awakener from Baris. Potipur knows he would give his life to get his hands on her. His search must have been out of phase. Evidently she has been behind him the whole time.'

'Behind him, or on the River, or hidden by Rivermen, what matter which,' Shavian sneered, annoyed with her. 'The fact is, she avoided him, him and all the others who were looking for her. She came to surface in a town where no Laughers were, a town from which your representative had only recently departed, a town ripe for ferment because of some damned statue the superstitious natives had found in the River.'

269

'The Jondarites should have stopped it,' growled Gendra through her teeth, glaring at the general. 'Why have Jondarites in all the towns otherwise . . .'

'The Jondarites have no orders concerning crusades,' said the general in an expressionless voice. 'They are ordered to put down insurrection. There was no insurrection. They are ordered to punish disrespect of the Protector of Man. No disrespect is being shown, rather the contrary. They are told to quell heresy. There has been no heresy they could detect. The woman spoke of lies told to the Protector, of plots against the Protector.' His eyes glowed red as he spoke. Who knew better than he of the lies that surrounded Lees Obol? Who knew better than he of the actuality of conspiracies? Scarcely a day went by that Jondrigar did not uncover a plot against the Protector. The mines had their share of Chancery conspirators he had unearthed.

'Enough,' rapped Shavian. 'Recriminations will not help us.'

'Where is the crusade now?' Tharius Don asked, knowing the answer already but wishing to get the conversation away from those around the table and onto something less emotionally charged. He was rigid in his chair, yet twitchy, full of nervous energy. New adherents to the cause were being reported almost daily. For reasons he could not admit even to himself, he had been delaying the strike for months, and it could not be put off much longer. With every week that passed, the fear of discovery grew more imminent and compelling. In his heart he thanked the gods for the crusade, even though it had put Pamra Don at risk. It had drawn the Chancery's attention, for a time. 'What's the name of the town?'

'A few days ago, she was in Chirubel,' Bossit answered in a weary, irritated voice. He did not want the fliers stirred up any more than they were, and though this matter had not yet seemed to upset them, who knew what it might mean in the future. And with Lees Obol failing so fast . . . though he had only the Jondarites' word for that. No one else could get nearer to him than across the room. He shook his head and

270

rasped, 'A watchtower relay brought word. The pits in Chirubel are full. There was a great storm there, and many of her followers died.'

'Died?' Tharius had not heard this.

'Old people, mostly. The great mob of them have no proper provision of food or shelter. The towns have been instructed to put their own surplus foodstuffs under guard, and the Jondarites have been ordered to prevent looting. So, there is a good deal of hunger. Which begets a regrettable tendency to eat off the land, as it were.'

'Violence?'

'Some. Fights break out. Mostly the deaths are old people dying of lung disease brought on by cold and hunger. Some younger ones, too, through accidents or violence. Some children and babies, the same.'

'So, the pits are full,' Gendra mused. 'Well, the fliers wanted the quota of bodies increased. They should be happy.'

'Ezasper Jorn,' queried Bossit, 'what mood are the fliers in?'

Jorn, huddled in his chair wrapped in three layers of blankets, blinked owlishly at them from his cavern of covers. 'Voiceless as mulluks. They may not understand what's going on so far as a crusade is concerned. They don't seem curious, but then they've seen these little skirmishes before. We've had intertown wars; we've had rebellions put down by the Towers. That kind of thing has filled the worker pits from time to time over the centuries, so they might not think much of it. In short, they do not seem to be concerned. It's a local phenomenon, after all.'

'They'll scarcely change their reproductive habits on the basis of this temporary glut, which, at most, affects ten or a dozen towns.' Koma Nepor was using his best pedant's voice, reserved for meetings such as this where chortle and giggle would not serve. 'I agree with Jorn. They'll stuff themselves for a time; then the movement or whatever it is will fizzle out as these things always do; and they'll go back to normal.'

271

'Hungry normal,' commented Gendra with a vast grinding of teeth. 'In those towns, at least. With all the oldsters gone, the death rate will be low for a time.' She reflected upon this. There was no reason the average life-span should not be somewhat shortened. For parents, say, fifteen years after the birth of the last child. Or even twelve. For nonreproducers, earlier, unless they filled some important niche in the town economy. She would send word to the Towers. Fuller pits around the world would please the fliers, and if she could start currying the favor of the Talkers even now . . .

'So, the Talkers will tell the fliers to move across town lines and share.' Shavian was heartily weary of the entire discussion. 'The point is not what the fliers will or will not do, though it may come to that later. The point is, what are we to do?'

Tharius stirred uneasily. He had been arguing the proper course of action with himself for days now, first yes, then no, both sides with reasons that seemed equally good. Now he must choose.

'Have her brought before me,' he said firmly, nothing in his voice betraying either how little faith he had in his own recommendation or how deeply he was invested in its success. 'Have her brought here. We know where she is. We do not need to wait for Laughers to find her. They were instructed, had they found her, to bring her here, so let us get on with it. Send word to the Jondarites in – what's the next town west, Gendra?' He knew perfectly well. Pamra Don had surfaced in a hotbed of the cause. The dozen towns west of Thou-ne were all rife with rebellion, and their Towers were full of Tharius's men.

'Rabishe-thorn,' she responded absently, even as she peered at him with searching eyes. What was he up to? 'Rabishe-thorn, then Falsenter. If we send word now, they should be able to intercept her in one or the other.'

'Send word she is not to be harmed,' Tharius went on in an emotionless voice, praying the quivering of his hands clasped in his lap could not be seen. 'As Propagator of the

Faith, I need to know everything she knows, and I won't get it if she's too frightened or abused or – forbid it – dosed with Tears. It will take months for her to reach us overland. During that time, the crusade will be effectively stopped since she will not be there to lead it.' And this was the bait he hoped would bring them. Though he was thankful for the distraction she had provided, he wanted Pamra safe. With the day of the strike approaching, with his own inevitable mortality close at hand, he wanted to know she was well. I want to leave something behind me, he told himself, as though talking to Kessie. Kessie, I want to leave a posterity – silly though that may seem. I want it.

None of this was the business of the gathering. He pulled himself into focus and said again, 'The crusade will dissipate while she is on her way here.'

Gendra would have liked to find something wrong with his reasoning, but she couldn't. Gendra wanted Pamra Don killed, both because it was her nature to dispose of wild factors in that way and because some instinct told her it would be a very good idea. Pamra Don and Tharius Don. And the lady Kesseret. An odd group, that. An untrustworthy group. When she, Gendra, became Protector of Man, her first order to the Jondarites would be to do away with certain of the Chancery staff. And certain Tower Superiors. And others. She smiled, a rare, awful smile, showing her teeth.

Shavian, his eyes darting between them as though watching a game of net-ball, nodded in approval. The general glared but did not object. Why would he? He would sooner believe in plots than in no plots.

Ezasper Jorn and Koma Nepor simply watched, listened, said little. Having plans of their own, they didn't care about these things. And as for Lees Obol, his voice came to them plaintively from the curtained niche behind them. 'Somebody get me my pot.'

The Jondarites outside the niche moved to the Protector's service. Gendra stood up and ordered tea in a loud voice, at least partly to disguise the sounds emanating from the curtained room. There was general babble for a few moments, for which Tharius Don was very grateful. A Jondarite brought the Protector's teapot into the hall and set it upon a distant table, over a lamp, ready when the Protector asked for it. Behind it, the curtain glowed red as blood in the light of the warmer. Tharius found his eyes fixed on it, as though it were an omen.

He joined the babble, adding to it. When they came to order once again, his suggestion would be remembered, but his own connection with it would be somewhat overlaid by later conversation. A subtlety, he felt, but nonetheless acceptable. Even subtlety was welcome.

And yet, except for his own emotional needs, why bother? He had asked himself this more than once in the preceding days and weeks, ever since the first word of the crusade had come via seeker bird and watchtower. Servants of the cause had passed the word along, knowing Tharius Don would want to know. Mendicants of the Jarb had passed the word along, for Chiles Medman had asked them to. The Jarb Houses were firm supporters of the cause, to Tharius's amazement, though Chiles had explained why.

They had met by chance on one of the outer walls of the Chancery compound, brought there by a day of inviting sun and more than seasonable warmth, encountering one another quite by accident and remaining together because not to have done so would have looked suspiciously like avoidance or disaffection. Avoidance was as suspect as propinquity. There were always watchers. They had fallen into conversation, the first they had ever held outside the context of the conspiracy. They had spoken of the nature of fliers.

'Look at a flier through the smoke sometime, Tharius Don.' Chiles Medman had held out his pipe, as though inviting Tharius to do it then and there. There were no fliers closer than Northshore that anyone had reported, though there might have been a dozen of them spying from the high peaks for all anyone knew.

'What do you see, Medman? A differing reality?' Tharius was touchy about this.

'We see them stripped of our own delusion, Tharius Don. Through the smoke they look like nothing much except winged incarnations of pride.'

'Pride?' He had not really been surprised. Everyone knew how stiff-necked the Talkers were.

'They would be happy to see every human dead if they did not need us for food. They would rend all intelligence but their own. They kill, not out of bloodthirstiness, but out of pride. They have a word for sharing, *horgho*. It means "to abase oneself." Their phrase for sharing food, *horgha sloos*, means also "dirtying oneself." Did you know they call us *sloosil*?'

Tharius Don could not help snorting at the word. 'No. What does it mean?'

'Meat. Simply that, in the plural. Meat. I met one of the Fourth Degree Talkers at a convocation once. His name was Slooshasill. "Meat manager." He was responsible for providing bodies for Fifth and Sixth Degree Talkers.'

'So you don't think they respect us?'

Chiles Medman had shaken his head, lit his pipe, and considered Tharius through the smoke. 'Why should they?'

'They've borrowed our craftsmen. They've learned writing from us.' Why shouldn't they? his hope had insisted. Why shouldn't they respect us?

'Well, they don't. If they didn't need us for food, they would slaughter us all tomorrow. They would not even keep us for slaves, because we remind them of *horgha sloos*. We remind them of abasement. They had an oral tradition and adequate housing for thousands of years before we came. Why do they need our writing? Or our craftsmen?'

Tharius had glanced around, assuring himself they were alone, then said softly, 'And yet you support the cause? Not, seemingly, because you share my dream of sharing this world in dignity?'

'You know I don't, Tharius. I support the cause because I believe it's the only chance for humanity. The track we are on is madness. We're a flame-bird's nest, waiting for the spark. Our self-delusion grows greater every generation.

275

We are moving farther and farther from our own truths.'

'We have twenty-four hundred townships. Every township has about forty thousand people in it. There are almost a hundred million of us and fewer than a hundred thousand of them,' Tharius had said in a mild voice.

'There are a hundred million blades of grass, and yet the weehar graze upon them all. The fliers could double their numbers in one year, Tharius. They're keeping their numbers down by breaking their eggs. They only incubate seven or eight a year in any given township, and they could incubate fifty or more. There's fifty percent mortality among the chicks. When the population grows too large, the Talkers kill the male chicks. If they could breed as they like, there would be a million of them in four or five years. All young. In fifteen years, when those came to breeding age, there would be hundreds of millions, all at once. The young may not be able to breed, but they can fight. They're carnivores, for gods' sake.'

'Necrovores, rather.'

'Not the Talkers. And none of the Thraish like eating dead meat.'

'How do you know all this about them? Their numbers? Their habits?'

'We look, Tharius. We listen. We pay kids to climb rocks and spy on their nests. We send spies into Talons and listen to what they say.'

'In contravention of the Covenant?'

'Oh, shit, Tharius. Come off it. Don't go all pompous on me. Who else is going to do it? Who except the Jarb Mendicants could be trusted to do it?'

Tharius's face had reddened. 'I get sick, sometimes, of your assumptions of omniscience, Medman. You see everything through the smoke, and that's supposed to be reality. It is not necessarily my reality, which I tend to believe has an equal right to exist!'

'We've never said it was the only reality,' Medman had said, putting away his pipe. 'We've only said we see without delusion. Without preconception. Without prejudice. The Jarb pipe does that for us. For some of us.'

'But only for you madmen.' It was unkind, and Tharius had repented of it at once.

'Yes.' Softly. 'Yes, Tharius Don. Only for us madmen. The smoke only works for those of us who are capable of alternate visions.' Chiles Medman had left him then, a little angry, only to return, speaking in a vehement whisper.

'Tharius Don, you have not been among the people of Northshore for a hundred years. When I am not here in the Chancery – which I am not, most times – I see them every day. I see those who are told to believe in Potipur and Abricor and Viranel. Potipur the Talker. Abricor the young male Thraish. Viranel the female Thraish. Three gods, Tharius Don, made in the likeness of their creators – the Thraish. Who eat humans. And I see mankind trying to believe in that . . .

'I see them trying valiantly to believe in the Sorters. Virtually every human knows in his heart it's a lie. They have seen the workers. You think boys don't sneak into the pits and look at the dead ones, just on a dare? You think people don't follow the Awakeners out to the pits sometimes, spying on them? You think people don't know? Aren't aware? Even those who believe the most, you think they don't suspect, down deep, that something is awry, that they are being fed on lies?'

'The Awakeners tell us most people believe,' Tharius had answered. It was lame, and he'd known it.

'The Awakeners tell you most people believe, and they tell the people the Holy Sorters exist, and they tell their colleagues one thing and their Superiors something else. I only knew one Awakener in all my years who would tell the truth. He's a man named Haranjus Pandel, from Thou-ne. He's a cynic, Tharius, and an honest man.

'But as for the rest of Northshore, it's a tinder pile, as I said. People have no hope for the future. They are ready to immolate themselves if it would hatch that hope. We have more Jarb Houses now than we had a hundred years ago, and we need twice as many. People see the workers shambling around, and something – perhaps the way one

277

of them moves or the tilt of a head – makes them think maybe Mother is under that wrapper, or Daddy, or sister or daughter or son. Or they think of themselves there, not peacefully laid away but staggering around, stinking, hated by everyone. Then madness, Tharius Don. Madness. And only the pipe gives them any hope then.'

'Your hallucinogenic pipe.' Tharius had smiled a little bitterly.

'The inverse of that,' Chiles Medman had replied. 'An inverse hallucinogenic, Tharius Don. A pipe that lets them see the dead for what they are, and the moons for what they are, and the fliers for what they are, so that they need not struggle to believe what their eyes and noses tell them is ridiculous. It is the struggle to believe which maddens, Tharius Don. The wildest of the Jarb House Mendicants come from the most devout homes . . .'

Something had happened then to interrupt their conversation, and Tharius had not talked with him since except for the odd word at ceremonial events. Still, and despite Tharius's own rudeness on that occasion, he counted on Medman's support. When the time came.

'If the time comes,' he said to himself bitterly. 'If the time comes.' The strike was as prepared at this moment as it would ever be. He was making excuses these days to delay it as he had been for months. He knew it. He didn't know why. 'When the time comes,' he said again, not convincing himself.

The council members resumed their places, now with tea steaming before them. The niche was silent. Shavian rubbed his forehead, reminding himself. 'Ah, what were we saying? Yes. Pamra Don to be summoned to the Chancery. Any comment?'

Chiles Medman rose, was noticed, said, 'I would support a meeting with Pamra Don here in the Chancery. The fact that this crusade has moved the people with such fervor indicates a level of disaffection among them we should be aware of. For our own sakes, as well as theirs.' He sat down again, having started them off like hunting birds after a swig-bug, darting here and there.

'Disaffection,' bellowed Gendra Mitiar. 'I'll give them disaffection!'

'Hush,' Bossit demanded. 'The governor general of the Jarb Mendicants has not said there is an insurrection. He has said "disaffection," and I agree we should know of any such. What do you hear of disaffection, Mendicant?'

'Murmurings,' Chiles replied, as though indifferent. 'The "disappearances" seem more noticed of late. Taken more account of.'

'There have been no more than usual,' Gendra said stiffly. 'About two a month from each township. Mostly old people.'

'They used to be mostly old people.' Chiles nodded. 'Of late, there have been many young ones. When old people vanish, it is a short wonder. When young ones go, people grieve longer. And talk longer.'

'The Towers have strict orders . . .' She fell silent, suddenly suspicious. Indeed, the Towers had very strict orders concerning those recruited for Talker meat. And yet, if the Talkers offered . . . if the Talkers offered a sufficient reward directly to the Superior of a Tower, might not that Superior be bought? The idea was shocking, and terrible and inevitable. Her eyes narrowed.

'Do you allege malfeasance?' she challenged Chiles Medman. 'If so, where? What Tower?'

He shook his head, took his pipe from his pocket, and lit it to peer at her through the smoke. What he saw evidently reassured him, for he smiled. 'I have no knowledge, Dame Marshal of the Towers. Only murmurings. Which is why I suggest bringing Pamra Don to the Chancery. Let us ask her.'

Gendra subsided, her teeth grinding. Shavian looked from one to the other of them awaiting further comment. Koma Nepor assented, Ezasper Jorn nodded. The general merely pivoted, keeping his eye on his men. 'No objection to that?' Shavian asked. 'Then let it be done.'

Now, Tharius thought to himself, let us send them off yet again in some other direction. 'Has any word come from the herdsmen? When last I spoke with you, Jorn, you said it was thought that fliers had made off with young weehar and thrassil. Is it still assumed that fliers have stolen a breeding stock? And did I hear there were herdsmen missing as well?'

Shavian reddened with chagrin. He could not fault the question, but it reflected upon his own purview. As Maintainer of the Household, the household herds were his responsibility. 'Yes,' he grated. 'There are herdsmen missing as well. Three of them, and among them the best men we had for understanding of the beasts.'

Tharius mused over this, looked up to catch Chiles's eye upon him through a haze of smoke. 'What do you see, Mendicant?' he asked.

'Herds,' the Jarbman replied. 'Stretching over the steppes of the Noor, in their millions.'

Koma Nepor snorted. 'From ten beasts? Hardly likely, Governor. The Talkers may guard a small herd. They will not be able to keep the fliers from depredations upon a large one. Eh, Jorn? Am I right?'

Ezasper Jorn nodded from his cocoon. 'Likely. They are voracious beasts, the fliers. Not sensible of much, according to the Talkers. I have been told that before the time of Thoulia they were warned to curtail their breeding and yet ignored the warnings until all the beasts were gone. What sensible beast would outbreed its own foodstock?'

'And yet,' brooded the Mendicant, 'I see herds.'

'And Noor?' asked the general, suddenly interested. 'If there will be herds, where are the Noor?'

The Mendicant put out his pipe, shaking his head. 'I see no Noor, General Jondrigar. None move upon the steppes in my vision. But then, who is to say when my vision will come true? In a thousand years, perhaps? Or ten times that.'

Tharius Don cleared his throat. 'It would be wise, General, to ask your balloon scouts to keep their eyes open for weehar and thrassil. If they are found upon the steppes, they should be slaughtered, at once. And I suppose a guard has been set upon the herds here behind the Teeth?'

Shavian gnawed his cheek, asserting to this without answering. Did the man think him a complete fool? Of course a guard had been set. Not only upon the household herds, but upon every herd in the northlands. All were being driven here, close by, where they could be watched.

'Have we anything more?' he asked, hoping fervently that what had already been discussed was enough.

'Hearing none,' he said, tapping the gavel perfunctorily once more, 'we are adjourned.'

'Somebody,' came a plaintive voice from behind the curtain. 'Bring me my tea.' The Jondarite across the room picked up the pot he had placed there and brought it forward. Ceremoniously, he entered upon service to Lees Obol.

They left the audience hall to go their various ways. Gendra Mitiar took herself off to the archives to harass old Glamdrul Feynt. The master of the files had not been diligent. When the time came, soon, she wanted proof or something that looked like proof, some reason for doing away with Tharius Don. Self-righteous prig! Staring at her as though she were less than nothing! She would show him who was nothing. Him, and his pretty cousin Kesseret, and his descendant, too, that Pamra Don . . .

Shavian Bossit went to his own suite and sent a messenger to Koma Nepor. It was time to talk seriously about what could be done to keep Talkers alive, but passive, while the elixir was made from their blood – not in these piddling quantities, but by the gallon! His spies told him Koma had been experimenting with the blight. Perhaps . . . He grinned in anticipation, a wicked mouse grin, then sat himself down to wait . . .

And Tharius Don took himself to the tower above his own quarters in the palace and brooded. He felt caught in a wrinkle in time, a place in which time was both too long and too short. Too short to do all his raging imagination told him he should have done long since; too long to wait, too long a time in which too many obstacles might be thrust up before the cause to inhibit the last great rebellion . . .

'Rebellion,' he whispered to himself. 'Since you were only a child, Tharius Don, you have dreamed of rebellion.' And yet, what else could he have been but a rebel?

He could have been nothing else, born into the family Don with its strong tendencies toward both repression and ambition. There had been many old people in the household. His mother's parents, the Stifes. His father's parents, the Dons. His own parents. An aunt. Seven of them, all artist caste. And against the seven of them, only Tharius and an adored, biddable younger sister who was happy to do whatever anyone said, at any time.

And they did say. Continually; contradictorily; adamantly. The Stifes were at knife's point with the Dons. The Stifes were clawing away at one another. The Dons elder were at the throats of the Dons junior, and the alliances among the seven swung and shifted, day to day. There was only one thing that could be depended upon, and that was that young Tharius would be both the weapon they used on one another and the battleground over which they fought. He was petted, praised, whipped, abused, slapped, ignored, only to be petted once more. He was of their nature, if not of their convictions, and at about age nine or ten – he could not remember the exact year, or even the incident that had provoked it – he had repudiated them all. He remembered that well, himself rigid against the door of the cubby in the attic which was his own, his face contorted as he stared into his own eyes in the mirror across the room, his utter acceptance of his own words as he said, 'I renounce you all. All of you. From now on, you can fight each other, but you will not use me.' Or perhaps those words had only come later, after he had had time to think about it. The renunciation, though, that had happened, just as he remembered it.

And from that time he was gone. An occasional presence. A bland, uninteresting person, hearing nothing, repeating nothing, unusable as a weapon because he did or said nothing anyone could use or repeat to stir up enmity or support.

Useless as a battleground because he did not seem to care. Not about anything at all.

As for Tharius, he did not care about them anymore. He had discovered books.

There had always been books, of course. There always were books, in the shops. Holy books. Accepted books. Bland histories in which there was never any violence or deviation of opinion. Devotional books in which there were never any doubts. Even storybooks, for children, in which obedient boys and girls obeyed their elders, learned their lessons, and became good, obedient citizens of their towns.

Life wasn't like that. Looking around him, Tharius saw hatred and violence, pain and dying. He saw workers. Awakeners. Grim, stinking fliers in the bone pits. Men and women vanishing, as though swallowed by evil spirits. None of that was in the books. Not the accepted books.

But there were other books.

A few days before Tharius's repudiation of his kin, the poultry-monger's shop across the alley was raided by the Tower. A great clatter of Awakeners and priests of Potipur came raging into the place, all blue in the face with their mirrors jagging light into corners. Tharius Don was on the roof above the alley when it happened, hiding from his grandmother Stife. There was noise, doors slamming, some shouting, some screaming, people moving around in the attics opposite him, barely seen through the filthy glass. Then the Awakeners burst through the back door and began throwing books into a pile. They were screaming threats at the poultry-monger and his wife, both of whom were protesting that they had only bought the house a year ago, that they'd never looked into the attic, that they didn't know the books were there. It was likely enough true. Tharius had never seen lights in the windows opposite his own.

'It's only that saves your life for you now, poulterer,' snarled an Awakener. 'That and the dust on these volumes. Don't touch them. There'll be a wagon here in an hour or so to haul them away for burning.'

They left a blue-faced priest of Potipur at the head of the

283

alley to keep watch, but he got bored with the waiting and fell alseep. Most priests were fat face-stuffers anyhow, half-asleep on their feet a good part of the time. Tharius had stared down at the pile of books, silent as a stalking stilt-lizard, judging how many of them he might take away and how long he had. His own attic room was at the top of a drainpipe, and getting them back would be a difficulty . . .

Inspiration struck him all at once. He found a sack, put all his own books in it, hung it over his shoulder, and climbed down the protruding drainpipe, his favorite road to freedom. The exchange was quick – his dull books for the ones in the alley – and he was back up the drainpipe again, sweating and hauling for all he was worth, hearing the creak of the wagon wheels even as he slid over the parapet onto the roof beside his own window.

When the wagon arrived, the books were loaded by some flunky who did not even look at them. From the roof, Tharius watched him as he took them down to the stone wharf at the Riverside and burned them. Everyone pretended not to notice, even one old man who was choked by the smoke and had to act as though it was from something else. So. There were books, and books. The forbidden books went on the shelf in the corner, just where the others had been. No one ever came up here except Grandmother Stife, once a month or so, to peek in the door and then shout at him to sweep the place out.

Tharius was hooked, confirmed in rebellion. The books were real ones. Stories of people as they were. A history of Northshore. A little book about the arrival, called *When We Came*. Tharius had been taught certain things as true, but they had always seemed senseless. Now, suddenly they began to connect.

Time went. Tharius became a book collector. Hidden in the attics of the Don home was a collection that would have condemned all the family to death had an Awakener got wind of it. Tharius found them in other attics, entering from the roofs, prowling dusty spaces by lantern light, old, shut-up places where no one came anymore but where books were sometimes found. In corners. Under floorboards. He found them in houses where people died, before the Awakeners or the kinfolk came to take inventory. He found them in the rag man's yard, buried at the bottom of stacks of old clothes. Fragments more often than whole volumes, but of whole volumes, three or four a year, perhaps. By the time he was eighteen and subject to the procreation laws, he had almost thirty of them.

Which was bad enough in itself. Worse, so far as Tharius was concerned, was the fact in these thirty books were references to hundreds of others. Somewhere on Northshore there were, or had been, more!

Sometimes late at night, when the moons lit the alleyway, Tharius Don had a waking dream of all those books. More and more. All the answers to all the questions anyone had ever asked would be there in the books.

And the books, he was convinced, were in the Towers. Why else would the Awakeners be so agitated about books, if it were not some kind of secret knowledge only they were supposed to have? Knowledge about how things really were. How things used to be. How they had been in some other place before humans had come here.

Influenced by a bit too much wine, Tharius broached that subject at dinner one night, hearing the words fall into a horrified silence.

'Before what?' his father snarled. 'Before what?'

'Before humans came to Northshore,' Tharius stuttered.

'Where did you get an ugly idea like that?'

'I just – I just thought we must have come from somewhere else, you know. Because there are so many things we can't eat.' Even in his half-drunken surprise at the words that had come from his own mouth, he was wary enough not to mention the books. 'It seemed obvious . . .'

He was sent from the table, in disgrace. Doctrine was clear on that point. Humans had always lived on Northshore and had always been governed by the gods. His bibulous remark was occasion for a loud, screaming battle among the Dons and the Stifes. Two days later when he returned home from a foray, he found a young woman named Shreeley at the table. He had seen her before. Not often. She was the daughter of a friend of his father's, a pamet merchant from the other side of Baris.

'Your wife-to-be,' his father said in a stiff, unrelenting voice. 'You have had entirely too much time on your hands to sit around dreaming up obscenities.'

Tharius Don was more amused than anything else. The girl wasn't bad looking; she had a sweet, rounded body, and Tharius Don had had some experience with sweet, rounded bodies. It would not be a bad thing to have one of his own to play with.

What he had not foreseen was the sudden loss of privacy. No more attic room. He had only time to hide the books before all his belongings were swept up and reinstalled in a room two stories below, one he would share. And after that, he found it difficult to be alone for a moment.

Shreeley made sure of that. She slept with him. She rose with him in the morning and walked with him to the job his grandparents Stife had obtained for him. 'You show none of the family talent for art, Tharius Don,' said Stife grandfather. 'We have apprenticed you, therefore, to Shreeley's father, the pamet merchant.'

'I thought it was custom for young people to choose their own professions,' Tharius complained.

'Had you done so in your fifteenth or sixteenth year, as is also customary, we would have acceded to your choice, Tharius Don. Since you did not do so, you lost that opportunity.'

Shreeley came to walk home with him after work. She ate with him. She sat with him or walked with him after dinner. Went to bed with him. He tried to read one of his books only once, but Shreeley caught him at it. 'Read to me,' she begged sweetly. 'Read to me, Tharius Don.' He made up something about Thoulia, and she fell asleep while he was reciting. He hid the book away, sweat standing on his brow.

Still, for a time it was not impossible. Sex was more than merely amusing. Tharius had a great deal of imagination about sex, and Shreeley was compliant. Until she became pregnant, at which time everything stopped.

'No,' she said. 'It might hurt the baby.'

'It won't hurt the baby. And you like it.'

'I don't like it. I only did it to get pregnant and comply with the laws, Tharius Don. I hope you don't think I *enjoyed* all that heaving about.'

'Shreeley's father says you have been neglecting your duties,' his father admonished. 'With a baby on the way, you'd better start attending to business.'

It was that night Tharius Don went to the Tower of Baris and begged admittance as a novice. When the family learned of it, they never spoke of him again. When Tharius's son was born, they named him Birald. When Tharius heard of it he uttered a heartfelt wish for the boy's sanity, but without much hope considering that he, Tharius, might be losing his own.

He had sacrificed everything in hope of books, and there were no books in the Tower except those of a shameless falsity and unmitigated dullness. There were no books, and there was no leaving the Tower. For a time Tharius considered killing himself, but he could not think of any foolproof way to do it. And as time wore on, one factor of Tower existence saved him — the rigid, unvarying discipline which allowed much time for thought. Tharius was in the habit of thought. And as the months wore away, he began to find links in the behavior and beliefs of the Awakeners to things he knew from books.

And he saw early on a thing that many in that place never saw. He saw that the seniors did not believe what the juniors were told to believe.

It was evident, once the first piece fell into place. There was knowledge here. Not among the juniors. Not taught to the juniors. Withheld from them, rather. Given to others later on.

With a grim persistence that would have astonished all factions among the warring Stifes and Dons, he persevered. Years went by. He achieved senior status, learned what he could, learned there was more yet that could be learned, in the Chancery!

He was thirty-eight, a cynical member of the trusted circle that actually ran the Tower of Baris, and a personal friend of the Superior, when he was responsible, all unwitting, for bringing Kesseret to the Tower.

One of his duties was the enforcement of the procreation laws. Women over the age of eighteen who were not readying for marriage or were not already mothers, whether married or no, came under his jurisdiction. A wealthy man – whose wealth did not exceed his age, decrepitude, or hideous ugliness – presented a petition together with a generous gift to the Tower. Tharius Don signed it as a matter of course. It ordered the nineteen-year-old woman named Kesseret to marry the merchant at once or present herself to the Tower as a novice. It was routine. Rarely did anyone come into the Tower as a result. Sometimes the one under orders made a generous gift and the petition was revoked for a time. Sometimes not. It was simply routine.

Except in this instance. Kessie had been unable to buy herself free. She had been unwilling to submit. She came to the Tower.

To the Tower, to Tharius Don, who asked for and received mentorship in her case. She was older than most novices, as he had been. It was harder for her than for most, as it had been for him. She rejected much of what she was taught, as he had done.

So he told her the truth. From the beginning. Comforting her, urging her, meeting her in quiet places away from the Tower, keeping her away from worker duty as much as possible. And one day she had said, 'You can protect me all you like, Tharius Don. That doesn't make it right, what we do.'

He had agreed. And from that the cause had been born. Not right away, not all at once. They did not know enough yet.

'I'm told the answers are at the Chancery,' he said. 'I'll have to get there.'

'How long?'

He shrugged. 'Twenty years, minimum, I should think. I'm in line to be Superior when Filch dies or moves up. If they don't give him the elixir pretty soon, there'll be no question about his moving up. Say five years there, either way. Then I have to make some kind of reputation for myself. In something.'

'Something safe,' she whispered. 'Apologetics, Tharius. The apologetics they feed us juniors is awful. It's dull. It's ugly. It wouldn't convince a swig-bug. Make your reputation in defense of the faith, Tharius. In scholarship. It takes only cleverness and a way with words. It's all mockery, all lies, but we can do it. I'll help you.'

And she had helped him, and he her. They had been lovers for twenty years, sometimes impassioned, never less than fond. Kessie was forty when she took Tharius's place as Superior of the Tower in Baris and he moved on to the Chancery. They had not known then that it was the last time they would make love to one another. Once at the Chancery, Tharius had advanced rapidly. He had been given the elixir. And after that was no passion, only the remembrance of their coupling, their ecstasy, though that remembrance had been full of nostalgic longing.

The books he had sought were at the Chancery. The palace was full of books, very old books. No one cared except Tharius. He read his way through centuries of books. Of all those at the Chancery, only Tharius knew the truth of the Thraish-human wars in all their bloody, vicious details. He rebelled against that viciousness. Only Tharius knew of the Treeci and dreamed of that gentle race – for so he interpreted what he read – as an answer not only for the Thraish, but for man. From these books came the cause, and in that long, long remembrance the cause had grown.

And now, now he had delayed long enough, and it must all soon come to pass. He leaned his face into his cupped hands and evoked the memory of Kessie. Kessie as he had seen her last, carried away over Split River Pass, smiling bravely back at him. Her life had been given to this thing. This secret thing. His own had been given, also.

For the two of them there could be no future, but perhaps he could save Pamra Don for some better fate. Perhaps she could live the life he and Kessie had not been able to live. Perhaps she could find someone to love; perhaps she could bear children as he and Kessie had never been allowed to do.

With such simple hopes he comforted himself, believing them. He would give up everything, the world itself, for this cause. But even while doing that, he would try to save Pamra Don.

5

Midday in the Temple on the first day of first summer, the year's beginning. In the wide, carved sand urns, sticks of incense burn away into curling smoke, gray-white wraiths, rising into the high vaults of blackened stone. On the floor the murmuring multitude shifts from foot to foot with a susurrus of leather upon rock. All is muted, the color leached away, all sharpness of sound reduced to this soft, formless whisper which runs from side to side of the Temple, like liquid sloshing in a bowl. 'Truth,' it says, 'Light,' lapping at the walls of the place like surf, returning again and again, tireless as water.

A pale blur of faces, staring eyes, gaped mouths, nostrils wide for the heaving, phthisic breath, indrawn by bodies that have forgotten to breathe for a time. Wonder piled on wonder as the crusaders parade with their blood-bright banners to the rumble-roar of the drums, rhythmless as thunder, rhymeless as pulse. Oh, Peasimy Flot has an eye for spectacle and an ear for the wry, discordant sound to set teeth on edge and wrench the ears away from ordinary concerns. See what drums he has manufactured from kettles and hides, what robes he has managed to scrounge from what can be begged or stolen; see what gilded crowns and jeweled scepters he has set in the followers' hands to confound and amaze the multitudes. Glass and shoddy may glitter with the best in the dim Temple light, as they do now, among the hundreds half-drunk on fragrant smoke.

And Peasimy himself, now mounting the steps of the Temple to stand as he always stands, as Pamra always

291

stood, before the carved moon faces, turning in his high coronal and rich-appearing vestments to call into that breathing silence.

'Thou shalt follow no creature except the Bearer of Light,' he calls in his little piping voice, from the Temple stairs in the twentieth town west of Rabishe-thorn. 'Thou shalt not earn merit except by crusade. Thou shalt not give to the Temple and the Tower what belongs to the Protector of Man.'

His voice is shrill, the high treble sound of a whistle. It cuts through the crowd murmur like a knife, leaving a throbbing wound of uncertainty behind. The voice is not of a piece with the display. They had expected other than this.

'Where is she?' someone brays in a trumpet voice. 'Where is the Light Bearer?' They have heard of her. Every township on this quadrant of Northshore has heard of her, and though the entertainment thus far has been better than expected, some few are irritated that she has not come herself, that this pumped-up little creature has come in her stead.

'Gone to the Protector of Man,' Peasimy replies, irritated to be so interrupted. 'Long ago. With many following after her to testify to truth.' He pauses, trying to remember his place in the usual speech, counting the thou-shalts in his head. 'And those who have gone will be first in her kingdom, and those who come later will be last, but even to the last will gifts be given which are greater than any gifts these devils have ever pretended to give.' His gesture at the carved moon faces is almost like Pamra Don's gesture, and these words are almost exactly something Pamra Don has said. Most of what Peasimy says is almost what Pamra has said. She has never referred to 'her kingdom,' though she has spoken of the kingdom of man. Peasimy points to the carved moon faces, flier faces, and waits until the babble dies down.

'Thou shalt not revere the Awakeners,' says Peasimy. 'Thou shalt not walk in darkness.'

'What does he mean?' a rugged, doubtful man grumbles

292

to one of the followers. 'What does he mean about walking in darkness?'

'It's symbolic,' whispers the follower. 'At night, when the lanterns are lit, you must walk in the patches of light as though splashing them into the darkness. It's symbolic of the Light Bearer.'

'What the hell good does it do?' the doubter persists.

'It's pious,' snarls the other. 'The Light Bearer does it. To concentrate her mind on the truth.' So Peasimy has said, and they have had no reason to doubt him. Or maybe what Peasimy said was that the Bearer of Truth had been found in that way. The follower can't remember. It doesn't matter.

'Oh.' The other subsides, twitching. None of this sounds like good sense to him, and he wonders what all the fuss has been about.

'Thou shalt love the Protector of Man with all thy heart,' Peasimy shouts. 'Thou shalt keep him safe from lies.'

'That's what the Light Bearer is going to the Chancery for,' the follower instructs. 'To advise Lees Obol of the lies which are done in his name.' The doubter grunts, unconvinced, though in this case the follower has quoted correctly.

'Thou shalt give generously to the followers of truth, in order that the world may be enlightened,' Peasimy goes on, ticking the commandments off on his fingers. Sometimes he remembers ten, sometimes more than that. Tonight the crowd is restive, he will only give them ten. 'Thou shalt not withhold food from those on crusade.' He is hungry, very tired, and his throat is sore from all the shouting. Tomorrow they will go on to a new town, and his voice can rest. He takes a deep breath. 'Thou shalt not make fuk-fuk.'

An embarrassed titter runs through the Temple, a break of laughter like light coming suddenly through clouds to astonish those beneath with a benison of gold. 'What the hell?' the doubter growls, doubled with laughter. 'Baby talk. What the hell!'

'The Mother of Truth commands it,' the follower says through gritted teeth, embarrassed himself by the word

Peasimy always uses and weary of having to explain it. 'If you want to be really Sorted Out, you don't do *that*.'

'Well, if we didn't do *that*, there wouldn't be any of us to be Sorted Out.' The man laughs in genuine amusement. 'Where the hell does he think babies come from, pamet pods?'

In which he is closer than he knows to Peasimy's true belief. The widow Flot had never found it necessary to tell Peasimy other than the pleasant myths of childhood, and Peasimy, who has discovered the facts beneath other myths by following and spying through windows, has never found the facts of this one. He has never seen a baby born. He would not believe the connection between that and the other were he told. Pamra Don, Mother of Truth, has said the strange, frightening act he has so often observed through windows at night is a mistake. It is therefore a perversion. A darkness.

The follower, elderly enough to have forgotten the urgencies of passion and much puffed up by his new position as expositor of truth, defends the revealed word. 'There's a lot more fucking going on than necessary for babies. That's what the Light Bearer means. The Mother of Truth says we don't do it, so we don't do it. Not and be a follower of hers.'

The questioner laughs himself out of the Temple, his healthily libidinous nature rejecting all of it. But in the vast echoing hall, there are others to whom the ideal of abstinence appeals. There are disenchanted wives who can do well without a duty that seems to consist mostly of discomfort, grunting, and sweat. There are husbands who consider it an onerous and sometimes almost impossible performance which seems to be demanded – in pursuance of the procreation laws – too frequently and at inconvenient times. There are young ones, drawn to a life of holiness like moths to a flame, easily willing to give up something they know nothing of. There are spinsters being forced into marriage or pregnancy by the procreation laws, and men being forced into unwanted associations by the same. There are those who resent the Tower saying yes and therefore choose to follow the Bearer saying no. For every lustful lover there is at least one juiceless stick, anxious to have his lack made into virtue. Thus, in the departing footprints of each mocker, a follower rises up, and Peasimy Flot leads them on to the next city west while a trickle of the formerly recruited ones move northward, then west, where Pamra Don has gone. The crusade has steadily been approaching Vobil-dil-go, the township through which Split River runs, the most direct route from Northshore to the Chancery.

'How long do we carry the word before we follow the Bearer?' one of the followers asks Peasimy. He is one of the dozen or so who have accumulated the status of leaders in the crusade, those to whom Peasimy habitually talks, those who know what is going on. His name is Joal

'Pretty soon now,' Peasimy answers him, though somewhat doubtfully. 'Pretty soon now I'll take some and go after the Bearer, and you must take some and go on.' He has dreamed this. The Bearer had gone a way, then turned north. Now Peasimy must go a way and then turn north. And so on, and on, like a chain. As he says it, he begins to like the idea. 'A chain,' he repeats. 'Like a chain. One, then another one, then another one.'

The follower to whom Peasimy speaks is an excellent speaker who has often itched to take Peasimy's place upon the Temple stairs. He has a loud, mellifluous voice, and, since he finds both women and sex utterly repugnant, he has wholly adopted Peasimy's doctrine. He will have sense enough not to speak of his repugnance directly to the multitudes, as he knows he must include women among his followers if he is to acquire the kind of power – and service – he desires. In his satisfaction at considering this not-so-distant future, he forgets to answer Peasimy's suggestion.

'You will do it if I tell you,' Peasimy asserts, interpreting the man's silence as unwillingness. 'Yes, you will.'

'If the Bearer of Light commands,' the man says, silently

exulting. 'When you leave us, how will you know which way to go?'

'North, until we see the mountains. Great tall mountains,' Peasimy replies proudly. The Jondarites had told him that, when they had taken Pamra Don away. Now he quotes them in a singsong voice, certain of the way he will go. 'Keep the mountains on the right.' He pats the arm on which he wears his glove. That is his right arm, Widow Flot had told him. 'The arm with the glove is your right arm, Peasimy. You eat with your right hand.' So he pats it now, quite sure. 'Keep the mountains on the right. Until we come to a big river with some high places with flat tops. That's Split River Pass, where we go through, to the Chancery.'

Joal makes note of it. He has no plans to lead the crusade anywhere but where he wants it to go, and at the moment that does not include going anywhere near to the Chancery.

6

Sometimes I wonder what I'm doing when I write these things down. I read what I wrote about what happened, and then I try to remember what happened, and sometimes I can't remember whether I'm remembering what really happened or only what I wrote about it. The words have a way of doing things on their own. They sneak around and say things I'm not sure are real.

I wrote something the other day about an order of food that came in from the east, and later I heard Taj Noteen talking with Medoor Babji about it as though it had been some other thing entirely. I always figured me and the men saw things pretty much the same way, but now there's others here who seem to look at this world as though they had eyes different from mine. If I hadn't written it down, I wouldn't have thought again about it, figuring I'd just missed something about it at the time. But I did write it down, and what I wrote wasn't what the Noor were saying at all.

Of course, I'm only an ignorant boatman. Maybe priests and Awakeners are taught to do it better, but words written down seem to me could be very dangerous things.

From Thrasne's book

While the *Gift* and the Noor waited for stores, Thrasne passed the time by doing things to the *Gift*. A new railing on the steering deck. A small cabin below for himself since the

Melancholics would be using his house. Reinforcement between the ribs in the fore and aft holds. And, though it cost him much thought and argument with himself, a tall mast mounted on the main deck, just behind the owner-house. This was decided soon after Obers-rom hired three new men who knew about sail.

'Used to run back and forth among the islands out there,' one of them told Thrasne. 'There's chains of islands out there, out of sight of Northshore, farther out than the shore boats go, Owner.'

'You ran *up*-River?' Thrasne asked in astonishment.

'Well – what I'd say about that would depend who I was talkin' to.'

And thus did Thrasne owner learn of whole tribes of boatmen who paid the tides no more attention than they paid the little pink clouds of sunset.

'You don't know how the tide works as far out as you plan to go, Thrasne owner,' the man said. 'You don't know and I don't know. You'll never row this flat bottom across World River, that's for sure, and I'm suggestin' it would be a good idea to have another way to move it.'

Thrasne regarded the mast with a good deal of suspicion, but he could not argue with what the man said. They surely couldn't row the *Gift* across the World River.

By the time they were ready to depart, Pamra had been gone for months. Still, word of her came to Thou-ne. The Towers evidently had a way of getting information, and Haranjus Pandel had conveyed certain information to the widow Flot, who conveyed it to half the town.

'She was in Chirubel,' Thrasne said to Medoor Babji in a carefully unemotional tone. 'There were thousands and thousands following her when she got there. I wonder how all those people are fed?' He wondered how Pamra herself was fed, but he did not mention it. Thoughts of her were like a wound which he knew could not heal unless he quit picking at it.

'Way I hear,' said Medoor, 'some aren't fed. Many dead, Thrasne. The worker pits in the towns between here

298

and Chirubel are full. Some of the Towers are recruiting extra Awakeners, so I hear it.'

'I'll bet the old bone eaters love that,' Thrasne said, turning his eyes to the wide wings that circled above the town.

'Well,' she said abstractedly, watching his face, 'if there are more dead people, there could be more fliers hatched, couldn't there? Probably the fliers like that idea.'

'You're not saying they think?' Thrasne objected. 'You mean more of their little ones would survive, that's all.'

'Did you ever hear of fliers who can talk?' she asked.

And he, driven into memory, remembered a time when old Blint had said something very much like that. Just before he died. He mentioned it to her, wondering.

'Talk to the Rivermen sometime, Thrasne. They know things.'

It was all she would say at the time, but it gave him something else to concern himself about. What was Pamra doing? Hadn't that Neff been a flier – well, sort of? Was she doing the will of the fliers? Without even knowing it!

These concerns were driven away in the flurry of departure.

It was almost at the end of first summer. The mists and breezes of autumn were beginning. Alternate days were chill and windy, and it was on one such that the *Gift* left the docks at Thou-ne. So far as the standabouts were concerned, the boat had been hired by the Melancholics for a Glizzee-prospecting voyage among the islands. It departed properly downtide, and only when it was out of sight of the town did it turn on the sweeps and press away from North-shore. Once well away, the new boatmen – sailors they called themselves – put up the bright, unstained sails and the boat moved on its own, cross-current, the wind pushing at it from up mid-River and yet somehow moving it across. It was the way the sail was slanted, the new men said, and Thrasne paid attention as they lectured him.

In the weeks that followed, he learned about tacking, though the new men laughed at the lumbering *Gift*, calling

299

her 'fat lady' and 'old barge bottom.' When Thrasne objected, they offered to show him the kind of boat that skipped among the islands, and he gave them leave to stop at a wooded isle they were passing at the time to spend two days cutting logs for ribbing and planks. It was to be a small thing, one that could be put together on the top of the owner-house. Thereafter the voyage was livened for all of them by their interest in the new boat.

Once they had passed the braided chains of islands, it was livened by little else.

Except for the sailors, none of them had ever been out of sight of land. Even the sailors had experienced this seldom and briefly, for the islands were thickly scattered in their chains, few of them isolated enough to require long sailing without a few rocky mountaintops or rounded hills in view. Now, however, they were beyond the last of the islands.

Each day at dusk, the winds began to blow from behind them, from Northshore. Then the sails would be set to take the wind almost full while the rudder slanted them against the tide, and all night long the watch would stand, peering ahead into nothing but water. In the mornings, the wind would reverse, blowing toward them, and the sailors would curse, setting the sail to let them move slightly forward and downtide. Thus they moved always away from Northshore, sometimes a little east, sometimes a little west, cleaving to a line that led southward – southward into what? None of them knew.

'This man who saw Southshore – Fatterday? Why didn't the Queen of the Noor hire him for this voyage?' Thrasne asked after a particularly frustrating bout of tacking.

'When they sought him, to send him to us, he was gone, Thrasne. Noor scouts looked everywhere for him. All the Melancholics were sent word to watch for him, but he has not appeared.'

'Sounds like a madman. Perhaps he is in a Jarb House somewhere.'

Medoor Babji shook her head at him. 'Then he will never come out, except as a Mendicant.'

'You won't know him then, if he does. All dressed up the way they are, with those pipes in their mouths most of the time.'

'Only when madness is about, Thrasne owner. So they say. They smoke the Jarb root only when madness is about, for they are vulnerable to visions.'

'The Mendicants? Truly? I thought they were supposed to be the only certifiably sane ones.'

Medoor Babji perched on the railing, teetering back and forth with a fine disregard for the watery depths below, setting herself to lecture, which she often enjoyed. 'The way I have heard it is this: There are two types of people in the wide world, Thrasne owner. There are those like you, and me, and most of those we know, who see the world the same. I say there is puncon jam on the bread, and you say it, too; we both taste it. Then there will be one who says there is an angel dancing on the bread, and another who says there is no bread at all but only starshine in the likeness of food. Those are the mad ones. So, the mad ones go to a Jarb House and live in the smoke, and they become like you and me, eating puncon on their bread. But if they come out of the house, they see angels again, or lose their bread entirely. But some of them come out with pipes in their mouths which they light when madness threatens. And they go throughout the world selling their vision of reality to those who are not sure whether they are mad or not.'

'And with the money they build Jarb Houses,' concluded Thrasne, amused despite himself. It was the first time he had been amused in a very long time.

'Don't laugh! It's all true. Moreover, those who come out as Mendicants can see the future of reality as well as the present. That's what they are paid for. So it is said. Now, I said don't laugh.'

'I wasn't laughing,' he said. 'I was wishing Pamra could come into a Jarb House, somehow.'

'No.' Babji shook her head, sending her tightly twisted strands of hair into a twirling frenzy around her back and being sure he heard what she said. 'That is a vain hope,

Thrasne. She would not stay. It is not our world she wishes to see.'

Upon the River day succeeded day upon the *Gift*. At the end of the first week they had made a modest festival, and this habit continued at the end of each week that followed. On the morning after one such celebration, a hail from the watchman brought them all on deck.

The creatures came out of the oily swell of the water like hillocks, lifting themselves onto the surface of the River to lie staring at the *Gift of Potipur*, a long row of eyes on a part of each one of them, that part lifted a little like a fish's fin, large eyes down near the body of the strangey and smaller eyes out at the tip. They blinked, but not in unison, those eyes, so that the people gathered at the ship's rail had the strange notion they were confronting a crowd, a committee rather than one creature. One of the oily hillocks swam close to the *Gift*, dwarfing it, and spat strangey bones onto the deck. 'A gift,' it sang in its terrible voice, turning onto its back and sinking into the River depths with a great sucking of water and roil of ivory underside, like a bellying sail of pale silk.

'What is that?' asked Medoor Babji, seeing how quickly the crew of the *Gift* moved about picking up the strangey bones.

'Glizzee spice,' said Thrasne. 'It grows within them. They spit it into ships, sometimes, or into the water near where ships are floating. Old Blint said they mean it as a gift. Strangeys watch ships a lot. Sometimes if a man falls overboard, a strangey will come up under him and hold him up until the boat can get to him, or even carry him downtide to the boat if it's gone on past.'

'They don't look like fish.'

'Oh, they aren't fish, Medoor Babji. Not shaped like them, not acting like them, not the size of fish. One time when old Blint was still alive, I saw one the size of an island. The whole crew could have gone onto his back and built a town there.'

'I never knew Glizzee was strangey bones.'

302

'Most people don't. They think it grows somewhere on an island, and that's why the boatmen have it rather than some land-bound peddler. And you know, there's some ships a strangey will not come near. Strange in look, strange in habit, strangey by name. That's what we say, we boatpeople.'

'How marvelous,' she breathed. 'And probably it isn't bones at all.'

'Likely,' he agreed. 'But it is something they make in their insides or swallow from some deep place in the River.'

He knew there was more to it than that. When night came, he wrote in his book, all his wonderings about it, but he said nothing of these to Medoor Babji.

7

Baris Tower shone in the light of first summer sun, its stones newly washed by rain. About its roof the fliers clustered, perching on the inner parapet, keeping watch as they had been commanded to do. Something about Baris had been doubtful for a considerable time now. From faroff Chancery word had come to the Talons. Baris was suspect. The one called Gendra Mitiar had sent the word. So much all the fliers knew. What was suspected, they did not know, except that it was something to do with the Superior of the Tower, with the human called Kesseret.

And yet it was Kesseret who had told them of the expedition over the River, to Southshore. 'It's only the Noor who are going,' she had said. 'And they are of no use to you, anyway. However, it might give other people bad ideas. You had best take word to the Talkers of this . . .'

This word had gone to the Talons, Black Talons and Gray, Blue and Red. In each it had led to much screaming argument on the Stones of Disputation. If a human was guilty of heresy, surely she would not have given such important information? If she had given such important information, then could she be guilty of heresy? Such nice distinctions, though they were the stuff of life to Talkers, were beyond fliers' comprehension or interest. They had been told to watch. Unwillingly, they watched.

Kessie, well aware of their constant surveillance, paid no more attention than was occasionally necessary. The story about the expedition of the Noor had done its planned work of distraction. She saw fliers constantly at the Riverside, spying on the boats that came and went. Reports would be going back to the Talons; speculation among the Talkers would be rife. So, their attention was where Tharius Don had wanted it. Now she had only to hang on, letting time wear by, praying he would not delay much longer, trying to figure out why he had delayed so long. Did he fear death that much? Surely not; surely not the idealist, Tharius Don. She could not answer the question that came back to her, again and again. Why had he delayed so long?

The business of the Tower crept on at the pace of a tree's growth, slow, unobservable. She tried to keep up appearances, with everything as it had been before. She let herself become a bit negligent in recruiting, but that could be laid to her experiences with the traitor junior, Pamra Don. Her servant, Threnot, seemed to spend more time than ever walking around Baristown in her veils and robes, but if the Superior wished to gather information, no one would question that too strongly. The Superior herself looked unwell, old, somehow, which might be explained by the strain of the long journey that had returned her to Baris.

Or could be explained by the fact that the elixir, sent from the Chancery through the office of Gendra Mitiar, was not efficacious. It seemed to have been adulterated. Kessie sent frantic word through secret routes. She did not mind dying, but she did not want to do it until after the strike. Her life had been given to the cause. She must see its fulfillment.

In time, another vial of elixir arrived from Tharius Don, but the damage had been done. She looked in the mirror at the lines graven around her eyes and mouth, the fine crepe of her skin. No pretense would convince her ever again that she was young. She regretted this. When the end came, she had wanted both of them to appear, at least for a time, as they had when they loved one another so dearly. It had been a culmination, a picture in her mind. A honeymoon. Ah, well; ah, well. She offered it up to the cause, along with her twisted fingers and toes.

'How long, lady?' begged Threnot. She was an old woman, eighty at least. She wished to live long enough to see the end, to see the Thraish confounded, to see the pits emptied. She was glad to see the lines around Kessie's eyes. They were like the lines around her own, confirming them sisters grown old in the cause.

'Soon, Threnot. Tharius Don tells me that Pamra Don is only a few weeks' journey from the Chancery. He admits to selfishness, but says he wishes to have her in his protection before the strike. There are one or two other things he's waiting on. If possible, he wants to locate the stolen herd beasts and eliminate them from consideration. He thinks if the Thraish have any beasts at all, they may place great weight upon some impossible future and delay acceding to reality.' And when he has done that, she thought despairingly, will he find some other reason for delay?

'They would.' Threnot nodded. 'Those filth bags would rather do anything than what good Tharius Don expects them to do.' Threnot had never met Tharius Don, but she had long been Kessie's confidante.

'When they are Treeci, they will not be filth bags anymore,' Kessie admonished, surprised that she had come to believe this. She had longed for this faith, the faith of Tharius Don, and perhaps it had come as a reward for her suffering. 'When they have become Treeci,' she said again, rejoicing in the calm confidence of her voice.

8

In the Tower at Thou-ne, Haranjus Pandel reflected on transiency. The sun was far sunk in the south. First summer had gone, and the rainy winds of autumn gathered about the tower, making the shutters creak and cold drafts creep through the stone corridors. Thunderheads massed over the River and surged over Northshore, sailing away into the north in mighty continents of cloud. Ill luck gathering, he thought. Like fliers. Dark and ominous. For days, weeks, fliers had been gathering upon the Black Talons to the east of the town, coming and going. He had never seen so many, not even at Conjunction when they came, so he believed, to breed. It was not the only strange thing to have happened recently.

A few weeks ago had come a Laugher, down from the northlands, cut off from further travel east, so he said, by the towering height of the Talons.

'I demand your assistance, Superior.'

He was like all of them, hot and bitter, his eyes like burning coals in the furnace of his face.

'How may I assist the servant of the Chancery?' Haranjus had asked, taking refuge in formality. It would not do to be indiscreet to a Laugher. It was not smart to relax convention or ritual. 'The Laugher's need is my command.'

'I need to get word to the Talkers, up there,' and he had pointed to the heights of the Talons, looming at Thou-ne's eastern border.

'I . . . I can summon a flier,' Haranjus had stuttered. He

had expected anything but this, anything at all. 'What is it you wish me to say?'

'I will say it myself. Just take me to the roof and summon one of them, however it is you do it.'

There was a way, of course. Twice each month, Haranjus was expected to provide a living body for the Talker's meat. He saw that these bodies were taken, almost always, from among the travelers through Thou-ne. The town was too small to accommodate the loss, otherwise. Certainly it was too small to accommodate it without comment. Now that the Temple attracted so many travelers, it was no trick to abduct one here, one there, as they traveled on westward. His few trusted seniors had become expert at the exercise.

And when the living bodies were ready, they were trussed up on the roof of the Tower and fliers were called. At evening. In the lowe of sunset, so the fliers might return to the Talons with their burden well after dark.

'Yes. There is a bell,' Haranjus said. 'But I don't have . . . I mean, there's no reason to call them. They may be very angry.'

'Leave their anger to me,' said Ilze. 'They will be more angry yet when they hear what I have to tell them.'

He went with Haranjus to the roof, not unlike the roof at Baris, surrounded by a low parapet, fouled with shit, littered with feathers, and reeking with the musty, permeating smell of Thraish. They waited there, not speaking, Ilze because he had no inclination to speak, Haranjus because he was afraid to. When the blaze of sunset was at its height, Haranjus struck the bell.

The plangent tone stole outward, away from the Tower, rising like a bird, lifted upon the air, winging to the Talons tops, a reverberation now softly, now loudly feeding upon itself, intensifying its own sound with echoes. When the blaze of the west began to dim, dark wings detached themselves from the distant peaks and came toward the tower. When those wings folded upon the tower top it was almost dark. The flier croaked, 'It is not time for meat.'

'This man asked for you,' Haranjus said. 'I have brought

him at his command, as I am sworn to do.' He turned then and left the roof. Whatever it was, he didn't want to be involved in it. Nothing could have stopped him from listening at the door, however. He leaned there, ear applied to the crack, holding his breath.

'I have a message for Sliffisunda of the Talons,' Ilze said. 'There is heresy abroad upon Northshore, and Sliffisunda of the Talons must be told of it.'

The fliers gabbled, croaked, not sure of whether they would or would not.

'Sliffisunda will command it if you tell him I am here,' Ilze said at last. 'He knows me. Return and ask him.'

Sliffisunda, it appeared, could be asked. He was at Black Talons. He had come there fairly recently. The fliers would return and ask him, albeit unwillingly. Sliffisunda was evidently in a temper.

'Tell him to send a basket for me!' shouted Ilze as the great wings lifted from the Tower. He stumped to the door and down the stairs, finding Haranjus somewhat out of breath in the study at their foot.

'Give me food,' Ilze commanded. 'And something to drink. They'll be back within the hour.'

'You're going to the Talons?' He could not help himself. Despite all promises to himself not to ask questions, his traitor tongue did it for him.

'One way or the other,' Ilze sneered. 'It was here the crusade started, wasn't it? I shouldn't wonder if you were involved in it.'

'Oh, no. No. A man came from the Chancery. He said I did right to ignore it . . .'

'Fools! What do they think is happening here? The roots of our society are being nibbled away, and they say to ignore it?'

'It seemed very – innocent.'

Ilze barked. It could have been a laugh. Like a stilt-lizard, ha-ha, ha-ha. 'When all the fliers are dead and the elixir gone forever, then tell me how innocent it was, fool.' Ilze, like many of the lower ranks of the Chancery staff, was naive enough to suppose that all Tower Superiors received the elixir. Haranjus Pandel did not disillusion him. Belatedly, firmly, he shut his mouth.

In an hour the fliers arrived with a large basket clasped in their claws. Moments later, the Laugher was gone, carried away in that same basket. Shortly after that, Haranjus sent a full account of his visit, via the signal towers, to Gendra Mitiar, knowing it would reach others as well.

9

Ilze was unceremoniously tumbled from the basket to sprawl upon a high, dung-streaked shelf of stone. Half a dozen fliers stood about, shifting from foot to foot and darting their heads at him as though he were prey. Ilze drew his knife and made a darting motion in return, at which there was a great outcawing of mockery. This, in turn, brought a Talker, who dismissed the fliers – to their evident annoyance – and escorted Ilze through a jagged opening in the cliffside along a rough, narrow corridor that appeared to be a natural cleft in the stone only slightly improved by artifice. A number of small rooms opened from this cleft, rooms with smoothed floors and blackened corners showing where fires had been laid in the past. Rough hangings closed each of these niches from the corridor, and piles of rugs along the walls made it clear the rooms were for the use of human visitors. Or slaves, Ilze told himself. Or meat.

He was left alone here, the Talker taking himself off without a word. Ilze was content with this. If they were interested in what he had to say, they would listen to him sooner rather than later. Though he feared them, it was worth the gamble to find and hold Pamra Don. He could not go on living until that was done.

A scrape at the doorway drew his attention, and he regarded the pallid man who entered with suspicion.

'Who are you?' They both asked it, at once. It was impossible for both of them to answer, and there was an itchy pause during which each waited for the other.

'You!' grated Ilze with an impatient gesture. 'Who are you?'

The pallid man answered, words tumbling over one another as though long dammed up behind the barrier of his throat. 'My name is Frule. Which tells you nothing much. I am a scholar. A student, you might say. I live here. I study the Thraish.'

Ilze snorted. 'And they allow that?'

'They might not, if they knew that's what I was really doing. However, I am an acceptable stonemason and a fair carpenter. The Thraish have a need for both.'

'For what?' Ilze stared around him, making an incredulous face. 'Do they live better than their guests?'

'Differently.' The other shrugged. 'Who are you?'

'I am Ilze, formerly of the Tower of Baris. I've come to bring the creatures news of something that much affects them,' he said in a challenging voice. 'In return for which I hope they will help me with my business.'

'Which is?'

'Finding and avenging myself on one Pamra Don.'

'Oh. The crusade woman.' The pallid man nodded wisely. 'We've heard of that business, even here. What has she done to you?'

'That's my business.' Had he tried, Ilze would have been unable to answer the question. It was one he had never asked himself. Pamra had been the cause of pain and unpleasantness. She was, therefore, fit subject for vengeance, no matter that she had done nothing at all to Ilze. 'My business,' he repeated abstractedly.

'Let it be your business, then,' said Frule. 'I only asked because it helps to know what brings humans here. The Thraish have few human visitors. I have seen only one or two. There are a few others like me, who pretend to be craftsmen. And a few who really are craftsmen, not that the Thraish can tell the difference.'

'Stupid animals,' Ilze snorted.

'No,' said the other in a calm, considering voice. 'Not, I think, stupid. Simply not very interested in most of the things humans are interested in. Though I can understand much of what they say to one another, when one has been here a time, one longs for human speech. And yet, as I remember it, we humans spend much time talking of sex or politics – that may not be true in the Chancery, of course.' This was a polite aside with a little bow to Ilze. 'The Talkers have no sex, and their politics are rudimentary. They do not talk of things most of us would find interesting. They talk of philosophical things. The nature of reality. The actuality of God. How Potipur differs in his essential nature from Viranel. Whether perception guarantees reality. Things of that kind . . .'

'I find that hard to believe,' Ilze said with a sneer. 'They do not look or behave like philosophers.'

'But then, how should philosophers look or behave? We cannot expect the Thraish to behave as if they were human. If human philosophers perched on high stones, engaging in screaming matches, shitting on each other's feet the while, they would be discredited, but for the Thraish that's ordinary enough behavior.'

'And they talk only of philosophy.'

'And food, of course. They talk a great deal about food.'

'Dead bodies,' snorted Ilze.

'No. They scarcely mention what they eat now. All their talk is of what was eaten long ago, when there were herdbeasts on the steppes. They recall the taste of weehar with religious fervor. There is something deeply and sincerely religious among the Thraish, and it wells up from that belief they call the Promise of Potipur.' The man nodded to himself, reflecting. 'Do you know that promise? "Do my will and ye shall have plenty." That seems to be the core of it. And the will of Potipur involves breeding large numbers of themselves, too many for this world to sustain, which destroyed their plenty before. I think sometimes how hard it must be for them to keep to that belief when there have been no herdbeasts on the steppes for centuries. But, I understand, there may be beasts soon again.'

Ilze had not heard this rumor. Frule enlightened him,

telling him what had been overheard. 'They don't seem to care what we overhear. Sometimes I don't think they believe we are sentient,' he commented, shaking his head. 'They don't seem to consider what we might tell other humans about them when we leave here.'

'Perhaps they have ethics which would make such a thing impossible,' Ilze suggested with a sneer.

'Possibly.' The man shrugged. 'It is true that the Thraish cannot conceive of a nest sibling giving anything of value to others outside that nest, and that would probably include information. They cannot conceive of it because no Thraish would do it, for any price. Perhaps they consider us human workers as a kind of nest sibling because they feed us. Perhaps they consider us an emotional equivalent to nestlings. On the other hand, there is a kind of scavenger lizard, the ghroosh, which lives in Thraish nests, feeding on the offal that is left there, and perhaps they consider us in that light. Perhaps we are merely tolerated. Ah, well, whatever the truth of that may be, it is interesting to meet you, good to see a new face.'

'How many humans are there here? And what do you eat?'

'Oh, we bring some food with us. And the fliers catch stilt-lizards for us, or we climb down to the River to catch fish. Though we have to eat it there. The Thraish will not allow it in the Talons. As for how many of us? A dozen or so, sometimes more, sometimes fewer. I've been here two years myself, building perches and feeding troughs, mostly. Though it's interesting, I've stayed long enough. It's getting time to go.'

'Go where?' Ilze was suddenly very interested. Did the Chancery know of these human lice, creeping among the feathers of the Thraish?

'Back home,' the scholar said with a vague gesture. He peered closely at Ilze, not reassured by what he saw in the Laugher's face. 'You wouldn't be of a mind to make trouble for me with the fliers, would you, Laugher? For my saying I'm studying the Thraish.'

'Is it in accord with doctrine?'

'I've never been told it's forbidden.'

'Which is not the same thing,' Ilze sneered. 'I've other stuff on my plate just now, *student*. I will remember you are here, however, when my current task is done.' He turned away in contempt, and when he turned again, the man was gone. Ilze threw himself down on the piled rugs and waited, not patiently. When the day had half gone, a flier pushed into the room, perhaps the same one who had led Ilze here.

'Sliffisunda of the Talons will see you, human. Follow me.'

Which Ilze was hard-pressed to do. Twice he had to be lifted in the claws of the fliers before he was deposited at last on an elevated ledge above a yawning gulf. A jagged hole led to a space among the stones where Sliffisunda stood before a curtained opening. Ilze was not invited to enter, and he shivered in the chill wind of the heights.

'You wish to report heresy,' it croaked at him. 'Heresy, Laugher?'

'There's that woman, Pamra Don,' Ilze snarled without preliminary chat. 'She's guilty of heresy. This crusade of hers is a heresy. The Talkers – all the Thraish – will soon learn to regret it.'

'We have listened to what she says, Laugher. It is nothing much. Meantime, pits are full. Fliers find much meat.'

'You have listened to what she says in the public squares, Sliffisunda. You have not heard what she says in the Temples.'

'Tower people tell us, nothing much.'

'Then Tower people lie.'

Sliffisunda hissed, head darting forward as though he would strike. 'Why would they lie?'

'Because they have been corrupted, stolen from the faith. They are not believers in Potipur. They dissemble, Talker. Pamra Don is a heretic, and she leads a band of heretics.'

'And yet pits are full.'

Ilze gestured impatiently. 'Of course. For a little time. Until she gains strength. Then there will be no more bodies in the pits at all.'

Ilze had expected rage. There was no rage. The Talker hissed once more, then turned his head away. For a time

315

there was silence. 'How long, Laugher, before this crusade does, as you say, "gain strength"?'

'Years,' Ilze admitted. 'It moves slowly, true. And yet, not many years. It will get all the way around the world in twelve or fifteen years, if it continues at its current pace.'

'And in that time, we may expect pits to be full?'

'Probably. But that's temporary, and purely local. Only where the crusade is passing at any given time.'

'Ah.' The Talker turned away again, hiding his face so the human would not see his expression. One might let the crusade alone. In fifteen years, when it had rounded the world, the Thraish would be ready to strike at them all. In the meantime, many humans would have died and been eaten, the fewer to fight later. However, Thraish numbers could not be increased on the basis of purely local plenty, and if some accident happened, if breeding stock were lost to winter cold, then fifteen years might be too soon.

On balance, it might be better if the crusade were stopped. On balance, it might be better if things were as usual for the next few years. Peaceful. The humans kept biddable and quiet. It was something for the Stones of Disputation, something he could discuss with his colleagues of the Sixth Degree.

'You wish to stop this thing, Laugher?'

'I can stop it, yes.'

'How?'

'Pamra Don is being taken by Jondarites to the Chancery. You Talkers must demand she be turned over to you. It was she, after all, who emptied the pits at Baris. You have just ground for complaint. Demand she be given to you. Then give her to me!'

If Sliffisunda could have smiled, he would have done so. Transparent, this one. And still as fiery as when the Talkers and Accusers had done with him, before he was made a Laugher. Set on the trail of Pamra Don, nothing would stay him, not even his fear of the Talkers.

'Do you not fear us?' he asked now. 'We gave you much pain.'

316

'Necessary,' Ilze said with an angry flush. 'It was necessary. Not your fault. Pamra's fault.' There was a little fleck of foam at the corner of his mouth. He felt it there, wiped it away, struggling to remain calm.

'And if we took this Pamra Don, but did not give her to you?'

'You owe her to me,' Ilze whined, the words vomited out unwillingly in a detested, shameful tone he could no more control than he could withhold. He willed himself to silence and heard his own voice once more. 'You set me looking for her. You owe her to me.'

'Perhaps,' soothed Sliffisunda, chuckling inwardly. 'Perhaps we do. We'll see, Laugher. Remain with us for now, while we discuss this matter.'

'If you will provide for me.' Sulkily, this.

'Oh, we will provide.' This time chuckling audibly, Sliffisunda turned away through the heavy curtain. In time some fliers came to take Ilze back to his room.

In a high, narrow shaft cut into the bones of the mountain, Frule edged himself away from the hole leading to Sliffisunda's aerie. It had taken him a year and a half to open the cleft wide enough that he could climb it. It was hidden on three sides and from above. Only the fourth side gaped toward the north, and Frule braced himself against the stone as he withdrew a small mirror from his pocket, breathing upon it, then polishing it vigorously upon his sleeve. He cocked an eye at the sun, then tilted the mirror to catch it and fling the dazzling beam into the empty northlands. Flash, flash, again and again, long and short, spelling out his message. After a time he stopped, waiting. From a distant peak came an answering flash, one, two, and three.

Frule sighed, hiding the mirror once more in his tunic. He had had more excitement in this one morning than in the last two years put together. Gratifying, in a way. There had been very little to report to Ezasper Jorn since the Ambassador to the Thraish had recommended him to Sliffisunda as a competent workman, luring his spy, Frule, to take the job by promise of much reward when the duty was done.

317

Much reward.

There could be only one reward. The elixir. Something of that magnitude was what it would take to pay him for these two cold, comfortless, stinking years! And yet, it would have been difficult to argue for such a reward had there been no results, no juicy, blood-hot information.

He shivered, half anticipation, half cold, drawing his cloak more closely around him. It would be some time before his message could be received at its ultimate destination and new instructions transmitted. Still, better wait where he was. Getting into the cleft required a hard climb up a rock chimney with his shoulders and feet levering him upward in increments of skin-scraping inches. He had managed to get into position today barely in time to hear the conversation between the visitor and the Talker. Better stay where he was. He lost himself in dreams of fortune, eyes glazing with thoughts of the elixir. He dozed.

He did not wake even when the claws dragged him out of the cleft and over the cliff to bounce upon a hundred projections before his pulped body came to rest far below.

'A spy,' said Sliffisunda mildly. 'I knew he was there, somewhere. I heard him breathing. And I smelled him. He was very excited about something.'

10

Looking at my carvings today, wondering which ones I ought to give away, I came across the little boat I'd carved, oh, fifteen years ago, maybe. The Procession boat. Always meant to get some gold paint for it, but never did.

I remember that Procession. I saw the Protector of Man with my own eyes. I don't know where I was when he came around before – I'd have been old enough to remember if I'd seen him, so I suppose I didn't. The golden boat was as long as a pier, and it shone like the sun itself, all full of Chancery people in robes and high feathers. It was a wonderful thing to see, and all the shore was lined with people chanting and waving. But when I saw it, I remember wondering what it was all those people did, there in the Chancery, there in the northlands. No farmers among them, that's for sure, nor boatmen, either. Soft hands and pale faces, all of them, so they aren't people who work. So I said to Obers-rom, what do you suppose they do with their time, those people? And he said, whatever it is, it won't help you or me, Thrasne. And I suppose that's right.

But I still wonder what they do.

From Thrasne's book

Word reached Ezasper Jorn late in the evening, carried down endless flights of stairs, through door after door, shut against the cold of polar winter, the message carefully transcribed onto handmade paper, the missive properly folded and sealed. Jorn liked these little niceties, the sense of drama conveyed in folded, sealed documents, ribbons dangling from the wax, the color of the ribbons betokening what lay within. These ribbons were red. Something vital. Something bloody, perhaps. He played with the heavy paper for a moment, sliding his thumbnail beneath the seal, teasing himself.

So, Frule had at last acquitted himself well! Ezasper Jorn had almost given up hope of receiving any sensible information from the man, not that it was his fault. Ezasper had visited an aerie in the Talons, once. They were not made for two-legged spies, and Ezasper had no source of winged ones. Frule must have carved himself a spy hole somewhere. Ezasper grinned, for the moment almost warm enough in the flush of his enthusiasm.

Now. Now. Where could the information best be used? He peered into the corridor for a long moment before slithering along to Koma Nepor's suite, knocking there for an unconscionable time before the Research Chief heard him and let him in. Ezasper gave him the letter, reading it again over his shoulder, jigging with pleasure.

'I think we'll give it to Gendra, don't you? Part of a package? Later we'll get old Glamdrul to tell her there's heresy all right, started in Baris. She'll like that. She's dying for a reason to get rid of the Superior in Baris, dying to rub Tharius Don's face in it, too. Then we'll suggest it would be a good idea if she went there herself.'

'She won't leave the Chancery,' Nepor objected. 'She won't leave the center of power when the power is looking for a center, old fish. No. Never. She won't.'

'Ah, but might she not go in order to obtain the support of the Thraish for her candidacy?'

'How would she do that?'

'Read what's in front of you, nit. She will gain the support of the Thraish by delivering Pamra Don into their claws. In return for supporting her, of course. All other things being equal, it's a strategy which just might work.

320

The assembly likes things peaceful between us and the Thraish. It would get her some votes, if she were around to get them – which she won't be.'

'Because while she's gone, we'll do away with Obol and see that you, old fish, that you're named Protector, is that it?' Nepor rubbed his hands together, jigging from foot to foot in his excitement. 'Oh, that will be a turn.'

Ezasper Jorn sat down ponderously, pulling his cap firmly down to cover his ears and stretching his legs toward the fire. Even in these vaults, far below the earth, the cold crept in as the winter lengthened. 'Well, Tharius will vote for himself, you may be sure of that. Obol will be dead. Gendra will be gone. That's three.'

'Bossit will vote for himself. You and I will vote for you, Jorn. That's six, and two votes for you.'

'Leaving Jondrigar.'

'Oh, that's a difficult one. I should think the general will not vote for anyone.'

'Ah, ah, but you see, I have this letter.'

'A letter? What letter, Jorn?'

'This letter from Lees Obol. To the general.'

'When did Lees Obol last write anything? Come now, Jorn. Would you try our credulity?'

'Nepor, if you ask the general, "Can the Protector of Man write a letter?" what will the general say?'

'He would say the Protector could write a letter, or ride a weehar bull over the pass, or thump down a mountain with his fists. He would say the protector could do anything at all. I think he believes it, too.'

'He does, yes. He has that happy faculty of never confusing reality with his preconceptions. General Jondrigar will believe in the letter, leave that to me.'

'And the letter will say?'

'That Lees Obol, feeling himself fading away, chooses to recommend to the general that he vote for Ezasper Jorn as the next Protector of Man.'

'That's three of you,' said Nepor admiringly. 'And only two against.'

'But a very strong two,' Ezasper mused, holding out his hands to the fire. 'Bossit. And Tharius Don. Perhaps I can find some reason that Tharius Don would consider it wise to support me . . .' He stared into the dancing flames, lost in contemplation. Koma Nepor, familiar with this state of reflective trance in his companion, snuggled more deeply into his chair to consider which of the several strains of blight he had available to him would be best to use in ridding themselves of Lees Obol.

Ezasper Jorn carried the message to Gendra Mitiar the following morning, wending his way through endless tunnels from the roots of the palace to the roots of the Bureau of Towers, finding Gendra Mitiar at last in a room warmed almost to blood heat by a dozen braziers, ventilated by the constant whir of great fans turned by her slaves. Gendra was undergoing a massage at the hands and feet of Jhilt, the Noor. Though Jhilt was sweating and panting from her exertions, the sheet-covered heap that was Gendra's ancient body showed no signs of perceiving her exhaustion.

'Message from the Talons,' he said, trying to fit his words between the slap, slap, slap, wrench, crunch, grunt that Jhilt continued.

'Ahum,' Gendra responded.

'Important, Gendra. You should listen.'

'Don't care about the stupid fliers.'

'Don't care about being the next Protector of Man, perhaps?'

'Enough, Jhilt,' Gendra said, slapping the woman's hands away. 'Get out of here.' She sat up, wrapped in the sheet, her ravaged face peering from the top of it like the head of an enshrouded worker, looking no less dead than many did. 'What was that you said?'

'I merely asked if you were not concerned with the possibility of being our next Protector. Koma Nepor and I have talked it over. In return for some arrangement which we can undoubtedly agree upon, we two would be willing to support you for that position. Entirely quid pro quo, Gendra.

You know me well enough to know I am not altruistic.' He made a long face, appearing both shamed and somehow ennobled by this admission, sighing deeply the while. She regarded him suspiciously, and he made a disarming gesture. 'I have no chance at the position myself, and making an arrangement to support you would be more profitable for me than seeing Tharius Don as Protector.' He turned away, watching her from the corner of his eye. It was not necessary to see her, for she ground her teeth at the mention of Tharius Don. He went on, 'Of course, this is all somewhat premature. I have every reason to believe Lees Obol will live for two or three years yet. Still, it is not too early to plan. Proper planning will, I am sure, assure your nomination. However, nomination by the council is only a first step. Election by the assembly is necessary. As Ambassador to the Thraish, I feel it would be important to convince the assembly you have the endorsement of the Thraish as well.'

'And how is that happy eventuality to be achieved?'

He handed her the message, its open seal still dripping red ribbons across the words. 'My spy, Frule, has overheard a conversation between the Laugher Ilze and our old friend Sliffisunda.'

She took the paper from his hand, screwing her eyes into it, pulling the content of the words out of the paper like a cork from a bottle, weighing, evaluating. When she had read it once, she cast Ezasper Jorn a suspicious glance and read it again.

'What here can be used to my advantage, Jorn? I don't see it.'

'If you were to deliver the woman to them yourself, Gendra? Having made somewhat of a bargain with them? Their support for yours. Tharius Don won't let this Pamra Don go easily, you know. He wants her in his own hands. So much was clear at our last meeting.'

'True. He has some unexplained interest there. I've asked Glamdrul Feynt to look into it, but the old bastard dithers and forgets. Still, I'll threaten Feynt a bit and see what emerges. So. So. You think my turning the woman

over to them would gain their favor, eh?' She had quite
another reason for wanting the favor of the Thraish, but she
did not intend to discuss that with Ezasper Jorn.

'Something for something, Gendra. If you want our support, Nepor's and mine, you'll have to offer something.
We'll talk again.' He left her chewing on that, figuring how
to outwit him in the long run, so taken with her own cleverness she couldn't think for a moment he had already out-
witted her.

The corridors of the Bureau of Towers were long and
echoing, the stairs even longer. When he came to the
bottom of the sixth flight, three levels below winter quarters, smelling the opulent dust of the files, he was too out
of breath to summon Glamdrul Feynt for a time. He contented himself with leaning on a table while his heart
slowed, then banged the nearest door in its frame three or
four times, hearing the echoes slam down the endless corridors, ricocheting fragments in an avalanche of sound.

When the sound died it was resurrected, coming from the
opposite direction, another door slammed somewhere far
away, and the sound of Feynt's voice, 'Hoo, hoo, hoo,' as
he stumbled nearer. When he saw who it was, he straight-
ened and stopped limping. 'So, Jorn. What's on your
mind?'

They sat on a filthy bench, staring at dust motes like
schools of silver fish in a slanting beam that struck from a
high lantern into the well of the files, talking of Gendra
Mitiar, of fliers, of this and that.

'So you've got it all planned, have you?'

'If you'll tell her there's heresy in Baris, yes. That'll do
the trick. She'll trot off to the fliers with Pamra Don, and
she'll keep right on going. Oh, she can't wait to set her claws
into that woman in Baris.'

'And you'll be the next Protector, then?'

'Sure as can be. We count three votes for it, against two at
the council. Of course, the assembly's something else, but
we can manage that.'

'And what's in it for old Feynt, Jorn? Oh, I know you've

talked dribs of this and drabs of that, but what's in it for me, I want to know?'

'Elixir, Feynt. All of that you want. What else can I do for you? Some other job? No reason you have to stick down here, is there?'

'Nobody else knows where anything is, you know that, Jorn.' It was said with a kind of belligerent pride.

'Does it matter?' It was said all unheeding, Jorn so drunk with his own plotting he didn't think. He was watching the dust motes, thinking of himself on the royal Progression, dressed all in gold and held up by the Jondarites to the acclaim of the mobs. He did not see the wrinkle come between Feynt's old eyebrows or the hateful gleam that winked once across his eyes. *Did it matter?* Did a man's life matter? Over a hundred years spent on these files, and did it matter?

When Ezasper Jorn left in a little time, he did not know he had made an enemy of what had been, at worst, a malicious but disinterested man.

11

Among the more respected followers of the crusade were
several scribes, including a light-colored spy sent by Queen
Fibji and at least one adventurer from the island chain.
Night found these assigned recorders, among others who
kept records for their own various reasons, hunched over
their individual campfires or crouched into the pools of their
lantern's light, scribbling an account of the day's sayings.
Some of them had not seen Pamra Don herself, so they
wrote what others said of her, of her and Lila.

'She shines with a holy radiance,' some wrote, confusing
the shining statue that had appeared in Thou-ne with the
woman it had likened. 'The child is a messenger of God,
sent into her keeping, an unearthly being, of an immortal
kind.' In which they were more accurate than they realized,
though Lila's unearthly nature came from a source closer to
them than the God of man.

'The Noor are personifications of the darkness,' they
scribbled. Queen Fibji's spy gritted his teeth as he made
note of this particular doctrine. It was a new teaching.
Peasimy Flot had been stopped by a troop of Melancholics
in a town market square as they were passing through.
Unwisely, the Melancholics had suggested the crusaders be
whipped for holiness's sake. Peasimy had peered into their
dark, grinning faces and had turned away with revulsion,
shivering. 'These are devils,' he cried. 'The darkness creeps
out of their skins.' The word had spread rapidly through the
following, and since that time, the crusade had gone out of
its way to surround and brutalize troupes of Melancholics,

beating them with their own whips. When the spy for Queen Fibji had written it all down, he rolled the account into a lightweight tube made of bone and attached it to the legs of a seeker bird. The Queen would soon have this news to add to her many burdens. The writer considered it more ominous than most information he had provided.

After sending the bird off, he went back into his little tent and shaved his head. His skin was light enough not to appear Noorish, but nothing could have disguised the long, crinkly strands of Noor hair. He would follow yet awhile. The whole movement had a feeling about it, as before a storm when the quiet becomes ominous. He slept badly, dreaming of that storm but unable to remember its conclusion when he wakened.

12

Out here, on the water, I think about things a lot, things that didn't bear thinking of when we were closer to shore. The nights are bigger here, and the daytimes, too. Space is bigger. I feel as though the inside of me – what's in my head – is bigger out here than it was on Northshore. Perhaps because it's quieter, here. Perhaps the quiet entices the shy thoughts out, ideas that never come out when there are people around . . .

Like the truth of what I felt . . . feel for Pamra Don. When she came, it was like there was a woman-shaped hole in my life, just waiting. Like a flower waits for a beetle to come along and land on it. Not doing anything, you understand. Just blooming, all that color around an emptiness. The emptiness has to be there, ready for something to move into. That's the way it was with me; all my bloom surrounded this Pamra-shaped hole. When she came along, that was the space that was empty. I guess things always nest or build or roost in spaces that are unoccupied, so that's where she roosted. You can't expect the beetle to love the flower or the bird to love the branch. The branch and the flower are just there, that's all. Does the flower need the bug? Maybe so. Maybe the branch needs the bird, too. But the bug and bird don't know that. Or care.

Maybe what happens between people, men and women, is often like that, one having a certain place that needs filling and another coming along who seems to fill it – for a while, at least.

From Thrasne's book

328

When Pamra Don arrived at the Split River Pass it was the beginning of second summer, the seventh month. Behind the Teeth of the North, polar winter had given way to thaw and the promise of spring. On the steppes, the rains of autumn made room for the balmier days to follow. Pamra went crowned with flowers, for each day some one among her followers created a chaplet for her, a task begun as one follower's happy inspiration and continued thereafter as custom. Each night the faded wreath was taken away by its creator to be pressed between boards and kept forever. Or so it was thought at the time.

The Jondarite captain, commander of her escort, had orders to bring her only so far as the cupped, alluvial plain at the foot of the pass. No one had known how long the journey would take, and it had been thought possible they might arrive during polar winter when the road to the Chancery was impassable. He sent word, therefore, upon arrival at the edge of Split River, and set up camp to await a reply. Pamra's followers, who had been strung out in a procession many days long upon the road, began to agglomerate on the banks of Split River and around the tall, flat-topped buttes that dotted this stretch of steppe with brooding, sharp-edged cliffs. Soon the vacant lands had the look of a settlement, with tents springing up like mushrooms, fishermen and washerwomen at the waterside, children climbing rocks and chasing birds, and small groups constantly coming and going from their search for food in the surrounding foothills and valleys.

When word came to the Chancery of the arrival of this mob, Tharius Don, after some deliberation, sent word for the Jondarite captain to see that the multitude was fed from the Chancery warehouse at the foot of the pass, 'for the prevention of disorder, and lest hunger lead large numbers of people to attempt an ascent of the pass.'

Not that Jondarites weren't quite capable of killing several thousand of them, but disposal of the bodies would be a problem, and there was no sense in letting scavengers ruin the surrounding countryside. So Tharius Don said, at some length, whenever anyone was inclined to listen.

Only then did he send a litter for Pamra Don, instructing the Jondarite captain to escort her to him, at the palace, as soon as might be. This order was countersigned by General Jondrigar. The captain would have ignored it, otherwise.

'What're you going to do with her?' the general wanted to know. 'Stirred up a lot of trouble, evidently, and showed up here with a mob. Better let me have the lot of 'em put down.' He said this with a flick of his curiously reptilian eyes. 'Save trouble.'

Tharius shook his head. 'No! We need to know many things about this crusade, General. We will not find them out by violence. Just get the young woman here, safely into my hands, please. As Propagator of the Faith, this is my province, and I have Lees Obol's instructions to take care of such matters.' As indeed he did, though the last such order had been issued fifty years before. Still, none of Obol's orders had ever been rescinded, and the least word of the Protector was supposed to be considered a command forever. Tharius used the Protector's name now in order to assure obedience from Jondrigar, knowing that unless Lees Obol himself contradicted what Tharius had just said, Pamra Don was as good as in his hands.

In which intention, Tharius succeeded better than he had planned. The general was so impressed by the use of the Protector's name – little enough referred to in recent years – that he decided to go over the pass and fetch the woman himself.

He set out upon the morning, riding a weehar ox, his plumed headdress nodding in time with the slow stride of the beast, as unvarying a pace as the sun's movement in its ponderous half circle above the mountains, from twilight to twilight. Soon this half-light would pass, and the Chancery lands would lie beneath a sun that did not set, but the general was content to relish this season of spring dusk. In it his accompanying men moved like shuffling shadows, their individuality lost, becoming one multilegged beast which tramped its way up the long, winding road toward Split River

Pass. At such times the general knew the immortality of now. There was no past, no future, and he was content to let time fade into nothing. There was only this plod, plod, plod, his own pulsebeat magnified into something mighty and eternal. Armies, he thought, turning the word over in his mind as though it had been the name of God. Armies. Mighty, inexorable, obdurate. It was as though his own body had been multiplied a thousand times, and he felt the multiplied strength bursting through his veins at each beat of the footfall drum. It was better, even, than battle, this slow marching, and in the dim light below the plumed helm, the general could have been seen to be smiling.

Behind him in the palace, Tharius Don supervised his servants in making ready the suite Pamra Don would occupy, vacant since Kessie's departure. It was chill from the winter, dusty from disuse. Out the window he could watch the slow snake of Jondarites as it wound its way up the pass. A day to the top, a day down the other side. A day there, changing the guard, seeing to the warehouses. Then two days to return.

'The cover on this chair is split,' he said to the housekeeper. 'Have it recovered and returned here within three days. Oh, and Matron, the paint on that window needs to be redone.' The window frame was blackened by fire. The ledge below, also, where the flame-bird's nest had burned. As he stood there, a flame-bird darted down the wall, the first bird of summer, shimmering across his sight like a vision, blurred by tears. 'Stupid,' he cursed at himself, wiping the moisture away. 'Stupid.' He had been thinking of Kessie.

Someone else at the Chancery also thought of the lady Kesseret. In her high solarium, still too cool for real enjoyment, though the view was, as always, enthralling, Gendra Mitiar stood peering out at the marching Jondarites. Shifting from bony buttock to bony buttock on a bench nearby, Glamdrul Feynt pretended a lack of interest. A litter of paper scraps around the bench testified to the fact he had been there for a time he considered unnecessary and unconscionable.

'I have to get back to the files, Mitiar,' he whined. 'Things are stacking up.'

'Oh, hush,' she snarled impatiently. 'I'm thinking.'

'Well, I can be doing my filing while you're thinking.'

'I want you here!' She ran her fingers down the crevasses of her face, once, twice, then scratched her balding pate vigorously, as though to stimulate thought. 'Tell me again, Feynt. You found evidence of heresy in Baris . . .'

'Some evidence there may be a hotbed of heresy in Baris, yes. I've said that. Go back a few generations and you find all sorts of things happening in Baris that spell unorthodoxy. Dating from the time of Tharius Don, when he was Superior of the Tower there. That was before you were Dame Marshal.' As it had been, though not by much, and Tharius had continued in that job for some time after Gendra had acquired her current position. Glamdrul Feynt did not dwell on that. Suspicion thrown on Tharius Don was merely lagniappe, thrown in for effect.

'Aha,' she muttered for the tenth time. 'Aha. And you have documentary evidence?'

'Sufficient,' he said. 'Sufficient.' He did have. Or would have, if he decided it was necessary, though chances were it would never be needed. Gendra was lazy. She wouldn't ask to see it. She was content to let underlings do the work, at risk of their heads if she was later displeased.

'All right,' she snarled. 'You can go.'

He closed the door behind him emphatically, then crouched to peer through the keyhole. Inside the solarium Gendra Mitiar was flinging her ancient body from side to side, jigging wildly, as though something had gotten inside her clothes and was biting her. It took him a moment to figure out what she was doing.

Gendra Mitiar was dancing.

The master of the files stumped away, limping ostentatiously until he was around the corner and a good way down the hall. The servant he had left there was sitting dejectedly on a bench, staring at nothing, and he snapped to attention when the old man struck at him.

'Wake up, you stupid fish. What do you think this is, your dormitory?' He fished in his clothing, shedding paper like

332

confetti, finding the folded, sealed packet at last in the bottom of a capacious pocket. 'Now, you take this to Tharius Don. Now. Not five minutes from now, but now. Got that? Then you come tell me you've done it or bring me an answer, one.'

He watched the man scurry off, then took himself below. 'So, Ezasper Jorn,' he snarled happily. 'So, Gendra Mitiar. So and so to both of you. Old shits. Old farts.' It became a kind of hum, te-dum, te-dum, and he sang it to himself as he went down the endless stairs. 'Old shits. Old farts. So and so.' Occasionally he interrupted this song to mutter, 'Does it matter?' to himself, screwing up his mouth in a mockery of Ezasper Jorn's usual speech. 'Does it matter, old fart? Does it, eh?'

Glamdrul Feynt was on his way to keep a very important, and secret appointment with Deputy Enforcer Bormas Tyle and with Shavian Bossit, Lord Maintainer of the Household.

When Feynt's servant arrived, Tharius was still at the window. Somehow he had not been able to leave it. He did not leave it when he opened the sealed packet, putting it before his blind eyes but not seeing it for long moments.

'Today Gendra Mitiar sends word to Jondarites in Baris for the arrest of Kesseret, Superior of the Tower at Baris.' He saw it without seeing it, and then it blazed into his consciousness all at once. *Arrest. Kessie.* Unsigned. He whirled. The man had gone. He ran to the door, looked down the hallway. Gone. He couldn't remember the man's face. Not one of his own servants. Whose? The packet was anonymous.

It was from someone in the Bureau of Towers, then. Someone Gendra had antagonized, perhaps. What matter who?

He left the room hastily, setting all thoughts aside but those of the message he must send. 'Highest priority, immediate attention, to Kesseret, Superior of Tower at Baris, Jondarites have order for your detention. Go at once to Thou-ne.' The message would be sent through his own secret channels, of course.

And then another. 'Highest priority, immediate attention, to Haranjus Pandel, Superior of Tower at Thou-ne.

Provide secret refuge for Kesseret, from Baris. Patience. Soon. Tharius Don.'

Only when these messages were sent did he sit down to try and figure out what was going on. The only message to reach Gendra lately, he assured himself, was one from Thou-ne saying that Ilze, the Laugher, had gone to the Talons. All messages from Haranjus Pandel – as from any member of the cause – were surreptitiously obtained and copied to Tharius as a matter of course. What other messages? What other messengers? In winter? None he knew of.

Ezasper Jorn was thought by Tharius – indeed, by every-one – to be so complete a fool that Tharius did not even con-sider him in passing.

At the top of the pass, General Jondrigar dismounted his beast and let the handlers take it away. Now that it was assumed the fliers knew there were weehar and thrassil behind the Teeth of the North, the general chose to ride an ox whenever he liked. Since last year's depredations on the herds, he had had crossbowmen stationed with the herdsmen, ready to bring down any flier who presumed to try such theft again. Making off with a weehar calf wasn't something that could be done quietly. One flier couldn't lift the creature, unless it was newborn, and the newborns were now carefully guarded. It would take two or three fliers, together with straps or some kind of basket, to carry a young beast, and that meant a certain amount of noise. The crossbowmen were alert. The general was fairly confident the fliers would get no more.

As for the beasts already gone, Koma Nepor had provided some clear flasks filled with a clinging liquid. Whenever the abducted herdbeasts were found, this liquid was to be thrown among them. 'It contains a special strain of . . . ah, let us say biological material? Eh? No matter what, exactly. It will do the job on the beasts. Additionally, it will infect any of the fliers who come into contact with them.'

Which, being a derivative of the blight, it would do. Nepor had not been successful in determining the life cycle of the blight. Something in it escaped him and his ancient microscopes. He had been able, however, to make from blighted fish a long-lived distillation that was very effective. This distillation, modified in various ways, had remarkable effects on people, and Koma Nepor had no reason to believe it would not work as well on weehar and thrassil.

Seeing the clutter on the plain below, the general's hand twitched as he considered using the flasks upon the herd of humans gathered there. 'Trash,' he muttered, reassuring himself with a glance at the expressionless Jondarites around him. 'Trash.' Indeed, the multicolored splotches at the foot of the pass could as well have been fruit rinds, paper scraps, shells, bones, and chips. It heaved like a garbage pit, too, alive with human maggots squirming along the River and among the buttes. 'Where is the woman?' he asked the messenger who awaited him. 'Pamra Don?'

The messenger pointed, offering his glass. On a slight hillock overlooking the River a wagon stood with a tall tent beside it. All around the hill, banners bloomed like flowers; red, green, blue, and Jondarite tents surrounded the whole. 'There,' said the messenger.

Through the glass, General Jondrigar stared into Pamra Don's face, At this great distance he could see nothing but the pale oval. A woman, carrying a child. Why was it, then, he asked himself in irritation, that she seemed to be looking directly into his eyes?

He did not hurry his trip down the pass. At the bottom of the pass there were warehouses to inspect. He received a report that worm had gotten into one that stored dried fish as well as roots and grain captured from the Noor. He specified the materials in that particular warehouse be used to feed the multitude. He was told what the spy balloons had seen from on high, a great number of approaching Noor, and also more crusaders, the steady trickle rising from Northshore into the northlands and thence to the place they stood.

'And a war party of young Noor, General. Just above Darkeldon. We could have a troop there in two days.'

The general shook his head. 'Not now, Captain. Not with all this nonsense going on. I want a battalion here, spaced out around this mob. I want crossbowmen stationed on the slopes of the Teeth and on some of those buttes. You'll have to scale some of them and let rope ladders down. No threats, mind, Tharius Don doesn't want this flock of nothings injured. Nonetheless, we won't take chances,' and he grinned his predator's smile, hard as iron, his gray, pitted skin twitching as though insects were crawling on it.

Only when all that business was attended to did he go on out onto the plain and to the tent his aides had set up at the foot of one of the buttes, protected from the wind. Evening was drawing down, and the cookfires were alight. They bloomed around him like stars, many nearby, fewer farther away, only a scatter at the far horizon and beyond, showing where the stragglers were.

A large fire marked the hill where Pamra Don's tent stood. He looked at it for a time, scornfully, then sent word to the commander of the troop guarding her. He wanted the woman brought to him tonight. As soon as he had eaten.

He had not finished when they brought her, carrying the child. He pointed with his chin at a chair across the tent, far from the fire. The soldiers escorted her there and stood at either side, calm and alert. General Jondrigar stared at her over his wine cup, waiting for her to say something. Prisoners always said something, started pleading sometimes, or offering themselves. Pamra Don said nothing. The child stared at him, but Pamra was not even looking at him but at something else in the room. The general swung his head to follow her line of vision. Nothing. A bow hung on the tent pole. His spare helmet. His spare set of fishskin armor with the wooden plates. She wasn't looking at those, surely. Nodding in that way. Seeming to murmur without actually making a sound. He went on chewing, suddenly uncomfortable.

'You can go,' he muttered to the soldiers. 'Wait outside.' For some reason he did not want them witness to this . . . this, whatever this was. Not rape. Even without Tharius Don's command, he would not have done that where anyone could see or hear him. Not good for discipline. When the men had gone, she still did not seem to see him.

'Do you know who I am?' he asked her at last.

She turned toward him eyes that were opaque, almost blind. They cleared, very gradually, and she focused upon him. 'I . . . they said you were General Jondrigar.'

'Do you know what I am?'

'You . . . no. I don't know.'

He rose to walk toward her, leaning forward a little, thrusting his face into hers. 'I am Lees Obol's right arm, his protection, leader of his armies . . .'

Her face lit up as though by fire. She leaned forward, across the child, to take him by the shoulders, and by surprise. He could not remember a woman ever having touched him willingly. Aunt Firrabel, of course, but only she. And now this one. Where she touched him burned a little, as though he were pressed against a warm stove, and he could not take his eyes from hers.

'General Jondrigar,' she said, 'the Protector of Man has need of you. Lees Obol has need of you.'

Of all the things she might have said, only this one could have been guaranteed to draw in his whole attention, focused as by a burning glass upon a radiant point. He lived for nothing but to meet the Protector's needs. Who could tell him what those needs were better than his own eyes, his own ears? Still, her eyes burned into his own with supernatural glow. Perhaps some messenger had conveyed something to her. Perhaps the soul of Lees Obol had spoken to her.

'What need?' he gurgled, barely able to speak. 'What need has the Protector?'

'The Protector has been misled by evil men,' she said, fulfilling all his fears and hopes at once. Had he not suspected plots against the Protector? Had he not prayed to forestall them all? 'They have told him that the fliers are more important than others. They have made his great title a trivial thing.'

'No,' he croaked. 'They would not dare.'

'They have,' she asserted, her face radiant with truth. 'I tell you they have! What is the Protector of Man if any man is nothing? Have you thought of that, General? If even a single man is nothing, of what value is the Protector of Man?'

'Man?' he asked, uncertain how she had meant it.

'Northshoremen,' she whispered, 'Jondarites. Chancery-men. Noor. Yes. Even the Noor. For if the Noor are made less, then their Protector is made less. A blow at the Noor is a blow at Lees Obol . . .

'And the workers, too, General. Were they not once men? If they are used and eaten, is not Lees Obol minimized by that?'

'Who does these things?' he asked, still a little uncertain, his slow, ponderous mind finding its way among the things she had said. Part of it had been clear the moment she said it. If a treasure was of no value, then he who guarded it was of no value, either. He could grasp that, all at once. It needed no explanation. 'Who?'

'You know who. Who here in the Chancery treats with the fliers, General? Who here in the Chancery maintains the Towers? Who goes ravaging among the Noor?'

'We?' he asked, uncertain, in growing horror. 'I?'

'You have said.' She nodded to him. 'You have said, General. All of you, here in the Chancery. You have betrayed Lees Obol!'

He roared then, striking her hands away, glaring at her with red, righteous eyes. How dared she? How dared she? And yet. Yet. The roar died in his throat. She stood there still, glowing, totally unafraid, looking at him with pity.

'It's not your fault,' she whispered. 'You didn't know. Not until I told you.'

'I know now,' he growled. It was a question, but it came forth as a statement of fact. 'I know now.'

'Yes.' She waited for a time while he stood there, immobile, the child on her shoulder, then turned and left him, without another word, walking out through the tent flaps where the soldiers waited. One of these men called, uncertainly, 'Shall we take her back to her tent, General?'

He muttered something affirmative unable to form words, standing there in silence, brooding beside his fire, slowly building the edifice his nature demanded, the structure that must properly house the Protector of Man. It could have no window or door to admit error. Monolithic, it must stand forever. Lees Obol could be better served only if man were better served.

What had she said to him? There were only those few words. He said them over to himself; again and again, seeking more. There must have been more. And yet, had she not said everything?

Late, past midnight, he sat there, getting up from time to time to add a stick to the fire, sitting down again. Very late in the night he rang the bell that summoned his aides. When they came, he astonished them with the messages he gave them, each signed with his own seal.

Then only one was left, he said, 'That woman, the prophetess. She is a warrior for Lees Obol.'

The man, not knowing what to say or if it was wise to say anything, merely nodded, attempting to look alert.

'She needs armor. A fighter needs armor. Tell my armorer. A helmet for her. Made to her measure. And a set of fishskin body armor, such as we wear. And boots. Have him plume the helmet with flame-bird plumes, like mine, and make her a spear.'

The man presumed to comment, 'Can she handle a spear, General?'

'No matter. Someone can carry it at her side. Let it bear a pennant. Tell the armorer. He will know. And bring one of the weehar oxen over the pass for her to ride, one of the young ones.'

The man went away, shaking his head, puzzled, wondering what the prophetess would think of all this.

She, when the armorer then came to measure her the next morning, thought it another sign. Neff from his shining cloud approved, and the radiance and the shadow both nodded.

339

13

Tharius Don's frantic message came to Baris at first dark. Each evening at this time, Threnot went for a walk along the parklands. From time to time on such forays she encountered wanderers who might, perhaps, have been accounted a little furtive if anyone had been inclined to care who a servant talked with during her frequent strolls. The wanderer encountered this night was less furtive and more in a hurry than most. Threnot returned swiftly to the Tower. Only an hour or so later, she might have been seen to leave once more, going down to town on some errand, her veils billowing in the light wind. The flier detailed to watch such comings and goings nodded, half-asleep. When Threnot was later seen to leave the Tower yet again that night, the flier scratched herself uncomfortably, for she had not seen the woman return from her second trip. Three trips in one night was not unheard-of, but it was rare. Perhaps she could mention it to the Talkers. Perhaps not. The ancient tension between Talker and flier had in no sense been changed by recent history.

Actually, only the first and third veiled women had been Threnot. The second had been Kesseret herself, fleeing to the house of a Riverman pledged to the cause. Threnot joined her there some hours later, and when dawn came, both women were on a boat halfway to the next town west. In the hours between Kessie's leaving the Tower and Threnot's leaving it, word had been spread in the Tower that the lady Kesseret was ill of a sudden fever, that she would stay in her rooms until healed of it, keeping Threnot with her to nurse her. Kesseret's deputy had been told to take charge of Tower affairs and asked not to bother the Superior for five or six days at least.

'I have taken water and food and all things needful to her rooms, Deputy,' Threnot had said in her usual emotionless voice. 'The Superior is anxious the Tower should avoid infection.' 'Infection' was a word generally used to mean any of several nasty River fevers that were occasionally epidemic and frequently fatal.

'She asks to be left alone until she is well recovered, which I have no doubt will occur in time.' Threnot looked appropriately grave, and the deputy – not an adherent of the cause – entertained thoughts of a possible untimely demise and his own ascension to the title.

Therefore, on the morrow when Jondarites came bearing orders for Kessie's arrest (emanating from Gendra, but countersigned by the general), the officious deputy told them of the Superior's illness in such terms as did not minimize the likelihood the sickness might prove fatal. The word 'infection' was used several times again, at which the Jondarites had second thoughts and departed. They would return, they said, in a week or so. Nothing in their instruction had indicated sufficient urgency in the matter to risk infecting a company of troops.

On board the *Shifting Wind*, the lady Kesseret, Superior of the Tower of Baris, became simply Kessie, marketwoman, one of the hundred thousand anonymous travelers on this section of River and shore. Her hair was not braided in the Awakener fashion; her clothes were ordinary ones long laid by for such a need; when she looked in the mirror, she did not see the lady Kesseret. If Gendra had looked her full in the face, she would not have seen Kesseret, either.

And Kessie amused herself bitterly, hour on hour, wondering whether Tharius Don would recognize her if he ever saw her again.

14

Rumor spread through the palace like a stain of oil on water, at first thick and turgid with unbelief, becoming thinner and brighter with each retelling, until at the end it was a mere rainbow film of jest, an iridescsent shining upon the surface of the day.

The general, accompanied by a woman. The general's weehar ox harnessed with another. His banner companied with another banner. Laughter burst forth at the thought, jests abounded, giggling servitors lost their composure when confronted by glum-faced Jondarites, themselves privy to the rumor but unable, because of the exigencies of discipline, to show any interest in it.

'True,' the palace whispered, cellar to high vault, 'it's true. The crusade woman has converted Jondrigar. She has put flowers on his head!'

Tharius Don shook his head, incredulous. Typical, he thought. The more outrageous the rumor, the more quickly it would spread in the Chancery, where excitements were few and urgencies infrequent. Any titillation was worth its weight in metal, and a laugh at the expense of the general was worth ten times even that. Flowers on his head, indeed. Tharius made his way to the high Tower, his powerful spyglass in hand, wanting to judge the progress of the procession now coming toward Highstone Lees, along Split River from the pass.

The drummers first, then the spearmen. Then the banner carriers – with two banners. And then . . .

Then, Tharius Don's eyes told him, then the general on a weehar ox with flowers on his head.

They came marching through the ceremonial gate, drummers, spearmen, banner carriers, then the general and Pamra Don, walking side by side while the weehar oxen were led off to be fed hay and groomed for another such occasion. Tharius Don so far recovered himself as to put on hierarchical garb and come out to meet them. While nothing had prepared him for this unlikely event, he had managed to survive the political climate of the Chancery for a hundred some years by reacting quickly to events no less improbable.

'General.' He bowed, waiting some explanation and trying not to stare at the chaplet of flowers that both the general and Pamra Don wore around their helms. Pamra Don carried a child. The child stared at him, smiling.

'Tharius Don,' boomed Jondrigar, 'Propagator of the Faith. This young person is a strong warrior for the faith, Tharius Don. She is a great soldier for Lees Obol.' This said, he peered intently at Tharius Don to see how it was received. The general had already determined that his view in the matter was to be the only one permitted.

From a window above them in the palace, Gendra Mitiar and Shavian Bossit stared down, Gendra's nails raking her face in agitation. Shavian, as usual, was inscrutably calm. Behind them in the room, Bormas Tyle strained for a glimpse of the ceremonial group assembled in the square, but his line of sight was obscured by the fountain which threw a curtain of spray across the assemblage. He grimaced, his knife sliding ominously in and out of its sheath as he stared at Gendra's back. No matter. Soon things would be arranged differently. Soon enough no one would get in the way of Bormas Tyle, or be so careless respecting his dignity. Shavian Bossit turned from the window and winked at him, only a twitch in that impassive face, but enough for Bormas Tyle to understand. He took his hand from his knife and went to find another window. Soon it would not matter. Meantime, he, too, would observe the spectacle.

In the square below, Tharius Don blinked away the spray

of the fountain and replied, 'I know she is a soldier for Lees Obol, General. Pamra Don cares greatly for the Protector of Man.' He stared at the child. It looked deeply into his eyes, making him uncomfortable.

The general shifted from foot to foot a little uncertainly. His imagination had carried him no further than this formal declaration, though he now felt that something more was warranted. He had feelings inside himself for which he had no name, feelings of anxiety, perhaps even of fear, as though recent events presaged dangers that would be inevitably derived from them, yet which he could not foresee.

'What is she to do here?' the general demanded, coming to practical matters.

'She is to be my guest,' said Tharius Don. 'She and the child. I have had a suite prepared for her . . . them. We will talk of her crusade. Perhaps she should meet with Lees Obol.'

'Yes.' The general nodded, his face clearing like a lowering sky after storm. 'Oh, yes, she should meet with Lees Obol.' Thus relieved of responsibility, he stepped back, satisfied for the moment, though Tharius Don knew his natural and chronic paranoia would overtake him before much time had passed.

Tharius Don offered his hand, courteously. Pamra Don took it, shining-faced. She turned to bow toward the general. 'Thank you for my armor, General Jondrigar. We will talk again of this great war we fight together.'

In the guest suite, high above the courtyard, Pamra Don went immediately to the windows to fling them wide. Neff had not followed her through the corridors, as her mother and Delia had, but he stood at once on the ledge outside the window, smiling through it at her, his radiance lighting the room.

'Would you like to put the baby down and put on something a little more comfortable?' Tharius Don suggested.

'I didn't bring any clothes,' she said simply, not seeming to care.

He opened the armoire, showing her a rack of soft robes and shoes. 'These would fit you, Pamra. They belonged to the lady Kesseret, of Baris. She wore them when she was here.'

'The Superior!' Her eyes flashed and her lips twisted. 'Liar!'

Tharius sighed. He had wondered whether Pamra held some such opinion. 'When did Kesseret ever lie to you, Pamra?'

'The Awakeners lied. About the Holy Sorters. They lied.'

'When did Kesseret ever lie to you?'

'Full of lies and filth about the workers, none of it true. I have come to appeal to Lees Obol, the Protector of Man. It is better if man knows the truth.'

'When,' Tharius repeated patiently, 'did Kesseret ever lie to you?'

The glaze left her eyes and she looked at him uncertainly. He said it again. 'When did Kesseret ever lie to you?'

'She was Superior.'

'When did she ever lie to you?'

'Not she,' Pamra admitted, 'but . . .'

'Kesseret would never have lied to you,' he concluded. 'Ilze lied to you, I have no doubt. But it is unfair of you to blame the lady Kesseret, my dear friend, your cousin.'

'Cousin?' She had not expected this, this homely word from a long-ago childhood, before the Tower. 'Cousin'.

'Cousin, yes. Can you remember your grandmother?'

Pamra's lips twisted again, but she nodded, yes.

'Her father was my son. And Kesseret is my cousin.'

She did not make the connection at once. It came only gradually, almost against her will. 'You are – you are my great-great-grandfather?'

'Say merely "ancestor", it is easier. Yes. Which is one of the reasons I have brought you here. We are family. Indeed, we are the only remnants of the family. Your half sisters are dead, so I am told. Without children. You and I, Pamra, are all the Dons.' He did not want to talk with her about her crusade. He did not want to talk with her about the lies told in

Towers or the obscene stupidity of the workers. He did not want to defend the status quo or to tell her the truth about the cause, for she might blurt it all out, unwittingly, even angrily, and then where would they be? He wanted to talk to her about the Dons, about Baris, about easy, sentimental things. It was a need in him.

But Pamra did not help him. She turned to the window where Neff blazed in the air, hearing his voice ringing in her ears. 'I must see Lees Obol,' she said, putting aside everything Tharius had said as though it had been wind sound, the chirping of swig-bugs, meaningless. 'Since you are family, you will help me see him.'

'Of course.' He sighed. 'Tomorrow. He is a very old man; he sleeps much of the time. Tomorrow morning, very early.' If one was to get any sense out of Lees Obol, the very early morning was the only possible time, though in recent months even that was unlikely.

'Not now?' She was disappointed, but not angry at the delay. She had come almost to welcome delay, so long as it was inevitable. Things had gone at such a pace, such a headlong plunge, that at times she felt she could not encompass all that was happening. Delay gave a space. Inevitable delay could not be questioned, not even by the voices. Sighing, she sat down.

'Would you like to take off your armor?' Tharius Don asked again. 'Put on one of these robes, Pamra Don, and we will have something to eat together. It is time you and I spoke, don't you think?'

Yet still she looked past him to the window, not seeing him, and he gave it up, sending in one of the servants instead, a heavy-bodied woman who would peel Pamra out of the tight fishskin armor and the high helm at Tharius Don's command. As she did, coming grim-lipped from the room.

'That's no dress for a woman. What kind of heretic is this? What's the matter with that child?'

'Never mind, Matron. Just see that the luncheon I've ordered is sent up promptly.' The thought of food made him

346

slightly ill. He had not eaten for days, perhaps for weeks. His body refused food, even though he was light-headed sometimes from hunger. He told himself it was only the imminence of the strike, the ultimate victory of the cause, but even telling himself this could not make his tongue enjoy the taste or his throat want to swallow. He had always felt his vision was clearer while he was fasting. Perhaps he fasted instinctively now, desiring the resultant clarity. Still, Pamra had to eat. The child had to be fed. Pamra seemed to be mostly skin stretched over slender bones. He did not look into the mirror to see how his description suited himself as well. 'Send up the luncheon,' he repeated to the servant's departing back.

She was gone with a fluster of skirts and a tight-lipped grunt. To spread more rumor, no doubt, thought Tharius. Rumor, the blood of the Chancery. Which we suck together, more, and yet more.

They sat together at a small table set by the window. The child drank water. Pamra ate almost nothing, and that little without any indication of enjoyment.

'What is the child's name?' he asked her.

'Lila,' she answered. She told him about Lila. He understood about one-tenth of what she said, and disbelieved most of that. The child was very strange. Its expression was not childlike. The way it moved was not childlike. It could not be her sister, and yet it could not be what she said it was, either. Tharius turned his eyes away to poke at the food without tasting it, watching this year's flame-bird as it built its tinder nest on the ledge, flying back and forth across the window with beakfuls of fiber from the pamet fields.

'Do you see him?' she asked suddenly, her eyes fixed on the open window.

'The flame-bird, yes.'

'Flame-bird,' she said. Yes. Neff was a flame-bird, born from the flame of his funeral pyre. How clever of this man, this ancestor, to have known. She reached out to take his hand, wanting to share with him what she knew, what she felt, about Neff, about Delia, about the God of man. Words poured from her, a spate of words, tumbling over one another in their haste to be spoken.

'Tell me,' he asked finally, marvelling at what he thought she was saying to him, 'is Neff in the keeping of the God of man?'

She nodded urgently. 'Yes, oh, yes.'

'But he is not a man. Neff, I mean. Treeci, didn't you say? Not human at all.' Treeci! His heart pounded. The Treeci existed. They really did. Just as the books had said, just as they needed to be. Beautiful. Civilized. As the Thraish would be, too. 'Neff was a Treeci. Not human?'

'Not then, no,' she said. 'But now, now he is . . .' She had not thought of this before, but of course he was. She saw him, radiantly winged, not the Neff of Strinder's Isle, but Neff with arms to hold her and a mouth that spoke to her, kissed her gently through the flames. 'He's a man now. Not like I am, or you, Tharius Don. Something finer than that.'

'An angel, perhaps.' He was trembling, awed, feeling himself in the presence of something exalted and marvelous.

She considered this. 'Angel' was a very ancient word, but one that every Northshoreman knew. A kind of beneficent spirit. Without sex or identity or kind. Suddenly she knew that was exactly what he was. 'An angel, yes,' in a tone of ringing rapture that made him want to weep.

'And the general saw all this, when you explained it to him!'

She tried to explain this as well, and Tharius Don's soul, ever eager for proof of his thesis, took it in like water upon sunparched earth. Even in this unlikely soil, goodness would grow! Oh, if Pamra Don could find a soul in Jondrigar and warm it to thaw, what might she not do for the Thraish! He longed for someone to discuss this with. Kessie. Kessie had told him the girl had this talent. Why had he not understood what Kessie meant? She had called it 'recruiting,' but it was so much more than that! Oh, if Kessie were here. But she was not! No one was. Only himself, and Pamra Don, and the world out there waiting a message from him.

Which he had dreaded to send. Which he had put off sending for some little time. The cause had been ready for a year or more, ready as it would ever be, and yet he had not sent the word. Why? He had asked himself this, morn and evening, wondering whether his own dedication was as great as it once had been. Was it failing purpose? Or did he fear his own inevitable death when the elixir was no longer available?

Or was his delay, his procrastination, foreordained, perhaps, in order to allow this thing, this miraculous thing, to happen.

'You told the general the truth,' he urged, 'and the general accepted that?'

She nodded. That was what had happened.

He shook his head, awestruck into silence. She had told the truth, and the general had accepted it. Tharius Don had never doubted the existence of the divine, and her statement confirmed his belief. Yes. He had delayed in ordering the strike because something greater than himself had chosen that he do so. Perhaps the Dons had indeed been chosen for something marvelous, for some great purpose. But it might be Pamra Don, not Tharius, who was to accomplish this great thing. He stared at her, watching the glitter of her eyes as though it had been stars, moving in the heavens to spell out a command.

There was a knock at the door, a knock too soft to break through his reverie, which was then repeated until he heard it.

A messenger with a letter from Shavian Bossit.

He broke the seal and read it, read it without really seeing it.

'The Jondarite captain at Split River Pass has received a delegation of Talkers, and they bear a written message as well. Sliffisunda demands Pamra Don be sent to him. The Thraish want her at the Talons for questioning. Gendra and I are inclined to agree it is a good idea, and Gendra offers to escort her and oversee her safety.'

Pamra was saying something, but he didn't hear her. He read the message again. At first it made no sense, but then its purpose bloomed in him like some gigantic, fiery flower, its perfume enwrapping him, spinning him in a sudden delirium. Pamra Don was wanted at the Talons, by the Thraish. Pamra Don, who had done a thing for the cause that Tharius Don had never thought of doing. Pamra Don, who had converted the general in one day. Pamra Don, who saw the souls of Treeci and people reborn as angels.

And yet, how could he know? How could he be sure? He turned to her with a fierce and longing love to demand the answer.

'If you were to speak to the Talkers – to the fliers, Pamra. If you were to tell them the truth, would they believe?'

She looked at him uncertainly, past him at the glowing figure of Neff, outside the window. Radiant. Breast stained with red, nodding to her as he always did. Yes, yes, anything was possible, anything was conceived. Yes.

'Talkers?' she asked.

'The fliers. The fliers who talk. You know.'

She did not know. Still, anything that talked should be told the truth. 'It's better to know the truth,' she said. Neff would know. Wasn't he kin to the fliers? Wouldn't he know?

'If I send you to them, Pamra? Can you convert them as you did General Jondrigar?

'It's better when people know the truth,' she said again, a thing she often said when nothing else seemed to fit, for that is what Neff often said to her. Her voice was calm, her face serene, still colored by the rapture that often came over it. 'It's better to know the truth.'

He took it for affirmation.

'Rest,' he told her with an exultant glad smile. 'I'll come back and talk with you more later.'

He went down to the council meeting, where Jorn and Mitiar, with their arguments for sending Pamra to the Thraish well rehearsed and arranged, were amazed to find such disputation unnecessary.

'I agree Pamra Don should go to the Thraish. Take her,' Tharius said. 'Keep her safe, Gendra, but take her along.

350

Take her, and the child, but be sure she talks to Sliffisunda himself.'

'I think Sliffisunda will require that,' Shavian interjected in a dry voice. 'There will be no problem.' He wanted to ask Tharius what had happened to him. The man was dizzy with joy, like a child on festival morning when the Candy Tree had grown in the night. Like a young Chanceryman at his first elixir ceremony. Full of light. Buoyed up. It was almost tempting to delay the meeting a little in order to find out why, but Gendra's offer to leave the Chancery was too much a godsend to risk losing. Easier on everyone if she's away for a while, he assured himself. Gives us time to get ready for it. And he glanced at the chairs against the wall where Glamdrul Feynt and Bormas Tyle huddled together, exchanging occasional whispered words. The perfect picture of conspirators, Shavian thought, shaking his head at them warningly.

The three of them had only the bare outline of a plot as yet. It would require three deaths: that of the general, that of Gendra Mitiar, and that of Lees Obol. One, two, three. Like a starting chant for a race. One to get steady, two to get ready, three to go.

Since Glamdrul Feynt was to end up as Lord Marshal of the Towers, he would dispose of Gendra Mitiar. Bormas Tyle wanted to be General of the Armies, which meant Jondrigar was his meat. Since Glamdrul and Bormas had charge of the elixir, nothing should be easier for them than a little selective adulteration. One, two. And then Lees Obol, with Shavian Bossit to take his place as Protector of Man – three votes in the council guaranteed: Bormas, Glamdrul, and his own – and the assembly already primed to vote for him.

Shavian started from agreeable visions of this future and was brought to himself.

'It's decided, then,' Gendra Mitiar intoned. 'I'll take her to Red Talons.'

'That's closest, yes,' Tharius Don approved.

'You'll keep her safe?' asked General Jondrigar, his voice

heavy and obdurate as iron, oily with suspicion. 'You, Mitiar, you'll keep her safe?'

Gendra smiled maliciously. 'Of course, General. Of course I will. That's why I'm going.'

The smile made Tharius wince, but only for the instant. Of course the old fish was up to something, but it didn't matter. What did she think of Pamra Don? Did she think anything at all? How could she know that Pamra Don was the divine intervenor, the peace bringer, the messenger of God, sent to mitigate violence and death? The messenger sent to Tharius Don to say he had been right in holding his hand, right to delay the strike. It would not be needed. The Thraish could be converted. The cause might be fulfilled without violence.

'It's settled, then,' said Gendra Mitiar. 'We'll leave in the morning.' She cast an enigmatic look at Ezasper Jorn, who had been silent throughout the meeting. He and Koma Nepor had exchanged two or three carefully casual glances, nothing more, though inwardly they were jubilant. The old crock had fallen for it. She thought she was going to gain support for herself. By the time she got back – it would be too late. If she got back at all.

So, the Council of Seven adjourned. Both they and their ancillary personnel rose to move about the room. Shavian Bossit rang a small bell, its sound hanging in the hall like a strand of tinsel, a bright shivering of metal. Through the high doors came screeching carts bearing tea; a dozen soft-footed servitors in gray livery to tend the tall silver and copper kettles with handles worked into nelfants and gorbons and other mythical animals, the charcoal stoves below them emitting a pungent smoke. Plates of cakes were passed: puncon tarts, nutcakes, sweetbean, and mince. The council members floated upon an ebullience that was infectious, every member of it assured that his or her own ambition was shortly to be fulfilled.

Ezasper would be Protector. Shavian would be Protector. Gendra would be Protector. Each of them knew it, was certain of it, glorying both in the absolute sureness of it and in the fact that no one else knew.

352

Koma Nepor would be Marshal of the Towers. Glamdrul Feynt would be Marshal of the Towers. They chatted with one another, laughing, each glorying in the other's eventual discomfiture.

The general would use his position to rectify distortions and lies. He thought of this as he listened to Bormas Tyle, who was certain he would soon become general. The two of them stood together in a window aperture with their cakes. General Jondrigar even made a little jest about the flower chaplet he had worn. They laughed.

And Tharius Don stood alone, happier than he had been in fifty years.

From behind the curtain a querulous old voice exclaimed, 'What's everyone laughing about? Tell me the joke. Tell me,' and several Jondarites went to busy themselves within.

To the assembled council, Lees Obol's command only seemed amusing, and even the general smiled. How could any one of them explain his joy? Each, knowing the reason for his own, thought better to pretend it was inexplicable.

The euphoria passed. Voices died down. The babble gave way to whispers, winks, nodded heads. Cups were set down on the waiting trays. Servitors scurried about with napkins to brush up the crumbs. The carts went screeching away, complaining into the vaulted silences. Ezasper Jorn hesitated in the doorway long enough to whisper to the Chief of Research, 'As soon as she's well gone, Koma. As soon as she's well gone.' And they, too, departed in good humor.

Above, in his guest suite, Tharius Don sat down with Pamra before the fire while Lila waved her hands at the flames and chortled in words he could not understand.

'Let me tell you about the Talkers,' he said gently, watching her face to be sure she paid attention.

But she, nodding and making sounds as though she were listening, heard very little that he said. She was far away, in some other world.

15

At the end of each month those aboard the *Gift* celebrated riotously on the extra day. Eenzie the Clown juggled hard melon and eggs on the main deck, discovering the eggs in the ears of the boatmen and losing them again down the backs of their trousers. On this occasion, Porabji brought out a great crock he had had fulminating in the owner-house and poured them all mugs of something that was almost wine and almost something else, cheering as Glizzee, though in a different way. Thrasne himself had taken a generous amount of the gift Glizzee from the locker and given it to the cook for inclusion in whatever seemed best. They played silly games and sang children's songs and ended by pouring wine on the new boat and naming it the *Cheevle*, which, said Eenzie, was the name of the delicious little fish that thronged the streams of the steppe. She mimed taking bites out of the new boat, making them all laugh. They took the canvas cover off the boat and sat in the hull, wrapped in blankets against the night chill, singing River chanteys and old heart-side songs. By the middle of the night they were all weary but wonderfully pleased, and most of them wandered off to their hammocks or bunks.

Thrasne came to himself atop the owner-house, staring at the stars, humming tunelessly, almost without thought. Medoor Babji found him there, came to stand beside him at the railing, leaning so close her bare arm was against his own and the warmth of them both made a shell around them.

'Babji,' he sang, more than half-drunk. 'Ayee, aroo,

Babji, Babji.' He smiled at her, putting an arm around her.

She did not answer, only pressed closer to him, knowing what would happen and willing that it happen. When he put his lips on hers, it was exactly as her body had anticipated. His mouth was sweet, wine smelling, his lips softly insistent. He cupped her bottom in his hands, pressing her close to the surging hardness of him. When he moved toward the *Cheevle*, toward the blankets piled in the bottom of it, she did not resist him. When he laid her down, himself above her, and found a way through their clothing, she did not say no. She cried out, once, at a pain that quickly passed, then all thought ceased.

It was a long time later she opened her eyes to see stars again. She was cradled on Thrasne's shoulder, his right arm under her and around her, blankets piled atop them like leaves over fallen fruit. No sound on the ship except the water sounds, the creak of timbers, the footsteps of the watch on the forward deck, the rattle of ropes against wood.

'Babji,' he said again, not singing, in a voice totally sober and a little disconsolate.

'What?' she said, knowing he had been awake while she slept. 'What are you thinking?'

'I was thinking about what you said the other day, Medoor Babji. About the two kinds of people in the world. Those like you and me, who see puncon jam on our bread, and those others who see other things. I have been thinking about that. Those of us who see jam are the most numerous, I know. But does that mean the jam is really there?'

She stared at the silhouette of his face against the night sky. 'Does it not, then?'

'I don't know. After a great, long time thinking of it, I could tell myself only that. I don't know.'

He brought her closer to him, reached down to arrange the blankets against the night's chill. The wind was cold, his voice was colder yet. 'It was Pamra's madness made me think of it. She does not see the world as we do. As you and I see it. As the boatmen see it. As your people see it. And so we call her mad. She will not come into the world I wanted

355

for her, so I call her mad. She will not love me and bear my children, so she's mad. She talks with dreams and consorts with visions, so she's mad. I was thinking of that as I lay here, listening to you sleep.'

She did not reply, halfway between sobbing and anger, not knowing which way to fall. After what had just passed between them, and it was Pamra in his mind still! She took refuge in silence.

He went on, 'The Jarb Mendicants could come with their blue smoke to sit beside me and tell me, "Yes, she's mad." But what would it mean, Medoor Babji? It would mean only that they see the same dream I see, not that the dream is real. So – so, if I were to share her dream, couldn't that be as real as my own?'

'How?' she asked him, moving from sadness to anger. 'Your good, sensible head wouldn't let you do that, Thrasne.'

'If the Jarb root gives one vision of reality, perhaps other things give other visions. Glizzee, perhaps.'

'Glizzee is a happy-making thing, truly, Thrasne, but I have never heard that visions come of it.'

'Then other things,' he said thoughtfully. 'Other things.' He looked down at his free hand, and she saw that he held a jug of the brew old Porabji had made. 'Other things.'

She moved away from him, less angry now, though he did not seem to care that she went, for he began to lace up the canvas cover of the little boat. In the owner-house she undressed and braided the long crinkles of her hair into larger braids to keep them from tangling while she slept. Perhaps tomorrow she would cry. There was a bleak hollow inside her full of cold wind. Perhaps she would not get up at all.

Eenzie stirred. 'Doorie? Where've you been? Up to naughty with the owner, neh?'

'Talking,' she said tonelessly, giving nothing away.

'About his madwoman, I'll wager,' Eenzie said with a yawn, turning back into sleep. 'He has nothing else to talk about.'

The morning found many less joyous than on the night before, with Obors-rom leaning over the rail to lose all he had eaten for a day or more.

'It's that brew of old Zynie's,' he gasped. 'I should have had better sense than to drink it.'

'Perhaps,' Thrasne suggested, 'you should only have had better sense than to try and drink it all.' Medoor Babji was passing as he said it. He saw her and looked thoughtfully at her, half remembering he had done something unwise, perhaps unkind. He needed to apologize to her for whatever it had been, if he could only have a moment to remember. She stared through him, as through a window.

'It is never wise to drink too much of old Porabji's brews,' she said. 'I have had a word with him.' She passed Thrasne by, not stopping, and he stared after her in confusion. The night before was not at all clear to him. Part of it, he thought, he might have dreamed. And yet something was owed because of it, he thought. Something needed to be done.

16

Late that afternoon came wind. It was no small breeze. At
first they welcomed it behind them, but the sailors soon
began to shake their heads. They reefed the big sail, leaving
only the small one at the top of the mast to maintain way. Later
the wind fell, but the sailors did not put the sail out again.

'Storm,' said one of them to Thrasne. His name was
Blange, a laconic, stocky man who looked not unlike
Thrasne himself.

'Last time I remember the clouds lookin' like that' – he
gestured to the horizon, where a low bank of cloud grew
taller with each passing hour – 'last time we were lucky
enough to get behind an island and ride it out. Five days'
blow it was, and the ship pretty battered when it was over. I
don't like the looks of that.'

Certainly if Thrasne had been near Northshore, he would
have tried to get behind something. He didn't like the looks
of it, either. The sky appeared bruised, livid with purpling
cloud, darted with internal lightning so that sections of the
cloud wall glowed ominously from time to time, a recurrent
pulse of pallid light that was absorbed by the surrounding
darkness as though swallowed.

The River surface looked flat and oily in that light, full of
strange, jellylike quiverings and skitterings, as though
something invisible ran across the surface. Swells began to
heave at the *Gift*, lifting and dropping, lifting and dropping.

'What's it likely to do?' Thrasne asked.

'It's likely to give us one hell of a beating,' Blange replied.

'Then let's get that little boat off the owner-house roof,'

358

Thrasne commanded. 'We don't need that banging around.'

They lowered the *Cheevle* into the water, running her out some distance from the *Gift* at the end of a stout rope. The two boats began a kind of minuet, bowing and tipping to one another across the glassy water between.

The wall of cloud drew closer even as they worked, still pulsing with intermittent light, muttering now in a growl that seemed almost constant. Obers-rom and the other boatmen were busy tying everything down that could be tied down and stowing everything else in the lockers and holds.

'Best take some of the spare canvas and nail it over the hatches,' one of the sailors told Thrasne.

'Surely that's extreme?'

'Owner, if you want to keep your boat and our lives, I'd recommend it. I'm tellin' you everything I know, and I don't know half enough.'

Thrasne stared at the wall of cloud. Perhaps the man was one of those doomsayers the River bred from time to time. On the other hand, perhaps he wasn't. Blange wasn't a young man. He had scars on his face and arms – from rope lashes, so he said. His hands were hard. One thing Blint had always said: 'You pay a man for more than his strong back, Thrasne. You pay him for his good sense if he's got any.'

So. 'Tell Obers-rom what you need, Blange. I'm going to see what's going on in the owner-house.'

What was going on was a card game among four of the inhabitants and naps for the other two.

'Thrasne,' burbled Eenzie the Clown. 'Come take my hand. I'm being beaten, but you could fight them off . . .'

'Yes, Thrasne,' Medoor Babji said in a chilly voice. 'Take Eenzie's cards and we'll do battle.'

He shook his head at her, scarcely noticing her tone. 'No time, Medoor Babji. The sailors tell me we are probably going to be hit by a storm. They say a bad storm. Anything you have lying around should be put away.' The sound of hammers came through the wall, and old Porabji sat up with a muffled curse.

359

'What're they doing?' Eenzie asked, for once in a normal tone of voice.

'Nailing canvas over the hatches to keep water out.'

'Waves?'

'I don't know. I've never been in a bad storm. Rain, I suppose. Waterspouts, maybe. I've seen those.' Thrasne was suddenly deeply depressed. The *Gift* was about to be assaulted and he had no idea how to protect her. 'If things get violent, you might rig some straps over the bunks and strap yourself in. Less likely to be hurt that way, I should think.' He turned and blundered out, needing to see what Blange was up to. Surely there would be something he could do.

When he emerged from the owner-house door, he was shocked into immobility by the wall of black that confronted him. The *Gift* rocked in a tiny pocket of clear water. Straight above them Potipur bulged toward the west, pushing his mighty belly toward the sunset in a tiny circle of clear sky. Elsewhere was only cloud and the ceaseless mutter of thunder. At the base of the cloud lay a line of agitated white, and Blange pointed this out, his face pale.

'There's the wind,' he said. 'Those are the wave tops, breaking up. It will be on us soon.' He turned away, shouting for men to help him cover the other hatch.

'The ventilation shafts,' Thrasne cried suddenly. 'We have to cover the ventilation shafts.'

'I'll help,' said a small voice at his side. Medoor Babji. 'Taj Noteen and I will help you. We can do the front shaft.' Indeed, she knew well where it was, for she had sat there many an hour during the voyage, watching as Thrasne himself had once watched. Birds. Waves. The floating stuff that the River carried past.

'Get tools from Obers-rom,' Thrasne said, hurrying away to the aft shafts, one eye on the rushing cloud.

Obers-rom gave them a hammer, nails – worth quintuple their weight in any nonmetal coin. 'Take care,' he growled at her. 'Don't drop them, Medoor Babji. These are all we have.' He sent one of the other men to carry the cleats.

She and Taj Noteen scrambled across the owner-house

roof and dropped onto the grating above the shaft. They would have to squat or lie on the grating and lean downward to nail the cleats across the canvas. There was not room for two of them.

'Get back up,' she grunted. 'You can hand me the cleats as I nail them.' She spread the canvas beneath her, holding it down with her body, pressing it against the outside of the square shaft, reaching behind her to take the cleat.

The wind struck. The *Gift* shuddered, began to tip. Medoor Babji cursed, thrust the hammer between her body and the canvas, and held on. Above her, Taj Noteen shouted, but she could not understand what he was saying.

The wind got under the canvas, lifted it. Her hands were clenched tight to it, her eyes shut. Only Taj Noteen saw her lifted on the bellying sail, lifted, flown, over the side and down into the chopping River. The water hit her and she screamed then, opening her eyes, seeing the loom of the *Gift* above her. Under her the canvas bulged like a bubble, air trapped beneath it, floating her. She was moving away from the boat. Away. She screamed again, soundless against the uproar of the sudden rain.

Then something struck the canvas, brushed it, away, brushed it again. The *Cheevle*. It bowed toward her once more, and she grabbed the side, lifted by it as it tilted away from her, pulling herself in. The canvas was tangled around her legs. It followed like a heavy tail, and she rolled onto the cover of the *Cheevle*. The wind stopped, all at once, and glassy calm spread across the waters.

Medoor Babji shouted. There were figures at the rail of the *Gift*, staring at her. Blange shouted at her. 'Get under the cover, Babji! Get under it and lace it up. The wind is coming back. There's no time to pull you in . . .'

She had scarcely time to comprehend what he had said and obey him, hurriedly loosening the lacing at one side of the little boat enough to crawl beneath it. She lay in the bottom of the boat, on the blankets tumbled there, and tugged at the lacing string with all her strength, pulling it tight again only moments before the wind struck once more.

It was like being inside a drum as the rain pounded down upon the tight canvas and she clung to the lacing strings, flung this way and that by the wind, protected from battering only by those tumbled blankets and the wet canvas that had almost killed her, then saved her from drowning.

There were sounds of thunder, muttering, growling, sharp cracks like the sudden breaking of great tree limbs. After one such crack her ears told her the *Cheevle* was moving, racing, driven by the wind. She imagined the *Gift* also driven, wondering briefly if one of them preceded the other or whether the wind sent them on this journey side by side. After a time the violent rocking stopped. The rain continued to fall in a frenzy of sound. Lulled by the noise, by the dark, by her fear and the pain of her bruises, she fell asleep, still clinging to the lacing strings of the cover as though they held her hope of life.

Aboard the *Gift*, darkness fell like a curtain, rain-filled and horrid. Wind buffeted them. The old boat creaked and complained, tilting wildly on the waves. They had seen Medoor Babji crawl beneath the cover of the *Cheevle*. They had no time to worry about her after that. In breaks in the storm they managed to cover the forward ventilation shaft. The hammer and nails were caught between the shaft and the forward wall of the owner-house. Except for Thrasne, and for the steersmen, struggling mightily to keep them headed into the waves and wind under only a scrap of sail, the others went into the owner-house and cowered there, waiting for something to happen. Thrasne lashed himself to the rail and peered into blackness, seeing nothing, nothing at all, rain mixed with tears running down his face. He could feel the pain in the *Gift*, and he was awash with guilt for having brought her on this voyage.

After an endless time, the wind abated. The rain still fell in a solid curtain of wet. Men went below and came back to say there were leaks – none of them large, but still, water was seeping into the holds. They set up a bailing line, using scoops to clear the water, chinking the seep holes with bits of rope dipped in frag sap. Night wore on. The rain softened to a mere downpour, then to a spatter of wind-flung drops. Far to the west the clouds parted to show Abricor, just off full, descending beneath the River. In the east, the sky lightened to amber, then to rose.

Thrasne untied the knots that held him to the railing, coiled the rope in his hands, and staggered up to the steering deck to relieve the men there and give orders for repairs. He was half through with it, Obers-rom busy in the hold, Blange and a crew restacking the cargo to make room for caulking, when he chanced to look over the railing to the place the *Cheevle* swam along in their wake.

Should have swum. The rope that had tied it lay frayed on the deck, broken in the storm. Of the *Cheevle* itself, or of Medoor Babji, there was no sign.

17

To most of the crew on the *Gift*, it seemed that Thrasne owner had gone mad. He was determined to search for the *Cheevle*. No matter what they said, he would not hear them. 'She'll be downtide,' he said, again and again. 'We have to look for her downtide.'

Taj Noteen had his own reasons for wanting the *Cheevle* found. He did not want to go to Queen Fibji and tell her the chosen heir had been lost upon the river, lost with no attempt made to find her. Still, looking about him at the measureless expanse of heaving water, searching seemed ridiculous and was made to seem more ridiculous still by the advice of the sailors, those men who had plied the island chains throughout much of their lives.

'Thrasne owner,' they begged. 'Making great circles here in the midst of the water will do no good! The *Cheevle* was blown as we were blown. The tide moved her as it moved us. If she is not near us now, and if she cannot be seen from the top of the mast, anything we do may merely take us farther from it.'

Thrasne would not hear it. Why it meant so much to him, he did not bother to figure out. Why his eyes filled at the thought of Medoor Babji alone, possibly injured upon the deep, he did not wonder. Why his gut ached at the idea of her lost, he did not put into words. He spoke often of finding the *Cheevle*. What he really longed to find was Medoor Babji herself, though he never said her name to himself. The name he had attached for so long to this feeling was Pamra. He had not brought himself to replacing the name, though her image had been replaced by another in his imaginings. In his sexual fantasies he would have whispered Pamra's name, though the woman in his mind would have been dark and fringe-haired, fire-eyed and silk-skinned as only Medoor Babji was. If he had realized this, he would have accounted this as being unfaithful to his dreams, his hopes, his vows, and therefore he did not admit to any change. If someone had asked him he would have said he loved Pamra Don as he always had, as Suspirra, as herself.

'She is as a member of the crew,' he wrote in his journal, in yet another of those many books he had filled over the years with *Thrasne's Thoughts*. 'We would not abandon a crew member until all hope was lost; so we may not abandon her.' As he wrote this, he was conscious that it was not quite the truth, but he could find no other words that satisfied him. 'It may be,' he continued, 'as the sailors say, that it is already hopeless.'

And yet he would not cease searching for the *Cheevle*.

They spent some days tacking, circling, up and down, back and forth, the sailors trying to keep some record of the way they had gone, shaking their heads and snarling at one another from time to time. During the storm several of the great water casks had been broken. Thrasne set the carpenter to repairing the casks, a job that did not take them long, but he either did not notice or did not see the implications of the fact that the casks were now empty. In this he was quite alone. The crew and the Noor saw well enough that the remaining water would not last them long. One could drink the brackish River water for a short time, a day or two, perhaps, the sailors said. Longer than that and people drinking the water doubled in cramps and fits and died.

On the evening of the fifth or sixth day of this aimless searching – during which every available pair of eyes had been stationed at the rail or on the steering deck or even aloft, at the top of the mast, the watchman having been hauled up there in a kind of swing – Taj Noteen made his way to the place Thrasne brooded atop the owner-house.

'Thrasne owner,' he said. 'Would you dishonor Medoor Babji?'

Thrasne turned on him, lips drawn back in a snarl. Then, seeing the quiet entreaty on the man's face, he subsided, wondering what ploy this was. 'I would not,' he growled. 'As you well know. Medoor Babji is my . . . friend.' He heard himself saying this, liked the sound of it, and repeated it firmly. 'My friend.'

'Then if you would honor your friendship, you should do as Medoor Babji would wish, Thrasne owner.'

'I would presume she would wish to be found,' he growled, becoming angry.

'Any of us would,' agreed Taj Noteen. 'Unless we were on a mission to which we would willingly sacrifice our lives. In that case, we might feel our mission more important than being found.' He sweated as he said this, and his mouth closed in a hurt, bitter line, for he revered Queen Fibji, as did most of the Noor. Blame for the loss of the Queen's daughter would fall on the leader of the group. Who else could be asked to bear it?

'So you say,' Thrasne argued. 'You, who lead this group. Perhaps those who follow you feel differently. Perhaps to them the mission is not more important than their lives.'

'We go at the Queen's command,' Noteen said softly. 'You have been told this.'

'I have been told. Yes.' It meant nothing to him.

'Medoor Babji is the Queen's daughter, her chosen heir. Medoor Babji is the real leader of this expedition, boatman. I speak with her voice when I tell you to give up this fruitless search.'

'How can you?' Thrasne cried. 'You know her! How can you?'

'Because there are ten thousand Medoor Babjis among the Noor,' he replied, gesturing wide to include all that world of suffering humanity. 'Ten thousand to be killed by Jondarites and taken slave in the mines. Ten thousand daughters to weep, ten thousand sons to die. We do not go to Southshore out of mere curiosity, Thrasne. We go because we must. The Noor are being slaughtered, day by day, week by week. Medoor Babji knows this! How do we honor her death if we perish of thirst here upon this endless water and the mission comes to nothing? Then she will have *died* for nothing! Would you dishonor her, Thrasne owner?'

Thrasne did not give up easily. Still, Noteen's words burned in his head. He went below to his airless little cubby and anguished to himself, thinking that everything he cared for was always reft from him, surprised at the thought, for it was only then he admitted to himself that he cared for Medoor Babji. Realizing it made his grief the worse, and he spent the night attempting to assign that grief some cause and function or to find some reasons in his own life for his being punished in this way. It was no good. He could not really believe in such punishment, though the priests and Awakeners taught it as a matter of course. It was nothing in his own life which controlled the lives of Pamra or Medoor Babji. They, too, were creatures who moved of their own will. He could only touch their lives a little, share their lives a little, if they would give him leave.

And Medoor Babji had given him leave where Pamra had not. The thought fled, like a silver minnow through his mind, elusive and yet fascinating.

Still, when morning came, he gave in to Taj Noteen's entreaties. The sailors turned the *Gift* toward the south, praying they would find water before many days had passed.

Despite his decision, Thrasne kept at the rail every hour of the light, or had himself hoisted to the top of the mast, or stood on the steering deck peering into the quivering glow of sun upon the waves for endless hours. He would resign himself to the need of the Noor to go south, he could not resign himself to the fact that she was gone. Something within him cried continuously that he would see the *Cheevle* dancing in the sun, beyond the next wave.

18

I remember when Blint first brought me aboard the *Gift*, sometimes at night I would wake from a dream of being lost upon the River. I was only twelve or thirteen, I suppose. Not a man yet, or anything near it. Perhaps they were a child's dreams, just as children dream of falling or flying but grown-ups seldom do. At least, I suppose that is true. I used to dream of falling all the time but don't anymore. I don't dream of being lost on the River anymore, either, but sometimes I dream of swimming – as though I were one of the strangeys . . .

From Thrasne's book

Medoor Babji woke to the slup-slup-slup of wavelets on the side of the boat, to the heat of the sun on the canvas above her. The air was stifling. She lay in a puddle of wet blankets, cozied into them like a swig-bug into water weed. It took her some minutes to extricate herself and untangle the lacing strings from fingers that were stiff and sticklike. 'Blight,' she cursed at herself, attempting cheer. 'My fingers have the blight.'

Her head came out of the *Cheevle*, bleary eyes staring around at the sparking wavelets on all sides, taking some notice of the clear amber of the sky and the high, seeking scream of some water bird before realizing, almost without surprise, that the *Gift* was gone. It was as though part of herself had been prepared for this eventuality – aware of it, perhaps, when the rope snapped, even during the fury of the storm – even as some other, less controlled persona prepared for panic.

'Now, now,' she encouraged herself, quelling a scream that had balled itself tight just below her breastbone and was pushing upward, seeking air. 'It may not be the *Gift's* gone. Maybe I'm gone. Separated, at any event. Oh, Doorie, now what?' Her insides were all melting liquid, full of confusion and outright fear, but the sound of her own voice brought a measure of control.

The persona in charge postponed answer of this question, postponed thought while she unlaced half the drum-tight covering of the *Cheevle* and folded it over the intact half. She wrung out the blankets as best she might and laid them over the loose canvas, seeing steam rise from them almost immediately. Her clothing followed. There was water in the bottom of the boat, though not much, and she sought the bailing scoops the sailors had carved, still tight on their brackets beneath the tiny bow deck. She postponed thought still further while bailing the boat dry, and further yet by turning and returning the blankets and clothing so that all were equally exposed to the drying rays of the sun.

And when all this was done, when she had dressed herself and taken a small drink of water from the River, brackish but potable – so Thrasne had told her, though one should drink very little at a time and not for long – there was no change in the circumstance at all. The *Cheevle* still bobbed on the wavelets, alone on the River, with no rock, no island, no floating flotsam in view.

'And no food,' she murmured to herself. 'And no really good water.' The taste of the River on her tongue was mucky, a little salty. It had done little to reduce her thirst.

The mast lay in the bottom of the boat. She had slept between it and the sharp rib corners all night. Now she considered it with a kind of fatalistic resignation. She had paid some attention when the sailors had demonstrated how the mast was to be stepped. It had, as she recalled, taken two of them to get it up. Still. If she had the wind, she might go somewhere. If she went on bobbing here, like some little wooden toy, lost in immensity by a careless child, she might float forever.

The mast was heavy. After using her strength to no purpose for a time, she stopped fooling with the thing and thought it through. She took the lines loose from the canvas cover, maneuvered the butt of the mast into position against its slanting block, then attached a line halfway up the mast, running it under and over two of the lacing hooks and using a third to take up the slack. She heaved, sweated, cursed, saw the mast rise a little. She tied it off and recovered, panting, then tried again. By alternately heaving and cursing at this primitive pulley arrangement, she managed to get the mast almost upright, at which point it slid into its slot with a crash that made her fear for the bottom of the boat. She felt around it gingerly, praying to find no water. There was water. Was it left over from bailing or from a new leak? She had no idea and spent several anxious moments measuring it with eyes and hands to see whether it got any higher.

When she had convinced herself – deluded herself, her other persona kept insisting – that the hull was sound, she restored the lacing to the cover and relaced half of it, folded the now dry blankets under this shelter, remembered to drop in the wedges that held the mast erect, and set about trying to recall what Blange had said about sail.

'If you cannot remember what you are told,' Queen Fibji had told her more than once, 'you must use trial and error. The thing to keep in mind about trial and error is that some errors are quite final. Therefore, it might be wise to listen carefully to the instructions of those who have experienced what they are trying to tell you about.'

'People are always telling me things,' Medoor Babji had complained. She had been about twelve at the time, coming into rebellion as inevitably as a flame-bird chick into its plumes.

'They don't even ask me what I think.'

The Queen had nodded, brow wrinkled a little at this. They were in the Queen's own tent, and her serving women were redoing the Queen's hair as well as Medoor Babji's. It was a long process, though infrequent. Each strand was carefully combed out, washed and rinsed, one by one, then rewound and decorated at the bottom with a bead of bone or faience. The serving women chatted between themselves, politely, pretending that the Queen and Medoor were not present, thus allowing the mother and daughter the same freedom.

'Ah,' Queen Fibji had said. 'Well, let us suppose you have broken your leg. Chamfas Muneen is sent for. Chamfas says to you, "Hold fast, this is going to hurt," and then sets your leg and binds it up. Do you want Chamfas to ask you what you think before doing it?'

'Chamfas is a bonesetter!'

'So?'

'So of course he won't ask me what I think! I don't know anything about bonesetting.'

'Well, let us suppose it is Aunty Borab. Suppose she tells you to eat your breakfast.'

'Yes, that's what I mean. She doesn't ask me if I want breakfast. She just tells me.'

'And what is Aunty Borab?'

'She's just an old woman.'

'Ah, no, Medoor Babji. There you are wrong. Aunty Borab is a life liver. She is a survivor. She is a power holder and a health giver. She is no less expert at what she does than is Chamfas Muneen. But you call her an old woman and disregard what she says.'

'She's bossy!'

'So is Chamfas, when he knows what is best for you. So am I when I seek to save my people hurt. And so is Borab when she knows it is best for you to eat your breakfast.'

The Queen's expression had been mild, but there had been obsidian in her eyes. Hard, black, and questioning. *Is this one to be my heir, or shall I choose some other?* After a pause, she continued. 'Instead of thinking of older folk as bossy persons with whom you must contend for control, Medoor Babji, think first what they are trying to tell you, or save you.

371

Indeed, they may only be attempting to assert the privilege of age, but it does no harm to listen, even to agree. They will die before you, and you will have time to do it your way.'

Medoor Babji had not wanted Queen Fibji to choose some other heir, so she had begun to save the rebellion for other targets and pay attention to Aunty Borab.

Now she wished she had paid as much attention to Blange and the other sailors.

'My fault,' she said, putting the rising sun on her right hand and bowing her head in the direction she assumed was north, toward the Noor lands, toward the Queen. 'I called them common sailors in my mind. I should have called them expert boat handlers and learned from them.' She closed her eyes in meditation. One had to meditate on mistakes when they were discovered. Otherwise, the opportunity to learn from them might pass one by. Another of the Queen's axioms that Medoor had adopted as her own.

When the meditation was over, she had remembered a few things. Other details came to her as she worked. There was a line to haul the triangular sail on its boom up and down the mast. There were lines to move the trailing end of it right or left. In the morning, they kept the wind behind them. That she remembered, for Thrasne had said it over and over. 'Morning wind to take us out, evening wind to bring us back.' After a time she got the hang of it, even remembering to steer a bit east of south. Then there was nothing to do but sit hot under the sun, watching a far bank of cloud in the west retreat below the horizon and disappear while other clouds formed out of nothing, fled away into shreds, and vanished. Around her the River heaved and pulsed, clucking against the boat's side. She grew half-blind from sun glimmer. She thought she saw things, strange winged figures larger than people, riding upon the waves. She blinked, and they were gone.

When the sun was directly overhead, something huge moved beside the boat. She felt the planks quiver and shift, not a natural, water-driven movement. Fish broke the surface of the water, leaping high to escape whatever was below. Two of them fell into the boat, flapping there with high-pitched squeals. Medoor Babji was not squeamish. She grasped them by their tails and banged them against the side of the boat. Her folding knife was in her sleeve pocket with her other essentials. She gutted the fish and filleted them, laying most of the strips of yellow flesh on the canvas to dry in the sun, eating the others slow mouthful by slow mouthful, grateful both for the sweet flesh and for the water in it.

'Strangey below,' she told herself. What else could be that size? Some monster of the mid-River? Had the provision of the fish been accidental? Somehow she didn't think so. What was it Thrasne had said? Sometimes strangeys picked up boatmen who had fallen overboard and returned them to their boats. Perhaps they fed stranded River wanderers as well.

By midafternoon she knew one thing more. Sometimes strangeys took small boats where they wanted them to go. In the lull after the morning wind had failed, Medoor Babji had attempted to set the sail as she remembered the sail on the *Gift* being set in the afternoons. She had accomplished this more or less and was headed westward once more when the boat shuddered, the sail flapped, and she found herself moving in a slightly different direction. Perhaps a bit more west of south than she had intended.

'When things are moving inexorably in a given direction,' Queen Fibji had told her, 'only foolish men attempt to move against the flow. And yet, those men who give themselves over entirely to the movement may also be foolish. The wise man works his way to an edge, if he can, and waits for opportunity to get ashore. From there he can observe what is happening without personal involvement.'

Having no other occupation, Medoor Babji meditated upon this saying of the Queen's. She had some time in which to do it. At sundown she ate some of the sun-dried fish. It was well after dark when the movement of the boat changed from one of being towed to a mere floating once again. Against the stars she saw the bulk of hills crowned with trees. The tidal current washed her onto a shelving beach, whether of sand or rock she could not tell, and all motion ceased. She crept into the blankets beneath the canvas cover and fell asleep.

Morning came with a twitter of birds, a bellow of lizards. By the shore stilt-lizards walked, their narrow heads darting into the shallows to bring up bugs and fishes, stopping now and then to utter their customary cry, 'Ha-ha, ha-ha,' without inflection. Stilt-lizard meat was edible, Medoor Babji told herself, coming out of sleep all at once, fully conscious of being somewhere new, different, unknown. This place could not be too foreign, she thought, if there were stilt-lizards. Edible. Yes. Hunger pinched her stomach and brought a flood of saliva into her mouth. She sat up in the boat, unwrapping herself. The lizards fled at sudden motion, then returned to stalk the shore once more, meantime keeping a wary eye on her.

The boat was halfway up a narrow beach, less sandy than stony, cut by a streamlet that bubbled down a shallow channel into a little bay. Contorted protrusions of black rock jutted from the beach and from the smooth surface of the bay, culminating in two writhing shapes, like a mighty arm and hand at each side of the entrance, reaching toward one another, braceleted with colonies of birds. Outside that embrace the River swept by, empty and endless.

Now the immediate danger was past. Now there was food and good water. Now that persona who had wished to cry for some time could cry.

It was some time before she realized what she was crying about, where the grief came from, boiling up from some deep well within her. It was not being lost, not being fearful for her life. It was being separated from Thrasne, lost from him, fearful for his life. And with that realization, she dried her tears, laughing at herself. The *Gift* was a strong, heavy boat, one that had plied the World River for generations. She thought of Thrasne fussing over it, repairing it at every opportunity, and of his crew of experienced men. Why had she assumed at once that he had met with some disaster? She was far more likely to have perished in the tiny *Cheevle*, and yet she lived. And if she lived, she could find the *Gift* again,

374

somewhere, if not on Southshore or mid-River, then on Northshore when it returned.

'If strangeys allow it,' she told herself with some asperity, trying to give herself something else to think about. It was a cheerless thought, yet it had the same strengthening force as one of Queen Fibji's lectures. 'Settle,' the Queen had said to her often. 'Settle, daughter. Consider calmly what you will do. Cry when it is done with, when you have the luxury of time.'

'How did you get to know absolutely everything?' Medoor had asked, somewhat bitterly.

There had been a long silence, then a humorless laugh. Medoor had looked up at her mother, startled, almost frightened. She had not heard that laugh before.

'I'll tell you a secret,' the Queen had said with a faraway, angry look on her face. 'I don't know. Much of the time I don't know anything. However, my not knowing will not help my people, so I must know. And I do. It is easier to correct a mistake than to be caught doing nothing. It is easier to beg forgiveness for a mistake than to beg permission to act. People will forgive you, child, but they will not risk allowing action. Go to a council and say, "Let me do this thing." They will think of ten thousand good reasons you should not. It could be wrong. Or it could be not quite right. Or it could be right, but of a strange rightness they are unfamiliar with. Oh, daughter, but they will talk and talk, but they will not say, "Do it." That is why I am Queen and they are my followers. Because they cannot risk anything nor take part in others doing so. They are herdbeasts, daughter. And yet I love them. When I speak to you of trial and error, Babji, whose experience do you think I am speaking of? . . .'

'So,' Medoor Babji told herself. 'If the Queen can prevail in such a way, so her daughter can also prevail.'

The resolution did not help her much in deciding what to do next. Securing food seemed most logical, and this decision was helped by a cramp of hunger that bent her in two. Fish was well and good, but it left one empty between meals.

It was important she not lose the *Cheevle*. She tugged it

375

farther up the beach and tied it firmly to a tree. A tidal bulge might come by; the presence of beaches argued for that probability. As she faced the bay, the sun was rising on her right hand, so the bay faced northward. Could this land be Southshore? Had the strangeys brought her to her journey's end? The beach extended on either hand as far as she could see, riven with tormented rock outcroppings here and there but interrupted by no headland, curving slightly outward at its western extremity to vanish in the River haze. She had come ashore in the only protected place within sight, though the haze prevented her from being sure she was on the only land in the vicinity.

The forest was made up almost entirely of one variety of tree, one unfamiliar to her, a short, thick-trunked tree, rather twisted in habit, with two or three main branches, also short and stout, with many graceful twigs bearing lacy clusters of pale green leaves that seemed almost pruned, so gracefully they barely overlapped one another, allowing each leaf its measure of sun.

Some of these trees carried large, waxy blooms of magenta and azure blue, fringed with silver. Others bore seed heads, drying, almost ready to open. Among these strange trees were other, more familiar ones. She found a puncon tree – a larger one than she had ever seen on North-shore – with fruit almost ripe. Not far from the fruit tree was a small grove of fragwood, and beyond that, inland, stood a gawky, feathery tree that looked and smelled almost like the thorn trees of the steppes. The leaf was more divided than in the trees she knew, and the fruit was larger. The scent pulled her halfway up the tree, stretched along a branch as she fumbled for ripe ones among the cluster, finding them sweeter than she was used to and more welcome for that. She ate a few bites, filling a sleeve pocket with more. She would stuff herself later, if she didn't get sick or die in the meantime.

Returning to the boat, she robbed it of enough line to make snares. By noon there were three stilt-lizards caught, killed, gutted, and drying in the smoke of a small fire. There were patches of white on many of the rocks, River salt dried by the sun, and she sprinkled this on the lizard meat. She had bought River salt in the markets of half a hundred towns but had never seen it in its natural state before. There had been no unpleasant result from eating the thorn tree fruit, so she ate a bit more, chasing it down with roast leg of lizard. The water in the streamlet was chill and pure. She felt less inclined to weep. 'Full stomachs,' Aunty Borab had been fond of saying, 'make calm judgements.' Or the reverse, sometimes. 'Hunger makes haste.'

It was time, she felt, for a slightly longer exploration. The boat could always be found so long as she kept the River within sight or hearing and went out with it on the one hand and returned with it on the other. The boat was safe enough. She piled brush over and around the lizard carcasses to let them dry a while longer in the smoke of the smothered fire, then strode off into the forest as far as she could without losing sight of the River through the trees, walking westward at a good pace, taking note of what she saw but making no effort to examine any aspect of the landscape in detail. There were more and more of the lacy-leafed trees interrupted by occasional groves of other kinds, some fruit bearing. She gathered the ripe fruit, filling her sleeve pockets as instinctively as a bird might gather seed. The Noor had been gatherers for generations. They did not pass bounty by.

Occasional outcroppings of the black stone broke the flatness of the land, peculiarly fluid-looking piles of it, as though it had been poured and then hardened. Medoor Babji found herself staring at it, trying to fathom what it made her think of, and realized it was like sugar candy poured out upon the slab, before it was worked and pulled. There were places on the steppes of the Noor, places near the Teeth of the North, where similar glossy stone was found. The wise men among her people said it came from the center of the earth, out of fiery vents, with great noise and plumes of ash. If so here, it had been long ago. Green lay over all, blanketing and softening.

There were many tiny streams. Once or twice she stopped, thinking she had heard something moving off in the woods among the recurrent bird noise. Once she looked shoreward between two groves to see a winged figure standing upon a rocky point, ready to dive into the sea. She blinked, and it was gone. It had not looked real, even at first, she told herself. Sun dazzle and weariness and being alone caused people to see things. The Noor were well aware of that. 'Steppe visions,' they called them. Well, these would be 'River visions.' When the sun had fallen before her, she turned to put it at her back, moving closer to the shore for the return trip.

Her mind was set on the outline of the boat, the stack of leafy branches she had placed over the fire. So it was she almost passed her campsite by, not recognizing it. The boat was shattered, great holes bashed through the planking as though by some heavy missile, a great spear, perhaps, thrust and withdrawn, thrust and withdrawn again. The fire was scattered into gray ash. The stilt-lizard meat was gone. All around the site and in the stream lay small blobs of guano, white and reeking.

Their footprints crosshatched the shoreline, coming out of nothing. Fliers. They had ruined her boat. They had stolen her meat. They had fouled her campsite and the stream. Two of them, she thought, who had walked side by side to do their hateful damage.

Worse, they had laid a trap for her. She put out her hand to coil some of the rope. She had almost touched it when a familiar glisten on the rough twist caught her eye. She put her hands behind her and bent forward, peering. A Tear of Viranel. Oh, hadn't the Noor learned long and long ago to watch for that glisten as they walked the steppes? The Tears could not kill them, but they made nasty sores where they touched, sores that were painful for a long time and took weeks to heal. Tears would grow anywhere, sometimes here, sometimes there. The Noor spread wood ashes on any patches they found, but the danger was always there. Medoor cursed, briefly, suddenly aware of danger from an active intelligence, out there, somewhere. They hadn't seen her except at a distance. They didn't know she was a Noor.

There were other Tears at the site. Not many she could find in the failing light. The destroyers had not bothered to rip the canvas cover away from the boat; the blankets were untouched. She took them. The light was too poor to do more than that. Tomorrow she would return to see what else could be salvaged. She stepped carefully away from the place, watching where she put her feet, scraping them again and again through the dry sand to remove any Tear that might have clung to her shoes.

Then she was back among the trees, looking up through the boughs into an empty, amber sky. They had spied on her, without doubt, seeing her easily on that barren beach. Now perhaps she could return the favor. Medoor Babji's lips parted in a snarl, an expression her mother would have recognized. When darkness came, she was well hidden in a copse of thick foliage, well wrapped against the night's chill, reasonably well fed on the fruit she had gathered during the day, and perhaps unreasonably set upon vengeance.

Inside her, shut away, someone grieved anew for Thrasne, for the near-kin, for all old, familiar, and much loved things. She had no way to repair the boat. Without it – without it her whole life might well be lived upon this shore. She shuddered with tears that she would not allow herself to shed, summoning anger instead.

In the earliest light of morning she went to the beach and salvaged all the rope she could lay hands on as well as all the canvas. They had been fairly clever in placing the Tears where she might have been expected to put her hands. She dragged her salvage through the ashes of her fire again and again, meantime protecting her hands with canvas strips cut from the boat cover. She would not cut the sail. Not yet. Morning and calm showed only four planks of the boat actually splintered. Perhaps, somehow, she would think of a way to restore them.

Heavily laden with her salvage, she went back into the woods and sought a cave, thrusting a long stick into every opening she found until she located a bottle-shaped hole in one of the black-rock outcroppings. The neck was almost too

379

narrow for her to wriggle through, but inside it opened out into a comfortable shape, smooth-walled. Here she stored the blankets, the rope, the canvas, her snares. The opening was hidden behind freshly cut branches. She brought out the snares to set them among the rocks where a streamlet rattled out of the forest onto the beach, hiding them with branches cut from the nearest tree. It trembled oddly when she cut it, but Medoor Babji had no time to pay attention to that. She picked fruit once more, filling her sleeve pockets. Then she went back to the shore to keep watch.

From a horizontal branch halfway up the largest tree in a small grove of frag trees, she could see the wrecked boat, the scattered ashes of her fire.

It was after noon when they came, spiraling down to land at the edge of the sand, their feet just above the waterline, as though fearful of it. They stalked into the campsite, examining each step of the way with nodding heads, peering eyes. One was of an unfamiliar type, taller and more slender than the other, better-groomed, with a shine to his feathers. The other was fusty and scurfy, feathers awry, and yet of the two, this one appeared the stronger and more vital.

'It came back,' croaked the taller one in harsh but understandable human language.

The other answered, making sounds Medoor Babji could not understand.

'Speak in meat talk,' the first croaked again. 'I don't understand your flier talk.'

'*Horgha sloos,* something-something,' the second said in a hideous, screeching tone. Then, in recognizable speech, 'Meat-talk soils my mouth.'

'Then let your mouth be filthy,' commanded the first. Though the shorter being croaked its speech, as though words were seldom used, the taller creature's words were clear and understandable. From her perch above them, Medoor Babji named it a Talker, unaware it was the name the whole class of creatures had chosen for themselves. It went on, 'At least I can understand meat talk. You barbarians from the wild lands talk like savages.'

The shorter flier deposited a blob of shit and held its wings at a threatening angle. 'Fliers not savages. Fliers important. We keeping meat animals in our care. Your highmost Talker commanded. We do. You, Slooshasill, nothing but Talons servant, do nothing, blat, blat, blat. Share meat. Dirty yourself.'

'Stop your words,' screamed the Talker in a rage. 'All that is unimportant. Do not speak of what is true on North-shore. We are not on Northshore. Thraish cannot fly over water, but storm can blow where Thraish cannot fly. Storm brought wind; wind brought us here. Now is only one importance. Food to keep us alive. Living or not living. Human meant much food, but human is gone.'

'Maybe got Tears on it. Maybe wandered off.' The flier opened its wings. For some reason, Medoor Babji thought it might be a female. Something in the way it moved, like a crouching barnyard fowl.

'No. Rope is gone. Cloth is gone. Ashes are spread around. Human took those things. Human saw and avoided Tears.'

The other cocked its head, took quick steps toward the waterside, then darted sideways with a hideous, serpentine stretch of the neck to snatch an unwary stilt-lizard that had poked its head from among the rocks. Medoor Babji watched in horrid fascination as the flier tossed the lizard up, caught it, tossed it again, each time cutting it as it struggled and shrieked, gulping it down at last while it still wriggled feebly, all its bones broken.

'Not enough of those, Esspill,' said the tall flier in a bleak tone. 'Not enough to keep us alive long.'

'Enough for me,' replied the other one. 'Enough for unimportant Esspill. Savage Esspill. Not enough for Slooshasill, important Slooshasill, Fourth Degree, that one can eat fish.'

The Talker darted his beak at the shorter bird, bloodying its head just above the beak. Dust rose around them as they fought, screamed, beat at one another with their wings. Then was silence. The dust settled. Medoor Babji could see

381

them crouched across from each other, panting. The taller one had had the worst of it. Hungry, her mind said to her in Aunty Borab's voice. That one's half-starved.

'Only filth eat fish,' the one called Slooshasill said at last. 'Only ground crawlers eat them.'

'Then catch lizards for yourself!'

'I am Talker.' In her hiding place, Medoor Babji's mouth twisted in amusement. She had named the creature correctly.

'You are flier. You are supposed to catch them. Fliers are supposed to bring food for Talkers. Females are to serve males!'

'Males,' the flier screamed in scorn. 'At mating time, Esspill will serve males. Talkers not males. And Slooshasill not even Talker now. Slooshasill nothing.'

They still crouched. 'When we get back to Northshore, Slooshasill will again be Talker. You will be punished, then, Esspill.'

'How get there? Cannot fly over water.'

'Did,' said the other in a hopeless tone. 'Did fly.'

'Didn't. Wind carried. Couldn't stop. Wind brought. Wind will have to take back again. Can't fly over water.'

A long silence. At last the Talker asked, in a tone that could only be the Thraish equivalent of a whine, 'What we do now, Esspill?'

'What you do, don't know. What I do is get more Tears. Then find human. Put Tears on. Eat it. I be strong then. Fly back. Fear or not.' It was an empty threat. Even to Medoor Babji, unused to the sound of flier talk, it came across as mere bluster. The wings came down in a hard buffet, throwing sand into a quickly falling cloud. Medoor dodged behind the trunk of the tree, afraid to be seen. When she came out again, both pairs of wings were above her, above the land, one in the lead, the other following. She watched them as they circled low above the forest, low above the beach, searching. Never, not even for a moment, did they fly out over the open water.

It seemed unwise, she felt, to stay in the vicinity of the

boat, though she did not want to risk losing it. She climbed higher in the tree and took a sighting. It was likely this small bay was unique. The bay lay midway on a line between two tallish hills, one crowned with a monstrous frag tree grove. There seemed to be no other hills within sight.

She came down the tree in a chastened mood, her desire for vengeance disciplined by reality. Esspill, the flier, was as large as she. Lighter, perhaps, but with talons and a sharp, hooked beak. Likely those talons could hold Tears without danger to Esspill herself. Herself. Medoor Babji would have been sure of it even without the verification of their speech.

But then what was the one called Slooshasill? A male? Not according to the other one. Not male or female. A kind of neuter thing. A Talker.

Who would have thought the fliers could talk? Queen Fibji had never spoken of any such thing. Of course, there were few fliers seen upon the steppes, but still it was odd that none among the Noor had known. If, in fact, they had not known.

And now? What?

She could hide indefinitely. She was confident of that. She had fruit and would eat fish, which the flier creatures would not. Even if Esspill caught every stilt-lizard on the place, which wasn't likely, Medoor Babji could be sure of food. But it would have to be a covert, sneaky kind of existence.

Or, she could fight. Reason said that odds against her would be reduced if she waited a while. That tall Talker creature was half-starved. The flier wouldn't feed it, and it didn't seem able to catch food for itself. Given only a little time, it would be dead or too weak to threaten her. So, patience was called for.

Still, it would be a difficult, nervous business, surviving with an eye in the sky looking for her. She went back to her cave, stopping at the snares on the way. Two stilt-lizards, not bad. She would smoke them . . .

She wouldn't smoke them. Medoor Babji cursed. Smoke would bring the damn feather mops on her in a moment. Smoke could be seen at great distances on any clear day or moonlit night. She would have to salt and sun-dry the meat. She could eat raw fish with resignation, perhaps even with a modicum of pleasure, but she could not face the idea of raw stilt-lizard. Hot bile stirred at the back of her throat. She needed a smoke oven. Perhaps one of the caves . . .

Smoke. She thought about that. It might be worth the effort, just to get the creatures away from here. Otherwise they would be haunting her. She thought about it for an hour and then decided upon it. She would begin today. There was no reason to wait.

One blanket and some food made a small pack. She headed east through the forest, moving as rapidly as possible while still keeping a fairly good watch on the land around her. When darkness came, she stopped on the beach to stack a large pile of wood with a smaller one next to it and then returned to the forest to build a small, smokeless fire of drift-wood under cover of a stone outcropping. She cooked a lizard over it, putting the fire out at once when she had eaten.

At early light, she lit the smaller pile of wood, connecting it to the larger one with a line of thin, dried sticks and shavings. Over the larger woodstack she laid leaves and grasses. By the time it caught and smoked, she should be some miles away to the east.

An hour later she climbed a tree and peered back the way she had come. A pillar of smoke rose straight into the windless sky, where two black dots swung and circled toward it. She allowed herself a brief moment of self-congratulation, then climbed down to walk east once more.

After the third smoke on the third morning, she went deeper into the woods and turned back the way she had come. If the fliers were not cleverer than she thought they were, they would go on east, looking for her there. The line of smokes had led them in that direction. There would be no smoke on the following morning, but they might think she had seen them and was hiding from them. If they kept on moving in that direction, she might be free of them for a very long time.

She slept in the woods for the two nights it took her to

return, each time awakened by stirrings and rustlings as though something or someone wandered in the leafy spaces. She was not foolish enough to call out. Her campsites were well hidden. She saw no evidence that anyone had wandered nearby when she woke. Still, it made a small itch of apprehension at the back of her mind.

When she returned to the boat, she unstepped the mast, laying it among fallen logs in the forest, half covering it with branches. The hull she drew deep into woods, tugging and hauling with much smothered cursing in between. It left a clear and unmistakable trail, one she took a great pains to eradicate. She raked away all the ashes of her earlier fire, gathered up the bits of charcoal, and built another fire half a mile down the beach, scattering it when it had burned out. If the fliers had not paid particular attention to the landmarks, they might assume that was the place the boat had been. She scattered some broken wood in that place and drew a heavy timber down the beach into the River. Now it looked as though she or someone had returned, had made some hasty repairs, perhaps, and then pulled the boat out into the water.

'Where it promptly sank, drowning me,' she said with a hopeless look at the carcass of the *Cheevle*. Two of the holes were small. They could be patched with wood whittled to size and pounded in, caulked with – well, caulked with something or other. Frag pitch. She knew where there were frag trees, and gathering the pitch was merely a matter of cutting the bark and collecting the hardening sap when it gathered in the scar, then melting it in – in something.

The remaining two holes, however, were sizable.

'When faced with a number of tasks,' Queen Fibji had said, 'so many that the mind balks at getting them done, pick one or two small ones and begin. When those are done, move on. Never consider all that must be done, for to do so is quite immobilizing . . .'

She began. Repairing the two small holes took five days, from dawn to dusk. She had caulked the wood with fresh frag sap, learning that it did quite well if applied in many thin coats and allowed to dry between. Using melted resin would have been quicker. It would also have been impossible. She had nothing she could use for a vessel and could find nothing that would serve. There were no gourds or hard-shelled nuts. Clay could be made into pots, of course, but that would have taken still longer.

While working, however, she had decided how to mend the larger holes. She would cut flat pieces of wood, glue them to the outside of the boat with frag sap, then cover the entire outside of the boat with the canvas boat cover.

It took five days more to complete the repairs. She dragged the hull back to the beach and into the water, where she managed to get the canvas under and around it, lacing the rope across the boat to catch the hooks on the opposite side. The mast was up, raised the same way she had raised it when on the River, with panting and grunts and a good deal of helpless cursing. She looked at the thing where it floated, shaking her head. It had a deck of rope, almost a net, where the lines laced across to hold the canvas. She would have to worm her legs between the ropes to sit at the rudder. She would have to wriggle herself beneath them to lie down at night. If there were another storm, she would probably sink.

In all that time, she had not seen the fliers. In all that time, she had almost forgotten them.

In the morning she could forget them completely, for she would be on the River once more, where they could not follow. Westward. To the end of this land, if it had an end. Then south. And if it had no end, then northward once more. Back to Northshore. She had a plentiful supply of dried fruit stored in canvas-sacks, an almost equal supply of sun-dried lizard meat. The last two days she had spent digging edible roots, which lay in well-washed succulence among the other provisions. She had raveled some rope to make a fishing line and curved some fragwood hooks. Even if the strangeys had forsaken her, she should be able to manage. She would not be out of sight of land unless she came to the end of this land and turned north or south once more.

So she built her small, smokeless fire under cover of the

rocks, ate fresh fruits and roots, freshly roasted meat, curled into sleep in satisfied exhaustion. There would be plenty of time to rest on the River.

During the night there was a tidal surge which washed the canvas-girdled *Cheevle* half back onto the shore. Medoor Babji, wanting an early start, was on the beach when the sun had barely risen, struggling to get the boat back into the water. Its canvas bottom did not wish to slide on the rough sand, and she swore at it fruitlessly, knowing she would need rollers to get it moving, which meant another day before she could leave.

The screech that came from behind turned her around, bent her backward over the *Cheevle* as though to protect it, before she even saw the fusty, raddled form of the flier stalking toward her over the sand. It carried a leaf-wrapped bundle in one set of rudimentary wing fingers. Without asking or being told, Medoor Babji knew they were Tears.

'So, human,' said Esspill. 'You tried to trick us.' It cawed laughter. 'You did trick stupid Talker. He went that way, long ago. Looking for you.'

'You weren't tricked?' she asked from a dry throat, the words croaked almost in the flier's own harsh tone.

Esspill shook her head, a mockery of human gesture. 'Oh, no. Was no meat in those fires. No bones. No reason for them.'

'You're very smart,' she gasped. 'Smarter than I thought.'

'Oh, fliers are smart. Smarter than Talkers think. Talkers think . . . think they are only smart ones. All words. No faith.'

'Faith?' She edged to one side, trying to get the boat between her and the flier.

'Stand still,' it commanded. 'Don't try to run. Tears won't hurt much. After that, humans don't feel.' It clacked its jaw several times, salivating onto its own feet, doing a little skipping dance to wipe the feet dry.

'Faith?' asked Medoor Babji again, thinking furiously. 'What do you mean, faith?'

387

'No faith in Promise of Potipur. Potipur says breed, grow, have plenty. Talkers say not breed, not grow, live on filth. Now Thraish have herdbeasts again. Soon have many. Then all humans will die. No more filth. No more *horgha sloos*.'

'But if you breed, your numbers will grow, and you'll eat all your animals and go hungry again.'

'Promise of Potipur,' it said stubbornly. 'Promise. You hold still now. For Tears.'

'Tears don't work on the Noor,' she cried. 'They don't work on blackskins.'

The fliers stopped, beak agape. 'Noor. You are Noor?'

'I am, yes. Medoor Babji. One of the Noor.'

'No. Dark from the sun. Humans turn dark from sun.'

'I am not dark from the sun, Esspill. I was born dark. Look at my hair. The Tears won't work on the Noor. It won't grow inside us.'

'Try,' the flier snarled. 'Try anyhow.'

She edged away again, feeling in her sleeve pocket for her knife. 'I'll fight,' she threatened. 'I may kill you.'

'Fight!' it commanded. 'Do that!'

Wings out, claw fingers stretched wide, talons lifted, beak fully extended, Esspill launched herself at Medoor, who dived in a long, flat dive into the River. It was instinct, not reason. It was the best thing she could have done. She came up in the water, clinging to the bowline of the *Cheevle*, began tugging at it, frantically working the boat into the water beside her. On the shore the flier danced up and down, pulling the boat away from her, screaming its rage.

Then it was gargling, its beak wide, eyes bulging. A long wooden shaft protruded from the flier's breast. She turned around, staring. Through the rocky arms that embraced the bay came another boat, no larger than the *Cheevle*. In it sat a man. In it stood a . . . a flier? Not a flier? Something very like, and yet not?

It had a bow in its wing fingers, an arrow nocked, the arrow pointed at the shore where Esspill still staggered to and fro, falling at last in a shower of dark blood onto the sand.

'Hello?' called the person. 'We saw your smoke. We've been looking for you for over a week.'

'Thraish,' cried the other, drumming his keeled breast with his wing fingers to make a hollow thumping. 'I have killed a Thraish.' Thumpy-thump, delight in that voice. 'Look, Burg, I've killed a Thraish!' It turned toward Medoor Babji, bowing. 'Happy day, woman. I have saved you.'

'We're called the Treeci,' he told her, working the sculling oar as they moved down the coast, westward, the *Cheevle* in tow. 'Have you heard of us?'

'I have,' she admitted. 'There are Treeci on a place called Strinder's Isle.'

'Oh, there are Treeci on half the islands in the River,' he said, making an expression that was very smilelike with a cock of head and flirt of eyes.

'That's possibly an exaggeration,' said the human person. He was a stout, elderly man with white hair that blew around his head like fluff.

'Possibly. Or possibly an understatement, so far as that goes. What was that Thraish trying to do to you, eat you?' The Treeci turned to Medoor Babji once more.

'She had Tears of Viranel wrapped up in a leaf. She wanted to put them on me and then eat me. Tears don't work on the Noor, though. Our skins are too dark.'

'I've heard that. Had you heard that, Burg?'

'Oh, it's probably written down somewhere. In the archives over on Bustleby. It's probably written down there.'

'You know about the Noor?'

'We have histories, young lady,' said Burg. 'We aren't savages. We're literate, human and Treeci both.'

'But where – where did you come from?'

'The same place you did, originally. Probably for the same reason. Trying to get away from the senseless conflict over there.' He jerked a thumb to the north. 'Long ago. At the time of the Thraish-human wars. They were eating

389

humans then. It's a wonder they haven't eaten them all by now.'

Medoor Babji shook her head. 'No. No, we have a – they have what my mother calls a detente. An agreement. They eat dead people. Northshore dead people, not Noor dead people.'

The Treeci spat. 'Carrion eaters,' he gasped. 'So I have heard, but I find it hard to believe, Medoor Babji.'

'Oh, come, Saleff, the Thraish were eating human dead during the wars. You know that.'

'Out of desperation, yes, but . . .'

'I presume they are no less desperate now.'

'They could do what we did.'

'We've talked about this a thousand times,' the human said irritably. 'The ones who could do what you did, *did* what you did. The ones who were left *couldn't* do it. They had offspring who also couldn't do it. The Thraish could no more eat fish and become flightless today than they could become sweet-natured and stop shitting all over their living space. It's called selective breeding, and they've done it.'

It was only argument, not even addressed to Medoor Babji, but the words rang inside her, setting up strange reverberations. Why? Something fled across her mind, trailing a scent of mystery and marvel. What? She tried to follow it, but it eluded her. She concentrated. Nothing. At least she would remember the words. *Selective breeding. Those who could do it, did it.* She would think about those words later.

'You know all about them?' Medoor Babji asked. 'How do you know all that?'

'Oh, some of us human islanders sneak back to Northshore every now and then. Young ones of us, boys with time on their hands and adventure in their blood. Some of them go and never return, some go and come back, enough to give us an idea what's going on. One of the more recent returnees was a slave for the Thraish for five years.'

'And they didn't eat him?'

'Would have, I suppose. He didn't give them a

chance.' Burg spoke proudly, almost boasting. 'My son.'

Silence fell, except for the sloshing of the sculling oar. After a time, Medoor Babji asked, 'You came to find my smoke?'

'You could have been one of ours,' said Burg. 'Lost. We use smoke signals. It looked like that, one fire each day for three days. We do that sometimes. Or sometimes three fires all at once.'

'Where are we going?'

'Down to Isle Point. West end of the island. You can look across the straits to the chain from there.'

'Who lives there?'

'Treeci, mostly. About a dozen humans, too. Most of our folk are down the chain, on Biddle Island, and Jake's.'

'How many?'

'A few thousand in this chain. The islands aren't that big. We have to spread out. Otherwise we'd overfish the River, kill off all the edible animals, the way the Thraish did during the hunger.'

'What edible animals?'

'The ones there aren't any more of on Northshore, girlie. Did you ever see an espot? Or a dingle? Little furry things? 'Course not. Thraish ate 'em all. They're extinct on North-shore. From what I understand, you've no mammals left at all on Northshore.'

'That flier, Esspill, she said they had herdbeasts again. I didn't know what she meant.'

The white-haired man pulled in his oar and stared at her, mouth working. 'Is that possible?'

'A few might have survived,' the Treeci responded. 'Somewhere. Perhaps behind the Teeth.'

'If they have herdbeasts again, it's the end of humans on Northshore,' the man snarled. 'You can depend on it. The Thraish will kill them all.'

Medoor Babji shook her head at him. 'I don't think the humans would let them do that,' she said. 'I think it might be the Thraish who would end up dead.'

'Hush,' said the Treeci. 'Don't upset yourself, Burg.

Northshore is none of our business. Don't we always say that, generation on generation? Northshore isn't our business.'

'How about Southshore?' Medoor Babji asked. 'That's what we were looking for.'

'Over there,' said Burg laconically, pointing over his shoulder. 'That way. About a month's travel or more.'

'It's really there?'

'Was the last time we looked. Bersdof's kids sailed there last year, just for the hell of it.'

'Is it empty, Burg? Is there room there for the Noor?'

'Room for the Noor and anybody else, far's I know. Nothing there but animals and plants. No human grain over there, though. You'd have to plant that.'

'Why? Why is it just sitting there? Why hasn't anyone gone there?' She tried to imagine an empty land, one without Jondarites. It was impossible.

'Well, those of us who fled with the Treeci landed here on the island chain first. Seeing what the Thraish had made of their world, we took it as kind of a religious thing to behave differently. We don't expand much. Small societies in small places. Closeness. That's why we haven't gone to Southshore. As for other people, I don't know. Maybe the place was just waiting for the Noor.'

The Treeci Saleff interrupted them with a long-drawn-out hooting call. There was a response in kind from the shore. 'There's Isle Point,' he said, turning to her with his cocked-head smile. She looked shoreward to see the water moving around the end of the island, and a little way west-ward another island, the long line of land broken only by this narrow strait. A village gathered itself beneath the trees, small wooden houses, curling smoke. A mixed group of humans and Treeci stood on the shore, old and young.

'Will you be my guest?' Saleff asked. 'Burg would ask you, I know, but he has a houseful just now. New grandchild.'

Medoor Babji bowed as best she could in the tilting boat. 'I would be honored, Saleff.'

'You'll be better off,' Burg snorted. 'Saleff's mama – Sterf, her name is – she's a finer cook than my wife is, that's honest.'

'My mother will welcome you. As will my nest sister and the young siblings.'

Medoor Babji bowed again. She was already lost. She had already told them about her need to find the *Gift*. It would seem rude and ungrateful to mention it again so soon. And yet their invitation had had an air of complacency about it, as though there could be no refusal nor any limit to her stay. She cast a quick look at the horizon. Where was Thrasne? And her people? She swallowed, smoothed the lines out of her forehead, and set herself to be pleasant. The boat was rapidly approaching the shore, and half a dozen people of various kinds were wading out to meet her.

* * *

Blint told me once there are fliers who can talk, or at least that some people say they can. At first this seemed a silly thing to believe, but as I got to thinking about it, I wondered if it wasn't sillier to believe that talk was something only men could do. I've heard the strangeys calling, and the sounds they make are so large and complicated they must be words of some terrible, wonderful kind. But the sounds the fliers make, if those are words, they are short words and hard words. And I wish I'd heard the Treeci talk, those Pamra spoke of, for if they can talk, then surely the fliers can, too, and all we've thought about them for all our lives must be lies.

It would be interesting to talk with fliers, and strangeys. Except their words may not mean what our words mean at all, and it would be worse to misunderstand them than to just have them a mystery.

From Thrasne's book

19

At Isle Point, the house of Saleff squatted beneath a grove of stout trees with ruddy-amber leaves that filtered golden light into the rooms and onto the many porches where Saleff's kin moved about like orderly ghosts. Medoor Babji was at first amused by and then solicitous of the silence.

'We have a habit of quiet,' Salef's mother, Sterf, told her. 'Originally adopted, I'm sure, out of rebellion against the cacophony of the Thraish. Later it became our own, particularly satisfying trait. The children tend to be a bit loud, of course, and must learn to go into the woods or out on a boat if they wish to shout or yodel or whatever it is they do.'

There were three children in the house, three young ones, at first alike as puncon fruit in Medoor's eyes, each then acquiring a mysterious individuality that she found difficult to define. Mintel was the serious one, the quietest. Cimmy was graceful, with a lovely voice. Taneff was the most delightful, curious, always present, full of whispered questions, ready to run quick errands, even without being asked. The three soon named her Cindianda, which meant in their language, they said, 'little dark human person.' Medoor Babji thought they might be fibbing to her, that the name might mean something very disrespectful, though Sterf assured her not.

'How old are they?' she asked, watching them cross the clearing with amazement. They moved like darting dancers, lithe as windblown grass.

'Oh, just fifteen,' Sterf said, a little wrinkle coming between the large orbs of her eyes. It was one of the things that made Treeci so like humans, the way their faces wrinkled around the eyes. If one looked only at the eyes, not at the flat, flexible horn of their beaks, they could have been humans in disguise, got up for some festival or other. 'Just fifteen.' There was something vaguely disquieting in her tone, and Medoor Babji thought back to everything Pamra had told her about the Treeci. Hadn't there been something? She shook her head, unable to remember. During that time Pamra Don and Medoor Babji had known one another – a misnomer of sorts, Medoor felt, since she did not feel she knew Pamra Don at all – Medoor had been so busy wondering what it was about Pamra that held Thrasne in such thrall she had paid too little attention to what Pamra had said.

'Trial and error,' she murmured to herself, being contrite. When Queen Fibji learned how many times Medoor Babji had remembered that particular lesson on this trip, she would no doubt be greatly gratified.

Also in the house was the mother of the young ones, Arbsen, who was also Sterf's daughter and Saleff's nest sister. Of them all, Arbsen was the most silent, the most withdrawn. Some days she sat on one of the porches, her eyes following the children, broodingly intent. Other days went by during which Medoor Babji did not see her at all. She seemed to spend a great deal of time shut up in her own room at the top of the house, carving things. They were not Thrasne kinds of things, not definable images, but rather strange, winding shapes which seemed to lead from the current and ordinary into realms of difference, strangeness. Several of these articles decorated the walls of the house, and seeing them, Medoor Babji thought of Jarb Houses, wondering if the Treeci had such things. 'Though I don't suppose Treeci ever go mad,' she commented.

'Of course we do,' said Saleff, amused. 'We are in all respects civilized.'

'You mean primitives don't go mad?'

'I mean they don't consider it madness. They would probably consider it being possessed by the gods, or in thrall to ghosts. Something of that kind.'

'How do you know all this? You've never seen a primitive.'

It came out as more of a challenge than she had intended, but Saleff did not take offense. 'The humans have books, Medoor Babji. There is a printing press on Shabber's Island. There are archives on Bustleby. There are men on Jake's Island who spend all their time collecting information and writing things down. During the hunger – that is, the period before and during the Thraish-human wars after the weehar were all gone – the humans who came here brought many things with them. Books. Musical instruments. Equipment for laboratories where they make medicines. It was part of the reason they came, to preserve their knowledge. The humans called what was happening on Northshore a "new dark age." You understand that? We have learned from men, but we have also taught them. It has been an equitable exchange.'

Medoor Babji had that flash of elusive thought again, as though someone had just told her the answer to a long-asked question, but it was gone before she could grasp it, leaving her shaking her head in frustration.

She walked in the groves with the children. 'Cindianda,' Taneff begged, 'tell us stories of Northshore.'

'What do you want to know?'

'Tell us of the Noor. Tell us of the great Queen.'

So, she invented, spinning incredible tales into the afternoon. Taneff was insatiable. Whenever she stopped, Taneff wanted more, more and more stories, and she began to look forward to these sessions under the trees during which she could let her imagination spin without fault. Nothing hung upon her stories but the day's amusement, and she relished that.

Each morning when she woke, she resolved to get the boat repaired and set out in search of Thrasne. Each evening, she resolved it anew. Still, the days went by in placid grace, full of quiet entertainment.

One morning she rose early, conscience stricken or dream driven, determined to go to the shore and examine the *Cheevle*. She was amazed to find it had been almost entirely repaired. Only one of the planks remained to be replaced. Saleff had said nothing to her of repairing her boat, and she felt shamed that so much had been done without her help or thanks. She looked up to find him beside her, head cocked in that smiling position.

'Soon,' he said. 'Some of the young people will want to go journeying soon, and they can go with you to find your friends.'

'When?' she begged, suddenly aware of how many days had passed.

He pointed skyward. 'After Conjunction. Not now. The tides will be treacherous for a time. When Conjunction passes, they will fall into a manageable state.'

She examined the moons, surprised she had not noticed how near to Conjunction they were. It would be weeks before she could go. 'I'll never find him,' she said hopelessly. 'Never.'

'Oh, we think you will. We've sent word by island messenger to all the settlements, east, west, south. The word is spreading among the island chains. Even the strangeys know we're looking for it. The *Gift of Potipur* will be spotted somewhere, don't fear.'

She went walking with the children. Cimmy and Mintel ran off into the woods, saying they smelled fruit ripening. Taneff stayed with her, leaping into the path, then out again, whirling about, seizing her by the hand to drag her, protesting, to the top of a pile of rocks.

'Ouch!' She bit the word off. 'Damn it, Taneff, that hurt.' There was a long graze on her arm where it had been dragged against the black stone. 'I'm bleeding.'

Taneff stood, looking at her stupidly, saying nothing, shifting from foot to foot, a dark shadow moving behind the eyes, utterly unlike their usual expression. Then the eyes cleared, and Taneff smiled, a little uncertainly. 'Sorry. I am sorry, Cindianda. I got carried away with the running and leaping, I guess. Everything in the village is so – so . . .'

'Circumscribed,' she offered with a wry laugh. 'Orderly.'

'Well, yes. Lately it just seems to irritate me.' Legs stamping, wings held slightly away from the body, Taneff began to gyrate, a mockery of a dance. 'I need to get it out of my system.'

Medoor Babji repeated this to Saleff with a laugh. 'I'm glad to know it isn't only among the Noor that young people get tired of order.'

Saleff received it in silence, with only a few murmured words of apology for Medoor Babji's injury. 'Yes. The young people need some excitement,' he said at last. 'We'll have some dances.'

They had one two days later, drumming and a lot of very elegant prancing on a dance floor, all the young mixed in together, leaping and jostling. Among the crowd were half a dozen who were magnificent dancers, the feathers around their eyes flushed a little with the unaccustomed noise.

'Cimmy and Mintel are going to visit some kinfolk,' old Burg announced one morning, apropos of nothing. 'Next island over. Would you like to go along?'

Medoor Babji allowed that she would. They left early in the morning, Sterf, Burg, Cimmy, and Mintel in a little, light boat with Medoor Babji perched in the stern like an afterthought, trailing her fingers in the water and humming to herself.

'I need to see some of my colleagues over on Jake's,' Burg told her. 'The Treeci are better with boats than I am, so I hitch a ride whenever anyone is going.'

'There are a lot of boats going,' she answered him, pointing them out, counting them off. Six boats from Isle Point, all setting out in various directions, all with young ones aboard.

'Bringing home the brides,' said Cimmy in a depressed little voice, at which Sterf said something sharp in admonition. Medoor Babji started to ask, but Burg shook his head at her. A taboo subject. Very well, she would not ask.

On Jake's she went with Burg to meet the humans on the island, spent the day, the night, and a greater part of the

398

next day doing so. They were many, garrulous, and eager for new faces and new information. Every word Medoor Babji uttered about Northshore was soaked up by an eager audience, and by afternoon her voice had given out.

Burg gave her puncon brandy and let her sit in a corner of the laboratory while he talked shop with his kinfolk. She dozed, warmly content after a night with almost no sleep.

'Arbsen was here last week,' someone was saying to Burg.

'Arbsen? She hardly ever leaves her room, except to walk with Taneff in the woods.'

'She was here, Burg. She wanted the blocker hormone.'

'That's illegal. Unethical, too.'

'It's only illegal for Treeci to use it, not for us to give it.'

'Don't be silly. We live with the Treeci; of course we obey the spirit of their laws. Have you told Saleff? Have you told *any* of the Talkers?'

'Not yet. I was waiting for you to come over. You know the family.'

'I'll talk to him. What did you tell Arbsen?'

'Just what you said. It's illegal.'

In her corner, Medoor Babji stirred uneasily. This was evocative of something she had heard before, something Pamra Don had said. Something.

Burg roused her sometime later, and they walked together to the shore. There was a strange youngster waiting with Sterf, wide-eyed and frightened looking.

'Treemi,' Sterf introduced her. 'Coming back with us to Isle Point.'

'Will Cimmy and Mintel be staying here long?' Medoor Babji asked. 'Will I have a chance to see them before I leave?'

The question somehow went unanswered in their bustle to load the boat. She did not ask it again. Taneff met them back at Isle Point. Taneff was carrying flowers for the visitor and was unwontedly silent. He did not even answer Medoor Babji's greeting.

There were other visitors. All the youngsters seemed to be

paired off, one local and one visitor, the locals wandering around a good part of the time with the visitors in attendance. Taneff, who had not let Medoor Babji alone in his demand for stories, now seemed almost to avoid her.

'All right, Burg,' she asked, seeking him out and peering around to be sure they were alone, human to human. 'What's going on?'

He shook his head at her, making a taciturn, pinch-lipped face.

'No, don't give me that. I know it's a taboo subject, but you've got to tell me what's going on or I may transgress. I don't want to do that.'

He sighed. 'I suppose you're right, Medoor Babji. It's Conjunction, that's all. Conjunction in a year in which some children in the community reach mating age.'

'Breeding age?' she asked, suddenly remembering something Pamra Don had said. 'Couldn't they put it off a few years? Gods, they're only children.'

He shook his head. 'No, actually, they're at exactly the right age. Biologically speaking, that is. Or so my friends over at the lab on Jake's tell me.'

'So the visitors are what? What was it Cimmy said, "brides"?'

'Yes. Cross-island mating, to prevent inbreeding. Do you know anything about that, Medoor Babji?'

'I know you breed champion seeker bird to champion seeker bird if you want the traits passed on. I know if you breed too close for too long, though, sometimes the chicks don't live.'

He nodded. 'It's the same for all creatures. Inbreeding intensifies characteristics, both desired and undesired. With seeker birds, you can destroy the faulty ones. The Treeci wouldn't approve of that, so, Cimmy and Mintel went over to Jake's Island to meet a couple of the young roosters over there, and little Treemi came back here to meet Taneff. That's really all there is to it.'

It was not all there was to it. There was a great deal more

400

to it than that, but someone came to the door of Burg's house, and the conversation ended.

As she was walking back to Saleff's house, she met Taneff on the path.

'Hear you've got a new friend,' she called, teasing him a little.

He looked at her, head down, wings slightly cocked. 'Friend,' he said. His eyes were glazed, dull as though a film lay over them. The visitor, Treemi, came out of the woods and took him by the wing, her fingers caressing him as she cast a quick, warning look at Medoor Babji.

'I've got fan fruit for you, Taneff,' she said. 'Fan fruit.'

'Fan fruit,' he said, turning toward her, feet dancing, wings lifting.

'Fan fruit,' she sang, leading him away, half dancing. Arbsen came out of the wood and followed them, at some distance, her eyes wild and haggard.

Medoor Babji stood looking after them, more troubled than she could explain. Of the three children, Taneff had been her favorite. Taneff, as he was, not this strange, withdrawn creature who talked in monosyllables. She shook her head, annoyed at herself.

That night she was wakened by voices. She rolled from her mat on the floor and went to the window to close it, only to stop as she recognized the voices coming from the room below her.

'I want you to give it to Taneff.' Arbsen's voice, husky with pain, anguish. 'Saleff, you've got to.'

'Arbsen, you've been eating Glizzee, haven't you.'

'What difference if I have? Glizzee is the only thing keeping me sane. That has nothing to do with what I asked you. I asked you to give the hormone to me. For Taneff. He's my child, Saleff. I can't let him die.'

'Arbsen. You, of all people, should know the folly of that. Remember Kora? Kora and her son, Vorn. Remember them?'

'Taneff isn't in the least like Vorn. I think Taneff's a Talker. Vorn wasn't.'

'No, Vorn wasn't. And Taneff isn't a Talker, either, Arbsen. I've been testing him myself, the last time just yesterday. Do you think I wouldn't do that, carefully, with a member of our own family?'

'You made a mistake,' she wept. 'I know you did. He's a Talker. I just know it.'

'If he were, my dear, I would know it. Can't you resign yourself, Arbsen? Go to Sterf. She'll help you.'

'How could she help me! She never had this happen to her. She had a *damn Talker*. She had you!' The sound of wild weeping erupted into the quiet glade. In the houses, lights went on. Silence fell below.

Medoor Babji shut the window, hideously uncomfortable. There were things she felt she should remember, things she wanted to ask Burg on the morning.

And on the morning, she could not. Burg had gone to Jake's for a time, she was told, taking his family with him. He would be back for her after Conjunction. There were only two human families left in Isle Point, neither of them with young people. Despite her affection for Saleff's family, Medoor Babji felt abandoned.

The whole settlement seemed to be under emotional strain. There was a sense of communal anguish which kept her from asking Saleff any questions. Several times over the succeeding days, she met Taneff and Treemi in the woods or on the beach paths. Taneff scarcely seemed to know her. His voice was only a croak, though the rest of him was becoming glorious, frilled with feathers, flushed with rose. Always, Arbsen followed them at a distance. She had grown gaunt, almost skeletal. Almost every night there were dances somewhere nearby. Medoor Babji was not invited to attend, but no one could hide the sound of the drums.

And Arbsen was suddenly much in evidence, a hectic flush around her beak, very talkative. Both Saleff and Sterf watched her with a worried grimace, and Medoor Babji wondered if she should not absent herself from the Treeci house.

Which point was decisively answered by Sterf herself.

402

'Mating time is difficult for us,' she said. 'Emotionally, you understand. Some of our loved children are far away, and we worry whether they are treated well. You are self-effacing and sensitive, Medoor Babji, but being so tactful is hard on you and us. Burg's house is empty. Would you mind using it for the next few days?'

To which Medoor Babji bowed and made appropriate expressions of sympathy and concern, all the while afire with curiosity.

There were drums that night, a fever in the blood. There were drums the night following. And on the third night, Conjunction came. Mindful of the laws of hospitality, Medoor Babji kept herself strictly within the Burg house, whiling the long, sleepless hours away by reading books. Burg had more of them than Queen Fibji had, and Queen Fibji had a good many. The drums went on most of the night, trailing away into a sad emptiness a few hours before dawn.

She woke late in the morning. The village was still silent, empty as a sucked puncon peel. Away in the woods somewhere, smoke rose, a vast, purposeful burning. The reek of it made the hairs on Medoor Babji's neck stand up – smoke, but more than smoke. Incense, too. And something else which the incense did not quite cover. There was a feeling of sadness, a smell of bittersweet horror. She sat on the porch with her book, drinking endless cups of tea, waiting for something to happen, half-afraid that something would.

What did happen was that Burg returned, with his family, grim-faced and white. Medoor walked down to meet him at the shore. 'Have you seen anyone today, Medoor Babji?'

'Not a soul, Burg. Forgive my trespassing on your home, but Sterf asked me to . . .'

He shook his head. 'Of no matter. I told her to send you over if things got tense. Which they have. Worse than I thought.'

He turned away to supervise the family – son, son's wife,

403

daughter, grandchild, baby – as the boat was unloaded.

'Turn it over, wash it out, and leave it here,' he told his son. 'Sterf will want to be taking Treemi home tonight or first thing in the morning. I'll go with her.' He said this as though he did not believe it, like a courtesy phrase, said out of habit, not out of conviction.

He trudged up to his house, pausing on the porch to feel the pot Medoor Babji had left there, pouring himself a cup when he found it still warm. She held her tongue, not wanting to distress him more than he obviously already was.

'Arbsen stole the stuff,' he said at last, looking over her shoulder into woods. 'The stuff we give young Talkers to get them through mating season without dying.'

'I – I don't understand.' And yet, she did. She remembered things Pamra had said. About Neff. Holy Neff. Her vision, the one that spoke to her all the time. Burg went on, confirming her recollection.

'Male Treeci – male Thraish, the whole species – they die after they mate. The breeding cycle triggers a kind of death hormone. Among the Thraish, the Talkers have learned to make an antidote from their own blood. They locate young Talkers before the breeding season, sequester them, give them the antidote, and it inhibits the breeding cycle.' He rubbed his forehead, rubbed tears from the corners of his eyes.

'When we first came here the technique had been lost or something. When young Talkers were born, they just died, along with all the rest of the males. A rare tragedy. Only about one in a thousand males is a Talker. Still, it was always a pity. Talkers don't lose their intelligence, you know, not like the others. The ordinary males – they go into it in a kind of anesthetized ecstasy. Not Talkers. Whatever it is that makes them different also makes them victims. So, we created an antidote in the labs, to save the Talkers. Ones like Saleff. It doesn't inhibit the breeding cycle as the Thraish medication did. It just inhibits the death hormone.'

'Then they can all live?' Medoor Babji said. 'Taneff can live! That's what Arbsen wanted from Saleff.'

404

'No. No, they can't. We tried that, out of compassion, a long time ago. It was a horrible mistake. But Arbsen was so crazy with grief, she stole the stuff. Now I have to find out what she did with it . . .'

'Why, she gave it to Taneff,' said Medoor Babji. 'What else would she do?'

'Oh, sweet girl, I pray you're wrong,' he said, the tears now running down his face in a steady stream. 'I know you're right, but I pray you're wrong.'

At the fall of evening, Treeci began to trickle back into the village, silent as shadows. Somewhere far away a bell began to ring, measured stroke after measured stroke. No one needed to say it was a mourning bell. The sound alone did that.

Saleff came to the house. 'Return to us, Medoor Babji. We need the distraction of your presence.' He was carefully not looking at Burg.

Burg would not allow the evasion. 'Arbsen stole the hormone, Saleff. Took it from the lab when she was over there a few weeks ago.' Burg was blunt, demanding a response.

Saleff didn't reply.

'Is Treemi all right?'

'We haven't found her,' the other said in a bleak, shattered voice. 'Tomorrow we will begin to look.'

'Is Arbsen around?'

'Not Arbsen, no. Nor Taneff.'

'Why wait until morning, Saleff? He has had them a full day. They could still be alive. If we look tonight, we may save Treemi's life. Otherwise you'll have blood guilt to pay her family, which will mean another life. You want to risk Cimmy, too? Or Mintel?'

The other looked up, an expression of despair on the strange, withdrawn face. 'If there is any chance she is alive, we will look tonight.'

They searched by torchlight, moving outward from the village, all the Treeci and all the human occupants, all but the youngest children.

They found Treemi first. Alive, but barely. Body

405

blooded, sexual parts ravaged and mutilated. Burg gathered the body into strong arms and carried it back toward the village, Sterf close behind him, weeping.

Later, down a long, leaf-strewn gully, they found Arbsen. Her body was broken, as though she had been buffeted with heavy clubs, but her eyes opened when they spoke to her.

'Arbsen, why?' Saleff murmured in a heartbroken voice.

'Why? You knew. You knew.'

'I didn't believe it,' she whispered, blood running from the corner of her mouth. 'He is my child. He loves me.'

'Oh, Arbsen, they only love if they die in the loving. If they live, it isn't love.' He leaned across her, weeping, not seeing her eyes, glazed and staring forever at the darkness.

It was dawn when they found Taneff at last, a golden dawn, gloriously alive. They heard him first, crowing at the sunrise. They saw him then, tumescent, flushed red as blood, eyes orbed with triumph, dancing upon a small elevation above the forest floor. Around him the trees were shredded; beneath his feet the earth was a ruin.

Medoor Babji was among the first to see him, all disbelieving. It could not be Taneff. She called his name in her disbelief, careless of her safety. When he turned toward her, she saw that it was he. Taneff as she had never seen him. He saw her, knew her, spoke her name with a kind of brute inevitability.

'Come,' he called. 'Come!'

He danced on the mound, beckoning.

She stopped, horrified at the sight of him. There was blood on his talons, blood on the wing fingers, which twitched and snapped.

'Why?' she cried, unable to contain it. 'Why did you kill Arbsen? Why did you kill your mother?'

'Told me to stop,' he crowed at her. 'Told me to stop. The young one said stop! Nobody tells Taneff to stop!'

He leaped high, rushed down the slope at her without warning. He attacked her, wings out, fingers clutching, sex organ bulging and throbbing. He did not see the torch she

406

held; she had forgotten she held it; her Noor-trained reflexes did the rest. It was not Taneff who blazed as he fought. It was horror.

Then there were men and Treeci all around. Someone had a spear. There was a long, howling struggle, and a body at the end of it. No one she knew. No one she had ever known.

'Why?' she sobbed on Saleff's breast. 'Why?'

The Talker stroked her as though she had been one of the Treeci young. 'Because they are meant to die, Medoor Babji. They are meant to die.'

He took her back to the house where Treemi lay, barely breathing, Burg working over her. They built a pyre on the shore for the other two, and somehow the night and the day following passed.

A few days later, Burg showed her the *Cheevle*, mended, as sound as when it had been built. 'Word has come,' he told her. 'We can lead you to the *Gift*. You will find it east of here, nearby a great island where our people do not go, but where the strangeys have brought your people.'

'Will someone go with me?' she asked, feeling suddenly very lonely at the thought of leaving them.

'Cimmy and Mintel are taking a boat out. They wish to be gone for a time. It is hard – hard for nest mates to lose one of their number at the time of mating. It is harder still to lose one as they lost Taneff.'

'He was mad,' she said sadly. 'Mad, Burg. The whole experience broke his mind.'

'Is that what you think?' He laughed harshly. 'Oh, Medoor Babji, you are far from the mark. No, no. Listen, I will tell you a little story. Something men have pieced together from tales told by the Treeci and excavations made long ago, before we left Northshore.

'Evidently in the long-ago, the males did not die when they bred. The male Thraish, that is; there were no Treeci then. They lived. As you saw Taneff, they lived. After the first mating their blood boiled with the desire for power.

They took females, more than they could possibly need, held them as slaves; they took territory and held that. And they fought. You saw. That is how they fought, competing with one another. Male against male. Tribe against tribe.

'In their violence, they didn't care whom they killed. In or out of season, they raped and mutilated. They killed infants. They killed females. Because the Thraish can lay large clutches of eggs, they managed to hang on for a long time, but in the end so many females died that those tribes could no longer survive.

'I have visions of them sometimes, the last few of those prehistoric Thraish, fighting one another in the skies of Northshore, already dead.'

'But the Thraish are not extinct,' she objected. 'What you are telling me is only a story.'

'No. It's the truth. Among all those wild, violent tribes there were some few, even then, in which the death hormone functioned. The males mated and died. There were no wars. Among these tribes was no rape, no slavery, no abuse of the young. And those groups survived. Such is their history. It is what we call a survival characteristic.'

After a time of silence, she asked, 'Treemi? What of her?'

'She will recover. She has blessedly forgotten what happened. She will even have young this season. There will be no blood price. Arbsen is dead. There can be no retribution.'

Medoor Babji nodded, overcome by sadness. Everything he had said was a heavy weight in her head, on her heart. She did not think she could bear the burden of it. There were lessons here she had not been taught by Queen Fibji, words she needed, instruction, comfort. And there was something more, fleeting like a silver minnow in her mind, something she herself could tell the Queen.

'Burg, you told me Southshore lies a month over the River. Do you swear it?'

He was startled. 'Why, I will swear it if you ask, Medoor Babji. Why do you ask?'

'Because I do not want to spend more time away from my

own kin. Because we were sent to find if Southshore is there, and if you will swear to me that you have seen it, with your own eyes, then I can go back and say so to the Queen.'

'I swear it, Medoor Babji. It is a great land. Empty, so far as we know, of any people, human or Thraish or Treeci. There are beasts there and familiar trees. I swear it. I have seen it with my own eyes.'

She surprised him by kissing him, then. It surprised her, as well. She was afire to reach Thrasne and the others. They would turn back now, racing home, home to the Noor. Something within her told her that only speed could prevent some hideous thing from happening. She remembered things Queen Fibji had said concerning the survival of the Noor, the lusty young warriors, the difficulty of holding them in check. She thought of the strutting Jondarites, their plumes nodding on their helms as the plumes had nodded on Taneff's head when he'd plunged into the spears. She thought of the mud graves of the warriors, and she longed to be home with every fiber of herself.

20

It was thirty days after the great storm, according to the journal of Fez Dooraz, that those on the *Gift of Potipur* saw the new island.

Though they could see no end to the land, yet they assumed it was an island, for it loomed up west of them like the prow of a great ship with water flowing on either side. Behind that mighty rock prow the land fell away west into lowlands and forests, with hills and mountains behind, seemingly limited both north and south but with no end to it they could see to the west, a long, narrow land where they had expected no land at all. Far off to the east a cloud hung over the water, and the sailors said this meant there was land there, as well. 'An island chain,' they said. 'It has been rumored there are island chains in mid-River.'

'Do we go ashore?' Obers-rom asked Thrasne. 'Is it possible this is Southshore?'

'Southshore or not, it is certainly a great land. And we have no choice if we are to get water.' Thrasne felt a bit doubtful, but with their need for water and with all the crew and the Noor hanging over the side, looking at the place, how could they go on by? They needed something to divert themselves from the thought of Medoor Babji. Even Eenzie the Clown was depressed, and Thrasne could not explain the feelings he had had since the storm. Now that she was gone, he realized who she had been. Not merely a queen's daughter – 'merely,' he mocked himself. More than that. To him, at least.

They lowered a man over the side to swim a line to the

land. When the light line was made fast, ropes were hauled in, tying them fast to trees ashore, and then the winch tugged the *Gift* in almost to the land's edge. The island fell sharply at this point, and the mooring was deep enough for the *Gift* to come very close. They built a small raft of empty kegs and planks to get back and forth, the sailors muttering meantime about the loss of the *Cheevle*.

Thrasne left a three-man watch aboard and went ashore with all the rest. He was heartily sick of the *Gift* himself, though the emotion made him feel guilty. The longest he could recall having traveled before without coming to land was a week or two, and that had been when sickness had struck a section of towns near Vobil-dil-go and all the boatmen had been warned away. Years ago, that had been, and then he had had the airy owner-house to live in. Now the little cabin he had squeezed himself out below was cramped and airless. He had considered slinging a hammock among the men a time or two, and would have except for the danger to discipline. It was hard to take orders from a man in his underwear, or so Thrasne had always believed.

At any rate, he was glad to walk on land again. He strolled along the narrow beach, really only a rocky shelf between the River and the cliffs, with a few hardy trees thrust through it. As he walked west, however, the shelf widened, dropped, became a real beach with sand on it, and the cliffs on their right hand also became lower, spilling at last into hillocks edged with dune grass and crowned with low, flat trees. The men of the *Gift* scattered toward the hills, into the woods, searching for water.

The Melancholics had dropped behind to poke among the tide pools at the island's edge, where they were finding brightly colored dye mulluks and flat coin fish. Thus it was only Thrasne at first who saw the carved man, buried to his knees in the sand.

'Ha,' Thrasne said, a shocked sound, as though he had been kicked in the stomach. 'That looks like old Blint.' He stopped short, knowing what he had said was ridiculous and yet filled with a horrible apprehension.

411

The carved man began to turn toward him, as though he had heard Thrasne speak. As though he had heard his name.

He turned so slowly that Thrasne had time to measure every familiar line of him, the undulating sag of the belly, the little hairy roll of fat at the back of the neck, the wiry ropes of muscle on the legs and arms where old rope scars still showed, the slant of the shoulders. When he was turned full toward him he saw it was Blint, Blint as though carved in dark fragwood, Blint with his mouth opening slowly, so slowly, to give him greeting.

'Thraaasneee,' the carved man said.

'Blint?' Thrasne bleated, terror stricken. What was this? His arms trembled, and the world darkened around him, shivering in a haze of red.

A voice in his mind said, 'Remember Suspirra, Thrasne. You were not afraid of Suspirra!'

For a time this was only mental noise with no sense to it. After a time his vision cleared, however, and he turned toward the strange figure in astonishment. Yes. He had taken Suspirra from the River, still living – in a way. She, too, had seemed carved. Now Blint – Blint, who had gone into the River that time long, long since, with weights tied to his ankles.

'I put you in the River,' Thrasne cried to the motionless figure.

'I know,' the carved man said, each word stretching into an infinitely long sound, fading into a silence more profound than had preceded it, as though other sounds upon the island stilled to allow this speech room in which to be heard. 'The blight, Thrasne. The strangeys came. Now I am here.'

'Where?' Thrasne begged. 'Where is here?'

'The Island of All of Us,' the carved man replied, his lips twisting upward into the ghost of a smile, the lids of his eyes moving upward also, the face lightening for that instant almost to a fleshly look. 'You have come to the Isle of Those Who Are Becoming Otherwise . . .'

412

Behind Thrasne the shouts of the searchers stilled. Before them on the long, pale beach there was movement. Lumps and piles that Thrasne had assumed were flotsam or clumps of grass stood up, turned, became men and women. On some, fragments of clothing still hung, as irrelevant as wind-driven leaves clinging on a fence. Though it was possible to tell that some were male, female, there was nothing sexual about them, as there had been nothing really sexual about Suspirra. In many, breasts or penises had dwindled into a general shapelessness. Or shapeliness, Thrasne thought half-hysterically, his artist's eyes assuring him that the shapes of those least human in appearance were also the most beautiful. As he thought these things, clinging tight to his sanity, willing himself to show no fear, the carved people approached him, slowly.

'Is he frightened of us?' one asked, the question seeming to take up most of the afternoon.

'Does he think we are ghosts?' asked another.

'What are they?' asked Taj Noteen from just behind him, his voice strained and shaking. 'I told all the others to get back to boat.'

Thrasne responded calmly, betrayed only by the smallest quiver in his voice. 'They are dead, Taj Noteen. Those whom the Rivermen have consigned to the River. Blighted then. And, seemingly, given a new life by the blight, as the workers in the pits are given life by the Tears of Viranel.'

'But these . . . these can talk.'

'Talk, yes,' said one of the carved people in long, slow syllables. 'And observe. And hear.'

'Cannot taste,' said one. It was a chant, an intonation, perhaps an invocation.

'Not smell,' said another.

'Not feel,' said Blint. 'Not much.'

Thrasne's immediate terror had begun to subside, and he looked closely at Blint. There was no fear or horror on that face. There was none on any face he could see. There was calm. Expressions that might betoken contentment. A kindly and very moderate interest, perhaps, though no

413

excitement. With this analysis, his heart slowed and he swallowed, conscious of a dry throat and scalp tight as a drumhead.

'Are you well, Blint?' he found himself able to ask, almost conversationally.

'Oh, yes, Thrasne. I am well.'

'Are all the River dead here, all of them?'

'Here. Or on some other island.'

'How did you get here?'

'The strangeys brought us. They bring us all.'

Throughout this last exchange the carved people had turned away and begun moving slowly back to the positions they had occupied before. There, they faded into the landscape once again, becoming mere manlike hillocks along the sand. Only Blint remained.

'Blint-wife is well.' Thrasne bethought himself that Blint might like to know this.

Blint did not seem to care. 'I'll leave it in your good hands,' he said, each word drawn into a paragraph of meaning. 'Thraaaasneee.' Blint's eyes were fixed on some more distant thing. They followed his gaze out across the waters to a swelling beneath the waves, a heaving, as some mighty creature rising from the depths, the great, glassy shells of its rising flowing with a tattered lace of sliding foam.

'The strangeys,' said Blint once again, his hands folded before him as though he had been in Temple. Though they spoke to him several more times, he did not answer. At last Taj Noteen tugged Thrasne away, back across the sands to the edge of the forest. By the time they arrived there, Thrasne was shaking as with an ague.

Taj held him, clasped him tightly, until he stopped shivering. Taj was as shaken as Thrasne. Among the dead he had seen were some he thought he knew, one he had known very well indeed.

'Come,' said Thrasne at last. 'We will explore a little.' He knew himself. In a moment his eyes would start to function, his fingers itch for the knife. In a little time, he would start to think. This shock had come only because he had

414

known the old man, known him almost as a father. So, let him move to let the shock pass. 'Come.' He moved away down a forest path.

They walked. Here and there along the way were others of the dead. Some, evidently the more recent, looked up as they passed. One or two of them spoke. Others did not seem to see them. And some, those who had been longest upon the island, Thrasne thought, were rooted in place like trees, stout trees with two or three stout branches, small tendrils of growth playing about their heads and shoulders and from their fingertips.

Thrasne stopped before an ancient tree, twisted and gnarled by a century's growth. 'The leaves are the same,' he said, pointing first at the tree, then at one of the dead a small distance away. 'The leaves. And see! It blooms.' At the tips of the twigs were blossoms like waxen crowns, magenta and sea blue, with golden centers.

'We bloom,' corrected a voice from behind them. 'And the seeds blow out upon the River and sink down. And grow there into a kind of water weed. Which grows, and after a time takes fins and swims. To become the blight. Which seeks a body to house it. And brings it to life again. And comes to the islands. To grow. To bloom . . .'

She who spoke had been a woman once. Now she fluttered with leaves, and her feet were deeply planted in the soil.

'And you,' Thrasne whispered, needing to know. 'Are you well?'

'Oh, yes. I am well.'

'There is no pain?'

'No pain.'

'Memories?'

'Memories?'

'Your name? Who you were?'

'I am,' the tree-woman replied. 'I am, now. It is enough.' She did not speak again.

'This tree does not grow on Northshore,' said Thrasne. 'You'd think somewhere, in the forests there. Some of them . . .'

415

'The strangeys probably don't take them there,' said Taj Noteen. 'Probably they bring them only here, or on other islands.'

'Why? How?'

'You will have to ask the strangeys, Thrasne,' he said. 'Those, swimming there in the deeps, with the foam around their faces.'

For they did swim there, south of the island, shining mounds lifting great, eyed fringes, sliding through the waters like mighty ships of flesh, calling to one another in their terrible voices, deep and echoing as caves.

'Come,' Taj Noteen urged him. 'Come back to the *Gift*, Thrasne. It will seem less strange tomorrow.' And in truth, he hoped it would, for his soul cowered in terror within him.

None of them felt they could leave on the day that followed, or the day after that. Thrasne did not find Blint again, though Taj Noteen found the woman he had once known, spoke to her, and returned to the *Gift* dazed and uncomprehending. On the third day, they wished to leave, tried to set sail, and were prevented from moving. Around them the strangeys moved, pushing the boat back against the shore each time they tried to move away. They had refilled all the water casks. Here and there among the strange trees on the island were some familiar fruiting kinds, and they had gathered all the fruits that were ripe. There was nothing more they could do, but the strangeys would not allow them to leave. It was time, Thrasne felt, to ask some questions.

What Thrasne wanted to know he could not ask from the crowded deck of the *Gift*, with all the crew clustered about thinking him crazy. He did not want to talk to the strangeys at a stone's throw, with old Porabji's cynical eye upon him. He wanted – oh, he wanted to be close to them. Close as their own skins or fins or whatever parts and attributes they had. He wanted to *see* them!

'Pull the raft around to the Riverside,' he ordered. 'And rig some kind of oarlocks on it.'

It was not a graceful craft. Still, it was sturdy enough, and he could maneuver it with the long oars in the high oarlocks, standing to them as he plied them to and fro.

Once he knew well enough what he was doing with the raft, he thought to sneak off at dawn, when the strangeys usually surfaced. He set his mind to wake himself early, a skill most boatmen had, and rose in the mist before the sun. As he slipped over the rail, he did not see Eenzie the Clown standing in the owner-house door watching him, wrapped tight in a great white robe over which her hair spilled in a midnight river of silken strands. As he left, she came to the railing to watch the raft heave away, clumsy as a basket.

It was dead slack tide with the moons lying at either horizon. Only a light wind blew into Thrasne's face from the south, laden with scents strange to him. 'There is more land there,' Thrasne breathed, assured of it for the first time. 'I smell it!'

He sniffed deeply, recognizing components of the odor as resinous, humusy, fecund smells. Swamps and forest. On the island the closer trees were only dark shadows against the mist behind them, a ground fog that rose only slightly above their tops to leave the taller trees outlined against the dawn. This retreating sequence of river mist, shore trees, mist again, taller trees, and yet again mist rising from some valley and the tallest trees on the hills behind it lent an appearance of great distance to the island, as though it had stretched away from him in the night, becoming a place in dream in which no distance could be measured. The far, hilltop trees were an open lacework against the opal sky, motionless in the morning light, with only an occasional flutter of wings among them to let one know they were not painted there, or carved.

He sculled through the rising fogs into the deep channel on the south side of the island. Behind him on the *Gift* the watchman raised his voice in a plaintive call, like a lonely bird. Moving through the shore mist, the dead men and women walked like an orchard come up from scattered seed. Though most of them stood or walked alone, there were a

417

few twos and threes of them who seemed to stay together. As though they had been friends or kin in life? Thrasne wondered, then gave up wondering as the River surged about him, bellying upward in huge arcs of shining water.

Upon that swelling wave were winged things, smaller than strangeys, peering at him from myriad eyes. Then they were gone.

'Perhaps they are strangey children,' said Thrasne in a conversational tone to himself. 'And here are the adults.'

They were all round him, their long, eye-decked fringes suspended above the raft, peering at it through the mists, monsters from dream.

'I need to talk with you,' Thrasne called. 'I want to ask some questions.'

A rearrangement took place among the fringes. Eyes were replaced by others. Water swirled, and from the top of a belled wave a comber of lace slid toward him, foaming around the boat. 'Yes,' said a terrible strangey voice. 'We will talk.'

'You are preventing our leaving the island,' he called. 'If we have offended you in some way, we wish to make reparation. We cannot stay here. We must go on. Southward.'

'No,' the strangey boomed, diving under the water to leave Thrasne bobbing above it, then emerging a little distance off. 'Your other one is coming to you.'

'Other one?'

'The one you lost. The one you have yet to find. Babji.'

'Coming here?' His heart swelled within him, suddenly joyous, leaping like a flame-bird chick from the nest. 'Here? Medoor Babji?'

'The Treeci are bringing her.'

This baffled him. It could not be the Treeci of Strinder's Isle. Some other Treeci. Before him the strangeys sank from sight, except for one.

'Do you have other questions?' it asked.

'Yes.' He licked dry lips. 'A long time ago, it was almost twenty years ago. A woman drowned herself off the piers at Baris. She was pregnant.'

418

There was no sound but the River sound, yet Thrasne had a feeling of colloquy, a vibration of the water beneath the boat, a great voice asking and answering in tones beneath his ability to hear them. 'Yes,' said the strangey voice at last. 'Her name was Imajh.'

'I don't know what her name was. I called her Suspirra. I thought she was only wood, you know. But she wasn't. She was alive.'

'She was alive in a way,' assented the voice. 'If you had not taken her from the River too soon, we would have brought her here and she would have been alive here, in a way. As the others are.'

Thrasne slumped. 'I killed her?'

Swirl of water. Sound as of what? Not laughter. No. Amusement. Something like amusement, but of so huge a kind that one could not call it that. Thrasne tried to identify the tone as the strangey spoke. It seemed important to know what the strangey felt as it answered. 'She was already dead, boatman. What she was given after that was the blessed time. Perhaps she used it better for her where she was than if she had come here.'

Thrasne, remembering, was not sure. 'She had a child. Suspirra did.'

'Yes. Our child. We want our child returned.'

Thrasne had meant Pamra. After a moment he realized it was Lila they spoke of. 'Why do you say Lila is your child, strangey? I meant her other child, Pamra Don.'

'Lila is our child because she carries our seed. We know of Pamra Don . . .' The voice trailed away in a sadness too deep to bear, the anguish beating at Thrasne's flesh like hammers.

Thrasne cried out against it. 'Don't. Oh, don't. Strangey! Don't you have another name I may call you for courtesy's sake?'

Again that indefinable emotion, the trembling of the water. And then, 'The name you call us does well enough. We are strangers, strangers to you and to this place. Aliens. Explorers. Though we were already here when your people

419

came, you will remain here when we go. When our examination – our crusade – is done.'

Strangers! Aliens? And yet, why not? If humans had come to this place, why not others, others with their own labyrinthine ways of thought, their own arcane judgments? It should have made no difference, yet it made all the difference. He tried to remember the questions he had wanted answers to. They did not seem so important now. The tone they had used in referring to Pamra Don closed that subject away. He did not want to hear Pamra's name spoken in that voice. There remained only one mystery, and stubbornly he asked about it.

'Why do you bring the blighted ones to these islands?'

Again that gigantic emotion that Thrasne could not identify. A troubling. A monstrous disturbance that had both laughter and tears in it. 'Blight is your word, Thrasne. We call it rather "extension." It seems a good thing. The human people do not live long; their ends come suddenly. They . . . look beyond too much. Or they refuse to look beyond at all. This gives them time . . .'

'The blight – you brought it?'

'We created it. Our gift. Just for you.'

Again that vastness, rolling around him. He could feel it without understanding it at all. He bent forward, trying to protect the core of himself from whatever it was. He did not understand anything they had said. The words they used were insufficient to explain what they had meant. The vast, rolling emotion came closer, overwhelming him, but he could not apprehend the content of the wave in which he drowned. It passed. He lay gasping on the raft, unsure he was alive.

They spoke again, sadly.

'Bring us our child, boatman. In payment for receiving your lost one back.'

Then the water flattened, all at once, as though oil had been poured upon it. There was no reaching swell, no tattered carpets of foam. Only silence, the flap of the sail, and from the distant *Gift*, muted by the mist, the sound of excited voices.

He steered toward it by sound. The cook banging on a pan. Taj Noteen's voice raised. Obers-rom giving an order. The clatter of wood and the loose flap of the sail. The sound of laughter, cries of joy. Then he saw it, saw the little boat with the *Cheevle* tied at its stern. He called out, in a great, hoarse voice, and saw Eenzie and Medoor Babji waiting at the rail.

'Have you finished with the strangeys? Come aboard, have your breakfast, then let us sail for home!'

He gaped at her, staring into her face, unbelieving. There was a lively intelligence there, a self-interested concern. She reached down and lifted him upward with a strong arm, and his skin woke at the feel of her own against it. He was aware of nothing but this as he took her hand and let her lead him toward the cooking smells, thinking only of what was at that moment and not at all, in that moment, of the strangeys or of Pamra. He had come to a place within himself where he could no longer bear to go back or to stay where he was, unchanging, and yet he hesitated to go forward. With that mighty, enigmatic emotion of the strangeys still washing through him, he hung upon the moment, poised, unmoving within himself, aware of a stillness within himself and at the core of all the liquid shifting of the River's surface, all the windblown agitation of the island, becoming part of it for a time, rather than choose – anything.

Two days later, after Medoor Babji had walked upon the Island of the Dead until she had seen what they had seen, they set sail for home.

21

No matter what I start out thinking about, I end up remembering what the strangeys said, and what they said seemed to me to be about sadness. The sadness of men – mankind, I guess you'd say. It's that we never have time to be what we know we should be, or could be. And it's not because of the time itself, the gods know we waste enough of it not doing anything at all, but because of what we are. And we don't have time, no matter how old we get, to be anything else. So they've brought this gift, so they called it, to let us be something else for a while. Something that *knows*, but doesn't care so much. It's caring so much that keeps us from being what we could be. Caring so much. About the wrong things, maybe. But still, if we didn't, what would we be?

From Thrasne's book

Word was sent to Sliffisunda that Pamra Don would be delivered up to the Thraish. In the Red Talons, Ilze danced his victory, a wild, frantic prancing upon the rocky height, then sat down upon a shelf of stone to wait, his eyes like polished pebbles, scanning the horizon for the first glimpse of those who would come from the Chancery. Though the message had said clearly that Gendra Mitiar would accompany the girl, Ilze cared nothing for that. It was Pamra Don he would see shortly; Pamra Don he would get into his own hands at last. He thought of her as he had used to think of her, tied to the stake, his whip falling across her shoulders as his caress, her voice rising up in screaming prayers to the empty sky. His body shook, twitched, spasmed with this thought, and the fliers on the rocks around him cast looks at one another, wondering what ailed him.

Sliffisunda was content to wait. There was no hurry about this business. His fliers told him the crusade went on, more massively than before, with great clots of people moving west and north. Wherever they moved, the pits were full, so he cared not whether they moved or not. In a hidden valley of the steppes known only to fliers, the herd-beasts were growing with each day that passed. Already the expedition to steal other young bulls had been planned. More than an expedition, almost an invasion, with enough surprise and numbers to succeed no matter what the humans did. It might prove expedient to stop this crusade; or again, it might not. It was a thing worthy of much screamed discussion, many loud sessions of the Stones of Disputation. Sliffisunda wiped his beak on the post of his feeding trough and was content.

And on the plains, moving southward and a little east, Pamra Don was content as well. 'A journey of a week or two,' she had been told. 'To the Red Talons. To meet the Talkers.' There were Jondarites and Chancery people escorting her. Once she felt a fleeting sadness that Tharius Don was not among them. There was scarcely room even for that emotion. She rode the weehar ox the general had given her, refusing to ride in the wagon pulled by Noor slaves. She abjured Gendra Mitiar with great passion to free these men as Lees Obol would require of her. Gendra listened, raked her face, ground her teeth, and said she would consider the matter. In truth, she found Pamra Don amusing in the same way Jhilt had been amusing during the early days of her captivity. So naive. So childishly convinced that her feelings mattered to anyone besides herself. So interestingly ripe to be disabused of that notion.

One day the escort paused on a low hill to let a procession of crusaders pass in the valley, banners, a wagon, a gorgeously robed figure in the wagon. Pamra looked down at it in wonder, not recognizing Peasimy Flot. Peasimy had decided to join Pamra Don at Split River, but he did not even see her riding in her bright armor in company with the Jondarites.

And as for the rest, it was merely travel. Creak of wheels. Plod of feet. Crack of whip. Wind in the grass. Murmur of voices. Fires at night gleaming like lanterns in the dark. Walking out into the grasses to pee, staring up at the moons which seemed to stare back in wonder, or threat, or admonition, depending upon one's point of view.

The slave Jhilt, walking each day away in a soft chinkle of chains. The Jondarites striding along, their plumes nodding over their impassive faces, their hands upon the butts of their spears, resting at night beside the fire, polishing their fishskin armor with oil. The captain himself, on orders from Jondrigar, polishing the armor of Pamra Don. Gendra Mitiar seeing this with amusement, but not interfering. Time for that. Time for everything.

In fact, Gendra Mitiar felt herself growing strangely weary from the journey, victim of an unaccustomed lassitude. She went to her strongbox and unlocked it with the key she carried around her neck to get at her reserve supply of elixir. Though it was a full season sooner than she had planned to take more of the stuff, she dosed herself liberally with the thick, brownish ichor, at which Jhilt smiled behind her hands and jangled her chains. On those chains, among a hundred other dangling charms and coins, hung a duplicate key to the strongbox. It had taken Jhilt over a year to file it to fit, but once it was done, it had taken only a minute to open the box, months ago, and taste the acrid stuff. When they set out upon this journey, it had taken only another minute to substitute for the elixir a vial of half-burned and diluted puncon jam. Who knew better than Jhilt that Gendra's aged mouth knew no savor, her aged nose knew no scent? 'Have some jam, old one,' she tittered to herself to the soft chankle-chankle of the chains. 'Live a little.'

Though she had sometimes forgotten it during her

captivity, here on the steppes Jhilteen Nobiji remembered she was Noor. If Noor could have justice, they would have vengeance. The key to the strongbox was not the only key that hung upon her chains, and her presence with this troop outside the barrier of the Teeth was one she had hoped for over many years.

There were twelve days like this before they sighted the Talons, looming redstone obelisks, contorted towers that broke the line of the steppes amid a dark forest. This out-cropping of redstone ran all the way from Northshore to the Teeth of the North, somewhere mere edges along the land, elsewhere squat cliffs lowering over the plain. Here the stone had been eaten by the wind and rain, chewed into monuments as full of holes as a worm-gnawed pod, and here the Talkers maintained one of their four strongholds. Black Talons, so they said, for strength; Gray Talons for wisdom; Blue Talons for vengeance; Red Talons for blood. Sliffisunda had come from Gray to Red, and the signifi-cance of that had not escaped him. 'From thought to action,' he cawed to himself when the human train was sighted. 'So, now we will have something interesting, per-haps some satisfaction.'

The Jondarites made camp some distance from the foot of the Talons, yet close enough that Talkers might come to them without exertion. The tents were set in a circle; the Jondarites took crossbows from their cases and placed quar-rels for them ready at hand, the heavy, square-headed bolts most efficacious against fliers. Though there had been little opportunity to use weapons against the Thraish in some hundreds of years, the stories of the last Thraish-human conflicts were well remembered among the soldiers of the Chancery, and the general had told them to be ready for any eventuality.

When all these preparations had been completed, Gendra Mitiar sent a messenger to the foot of the Talons with a letter for Sliffisunda. He might come, she said, to their camp. To question Pamra Don. And to discuss certain matters with her, Gendra Mitiar.

425

Sliffisunda did not come himself. He sent a Fourth Degree underling and the human, Ilze. It amused him to do this, setting the humans one against the other. He did it sometimes with slaves or craftsmen, making one's safety dependent upon betrayal of the other. So, now, he thought Ilze might work against Gendra Mitiar to obtain the person of Pamra Don.

But she, remembering Ilze in the Accusatory, was disinclined to pay him attention.

'I must speak with the Talker,' she said. 'I don't know what he was thinking of, sending you.' She sniffed, raking her face, staring at him as though he had been some kind of bug. Her teeth ground, and he tensed in every nerve, expecting pain. That sound had accompanied pain before, and he wanted to scream at her.

'Sliffisunda wants to see her,' he grated.

'Fine,' Gendra said. 'Let him come to see her. Talk with her. Question her, if he likes. I need to talk with him, too, and I'll not be hauled up there like some sack of laundry.'

Taking a quick look at the alert Jondarites, Ilze retreated, quelled for this time. He had not laid eyes on Pamra Don. For all he knew, she was not even with the group. She, however, spying through a slit in the tent side, had seen him very well, seen him and disregarded him as an irrelevancy. He would hurt her if he could, but he would not be allowed. The Chancery folk would not allow it. Her great-great-grandfather, Tharius Don, would not allow it, She explained this to Neff and her mother and Delia as all of them nodded and smiled.

Back at the Talons Ilze's failure was reported to Sliffisunda, who cawed laughter. 'I did not think he would do any good!' The Fourth Degree Talker who had reported on Ilze kept his beak shut, wisely. Sliffisunda shuffled back and forth on his perch, darting his head from side to side. 'Well, I will go talk to this old human. Tomorrow, perhaps. Or next day.'

He let two days pass before going to the camp. Gendra, who had studied the fliers for some time, was not concerned

426

about the delay. The lassitude that had bothered her on the journey had not yet abated, and she remained in her tent, ministered to by Jhilt. Pamra, meantime, preached to the Jondarites. They, remembering how their general had responded to her, varied in their response from polite to enthusiastic.

And at last Sliffisunda arrived. The Talkers had lately taken to regalia, a tendency borrowed from humans, and Sliffisunda wore a badge of degree slung about his neck as well as various sparkling ornaments on his legs, feet, and wing fingers. Warned of his coming, Gendra had Pamra brought out of her tent, fully accoutred in her Jondarite armor, and set in a chair beside the fire with Jondarites at either side. If the old rooster wanted this one, Gendra thought, he would have to give something significant in return, though nothing of this appeared in her face or voice as she first greeted the Talker.

'I am honored,' she said. 'We grant the request of Sliffisunda to talk with – even question – the woman, Pamra Don.'

'She was to have been sent to us,' the Talker cawed, depositing shit on Gendra's words.

Gendra's fingers twitched toward her face, then stilled, knotted. So, it was to be a battle of insults. 'One pays little attention to what Talkers demand,' she replied in a bored voice. 'Unless one is given reason to listen.'

Sliffisunda almost crouched in surprise. So, the humans could engage in Talkerly disputation! Almost always the humans were like spoiled eggs, stinking soft. This one was not. He turned away from her, showing his side – not quite a fatal insult, though close. 'What reason would humans understand?' he cawed.

'More subtle reasons than a Talker could ascertain, perhaps,' she replied, turning her shoulder toward him to signal the Jondarites. 'The Thraish have not been noted for good sense.'

He stretched his wings wide and threatened her. She gestured again at the Jondarites. He looked up to see a dozen crossbows centered on his chest. He laughed and subsided. 'So. So, Gendra Mitiar. What have you to say?'

'I have to say your interest and mine are the same, Sliffisunda. Do you speak for the Talkers?'

'I speak to Talkers,' he boasted. 'And they listen.'

'Ah,' she murmured. So, he could not commit the Talkers to anything, but he could argue a case. If she succeeded in acquiring an alliance with him, she would buy an advocate, not a potentiary. Still, what matter? Those in the assembly would accept a Talker's interest as representative of the Thraish. They would not know the difference.

She turned full face toward him and said, 'I have a case to put to you, Uplifted One . . .'

She spoke of her desire for the post of Protector of Man. She spoke of her intentions, once that post was hers.

'There is no reason the Thraish cannot increase in numbers. Human numbers can be increased to feed them. The Noor are no good to you because the color of their skins will not allow the Tears of Viranel to grow properly within them. Let us eradicate the Noor. Let us replace them with settlers from Northshore.'

Behind the tent flap, Jhilt quivered in shock. This she had not heard before.

'How will you convince the Chancery to do this?' Sliffisunda asked, interested despite himself. Even though none of this would be needed when the herdbeasts multiplied, it was still an interesting concept.

'If your numbers are increased, the amount of elixir can be increased. More humans can receive it. Those whose votes are needed in the Chancery assembly will be promised elixir. A simple thing, Sliffisunda.'

'How will you wipe out Noor?'

'War.' She shrugged. 'General Jondrigar needs opportunity for war.'

'Not enough Jondarites.' This was said as mere comment, not as objection.

'True.' Again she shrugged. 'We will need to conscript men from Northshore as well. Any man, I should

428

think, who has not fathered a child in a few years.'

Who will then not be available to support children he has fathered, Sliffisunda thought, while keeping silent. The Thraish understood nestlings. Even Talkers understood nestlings. When the parent was lost, the nestlings were lost. Many would die if this woman came to power. The pits would be full. And if that went on for a long time, the Thraish could expand in advance of the day he had planned. The woman was ambitious, but not wise. He could use her, despite her disputatious nature.

'Let us talk,' he said, smiling inside himself.

On the day following, Sliffisunda arrived to question Pamra. This was a simple feint or, as the fliers put it, *hadmaba*, a threatening posture designed to bluff rather than injure. Sliffisunda wanted to support Gendra Mitiar; he did not want her to think he did it willingly or for his own purposes. So, let her think he was really interested in this pale, thin woman with the blazing eyes with the child on her lap.

'Tell me of your crusade,' he said, expecting nothing more than ranting or evasions.

'You do an evil thing,' she said in a level tone, fixing him with her eyes. 'All you fliers.' The child fixed him with her eyes, strangely.

He hunched his shoulders, staring at her, ignoring her young. 'What evil is that?'

'It is for you the workers are raised up,' she said. 'I did not know that until I came to the Chancery, until my great-great-grandfather Tharius Don told me. I thought it was for the work they did, as we were taught. I thought it was Potipur's will. I had been taught that. It was false.'

'It is Potipur's will,' Sliffisunda replied, amused. 'Potipur has promised the Thraish plenty. The bodies of your dead are the plenty he promised.'

'A true god would make no such promise. A true god would not do evil. Therefore, Potipur is not a true god, he is merely your god, a Thraish god. Not a god of man.'

'Does man have a god?' Considering the trouble the

priests and Towers had been to to suppress all humanish religions, it was amazing that she had come up with this. Despite himself, he was intrigued.

'If the Thraish have a god, then men, also, have a god. My voices tell me that if there is not One, over us all, then there are several, for each race of creatures.'

'Or none?' he asked. 'Have you thought of that?'

She shook her head at him. 'My voices say there is. A god. Of humans and Treeci, for we are like.'

Sliffisunda shat, offended, turning his back on her. She did not seem to notice but merely stared at him as though he were some barnyard fowl. He screamed at her, wings wide, and she merely blinked. 'Foul Treeci. Offal. Fish eaters.'

'The Treeci are wise and benevolent creatures,' she said. 'As man can be if not brutalized by wickedness. Raising up the workers is a wicked thing to do, Sliffisunda. We know their pain and do nothing. Thereby we condone it. Thereby we are made brutes. Not by the workers themselves, but by the Thraish, who require they be raised. So my voices say.'

Gendra, sitting on the other side of the fire, blinked in amazement. She had not heard more than five words from Pamra Don during the entire trip. Now this! What had gotten into the woman?

'Heretic!' Sliffisunda cawed. 'Unbeliever in Potipur.'

'If Potipur is only a Thraish god, why should I believe in him?' she asked. 'If the weehar had a god, would it be the god of the Thraish?'

Theology dictated that the weehar could have no god except the Thraish god, but Sliffisunda had his own doubts about that. He recalled the quasi-racial memories of the fliers' last hunt, as he taught them to nestlings. Certainly the weehar had not seemed to rejoice in Potipur. Perhaps the weehar did not rejoice because they were being punished. But for what? What sins could a weehar commit? The sin of offal eating? The sin of debasement? The sin of doubt in Potipur's care for the Thraish? The sin of failing to breed? The sin of failing to give honor? How could the weehar or thrassil commit any of these? More likely the

430

weehar were only things, needing no god at all. As the humans were things. Sliffisunda shook his head. The woman didn't talk like a thing, which was troubling. Abruptly he rose, stalked to the edge of the encampment, and raised himself into the air. Too troubling. Too much talk.

Behind him, Pamra watched him go, a little wrinkle between her eyes. It was hard, so hard. She could not reach him. She looked around for Neff, for her mother. They would have to help her with this one. She could not feel her way into his heart, not at all. They stood remote, their effulgence dimmed in the light of the day, hard to see. She listened for their voices and was not rewarded. Nothing. Tears crept into her eyes, and she shook them away angrily. If they did not speak to her, it was because they didn't need to. She could not expect them to be with her every minute. Perhaps they had other things to do, other people to guide as well.

Sliffisunda arrived at the Talons in a foul mood. He stalked into his aerie, snatching a mouthful of food as he passed the trough, ripping an arm from the twitching meat and cracking it for the marrow. It had no savor. The human, Ilze, was waiting outside. Sliffisunda could smell him, that sweetish, human stink which only the Tears of Viranel softened and ameliorated into something almost satisfying. Almost. Sliffisunda drooled, thinking of weehar.

A human god? To believe in a human god, that would be a sin. But if weehar believed in a god at all, what god would it be? Sliffisunda made a noise like a snarl in his throat. Under the Thraish, the weehar had ended. Under the humans, they had multiplied. Which god would the weehar accept? And that could be the sin for which they were punished – except that the punishment had come first.

Ignoring the crouching human on his porch, Sliffisunda launched himself toward the Stones of Disputation. This was not a matter he cared to think about by himself.

Behind him, Ilze pounded his knee with his fist, livid with

431

frustration. Where was Pamra Don? Why hadn't this Talker brought him Pamra Don?

In the camp, Gendra Mitiar watched Pamra Don, her eyes narrowed. She had noticed for the first time that Pamra Don ate almost nothing. The woman seemed built of skin tightly drawn over her bones, like a stilt-lizard, all angles, with eyes like great glowing orbs in her face.

'Doesn't she ever eat?' she asked the Jondarite captain.

'Very little,' he admitted. 'A little bread in the morning. She seems to like Jarb root, and one of the men sought it for her during the journey.'

'You'd better detail him to find more,' she said. 'The woman may not last a week if she doesn't eat something.'

'I can force her if you like,' the captain suggested. It was sometimes necessary to force-feed captives, particularly Noor captives, who often tried to starve themselves when their families had been killed before their eyes.

Gendra shook her head. 'No. I need her cooperative with the Thraish. If she will eat Jarb root, see she gets it. At least enough of it to keep her alive.' She looked up, drawn by a distant cacophony. 'What's that?'

'The Talkers on the top of the Talons, Dame Marshal. They do that sometimes, late into the night – sometimes all night long.'

'What are they doing?'

'Arguing, so I've been told. Only the high-mucky-muck ones like the one who was here. Sixth Degree ones. They have the highest pillars all to themselves. The less important ones, they meet lower down. Some nights there will be three or four bunches of them, all going at it. Not always this loud, though. Sliffisunda must have a bone in his craw!' The captain laughed, unawed.

Gendra's eyes narrowed once more. So. Sliffisunda had talked to Pamra Don, and then some great argument followed among the Thraish. Perhaps Gendra's case was even now being argued. She smiled. Good. Very good.

As she rose from her chair and moved toward the tent,

she stumbled, a sudden dizziness flooding over her.

'Jhilt,' she gasped, feeling the slave's hands fasten around her arms and shoulders.

'The Dame Marshal has been sitting too long near the fire,' the slave soothed, hiding a smile behind her hand. 'It makes one dizzy.'

'You get dizzy, sitting by the fire?' Gendra said childishly. 'You do?'

'Of course. Everyone does.' Jhilt half-carried the woman into her tent and eased her onto the bed. 'Everyone does.' Especially, Jhilt said to herself, when one is some hundreds of years old and is no longer getting any elixir. The woman on the bed looked like a corpse, like something in the pits, gray, furrowed skin gaped over yellow teeth, like a skull. 'Everyone does,' she soothed, wondering how long it would take. Jhilt had a small supply of Tears in a vial hanging on her chains. She had toyed with the idea of using the Tears before rather than after Gendra's death. She amused herself by thinking of this now, weighing the idea for merit.

'No,' she sighed at last. 'The captain would know what I had done. If she merely dies, he will know.'

Perhaps she could use the Tears on someone else. That Laugher, perhaps. That would be amusing, too.

The disputation on the stones went on until almost dawn, not merely acrimonious, which most disputations were, but becoming increasingly enraging as the night wore on. Blood was drawn several times before the argument broke up, and only Sliffisunda's quickness in parrying attacks kept him from being among the injured. It was clear the Talkers would not accept the idea of a human god or any weehar god. Only the Thraish had a god, and the god of the Thraish was the god of all. The Thraish were the chosen of Potipur, who set aside all other creatures for the service of the Thraish. So the Talkers believed.

Sliffisunda, bruised and tired, was not so sure. The other Talkers of the Sixth Degree had not heard Pamra Don. He did not like to think what might have happened if they had

433

heard Pamra Don. It might be better if none of them heard her, ever. Better if Sliffisunda had not heard her himself. He settled upon his perch, head resting upon his shoulder. In the afternoon, he would talk with the human, Ilze. In the evening, he would go to the camp of the humans again and make an agreement with Gendra Mitiar. It did not matter what agreement with her was made. The woman stank of death. She would not live long enough to worry him.

'What will you do with Pamra Don?' he asked Ilze.

Ilze's mouth dropped open. He salivated. The stench of him rose into Sliffisunda's nostrils, sickeningly sweet. 'Teach her,' he said at last, a low, gargling sound. 'Teach her she cannot do this to me.'

'Where?' Sliffisunda asked. 'Where will you do this?'

'Here. In the Talons. Anywhere. It doesn't matter.'

'Before those from the Chancery?' Sliffisunda was watching him closely. If, as Sliffisunda thought likely, all those in the crusade had been contaminated by Pamra Don's ideas, then some private vengeance against the woman would not suffice. Her followers would have to be convinced that Pamra Don was wrong. 'Would you punish her before those from the Chancery and all her followers?'

Ilze shivered. He wanted to say yes, but his soul shrank from it. He had orders not to touch her. If he punished her in public, they would kill him. He knew that. They would kill him at once. Those from the Chancery would do it. Her followers would do it. And no one would care enough to save him from them. 'If you would protect me,' he whined, hearing the whine and hating it.

'Ah. Well, suppose you don't do it. Suppose we do it, the Thraish. How should it be done?'

Ilze had only thought of whips, of stakes. 'Tie her to a stake,' he said, then stopped. The Talkers didn't use whips. 'Eat her?' he offered.

Sliffisunda cawed his displeasure, pecking Ilze sharply on one side of his head so the blood flowed. 'Take into our bodies the foul flesh of a heretic? Stupid human!'

'Well, do whatever you do, then,' Ilze sulked, trying to stanch the blood.

'We have a ceremony,' Sliffisunda said. 'A ceremony.'

Night came. Sliffisunda came again. Pamra Don came again, to the fireside.

'Do your followers believe as you do?' the Talker asked her, already certain of the answer.

'Yes. Most of them. All of them, in time. All mankind, in time.' It was not the question she had expected, not one of the questions she was ready for, but the Talker asked nothing else. He turned and left her, going to Gendra Mitiar to carry on a lengthy, soft-voiced conversation which Pamra could not hear.

Jhilt could hear it.

'You wish to be Protector of Man?'

Gendra Mitiar nodded. Her voice was very husky tonight, and it tired her to talk.

'What can Thraish do to guarantee this?' he purred.

'Wait until Lees Obol dies. I will let you know. Then send a messenger. Tell the assembly the elixir will be decreased unless I am elected. In which event it will be increased.'

'And when you are Protector, you will increase the quota of humans? You will eradicate the Noor for this?'

'You have my word.'

'And in return for this agreement, you will give me the person of this woman, this Pamra Don?'

'As you like, Uplifted One. She is nothing to me. What do you want her for?'

'To prove she is a false prophet, Dame Marshal. In ceremony before all her followers at Split River Pass. To show them Potipur will not be mocked.'

Gendra laughed, thinking of Tharius Don. 'How may I assist you, Uplifted One?'

Jhilt heard all this, her ear tight to the tent flap.

When Sliffisunda had gone, when Gendra Mitiar was asleep, an uneasy sleep in which her heart faltered and her lungs seemed inclined to stop working, Jhilt walked out to the cage of seeker birds that every Jondarite troop carried with it. The message bone was already in her hands.

'A message for Tharius Don,' she said, keeping her voice bored and level. 'From the Dame Marshal.'

The Jondarite keeper made a cursory examination of the seal. It looked like the Dame Marshal's seal, and who else's would it be? The bird came into his hands willingly, accepted the light burden as trained to do, and launched itself upward to turn toward the north without hesitation, strong wings beating across Potipur's scowling face.

Jhilt shivered, thinking of what was in that message.

'You cold?' leered the soldier, opening his cloak in invitation.

She shook her head. 'The Dame Marshal needs me,' she said, turning back toward the tent. Though, indeed, if the Dame Marshal needed her at all, it would not be for much longer. Queen Fibji should be told of this conspiracy against the Noor. Jhilt had no seeker birds for the Queen; therefore she must find some Noor signal post that would have them. Gendra would not spend time looking for a slave, not now, not as weak as she was and with so much going on. Jhilt fumbled among her chains for the other key, the one that unlocked her jingling manacles. Moments later she moved off across the steppes, silent as the moons.

22

A yawning servant brought word to Tharius Don in the middle of his sleep time. 'The general asks for you at once in the audience hall, Lord Propagator. Most urgently.' He waited for some reply, and when Tharius waved him off, he scurried away into darkness. The midnight bell had only lately struck. Tharius had heard it in his sleep, through the purple dusk that was night in this season.

He wrapped himself in a thick robe with a hood and made his way down the echoing corridors and endless flights of stairs to the audience hall. Muslin curtains hung limp against the closed shutters, like so many wraiths in the torchlight. At the side, where Lees Obol's niche was, the curtains were flung wide, and General Jondrigar stood there, face impassive and his hand upon his knife. Something in his stance recommended caution to Tharius Don, who approached softly, pausing at some distance to ask, 'You needed me, General?'

'Dead,' Jondrigar replied. 'I think. Dead.'

'Dead? Who?' Only to understand at once who it was and why this midnight summons. 'The Protector?'

The general nodded, standing aside to gesture Tharius forward. In the niche, still overheated by the little porcelain stove which was only now burning itself out, the bed stood with its coverlets thrown back. On the embroidered sheet the body of Lees Obol lay immobile. His eyes were open. One arm was rigidly extended above him, as though petrified, pointing.

'Telling me, go!' Jondrigar said, indicating the hand. 'Telling me. As he always did.'

'Rigor,' Tharius murmured. 'All dead men get rigor, General. It doesn't mean—'

'Telling me go,' the general repeated, his eyes glowing. 'Rigor comes long after. He died like this. The message for me.'

Tharius moved to the bed, put his hands gently upon the ancient face, the neck, the arms. Rigid. All. Like rigor, yes. Or blight. His face darkened. So. Plots. Perhaps.

'When was he last seen alive?'

'You were here one time.'

'Yes. Last evening. Shavian Bossit and I met in the hall for a few moments. I didn't look in on Lees Obol, though Shavian may have done.'

'He did. Through the curtains. Jondarite captain reports this to me.' Jondrigar took off his helmet and ran a trembling hand across his mane. 'Jondarite captain looked in every hour. Served tea late, as Protector wanted. Then, at midnight bell, he looked in again. This is what he found.'

We could have a bloodbath here, Tharius thought. Better defuse that. 'We have been surprised he has lived this long, General. We all knew he would die very soon. The elixir does not give eternal life. Only more years, not an eternity.'

'No one killed him.'

It could have been a question, or a statement. Tharius Don chose to interpret it as both.

'No one killed him. Age killed him. As it will all of us.'

'But he left a message for me,' the general said again. 'He told me to go.'

Tharius thought it wiser to say nothing. He had no idea what was in the general's mind and chose to take no chance of upsetting him.

'The Noor Queen. She is coming to Split River Pass,' the general said suddenly. 'I need to go there.'

Tharius thought the general's mind had slipped and said soothingly, 'There will be a council meeting within hours. You should be here for that.'

The general nodded. 'Yes. Then I will go to Split River Pass.' He turned and made his way out of the hall, unsteadily, as though under some great pressure. Tharius felt a fleeting pity. Lees Obol had been all Jondrigar's life. What would he do now?

He put the question away. There were customs to comply with. 'Send someone to Glamdrul Feynt,' he said to the Jondarite captain who hovered against the wall. 'Tell him to look up what funeral arrangements were made the last time a Protector died, then come tell me what they were. Send someone else for servants. Wash the body and clothe it properly. Then get the messengers moving. Let them know at the Bureau of Towers. Tell them to get the word out to the towns. There will probably be some period of mourning. Find out who's running things over there while Gendra's gone, and send them to me. Oh, and find my deputy, Bormas Tyle, and send him to me as well.'

Tharius chewed a thumbnail. Should a seeker bird be sent to Gendra Mitiar? Suppose Pamra Don was just now having success with the Talkers? Suppose this message interrupted something vital? He shivered. Better let it alone. Send a message later, if at all.

He turned, catching a glimpse of a scurrying figure out of the corner of one eye? Nepor? Here? Surely not. Probably a curious servant, fearful of being caught away from his assigned duties. Well, they would all have their curiosity satisfied soon enough.

23

'Done,' whispered Koma Nepor, pausing at a shadowed doorway.

'Dead? Ah. How did he look?'

'Who can say, Jorn? I didn't look at him. The Jondarite put the tea kettle down on the table by the curtain as he always does. From my hiding place behind the curtain, I put the blight in the kettle. The old man called for tea; tea he was served. An hour later, off goes the captain, here comes the general. Then here comes Tharius Don, much whispering and sending of this one and that one. I didn't stay to listen.'

'What happened to the kettle?'

'The servants are in there now, cleaning up. They'll take the kettle and cups away. The blight's only good for an hour or so. All gone now, I should think. That's what took me so long to develop, finding a strain that wouldn't last.'

'No evidence to connect you, then.'

'No evidence to connect *us*, Jorn. None. Shall we go to our beds now, so's to hear it properly, wakened from sleep?'

They went off down the twisting corridor, two shadows in the shuttered gloom, whispering, heads bent toward one another like Talkers, plotting on the stones.

'When will you give General Jondrigar the letter?'

'Later. There'll be a meeting to discuss the funeral. After that.'

Their forms dwindled into shadowed silence.

Shavian Bossit was wakened from sleep to receive the news. He sent a message at once to Bormas Tyle, awaiting his arrival with some impatience.

'Where've you been?' he damanded when the other arrived. 'I sent for you over an hour ago.'

'So did my superior,' the other replied, glaring at him. 'Tharius Don. It seems we have lost a Protector. Are we about to gain another?'

'It's sooner than we'd planned.'

'Nonetheless welcome.'

'True. But we're hardly ready. Gendra's still alive. So is Jondrigar.'

'So they're still alive. For a few weeks, perhaps. Support one of them for the post.'

'The general? Ha!'

'Well, Gendra, then. In her absence. Elect Gendra as Protector, which will vacate the position of Marshal of the Towers. Feynt will take over there, as we've planned, and that will give you two votes. Meantime, the general will not last long. I will take his position when he dies. Last, Gendra will fade away, you will have Feynt's vote, my vote, and your own. Enough, Bossit.' Bormas Tyle slid his knife in and out of its holster, a whisper of violence in the room. 'A few weeks or months more and we will have succeeded.'

'I suppose. Still, something's bothering about all this. The servants are whispering about Obol's death.'

'Did you expect them not to?' Bormas snorted. 'Servants whisper about everything.'

'Just the way he died. As though he'd been frozen. One arm pointed out like a signpost.'

'Some deaders do that.'

'I suppose,' Shavian said again. 'Very well. We proceed as planned. The council will meet in the morning, an hour before noon. And what about the funeral?'

'I don't know. Tharius has our old charlatan in the files looking up what happened last time. I can't even remember who the Protector was before Lees Obol.'

'His name was Jurniver,' Shavian said, abstractedly. 'Jurniver Quyme. He lived four hundred and sixty-two years. He came to office in his two hundredth year. He made fifteen Progressions. He died long before I was born. Feynt knows all about him. It'll be in the files.'

'Old faker.'

'Why do you say that?'

'He pretends to be ancient and crippled whenever anyone wants anything. Watch him, though, when he thinks no one's looking. He moves like a hunting stilt-lizard, quick as lightning.'

'It's a game he plays for Gendra's benefit.'

'It's a game he plays for his own. Keep it in mind, Bossit, when he's Marshal of the Towers. Feynt's no fool.'

'Would we be planning together if he were?' Shavian made an impatient gesture. 'Get on with it. I'll have to see what happens at the council meeting. If you can find Feynt, tell him we've talked.' And he turned away across his room, groping his way to the shutters and throwing them wide. The sweet breezes of summer dawn immediately raised the muslin curtains, flinging them like perfumed veils into the room, where he struck at them impatiently. Outside in the plaza the trees' leaves had unrolled to their fullest extent, glistening in the amber sun, a bronzy green light that covered everything like water, flowing and changing, rippling along the stones and over the walls in a constant tide. 'Riverlight,' it was called. 'Summer Riverlight,' created by the wind and the trees.

The fountain played charmingly, the little bells hung in its jet tumbling and jingling. On the nearest meadows the weehar lowed and the thrassil neighed, gentle sounds. With the wind in this direction, one could scarcely hear the axes, far off in the hills.

At the center of the plaza, near the fountain, Tharius Don and Glamdrul Feynt stood in the midst of a crowd of servants and craftsmen, hands pointing, voices raised. Funeral arrangements, Shavian told himself, yawning. Evidently there was to be a catafalque in the ceremonial square prior to entombment. Respected members of the Chancery were not put into pits on their deaths. It was presumed the Holy Sorters would take them directly from their roofless tombs into Potipur's arms. Shavian yawned again. The truth of

442

which would be easy to ascertain, he thought, if anyone wanted to climb over a tomb wall and look. Since he was reasonably certain of what he would find – considering the number of small birds and vermin that congregated around tombs – Shavian was not tempted to do so.

He rang for his servants. There was time for a bath and a massage before the meeting of the council. He ordered perfumes for his bath and others sprinkled upon his clothing. The chamber of meeting would stink of death.

When they met, the body of Lees Obol had already been removed and there was no smell at all. They sat about impatiently, waiting for Jondrigar to arrive. Jorn and Nepor were side by side, pretending no interest in one another, though usually they were collusive as heretics. Shavian watched this, mildly amused. They were up to something. Across the table, in the secondary row of chairs, Bormas Tyle and Glamdrul Feynt bore similar expressions of disinterest. No doubt if Gendra had been present, she would have looked the same. Shavian adjusted his face to one of polite alertness. Why not break the mold, behave somewhat differently, confuse them all?

Tharius Don brooded, but then he always brooded. He had not sent a message to Gendra. He hoped no one else had, though there was no guarantee someone in the Bureau of Towers had not. Or Bormas Tyle, perhaps. Tharius had no illusions about his deputy's sense of loyalty. Bormas Tyle had none, except to himself.

A clatter of feet in the hall, more than one. The doors at the end of the great chamber were flung wide, and General Jondrigar entered at the head of a company of troops. The others stared. Ezasper Jorn bit off an exclamation, throwing a sideways glance at Nepor. What was this?

Shavian, no less surprised than the others, decided to treat it as a normal occurrence. 'We have been waiting for you, Jondrigar. Do you wish to sit down?'

'I'll stand,' he boomed. 'There is little time to do what must be done. I have received the message Lees Obol meant

443

for me. "Go," he said to me, and go I must. He wishes me to finish the work he could not finish. He desires I take upon myself the title of Protector of Man.'

There was a stunned silence. Into that silence crept the sound of Bormas Tyle's knife, sliding in its scabbard. Shavian Bossit swallowed, tried to concentrate, torn between laughter and shock. What had he and Bormas Tyle said only that morning? Support either the general or Gendra for the position of Protector. Soon both would be dead. He swallowed his surprise and found his voice.

'I would support you in that, Jondrigar.' He turned to find two faces frozen upon his own, Jorn's and Nepor's. Ah, so they had been up to something. 'Tharius, you would support Jondrigar's accession to the title, would you not?'

'I would,' said Tharius in a strangely husky voice. It was another sign. A sign from heaven. From the God to man, if one cared to say it that way. From Pamra Don. 'I would support General Jondrigar. He knows what is needed to protect mankind.'

'I have already begun,' the general boomed. 'When I returned with Pamra Don from the pass, I sent commands to all the mines that slaves should be released and taken over the mountains to their homeland.'

There were gasps from around the table. Shavian bit his tongue. Tharius looked upon the general with loving, glowing eyes.

'Now I must go to the place Queen Fibji is, to beg her forgiveness. And when that is done, I will return to take up this great office, which Lees Obol intended from my birth.' He turned away, strode away, the feet of his troops drumming behind him, the chamber echoing with sound. Behind him was silence.

'No slaves in the mines?' Bormas breathed at last.

Shavian shook his head warningly. 'There is metal in the warehouses. Enough for a very long time. We can bear a hiatus.'

'Queen Fibji will have evidence of slavery when her people come home.'

'Cross that stream when it splashes us.'

Ezasper Jorn and Koma Nepor said nothing. They were frozen with shock.

'Let be,' said Tharius Don. 'It may be we are entering a new age.' Jondrigar had not said anything about the fliers, but if he had truly understood Pamra Don, it would not be long before he moved in that direction as well. First the Noor, then the fliers. First those close by, then those more remote. Tharius Don placed his hand over his eyes, covering the weak tears that gemmed the corners. Almost he could see through those hands, so thin they were, so translucent. He should eat. He should. There were things he had to do. His stomach turned at the thought. No. No, he would eat after everything was done.

And everything would soon be done. After which he could die – die in thankfulness that it had not been necessary to invoke the strike, in gratitude that Pamra Don would be safe in the general's care . . .

As would the world of man.

24

Seeker birds had been bred originally by the Noor. On the vastness of the steppes, messages could be sent, as they were from the signal towers of the Chancery, by heliograph during the day or by reflector lantern at night. Information was exchanged in these ways on a more or less regular and formal basis among Queen Fibji's guards and outliers. For more spontaneous sharing of information or to carry greetings among near-kin, seeker birds were used, flying back and forth between their two masters, sometimes over enormous distances. Possession of a seeker bird was no longer considered de facto proof that the owner was a Noor or Noor sympathizer, though that had once been the case. Many merchants used them now. Medoor Babji had taken half a dozen Fibji seekers with her when she sailed away on the *Gift*. Every troop of Melancholics had two or three home seekers, imprinted to seek some near-kin on the steppes. And, of course, Fibji's spies had seeker birds.

One of these arrived in the cage late in the afternoon, after the audiences for the day were done. Strenge thrust his little finger into the bone message tube and twirled it around, bringing the paper out in a crackling cylinder, frowning as he did so.

'Which one of our people sent that?' the Queen asked, splashing her footbath at him with one toe. The attendant looked reproachfully at the Queen, pumice stone held ready. 'That's all right, Jenniver.' She smiled. 'Give me the towel. You don't need to rub at my horny feet tonight. After half a century walking on them, it's no wonder they're tough as old fish hide.'

446

He put the message he had just received into his sleeve and took another instead, twirling a finger into the end of it. 'This one first, Fibby. It's from Medoor Babji.'

'Doorie! Oh, how wonderful. We haven't had word from her in months, months!' The Queen held out her hands, seeing that they trembled a little, to unroll the tight scroll and lay it flat on the little table by her cushions.

'Dear Mother and most honored Queen,' she read. 'Today the *Gift of Potipur* turns northward. We have found an island chain in center River where men and Treeci live. Many of the men here have seen Southshore with their own eyes. It is there, about a month's sail farther south. There is no question. It is a huge land, empty of men, so these men believe.

'We do not know when or where we will strike land on Northshore, though it will be at least two months, one hundred long days, from now, and probably some distance west of Thou-ne from where we departed. Send a message to me through all the Melancholics of Northshore from Thou-ne at least so far as Vobil-dil-go.

'I have learned that the fliers have found some herdbeasts. They have a plan to raise the herdbeasts on the steppes until there are great herds and then kill all humans. Two fliers were blown to an island in a mighty storm, and I overheard them. I have not told anyone of this but you.

'The Noor must make plans at once to leave for the south. If the Thraish go on with their plans, the plan we have so long depended upon will be only another kind of grave.

'I have found the answer to Grandfather's riddle.

'Your loving and obedient daughter, Medoor Babji.

'P.S. I think I am pregnant.'

'Ah,' said Strenge, looking perplexed, gulping a little, hardly knowing which part of the message to think of first. 'Well, if she only thinks she is pregnant, it happened after she left.'

'Rape,' snarled the Queen.

'I think not,' Strenge said soothingly. 'She would not have used those words had it resulted from rape. No. I have had seeker birds from those who were with the troupe in Thou-ne, and they tell me Medoor Babji was fascinated by the boat owner, Thrasne.'

'That is not a Noor name!'

'No. And Noor do not own boats. Shh, shh, Fibji. We have children among our near-kin who are not wholly Noor.'

The Queen snarled. Strenge petted her and she wept in pain, anger, and frustration.

When she had finished weeping, he said, 'And now, Queen of the Noor, you must hear evil news.' He took the just received message bone from his sleeve, turning it in his hands for some moments, a sour expression on his face.

'Well?'

'It's from one of our people long enslaved in the Chancery,' he replied in a strained, tight voice. 'From a sentinel post near the Red Talons. Things are taking a nasty turn, Fibji.'

She took the paper and read from it. 'Oh, by all the gods. We heard from the scribe that the leader of the crusade was readying for racial persecution. Now some faction in the Chancery plots our extermination in order to settle our lands with paler skins! Have there been any reports of such action against us?'

'We've had no reports, but the Melancholics may not realize what's going on. There's always the chance of more or less random harassment in the cities.'

'Get some inquiries out, Strenge. It's unlikely there's been time for the Chancery to act on this, but they may move more swiftly than usual.'

'No matter how swiftly or how slowly, Fibby, we must act now, no matter what they do. One message told you a persecution is being built as a fire is laid, with fuel added each place the crusade stops. Another says that now Gendra Mitiar connives at persecution. If her connivance succeeds, our people may find it impossible to gather coin on Northshore. Now comes word from your daughter to say Southshore exists. It is actual, real. It is accessible, too, without such arduous effort as to make it impractical.'

'Then why haven't people gone there?'

'Why should they? The journey is very long. There are vast unsettled stretches on Northshore, to say nothing of the steppes. The Towers have long forbidden exploration of the River.'

'But she says there are men living there, in mid-River!'

'Who may have been there for countless generations. What I find more interesting is that she says there are Treeci, but she does not tell us what those are. Another race of creatures, however. That must be what she means!'

'It is unfathomable to me that men would not have settled another land if that land were reachable by any means,' she grumbled, still preoccupied with Medoor Babji's possible pregnancy and not thinking of exploration or settlement at all.

'And perhaps they did,' he replied. 'And perhaps they are there now. And perhaps they did, and perhaps they all died. And perhaps they did, and some other thing happened. And perhaps, just perhaps, the men who are meant to settle that other land are the Noor.'

She bowed her head, whispered, 'You're right, Strenge. As you often are. So. Send word to all the Noor. They are to leave for Southshore by the quickest route, every tribe in its own way. Empty the coffers of the Queen. Hire boats where we can. Take them where we cannot. Arrange provisions. And send word, as Medoor Babji has suggested, to all Melancholics between Thou-ne and Vobil-dil-go. There must be some plan made for the assembly of our people when we reach Southshore. If we do . . .' She took a deep breath, drew herself up.

'We will leave in the morning! We will forget our plans to seek any agreement with the Chancery. It was always a vain hope. Since we are very near to Split River already, we will go down along the river to Northshore. Forced march. We Noor can march in three months or four what would take the Northshoremen a year. She bids us hurry. We will hurry.'

449

She was silent a time, thinking. With all this threat to her people, still she longed to have Medoor Babji beside her at this time. But pregnant?

'Ah. I am to be a grandmama again. My heir is to have a child. Ah, Strenge, what message shall my heart have for my daughter when she returns?'

Tharius Don slept, deep in the sleep of angels, where no trouble was nor anguish. He flew, as with his own wings, alight with holy fire.

Someone shook him by the shoulder.

He opened his eyes, struggling to penetrate the gloom.

'Your Grace.'

'Ah?'

'A message, sir. It came in this afternoon, but with everything that was going on, it got mislaid. When I came on duty, I knew it should be brought to you at once. It's from the Dame Marshal.'

The young officer looked haggard. He offered the message bone with a shaking hand.

'Open it,' Tharius ordered, pulling himself up in the bed. Even when the message was unrolled before him, he had trouble focusing on it. It wasn't Gendra's hand . . .

The thing wasn't from Gendra. The words within were signed by the Noor slave, Jhilt. They spoke briefly of the Noor, and then they spoke of Pamra Don, who was to be given to the Thraish for some kind of ceremonial degradation at Split River Pass. The Thraish had not been convinced or in anywise changed by Pamra Don. They planned this thing in order to discredit her before all her followers.

When he had read the words over for the fourth or fifth time, Tharius Don dried the weak, futile tears that were flowing unbidden down his face, dripping off his chin.

'So,' he said, reaching for the bell at his hand. 'So is my pride humbled.'

'Bring me food,' he said to the yawning servant who came in response to the sound. 'Something hot and strengthening. Find my musician, Martien, and ask him to come to me here.'

When Martien arrived, breathless, he found Tharius Don wrapped in a blanket, eating with single-minded compulsion. His face was drawn into an expression of concentration and pain.

'I am not staying here for the funeral,' Tharius said. 'I'm going over the pass, leaving almost immediately. Send the alert for the strike, Martien. Have watchmen posted on the heights. Though I pray it will not be needed, I will carry the green banner. When it falls, the word is to go out.'

'When the green banner falls, the word is to go out,' Martien repeated, himself in shock. He had heard so often of this day; he had thought it would never come to pass.

'I may have been a great fool,' said Tharius Don. 'A weak, prideful fool. Medman tried to tell me . . .'

'Oh, well, Mendicants,' Martien said, trying to comfort him.

'Yes. Mendicants. They tell us what we don't want to hear, so we don't hear. Oh, another thing, Martien. Send word through my secret channels to Queen Fibji that Mitiar is conspiring with the Thraish to wipe out the Noor. This slavewoman Jhilt may have already told her, but I won't take that chance. Nothing may come of Gendra's plotting, but the Queen must be warned, if she'll believe me. Tell her also that General Jondrigar in on his way to her. To beg her pardon. She may not believe that, either.'

'Queen Fibji?'

'She is somewhere near Split River Pass. She's been journeying toward it for some time now. I don't know why. Perhaps she planned another visit to the Chancery.' He fell silent, drinking the last of the soup, half-choking on it, a sickness in his stomach at the unaccustomed food. 'Half the world is at Split River Pass. The crusade. The general. Fibji. And soon, according to the message I have received, the Thraish.'

He stood up, staggering a little. Martien looked at him with concern and offered a supporting arm, which Tharius shrugged away.

451

'It's all right, Martien. I've been forcibly recalled to myself. Late in life to be taught a lesson like this, but not too late, perhaps. Go now. I trust you to see to everything.'

He watched his trusted friend go out, thinking he would not see him again, remembering the flat harp music, the flame-bird, Kessie.

'I am thankful,' he told himself resolutely. 'Thankful that if I have misjudged, I will have an opportunity not to betray myself, my cause, and those whose lives have been given to it.' It was a kind of litany, though he did not think of it in those terms. When the room had steadied around him a little, he went up the endless stairs to make his preparations, wondering what kind of ceremony it was the Thraish planned at Split River Pass and how he could comfort and heal Pamra Don when it was over.

25

Watching Medoor Babji and Eenzie the Clown today. They were washing their hair on the deck, flinging water about, dancing in their small clothes like festival whirlers, making all the men stand there with their mouths open. Some of the men lusting, I'm sure, we've been so long from shore. Medoor Babji has sent all her birds away, and it's as though someone took a heavy burden from her, for she laughs, giddy, like a child, and she comes teasing me during the daytime and inviting me up to the owner-house roof after dark. Sometimes I go, too.

I'm careful not to talk about Pamra Don. I did that once, to Babji's hurt, so I'll not do it again. Still, each time there is happiness with Babji, it makes me ache for Pamra. At first I thought it meant I would rather it *was* Pamra, but that isn't so. If it was Pamra, it would be all tears and pain and sadness instead of this joyousness, and I'm not so silly as to wish that for myself. But I can wish it for Pamra herself, and that's where the hurt is.

Times like this, it would be nice to believe in gods somewhere who took care of things. I could pray, 'See to Pamra. Give her joy. Take away whatever the pain is that festers in her.'

But there isn't a god to do that. I still love her. I feel unfaithful to her, too, in a strange kind of way, as though it's wrong for me to have pleasure or take joy in life. Good sense tells me that's a wrong kind of feeling. Death lies that way, and I'm no death courter.

So, I'll try to put her and all her pain away, some-where inside a protected place. I won't throw it away, or forget it, but I can't go on waving it about like a banner, either, to make Medoor Babji cry.

So, I'll keep it. Quietly. Until I don't have to anymore.

From Thrasne's book

To one coming down Split River Pass toward the cupped, alluvial plain at its foot, the buttes seemed to spread fanwise toward the southern horizon, lines and clusters of level-topped, sheer-sided mountains, all that was left of the great mesa that had lain at the foot of the mountains in time immemorial, now chewed by the river into these obdurate left-overs. Higher up, the pass itself wound along towering canyons and through one enormous valley, more than half-filled by the lake called Mountain's Eye, fed at this season by a thousand hurrying streams carrying melted snow from the heights, itself the source of Split River's flowing both north and south. The south-flowing stream was the larger one, in this season capable of violent excess, sometimes tumbling great boulders into its own path, detouring itself east or west at the foot of the pass to flow in any of a hundred ancient channels among the buttes. This year it had ramified into a braid of smaller streams on either side of the vastly swollen main river, and Tharius Don looked down from the pass to see the buttes glittering among tinsel ribbons of water in the late sun.

Tents were thickly scattered among the buttes, an agglomeration and tumult of peoples. Tharius put his glass to his eye and scanned the multitude. To the south, at some distance down the main stream, were the tents of the Noor, a large party of them with more arriving. Near the Noor, the banners of the Jondarite select guard and the tent of the general. Nearest the pass, the crusaders, thickly sown, like fruit fallen beneath a tree. To the east, not far, a party of Jarb Mendicants, their distinctive round tents identifiable even at this distance, surrounded themselves in a haze of smoke. Tharius put the glass away and went on down the pass, toward a Jondarite guardpost.

Near Red Talons there had been two days of argument, stretched out partly by Gendra Mitiar and partly by Sliffisunda, who wanted to be sure there were plenty of witnesses present at Split River Pass. When his scouts returned to say that a vast multitude of crusaders and Noor and even Mendicants were gathered there, Sliffisunda delayed no longer.

'I will take the woman now,' he said.

'You'll take me, too,' said Gendra grimly, drawing on her last reserves of strength. 'I must return to the Chancery the fastest way.' Jhilt's defection had made her think of treachery, and treachery had made her think of the elixir. Though the bottle did not look in any wise different, its effects were not what she had counted on. She had to get back to the Chancery and a new supply, bartered off old Feynt.

'Take me, too, Sliffisunda.'

He had consented, not caring greatly, rather more amused by the request than not. He would take her and the Laugher, Ilze. He wanted to watch Ilze during the cere-mony with Pamra Don, see what he did. Abnormal human behavior was very interesting to Sliffisunda, and there would not be many more years of humans in which to study it.

'Very well,' he said in a calm voice that any flier would have recognized as dangerous, 'I will take all three of you. The others may follow after.' He did not like the Jondarites with their crossbows this close to the Talons and was glad to hear Gendra order them to return to the Chancery.

Three of the coarse flier-woven baskets were brought. Pamra Don would not give up the child, which Sliffisunda thought odd, but it added little to the load. There was no hurry. Fliers had gone on ahead to prepare, and Sliffisunda himself had ordered what was to follow. There would be an

455

announcement first, to get the attention of the mob. Then the ceremony with the rest. Then the woman from the Chancery would order the mob to disperse. It was all agreed.

Pamra heard only that they were returning to the Chancery. She rejoiced in this. It did no good to talk to these fliers. Neff comforted her by telling her she had not been sent to the fliers, but to man, which she understood. 'We're going back now,' she said to Lila, jouncing the child on her knee.

'Back where?' Lila asked. 'Do you know where, Pamra Don?'

It was the first time the child had called her by name, and Pamra looked into her face, wondering at this adult, understanding tone. 'Why, to the Chancery,' she said. 'We will see Great-Great-Grandfather again.'

The child shook her head, reaching up to pat Pamra's face. 'Pamra Don,' she said. 'You don't listen.'

'Where are the Thraish?' Tharius asked the Jondarite officer who was stationed at the guardpost.

'The fliers are mostly on those two buttes over there, Lord Propagator,' the man answered, pointing them out. The rocky elevations he indicated were so near the pass that the river washed their feet. They were about forty or fifty feet high, very sheer-walled, their bases carved inward into low, smooth-walled caves by the water's flow. Tharius put the glass to his eye and stared at their slightly sloping tops. There were fliers there, certainly, quite a mob of them on both butte tops, but there were fliers on several of the farther buttes as well, coming and going, all of them staying well away from the edges.

'Did you plan to shoot at them?' he asked the Jondarite, noting the crossbow case on the man's back.

The Jondarite shook his head. 'Not unless ordered to, sir, and even then not so long as they stay in the middle of the butte that way. It's too far from here, and we can't get them from below unless they come to the edge. They're too smart for that.'

Tharius shook his head, wondering why they always

thought of weapons first and talking later. 'Do you have any seeker birds for the general?'

The Jondarite saluted and ran off to get one from the cage. Tharius laid paper on his knee and wrote out the message. 'To the Protector of Man. The Thraish plan some ceremony to discredit Pamra Don because she defends the Protector of Man. They seem to be gathering on the buttes at the entrance to the pass. Tharius.' They sent the bird off, watching it winging down the river toward the Jondarite tents.

'I've sent three messages by that bird already today,' the Jondarite said. 'That bird knows right where he is.'

Tharius reached into his pocket for bread. He had been eating constantly since he left the Chancery, trying to convince himself he had strength enough to do whatever would need doing. 'Can you get on top of that thing?' He indicated the nearest butte. If the ceremony was to occur on that height, it might be necessary for them to get close in order to talk with Sliffisunda.

'With grappling ladders, sure. Trouble is, we start to climb it, they'll just move to another one. We don't have enough men here to put a guard on all of them. The general's already sent a message for all troops at Highstone Lees to join him here.'

All the troops? Tharius stared at the man in amazement. There had never been a time when all the Jondarites had left Highstone Lees. 'What are the fliers up to?'

'I don't know. They've been coming and going all day. Carrying trash. Look like a bunch of birds building a nest.'

A nest, Tharius thought. For nestlings. Juveniles. One could be discredited in the eyes of a multitude by being reduced to the status of a juvenile. Would the mob understand that? Or would Sliffisunda explain it to them? He was too shrewd to let them misunderstand it, that was certain.

'Have any of them come in carrying people?'

The Jondarite shook his head. 'Not that I've seen.'

Tharius sighed. If Pamra Don was not yet here, then he was in time. There could still be negotiations. He gave

457

quick instructions to the Jondarite. 'You can see better from here than I'll be able to from below. The minute you see any fliers carrying people – or any people approaching across the valley from the directions of the Red Talons – send me word. I'll leave a man here with half a dozen of my birds.'

He took another bite of the bread and started on down the pass, Martien close behind him. Martien was holding the green banner. Somewhere high above them among the encircling peaks there were signal posts and watchers, their eyes on that banner. Since Pamra Don had failed, he would have to send the signal for the strike soon. Better for everyone if he had sent it a year ago. 'Weak,' he castigated himself. 'You're weak, Tharius Don.'

'What are you going to do?' Martien asked.

'I don't know. Try to get to whoever's in charge. Sliffisunda, maybe. Gendra, maybe. Or that Laugher, Ilze. The message I got said he was involved.'

'How did the general get so far down the river? He couldn't have left more than a few hours before you.'

'He's in better shape than I am, Martien. I have to face it. I've been a fool. Starving myself. It felt right, you know. Light. As though I were taking off weights, enabling myself to fly. I saw everything so clearly. The light was limpid. Nothing was complicated. I'd half convinced myself God was talking to me through Pamra Don. All the time it was only pride pretending to be something else. And Pamra Don the same. Familial stupidity, maybe. Well, I sent her into this. Now I have to get her out.'

Far down the valley, Queen Fibji heard the reports of her own scouts. They had not expected this great mob of people. They had not expected to find the originator of the anti-Noor doctrine here, either, but Peasimy Flot was said to be present as well.

Though mobs were always dangerous in the Queen's opinion, and Strenge agreed with her, this one on this occasion was doubly, trebly dangerous. No matter what the general had said. She was not sure she believed him. If she believed him, she was not sure he could do what he promised. Too late, she told herself. His pleas for forgiveness had come too late.

'I think we'd better move south, away from this, don't you?' she said to Strenge, breaking into his musing.

'I think it would be wise,' he agreed soberly. 'I'll call Noor-count and march.' He was out of the tent before she could say anything more, and she had to summon her own people with a trembling hand on the bells. 'Pack it up,' she said. 'We're moving within the hour.'

She did not want to think about the mob. General Jondrigar had just left her, and she did not wish to think of what they had said to one another, either. She distracted herself by helping with the packing, scandalizing her people thereby.

From the air, the steppe looked like a carpet of ash and dun and grayed green. Pamra Don stared down at it, fascinated despite herself. If she could convince some of the fliers to carry her like this, her crusade could grow that much faster. Less time would be spent in travel. Though perhaps it was not necessary for the crusade to grow any more than it had. She had not spoken to Lees Obol yet, and when she did, perhaps he would believe her all at once as the general had done. Neff flew beside her, turning his shining face toward hers in the high, chill air. 'Don't you think so?' she cried. 'Neff?'

He didn't answer but merely sailed there, driven on the wind, just out of her reach.

Tharius and his men continued their descent, the plain coming up to meet them as they twisted back and forth along the downward road. When they arrived at the bottom, a breathless runner confronted them with the general's message. 'Wait for him here, Lord Propagator. He follows close behind me.'

It was an hour before the general arrived at the head of his battalions, during which time the fliers went on clustering at the butte tops and nothing changed.

'Did you see Queen Fibji?' Tharius asked, wondering at the expression on the man's face. It was full of pain.

'I saw her,' heavy, without intonation. For a time Tharius thought he would not explain, but then he went on, 'She heard me. She said if the God of man forgave me, ever, then so would she and her people. I do not know if the God of man has forgiven me or ever will, Tharius Don.'

'I think – I think he probably has,' Tharius said, astonished. Whether the God of man had forgiven Jondrigar or not; whether there was any such deity, they could not afford the time to worry about it now. 'What is Queen Fibji doing here?'

'It was the shortest route to Northshore from where they were, because of the good roads along Split River. The Queen said they would be leaving very soon. South. While there is time.'

'Time?'

'She says the crusaders plan to kill the Noor because the Noor are black. She says the crusaders have betrayed Pamra Don. A devil has come to lead them. So says Queen Fibji. She called upon me, the Protector of Man, to put an end to him.'

Oh, clever Queen, Tharius thought half-hysterically. Turning her enemies or former enemies against one another. 'What is this devil's name?'

'Peasimy Flot. He calls himself Peasimy Prime. He teaches no breeding, no children, no Noor. He cries, "Light comes," and brings only darkness and death. So says Queen Fibji.'

'Where is he?'

The general gestured toward the west. 'There. She showed me where. His people and wagons have recently arrived. If you will look with your glass, you can see him between those two buttes, high in his wagon, a crown on his head. I have looked at him. When we have talked, I will go kill him.'

Tharius laid a hand upon his shoulder. 'First we must take care of Pamra Don.' He pointed out the buttes, showed

460

the general the message he had received. 'Two days ago, Jondrigar. Almost three. They would be here by now, wouldn't you think?'

'If they flew. Perhaps they didn't. Perhaps they sent her back as she came to them, traveling over the steppe with Gendra Mitiar.'

Tharius stared at the high buttes. They couldn't have picked a more visible place to do whatever they planned. Accessible only from the air, only by fliers, yet sloped enough to be unconcealed to all except those at the foot of the butte. Even as he stared, the seeker bird arrived.

'Fliers carrying baskets, slow, coming this way.'

From the air, the butte tops looked like tables above the colorful carpet of the valleys. Nearest the pass were two where many fliers clustered, and it was to one of these that Gendra and Ilze were carried and tumbled out with no ceremony. Ilze was on his feet at once, shaking his fist and screaming, but Gendra lay where she had rolled, unable to move. Some link within her was broken, she thought dully. Some vital connection. At last she gathered her remaining strength and struggled to her feet. At the very center of the space they stood upon, Sliffisunda crouched among a few weathered boulders, invisible to anyone looking from below, staring across Gendra's shoulder. She turned. Across from her, level with her eyes, was another butte, perhaps a hundred yards away. Fliers clustered on it like flies on puncon jam, getting in each other's way.

They are building a nest, she thought to herself. The stupid fliers are building a nest. She looked down. Thousands of faces stared back at her, white ovals, mouths open. A ripple moved from the base of the butte outward as people turned, staring, faces and faces. A murmur came, like a murmur of waves. She had not expected this many, not this many.

A new emotion came to her, all at once. Dismay. There should not have been this many crusaders. And there should have been only a few Jondarites, but there were Jondarites

461

everywhere. With their bows. Why were there so many Jondarites?

Beside her Ilze stood, still waving his fists at the crouching Talker, screaming at him. 'You owe her to me, Sliffisunda. You owe me!'

A flier came screaming low over the crowd below. Gendra could not understand what it said, but the crowd seemed to understand, for the murmur deepened, became a roar.

Tharius crumpled the message and raised his glass. The fliers had reached one of the buttes near the pass and dumped the basket on it. Someone stood up, shaking his fist. 'Ilze,' Tharius breathed. 'The Laugher. They've brought him. There's another one.' This time the tumbled figure did not stand up at once; when it did, Tharius could hardly recognize it. Gendra Mitiar? It looked dead, a staggering corpse. An errant wind brought Ilze's shouts to their ears, though they could not see whom he was shouting at.

'You owe her to me, Sliffisunda. She's mine!'

'Where are the Jondarites who were with Gendra?' the general asked. 'What has happened to them?'

'I don't know,' Tharius answered. 'Gendra and Ilze seem to have come willingly. They haven't been hurt.'

He tried to think. He had to get a message to Sliffisunda somehow, get him to talk. But where was Sliffisunda? Was he even here? His frantic thought was interrupted by a harsh cawing as a flier came over them from the east, flying low, screaming its message so that all could hear: 'Pamra Don is a heretic. Pamra Don denies Potipur. See how the Thraish deal with heretics!' Elsewhere upon the plain other fliers soared, all screaming the same message.

The flier turned and came over once more, still screaming. The general spoke to his aide. Before Tharius could intervene, men reached for their crossbows and quarrels flew. The flier choked, sideslipped, tumbled from the sky in a crumpled heap. Elsewhere on the plain, other crossbowmen began to shoot and other fliers fell. From the butte came a cry of rage. The Talkers had not expected this. Fliers and Talkers rose from it in a cloud, straight up, offering no further targets.

Oh, gods, Tharius thought. Now they won't listen to any offer of talk.

The roar became a howl. Gendra sank to her knees. The stupid fliers shouldn't have done it. Shouldn't have threatened Pamra Don. It was all going wrong, all wrong. 'Sliffisunda,' she croaked, trying to warn him. He ignored her, his eyes glowing. 'Don't,' she croaked. 'You'd better take the woman down to them and let her alone.'

He turned his back on her, shat, walked closer to the edge of the butte, eyes still fixed on the other tabletop.

When they began to descend, Pamra leaned over the basket side, seeing everything from above, a great, scattered carpet of followers, her followers. She took a deep breath and the rapture came, glowing. All her followers, waiting for her.

'Pamra Don,' said Lila again.

She scarcely heard the child. Above her, wings tilted toward one of the flat-topped mountains. It had a huge nest built on it, a flier nest.

Before she could think about that, they had taken her out of the basket and tied her to something in the nest. What did they think she was? A nestling? The fliers were screaming in rage. They wanted her to look like a nestling, that was it. Wings lifted in a cloud, leaving only one or two of the fliers behind her. She could not see them. She could not see the nearby followers either, only the distant ones, a wave of faces, turning toward her, thousands of faces.

She smelled smoke. Smelling smoke always made her think of flame-birds. In her arms, Lila grew very still. Still and hard.

Tharius had no more time to think of talking with the Thraish. A laboring pair of fliers appeared high above the butte and dropped onto it, burdened by the load they carried. 'Tell your men not to shoot,' Tharius cried. 'That's Pamra Don.'

Too late. The bowmen were already shooting, but it had no

463

effect. The edges of the butte effectively blocked the bolts, which rattled harmlessly on the rocks. Tharius focused his glass upon the butte top. There was a huge pile of twigs and branches there, an untidy cupped mass, as all Thraish nests were. His stomach heaved, and he vomited violently, Martien holding his shoulders. 'Stop them,' he croaked. 'We've got to stop them!' Suddenly he knew what they were about to do.

There was no time. There was scarcely time to feel horror. The distant figure was tied upright in the nest and it was set alight, all in a moment. A moment. They could scarcely see her through the smoke. 'She's carrying the baby,' Tharius cried, as horrified at this as at the distant puff of smoke. Flames rose up, almost invisible in the sunlight. Word spread among the crusaders, and they turned toward the butte, seeing the fliers circling above it, the flames, the struggling form there disclosed, then hidden by blowing smoke. A cry rose up, a great shout. One of the bowmen made a lucky shot, and a Talker tumbled from the sky. The fliers rose, screaming, then darted downward, claws extended, only to fall victim to the cloud of bolts. Some fell into the plain still alive and were beaten to death by crusaders as the shout rose, louder and louder.

Ilze watched, his eyes bulging, his body twitching. 'Oh, yes,' he said. 'Oh, yes.'

'Don't,' Gendra begged. 'We've made a mistake, Uplifted One. It won't happen as you expected it to. Put out the fire . . .'

The first flames touched Pamra Don. Neff, she thought. She tried to look over her shoulder to see his face, but she couldn't. He was there, she felt his blazing glory. Before her on the rimrock were her mother and Delia, but Neff was behind her. He was hurting her. 'Neff,' she cried. The flames were all around her, and she cried his name again, the word rising up in an agonized howl to fill a silence that had fallen over all that multitude, rising and rising from a throat that could not stop it nor end it nor consider what it was doing, on and on and on into a silence that seemed to resound with it still when it had ended.

'Get grappling ladders onto that butte,' the general shouted, not seeing that Jondarites had already done so and were scaling the sheer wall, being attacked by furious fliers, thrown down, replaced by others, with the smoke still blowing. The first man reached the top, was pitched off by buffeting wings, was replaced by two more who flailed with their hatchets at the fliers guarding the fire. Other men poured up the ladders after them. The wind stilled for a moment, falling into an enormous, awful silence. Into this silence the scream insinuated itself as though dropping from the heights of the sky itself to fill all the world. It had all agony in it, all pain, all loneliness. Pamra's voice. One endless scream. Then again the silence.

And after the silence a roar of fury which moved across the multitudes like a mighty wave, from the base of the butte to the farthest edges of the encampment. Fliers had landed here and there to strut and crow before crowds of unarmed crusaders. They were clubbed to the earth, clubbed into the earth, pounded into bloody soil and scraps of feathers.

'You should not have done it,' Gendra muttered, falling to the stone. She had no more strength. Nothing mattered now. She knew what would happen next. It was inevitable. From beside her, Sliffisunda watched, amazed and wild-eyed. This was not the way it should have gone. The humans should have cowered before this. On the Stones of Disputation it had been decided, they would be frightened, they would be abased, obedient. But they were not. They screamed. They howled. Sliffisunda felt a strange, unfamiliar emotion. Terror.

'Hostages,' he screamed to three fliers near him in the sky. 'Take these two humans. We may need hostages.'

Obedient, as frightened as Sliffisunda himself, they dropped straight down and took off again, Ilze struggling in their claws, Gendra Mitiar hanging limp, unconscious. They tilted, spun, flew toward the Red Talons. Behind them, bolts filled the air and other, less wary fliers fell from the sky.

Tharius Don found himself running, not remembering when he had started running, only that he was. The general pounded along beside him, both of them headed for the butte that was about a quarter mile away, close to the main river. Without the glass, they could not see its top. They panted their way to its bottom, leaned against the stone, puffing. A Jondarite came down the ladder.

'The woman?' the general asked. 'Pamra Don?'

'I think she's dead, General.'

'You think?'

'Something there. Strange. The men won't go near it.'

They were climbing the ladder then, swaying. Tharius had never liked heights. He didn't think he could climb this ladder, but he was being pulled over the rimrock before he could determine whether it was possible or not. A smoking pyre was before him, a great heap of glowing wood. In the center what remained of Pamra Don, black, contorted, its teeth showing between charred lips, held upright by a partially burned stake.

And in its arms a sphere of softly moving light which pulsed. And pulsed. And breathed.

And broke.

Something came out of it. Winged. Or perhaps finned. Or both. Whatever it was spoke to Tharius Don. 'Poor Tharius. She was the last of your line.' Then it was gone, falling or flying from the edge of the rock to the river below, entering it with scarcely a splash, moving in it as though born to it, south, southward, away toward the River that encircled the world.

'Lila?' breathed Tharius Don. 'Lila?'

The general did not seem to have seen. He leaned from the rimrock to shout in a stentorian voice, 'The fliers have burned Pamra Don.'

From far off came a treble shout. 'The Mother of Truth

466

has been killed. War against the fliers. Night comes, night comes, night comes!'

Tharius looked across the plain to the place Martien waited. He made a chopping gesture, made it again, and again and again. Four times. The far green speck that was his banner dropped and then rose, four times. So. Let it begin. Let it all begin. Let it all come to a bloody end. Let the damn Thraish die as they deserved. He began to weep.

Below he could see Jondarites fighting against a party of crusaders. 'Why?' he demanded of the general.

'Someone has said it was Jondarites who killed Pamra Don,' he growled. 'Perhaps the devil with the crown has set his people against the Jondarites. I go to lead my armies. See, he flees!'

The cart that Peasimy Flot had traveled in was moving away, pulled by a dozen running men. Voices were calling out, wanting to know who it was who had killed Pamra Don. 'Jondarites,' said some, attacking the nearest ones and falling in their blood. 'Fliers,' said others, marching off toward the Red Talons, clubs and bows in their hands. And still others said, 'Chancery. Those of the Chancery.'

'The Noor,' cried some, looking around for dark faces. 'The blackfaces.' Tharius stared out over valley. The Noor were moving rapidly south, visible now only as a trail of dust upon the horizon, too far away to become victims of this general holocaust. Below him a thousand battles were being waged, generalized slaughter was going on, and Jondrigar moved ponderously down the ladder to get his troops around him.

Tharius sat down where he was, staring at the blackened corpse of Pamra Don. The pyre still smoked.

The Jarb Mendicants left their encampment and began to move onto the battlefield, their pipes smoking, the haze around them thickening. Slowly, slowly, as the Mendicants covered the field, the fighting stopped. Shouting stopped. Cries of fury stopped. Sobbing and cries of pain and grief came after. Beside Tharius Don the ladder quivered, and

467

Chiles Medman climbed onto the stone to regard him with calm, awful eyes.

'She was mad,' Tharius said, his eyes red-lined with weeping. 'Mad, and I did not see it.'

'Was she?' asked Chiles Medman, glancing at the blackened corpse, shuddering, turning his eyes away.

'Of course! Look at the slaughter down there. All madness. Madness.'

'Oh, that is probably true, Tharius Don.'

'Let it end.'

'I do not think it will end, no. Peering through the smoke, I see what is to be.' He stood at Tharius's side, taking the oracular stance: hands held out, facing the weeping multitude, head thrown back, the pipe between his teeth so the smoke rose before his eyes. He called in a trumpet voice, 'Millions will die in her name. The steppes will be soaked in blood. I see a future in which women are herded into one set of cities, men into another. I see endless processions, mindlessly stamping puddles of light. I see age, coming inexorably, with no youth to soften it, no children to bless it. I see Peasimy Prime immolating himself at last when death draws near, in order to assure for himself the immortality promised by Pamra Don.'

'Millions?' Tharius faltered. 'What would be left?'

'I see a dozen, a hundred interventions, heresies, rebellions, all of which might succeed, any of which might fail. Still, the Jarb Houses will try, and try. And in the end die or flee, as all else dies or flees. Then there will be remnants, scratching in the ashes, ready to begin again.' He lowered his hands, took the pipe from his mouth, put his hand on Tharius's shoulder as though in comfort.

'Madness!'

'Not to Peasimy Flot,' he said calmly. 'Not to the fanatics who follow him. They do not see this world at all, but only their hope of the next. He has crossbowmen, did you know that? Men he has hired. They have instructions to shoot any Jarb Mendicant who comes anywhere near. He has named us the ultimate heretics. Us, and the Noor, and the

Jondarites, for he has heard that General Jondrigar has been named the Protector of Man. Peasimy says no, the general is not Protector. He, Peasimy, is the Protector.'

'No hope.' Tharius clutched at himself, as though he had been stabbed.

Chiles Medman laughed bitterly. 'Oh, there is always hope. Even now Noor are marching toward the Rivershore. Every boat able to float will soon be headed south with Noor abroad. I do not know why, but they are a saner race than most. There is a riddle there. With the great numbers they have lost to slavery and war, one would think quite otherwise, and yet because of some chance they seem inclined, particularly in recent generations, toward peace and good sense. Medoor Babji has begged a boon of her mother, the Queen, so the smoke tells me. Because of the love she bears for a certain Northshoreman, the Noor have said they will take certain – peaceful – others, as well. That proud, persecuted people will take others as well. It is remarkable.'

'Ah.'

'So I suggest you go with them, Tharius Don. There is a future for you, too. It is not long, but I see it in the smoke.'

'Kessie,' he murmured.

'Kessie as well. She is in Thou-ne, where you sent her, where all of this might be said to have begun. Send word for her to meet you in Vobil-dil-go.'

'Your sources of information are better than mine, Medman. But this did not begin in Thou-ne. It began in Baris, long and long ago.'

'Well, if you must talk of ultimate beginnings, it began long before that.'

'Why? Why? Medman, I read the books in the palace, again and again. They are old books. If they tell the truth, our history is full of this. We humans have done this again and again. In the face of truth we choose madness! Over and over. We choose madmen as leaders, clever players who will tell us pretty lies. We repudiate those who promise us honesty and cleave to those who promise us myths. Never the truth, always the Candy Tree. Like flame-birds, we do

469

not feel the flames even while they burn us, as we hatch our like to make the same mistakes in their time. And I, I who sought to do everything in my power to achieve life and peace, I have fallen into the trap. Why? Why?'

'Ask the strangeys, Tharius Don. Perhaps they know. I don't.' Chiles Medman stretched wearily, his nostrils flaring at the stench of the fires. Among the dead and dying moved the Mendicants, hazing the valley with smoke. On the far green horizon, Peasimy Flot's cart gleamed in the sun, its bright banners fluttering as the men drawing it ran at top speed away from the battle. 'Do not let that one get hold of you,' said Chiles in a conversational tone. 'Power has come to him, and he will drive it as a child drives a hobby. He has it between his legs, and he will make it take him where he will.'

'The general will catch him,' Tharius said wearily. 'He cannot run forever.'

'So reason says, and yet that is not what I see,' said Medman, putting his pipe away as he started down the slope. 'Vobil-dil-go, Tharius. Now. Do not return behind the Teeth. There is nothing there for you.

And indeed, there was little enough left behind the Teeth for anyone. The Jondarites had flowed from Highstone Lees like water; after them the servants, for who would stay if there were no Jondarites to enforce discipline? Split River Pass ran like a river with soldiers and slaves and servants and all, out and away. Tharius Don was gone; Gendra Mitiar gone; the general gone; Lees Obol dead, and none caring that he lay all alone on the catafalque in the ceremonial square.

Shavian Bossit wandered through the empty rooms, wondering where everyone had gone, down the long, echoing corridors to winter quarters, through those to the deeper caverns of the files. 'Feynt!' he called, hearing his own voice shattering the silences. 'Feynt!'

There was no answer. Glamdrul Feynt and Bormas Tyle were together in a deep, hidden room of the place, unaware

470

of their abandonment, plotting. In another room, distant from the first, Ezasper Jorn and Koma Nepor were doing likewise. They knew nothing of the slaughter beyond the pass, nothing of the strike that had begun, nothing of the war that had started while they whispered, all unwitting, in the dark cellars of the Chancery.

'Jorn!' cried Shavian Bossit. 'Nepor!'

There was no answer, and he struggled up the endless stairs to a high terrace, where he stepped into the light once more. In the ceremonial square a herd of weehar milled about the unguarded catafalque. Around them lay the scattered bodies of dead herders, and over the bawling animals fliers struck and struck again.

'Stop that!' he howled, unthinking that there were no Jondarites to enforce his commands. 'Stop that!'

He scarcely felt the claws that seized him from behind and lifted him into the high, chill air. Sliffisunda had told the raiding party to bring bull calves, but also, if they had an opportunity, to bring hostages.

In the deepest corridors below the Chancery, those on whom Koma Nepor had tested his improved strain of the blight began to stir. Bodies began to twitch, to move, to stand up and look curiously about themselves. The incubation period was over. Now they moved, seeking others to touch, to infect, to make as themselves. In all of the Chancery, there were only four live persons remaining. All else had been taken, or had fled.

26

When Tharius Don stood upon the height where Pamra Don had been burned, it was the fifth day of the week. He raised and dropped his arm as a signal four times. Four days later, on the ninth day, that which had been long planned would take place. With that gesture, the signal so long awaited had been sent.

From a ledge high upon the Teeth of the North the birds went out near dusk, a flurry of them, like windblown flakes of white, twirling for the moment on their own wingtips with a murmur of air in feathers, a light rustling as of satin, a sound so innocent, so quiet, that no apprehension could attach to it. They were only birds, silver in the light of late afternoon, a little cloud of wings breaking into dots of fleeing light which beat away and away, some along the precipices east and west, others southward, still others in long diagonals away from the wall of mountains.

After the first flurry came a second and a third, glittering spirals, fleeing jots of amber and rose as the sun dropped still lower, and finally a fourth cloud of wings, blood red in the last of the light, darkening to ominous purple as they fled into the waiting dark.

There were thousands of birds, gathered over the years for this purpose alone. Each bird sought a separate person in a separate place. Each bird carried the same message. 'On the ninth day, let the strike begin.'

Below the ledge from which the birds went out was another on which a signal tower stood, and from here went winking lights like spears cast into the dusk, to be answered by other gleamings in the distance east and west, and then by others farther still, twinkling stars in the dark void of earth's night.

There were many thousands of towers transmitting the lights, ranks and files of them marking the edges of areas and zones, of townships and rivers, manned by newly volunteered zealots for the cause or by rebel Awakeners or by Rivermen, and it was to these the word came.

'On the ninth day, let the strike begin.'

In far-off places, villages remote from the River, and to the townships themselves, the birds came bearing the same words. 'On the ninth day, let the strike begin.'

To the nearer places first, to the farther places only after days had passed, still the word ran like fever in the veins of Northshore, corrupting the blood of the world into a fatal hemorrhage.

In Zephyr, the husband of her who had been Blint-wife went to his bird cote at dawn. It was the morning of the ninth day. He read the message almost with disbelief. So long, so long planned. So long in the coming. And so suddenly was it *now*. This coming night. He went down the stairs, the message in his hands. 'Murga?'

She was bustling about in the kitchen, making a cheerful clack with her tongue as she fed stewed fruit and grain to the grandchildren. 'Murga.'

She appeared at the door, wiping her hands. 'Raffen? What is it? Are you ill?'

He realized his voice had betrayed him, edged with half excitement, half fear; like a knife, it had cut into her contentment. 'The word has come.'

She shivered. She had had to know, as all the Rivermen knew, and yet she had kept it closed away in the back of her mind somewhere, along with other unwanted and dangerous lumber. 'When?'

'Tonight.'

'So soon!'

'Once the word came, it had to be soon. Immediate. We

473

could not expect to keep it quiet after the word was given. Too many birds. Too many messages.'

'So.' She wiped her hands again, as though by wiping them she might wipe away the need for acting, for responding, 'What am I to do?'

'You are to stay here, in the house. I'll need the children as messengers for a time, then they must come in and stay close. I will spread the word now. We will spy out the pits during the day to see how many men will be needed.'

'The River?'

'Yes. The barge is ready. The stone sacks are ready. We have men to man the lines.'

'I worry,' she said, tears in the corners of her eyes. 'I worry the barge may break loose. You may end up west of here. You could not return to me. How would I find you?'

He laughed, a quick, unamused bark of laughter. 'Silly woman. Such a silly Murga. After tonight, dear one, it will not matter east or west. When we have done with the Servants of Abricor, do you not think we will have done with their gods? And then do you not think we may walk where we choose? East or west?'

That night he came with others to the pit, well after dark, to pile the bony remnants and twitching corpses into barrows, careful not to touch them with naked skin lest there be some infection from the Tears of Viranel. The barrows creaked down through the town and were emptied into the barge, and there the heavy sacks of stone were tied to the bodies while the barge made its laborious way out into the River, sweeps creaking and men cursing at the unaccustomed labor. The line that connected them to shore reeled out, span after span, and at last Raffen gave the word they had waited for. The bodies went overboard, into the massive currents of the ever-moving River, and the Rivermen turned to the winch to take up the line and bring the barge back to the place it had left.

When morning came, there was nothing different,

474

nothing remarkable, nothing to show that the world had changed. Except that the worker pits were empty.

In Xoxxy-Do, where there were no piers and great rocks encumbered the Riverside, a great pit had been prepared, dug by Rivermen over the decades, deeper and deeper with each succeeding year, the stones taken from it piled above it on teetering platforms of poised logs, the earth piled behind the stones. 'A quarry,' they had called it, taking from it small quantities of carefully crafted blocks, chosen, so it was said, for their veining and color. There the Rivermen came to the quarry late, bringing with them the harvest of the worker pits of towns both east and west, their wagon wheels creaking in the dark and lanterns gleaming. It was early morning when the last of the bodies was laid in the great stone hollow, almost day, with the green lines of false dawn sketched flatly on the eastern plains. Then the engineers moved certain logs that braced certain others in place, and the mountain of piled rubble fell, the accumulation of years fallen into the place from which it had been taken.

If the Rivermen were to try to dig it up, it would take a generation. The Servants of Abricor could not unearth the bodies in a thousand years.

In the towns of Azil and Thrun and Cheeping Wells, the Rivermen carried the corpses to the ends of the long piers, weighted them well, and tossed them out into the River's deep currents.

In Crisomon a great pyre had been built, and in that township every man, woman, and child danced around the pyre as the bodies of the workers were burned to ashes. In Crisomon, conversion to the cause had been total and unanimous.

Elsewhere that was not so. In some townships the Awakeners were vigilant or wakeful and came out of the Towers to defend the pits. In a few places the Awakeners prevailed, but in most the Rivermen won and the corpses of Awakeners were merely added to other corpses which had to be disposed of before dawn.

Dawn.

475

Worker pits empty when the sun rose. In B'for, just east of Thou-ne, an Awakener returned in some haste to the Tower to speak with the Superior, who was in company with the lady Kesseret, said to be Superior of a Tower farther east who had come to B'for on urgent business and was receiving Lord Deign's hospitality before going on.

The Awakener was panting so much it was hard to discern the message that the pit was empty.

The Superior was silent, but the lady Kesseret seemed to understand what had been said.

'Then you will not need to go to the fields today,' she said calmly. There were great wrinkles around her eyes and lips, and her voice was thready. 'Rejoice.'

'But, but,' the young Awakener stuttered, 'but, what shall I do?'

'Go to the chapel and pray,' she suggested.

'What should I pray for?'

'Enlightenment. Patience. Resignation.'

Were these not what she herself had prayed for? She searched Deign's face for signs of shock. None. Both of them had been ready for this. Now it had happened, and she must plan to leave B'for to travel westward to Thou-ne. In a few days or weeks, if they were permitted to live that long. She would not fail to be in that place where Tharius Don would come for her or send her word.

In a few towns the word had not arrived in time, or there had been no Rivermen to receive it. In a few towns there had been no strike, no disturbance at all. The Servants of Abricor fed as usual in the bone pits, looking up with surprise to see their fellows from neighboring townships circling high above, dropping down to sit with them in long, dusty lines upon the pit edges, talking of this thing.

'No workers in our town,' the fliers said. 'No workers.'

'Sometimes there are no workers,' they told one another. 'Sometimes it happens.'

'Not often,' they agreed. 'Not so many places all at once.'

476

It was almost noon of the day after the strike before they sent some among them off to tell the Talkers at the Talons.

'How long?' the Rivermen asked one another. 'How long will it take before they do something?'

'Pile the fish upon the wharves and wait,' they said to each other. 'Each day, fresh fish, there for the eating.'

It took only another day before Servants descended upon the towns, snatching at children or smaller adults. In Baris one among them distracted a group of townsmen while others made off with a living, pleading victim. In some towns, the Rivermen were ready for this; ready with crossbows and stone-tipped bolts, ready with nooses and obsidian clubs. In other towns the victims screamed into unheeding air, were flown away to be dosed with Tears and left in some pit or other until ready for eating.

The Servants had never considered human anger. In the wake of these seizings, anger rose like a veil of smoke around the towns, palpable as wind. Even they who had not been Rivermen, who had revered the Awakeners, even they could feel nothing but anger as they saw their children hoisted aloft, blood dripping from sharp talons as the screaming prey were carried away. Towns in which the first victims were easily taken proved to be impregnable on the second try. Doors and windows were closed. Farmers were not working in their fields. Children were not playing in the streets. Where groups moved, armed men moved with them.

On the wharves the fishermen, guarded by bowmen, drew in their nets and piled the bounty of the River upon the wharves.

On the third day after the strike, Servants attacked some of the towns, tearing at shutters with their talons and beaks, screaming rage at the inhabitants, making short flights to the Riverside to attack the fishermen and to drop tiny blobs of stinking shit upon the fish piled there. The bowmen were practiced by now and used their bolts to advantage. The fliers, in their rage, scarcely noticed how their numbers were being reduced.

In Zephyr, Murga and Raffen sat in their kitchen, listening to a fury of wings outside, like the sound of a great, windy storm. The children cowered beside them, both frightened and excited by this frenzy. 'When will it be over?' they asked, not sure whether they wanted the excitement to end.

'Soon,' said Raffen. 'They will weaken soon.' He sighed. Thus far, not a single one of the fliers had taken any of the fish from the shore. Though many of the Rivermen were not unhappy about this, Raffen believed in the purity of the original cause. He had not wanted the flier folk to die. 'They will weaken soon,' he repeated, hoping they would grow weak enough to succumb at last to reality and eat what was offered them.

In most Towers, Superiors ordered their Awakeners to stay within. Even those most dedicated to the worship of Potipur, and to the virtual immortality that worship might have gained them, learned that discretion was needed. Blinking lights told them of Awakeners in neighboring towns beaten to death by mobs of outraged citizens. Seeker birds arrived to tell them of Awakeners burned in their Towers because they had seemed to favor the Servants of Abricor. These messages had been planned by Tharius Don and long arranged for, designed to be sent a day after the strike to prevent the Awakeners from interfering with what was going on.

And in the Talons was a fury such as Northshore had not seen in a thousand years. Upon the Stones of Disputations the Talkers sat in their tattered feathers, screaming at one another of fault and blame and guilt and shame, while below them in the aeries the last of the Talkers' meat struggled mindlessly in the troughs. Sliffisunda brooded alone in his own place, considering the likelihood of survival, his mind sharpened by the knowledge that there had indeed been a heresy afoot.

478

'Promise of Potipur,' the surviving fliers cried, dropping from the sky like knives of black fire upon the Stones of Disputation while the Talkers scurried for cover. 'Promise of Potipur!' From his concealed room, Sliffisunda heard them, heard the shrieks of pain and rage as those like himself were slaughtered by the angry flocks, his mind working relentlessly as he determined to go on living whether any other of the Thraish lived or not. He would wait until dark. He would fly into the north, to the Chancery, to that place he had flown once before, against his own will, where the herds of thrassil and weehar still grazed on the grasses of Potipur's Promise. Enough to feed himself, he thought. For years. The hot, lovely blood of thrassi. In the north.

He forgot that others of the Thraish had already been sent to hunt among the herds beyond the Teeth.

On the great moors of the Noor, Peasimy Flot learned of the conflagration to the south. Some among his entourage could read the flicking lights. There was even one who was sought out by a seeker bird. The days brought increasing information, until even Peasimy could not but be aware of what was happening.

'Light comes?' he asked, almost whimpering in his hatred for whoever had done this without him. 'Light comes?' He had sworn vengeance upon those who had burned Pamra Don, and now those who had burned Pamra Don were dead or dying without any action by Peasimy Flot. Without his hand in their guts, his knife in their throats. He had fled – though, he told himself, he had done so only to consolidate his strength – but still they died. How dared they?

'Who did it?' he asked at last, while they conferred and tried to come up with an answer. 'Who killed them?'

'Someone in the Chancery,' they said. 'It had to be someone in the Chancery.'

'Heretics,' he hissed. 'All those in the Chancery. We go to war!' For it had been near the Chancery that Pamra Don had died. And near the Chancery that the great assembly had seen him flee away. And from the Chancery that some troop of soldiers had been seeking him ever since. He would make sure there were no witnesses to that defection left to speak of it.

'War,' he said again, telling his close advisers to make that message manifest among the multitude.

During the night some among the followers faded away to the south, but enough others were still there when the sun rose, polishing their axes and making ready new bolts for their bows, to make a great army.

Not far to the east, General Jondrigar pursued Peasimy Flot, eager to chastise him for his insults to the Noor.

After about a week, and in only a few towns, a flier or two descended upon the wharves to gorge themselves on the fish piled there. They did not return for another meal. Scarcely had they time to arise from their feasting before the talons of other, more traditional Thraish hurled them from the sky. Then there was screaming and feasting of flier upon flier, with much buffeting of wings and thrusting of beaks. For the most part the Rivermen were faithful to the instructions of Tharius Don, taking no action against the fliers unless they themselves were attacked – they or other humans in the towns. In some, however, it was an excuse for general slaughter, and more of the fliers died.

'When?' asked the children. 'We don't hear anything anymore.'

'Now, I think,' said Raffen the Riverman. 'Let us go out.'

The streets were littered with bits of broken shutter, with blown feathers, with the wind-tossed refuse that accumulates in every town unless swept away daily by those whose business it is to keep the streets. People wandered here and there, peering around them as though to see whether there might not be just one Awakener among them, just one group of workers. There were none. The Tower stood in its

480

park. No one had looked inside it yet, but it gave the appearance of a place that was tenantless. Empty. Like a shell when the nut had been eaten away.

A bustling man came to Raffen for advice. There were dead in the town to be disposed of, and Raffen went away with him to instruct the townsfolk how this should be done in the future.

Murga and the children went on wandering the streets. On the highest point of the town, the Temple still stood, its high dome gleaming white with paint. From inside came the sound of hammers.

'What are they doing?' Murga asked a passerby.

'Taking the moon faces off the wall,' came the answer. 'They are setting up an image of the Light Bearer instead.'

Murga took the children by the hands and led them to the Temple to see what was going on. The Temple floor was littered with shattered stone before the wall where the masons' hammers were at work, but the image that stood at the top of the stairs was one Blint-wife had known well. She was carved in ivory stone, her arms curved around a child. It was a copy of the statue in Thou-ne.

'Thrasne's woman!' Murga whispered to herself. 'That's Thrasne's woman!'

The serene face gleamed down at her, unmoved, unmoving, just as it had always seemed aboard the *Gift*.

'Well, at least she's got her baby,' said Murga, unawed by this elevation to divinity. 'At least that.'

27

The *Gift* had returned to Northshore, thanks to the skill of the sailors, three towns east of Thou-ne. Those who had sailed in her gathered at the rail, watching the familiar shoreline grow closer, each of them aware that something was wrong, was missing, without knowing precisely what until Medoor Babji said, 'There aren't any fliers!'

It was true. There were no wings aloft except for the little birds. There were no great, tattered shapes floating above the Talons.

There were great heaps of fresh-caught fish on the piers, which no one seemed to be eating or selling. Within an hour of their arrival, they had been told why and how, and Thrasne had gone to the Temple to see the wall where the moon faces had been. A stone carver was there, working on a large figure. When Thrasne asked what it was to be, he said it was to be the Light Bearer. A woman, with a child in her arms. It did not look at all like Suspirra, but then the carver was not very talented. Or so Thrasne thought, wondering what Pamra would think of this image. He said something of this to the carver, twitting him only a little, saying the image was not really like unto her.

'Well, as to that' – the man spat rock dust at him – 'likely she will be carved in a hundred fashions or more. What was left of her after they burned her, so I'm told, didn't leave much for us to model from.'

Thrasne had him by the throat before the poor man knew what he had set off, and it was only when two people came up from the Temple floor, pulling at him and screaming in his ear, that he let the carver go. They told him then what they knew, which was not much and already overlaid with myths.

'She rose,' one woman whispered. 'Like the flame-bird, burning, into the very heavens, singing like an angel.'

Thrasne stumbled out of the place.

There was a hurt place inside him, one he could cover with his outspread hand, a hot burning as though he were being consumed from within. He burned as Pamra Don had burned. The fiery spot widened, spread, reached the limits of his body, and then erupted through his skin in a fleeing cloud of spiritual flame, vaguely man-shaped, the heat of it an emotional blast which fled away as a hot wind flees. He could feel it as a presence departing, an actuality with motivations of its own, now vanishing from his understanding. In that momentary excruciation he felt he had emitted an angel which now expanded to fill all the universe, becoming more tenuous with every breath until all connection with Thrasne was teased away into nothing.

He flexed his hand across the place the angel had left, somewhere near his stomach or heart, an interior place that had nothing to do with thought but only with the tumbling of liquors and the rumbling of guts, the living heart-belly of his being. Where the fire had burned was a vacancy. A hole. He poked a finger at himself, half expecting it to penetrate into that emptiness, but he encountered only solid muscle and the hard bones of his ribs. Whatever the emptiness might be, it was not physical, and there was no pain associated with it. The angel had taken the pain with it when it departed.

'Pamra Don,' he said, testing himself for a response. There was none. Perhaps a twinge of bittersweet sadness, like dawn mist blown across one's face, carrying the scent of wet herbs, evocative of nothing but itself. 'Pamra Don?'

And then again he tried, 'Suspirra?'

To find her gone as well.

So, what was it that had fled? A ghost? A fiery spirit? A succubus who had lived beneath his heart?

Or was it some soul-child of his own, self-created, dreamed, hoped-for, stillborn in this world but released into some wider universe?

Whatever it might have been, it would not be. 'I can do nothing,' he said to himself in wonder. 'There is nothing I can do for Pamra Don.'

Except perhaps, his hands said of themselves, twitching for his knife or a chisel as he remembered what the carver was making in the Temple. Except perhaps. Whatever she was, whatever she had become, Thrasne could show her as she had been.

'I knew her, after all,' he said to himself wonderingly. 'I knew her.'

28

The days of the strike had fallen into memory. In Vobil-dil-go, order had been restored. The heights of the Talons on the eastern skyline were empty of wings. The Tower was empty of Awakeners. Only Haranjus Pandel had occupied a room there when he had come with the lady Kesseret and the widow Flot from Thou-ne. He came down to the town occasionally to greet this one and that one, well accepted by all. To the north, it was said, great armies moved, but at the Riverside there was a precarious calm, like that at the eye of a storm before the great winds come again.

On a stone above the River, Queen Fibji drew her feet beneath her and sat thus, cross-legged, looking across all that mighty water to the place she hoped to arrive with her people in a little time. Below her the Noor and some North-shoremen toiled among the boats, carrying endless bales and barrels into the holds. She approved this, searching among the busy forms for the tall bulky one her daughter just mentioned. Thrasne. Boatman. Not a Noor and, to hear Medoor Babji tell it, in love with someone else to boot. And yet, her daughter's choice.

'How long before we leave?' she asked for the tenth time.

'Three hours,' answered Medoor Babji. 'Perhaps four.'

'And how many boats?'

'A dozen have gone that we know of. Fifteen are readying to go. There will be more. There are Noor in every town, buying boats, hiring boats. There will be hundreds, thousands.'

'If we get away before they kill us all.'

'We will. The battles are all on the steppes, behind us where the Jondarites are fighting the crusaders. The towns are not involved.'

'Not yet!'

'Oh, I agree, great Queen. They will be. But they are not, yet.'

'How will we find one another, when we get there?'

'Those who leave from towns west of Vobil-dil-go are to march east when they arrive at Southshore. Those who leave from towns east of Vobil-dil-go are to march west. When we arrive on Southshore, we will build a great tower upon the shore. We will light beacons on the top of it at night. We will leave messages in cairns upon the beaches. We will send runners. We will find one another, great Queen.'

'And the islands of the River . . .'

'Are full of friendly folk, human and Treeci. And the strangeys of the depths are not to be feared.'

'And Southshore waits.'

What they said to one another was a litany. A ritual. They had repeated it a hundred times. Perhaps the Queen would say it a hundred times more on the boat, convincing herself.

'Does that man know you're pregnant?'

Medoor Babji looked at her swollen belly and laughed. 'It would be very hard for him not to know.'

'What does he say about that?'

'Thrasne says very little about anything. I have told him it is his. He got a strangely bemused expression on his face. It seems to me he smiles a great deal more recently, though he still goes into those old abstractions and stares at the water. I know then that he is thinking of Pamra Don.'

The Queen had resolved not to remonstrate, and now she shut her teeth firmly upon her tongue. Her whole self writhed at this self-imposed silence, and she sought a subject that was not – or would not seem to be – related. She would talk about . . . about something global.

'Medoor Babji, since you are my heir, let me share my

mind with you as my father once shared his mind with me. Since I received your message, I have spent much time in thought. Perhaps my thoughts will interest you.

'When I was very young, I often wondered what I was for. The boys, most of them, seemed to know. They were to be warriors. The girls were to bear children. But my father told me I was to be Queen, and we did not have a queen then, so I could not see what one was. Whatever it might be, I was quite sure it was something wonderful and eternal. Then, when I was about seven or eight – with some it happens earlier, I suppose; there may be some with whom it never happens – the understanding came all at once, in one hot burst, that Queen or no, I would not always be, that someday I would die and stop being. I screamed and wept. I thought I knew something no one else knew, but my father comforted me. He told me it was the first accomplishment of mankind, to know our own mortality, a thing that beasts and fishes never know.

'So, it seemed my father knew all about it. At that age, grown people seem to know everything about everything – you accused me of that once, I remember.

'Well, when it was time to sleep, back then when I was a child, I would lie on my blankets and go drifting into a certain world. I remember little of it now, except that there was music everywhere, and fountains of pearl, and beasts one could ride, and funny little furry things that talked . . .

'So, one day I said to my father that I wished he would get me a – what was it I called them? a foozil or some such – get me a foozil. And he asked me what a foozil was, and I explained that it was one of the furry, talking animals, and he told me I had made it all up. Imaginary, he said.

'Well, I had not known that the world I drifted in before sleep was only my own. I had thought it was a world everyone knew of. I thought we shared it, other people and I. It was the first time I knew that we all have separate worlds, Medoor Babji. No one else knew of my foozil. No one else had seen my fountains of pearl, or my wondrous beasts. How sad for them, I thought. Until I realized that they, each of them, had a world of his own.

487

'And I was shut out of them, daughter! Oh, the tragedy and wonder of that! The wonder of knowing that my own universe, much of it unexplored, bright or dim, shadowed or sunlit, full of every possible expression of dream and imagination – that the universe I have inside me was *not shared*. But more tragic, to know that all around me were a hundred thousand others, also dim or bright, full of dream, none of which I could ever see or know. The tragedy of knowing I would never know! Do you understand what I mean, Medoor Babji?'

Medoor nodded, thinking perhaps she did, perhaps she did not. Her mother did not wait for a response.

'I was a child. I didn't realize how limited our lives really are. I decided to learn all about the worlds of others. I asked them to tell me stories of their worlds, and they gave me words, daughter. Do you know how limited words are? People try to describe their worlds to you, but their words are like a map drawn with a burned stick beside a campfire. At best they let you in a little; at worst they hide the way entirely. I found that people go through life giving each other these little maps and little passwords. We explore one another, and gradually the maps accumulate, the passwords become more numerous. The more we are alike, the more we share, the more we understand. So, we Noor can see further inside one another than most. We can share each other's worlds better than most. But we can never really see it all. . . .

'So, you have a world inside you, child of my heart, which I can see a little. And the one you love, this Thrasne, he has a world as well, and it is utterly strange to me, to all the Noor. You ask me to love him for your sake. And I have not even a little map drawn with a burned stick to find my way to that.' She smiled at Medoor Babji, shaking her head ruefully, receiving an equally rueful smile in return.

'So, I must do what we all do. I will take it on faith. His world is real because you tell me so. I cannot perceive it. I can only assume it. I will love him for your sake, Doorie.'

Medoor Babji took her hand and held it tightly. There

were tears on the Queen's cheeks as she went on.

'Perhaps you will ask him to show me what he can of his world. Perhaps he will give me a map. From his map, I will travel in his strange world of water and boats if I can.'

'Oh, great Queen . . .'

'Call me "Mother," child. There may be no Queen of the Noor where we are going. There may be no throne for you to ascend.'

'I think he is afraid of you, Queen Fibji.'

'Well, so, and I am afraid of him as well. We must do what we can about that. I will give him passwords to walk in my world, and he must give me passwords to walk in his, so we can pass each other by without disruption. There are many passwords, child. "Be careful," or "Forgive me," or "I love you," or "Take care of my child." '

'What do I do if he still loves Pamra the Prophetess? Or believes he does? Or remembers doing so?'

'You have told me he is an artist, and she was beautiful. I never saw her, but I have seen the image of her in the Temple here. He may always love that image of her. But it will not matter. Pretend it is God he loves, or his art. It is much the same thing.'

'And you will give me your blessing?'

'You have had my blessing since I conceived you, Doorie. It is not something one can take back. But if you want it renewed, so be it. Have your Thrasne, child. To whatever extent you can. Take whatever password he gives you, and be grateful.'

The Queen brushed at her trousers and threw back the long tassels of her hair. 'It is time we were done with this serious talk. All day has been full of weeps and moans. I cried this morning, thinking of all those who would not come with us to this River. How many there were who would not follow me! How many there were who stayed, to revenge them-selves upon those who had persecuted us. How many there were who chose that, rather than this . . .'

'The River is frightening,' Medoor admitted. 'I was frightened by it.'

'They were not frightened of the River,' Queen Fibji contradicted. 'They were frightened of going where there would not be any enemies to fight. These were the young men with battle in their blood. They thumped their spears on the ground and leapt high in a battle dance and sent their spokesmen to me to explain. They spoke of honor. Of glory. I tried to tell them what I have told you, but it meant nothing to them. I told them of my father. I told them the riddle he had given me as a child. "Of what good are dead warriors?" I asked them. It did no good. They stayed behind. They did not see my world, child. They would not see my world . . .'

She gazed out over the water, not seeing Medoor Babji's eyes fixed on her, wide and terrible.

And she, Medoor, within herself but without speaking, said to her mother, 'Mother, I found the answer to your father's riddle. I sent a message to tell you . . .'

She imagined that the Queen was silent for a moment, thinking, 'Of course you did. And you told me you were pregnant. And that Southshore awaited. And those things drove the other from my mind. So. You have the answer. Will you tell it to me?'

'It is the answer to your riddle of long and long ago. The riddle your father set you. "Of what good are dead warriors?" I found the answer to that.'

'Where did you find it?'

'I learned it from the Treeci, by chance.'

'So? Come, child. Why this hesitation? Tell me!'

Medoor imagined herself delaying, knowing she was right, and yet the answer was a hard and hurtful one. 'Warriors are those who desire battle, Mother.'

'Yes?' The Queen would be puzzled.

'Warriors are those who desire battle more than peace. Those who seek battle despite peace. Those who thump their spears on the ground and talk of honor. Those who leap high in the battle dance and dream of glory . . .

'The good of dead warriors, Mother, is that they are dead.'

The Queen would stand staring at her for a long time. After that time, tears would begin to run down her cheeks. Medoor saw them clearly. If she told her mother the answer to the riddle, her mother would cry once more and there had been enough tears today. She would not tell her mother the answer. Not today. Perhaps not ever. It was a stony answer, a hard answer.

When all the warriors were dead, when they made no more children like themselves, then others might live in peace. She would not tell the answer, but she would keep it in her heart.

'Let us go down to the River,' said the Queen.

They walked together down toward the *Gift*, the ship that was to take them to Southshore.

29

There were some others who would sail aboard the *Gift* as well: Haranjus Pandel, the widow Flot, and two very old and feeble people, Tharius Don and the lady Kesseret. Tharius had sent word for her to meet him in Vobil-dil-go, and here he had begged passage for them both from Thrasne.

'I have not seen a flier in weeks,' the lady said, her voice quavering. 'I think the last was a month ago.'

'They are probably all dead,' answered Tharius, his voice emotionless. He had done grieving for the Thraish. His grief over Pamra Don had been all the grief he had left. 'I was wrong, that's all. A few survived for a time, eating stilt-lizards and the lesser birds, until there were no more. Except for a few, they wouldn't eat fish, even to save their lives.'

'Medoor Babji told me a strange thing,' the lady said. 'She said that at the time of the hunger, long and long ago, all the Thraish who could eat fish had done so. They left Northshore then, in fear of their lives. Only those who couldn't do it had remained here on Northshore, and there were very few of them. And all those who lived here on Northshore were descendants of those few who could not. It wasn't your fault, Tharius. It was bred in them. They couldn't. That's all.'

'It's no one's fault,' he said.

'Medoor Babji told me something else. She says that when the dead are put in the River, they are touched by blight and then taken by the strangeys to the islands. They go on living there, Tharius. They grow slower and slower, rooting themselves like trees, time all quiet around them. I want to go there.'

'Why? Why?'

'Because there has never been time for me. Only for the cause. It would be nice to have time for me.'

He buried his face in her hair and said nothing. He would grow roots beside her if she liked. He didn't know whether to believe Medoor Babji's tale or not.

'It's a pity Pamra Don could not have been put in the River. What did you do with her body, Tharius?'

'Buried it,' he said. 'Wrapped it in a robe and buried it beneath a thorn tree. There was nothing but bones. And a kind of child-shaped shell that Lila hatched out of. I think it was Lila.'

'Lila?'

He told her of Lila. He had heard more about Lila from Thrasne, though he wasn't sure how much of that he believed, either. 'I don't know what it was that went into the River,' he said. 'The strangeys called her their child. She was something strange.'

'They're taking up the plank,' she said. 'The oars are beginning to sweep.'

He looked out across the railing. The River slid between the *Gift* and the shore, and they began to move out onto the waters. All the deck was crowded with Noor amid a sprinkling of other folk. 'Half a year,' he said. 'To Southshore.'

'It is unlikely we will see it,' she said, contented. 'I don't care.'

Behind them on the bank, a few standabouts stood watching their slow progress. Most of them paid little attention. Too much else was happening. There were no workers anymore. The Towers were empty. There were no fliers, not anywhere. All of them had starved to death, it was said, though a good many had been killed when they'd attacked humans, trying to dose them with Tears or carry them off to the Talons. If one wanted excitement, one might think about joining the war going on, back on the steppes. Two Protectors of Man, one true, one false, fighting each other, and who knew which was which? There was even talk that one side wanted to kill off all the Noor. People were taking sides, joining up with one or the other, getting irate about one side or the other in taverns. Some were Peasimites, some Jondarites, and the gods knew where it would all end.

The gods knew; not that anyone meant the old gods. Potipur was finished. His image was scratched right off the Temple walls, and so were Viranel and Abricor. The Mother of Truth stood there now, shining, and people came from far away to make measurements of her so they could carve copies for their own Temples. The man who had carved her had actually known her, so it was said, before she was the Light Bringer. He had written it, right there on the image, for all the doubters to see.

Still, other carvers carved her differently. Sometimes they carved her with a child in her arms, sometimes with a flame-bird chick, for it was told how a flame-bird had hatched in her arms when she was put in the fire. Her soul, some said, which flew straight to the God of man. Something else, others said, which had not looked like a flame-bird at all. She had been burned by Jondarites, some said. By Peasimites, said others. By the fliers, said others yet. But who knew the truth? Priests used to answer the questions like that, but they were gone, along with the Awakeners. Who knew where? They unbraided their hair, laid down their staffs, wiped the paint from their faces, and disappeared. Just like anyone else, now.

The gates were gone now. People went east if they felt like it, though some felt very uncomfortable about it. And sure as sure, some oldsters couldn't stand the changes and had to carry their dead west for the Holy Sorters, even though everyone knew there weren't any such things. The Rivermen kept watch, though. There weren't any bodies left lying around to attract fliers, even though no one had seen any fliers for weeks. Sooner or later, everyone ended up in the River.

Or across it. For there was word of a new land there, a far land, a land where the Noor were going – and smart of 'em, too, if the Peasimites were coming. Now and then someone might stop a moment and look in that direction, saying the word over as though it had some magical meaning.

Southshore.

30

They were somewhere near the Island of the Dead when the two old people died. First Tharius Don, all at once, with one deep, heaving breath; then Kessie, calling his name once and then not breathing again, as though there were no reason to breathe once the other was gone. Thrasne found Medoor Babji crying over them, the tears lying on her cheeks like jewels, and he kissed them away, comforting her.

'Aiee, Medoor Babji, but those were old, old folk. Tharius Don told me he'd lived hundreds of years. More than you and me put together ever will.'

'I know,' she wept. 'It's just they loved each other, Thrasne.'

She would not be comforted, but she did stop crying. The late evening mist hid the waters, and he couldn't see whether the island was really near or not, though he smelled it, or another one like it, and had been doing so all day. There was a peculiar odor about the Island of the Dead, a tree fragrance unlike any other, and he could detect it now, faintly borne on the light wind. The two old people lay on the deck, side by side, and the Noor Queen came out of the owner-house to say some words over them in a high, sing-song voice before Obors-rom slid their bodies into the River.

They sank down, out of sight, quickly, as though eager to depart. Medoor Babji clung to Thrasne almost fearfully, and he held her close beside him, bringing her into his bed that night, big belly and all, feeling the babe kicking inside her with a kind of quiet joy and fear all at once. There had still been no words, no real words, between them. They had not talked of Pamra Don or of Thrasne's feelings. He did not know how she felt about him, really, or how a queen's daughter would be allowed to feel. He was afraid to ask. And yet she lay there beside him, deeply asleep, and he took it to mean something.

In the night he dreamed of Lila.

She had become a creature wholly strange, not human at all and yet, one could have said, not totally unlike. There was something one thought of as a head, with organs of sight and smell and perhaps taste and hearing, this part already fringed at the edges. There were parts that could have been arms and legs on their way to being something else, not flippers or fins, precisely, and yet fulfilling those functions as well as other, unimaginable ones. Her voice, when she spoke, was Lila's voice, a child's chuckling voice using words that set up unfamiliar chains of association in his mind as he heard her demanding to know why Medoor Babji was grieving.

'Medoor Babji was crying because they died, and they loved one another,' he explained to her.

'My people tell me humans are maddened by death,' she said. 'It comes too quickly, severing love. People need time to become accustomed to it. Either they dwell on it all the time, worrying their lives away to make monuments to themselves, or they refuse to think of it at all, like Queen Fibji's young warriors. It becomes an obsession with men, one way or the other, so they forget to live. Like you, Thrasne.'

'I don't understand,' Thrasne said in his dream. 'What has that to do with me?'

'Your mother died, Thrasne, and you could not bear that she was gone. So you created her again, as Suspirra, a carving, which was safe because it could not die. And then you found the drowned woman, and she was safe, too, because she was already dead. Then, when she fell into dust – I know; I was there – when she fell into dust you

496

chose Pamra to continue to be Suspirra. You told yourself you wanted her to love, to bear your children. In truth you only wanted her never to change. You wanted her to be Suspirra.

'It is easier to honor the dead than it is to love the living.'

'That's crazy,' he said in his dream, but weakly.

'Oh, but men are crazy,' Lila said in her bubbling voice. 'Only crazy people would have had things like Awakeners and workers. Only crazy people would dream of an eternal life in Potipur's arms.' She laughed. 'A baby, held in arms, rocked to and fro, unchanging. Ah, ah, that is not eternal life, Thrasne. That is eternal death. Only a crazy man would have loved Pamra. . . .'

'But I did love her,' he argued, angry even in his dream, knowing he did not quite believe it.

'Only because she was Suspirra. What was she other-wise? A narrow, ignorant woman. Maddened by death into rejecting life. Holding fast to a childish naiveté which protected her from seeing reality. A believer in impossible futures. A simple, totally selfish woman who saw no one's need but her own, who invented a doctrine to meet that need and voices to validate it, who walked a way upon the world convincing others her myth was better than their myths, letting others suffer and die in the service of her madness, starving herself into spasms of self-generated rapture, not seeing, not hearing, only to be burned at last by that which she would not hear or see.'

'She wanted to free the slaves. She wanted to stop the workers. She was a saint,' he muttered.

'There are those who say so now. There are those who will say so,' Lila whispered. 'What is a saint? Delia was a saint.'

'You're saying she never could have loved me!' he cried, angry at this in the dream, though he knew it was true.

'I'm saying you never should have loved her,' Lila said, her voice somehow changed into something remote and terrible. 'For she was like the blight, a terrible thing that kills . . .'

'And preserves,' whispered Thrasne in his dream.

'And preserves,' whispered Lila as the dream whirled about him, giving way to the sounds of the River, the soft, eternal sluff of water.

He woke then, the dream at first clear, then fading from his mind. Medoor Babji lay heavily beside him, her cheek flushed and warm where it had rested against his own. He rose without waking her and went out of the owner-house onto the deck. In the dawn light the Island of the Dead loomed to the south, mist and tree behind mist and tree and yet again, mist and tree to the limit of sight, with the blessed ones – for so he now called them in his mind – the blessed ones moving slowly in the mists, like swimmers. There on the water the strangeys danced, calling to one another in their terrible voices, and among them their young sported themselves, standing winged upon the waves.

One of these came very close to the ship and looked up at Thrasne with eyes that seemed somehow familiar.

'Thrasne,' it said to him in a bubbling voice. 'Kesseret is here, Thrasne. And Tharius Don. They have been given the time we created for them. They live. You live, too, Thrasne. And come to us.' It sank beneath the flowing surface, its eyes still fixed on Thrasne's face.

There was a hand on his shoulder.

'Come,' said Medoor Babji, her dry and watchful eyes on the waves where the strangeys danced. 'Let us go on to Southshore, Thrasne. This is not the place for us.'

He heard the rattle of the anchor tackle, the call of the sailors as the sails were raised. On the shore of the island, one of the blessed raised its hand to wave. Tharius Don? Too soon for Tharius Don. Someone else. Bending across the rail, Thrasne let a few tears come and fall and wash away the last of whatever thing there had been tight inside himself.

And then he stood to take Medoor Babji's hand and nod acceptance. 'To Southshore.'

31

As they sailed on into the south, Thrasne rigged a chair over the bow and laboriously chiseled away two of the three words that had been carved into the prow of the ship. The *Gift of Potipur* became simply the *Gift*. The winged figure that had leaned into the wavelets of the River for decades was replaced with another carving, one that Medoor Babji called, only to herself, 'Suspirra in ecstasy,' taking comfort in the fact that Thrasne had carved it, for it was not a face or figure any living man would lust for. It was Pamra's face, but a face beatified, glorious, and inhuman, the face of a departing spirit. Before her in her wooden hands she held the gift, a strangely shaped being that might have had either wings or flippers and was carved as though eternally poised to drop into the waters below. Tharius Don, before his death, had told Thrasne about Lila as he had seen her, Lila transformed, the child of the strangeys.

On a calm and starry night when there were no moons, the child was born. When it had been cleaned and wrapped and laid in a basket, Thrasne stood by the basket and the baby grasped his hand, curling infant fingers around one of his own in a gesture as old as time and demanding as life itself. 'Mine,' said Thrasne wonderingly. 'This is mine.'

'Ours,' said Medoor Babji firmly. 'He belongs to us, and to the Noor.'

'And to the *Gift*,' said Thrasne stubbornly. 'And to Southshore.'

'That, too. I pray we find good fortune there, for our ancestors alone know what is happening behind us.' She

499

reached for Thrasne's other hand. The birth had been more than she had expected; more in the way of pain, of effort, and of fulfillment when it was done. It was time to say. Time for words. 'And what of the baby's mother, Thrasne? Do you claim her, too, or only the child?'

'Oh yes,' he said, suddenly surprised that it should need saying. 'Oh, yes! She, too, is mine if she will be.'

'And Suspirra?'

He shrugged, rather more elaborately than the question warranted at this stage, but he needed to be sure that both of them understood what he meant. 'At the prow of the *Gift*, Doorie. Where dreams are put. That was a different thing from this.'

She was content, and Queen Fibji, hearing this exchange from outside the door, sighed a great sigh of relief.

They had come to the baby's tribal day, that day on which he was to be given a name, when the hail came from the steering deck. They thought it might be only another island and sent someone scurrying up the mast to spy out the cloudy land. He came back down to say there was no end to the land he could see, not south nor east nor west, but ahead of them were white beaches and a great, towering smoke. They gave up any thought of ceremony then, preferring to crowd the rails for the earliest glimpse of the new land.

By the time dusk came they had anchored in a shallow bay rimmed with pale dunes. On the beach were three boats that Thrasne recognized, and scattered across the dunes were the tents of many earlier arrivals. High above them to the west was a towering scaffold bearing a clay firefox, and in this a great beacon burned, smoke rolling above it as from a chimney.

Some of those aboard the *Gift* splashed into the water and swam ashore while others plied to and fro on hastily rigged rafts. The *Cheevle* bore Queen Fibji, Medoor Babji, Thrasne, and the child, with Strenge plying the rudder as they ran the little boat up on the sand. The Noor crowded around, not too closely, making obeisance, pointing at the

500

child, who regarded them with wide, wondering looks from his not altogether Noorish eyes.

'Let me see this land,' the Queen called, waving them aside as she staggered toward the tops of the dunes to peer inland, seeing there a vast prairie of grass and scattered copses in the light of the moons.

Thrasne came up behind her, one arm around Babji's shoulders, the baby in the other. From behind them, far down the beach, came a hail, and they turned to see another ship against the darkening sky, and beyond that one still another.

'The Noor are gathering. On Southshore,' said the Queen. 'We have made landfall. All my hopes, Doorie. All my hopes. I feel – oh, I feel I might die now, knowing the best thing I could have done is done.'

'Do not talk of dying,' said Thrasne, shaking her by one shoulder, much to her astonishment, for the Noor did not presume to touch their Queen. 'There is much planting to do if all this mob is to be fed, and who will see to that if not you?' He sounded, she thought, really angry at her. 'And this one is a month old today and still has no name. Who will name him if you go dying?'

'Ah, babe, babe.' She laughed, half crying as she turned to take the child. 'Your father speaks the truth. You have no name.' She held the baby high so he might peer away, as she did, toward the wide plains before her and the nearest line of hills. She wondered what mysteries would lie behind them, for it was sure that something wonderful awaited, just beyond the horizon. Then she turned to look into Medoor Babji's eyes, full of trust and pain, wonder and joy intermixed, then to Thrasne's craggy face, which held the same mixture of feelings. So they stood for some time, regarding each other without speaking.

'I name this child Temin M'noor,' she said at last, passing him into Thrasne's keeping as she moved away from them down the hill. 'Temin M'noor,' she called again, her voice like that of a shore bird, hunting.

'What does it mean?' Thrasne asked, thinking he had heard the words somewhere before.

Medoor Babji was smiling at him, holding out her arms for the child, her eyes swimming with tears.

'Temin, which is to say *a key*, and M'noor, that which is *spoken* . . .'

He did not understand, and she explained it to him.

'We have given him to one another between our worlds, Thrasne.

'His name is Password.'

GLOSSARY

Significant Individual People

Arbsen: One of the Treeci of Isle Point, Saleff's sister, Taneff's mother.

Binna: One of the Treeci on Strinder's Isle.

Blint: Owner of the Riverboat the *Gift of Potipur*.

Bormas Tyle: Chancery official, Deputy Enforcer to Tharius Don, conspirator with Shavian Bossit.

Burg: A human resident of Isle Point.

Chiles Medman: Governor General of the Jarb Mendicants. A frequent visitor at Chancery.

Delia: Nanny to Pamra Don, called Saint Delia by the townsfolk of Baris.

Drowned Woman, the: The drowned wife of Fulder Don, taken from the River in a blighted state and kept by Thrasne. Her given name was Imajh.

Eenzie the Clown: Member of a group of Melancholics to which Medoor Babji belongs.

Esspill: A flier, blown by storm to an island far in the River.

Ezasper Jorn: Ambassador to the Thraish; member of the Council of Seven in the Chancery, Conspirator with Koma Nepor.

Fibji: Queen of the Noor.

Fulder Don: A man of the artist caste in the town of Baris. Father of Pamra Don.

Gendra Mitiar: Dame Marshal of the Towers, member of the Council of Seven in the Chancery. Conspirator with Ezasper Jorn.

Glamdrul Feynt: Master of the files in the Bureau of Towers, Chancery. Conspirator with Shavian Bossit.

Haranjus Pandel: Superior of the Tower in Thou-ne.

Ilze: Senior Awakener in the Tower of Baris, mentor to Pamra Don. Becomes a Laugher.

Jhilt: Noor slave of Gendra Mitiar.

Jondrigar: General Jondrigar, member of the Council of Seven in the Chancery; leader of the armies of the Protector.

Joy: Surviving resident of Strinder's Isle.

Kesseret: 'Kessie', 'the lady Kesseret', Superior of the Tower in Baris.

Koma Nepor: Director of Research, member of the Council of Seven in the Chancery.

Lees Obol: Protector of Man, member of the Council of Seven in the Chancery.

Lila: The slow-baby. Born from the drowned woman.

Martien: Musician, close friend and follower of Tharius Don.

Medoor Babji: Daughter of Queen Fibji; chosen heir of the throne of the Noor.

Murga: Wife of owner Blint. Called Blint-wife.

Neff: A young male Treeci living on Strinder's Isle.

Obers-rom: Thrasne's trusted assistant, first owner's man after Thrasne takes over the *Gift of Potipur*.

Pamra Don: Awakener in the Tower of Baris, who leaves the Tower to begin the great crusade.

Peasimy Flot: Resident of Thou-ne, childlike adult son of the widow Flot. Follower of Pamra Don. Also called Peasimy Prime.

Prender: Half sister to Pamra Don.

Raffen: A Riverman in the town of Zephyr. Second husband to Murga, Blint-wife.

Saleef: A Treeci talker, resident of Isle Point, brother of Arbsen and son of Sterf.

Shavian Bossit: Maintainer of the Household; member of the Council of Seven in the Chancery.

Shishus: A semimythical typical flier of the past, used as an eidolon for young Talkers.

Sliffisunda: A Talker of the Sixth (highest) Degree among the Thraish.

Slooshasill: A Thraish Talker of the Fourth Degree, blown by storm to an island in the River.

Sterf: A Treeci resident of Isle Point, mother of Saleff and Arbsen.

Stodder: Resident of Strinder's Isle.

Strenge: Favorite consort of Queen Fibji.

Suspirra: The idealized woman of Thrasne's dreams. A carved image of that woman.

Taj Noteen: Leader of a group of Melancholics to which Medoor Babji belongs.

Taneff: Young male Treeci, resident of Isle Point, son of Arbsen.

Tharius Don: Propagator of the Faith; member of the Council of Seven in the Chancery. Ancestor of Pamra Don. Leader of the cause.

Thoulia: Semimythical 'Sorter', the Talker who first discovered the efficacy of the Tears of Viranel.

Thrasne: Third assistant owner's man aboard the Riverboat the *Gift of Potipur*. An orphan, adopted by the owner, Blint. Later owner of the *Gift*.

Threnot: Servant to Kesseret.

Werf: One of the Treeci on Strinder's Isle.

Groups, Places, and Things

Abricor: Male, second god in the Thraish trinity. Also the second-largest moon.

Awakeners, the: Religious order living in the Towers who oversee disposal of the dead.

Baris: Township. Homeplace of Pamra Don, Tharius Don, and the lady Kesseret.

Blight, the: A fungus living in the World River that seems to turn living flesh to wood.

Boatmen: Those who make their living on the boats that travel westward on the World River. Merchants. Not to be confused with Rivermen, q.v.

Chancery, the: The administrative center of Northshore, including the offices, buildings, and bureaucracy, located at Highstone Lees, behind the Teeth of the North.

Direction of Life, the: Movement to the west, as the sun, tides, and moons move. Movement to the east is considered antilife and forbidden.

Flame-bird: A species of Northshore bird that sets its nest afire in order to hatch its eggs.

Fliers, the: Ordinary – nontalker – members of the Thraish.

Gift of Potipur: Riverboat belonging first to Blint, then to Thrasne.

Glizzee; Glizzee spice: euphoric substance of pleasant flavor, provided by strangeys, sold in the markets as a food additive.

Highstone Lees: The name given to the Protector's palace, as well as the Chancery offices and residence grounds in the lands behind the Teeth.

Holy Sorters: Those human or superhuman creatures who sort the dead into categories of worthy or unworthy.

Isle of the Dead: Any one of many islands to which the Strangeys bring blighted humans.

Isle Point: An island of mixed Treeci, human population in mid River.

Jakes Island: An island of mixed Treeci, human population in mid River.

Jarb Houses: Places of residence set up by the order of Mendicants for the treatment and housing of madmen.

Jarb Mendicants: Madmen enabled to see the truth by smoking Jarb root; visionaries; oracles.

Jarb Root: A food root often eaten by the Noor whose toasted peel contains an anti-illusory drug.

Jondarites: The military personnel under the command of General Jondrigar.

Laughers: Pursuivants and inquisitors sent from the Chancery to find heretics in Northshore.

Light Bringer, the: The name given to Pamra Don by the crusaders, particularly by Peasimy Flot. Also, 'Mother of Light'.

Melancholics: Wandering pseudoreligious bands of the Noor who collect coin for the Queen of the Noor in the cities of Northshore.

Noor, the: The black people of the northern moors, from whom the Melancholics come.

Northshore: That area of land immediately to the north of the World River which is occupied with separated townships.

Pamet: A fiber crop in which armlong pods open to reveal sheaves of white strands used in making cloth.

Potipur: Chief god in the Thraish trinity. Also the largest moon.

Priests of Potipur: Awakeners assigned to Temple duty, distinguished by blue-painted faces and mirror-decked garb.

510

Progression: The circumnavigation of the planet done once every eighteen years by the Protector of Man. Ship of the Progression: the gilded and highly ornamented ship on which this journey is made.

Puncon: A spicy fruit, most often used in jam and confections. The bloom of the puncon tree.

Rivermen: A heretical group who put their dead in the River.

Servants of Abricor: Another name for the fliers who frequent the bone pits. The Thraish.

Shorefish: Derogatory term used by the Noor to describe the non-Noor inhabitants of Northshore. Term also used by the Talkers to describe all humans. The implication is of a thing which can be easily caught or eaten.

Song-Fish: A shallow-water fish that grows to great size and which sings in the evenings and early mornings, the pitch and tempo dependent upon the size of the fish (smaller fish having higher, more frequent tonal eruptions).

Sorting Out: Theologically, that process by which the dead are sorted into categories of worthy and unworthy.

Southshore: The land to the south of the World River, considered almost mythical.

Split River; Split River Pass: A river originating in a mountain lake in the Teeth of the North, running both north and south from that point. The pass cut by that river. The shortest route from the Chancery to Northshore, ending in the town of Vobil-dil-go.

Stilt-lizard: A lizard with very long rear legs that stalks the shallow waters of the River or swamps, snapping up small fish or aquatic bugs.

Strangeys, the: Creatures of vast size and unknown habits living in the World River.

Strinder's Isle: An island not far from Northshore that is occupied by a tribe of Treeci and a few surviving members of the Strinder family.

Talkers, the: Infrequently hatched members of the Thraish who have the talent of articulate speech over and above that found in ordinary Thraish.

Tears of Viranel: A fungus that reanimates recently dead bodies or takes over live ones, changing the composition of the flesh.

Teeth of the North: The mountain range separating Chancery lands from the moors of the Noor and Northshore.

Thou-ne: Township. Birthplace of Peasimy Flot. Site of the origin of the crusade.

Thraish, the: Race of large, carnivorous fliers in the world north of the World River. A flier can lift a small person easily. Two or more of them can carry a large adult human. While light-boned, their talons and beaks are formidable weapons.

Towers, the: One in each township, residences of the Awakeners.

Towns, the: Areas along Northshore, each approximately thirty miles wide, largely agricultural, usually centered on a village or urban area, extending northward into unsettled or Noor country. Typical towns are Thou-ne, Baris, Cheeping Wells, Xoxxy-Do, and so forth. There are 2,400 towns on Northshore.

Treeci: A race of ground-dwelling Thraish whose wings have atrophied because of their diet. Their wings, however, are still large and their wing-fingers are capable of adroit manipulation.

Viranel: Third, female, deity in the Thraish trinity. Also the third moon.

Vobil-dil-go: Township. Some distance west of Thou-ne. Historically called the site of the embarkation of the Noor.

Xoxxy-Do: Township. Birthplace of Thrasne.

RAINBOW CLASSICS

General Editor: May Lamberton Becker

JOHANN WYSS

The Swiss Family Robinson

EDITED BY WILLIAM H. G. KINGSTON

ILLUSTRATIONS BY JEANNE EDWARDS

INTRODUCTION BY MAY LAMBERTON BECKER

Cleveland and New York

The World Publishing Company

Rainbow Classics

are published by THE WORLD PUBLISHING COMPANY

2231 West 110th Street · Cleveland 2 · Ohio

Contents

We pack up–A family removing in patriarchal style–A prickly enemy–Jack shoots it–We reach our new home–Fritz rids our poultry of an enemy–Little Franz finds the figs–Dinner–We prepare materials for our nest–Flamingoes–Roast and tame–The use of trigonometry–A cord carried over the bough–The rope ladder made–We mount our tree–Sleep under the roots–The building of the nest–Retire to roost for the first time

A day of rest–A parable for the young people–Quiet recreation– Geographical nomenclature–The margay and porcupine skins made of use–An expedition to Tentholm–Potatoes, potatoes– Tropical vegetation–The use of the karatas–Jack's greediness and its punishment–Ernest discovers cochineal–Arrive at Tentholm– The poultry rebellious–Return to Falconhurst–Ernest roused out early–We collect wood for a sledge–Master Knips turns thief– Franz's plan for the saving of ammunition–Ernest and I take the sledge to Tentholm–Ernest's laziness exemplified–He catches a salmon–We start for home–Kill a kangaroo–And cook it

Jack and Ernest disappear–Fritz and I start for the wreck–The boys' ambuscade–We form a raft–Ransack the vessel–Again embark–A turtle in sight–Fritz harpoons it–The turtle acts as "steam tug"–Safe ashore–Return home–Jack's clay field–A fresh discovery–The mother's cellar–A trip to the wreck–The pinnace– Jack's raid on the Lilliputians–A secret revealed–A new method of grinding flour–Wholesome or poisonous?–Bread-making in earnest

Now for the pinnace–Repeated visits to the wreck–The pinnace built–How shall we cut her out?–The difficulty solved–We fit her out–Fire a salute–The mother's surprise–We visit Falconhurst– Attend to our fruit trees–Athletics–The lasso–An excursion–A bustard captured–Ernest discovers a magician–Jack fights him– The liane rouge–We turn carvers–Ernest's alarm–The old sow again–We discover a sleeping beauty–Return with it to the camp –Knips pronounces our apples "good"–Return to Falconhurst

Fritz and I return to the Calabash Wood–Fritz shoots a ruffed grouse–We come across waxberry bushes–Sociable grosbeaks–Fritz

captures a parrot–A lecture on ants–Caoutchouc trees–The sago-
palm and the edible worms–Return with sugar-canes to Falconhurst–Candle-making–How to make butter without a churn–
Plant trees and adorn Tentholm–Last visit to the wreck–The first
ducklings on the island–Falconhurst again–An excursion–We
pitch our tent–Fritz and Jack ascend the cocoanut trees–Ernest
brings us a delicacy–Loss of Grizzle–Jack and I go in pursuit–
Giant bamboos–Encounter with buffaloes–The buffalo calf–Find
a jackal's lair–Reach our camp–What happened in our absence–
Fritz's pet–Sago manufacture–Meet with our sow and her family
again–How Ernest tamed the eagle

CHAPTER EIGHTEEN   354

Introduction

HOW THIS BOOK CAME TO BE WRITTEN

by May Lamberton Becker

IT IS a wonder that *The Swiss Family Robinson* has always been so popular with boys, because from the first they were told it was good for them. Even as late as the Philadelphia edition of 1856 and the Boston one of the 1860's, its title page continued to state that the story was "a clear illustration of the first principles of natural history and many branches of science which most immediately apply to the business of life." You might think that would scare off any ten-year-old looking for a good yarn, especially as it went on, "to which are added notes of reference explanatory of the subjects treated of."

The author, Johann Wyss (1743–1818), a Swiss army chaplain of whom we know very little, wrote the story for his own sons, and one of them published it at Zurich in two parts in 1812 and 1813. Very soon, it was translated from the original German into English by William Godwin, afterward the father-in-law of Percy Bysshe Shelley. Some people think the poet may have had a hand in the translation. However, that is unimportant to present readers of the book, because as it was then, it was much shorter than it is now, and quite different. The first French translator, Mme. de Montholieu, asked permission of Wyss's son not only to change the original ending, but to add to the story at her discretion, and what she added contains some of the episodes for which it is best remembered–the adventure with the boa-constrictor, for example, that swallowed the donkey whole. By 1849 this patchwork, somewhat altered by W. H. G. Kingston, had become what is generally considered the authoritative English version. I put in this fact just for the record, because only a bibliographer can tell his way around among the versions that have been made by continuations and alterations, and anyone who reads it when young prefers for the rest of his life the version on which he was brought up.

For, all this time, whatever was done to it, the story kept that enthralling sense of reality that makes it amount to a personal experience. It was always the story that counted, not the style: the tale of the Swiss pastor who lost his fortune in the Revolution of 1798, set out with his wife and family on a mission to Otaheite, and was shipwrecked on an island with more unusual things on it than any in fiction—until Jules Verne created his mysterious island in the sequel to *Twenty Thousand Leagues under the Sea.*

Whoever reads this book as a child never forgets it, but when you ask him what it was like, years after, you find that each man remembers it for a different reason. Captain Marryat, a famous writer for young folks who had been a great sailor, complained that "it does not adhere to the probable, or even the possible," but his own children, who did not know so much about navigation, demanded that he write them more of the same, because they couldn't ever get enough of the Swiss Family. So he wrote *Masterman Ready* in three volumes, but he had to make it a quite different book.

F. J. Harvey-Darton, greatest English authority on children's books, said he did not notice, until he read it again as a grownup, that the *Swiss Family* was full of piety: he just slid over that at the time. He didn't realize, either, that one island would scarcely have the fruits and creatures of half the globe; it was enough for him that in the book it did. One person remembers all those ostriches; and another—oh, so many others!—remembers the house in the tree. I myself remember the wreck and their excursions to it, because at the time I read the book I was marooned on an island myself—every afternoon out of school hours—in a house built in an angle of a high board fence. For my grandfather, who loved to make things grow and had filled our front yard and back garden with flowers, leased a large plot back of our city house, cut a door through the back fence, and set up a vegetable garden that was the admiration of the neighborhood and the center of the world for me and for the two boys next door who helped bring me up. My grandfather, who understood small fry, let us take over each patch as it was harvested. In front of our fence board house, with the assistance of every small boy in the neighborhood, we cooked Grandpa's vegetables on a fireplace whose bricks were baked in our own kiln; as for cooking utensils, you'd be surprised to find how many tin cans you can salvage on a back lot, and for anything we couldn't raise–such as pepper or cookies–it was always possible to fall back on my grandmother's kitchen. In those blissful months, *The Swiss Family Robinson* came my way, and I was thrilled to find I was living as they were. It was the wreck that charmed me most: at the beginning, whenever they had to have something they couldn't produce, they could make their way, although with difficulty, out to the wreck, and there it was. It was my grandmother's kitchen translated to the tropics.

Johann Wyss was no Daniel Defoe; Pastor Robinson never thought so deeply as Robinson Crusoe did; everyone rejoices when Crusoe is rescued from his island, lovely as it is; but so far as most of us are concerned the Swiss Family are on their island yet, for all we remember of how they got off. But their hold on us as children is shown by the way we wanted them to stay on.

There have been later variants on the theme of being stranded–and good ones, too. Owen Wister's *The New Robinson Crusoe* came out in 1882 in the *Harvard Lampoon*, and in 1932 Christopher Morley's *Swiss Family Manhattan* was published here and in England, a gay little fantasy with ironic undertones, in which a Swiss family, on a ten-day airship vacation from the League of Nations, is marooned on the top of the Empire State Building.

If you wonder where on earth Johann Wyss collected all the general information for which the original story called, although we do know little about him, we are told that the regiment of which he became chaplain in 1766, and to which he had to preach in French and German, was stationed for a while in Sardinia where he learned to speak Italian and studied general literature, science, military tactics and fortification. That, we imagine, must be where and when he packed in the information which his first editors so highly commended. But what makes his book live is not its information but the living, lively use he made of it.

Jeanne Edwards, who illustrated this edition of *The Swiss Family Robinson,* was born in 1921, and if you subtract that date from the present year you will find that she is still a very young lady. I am glad of that, for her illustrations possess the sort of youthful exuberance and vitality that the story itself possesses. She is capable of a much more restrained type of illustration, as you will see if you look at the pictures she did for an edition of *A Shropshire Lad.* But in doing these pictures she has remembered that she is young, and that this is a book for all those who are themselves young, in body or in spirit.

She says that she started drawing when she was four, and has been at it ever since. In high school she studied life drawing at night. After high school she went to New York City and studied at the National Academy of Design, and then with Moses Soyer and De Hirsh Margules. It was not always easy to pursue her career, and she says that "in order to continue painting I have taken many strange jobs—from carving buttons and painting postcards to teaching children and working for a radiologist."

Most of us grownups have long since forgotten the illustrations that were in our own copies of *The Swiss Family Robinson.* The story has suffered from a long line of indifferent illustrators. I think you will remember Miss Edwards' pictures for this edition. I think even Pastor Wyss would approve of his Swiss Family as they are presented in her warm and imaginative drawings.

The Swiss Family Robinson

Chapter One

F OR many days we had been tempest-tossed. Six times had the darkness closed over a wild and terrific scene, and returning light as often brought but renewed distress, for the raging storm increased in fury until on the seventh day all hope was lost.

We were driven completely out of our course; no conjecture could be formed as to our whereabouts. The crew had lost heart, and were utterly exhausted by incessant labor.

The riven masts had gone by the board, leaks had been sprung in every direction, and the water, which rushed in, gained upon us rapidly.

Instead of reckless oaths, the seamen now uttered frantic

cries to God for mercy, mingled with strange and often ludicrous vows, to be performed should deliverance be granted.

Every man on board alternately commended his soul to his
Creator, and strove to bethink himself of some means of saving his life.

My heart sank as I looked round upon my family in the
midst of these horrors. Our four young sons were overpowered
by terror. "Our dear children," said I, "if the Lord will, he
can save us even from this fearful peril; if not, let us calmly
yield our lives into his hand, and think of the joy and blessedness of finding ourselves forever and ever united in that happy
home above."

At these words my weeping wife looked bravely up, and, as
the boys clustered round her, she began to cheer and encourage them with calm and loving words. I rejoiced to see her
fortitude, though my heart was ready to break as I gazed on
my dear ones.

We knelt down together, one after another praying with
deep earnestness and emotion. Fritz, in particular, besought
help and deliverance for his dear parents and brothers, as
though quite forgetting himself.

Our hearts were soothed by the never-failing comfort of
child-like, confiding prayer, and the horror of our situation
seemed less overwhelming. "Ah," thought I, "the Lord will
hear our prayer! He will help us."

Amid the roar of the thundering waves I suddenly heard
the cry of "Land, land!" while at the same instant the ship
struck with a frightful shock, which threw everyone to the
deck, and seemed to threaten her immediate destruction.

Dreadful sounds betokened the breaking up of the ship, and
the roaring waters poured in on all sides:

Then the voice of the captain was heard above the tumult,
shouting, "Lower away the boats! We are lost!"

"Lost!" I exclaimed, and the word went like a dagger to
my heart; but seeing my children's terror renewed, I composed
myself, calling out cheerfully, "Take courage, my boys! we
are all above water yet. There is the land not far off; let us
do our best to reach it. You know God helps those that help
themselves!" With that, I left them and went on deck. What
was my horror when through the foam and spray I beheld the

only remaining boat leave the ship, the last of the seamen spring into her and push off, regardless of my cries and entreaties that we might be allowed to share their slender chance of preserving their lives. My voice was drowned in the howling of the blast; and even had the crew wished it, the return of the boat was impossible.

Casting my eyes despairingly around, I became gradually aware that our position was by no means hopeless, inasmuch as the stern of the ship containing our cabin was jammed between two high rocks, and was partly raised from among the breakers which dashed the forepart to pieces. As the clouds of mist and rain drove past, I could make out, through rents in the vaporous curtain, a line of rocky coast, and rugged as it was, my heart bounded toward it as a sign of help in the hour of need. Yet the sense of our lonely and forsaken condition weighed heavily upon me as I returned to my family, constraining myself to say with a smile, "Courage, dear ones! Although our good ship will never sail more, she is so placed that our cabin will remain above water, and to-morrow, if the wind and waves abate, I see no reason why we should not be able to get ashore."

These few words had an immediate effect on the spirits of my children, who at once regarded our problematical chance of escaping as a happy certainty, and began to enjoy the relief from the violent pitching and rolling of the vessel.

My wife, however, perceived my distress and anxiety, in spite of my forced composure, and I made her comprehend our real situation, greatly fearing the effect of the intelligence on her nerves. Not for a moment did her courage and trust in Providence forsake her, and on seeing this, my fortitude revived.

"We must find some food, and take a good supper," said she, "it will never do to grow faint by fasting too long. We shall require our utmost strength to-morrow."

Night drew on apace, the storm was as fierce as ever, and at intervals we were startled by crashes announcing further damage to our unfortunate ship.

"God will help us soon now, won't he, father?" said my youngest child.

"You silly little thing," said Fritz, my eldest son, sharply, "don't you know that we must not settle what God is to do for us? We must have patience and wait his time."

"Very well said, had it been said kindly, Fritz, my boy. You too often speak harshly to your brothers, although you may not mean to do so."

A good meal being now ready, my youngsters ate heartily, and retiring to rest were speedily fast asleep. Fritz, who was of an age to be aware of the real danger we were in, kept watch with us. After a long silence, "Father," said he, "don't you think we might contrive swimming belts for mother and the boys? with those we might all escape to land, for you and I can swim."

"Your idea is so good," answered I, "that I shall arrange something at once, in case of an accident during the night."

We immediately searched about for what would answer the purpose, and fortunately got hold of a number of empty flasks and tin canisters, which we connected two and two together so as to form floats sufficiently buoyant to support a person in the water, and my wife and young sons each willingly put one on. I then provided myself with matches, knives, cord, and other portable articles, trusting that, should the vessel go to pieces before daylight, we might gain the shore not wholly destitute.

Fritz, as well as his brothers, now slept soundly. Throughout the night my wife and I maintained our prayerful watch, dreading at every fresh sound some fatal change in the position of the wreck.

At length the faint dawn of day appeared, the long, weary night was over, and with thankful hearts we perceived that the gale had begun to moderate; blue sky was seen above us, and the lovely hues of sunrise adorned the eastern horizon.

I aroused the boys, and we assembled on the remaining portion of the deck, when they, to their surprise, discovered that no one else was on board.

"Hallo, papa! what has become of everybody? Are the sailors gone? Have they taken away the boats? Oh, papa! why did they leave us behind? What can we do by ourselves?"

"My good children," I replied, "we must not despair, although we seem deserted. See how those on whose skill and good faith we depended have left us cruelly to our fate in the hour of danger. God will never do so. He has not forsaken us, and we will trust him still. Only let us bestir ourselves, and each cheerily to do his best. Who has anything to propose?"

"The sea will soon be calm enough for swimming," said Fritz.

"And that would be all very fine for you," exclaimed Ernest, "but think of mother and the rest of us! Why not build a raft and all get on shore together?"

"We should find it difficult, I think, to make a raft that would carry us safe to shore. However, we must contrive something, and first let each try to procure what will be of most use to us."

Away we all went to see what was to be found, I myself proceeding to examine, as of great consequence, the supplies of provisions and fresh water within our reach.

My wife took her youngest son, Franz, to help her to feed the unfortunate animals on board, who were in a pitiful plight, having been neglected for several days.

Fritz hastened to the arm chest, Ernest to look for tools; and Jack went toward the captain's cabin, the door of which he no sooner opened than out sprang two splendid large dogs, who testified their extreme delight and gratitude by such tremendous bounds that they knocked their little deliverer completely head over heels, frightening him nearly out of his wits. Jack did not long yield either to fear or anger; he presently recovered himself; the dogs seemed to ask pardon by vehemently licking his face and hands, and so, seizing the larger by the ears, he jumped on his back, and, to my great amusement, coolly rode to meet me as I came up the hatchway.

When we re-assembled in the cabin, we all displayed our treasures.

Fritz brought a couple of guns, shot belt, powder flasks, and plenty of bullets.

Ernest produced a cap full of nails, an ax, and a hammer, while pincers, chisels, and augers stuck out of all his pockets.

Little Franz carried a box, and eagerly began to show us the "nice sharp little hooks" it contained. "Well done, Franz!" cried I; "these fish hooks, which you, the youngest, have found, may contribute more than anything else in the ship to save our lives by procuring food for us. Fritz and Ernest, you have chosen well."

"Will you praise me too?" said my dear wife. "I have nothing to show, but I can give you good news. Some useful animals are still alive; a cow, a donkey, two goats, six sheep, a ram, and a fine sow. I was but just in time to save their lives by taking food to them."

"All these things are excellent indeed," said I; "but my friend Jack here has presented me with a couple of huge, hungry, useless dogs, who will eat more than any of us."

"Oh, papa! they will be of use! Why, they will help us to hunt when we get on shore!"

"No doubt they will, if ever we do get on shore, Jack; but I must say I don't know how it is to be done."

"Can't we each get into a big tub, and float there?" returned he. "I have often sailed splendidly like that, round the pond at home."

"My child, you have hit on a capital idea," cried I. "Now, Ernest, let me have your tools, hammers, nails, saws, augers, and all; and then make haste to collect any tubs you can find!"

We very soon found four large casks, made of sound wood, and strongly bound with iron hoops; they were floating with many other things in the water in the hold, but we managed to fish them out, and drag them to a suitable place for launching them. They were exactly what I wanted, and I succeeded in sawing them across the middle. Hard work it was, and we were glad enough to stop and refresh ourselves with wine and biscuits.

My eight tubs now stood ranged in a row near the water's edge, and I looked at them with great satisfaction; to my surprise, my wife did not seem to share my pleasure!

"I shall never," said she, "muster courage to get into one of these!"

"Do not be too sure of that, dear wife; when you see my contrivance completed, you will perhaps prefer it to this immovable wreck."

I next procured a long, thin plank, on which my tubs could be fixed, and the two ends of this I bent upward so as to form a keel. Other two planks were nailed along the sides of the tubs; they also being flexible, were brought to a point at each end, and all firmly secured and nailed together. I felt satisfied that in smooth water this craft would be perfectly trustworthy. But when we thought all was ready for the launch, we found, to our dismay, that the grand contrivance was so heavy and clumsy, that even our united efforts could not move it an inch.

"I must have a lever," cried I. "Run and fetch the capstan bar!"

Fritz quickly brought one, and, having formed rollers by cutting up a long spar, I raised the fore part of my boat with the bar, and my sons placed a roller under it.

"How is it, father," inquired Ernest, "that with that thing you alone can do more than all of us together?"

I explained, as well as I could in a hurry, the principle of the lever; and promised to have a long talk on the subject of Mechanics, should we have a future opportunity.

I now made fast a long rope to the stern of our boat, attaching the other end to a beam; then placing a second and third roller under it, we once more began to push, this time with success, and soon our gallant craft was safely launched: so swiftly indeed did she glide into the water that, but for the rope, she would have passed beyond our reach. The boys wished to jump in directly; but, alas, she leaned so much on one side that they could not venture to do so.

Some heavy things being thrown in, however, the boat righted itself by degrees, and the boys were so delighted that they struggled which should first leap in to have the fun of sitting down in the tubs. But it was plain to me at once that something more was required to make her perfectly safe, so I contrived out-riggers to preserve the balance, by nailing long poles across at the stem and stern, and fixing at the ends of each empty brandy casks. Then the boat appearing steady, I got in; and turning it toward the most open side of the wreck, I cut and cleared away obstructions, so as to leave a free passage for our departure, and the boys brought oars to be ready for the voyage. This important undertaking we were forced to postpone until the next day, as it was by this time far too late to attempt it. It was not pleasant to have to spend another night in so precarious a situation; but yielding to necessity, we sat down to enjoy a comfortable supper, for during our exciting and incessant work all day we had taken nothing but an occasional biscuit and a little wine.

We prepared for rest in a much happier frame of mind than on the preceding day, but I did not forget the possibility of a renewed storm, and therefore made every one put on the belts as before.

I persuaded my wife (not without considerable difficulty), to put on a sailor's dress, assuring her she would find it much more comfortable and convenient for all she would have to go through. She at last consented to do this, and left us for a short time, reappearing with much embarrassment and many blushes, in a most becoming suit, which she had found in a midshipman's chest. We all admired her costume, and any awkwardness she felt soon began to pass off; then retiring to our berths, peaceful sleep prepared us all for the exertions of the coming day.

We rose up betimes, for sleep weighs lightly on the hopeful, as well as on the anxious. After kneeling together in prayer, "Now, my beloved ones," said I, "with God's help we are about to effect our escape. Let the poor animals we must leave behind be well fed, and put plenty of fodder within their reach: in a few days we may be able to return, and save them likewise. After that, collect everything you can think of which may be of use to us."

The boys joyfully obeyed me, and I selected from the large quantity of stores they got together, canvas to make a tent, a chest of carpenter's tools, guns, pistols, powder, shot, and bullets, rods and fishing tackle, an iron pot, a case of portable soup, and another of biscuit. These useful articles, of course, took the place of the ballast I had hastily thrown in the day before.

With a hearty prayer for God's blessing, we now began to take our seats, each in his tub. Just then we heard the cocks begin to crow, as though to reproach us for deserting them. "Why should not the fowls go with us!" exclaimed I. "If we find no food for *them*, they can be food for *us!*" Ten hens and a couple of cocks were accordingly placed in one of the tubs, and secured with some wire-netting over them.

The ducks and geese were set at liberty, and took to the water at once, while the pigeons, rejoicing to find themselves on the wing, swiftly made for the shore. My wife, who managed all this for me, kept us waiting for her some little time, and came at last with a bag as big as a pillow in her arms. "This is *my* contribution," said she, throwing the bag to little Franz, to be, as I thought, a cushion for him to sit upon.

All being ready, we cast off, and moved away from the wreck. My good, brave wife sat in the first compartment of the boat; next to her was Franz, a pretty little boy, nearly eight years old. Then came Fritz, a handsome, spirited young fellow of fifteen; the two center tubs contained the valuable cargo; then came our bold, thoughtless Jack; next him Ernest, my second son, intelligent, well-formed, and rather indolent. I myself, the anxious, loving father, stood in the stern, endeavoring to guide the raft with its precious burden to a safe landing place.

The elder boys took the oars; everyone wore a float belt, and had something useful close to him in case of being thrown into the water.

The tide was flowing, which was a great help to the young oarsmen. We emerged from the wreck and glided into the open sea. All eyes were strained to get a full view of the land, and the boys pulled with a will; but for some time we made no progress, as the boat kept turning round and round, until I hit upon the right way to steer it, after which we merrily made for the shore.

We had left two dogs, Turk and Juno, on the wreck, as being both large mastiffs we did not care to have their additional weight on board our craft; but when they saw us apparently deserting them, they set up a piteous howl, and sprang into the sea. I was sorry to see this, for the distance to the land was so great that I scarcely expected them to be able to accomplish it. They followed us, however, and, occasionally resting their fore-paws on the outriggers, kept up with us well. Jack was inclined to deny them this, their only chance of safety. "Stop," said I, "that would be unkind as well as foolish; remember, the merciful man regardeth the life of his beast."

Our passage, though tedious, was safe; but the nearer we approached the shore the less inviting it appeared; the barren rocks seemed to threaten us with misery and want.

Many casks, boxes, and bales of goods floated on the water around us. Fritz and I managed to secure a couple of hogsheads, so as to tow them alongside. With the prospect of famine before us, it was desirable to lay hold of anything likely to contain provisions.

By and by we began to perceive that, between and beyond the cliffs, green grass and trees were discernible. Fritz could distinguish many tall palms, and Ernest hoped they would prove to be cocoanut trees, and enjoyed the thoughts of drinking the refreshing milk.

"I am very sorry I never thought of bringing away the captain's telescope," said I.

"Oh, look here, father!" cried Jack, drawing a little spyglass joyfully out of his pocket.

By means of this glass, I made out that at some distance to the left the coast was much more inviting; a strong current, however, carried us directly toward the frowning rocks, but I presently observed an opening, where a stream flowed into the sea, and saw that our geese and ducks were swimming toward this place. I steered after them into the creek, and we found ourselves in a small bay or inlet where the water was perfectly smooth and of moderate depth. The ground sloped gently upward from the low banks to the cliffs, which here retired inland, leaving a small plain, on which it was easy for us to land. Everyone sprang gladly out of the boat but little Franz, who, lying packed in his tub like a potted shrimp, had to be lifted out by his mother.

The dogs had scrambled on shore before us; they received us with loud barking and the wildest demonstrations of delight. The geese and ducks kept up an incessant din, added to which was the screaming and croaking of flamingoes and penguins, whose dominion we were invading. The noise was deafening, but far from unwelcome to me, as I thought of the good dinners the birds might furnish.

As soon as we could gather our children around us on dry land, we knelt to offer thanks and praise for our merciful escape, and with full hearts we commended ourselves to God's good keeping for the time to come.

All hands then briskly fell to the work of unloading, and oh, how rich we felt ourselves as we did so! The poultry we left

at liberty to forage for themselves, and set about finding a suitable place to erect a tent in which to pass the night. This we speedily did; thrusting a long spar into a hole in the rock, and supporting the other end by a pole firmly planted in the ground, we formed a framework over which we stretched the sailcloth we had brought; besides fastening this down with pegs, we placed our heavy chest and boxes on the border of the canvas, and arranged hooks so as to be able to close up the entrance during the night.

When this was accomplished, the boys ran to collect moss and grass, to spread in the tent for our beds, while I arranged a fire-place with some large flat stones, near the brook which flowed close by. Dry twigs and seaweed were soon in a blaze on the hearth; I filled the iron pot with water, and giving my wife several cakes of the portable soup, she established herself as our cook, with little Franz to help her.

He, thinking his mother was melting some glue for carpentering, was eager to know "what papa was going to make next?"

"This is to be soup for your dinner, my child. Do you think these cakes look like glue?"

"Yes, indeed I do," replied Franz, "and I should not much like to taste glue soup! Don't you want some beef or mutton, mamma?"

"Where can I get it, dear!" said she, "we are a long way from a butcher's shop! but these cakes are made of the juice of good meat, boiled till it becomes a strong, stiff jelly—people take them when they go to sea, because on a long voyage they can only have salt meat, which will not make nice soup."

Fritz, meanwhile, leaving a loaded gun for me, took another himself, and went along the rough coast to see what lay beyond the stream; this fatiguing sort of walk not suiting Ernest's fancy, he sauntered down to the beach, and Jack scrambled among the rocks, searching for shellfish.

I was anxious to land the two casks which were floating alongside our boat, but on attempting to do so, I found that I could not get them up on the bank on which we had landed, and was therefore obliged to look for a more convenient spot. As I did so, I was startled by hearing Jack shouting for help, as though in great danger. He was at some distance, and I hurried toward him with a hatchet in my hand. The little fellow stood screaming in a deep pool, and as I approached, I saw that a huge lobster had caught his leg in its powerful claw. Poor Jack was in a terrible fright; kick as he would, his enemy still clung on. I waded into the water, and seizing the lobster firmly by the back, managed to make it loosen its hold, and we brought it safe to land. Jack, having speedily recovered his spirits, and anxious to take such a prize to his mother, caught the lobster in both hands, but instantly received such a severe blow from its tail that he flung it down, and passionately hit the creature with a large stone. This display of temper vexed me. "You are acting in a very childish way, my son," said I; "never strike an enemy in a revengeful spirit." Once more lifting the lobster, Jack ran triumphantly toward the tent.

"Mother, mother! a lobster, Ernest! look here, Franz! mind, he'll bite you! Where's Fritz?" All came crowding round Jack and his prize, wondering at its unusual size, and Ernest wanted his mother to make lobster soup directly, by adding it to what she was now boiling.

She, however, begged to decline making any such experiment, and said she preferred cooking one dish at a time. Having remarked that the scene of Jack's adventure afforded a convenient place for getting my casks on shore, I returned thither and succeeded in drawing them up on the beach, where I set them on end, and for the present left them.

On my return I resumed the subject of Jack's lobster, and told him he should have the offending claw all to himself, when it was ready to be eaten, congratulating him on being the first to discover anything useful.

"As to that," said Ernest, "I found something very good to eat, as well as Jack, only I could not get at them without wetting my feet."

"Pooh!" cried Jack, "I know what he saw—nothing but some nasty mussels; I saw them too. Who wants to eat trash like that! Lobster for me!"

"I believe them to be oysters, not mussels," returned Ernest calmly.

"Be good enough, my philosophical young friend, to fetch a few specimens of these oysters in time for our next meal," said I; "we must all exert ourselves, Ernest, for the common good, and pray never let me hear you object to wetting your feet. See how quickly the sun has dried Jack and me."

"I can bring some salt at the same time," said Ernest, "I remarked a good deal lying in the crevices of the rocks; it tasted very pure and good, and I concluded it was produced by the evaporation of sea water in the sun."

"Extremely probable, learned sir," cried I; "but if you had brought a bagful of this good salt instead of merely speculating so profoundly on the subject, it would have been more to the purpose. Run and fetch some directly."

It proved to be salt, sure enough, although so impure that it seemed useless, till my wife dissolved and strained it, when it became fit to put in the soup.

"Why not use the sea water itself?" asked Jack.

"Because," said Ernest, "it is not only salt, but bitter too. Just try it."

"Now," said my wife, tasting the soup with the stick with which she had been stirring it, "dinner is ready, but where can Fritz be?" she continued, a little anxiously.

"How are we to eat our soup when he does come?" I asked; "we have neither plates nor spoons, and we can scarcely lift the boiling pot to our months. We are in as uncomfortable a position as was the fox to whom the stork served up a dinner in a jug with a long neck."

"Oh, for a few cocoa-nut shells!" sighed Ernest.

"Oh, for half a dozen plates and as many silver spoons!" rejoined I, smiling.

"Really though, oyster-shells would do," said he, after a moment's thought.

"True, that is an idea worth having! Off with you, my boys; get the oysters and clean out a few shells. What though our spoons have no handles, and we do burn our fingers a little in baling the soup out."

Jack was away and up to his knees in the water, in a moment, detaching the oysters. Ernest followed more leisurely, and still unwilling to wet his feet, stood by the margin of the pool and gathered in his handkerchief the oysters his brother threw him; as he thus stood he picked up and pocketed a large mussel shell for his own use. As they returned with a good supply

We reached a bold promontory. (Page 40)

we heard a shout from Fritz in the distance; we returned it joyfully, and he presently appeared before us, his hands behind his back, and a look of disappointment upon his countenance.

"Unsuccessful!" said he.

"Really!" I replied; "never mind, my boy, better luck next time."

"Oh, Fritz!" exclaimed his brothers, who had looked behind him, "a sucking-pig, a little sucking-pig. Where did you get it? How did you shoot it? Do let us see it!"

Fritz then with sparkling eyes exhibited his prize.

"I am glad to see the result of your prowess, my boy," said I; "but I cannot approve of deceit, even as a joke; stick to the truth in jest and earnest."

Fritz then told us how he had been to the other side of the stream. "So different from this," he said; "it is really a beautiful country, and the shore, which runs down to the sea in a gentle slope, is covered with all sorts of useful things from the wreck. Do let us go and collect them. And, father, why should we not return to the wreck and bring off some of the animals? Just think of what value the cow would be to us, and what a pity it would be to lose her! Let us get her on shore, and we will move over the stream, where she will have good pasturage, and we shall be in the shade instead of on this desert, and father, I do wish——"

"Stop, stop, my boy!" cried I. "All will be done in good time. To-morrow and the day after will bring work of their own. And tell me, did you see no traces of our shipmates?"

"Not a sign of them, either on land or sea, living or dead," he replied.

"But the sucking-pig," said Jack, "where did you get it?"

"It was one of several," said Fritz, "which I found on the shore; most curious animals they are; they hopped rather than walked, and every now and then would squat down on their legs and rub their snouts with their fore-paws. Had not I been afraid of losing them all, I would have tried to catch one alive, they seemed so tame."

Meanwhile Ernest had been carefully examining the animal in question.

"This is no pig," he said; "and except for its bristly skin, does not look like one. See, its teeth are not like those of a pig, but rather those of a squirrel. In fact," he continued, looking at Fritz, "your sucking pig is an agouti."

"Dear me," said Fritz; "listen to the great professor lecturing! He is going to prove that a pig is not a pig!"

"You need not be so quick to laugh at your brother," said I, in my turn; "he is quite right. I, too, know the agouti by descriptions and pictures, and there is little doubt that this is a specimen. The little animal is a native of North America, where it makes its nest under the roots of trees, and lives upon fruit. But, Ernest, the agouti not only looks something like a pig, but most decidedly grunts like a porker."

While we were thus talking, Jack had been vainly endeavoring to open an oyster with his large knife. "Here is a simpler way," said I, placing an oyster on the fire; it immediately opened. "Now," I continued, "who will try this delicacy?" All at first hesitated to partake of them, so unattractive did they appear. Jack, however, tightly closing his eyes and making a face as though about to take medicine, gulped one down. We followed his example, one after the other, each doing so rather to provide himself with a spoon than with any hope of cultivating a taste for oysters.

Our spoons were now ready, and gathering round the pot we dipped them in, not, however, without sundry scalded fingers. Ernest then drew from his pocket the large shell he had procured for his own use, and scooping up a good quantity of soup he put it down to cool, smiling at his own foresight.

"Prudence should be exercised for others," I remarked; "your cool soup will do capitally for the dogs, my boy; take it to them, and then come and eat like the rest of us."

Ernest winced at this, but silently taking up his shell he placed it on the ground before the hungry dogs, who lapped up its contents in a moment; he then returned, and we all went merrily on with our dinner. While we were thus busily employed, we suddenly discovered that our dogs, not satisfied with their mouthful of soup, had espied the agouti, and were rapidly devouring it. Fritz, seizing his gun, flew to rescue it from their hungry jaws, and before I could prevent him, struck one of them with such force that his gun was

bent. The poor beasts ran off howling, followed by a shower
of stones from Fritz, who shouted and yelled at them so fiercely
that his mother was actually terrified. I followed him, and as
soon as he would listen to me, represented to him how
despicable, as well as wicked, was such an outbreak of temper:
"for," said I, "you have hurt, if not actually wounded, the
dogs; you have distressed and terrified your mother, and
spoiled your gun."

Though Fritz's passion was easily aroused, it never lasted
long, and speedily recovering himself, immediately he en-
treated his mother's pardon, and expressed his sorrow for his
fault.

By this time the sun was sinking beneath the horizon, and
the poultry, which had been straying to some little distance,
gathered round us, and began to pick up the crumbs of biscuit which had fallen during our repast. My wife hereupon
drew from her mysterious bag some handfuls of oats, peas,
and other grain, and with them began to feed the poultry.
She at the same time showed me several other seeds of various
vegetables. "That was indeed thoughtful," said I; "but pray
be careful of what will be of such value to us; we can bring
plenty of damaged biscuits from the wreck, which, though of
no use as food for us, will suit the fowls very well indeed."

The pigeons now flew up to crevices in the rocks, the fowls
perched themselves on our tent pole, and the ducks and geese
waddled off, cackling and quacking, to the marshy margin of
the river. We, too, were ready for repose, and having loaded
our guns, and offered up our prayers to God, thanking him
for his many mercies to us, we commended ourselves to his
protecting care, and as the last ray of light departed, closed our
tent and lay down to rest.

The children remarked the suddenness of nightfall, for
indeed there had been little or no twilight. This convinced
me that we must be not far from the equator, for twilight results from the refraction of the sun's rays: the more obliquely
these rays fall, the farther does the partial light extend; while
the more perpendicularly they strike the earth, the longer do
they continue their undiminished force, until, when the sun
sinks, they totally disappear, thus producing sudden darkness.

Chapter Two

We should have been badly off without the shelter of our tent, for the night proved as cold as the day had been hot, but we managed to sleep comfortably, everyone being thoroughly fatigued by the labors of the day. The voice of our vigilant cock, which, as he loudly saluted the rising moon, was the last sound I heard at night, roused me at daybreak, and I then awoke my wife, that in the quiet interval while yet our children slept, we might take counsel together on our situation and prospects. It was plain to both of us that, in the first place, we should ascertain if possible the fate of our late companions, and then examine into the nature and resources of the country on which we were stranded.

We therefore came to the resolution that, as soon as we had breakfasted, Fritz and I should start on an expedition with these objects in view, while my wife remained near our landing-place with the three younger boys.

"Rouse up, rouse up, my boys," cried I, awakening the children cheerfully. "Come and help your mother to get breakfast ready."

"As to that," said she smiling, "we can but set on the pot, and boil some more soup!"

"Why, you forget Jack's fine lobster!" replied I. "What has become of it, Jack?"

"It has been safe in this hole in the rock all night, father. You see, I thought, as the dogs seem to like good things, they might take a fancy to that, as well as to the agouti."

"A very sensible precaution," remarked I. "I believe even my heedless Jack will learn wisdom in time. It is well the lobster is so large, for we shall want to take part with us on our excursion to-day."

At the mention of an excursion, the four children were wild with delight, and capering around me, clapped their hands for joy.

"Steady there, steady!" said I, "you cannot expect all to go. Such an expedition as this would be too dangerous and fatiguing for you younger ones. Fritz and I will go alone this time, with one of the dogs, leaving the other to defend you."

We then armed ourselves, each taking a gun and a game bag; Fritz in addition sticking a pair of pistols in his belt, and I a small hatchet in mine; breakfast being over, we stowed away the remainder of the lobster and some biscuits, with a flask of water, and were ready for a start.

"Stop!" I exclaimed, "we have still left something very important undone."

"Surely not," said Fritz.

"Yes," said I, "we have not yet joined in morning prayer. We are only too ready, amid the cares and pleasures of this life, to forget the God to whom we owe all things." Then having commended ourselves to his protecting care, I took leave of my wife and children, and bidding them not wander far from the boat and tent, we parted not without some anxiety on either side, for we knew not what might assail us in this unknown region.

We now found that the banks of the stream were on both sides so rocky that we could get down to the water by only one narrow passage, and there was no corresponding path on the other side. I was glad to see this, however, for I now knew that my wife and children were on a comparatively inaccessible spot, the other side of the tent being protected by steep and precipitous cliffs. Fritz and I pursued our way up the stream until we reached a point where the waters fell from a considerable height in a cascade, and where several large rocks lay half covered by the water; by means of these we succeeded in crossing the stream in safety. We thus had the sea on our left, and a long line of rocky heights, here and there adorned with clumps of trees, stretching away inland to the right. We had forced our way scarcely fifty yards through the long rank grass, which was here partly withered by the sun and much tangled, when we heard behind us a rustling, and on looking round saw the grass waving to and fro, as if some animal were passing through it. Fritz instantly turned and brought his gun to his shoulder, ready to fire the moment the beast should appear. I was much pleased with my son's coolness and presence of mind, for it showed me that I might thoroughly rely upon him on any future occasion when real danger might occur; this time, however, no savage beast rushed out, but our trusty dog Turk, whom in our anxiety at parting we had forgotten, and who had been sent after us, doubtless, by my thoughtful wife.

From this little incident, however, we saw how dangerous was our position, and how difficult escape would be should any fierce beast steal upon us unawares: we therefore hastened to make our way to the open seashore. Here the scene which presented itself was indeed delightful. A background of hills, the green waving grass, the pleasant groups of trees stretching here and there to the very water's edge, formed a lovely prospect. On the smooth sand we searched carefully for any trace of our hapless companions, but not the mark of a footstep could we find.

"Shall I fire a shot or two?" said Fritz; "that would bring our companions, if they are within hearing."

"It would indeed," I replied, "or any savages that may be here. No, no; let us search diligently, but as quietly as possible."

"But why, father, should we trouble ourselves about them at all? They left us to shift for ourselves, and I for one don't care to set eyes on them again."

"You are wrong, my boy," said I. "In the first place, we should not return evil for evil; then, again, they might be of great assistance to us in building a house of some sort; and lastly, you must remember that they took nothing with them from the vessel, and may be perishing of hunger."

Thus talking, we pushed on until we came to a pleasant grove which stretched down to the water's edge; here we halted to rest, seating ourselves under a large tree, by a rivulet which murmured and splashed along its pebbly bed into the great ocean before us. A thousand gayly-plumaged birds flew twittering above us, and Fritz and I gazed up at them.

My son suddenly started up.

"A monkey," he exclaimed; "I am nearly sure I saw a monkey."

As he spoke he sprang round to the other side of the tree, and in doing so stumbled over a round substance, which he handed to me, remarking, as he did so, that it was a round bird's nest, of which he had often heard.

"You may have done so," said I, laughing, "but you need not necessarily conclude that every round hairy thing is a bird's nest; this, for instance, is not one, but a cocoanut."

We split open the nut, but, to our disgust, found the kernel dry and uneatable.

"Hullo," cried Fritz, "I always thought a cocoanut was full of delicious sweet liquid, like almond milk."

"So it is," I replied, "when young and fresh, but as it ripens the milk becomes congealed, and in course of time is solidified into a kernel. This kernel then dries as you see here, but when the nut falls on favorable soil, the germ within the kernel swells until it bursts through the shell, and, taking root, springs up a new tree."

"I do not understand," said Fritz, "how the little germ

manages to get through this great thick shell, which is not like an almond or hazel nut-shell, that is divided down the middle already."

"Nature provides for all things," I answered, taking up the pieces. "Look here, do you see these three round holes near the stalk? It is through them that the germ obtains egress. Now let us find a good nut if we can."

As cocoanuts must be over-ripe before they fall naturally from the tree, it was not without difficulty that we obtained one in which the kernel was not dried up. When we succeeded, however, we were so refreshed by the fruit that we could defer the repast we called our dinner until later in the day, and so spare our stock of provisions.

Continuing our way through a thicket, which was so densely overgrown with lianas that we had to clear a passage with our hatchets, we again emerged on the seashore beyond, and found an open view, the forest sweeping inland, while on the space before us stood at intervals single trees of remarkable appearance.

These at once attracted Fritz's observant eye, and he pointed to them, exclaiming:

"Oh, what absurd-looking trees, father! See what strange bumps there are on the trunks."

We approached to examine them, and I recognized them as calabash trees, the fruit of which grows in this curious way on the stems, and is a species of gourd, from the hard rind of which bowls, spoons, and bottles can be made. "The savages," I remarked, "are said to form these things most ingeniously, using them to contain liquids: indeed, they actually cook food in them."

"Oh, but that is impossible," returned Fritz. "I am quite sure this rind would be burnt through directly it was set on the fire."

"I did not say it was set on the fire at all. When the gourd has been divided in two, and the shell or rind emptied of its contents, it is filled with water, into which the fish, or whatever is to be cooked, is put; red hot stones are added until the water boils; the food becomes fit to eat, and the gourd-rind remains uninjured."

"That is a very clever plan: very simple too. I daresay I should have hit on it, if I had tried," said Fritz.

"The friends of Columbus thought it very easy to make an egg stand upon its end when he had shown them how to do it. But now suppose we prepare some of these calabashes, that they may be ready for use when we take them home."

Fritz instantly took up one of the gourds, and tried to split it equally with his knife, but in vain: the blade slipped, and the calabash was cut jaggedly. "What a nuisance!" said Fritz, flinging it down, "the thing is spoiled; and yet it seemed so simple to divide it properly."

"Stay," said I; "you are too impatient, those pieces are not useless. Do you try to fashion from them a spoon or two while I provide a dish."

I then took from my pocket a piece of string, which I tied tightly round a gourd, as near one end of it as I could; then tapping the string with the back of my knife, it penetrated the outer shell. When this was accomplished, I tied the string yet tighter; and drawing the ends with all my might, the gourd fell, divided exactly as I wished.

"That is clever!" cried Fritz. "What in the world put that plan into your head?"

"It is a plan," I replied, "which the Negroes adopt, as I have learned from reading books of travel."

"Well, it certainly makes a capital soup-tureen, and a soup-plate too," said Fritz, examining the gourd. "But supposing you had wanted to make a bottle, how would you have set to work?"

"It would be an easier operation than this, if possible. All that is necessary is to cut a round hole at one end, then to scoop out the interior, and to drop in several shot or stones: when these are shaken, any remaining portions of the fruit are detached, and the gourd is thoroughly cleaned, and the bottle completed."

"That would not make a very convenient bottle though, father; it would be more like a barrel."

"True, my boy; if you want a more shapely vessel, you must take it in hand when it is younger. To give it a neck, for instance, you must tie a bandage round the young gourd while it is still on the tree, and then all will swell but that part which you have checked."

As I spoke, I filled the gourds with sand, and left them to dry; marking the spot that we might return for them on our way back.

For three hours or more we pushed forward, keeping a sharp lookout on either side for any trace of our companions, till we reached a bold promontory, stretching some way into the sea, from whose rocky summit I knew that we should obtain a good and comprehensive view of the surrounding country. With little difficulty we reached the top, but the most careful survey of the beautiful landscape failed to show us the slightest sign or trace of human beings. Before us stretched a wide and lovely bay, fringed with yellow sands, either side extending into the distance, and almost lost to view in two shadowy promontories; inclosed by these two arms lay a sheet of rippling water, which reflected in its depths the glorious sun above. The scene inland was no less beautiful; and yet Fritz and I both felt a shade of loneliness stealing over us as we gazed on its utter solitude.

"Cheer up, Fritz, my boy," said I presently. "Remember that we chose a settler's life long ago, before we left our own dear country; we certainly did not expect to be so entirely alone—but what matters a few people, more or less? With God's help, let us endeavor to live here contentedly, thankful that we were not cast upon some bare and inhospitable island. But come, the heat here is getting unbearable; let us find some shady place before we are completely broiled away."

We descended the hill and made for a clump of palm trees, which we saw at a little distance. To reach this, we had to pass through a dense thicket of reeds, no pleasant or easy task; for, besides the difficulty of forcing our way through, I feared at every step that we might tread on some venomous snake. Sending Turk in advance, I cut one of the reeds, thinking it would be a more useful weapon against a reptile than my gun. I had carried it but a little way, when I noticed a thick juice exuding from one end. I tasted it, and to my delight found it sweet and pleasant. I at once knew that I was standing among sugar-canes. Wishing Fritz to make the same discovery, I advised him to cut a cane for his defense; he did so, and as he beat the ground before him, the reed split, and his hand was covered with the juice. He carefully touched the cane with the tip of his tongue, then, finding the juice sweet, he did so again with less hesitation; and a moment afterward sprang back to me exclaiming:

"Oh, father, sugar-canes! sugar-canes! Taste it. Oh, how delicious, how delightful! do let us take a lot home to mother," he continued, sucking eagerly at the cane.

"Gently there," said I, "take breath a moment, moderation in all things, remember. Cut some to take home if you like, only don't take more than you can conveniently carry."

In spite of my warning, my son cut a dozen or more of the largest canes, and stripping them of their leaves, carried them under his arm. We then pushed through the cane-brake, and reached the clump of palms for which we had been making; as we entered it a troop of monkeys, who had been disporting themselves on the ground, sprang up, chattering and grimacing, and before we could clearly distinguish them were at the very top of the trees.

Fritz was so provoked by their impertinent gestures that he raised his gun and would have shot one of the poor beasts.

"Stay," cried I, "never take the life of any animal needlessly. A live monkey up in that tree is of more use to us than a dozen dead ones at our feet, as I will show you."

Saying this, I gathered a handful of small stones, and threw them up toward the apes. The stones did not go near them, but influenced by their instinctive mania for imitation, they instantly seized all the cocoanuts within their reach, and sent a perfect hail of them down upon us.

Fritz was delighted with my stratagem, and rushing forward picked up some of the finest of the nuts. We drank the milk they contained, drawing it through the holes, which I pierced, and then, splitting the nuts open with the hatchet, ate the cream which lined their shells. After this delicious meal, we thoroughly despised the lobster we had been carrying, and threw it to Turk, who ate it gratefully; but far from being satisfied, the poor beast began to gnaw the ends of the sugar-canes, and to beg for cocoanut. I slung a couple of the nuts over my shoulder, fastening them together by their stalks, and Fritz having resumed his burden, we began our homeward march.

I soon discovered that Fritz found the weight of his canes considerably more than he expected: he shifted them from shoulder to shoulder, then for a while carried them under his arm, and finally stopped short with a sigh. "I had no idea," he said, "that a few reeds would be so heavy."

"Never mind, my boy," I said, "patience and courage! Do you not remember the story of Æsop and his bread-basket, how heavy he found it when he started, and how light at the end of his journey? Let us each take a fresh staff, and then fasten the bundle crosswise with your gun."

We did so, and once more stepped forward. Fritz presently noticed that I from time to time sucked the end of my cane.

"Oh, come," said he, "that's a capital plan of yours, father, I'll do that too."

So saying, he began to suck most vigorously, but not a drop of the juice could he extract. "How is this?" he asked. "How do you get the juice out, father?"

"Think a little," I replied, "you are quite as capable as I am of finding out the way, even if you do not know the real reason of your failure."

"Oh, of course," said he, "it is like trying to suck marrow from a marrow-bone, without making a hole at the other end."

"Quite right," I said, "you form a vacuum in your mouth and the end of your tube, and expect the air to force down the liquid from the other end which it cannot possibly enter."

Fritz was speedily perfect in the accomplishment of sucking sugar-cane, discovering by experience the necessity for a fresh cut at each joint or knot in the cane, through which the juice would not flow; he talked of the pleasure of initiating his brothers in the art, and of how Ernest would enjoy the cocoa-nut milk, with which he had filled his flask.

"My dear boy," said I, "you need not have added that to your load; the chances are it is vinegar by the time we get home. In the heat of the sun, it will ferment soon after being drawn from the nut."

"Vinegar! Oh, that would be a horrid bore! I must look directly, and see how it is getting on," cried Fritz, hastily swinging the flask from his shoulder, and tugging out the cork. With a loud "pop" the contents came forth, foaming like champagne.

"There now!" said I, laughing as he tasted this new luxury, "you will have to exercise moderation again, friend Fritz! I daresay it is delicious, but it will go to your head, if you venture deep into your flask."

"My dear father, you cannot think how good it is! Do take some. Vinegar, indeed! This is like excellent wine."

We were both invigorated by this unexpected draught, and went on so merrily after it, that the distance to the place where we had left our gourd-dishes seemed less than we expected. We found them quite dry, and very light and easy to carry.

Just as we had passed through the grove in which we had breakfasted, Turk suddenly darted away from us and sprang furiously among a troop of monkeys, which were gamboling playfully on the turf at a little distance from the trees. They were taken by surprise completely, and the dog, now really ravenous from hunger, had seized and was fiercely tearing one to pieces before we could approach the spot.

His luckless victim was the mother of a tiny little monkey, which, being on her back when the dog flew at her, hindered her flight. The little creature attempted to hide among the grass, and in trembling fear watched its mother. On perceiving Turk's bloodthirsty design, Fritz had eagerly rushed to the rescue, flinging away all he was carrying, and losing his hat in his haste. All to no purpose as far as the poor mother ape was concerned, and a laughable scene ensued, for no sooner did the young monkey catch sight of him, than at one bound it was on his shoulders, and, holding fast by his thick curly hair, it firmly kept its seat in spite of all he could do to dislodge it. He screamed and plunged about as he endeavored to shake or pull the creature off, but all in vain; it only clung the closer to his neck, making the most absurd grimaces.

I laughed so much at this ridiculous scene, that I could scarcely assist my terrified boy out of his awkward predicament.

At last, by coaxing the monkey, offering it a bit of biscuit; and gradually disentangling its small sinewy paws from the curls it grasped so tightly, I managed to relieve poor Fritz, who then looked with interest at the baby ape, no bigger than a kitten, as it lay in my arms.

"What a jolly little fellow it is!" exclaimed he, "do let me try to rear it, father. I daresay cocoanut milk would do until we can bring the cow and the goats from the wreck. If he lives he might be useful to us. I believe monkeys instinctively know what fruits are wholesome and what are poisonous."

"Well," said I, "let the little orphan be yours. You bravely and kindly exerted yourself to save the mother's life; now you must train her child carefully, for unless you do so its natural instinct will prove mischievous instead of useful to us."

Turk was meanwhile devouring with great satisfaction the little animal's unfortunate mother. I could not grudge it him, and continued hunger might have made him dangerous to ourselves. We did not think it necessary to wait until he had dined, so we prepared to resume our march.

The tiny ape seated itself in the coolest way imaginable on Fritz's shoulder, I helped to carry his canes, and we were on some distance before Turk overtook us, looking uncommonly well pleased, and licking his chops as though recalling the memory of his feast.

He took no notice of the monkey, but it was very uneasy at sight of him, and scrambled down into Fritz's arms, which was so inconvenient to him that he devised a plan to relieve himself of his burden. Calling Turk, and seriously enjoining obedience, he seated the monkey on his back, securing it there with a cord, and then putting a second string round the dog's neck that he might lead him, he put a loop of the knot into the comical rider's hand, saying gravely: "Having slain the parent, Mr. Turk, you will please to carry the son."

At first this arrangement mightily displeased them both, but by and by they yielded to it quietly; the monkey especially amused us by riding along with the air of a person perfectly at his ease.

"We look just like a couple of mountebanks on their way to a fair with animals to exhibit," said I. "What an outcry the children will make when we appear!"

My son inquired to what species of the monkey tribe I thought his *protégé* belonged, which led to a good deal of talk on the subject, and conversation beguiling the way, we found ourselves ere long on the rocky margin of the stream and close to the rest of our party.

Juno was the first to be aware of our approach, and gave notice of it by loud barking, to which Turk replied with such hearty good will, that his little rider, terrified at the noise his steed was making, slipped from under the cord and fled to his refuge on Fritz's shoulder, where he regained his composure and settled himself comfortably.

Turk, who by this time knew where he was, finding himself free dashed forward to rejoin his friends, and announce our coming.

One after another our dear ones came running to the opposite bank, testifying in various ways their delight at our return, and hastening up on their side of the river, as we on ours, to the ford at which we had crossed in the morning. We were quickly on the other side, and, full of joy and affection, our happy party was once more united.

The boys suddenly perceiving the little animal which was clinging close to their brother, in alarm at the tumult of voices, shouted in ecstasy:

"A monkey! a monkey! oh, how splendid! Where did Fritz find him? What may we give him to eat? Oh, what a bundle of sticks! Look at those curious, great nuts father has got!"

We could neither check this confused torrent of questions, nor get in a word in answer to them.

At length, when the excitement subsided a little, I was able to say a few words with a chance of being listened to. "I am truly thankful to see you all safe and well, and, thank God, our expedition has been very satisfactory, except that we have entirely failed to discover any trace of our shipmates."

"If it be the will of God," said my wife, "to leave us alone on this solitary place, let us be content; and rejoice that we are all together in safety."

"Now we want to hear all your adventures, and let us relieve you of your burdens," added she, taking my game bag.

Jack shouldered my gun, Ernest took the cocoanuts, and little Franz carried the gourds; Fritz distributed the sugarcanes amongst his brothers, and handing Ernest his gun replaced the monkey on Turk's back. Ernest soon found the burden with which Fritz had laden him too heavy for his taste.

His mother perceiving this, offered to relieve him of part of the load. He gave up willingly the cocoanuts, but no sooner had he done so than his elder brother exclaimed:

"Hullo, Ernest, you surely do not know what you are parting with; did you really intend to hand over those good cocoanuts without so much as tasting them?"

"What? ho! are they really cocoanuts?" cried Ernest. "Do let me take them again, mother, do let me look at them."

"No, thank you," replied my wife with a smile. "I have no wish to see you again overburdened."

"Oh, but I have only to throw away these sticks, which are of no use, and then I can easily carry them."

"Worse and worse," said Fritz; "I have a particular regard for those heavy, useless sticks. Did you ever hear of sugar-canes?"

The words were scarcely out of his mouth when Ernest began to suck vigorously at the end of the cane, with no better result, however, than Fritz had obtained as we were on the march.

"Here," said Fritz, "let me show you the trick of it," and he speedily set all the youngsters to work extracting the luscious juice.

My wife, as a prudent housekeeper, was no less delighted than the children with this discovery; the sight of the dishes also pleased her greatly, for she longed to see us eat once more like civilized beings. We went into the kitchen and there found preparations for a truly sumptuous meal. Two forked sticks were planted in the ground on either side of the fire; on these rested a rod from which hung several tempting looking fish; opposite them hung a goose from a similar contrivance, slowly roasting while the gravy dropped into a large shell placed beneath it. In the center sat the great pot, from which issued the smell of a most delicious soup. To crown this splendid array, stood an open hogshead full of Dutch cheeses. All this was very pleasant to two hungry travelers, but I was about to beg my wife to spare the poultry until our stock should have increased, when she, perceiving my thought, quickly relieved my anxiety. "This is not one of our geese," she said, "but a wild bird Ernest killed."

"Yes," said Ernest, "it is a penguin, I think; it let me get quite close, so that I knocked it on the head with a stick. Here are its head and feet, which I preserved to show you; the bill is, you see, narrow and curved downward, and the feet are webbed. It had funny little bits of useless wings, and its eyes looked so solemnly and sedately at me that I was almost ashamed to kill it. Do you not think it must have been a penguin?"

"I have little doubt on the matter, my boy," and I was about to make a few remarks on the habits of this bird, when my wife interrupted me and begged us to come to dinner, and continue our natural history conversation at some future time. We then sat down before the appetizing meal prepared for us, our gourds coming for the first time into use, and having done it full justice, produced the cocoanuts by way of dessert.

"Here is better food for your little friend," said I to Fritz, who had been vainly endeavoring to persuade the monkey to taste dainty morsels of the food we had been eating; "the poor little animal has been accustomed to nothing but its mother's milk; fetch me a saw, one of you."

I then, after extracting the milk of the nuts from their natural holes, carefully cut the shells in half, thus providing several more useful basins. The monkey was perfectly satisfied with the milk, and eagerly sucked the corner of a handkerchief dipped in it. Fritz now suddenly recollected his delicious wine, and producing his flask, begged his mother to taste it. "Try it first yourself," said I; Fritz did so, and I instantly saw by his countenance that the liquor had passed through the first stage of fermentation and had become vinegar.

"Never mind, my boy," said my prudent wife, when she learned the cause of his wry faces, "we have wine already, but no vinegar; I am really pleased at the transformation."

The sun was now rapidly sinking behind the horizon, and the poultry, retiring for the night, warned us that we must follow their example. Having offered up our prayers, we lay down on our beds, the monkey crouched down between Jack and Fritz, and we were all soon fast asleep.

We did not, however, long enjoy this repose; a loud barking from our dogs, who were on guard outside the tent, awakened us, and the fluttering and cackling of our poultry warned us that a foe was approaching. Fritz and I sprang up, and seizing our guns rushed out. There we found a desperate combat going on; our gallant dogs, surrounded by a dozen or more large jackals, were fighting bravely. Four of their opponents lay dead, but the others were in no way deterred by the fate of their comrades. Fritz and I, however, sent bullets through the heads of a couple more, and the rest galloped off. Turk and Juno did not intend that they should escape so cheaply, and pursuing them, they caught, killed, and devoured another of the animals, regardless of their near relationship. Fritz wished to save one of the jackals that he might be able to show it to his brothers in the morning; dragging, therefore, the one that he had shot near the tent, he concealed it, and we once more returned to our beds.

Soundly and peacefully we slept until cock-crow next morning, when my wife and I awoke, and began to discuss the business of the day.

"It seems absolutely necessary, my dear wife," I began, "to return at once to the wreck while it is yet calm, that we may save the poor animals left there, and bring on shore many articles of infinite value to us, which, if we do not now recover, we may finally lose entirely. On the other hand, I feel that there is an immense deal to be done on shore, and that I ought not to leave you in such an insecure shelter as this tent."

"Return to the wreck by all means," replied my wife, cheerfully. "Patience, order, and perseverance will help us through all our work, and I agree with you that a visit to the wreck is without doubt our first duty. Come, let us wake the children, and set to work without delay."

They were soon roused, and Fritz, overcoming his drowsiness before the others, ran out for his jackal; it was cold and stiff from the night air, and he placed it on its legs before the tent, in a most life-like attitude, and stood by to watch the effect upon the family. The dogs were the first to perceive their enemy, and growling, seemed inclined to dispose of the animal as they had disposed of its brethren in the night, but Fritz called them off. The noise the dogs made, however, had the effect of bringing out the younger children, and many were the exclamations they made at the sight of the strange animal.

"A yellow dog!" cried Franz.

"A wolf!" exclaimed Jack.

"It is a striped fox," said Ernest.

"Hullo," said Fritz. "The greatest men may make mistakes. Our Professor does not know a jackal when he sees one."

"But really," continued Ernest, examining the animal, "I think it is a fox."

"Very well, very well," retorted Fritz, "no doubt you know better than your father! He thinks it is a jackal."

"Come, boys," said I, "no more of this quarreling; you are none of you very far wrong, for the jackal partakes of the nature of all three, dog, wolf, and fox."

The monkey had come out on Jack's shoulder, but no sooner did it catch sight of the jackal, than it fled precipitately back into the tent, and hid itself in a heap of moss until nothing was visible but the tip of its little nose. Jack soothed and comforted the frightened little animal, and I then summoned them all to prayers, soon after which we began our breakfast. So severely had we dealt with our supper the previous night that we had little to eat but the biscuits, which were so dry and hard, that, hungry as we were, we could not swallow much. Fritz and I took some cheese to help them down, while my wife and the younger sons soaked theirs in water. Ernest roamed down to the shore, and looked about for shell-fish. Presently he returned with a few whelks. "Ah," said he, "if we had but some butter." "My good boy," I replied, "your perpetual IF, IF, quite annoys me; why do you not sit down and eat cheese like the rest of us." "Not while I can get butter," he said; "see here, father," and he pointed to a large cask, "that barrel contains butter of some sort or another, for it is oozing out at the end."

"Really, Ernest," I said, "we are indebted to you. I will open the cask." So saying, I took a knife and carefully cut a small hole, so that I could extract the butter without exposing the mass of it to the effects of the air and heat. Filling a cocoa-nut shell, we once more sat down, and toasting our biscuits before the fire, spread them with the good Dutch butter. We found this vastly better than the dry biscuits, and while we were thus employed I noticed that the two dogs were lying unusually quiet by my side. I at first attributed this drowsiness to their large meal during the night, but I soon discovered that it arose from a different cause; the faithful animals had not escaped unhurt from their late combat, but had received several deep and painful wounds, especially about the neck. The dogs began to lick each other on the places which they could not reach with their own tongues, and my wife carefully dressed the wounds with butter, from which she had extracted the salt by washing.

A sudden thought now struck Ernest, and he wisely remarked, that if we were to make spiked collars for the dogs, they would in future escape such dangerous wounds. "Oh, yes," exclaimed Jack, "and I will make them; may I not, father?"

"Try, by all means, my little fellow," said I, "and persuade your mother to assist you; and now, Fritz," I continued, "we must be starting, for you and I are to make a trip to the wreck." I begged the party who were to remain on shore to keep together as much as possible, and having arranged a set of signals with my wife, that we might exchange communications, asked a blessing on our enterprise. I erected a signal post, and, while Fritz was making preparations for our departure, hoisted a strip of sailcloth as a flag; this flag was to remain hoisted as long as all was well on shore, but should our return be desired, three shots were to be fired and the flag lowered.

All was now ready, and warning my wife that we might find it necessary to remain all night on the vessel, we tenderly bade adieu and embarked. Except our guns and ammunition, we were taking nothing, that we might leave as much space as possible for the stowage of a large cargo. Fritz, however, had resolved to bring his little monkey, that he might obtain milk for it as soon as possible. We had not got far from the shore, when I perceived that a current from the river set in directly for the vessel, and though my nautical knowledge was not great, I succeeded in steering the boat into the favorable stream, which carried us nearly three-fourths of our passage with little or no trouble to ourselves; then, by dint of hard pulling, we accomplished the whole distance, and entering through the breach, gladly made fast our boat and stepped on board. Our first care was to see the animals, who greeted us with joy—lowing, bellowing, and bleating as we approached; not that the poor beasts were hungry, for they were all still well supplied with food, but they were apparently pleased by the mere sight of human beings. Fritz then placed his monkey by one of the goats, and the little animal immediately sucked the milk with evident relish, chattering and grinning all the while; the monkey provided for, we refreshed ourselves with some wine and biscuits. "Now," said I, "we have plenty to do; where shall we begin?"

"Let us fix a mast and sail to our boat," answered Fritz; "for the current which brought us out will not take us back, whereas the fresh breeze we met would help us immensely had we but a sail."

"Capital thought," I replied; "let us set to work at once."

I chose a stout spar to serve as a mast, and having made a hole in a plank nailed across one of the tubs, we, with the help of a rope and a couple of blocks, stepped it and secured it with stays. We then discovered a lug-sail, which had belonged to one of the ship's boats; this we hoisted; and our craft was ready to sail. Fritz begged me to decorate the masthead with a red streamer, to give our vessel a more finished appearance. Smiling at this childish but natural vanity, I complied with his request. I then contrived a rudder, that I might be able to steer the boat; for though I knew that an oar would serve the purpose, it was cumbrous and inconvenient. While I was thus employed, Fritz examined the shore with his glass, and soon announced that the flag was flying and all was well.

So much time had now slipped away that we found we could not return that night, as I had wished. We signaled our intention of remaining on board, and then spent the rest of our time in taking out the stones we had placed in the boat for ballast, and stowed in their place heavy articles of value to us. The ship had sailed for the purpose of supplying a young colony, she had therefore on board every conceivable article we could desire in our present situation; our only difficulty, indeed, was to make a wise selection. A large quantity of powder and shot we first secured, and as Fritz considered that we could not have too many weapons, we added three excellent guns, and a whole armful of swords, daggers, and knives. We remembered that knives and forks were necessary, we therefore laid in a large stock of them, and kitchen utensils of all sorts. Exploring the captain's cabin, we discovered a service of

silver plate and a cellaret of good old wine; we then went over
the stores, and supplied ourselves with potted meats, portable
soups, Westphalian hams, sausages, a bag of maize and wheat,
and a quantity of other seeds and vegetables. I then added a
barrel of sulphur for matches, and as much cordage as I could
find. All this—with nails, tools, and agricultural implements—
completed our cargo, and sank our boat so low that I should
have been obliged to lighten her had not the sea been calm.

Night drew on, and a large fire, lighted by those on shore,
showed us that all was well. We replied by hoisting four ship's
lanterns, and two shots announced to us that our signal was
perceived; then, with a heartfelt prayer for the safety of our
dear ones on shore, we retired to our boat, and Fritz, at all
events, was soon sound asleep. For a while I could not sleep;
the thought of my wife and children—alone and unprotected,
save by the great dogs—disturbed my rest.

The night at length passed away. At daybreak Fritz and I
arose and went on deck. I brought the telescope to bear upon
the shore, and with pleasure saw the flag still waving in the
morning breeze; while I kept the glass directed to the land,
I saw the door of the tent open, and my wife appear and look
steadfastly toward us.

I at once hoisted a white flag, and in reply the flag on shore
was thrice dipped. Oh, what a weight seemed lifted from my
heart as I saw the signal!

"Fritz," I said, "I am not now in such haste to get back,
and begin to feel compassion for all these poor beasts. I wish
we could devise some means for getting them on shore."

"We might make a raft," suggested Fritz, "and take off one
or two at a time."

"True," I replied; "it is easy enough to say, 'make a raft,'
but to do it is quite another thing."

"Well," said Fritz, "I can think of nothing else, unless indeed we make them such swimming belts as you made for the
children."

"Really, my boy, that idea is worth having. I am not joking,
indeed," I continued, as I saw him smile; "we may get every
one of the animals ashore in that way."

So saying, I caught a fine sheep, and proceeded to put our
plan into execution. I first fastened a broad piece of linen

round its belly, and to this attached some corks and empty tins; then, with Fritz's help, I flung the animal into the sea— it sank, but a moment afterward rose and floated famously.

"Hurrah!" exclaimed Fritz, "we will treat them all like that." We then rapidly caught the other animals and provided them, one after the other, with a similar contrivance. The cow and ass gave us more trouble than did the others, as for them we required something more bouyant than the mere cork; we at last found some empty casks and fastened two to each animal by thongs passed under its belly. This done, the whole herd were ready to start, and we brought the ass to one of the ports to be the first to be launched. After some maneuvering we got him in a convenient position, and then a sudden heave sent him plunging into the sea. He sank, and then, bouyed up by the casks, emerged head and back from the water. The cow, sheep, and goats followed him one after the other, and then the sow alone remained. She seemed, however, determined not to leave the ship; she kicked, struggled, and squealed so violently, that I really thought we should be obliged to abandon her; at length, after much trouble, we succeeded in sending her out of the port after the others, and when once in the water, such was the old lady's energy that she quickly distanced them, and was the first to reach the shore.

We had fastened to the horns or neck of each animal a cord with a float attached to the end, and now embarking, we gathered up these floats, set sail, and steered for shore, drawing our herd after us.

Delighted with the successful accomplishment of our task, we got out some biscuits and enjoyed a midday meal; then, while Fritz amused himself with his monkey, I took up my glass and tried to make out how our dear ones on shore were employing themselves. As I was thus engaged, a sudden shout from Fritz surprised me. I glanced up; there stood Fritz with his gun to his shoulder, pointing it at a huge shark; the monster was making for one of the finest sheep; he turned on his side to seize his prey; as the white of his belly appeared Fritz fired. The shot took effect, and our enemy disappeared, leaving a trace of blood on the calm water.

"Well done, my boy," I cried, "you will become a crack shot

one of these days; but I trust you will not often have such dangerous game to shoot." Fritz's eyes sparkled at his success and my praise, and reloading his gun carefully watched the water. But the shark did not again appear, and, borne onward by the breeze, we quickly neared the shore. Steering the boat to a convenient landing place, I cast off the ropes which secured the animals, and let them get ashore as best they might.

There was no sign of my wife or children when we stepped on land, but a few moments afterward they appeared, and with a shout of joy ran toward us. We were thankful to be once more united, and after asking and replying to a few preliminary questions, proceeded to release our herd from their swimming belts, which, though so useful in the water, were exceedingly inconvenient on shore. My wife was astonished at the apparatus.

"How clever you are!" said she.

"I am not the inventor," I replied; "the honor is due to Fritz. He not only thought of this plan for bringing off the animals, but saved one, at least, of them from a most fearful death." And I then told them how bravely he had encountered the shark.

My wife was delighted with her son's success, but declared that she would dread our trips to the vessel more than ever, knowing that such savage fish inhabited the waters.

Fritz, Ernest, and I began the work of unloading our craft, while Jack, seeing that the poor donkey was still encumbered with his swimming belt, tried to free him from it. But the donkey would not stand quiet, and the child's fingers were not strong enough to loosen the cordage; finally, therefore, he scrambled upon the animal's back, and urging him on with hand and foot, trotted toward us.

"Come, my boy," I said, "no one must be idle here, even for a moment; you will have riding practice enough hereafter; dismount and come and help us."

Jack was soon on his feet. "But I have not been idle all day," he said; "look here!" and he pointed to a belt round his waist. It was a broad belt of yellow hair, in which he had stuck a couple of pistols and a knife. "And see," he added, "what have I made for the dogs. Here, Juno! Turk!" the dogs came bound-

ing up at his call, and I saw that they were each supplied with
a collar of the same skin, in which were fastened nails, which
bristled round their necks in a most formidable manner.

"Capital, capital! my boy," said I, "but where did you get
your materials, and who helped you?"

"Except in cutting the skin," said my wife, "he had no assistance, and as for the materials, Fritz's jackal supplied us
with the skin, and the needles and thread came out of my
wonderful bag. You little think how many useful things may
be had from that same bag; it is woman's duty and nature, you
know, to see after trifles."

Fritz evidently did not approve of the use to which his
jackal's hide had been devoted, and holding his nose, begged
his little brother to keep at a distance; "Really, Jack," he said,
"you should have cured the hide before you used it; the smell
is disgusting; don't come near me."

"It's not the hide that smells at all," retorted Jack, "it is
your nasty jackal itself, that you left in the sun."

"Now, boys," said I, "no quarreling here; do you, Jack,
help your brother to drag the carcase to the sea, and if your
belt smells after that you must take it off and dry it better."

The jackal was dragged off, and we then finished our work
of unloading our boat. When this was accomplished we started
for our tent, and finding no preparation for supper, I said,
"Fritz, let us have a Westphalian ham."

"Ernest," said my wife, smiling, "let us see if we cannot
conjure up some eggs."

Fritz got out a splendid ham and carried it to his mother
triumphantly, while Ernest set before me a dozen white balls
with parchment-like coverings.

"Turtles' eggs!" said I. "Well done, Ernest! where did you
get them?"

"That," replied my wife, "shall be told in due course when
we relate our adventures; now we will see what they will do
toward making a supper for you; with these and your ham I
do not think we shall starve."

Leaving my wife to prepare supper, we returned to the shore
and brought up what of the cargo we had left there; then,
having collected our herd of animals, we returned to the tent.
The meal which awaited us was as unlike the first supper

we had there enjoyed as possible. My wife had improvised a table of a board laid on two casks; on this was spread a white damask tablecloth, on which were placed knives, forks, spoons, and plates for each person. A tureen of good soup first appeared, followed by a capital omelette, then slices of the ham; and finally some Dutch cheese, butter, and biscuits, with a bottle of the captain's Canary wine, completed the repast.

While we thus regaled ourselves, I related to my wife our adventures, and then begged she would remember her promise and tell me all that had happened in my absence.

Chapter Three

"I WILL spare you a description," said my wife, "of our first day's occupations; truth to tell, I spent the time chiefly in anxious thought and watching your progress and signals. I rose very early this morning, and with the utmost joy perceiving your signal that all was right, hastened to reply to it, and then, while my sons yet slumbered, I sat down and began to consider how our position could be improved. 'For it is perfectly impossible,' said I to myself, 'to live much longer where we are now. The sun beats burningly the lifelong day on this bare, rocky spot; our only shelter is this poor tent, beneath the canvas of which the heat is even more oppressive than on the open shore. Why should not I and my little boys exert ourselves as well as my husband and Fritz? Why should not we too try to accomplish something useful? If we could but exchange this melancholy and unwholesome abode for a pleasant, shady dwelling place, we should all improve in health and spirits. Among those delightful woods and groves where Fritz and his father saw so many charming things, I feel sure there must be some little retreat where we could establish ourselves comfortably; there must be, and I will find it.'

"By this time the boys were up, and I observed Jack very quietly and busily occupied with his knife about the spot where Fritz's jackal lay. Watching his proceedings, I saw that he had cut two long, narrow strips of the animal's skin, which he cleaned and scraped very carefully, and then taking a handful of great nails out of his pocket, he stuck them through the skin, points outward, after which he cut strips of canvas sailcloth, twice as broad as the thongs, doubled them, and laid them on the raw side of the skin, so as to cover the broad, flat nail heads. At this point of the performance, Master Jack came to me with the agreeable request that I would kindly stitch the canvas and (moist) skin together for him. I gave him needles and thread, but could not think of depriving him of the pleasure of doing it himself.

"However, when I saw how good-humoredly he persevered in the work with his awkward, unskillful fingers, I took pity on him, and conquering the disgust I felt, finished lining the skin dog-collars he had so ingeniously contrived. After this, I was called upon to complete in the same way a fine belt of skin he had made for himself. I advised him to think of some means by which the skin might be kept from shrinking.

"Ernest, although rather treating Jack's manufacture with ridicule, proposed a sensible enough plan, which Jack forthwith put into execution. He nailed the skin, stretched flat, on a board, and put it in the sun to dry.

"My scheme of a journey was agreed to joyously by my young companions. Preparations were instantly set on foot: weapons and provisions provided; the two elder boys carrying guns, while they gave me charge of the water flask, and a small hatchet.

"Leaving everything in as good order as we could at the tent, we proceeded toward the stream, accompanied by the dogs.

Turk, who had accompanied you on your first expedition, seemed immediately to understand that we wished to pursue the same route, and proudly led the way.

"As I looked at my two young sons, each with his gun, and considered how much the safety of the party depended on these little fellows, I felt grateful to you, dear husband, for having acquainted them in childhood with the use of firearms.

"Filling our water-jar, we crossed the stream, and went on to the height, from whence, as you described, a lovely prospect is obtained, at the sight of which a pleasurable sensation of buoyant hope, to which I had long been a stranger, awoke within my breast.

"A pretty little wood in the distance attracted my notice particularly, and thither we directed our course. But soon finding it impossible to force our way through the tall, strong grass, which grew in dense luxuriance higher than the children's heads, we turned toward the open beach on our left, and following it, we reached a point much nearer the little wood, when, quitting the strand, we made toward it.

"We had not entirely escaped the tall grass, however, and with the utmost fatigue and difficulty, were struggling through the reeds, when suddenly a great rushing noise terrified us all dreadfully. A very large and powerful bird sprang upward on the wing. Both boys attempted to take aim, but the bird was far away before they were ready to fire.

" 'Oh, dear, what a pity!' exclaimed Ernest; 'now if I had only had my light gun, and if the bird had not flown quite so fast, I should have brought him down directly!'

" 'Oh, yes,' said I, 'no doubt you would be a capital sportsman, if only your game would always give you time to make ready comfortably.'

" 'But I had no notion that anything was going to fly up just at our feet like that,' cried he.

" 'A good shot,' I replied, 'must be prepared for surprises; neither wild birds nor wild beasts will send you notice that they are about to fly or to run.'

" 'What sort of bird can it have been?' inquired Jack.

" 'Oh, it certainly must have been an eagle,' answered little Franz, 'it was so very big!'

" 'Just as if every big bird must be an eagle!' replied Ernest, in a tone of derision.

" 'Let's see where he was sitting, at all events!' said I.

"Jack sprang toward the place, and instantly a second bird, rather larger than the first, rushed upward into the air, with a most startling noise.

"The boys stood staring upward, perfectly stupefied, while I laughed heartily, saying, 'Well, you are first-rate sportsmen, to be sure! You certainly will keep my larder famously well supplied!'

"At this, Ernest colored up, and looked inclined to cry, while Jack put on a comical face, pulled off his cap, and with a low bow, called after the fugitive:

" 'Adieu for the present, sir! I live in hopes of another meeting!'

"On searching the ground carefully, we discovered a rude sort of nest made untidily of dry grass. It was empty, although we perceived broken egg shells at no great distance, and concluded that the young brood had escaped among the grass, which, in fact, we could see was waving at a little distance, as the little birds ran through it.

" 'Now look here, Franz,' said Ernest, presently, 'just consider how this bird could by any possibility have been an eagle. Eagles never build on the ground, neither can their young leave the nest and run as soon as they are out of the egg. That is a peculiarity of the gallinaceous tribe of birds alone, to which then these must belong. The species, I think, is indicated by the white belly and dull red color of the wing coverts which I observed in these specimens, and I believe them to be bustards, especially as I noticed in the largest the fine mustache-like feathers over the beak, peculiar to the great bustard.'

" 'My dear boy!' I said, 'your eyes were actively employed, I must confess, if your fingers were unready with the gun. And after all, it is just as well, perhaps, that we have not thrown the bustard's family into mourning.'

"Thus chatting, we at length approached my pretty wood. Numbers of birds fluttered and sang among the high branches, but I did not encourage the boys in their wish to try to shoot any of the happy little creatures. We were lost in admiration of the trees of this grove, and I cannot describe to you how wonderful they are, nor can you form the least idea of their enormous size without seeing them yourself. What we had been calling a wood proved to be a group of about a dozen trees only, and, what was strange, the roots sustained the massive trunks exalted in the air, forming strong arches, and props and stays all around each individual stem, which was firmly rooted in the center.

"I gave Jack some twine, and scrambling up one of the curious open-air roots, he succeeded in measuring round the trunk itself, and made it out to be about eighteen yards. I saw no sort of fruit, but the foliage is thick and abundant, throwing delicious shade on the ground beneath, which is carpeted with soft green herbage, and entirely free from thorns, briars, or bushes of any kind. It is the most charming resting place that ever was seen, and I and the boys enjoyed our midday meal immensely in this glorious palace of the woods, so grateful to our senses after the glare and heat of our journey thither. The dogs joined us after a while. They had lingered behind on the sea-shore, and I was surprised to see them lie down and go comfortably to sleep without begging for food, as they do usually when we eat.

"The longer we remained in this enchanting place, the more did it charm my fancy; and if we could but manage to live in some sort of dwelling up among the branches of those grand, noble trees, I should feel perfectly safe and happy. It seemed to me absurd to suppose we should ever find another place half so lovely, so I determined to search no further, but return to the beach and see if anything from the wreck had been cast up by the waves, which we could carry away with us.

"Before starting, Jack persuaded me to sit quietly a little longer, and finish making his belt and the spike-collars for the dogs, for you must know that the child had actually been carrying the board on which these were stretched all this time, so that they should get the full benefit of the sun. As they were now quite dry, I completed them easily, and Jack girded on the belt with great pride, placing his pistols in it, and marching about in the most self-important style, while Ernest fitted the collars on the two dogs.

"On reaching the shore, we found it strewed with many articles, doubtless of value, but all too heavy for us to lift. We rolled some casks, however, beyond high-water mark, and dragged a chest or two also higher on the beach; and, while doing so, observed that our dogs were busy among the rocks. They were carefully watching the crevices and pools, and every now and then would pounce downward and seize something which they swallowed with apparent relish.

" 'They are eating crabs,' said Jack. 'No wonder they have not seemed hungry lately.'

"And, sure enough, they were catching the little green crabs with which the water abounded. These, however, did not apparently entirely satisfy them.

"Some time afterward, just as we were about to turn inland toward the ford, we noticed that Juno was scraping in the sand, and turning up some round substances, which she hastily devoured. Ernest went to see what these were, and reported in his calm way that the dog had found turtles' eggs.

" 'Oh,' cried I, 'then let us by all means share in the booty!' Mrs. Juno, however, did not at all approve of this, and it was with some difficulty that we drove her aside while we gathered a couple of dozen of eggs, stowing them in our provision bags.

"While thus employed, we caught sight of a sail which appeared to be merrily approaching the shore beyond the cliffs. Ernest declared it must be our raft. Little Franz, always having the fear of savages before his eyes, began to look frightened, and for a moment I myself was doubtful what to think.

"However, we hastened to the stream; and crossing it by the stepping-stones, came in sight of the landing place, where we joyfully met you.

"Now I hope you approve of the proceedings of your exploring party, and that to-morrow you will do me the favor of packing everything up, and taking us away to live among my splendid trees."

"Aye, little wife," said I; "so that is your idea of comfort and security, is it! A tree, I do not know how many feet high, on which we are to perch and roost like the birds? If we had but wings or a balloon, it would, I own, be a capital plan."

"Laugh as much as you like," returned my wife, "my idea is not so absurd as you make it out. We should be safe up there from jackals' visits during the night. And I know I have seen at home, in Switzerland, quite a pretty arbor, with a strong floor, up among the branches of a lime tree, and we went up a staircase to reach it. Why could not we contrive a place like that, where we could sleep safely at night?"

"I will consider the idea seriously, my wife," said I; "perhaps something may come of it, after all! Meantime, as we have finished our supper, and night is coming on, let us commend ourselves to Almighty protection and retire to rest."

Beneath the shelter of our tent, we all slept soundly, like marmots, until break of day; when, my wife and I awaking, we took counsel together as to future proceedings.

Referring to the task she had the previous evening proposed for me, I remarked that to undertake it would involve so many difficulties that it was highly necessary to look closely into the subject.

"In the first place," said I, "I am unwilling hastily to quit a spot to which I am convinced we were providentially led as a landing place. See how secure it is; guarded on all sides by these high cliffs, and accessible only by the narrow passage to the ford, while from this point it is so easy to reach the ship that the whole of its valuable cargo is at our disposal. Suppose we decide to stay patiently here for the present—until, at least, we have brought on shore everything we possibly can?"

"I agree with you to a certain extent, dear husband," replied she; "but you do not know how dreadfully the heat among the rocks tries me. It is almost intolerable to us who remain here all day, while you and Fritz are away out at sea or wandering among the shady woods, where cool fruits refresh, and fair scenes delight you. As to the contents of the ship, an immense deal has been cast ashore, and I would much rather give up all the remainder, and be spared the painful anxiety it gives me when you even talk of venturing again on the faithless deep."

"Well, I must admit that there is much right on your side," I continued; "suppose we were to remove to your chosen abode, and make this rocky fastness our magazine and place of retreat in case of danger. I could easily render it more secure, by blasting portions of the rock with gunpowder. But a bridge must be constructed in the first place, to enable us to cross bag and baggage."

"Oh, I shall be parched to death before we can leave this place if a bridge has to be made," cried my wife impatiently. "Why not just take our things on our backs and wade across, as we have done already? The cow and the donkey could carry a great deal."

"That they will have to do, in whatever fashion we make the move," said I; "but bags and baskets we must have, to put things in, and if you will turn your attention to providing those, I will set about the bridge at once. It will be wanted not once but continually; the stream will probably swell and be impassable at times, and even as it is, an accident might happen."

"Well! well!" cried my wife, "I submit to your opinion; only pray set about it without delay, for I long to be off. It is an excellent idea to make a strong place among the cliffs here; the gunpowder especially, I shall be delighted to see stored here when we go away, for it is frightfully dangerous to keep so much as we have close to our habitation."

"Gunpowder is indeed the most dangerous and at the same time the most useful thing we have," said I, "and for both these reasons we must be especially careful of it. In time I will hollow out a place in the rock where we can store it safe from either fire or damp."

By this morning's consultation we had settled the weighty question of our change of abode, and also chalked out work for the day.

When the children heard of the proposed move their joy was boundless; they began at once to talk of it as our "journey to the Promised Land," and only regretted that time must be "wasted," as they said, in bridge-building before it could be undertaken.

Everyone being impatient for breakfast that work might be begun at once, the cow and goats were milked, and, having enjoyed a comfortable meal of biscuit boiled in milk, I prepared to start for the wreck, in order to obtain planks for the proposed bridge. Ernest, as well as Fritz, accompanied me, and we were soon within the influence of the current, and were carried swiftly out to sea. Fritz was steering, and we had no

sooner passed beyond the islet at the entrance of the bay, so as
to come in sight of its seaward beach, than we were astonished
to see a countless multitude of sea birds, gulls, and others,
which rose like a cloud into the air, disturbed by our approach,
and deafened us by their wild and screaming cries. Fritz caught
up his gun, and would have sent a shot among them had I permitted it. I was very curious to find out what could be the great
attraction for all this swarm of feathered fowl; and, availing
myself of a fresh breeze from the sea, I set the sail and directed
our course toward the island.

The swelling sail and flying pennant charmed Ernest, while
Fritz bent his keen eyes eagerly toward the sandy shore, where
the flocks of birds were again settling.

Presently he shouted: "Aha! now I see what they are after!
They have got a huge monster of a fish there and a proper feast
they are making! Let's have a nearer look at it, father!"

We could not take our boat very close in, but we managed
to effect a landing at a short distance from the festive scene;
and, securing the raft by casting a rope round a large stone, we
cautiously drew near the object of interest.

It proved to be a monstrous fish on whose flesh these multitudes of birds were ravenously feeding; and it was extraordinary to watch the ferocity, the envy, the gluttony, and all
manner of evil passions, exhibited among the guests at this
banquet.

"There was nothing on this sandy beach when we passed
yesterday, I am certain, father," said Fritz. "It seems strange
to see this creature stranded here."

"Why, Fritz!" cried Ernest, "It must be the shark! your
shark, you know! I believe I can see where you hit him in
the head."

"You are right, I do believe, Ernest," said I, "though I
think your imagination only can distinguish the gunshot
wounds among all the pecking and tearing of the voracious
birds there. Just look, boys, at those terrific jaws, beneath the
strangely projecting snout. See the rows upon rows of mur-
derous teeth, and thank God we were delivered from them!
Let us try if we can induce these greedy birds to spare us a bit
of the shark's skin; it is extremely rough, and when dry may
be used like a file."

Ernest drew the ramrod from his gun, and charged so manfully into the crowd, that striking right and left he speedily killed several, while most of the others took to flight. Fritz detached some broad strips of skin with his knife, and we returned toward the boat.

Perceiving with satisfaction that the shore was strewn with just the sort of boards and planks I wanted, I lost no time in collecting them; and, forming a raft to tow after us, we were in a short time able to direct our course homeward, without visiting the wreck at all. As we sailed along, extremely well pleased with our good fortune, Fritz, by my direction, nailed part of the shark's skin flat on boards to dry in the sun, and the rest on the rounded mast.

"Will that be a good plan, father?" inquired he, "it will be quite bent and crooked when it hardens."

"That is just what I want it to be," said I, "we may happen to find it useful in that form as well as flat. It would be beautiful shagreen if we could smooth and polish it."

"I thought," remarked Ernest, "that shagreen was made from asses' hide."

"And you thought rightly," said I. "The best shagreen is prepared in Turkey, Persia, and Tartary, from the skins of horses and asses. In these skins, the roughness is produced artificially; while the skin is newly flayed and still soft, hard grains of corn are spread on the under surface, and pressed into it as it dries. These grains are afterward removed, and the roughnesses imparted to the appearance of the skin remains indelibly; shagreen is useful in polishing joiners' work, and it is made in France from the rough skin of a hideous creature called the angel-fish."

"Angel-fish!" exclaimed Fritz; "what a name to give to anything 'hideous,' father!"

"There are bad angels as well as good ones," observed Ernest, in his dry, quiet way; "it is better to leave people to see for themselves which is meant."

By this time we were close in shore; and, lowering the sail, we soon had our craft, with the raft in tow, safely moored to the bank.

No one was in sight, not a sound to be heard, so with united voice we gave a loud, cheery halloo, which after a while was answered in shrill tones, and the mother, with her two boys, came running from behind the rocks between us and the stream, each carrying a small bundle in a handkerchief, while little Franz held aloft a landing net.

Our return so soon was quite unexpected, and they anxiously inquired the reason, which we soon explained; and then the mysterious bundles were opened, and a great number of fine crawfish displayed; whose efforts to escape by scuttling away in every direction, directly they were placed in a heap on the ground, caused immense fun and laughter as the boys pursued and brought them back, only to find others scrambling off in a dozen different ways.

"Now, father, have we not done well to-day!" cried Jack, "did you ever see such splendid crawfish? Oh, there were thousands of them, and I am sure we have got two hundred here at least. Just look at their claws!"

"No doubt you were the discoverer of these fine crabs, eh, Jack?" said I.

"No! fancy young Franz being the lucky man!" answered he. "He and I went toward the stream while mother was busy, just to look for a good place for the bridge. Franz was picking up pebbles and alabasters, some because they were so pretty, some to strike sparks with in the dark, and some, he insisted, were 'gold.' 'Jack! Jack!' cried he presently, 'come and see the crabs on Fritz's jackal!' You know we threw it away there, and to be sure it was swarming with these creatures. Are you glad we have found them, father? Will they be good to eat?"

"Very excellent, my boy, and we may be thankful that food for our wants is thus provided day by day."

When each party had related the day's adventures, and while the mother was cooking the crawfish, we went to bring our store of planks to land. Even this apparently simple operation required thought, and I had to improvise rope-harness for the cow and the donkey, by which we could make them drag each board separately from the water's edge to the margin of the stream.

Jack showed me where he thought the bridge should be, and I certainly saw no better place, as the banks were at that point tolerably close to one another, steep, and of about equal height.

"How shall we find out if our planks are long enough to reach across?" said I. "A surveyor's table would be useful now."

"What do you say to a ball of string, father?" said Ernest. "Tie one end to a stone, throw it across, then draw it back and measure the line!"

Adopting my son's idea, we speedily ascertained the distance across to be eighteen feet. Then allowing three feet more at each side, I calculated twenty-four feet as the necessary length of the boards.

The question as to how the planks were to be laid across was a difficult one. We resolved to discuss it during dinner, to which we were now summoned. And my wife, as we sat resting, displayed to me her needlework. With hard labor she had made two large canvas bags for the ass to carry. Having no suitable needle, she had been obliged to bore the hole for each stitch with a nail, and gained great praise for her ingenuity and patience. Dinner was quickly dispatched, as we were all eager to continue our engineering work. A scheme had occurred to me for conveying one end of a plank across the water, and I set about it in this way. There fortunately were one or two trees close to the stream on either side. I attached a rope pretty near one end of a beam, and slung it loosely to the tree beside us; then, fastening a long rope to the other end, I crossed with it by means of broken rocks and stones, and having a pulley and block, I soon arranged the rope on a strong limb of the opposite tree, again returning with the end to our own side.

Now putting my idea to the proof, I brought the ass and the cow, and fastening this rope to the harness I had previously contrived for them, I drove them steadily away from the bank. To my great satisfaction, and the surprise and delight of the boys, the end of the plank which had been laid alongside the stream began gently to move, rose higher, turned, and soon projecting over the water, continued to advance, until, having described the segment of a circle, it reached the opposite bank; I stopped my team, the plank rested on the ground, the bridge was made! So at least thought Fritz and Jack, who in a moment were lightly running across the narrow way, shouting joyfully as they sprang to the other side.

Our work was now comparatively easy. A second and third plank were laid beside the first; and when these were carefully secured at each end to the ground and to the trees, we very quickly laid short boards side by side across the beams, the boys nailing them lightly down as I sawed them in lengths; and when this was done, our bridge was pronounced complete. Nothing could exceed the excitement of the children. They danced to and fro on the wonderful structure, singing, shouting, and cutting the wildest capers.

I must confess I heartily sympathized with their triumphant feelings.

Now that the work was done, we began to feel how much we were fatigued, and gladly returned to our tent for refreshment and repose.

Next morning, while we breakfasted, I made a little speech to my sons on the subject of the important move we were about to make, wishing to impress them with a sense of the absolute necessity of great caution.

"Remember," said I, "that, although you all begin to feel very much at your ease here, we are yet complete strangers to a variety of dangers which may surprise us unawares. I charge you, therefore, to maintain good order, and keep together on the march. No darting off into by-ways, Jack. No lingering behind to philosophize, Ernest. And now all hands to work."

The greatest activity instantly prevailed in our camp. Some collected provisions, others packed kitchen utensils, tools, ropes, and hammocks, arranging them as burdens for the cow and ass. My wife pleaded for a seat on the latter for her little Franz, and assuring me likewise that she could not possibly leave the poultry, even for a night, nor exist an hour without her magic bag, I agreed to do my best to please her, without downright cruelty to the animals.

Away ran the children to catch the cocks and hens. Great chasing, fluttering, and cackling ensued; but with no success whatever, until the mother recalled her panting sons, and scattering some handfuls of grain within the open tent, soon decoyed the fowls and pigeons into the enclosure; where, when the curtain was dropped, they were easily caught, tied together, and placed on the cow. This amiable and phlegmatic animal had stood calmly chewing the cud, while package after package was disposed of on her broad back, nor did she now object even to this noisy addition to her load. I placed a couple of half-hoops over all; and, spreading sailcloth on them, put the fowls in darkness, and they rapidly became quiet; and the cow, with the appearance of having a small wagon on her back, was ready to start.

Franz was firmly seated on the ass, amidst bags and bundles of all sorts and sizes; they rose about him like cushions and pillows, and his curly head rested on the precious magic bag, which surmounted all the rest.

Having filled the tent with the things we left behind, closing it carefully, and ranging chests and casks around it, we were finally ready to be off, each well equipped and in the highest spirits.

Fritz and his mother led the van.

Franz (the young cavalier) and the sober-minded cow followed them closely.

Jack conducted the goats; one of these had also a rider, for Knips, the monkey, was seated on his foster-mother, whose patience was sorely tried by his restlessness and playful tricks.

The sheep were under Ernest's care, and I brought up the rear of this patriarchal band, while the two dogs kept constantly running backward and forward in the character of aides-de-camp.

"We seem delightfully like those simple and pastoral tribes I have read of," said Ernest, as we proceeded, "whose whole lives are spent in shifting from place to place, without any wish to settle."

"Yes," said I. "Among the Arabs, Tartars, and some other Eastern nations, this mode of life is natural. They for that reason are called Nomads.

"These tribes are amply provided with camels and horses, and effect their journeys more quickly and conveniently than we are likely to do with these deliberate quadrupeds of ours. Whatever you young folks may think, I suspect your mother and I will be quite satisfied with one such undertaking. At least I hope she will be contented with the nest she intends me to build for her up in her wonderful trees."

With honest pride I introduced my wife to my bridge, and after receiving from her what I considered well-merited praise for my skill in its construction, we passed over it in grand procession, re-enforced unexpectedly on the opposite side by the arrival of our cross-grained old sow. The perverse creature had obstinately resisted our attempts to bring her with us, but finding herself deserted, had followed of her own accord, testifying in the most unmistakable manner, by angry grunts and squeals, her entire disapproval of our proceedings.

I soon found we must, as before, turn down to the sea beach, for not only did the rank grass impede our progress, but it also tempted the animals to break away from us, and, but for our watchful dogs, we might have lost several of them.

On the firm open sands we were making good way, when, to my annoyance, both our dogs suddenly left us, and springing into the thick cover to our right, commenced a furious barking, followed by howling as if in fear and violent pain.

Not for a moment doubting that some dangerous animal was at hand, I hastened to the spot, remarking as I went the characteristic behavior of my three sons.

Fritz cocked his gun and advanced boldly, but with caution.

Ernest looked disconcerted, and drew back, but got ready to fire.

While Jack hurried after Fritz without so much as unslinging his gun from his shoulders.

Before I could come up with them, I heard Jack shouting excitedly:

"Father! father! come quickly! a huge porcupine! a most enormous porcupine!"

Sure enough, the dogs were rushing round and round a porcupine, and having attempted to seize it, were already severely wounded by its quills. Each time they came near, the creature, with a rattling noise, bristled up its spines.

Somewhat to my amusement, while we were looking at the curious defense this creature was making, little Jack stepped close up to it, with a pocket pistol in his hand, and shot it dead, making sure of it by a couple of hearty raps on the head, and then giving way to a burst of boyish exultation, he called upon us to help to convey his prize to his mother. This it was not by any means easy to do. Sundry attempts resulted in bloody fingers, till Jack, taking his pocket handkerchief, and fastening one corner round its neck, ran off, dragging it after him to where his mother awaited us.

"Hullo, mother! here's a jolly beast, isn't it? I shot it, and it's good to eat! Father says so! I only wish you had seen how it terrified the dogs, and heard the rattling and rustling of its spines. Oh, it is a fearful creature!"

Ernest, examining it carefully, pronounced its incisor teeth, its ears and feet, to resemble those of the human race, and pointed out the curious crest of stiff hairs on its head and neck.

"I have read of another species," said he, "called the tuft-tailed porcupine, which must be even more curious looking than this is. It has short, flat quills, and a scaly tail ending in an extraordinary tuft, like a bunch of narrow strips of parchment. It cannot be such a disagreeable enemy to encounter as this fellow."

"Were you not afraid, Jack," asked I, "lest the porcupine should cast some of his quills like darts at you?"

"Of course not," returned he, "I know well enough that is nothing but a fable!"

"A fable!" said I; "why, look at your mother! she is drawing five or six spines out of each of the dogs!"

"Ah, those stuck into them when they so fiercely fell upon it in their attack. Those are the shortest quills, and seem very slightly fixed in its skin. The long quills bent aside when Juno pressed against them."

"You are perfectly right, my boy," said I; "there is no truth in the old idea of shooting out the spines. But now, shall we leave this prickly booty of yours, or attempt to take it with us?"

"Oh, please, father, let us take it! Why, it is good to eat!"

Smiling at the child's eagerness, and willing to please him, I made a somewhat awkward bundle of the porcupine, wrapping it in several folds of cloth, and added it to the donkey's load.

Our party then resumed the march, which, with little interruption, was continued steadily, until we came in sight of our future place of residence.

The wonderful appearance of the enormous trees, and the calm beauty of the spot altogether, fully came up to the enthusiastic description which had been given me. And my wife gladly heard me say that, if an abode could be contrived among the branches, it would be the safest and most charming home in the world.

We hastily unloaded the ass and cow, securing them, as well as the sheep and goats, by tying their fore-feet closely together. The doves and poultry were set at liberty, and we sat down to rest among the soft herbage while we laid our plans for the night.

Fritz soon left us, but presently two shots were fired, and he appeared holding a fine tiger cat by the hind legs, which, with the intensest delight, he exhibited to each in turn.

"Well done, Fritz!" cried I. "Our cocks and hens would have had an unfortunate night of it but for this lucky shot of yours. It is to be hoped he has left no companion near at hand. You must be on the lookout."

"How curious it seems," remarked Ernest, "that God should create hurtful animals like this."

"To our feeble and narrow vision many of the ways of the Infinite and Eternal Mind are incomprehensible," I replied. "What our limited reason cannot grasp, let us be content to acknowledge as the workings of Almighty power and wisdom, and thankfully trust in that 'Rock,' which, were it not higher than we, would afford no sense of security to the immortal soul. That animals should prey upon one another is a means of preserving a due balance in the world of nature, and in many ways these beasts of prey are also useful to man. What beautiful and warm furs are procured by hunters just in those countries where no other covering would defend the inhabitants from the wintery cold!—as, for instance, the skins of bears, wolverines, and arctic foxes, wild cats, and many others."

"The skin of the seal, or sea dog, is also valuable," said Ernest.

"It is," I replied, "and in its own element that creature preys on fish as the dog did on land animals before his race became domesticated by man. But now, Fritz, tell us how you obtained your prize."

"Observing that something moved among the branches," said he, "I went softly around the tree with my gun, and making sure the creature was a wild cat, I fired and brought it down. It was severely wounded, but, rising in a fury, it attempted to climb the tree, when I, luckily having a loaded pistol, gave it a quietus. And do tell me, father, what sort of a cat it is."

"It is a mercy the brute did not fly at your throat instead of attempting to escape," said I. "It belongs to a fierce and blood-thirsty race—that of the ocelots or tiger cats, natives of the tropical parts of America. I should say this was a margay, and it would have proved a cruel foe, not only of our poultry, but also of our sheep and goats. I am well pleased that you have rid us of it."

"May I have the beautiful skin, father? And will you tell me what will be the best use to make of it?"

"I advise you to skin the animal very carefully, and of the handsome black and yellow tail make a hunting-belt for yourself. The paws—let me see—why, I fancy the paws might be made famous cases for knife, fork, and spoon, and look well hanging from the belt. The skin of the body you had better preserve until you find some suitable use for it."

"Oh, father, what a splendid plan!" cried Jack; "do tell me some good use for my porcupine."

"I think its feet may make cases also; at least, you may try. The quills, I am sure, may be used for packing needles, and for tipping arrows, and I should try to make defensive armor for the dogs out of the rest. They may fall in with foes more dangerous than any we have yet seen."

"To be sure, father, the very thing!" shouted Jack in high glee. "I have seen pictures of boar hunts, in which the dogs were protected by a sort of leather coat of mail. That will be grand!"

After giving this advice, I got no peace until I had shown my boys how to act upon it, and in a short time each had his prize fastened up by the hind legs, and carefully slitting the skin, was stripping it from the carcase.

Ernest, meanwhile, was fetching large flat stones in order to form a fireplace, while Franz gathered sticks, as his mother was anxious to prepare some food.

"What sort of a tree do you suppose this to be, father?" inquired Ernest, seeing me examining that under which we were encamping. "Is not the leaf something like the walnut?"

"There is a resemblance, but in my opinion these gigantic

trees must be mangroves or wild figs. I have heard their enormous height described, and also the peculiarity of the arching roots supporting the main trunk raised above the soil."

Just then little Franz came up with a large bundle of sticks, and his mouth full of something he was eating with evident satisfaction.

"Oh, mother!" cried he, "this is so good! So delicious!"

"Greedy little boy!" exclaimed she in a fright. "What have you got there? Don't swallow it, whatever you do. Very likely it is poisonous! Spit it all out this minute!" And the anxious mother quickly extracted from the rosy little mouth the remains of a small fig.

"Where did you find this?" said I.

"There are thousands lying among the grass yonder," replied the little boy. "They taste very nice. I thought poison was nasty. Do you think they will hurt me? The pigeons and the hens are gobbling them up with all their might and main, papa!"

"I think you have no cause for alarm, dear wife," I said. "The trees seem to be the fig-bearing mangrove of the Antilles. But remember, Franz, you must never eat anything without first showing it to me, never mind how good it seems. If birds and monkeys eat a fruit or vegetable, it is usually safe to believe it wholesome," added I, turning to the other boys, who, instantly taking the hint, coaxed Franz to give them the figs he still had in his pocket, and ran to offer them to Knips, who was closely watching the skinning of the tiger cat and porcupine, apparently giving his opinion on the subject with much chattering and gesticulation.

"Here, Knips, allow me to present you with a fig!" cried Jack, holding one out to the funny little creature.

Knips took it readily, and after turning it about, and sniffing and smelling it, he popped it into his mouth, with such a droll grimace of delight and satisfaction that the boys all laughed and clapped their hands, crying "Bravo, Knips! you know a good thing when you see it, don't you, old fellow! Hurrah!"

My wife, with her mind set at rest on the question of the figs, now continued her preparations for dinner.

The flesh of the margay was given to the dogs, but part of the porcupine was put on the fire to boil, while we reserved the rest for roasting.

I employed myself in contriving needles for my wife's work, by boring holes at one end of the quills, which I did by means of a red hot nail, and I soon had a nice packet of various sizes, which pleased her immensely. I also laid plans for making proper harness for our beasts of burden, but could not attempt to begin that while so many wants more pressing demanded attention.

We examined the different trees, and chose one which seemed most suited to our purpose. The branches spread at a great height above us, and I made the boys try if it were possible to throw sticks or stones over one of these, my intention being to construct a rope ladder if we could once succeed in getting a string across a strong bough.

Finding we could not succeed in that way, I resolved other schemes in my mind, and meantime went with Jack and Fritz to a small brook close by, where I showed them how to place the skins to steep and soften in the water, with stones placed on them to keep them beneath the surface.

When dinner was over, I prepared our night quarters. I first slung our hammocks from the roots of the tree, which, meeting above us, formed an arched roof, then covering the whole with sailcloth, we made a temporary tent, which would at least keep off the night damps and noxious insects.

Leaving my wife engaged in making a set of harness for the ass and cow, whose strength I intended to employ the following day in drawing the beams up to our tree, I walked down with Fritz and Ernest to the beach to look for wood suitable for building our new abode, and also to discover, if possible, some light rods to form a ladder. For some time we hunted in vain, nothing but rough drift wood was to be seen, utterly unfit for our purpose. Ernest at length pointed out a quantity of bamboos, half buried in the sand. These were exactly what I wanted, and stripping them of their leaves I cut them into lengths of about five feet each; these I bound in bundles to carry to the tree, and then began to look about for some slight reeds to serve as arrows.

I presently saw what I required in a copse at a little distance.

We advanced cautiously lest the thicket should contain some wild beast or venomous serpent. Juno rushed ahead; as she did so a flock of flamingoes, which had been quietly feeding, rose in the air. Fritz, instantly firing, brought a couple of the birds to the ground, the rest of the squadron sailing away in perfect order, their plumage continually changing, as they flew, from beautiful rose to pure white, as alternately their snowy wings and rosy breasts were visible. One of those which fell was perfectly dead, but the other appeared only slightly wounded in the wing, for it made off across the swampy ground. I attempted to follow, but soon found that progress was impossible on the marsh; Juno, however, chased the bird and, seizing it, speedily brought it to my feet. Fritz and Ernest were delighted at the sight of our prize.

"What a handsome bird!" exclaimed they. "Is it much hurt? Let us tame it and let it run about with the fowls."

"Its plumage is much more brilliant than that of the dead one," remarked Fritz.

"Yes," said Ernest, "this is a full grown bird, while yours is younger; it is some years before they reach perfection. See what long active legs it has, like those of a stork, while with its great webbed feet it can swim faster than a goose. Earth, air, or water is all the same to the flamingo, it is equally at home in any one of the three."

"Well," said Fritz, "let us take the dead one to mother and get her to introduce it to the other element, and see what it will make of that; if it is young and tender, as you say, it should make a delicious roast."

Fritz and Ernest then carried the birds and bamboos to the tree, while I proceeded to cut my reeds. I chose those which had flowered, knowing that they were harder, and having cut a sufficient quantity of these, I selected one or two of the tallest canes I could find to assist me in measuring the height of the tree. I then bound them together and returned to my family.

"Do you mean to keep this great hungry bird Fritz has brought?" said my wife, "it is another mouth to feed, remember, and provisions are still scarce."

"Luckily," I replied, "the flamingo will not eat grain like our poultry, but will be quite satisfied with insects, fish, and little crabs, which it will pick up for itself. Pray reassure yourself, therefore, and let me see to the poor bird's wound."

So saying, I procured some wine and butter and anointed the wing, which though hurt was not broken. I bound it up, and then took the bird to the stream, where I fastened it by a long cord to a stake and left it to shift for itself. In a few days the wound was healed, and the bird, subdued by kind treatment, became rapidly tame.

While I was thus employed my sons were endeavoring to ascertain the height of the lowest branch of the tree from the ground. They had fastened together the long reeds I had brought, and were trying to measure the distance with them, but in vain; they soon found that were the rods ten times their length they could not touch the branch.

"Hullo, my boys," I said, when I discovered what they were about, "that is not the way to set to work. Geometry will simplify the operation considerably; with its help the altitude of the highest mountains are ascertained. We may, therefore, easily find the height of the branch."

So saying, I measured out a certain distance from the base of the tree and marked the spot, and then by means of a rod whose length I knew, and imaginary lines, I calculated the angle subtended by the trunk of the tree from the ground to the root of the branch. This done, I was able to discover the height required, and, to the astonishment of the younger children, announced that we should henceforth live thirty feet above the ground. This I wanted to know, that I might construct a ladder of the necessary length.

Telling Fritz to collect all our cord, and the others to roll all the twine into a ball, I sat down, and taking the reeds, speedily manufactured half a dozen arrows and feathered them from the dead flamingo. I then took a strong bamboo, bent it, and strung it so as to form a bow. When the boys saw what I had done they were delighted, and begged to have the pleasure of firing the first shot.

"No, no!" said I, "I did not make this for mere pleasure, nor is it even intended as a weapon, the arrows are pointless. Elizabeth," I continued to my wife, "can you supply me with a ball of stout thread from your wonderful bag?"

"Certainly," replied she, "I think a ball of thread was the

first thing to enter the bag," and diving her hand deep in, she drew out the very thing I wanted.

"Now, boys," I said, "I am going to fire the first shot," and I fastened one end of the thread to one of my arrows and aimed at a large branch above me. The arrow flew upward and bore the thread over the branch and fell at our feet. Thus was the first step in our undertaking accomplished. Now for the rope ladder!

Fritz had obtained two coils of cord, each about forty feet in length; these we stretched on the ground side by side; then Fritz cut the bamboos into pieces of two feet for the steps of the ladder, and as he handed them to me, I passed them through knots which I had prepared in the ropes, while Jack fixed each end with a nail driven through the wood. When the ladder was finished, I carried over the bough a rope by which it might be hauled up. This done, I fixed the lower end of the ladder firmly to the ground by means of stakes, and all was ready for an ascent. The boys, who had been watching me with intense interest, were each eager to be first.

"Jack shall have the honor," said I, "as he is the lightest; so up with you, my boy, and do not break your neck."

Jack, who was as active as a monkey, sprang up the ladder and quickly gained the top.

"Three cheers for the nest!" he exclaimed, waving his cap. "Hurrah, hurrah, hurrah for our jolly nest! What a grand house we will have up here; come along, Fritz!"

His brother was soon by his side, and with a hammer and nails secured the ladder yet more securely. I followed with an ax, and took a survey of the tree. It was admirably suited to our purpose; the branches were very strong and so closely interwoven that no beams would be required to form a flooring, but when some of the boughs were lopped and cleared away, a few planks would be quite sufficient.

I now called for a pulley, which my wife fastened to the cord hanging beside the ladder. I hauled it up, and finding the boys rather in my way, told them to go down, while I proceeded to fasten the pulley to a stout branch above me, that we might be able to haul up the beams we should require the next day. I then made other preparations, that there might be no delay on the morrow, and a bright moon having arisen, I by its light continued working until I was quite worn out, and then at length descended. I reached the ground, but to my surprise found that the two boys were not there. They had not been seen. A moment afterward, however, all anxiety was dispelled, for among the topmost boughs I heard their young voices raised in the evening hymn. Instead of descending, they had, while I was busy, climbed upward, and had been sitting in silent admiration of the moonlight scene, high above me. They now joined us, and my wife showed me the results of her labor. She had made two complete sets of harness. I congratulated her upon her success, and we then sat down to supper. On a cloth spread out upon the grass were arranged a roast shoulder of porcupine, a delicious bowl of soup made from a piece of the same animal, cheese, butter, and biscuits, forming a most tempting repast. Having done this ample justice, we collected our cattle, and the pigeons and fowls having retired to roost on the neighboring trees, and on the steps of our ladder, we made up a glorious fire to keep off any prowling wild beasts, and ourselves lay down. The children, in spite of the novelty of the hammocks, were quickly asleep. In vain I tried to follow their example; a thousand anxious thoughts presented themselves, and as quickly as I dispelled them others rose in their place. The night wore on, and I was still awake; the fire burned low, and I rose and replenished it with dry fuel. Then again I climbed into my hammock, and toward morning fell asleep.

Early next morning we were astir, and dispersed to our various occupations. My wife milked the goats and cow, while we gave the animals their food, after which we went down to the beach to collect more wood for our building operations. To the larger beams we harnessed the cow and ass, while we ourselves dragged up the remainder. Fritz and I then ascended the tree, and finished the preparations I had begun the night before, all useless boughs we lopped off, leaving a few about six feet from the floor, from which we might sling our hammocks, and others still higher, to support a temporary roof of sailcloth. My wife made fast the planks to a rope passed through the block I had fixed to the boughs above us, and by this means Fritz and I hauled them up. These we arranged side by side on the foundation of boughs, so as to form a smooth solid floor, and round this platform built a bulwark of planks, and then

throwing the sailcloth over the higher branches, we drew it
down and firmly nailed it. Our house was thus enclosed on
three sides, for behind the great trunk protected us, while the
front was left open to admit the fresh sea breeze which blew
directly in. We then hauled up our hammocks and bedding
and slung them from the branches we had left for that purpose.
A few hours of daylight still remaining, we cleared the floor
of leaves and chips, and then descended to fashion a table
and a few benches from the remainder of the wood. After
working like slaves all day, Fritz and I flung ourselves on the
grass, while my wife arranged supper on the table we had
made.

"Come," said she at length, "come and taste flamingo stew,
and tell me how you like it. Ernest assured me that it would
be much better stewed than roasted, and I have been following
his directions."

Laughing at the idea of Ernest turning scientific cook, we
sat down. The fowls gathered round us to pick up the crumbs,
and the tame flamingo joined them, while Master Knips
skipped about from one to the other, chattering and mimick-
ing our gestures continually. To my wife's joy, the sow appeared shortly after, and was presented with all the milk that
remained from the day's stock that she might be persuaded to
return every night.

"For," said my wife, "this surplus milk is really of no use
to us, as it will be sour before the morning in this hot climate."

"You are quite right," I replied, "but we must contrive to
make it of use. The next time Fritz and I return to the wreck
we will bring off a churn among the other things we require."

"Must you really go again to that dreadful wreck?" said my
wife, shuddering. "You have no idea how anxious I am when
you are away there."

"Go we must, I am afraid," I replied, "but not for a day or
two yet. Come, it is getting late. We and the chickens must go
to roost."

We lit our watch-fires, and, leaving the dogs on guard below,
ascended the ladder. Fritz, Ernest, and Jack were up in a moment. Their mother followed very cautiously, for though she
had originated the idea of building a nest, she yet hesitated
to entrust herself at such a terrific height from the ground.

When she was safely landed in the house, taking little Franz on my back, I let go the fastenings which secured the lower end of the ladder to the ground, and swinging to and fro, slowly ascended.

Then for the first time we stood all together in our new home. I drew up the ladder, and, with a greater sense of security than I had enjoyed since we landed on the island, offered up our evening prayer, and retired for the night.

Chapter Four

NEXT morning all were early awake, and the children sprang about the tree like young monkeys.

"What shall we begin to do, father?" they cried. "What do you want us to do to-day?"

"Rest, my boys," I replied, "rest."

"Rest?" repeated they. "Why should we rest?"

" 'Six days shalt thou labor and do all that thou hast to do, but on the seventh, thou shalt do no manner of work.' This is the seventh day," I replied, "on it, therefore, let us rest."

"What, is it really Sunday?" asked Jack; "how jolly! oh, I

won't do any work; but I'll take a bow and arrow and shoot, and we'll climb about the tree and have fun all day."

"That is not resting," said I, "that is not the way you are accustomed to spend the Lord's day."

"No! but then we can't go to church here, and there is nothing else to do."

"We can worship here as well as at home," said I.

"But there is no church, no clergyman, and no organ," said Franz.

"The leafy shade of this great tree is far more beautiful than any church," I said; "there will we worship our Creator. Come, boys, down with you: turn our dining hall into a breakfast room."

The children, one by one, slipped down the ladder.

"My dear Elizabeth," said I, "this morning we will devote to the service of the Lord, and by means of a parable, I will endeavor to give the children some serious thoughts; but, without books, or the possibility of any of the usual Sunday occupations, we cannot keep them quiet the whole day; afterward, therefore, I shall allow them to pursue any innocent recreation they choose, and in the cool of the evening we will take a walk."

My wife entirely agreed with my proposal, and having breakfasted, the family assembled round me, as we sat in the pleasant shade on the fresh, soft green grass.

After singing some hymns and offering heartfelt prayers to the Almighty Giver of all good, I told the children I would relate to them a parable instead of preaching a sermon.

"Oh, that would be delightful! I like the parables in the Bible better than anything," said Franz. "When can we hear you read out of the Bible again, father?"

"Ah, my little boy, your words reproach me," returned I. "While eagerly striving to procure from the ship what would feed our bodies and provide for *their* comfort, I blush to think that I have neglected the Bread of Life, the word of God. I shall search for a Bible on my next return to the wreck: although our own books were nearly all destroyed, I am pretty sure to find one."

At these words my wife arose, and, fetching her magic bag,

she drew from it a copy of the Holy Scriptures, which I thankfully received from her hand; and, after reading aloud from its sacred pages, I spoke as follows:

"A Great King, ruling in power and splendor over a vast realm of light and love, possessed within its boundaries a desolate and unfruitful island. This spot he made the object of his special care; and, lavishing on it all the varied resources of his might and goodness, it bloomed in beauty, and became the happy residence of a band of colonists, who were charged not only with the cultivation and improvement of the soil, but each, individually, was bound to cherish in his soul the spirit of love and true allegiance to his Sovereign. While this faithful union was maintained, the colony flourished; and the noblest virtues exalted and rendered happy the existence of every member of the race. That a discontented and rebellious spirit should ever have infected these fortunate subjects of so loving a master, seems incredible, yet so it was; disobedience and pride brought misery and punishment, the fair prospects of the colony were blighted, the labors of the colonists were unblessed, and total separation from the parent kingdom seemed inevitable. A message of pardon—of free forgiveness —was nevertheless accorded to these rebels; and to all who, humbly accepting it, molded their future lives to the will of the Great King (now revealed in a character even more gracious than before), was held out the promise of removal at last from among the ruins caused by the great rebellion, to the glory and undimmed splendor of the realm of Light and Blessedness."

Having interested the children, I then, leaving allegory, pressed simply and earnestly home to each young heart the truths I sought to teach; and, with a short prayer for a blessing on my words, brought the service to a close.

After a thoughtful pause, we separated, and each employed himself as he felt disposed.

I took some arrows and endeavored to point them with porcupine quills.

Franz came to beg me make a little bow and arrow for him to shoot with, while Fritz asked my advice about the tiger cat skin and the cases he was to contrive from it. Jack assisted

with the arrow making, and inserting a sharp spine at one end
of each reed made it fast with pack-thread, and began to wish
for glue to ensure its remaining firm.

"O Jack! Mamma's soup is as sticky as anything!" cried
Franz; "shall I run and ask for a cake of it?"

"No, no, little goose! better look for some real glue in the
tool-box."

"There he will find glue, to be sure," said I, "and the soup
would scarcely have answered your purpose. But Jack, my boy,
I do not like to hear you ridicule your little brother's ideas.
Some of the most valuable discoveries have been the result of
thoughts which originally appeared no wiser than his."

While thus directing and assisting my sons, we were surprised by hearing a shot just over our heads; at the same moment two small birds fell dead at our feet, and looking up,
we beheld Ernest among the branches, as bending his face
joyfully toward us, he cried, "Well hit! well hit! a good shot,
wasn't it?"

Then slipping down the ladder, and picking up the birds,
he brought them to me. One was a kind of thrush, the other
a small dove called the ortolan, and esteemed a very great
delicacy on account of its exquisite flavor. As the figs on
which these birds came to feed were only just beginning to
ripen, it was probable that they would soon flock in numbers
to our trees; and by waiting until we could procure them in
large quantities, we might provide ourselves with valuable
food for the rainy season, by placing them, when half cooked
in cases with melted lard or butter poured over them.

By this time Jack had pointed a good supply of arrows, and
industriously practiced archery. I finished the bow and
arrows for Franz, and expected to be left in peace; but the
young man next demanded a quiver, and I had to invent that
also, to complete his equipment. It was easily done by stripping a piece of bark from a small tree, fitting a flat side and a
bottom to it, and then a string. Attaching it to his shoulders,
the youthful hunter filled it with arrows and went off; looking, as his mother said, like an innocent little Cupid, bent on
conquest.

Not long after this, we were summoned to dinner, and all
right willingly obeyed the call.

During the meal I interested the boys very much by proposing to decide on suitable names for the different spots we had visited on this coast.

"For," said I, "it will become more and more troublesome to explain what we mean, unless we do so. Beside which, we shall feel much more at home if we can talk as people do in inhabited countries: instead of saying, for instance, 'the little island at the mouth of our bay, where we found the dead shark,' 'the large stream near our tent, across which we made the bridge,' 'that wood where we found cocoanuts, and caught the monkey,' and so on. Let us begin by naming the bay in which we landed. What shall we call it?"

"Oyster Bay," said Fritz.

"No, no!—Lobster Bay," cried Jack, "in memory of the old fellow who took a fancy to my leg!"

"I think," observed his mother, "that, in token of gratitude for our escape, we should call it Safety Bay."

This name met with general approbation, and was forthwith fixed upon.

Other names were quickly chosen. Our first place of abode we called Tentholm; the islet in the bay, Shark's Island; and the reedy swamp, Flamingo Marsh. It was some time before the serious question of a name for our leafy castle could be decided. But finally it was entitled Falconhurst; and we then rapidly named the few remaining points: Prospect Hill, the eminence we first ascended; Cape Disappointment, from whose rocky heights we had strained our eyes in vain search for our ship's company; and Jackal River, as a name for the large stream at our landing place, concluded our geographical nomenclature.

In the afternoon the boys went on with their various employments. Fritz finished his cases, and Jack asked my assistance in carrying out his plans for making a cuirass for Turk out of the porcupine skin. After thoroughly cleansing the inside, we cut and fitted it round the body of the patient dog; then when strings were sewn on and it became tolerably dry, he was armed with this ingenious coat of mail, and a most singular figure he cut!

Juno strongly objected to his friendly approaches, and got out of his way as fast as she could; and it was clear that he would easily put to flight the fiercest animal he might encounter, while protected by armor at once defensive and offensive.

I determined to make also a helmet for Jack out of the remainder of the skin, which to his infinite delight I speedily did.

Amid these interesting occupations the evening drew on, and after a pleasant walk among the sweet glades near our abode, we closed our Sabbath day with prayer and a glad hymn of praise, retiring to rest with peaceful hearts.

Next morning, I proposed an expedition to Tentholm, saying I wished to make my way thither by a different route. We left the tree well armed; I and my three elder sons each carrying a gun and game bag, while little Franz was equipped with his bow and quiver full of arrows. A most curious party we formed: Fritz, adorned with his belt of margay skin, and Jack, with his extraordinary head-dress, looked like a couple of young savages. Their mother and I walked together: she, of the whole party, being the only one unarmed, carried a jar in which to get butter from Tentholm; we were preceded by the dogs—Turk armed most effectually with his cuirass of porcupine skin, and Juno keeping at a respectful distance from so formidable a companion. Master Knips fully intended to mount his charger as usual; but when he saw him arrayed apparently in a new skin, he approached him carefully, and touching him with one paw, discovered that such a hide would make anything but an agreeable seat; the grimace he made was most comical, and chattering vociferously he bounded toward Juno, skipped on her back, seated himself, and soon appeared perfectly reconciled to the change of steed. The flamingo saw us starting, and, having been much petted during the last day or two, considered himself entitled to accompany us; for some time he kept beside the children, following first one and then another as they explored the wood on either side; their irregular course, however, at length disgusted him, and, abandoning them, he walked sedately by my side. We strolled on in the cool air, following the course of the stream; the great trees overshadowed us, and the cool, green sward stretched away between them at our feet. The boys roamed ahead of me, intent on exploration. Presently I heard a joyful shout, and saw Ernest running at full speed toward me, followed by his brothers. In his hand he held a plant, and, panting for breath, and with sparkling eyes, he held it up to me.

"Potatoes! potatoes! father," he gasped out.

"Yes," said Jack, "acres and acres of potatoes!"

"My dear Ernest," said I, for there was no mistaking the flower and leaf, and the light clear-green bulbous roots, "you have indeed made a discovery; with the potato we shall never starve."

"But come and look at them," said Jack, "come and feast your eyes on thousands of potatoes."

We hurried to the spot: there, spread out before us, was a great tract of ground, covered with the precious plant.

"It would have been rather difficult," remarked Jack, "not to have discovered such a great field."

"Very likely," replied Ernest, smiling; "but I doubt if you would have discovered that it was a potato field."

"Perhaps not," said Jack, "you are quite welcome, at all events, to the honor of the discovery; I'll have the honor of being the first to get a supply of them." So saying, he dug up, with hands and knife, a number of plants, and filled his game bag with the roots. The monkey followed his example, and scratching away with his paws most cleverly, soon had a heap beside him. So delighted were we with the discovery, and so eager were we to possess a large supply of the roots, that we stopped not, digging until every bag, pouch, and pocket was filled. Some wished to return at once to Falconhurst, to cook and taste our new acquisition; but this I overruled, and we continued our march, heavily laden, but delighted.

"How," said I, "can we thank the Giver of all these blessings, sufficiently?"

"Oh," said Franz, "we can say, 'We thank thee, O Lord, for all thy goodness and mercy; and bless us for Jesus Christ's sake. Amen.'"

"That would not be sufficient," said Fritz. "Do you think it would be enough, just to say to father and mother: 'Thank you for all you do,' and not to show that we were really thankful, by loving them and doing what we can to please them?"

"You are quite right, Fritz," said I; "Franz did not say all that was necessary, he should have added, 'Give me grace to do Thy will, and to obey Thee in all things.'"

As we thus talked, we reached the head of our streamlet, where it fell from the rocks above in a beautiful, sparkling, splashing cascade. We crossed and entered the tall grass on the other side. We forced our way through with difficulty, so thick and tangled were the reeds. Beyond this, the landscape was most lovely. Rich tropical vegetation flourished on every side: the tall, stately palms, surrounded by luxuriant ferns; brilliant flowers and graceful creepers; the prickly cactus, shooting up amidst them; aloe, jasmine, and sweet-scented vanilla; the Indian pea, and above all the regal pine-apple, loaded the breath of the evening breeze with their rich perfume. The boys were delighted with the pine-apple, and so eagerly did they fall to, that my wife had to caution them that there were no doctors on our territory, and if they became ill, they would have to cure themselves as best they might.

This advice, however, seemed to have small effect on my sons, and showing Knips what they wanted, they sent him after the ripest and best fruit.

While they were thus employed, I examined the other shrubs and bushes. Among these I presently noticed one which I knew well from description to be the karatas.

"Come here, boys," I said; "here is something of far more value than your pine-apples. Do you see that plant with long pointed leaves and beautiful red flower? That is the karatas. The filaments of the leaves make capital thread, while the leaves themselves, bruised, form an invaluable salve. The pith of this wonderful plant may be used either for tinder or bait for fish. Suppose, Ernest, you had been wrecked here, how would you have made a fire without matches, or flint and steel?"

"As the savages do," replied he; "I would rub two pieces of wood together until they kindled."

"Try it," I said; "but, if you please, try it when you have a whole day before you, and no other work to be done, for I am certain it would be night before you accomplished the feat. But see here," and I broke a dry twig from the karatas, and peeling off the bark, laid the pith upon a stone. I struck a couple of pebbles over it, and they emitting a spark, the pith caught fire.

The boys were delighted with the experiment. I then drew some of the threads from the leaves, and presented them to my wife.

"But what," said Fritz, "is the use of all these other prickly plants, except to annoy one? Here, for instance, is a disagreeable little tree."

"That is an Indian fig," said I. "It grows best on dry, rocky ground; for most of its nourishment is derived from the air. Its juice is used, I believe, medicinally, while its fruit is pleasant and wholesome."

Master Jack was off in a moment when he heard of a new delicacy, and attempted to gather some of the fruit, but in vain; the sharp thorns defied his efforts, and with bleeding hands, and rueful countenance, he returned. I removed the thorns from his hands, and making a sharp wooden skewer, I thrust it into a fig, and quickly twisted it from its branch and split it open with a knife, still holding it upon the skewer. The rest followed my example, and we regaled ourselves upon the fruit, which we found excellent. Ernest carefully examined the fig he was eating. "What are these," he exclaimed presently; "little red insects! they cling all over the fruit, and I cannot shake them off. Can they be cochineal?"

He handed me the fig, and I examined it attentively.

"You are quite right, my boy," I said; "there is no doubt this is the real cochineal. However, though it is worth its weight in gold to European traders, it is of little use to us, I am afraid, unless any of you care to appear in gay colors. The cochineal, you know, forms the most lovely scarlet dye."

"No, thank you," said Jack, "but we will take a lot of it when we go home again. Now let us find something more useful to us." And they thereupon plied me incessantly with questions concerning every plant and shrub we passed.

"Stop, stop," I said at length; "the most learned naturalist would be much puzzled with many of these trees, and I who have never seen any of them before, and know them merely by description, cannot pretend to tell you the names, or explain to you the use of one-quarter of them."

Discussing, however, the properties of such shrubs as I did know, we at length reached Tentholm. Everything was safe, and we set to work to collect what we wanted. I opened the butter cask, from which my wife filled her pot. Fritz saw after the ammunition, and Jack and Ernest ran down to the beach to capture the geese and ducks. This they found no easy matter, for the birds, left so long alone, were shy, and nothing would induce them to come on shore and be caught. Ernest at length hit upon an ingenious plan. He took some pieces of cheese, and tied them to long strings. This bait he threw into the water, and the hungry ducks instantly made a grab at it; then with a little skillful maneuvering he drew them on shore. While Jack and he were thus busily employed catching and tying the rebels together by the feet, we procured a fresh supply of salt, which we packed upon Turk's back, first relieving him of his coat of mail. The birds we fastened to our game bags, and carefully closing the door of our tent, started homeward by the seashore. After a cheerful and pleasant walk, we once more reached our woodland abode. I released the birds and, clipping their wings to prevent their leaving us, established them on the stream. Then, after a delicious supper of potatoes, milk, and butter, we ascended our tree and turned in.

Having remarked a great deal of driftwood on the sands the preceding evening, it occurred to me that it would be well to get some of it, and make a kind of sledge, so that the labor of fetching what we wanted from our stores at Tentholm might not fall so heavily on ourselves.

I awoke early, and roused Ernest as my assistant, wishing to encourage him to overcome his natural fault of indolence. After a little stretching and yawning, he got up cheerfully, pleased with the idea of an expedition while the others still slept, and we made our way to the beach, taking with us the donkey, who drew a large broad bough, which I expected to find useful in bringing back our load.

As we went along, I remarked to Ernest that I supposed he was rather sorry for himself, and grudged leaving his cozy hammock and pleasant dreams at this untimely hour.

"Oh, father, do not laugh at my laziness! Indeed, I mean to cure myself of it. I am very glad to go with you. I intended to shoot some more of the ortolans this morning, but there will be plenty of time afterward. The boys will be shooting at them, I daresay, but I don't expect they will have any great luck."

"Why not, pray?" inquired I.

"I don't believe they will know what shot to use at first, and, besides, they will most likely shoot upward at the birds and be sure to miss them, on account of the great height and thickness of the branches and foliage."

"Well, Ernest, you certainly possess the gifts of prudence and reflection, as well as observation. These are valuable; but sudden action is so often necessary in life, that I advise you to cultivate the power of instantly perceiving and deciding what must be done in cases of emergency. Presence of mind is a precious quality, which, although natural in some characters, may be acquired in a certain degree by all who train themselves to it."

Once on the seashore, our work was quickly accomplished, for, selecting the wood I thought fit for my purpose, we laid it across the broad, leafy branch, and, with some help from us, the donkey dragged a very fair load of it homeward, with the addition of a small chest, which I raised from among the sand, which nearly covered it.

We heard the boys popping away at the birds as we drew near. They hastened to meet us, and inquired where we had been, looking curiously at the chest, which I allowed them to open, while I asked my wife to excuse our "absence without leave," and after submitting to her gentle reprimand, I explained my plan for a sledge, which pleased her greatly, and she already imagined it loaded with her hogshead of butter, and on its way from Tentholm to Falconhurst.

The chest proved to be merely that of a common sailor, containing his clothes, very much wetted by the sea water.

The boys exhibited an array of several dozen birds, and related, during breakfast, the various incidents of failure and success which had attended their guns. Ernest had rightly guessed the mistakes they would make, but practice was making them perfect, and they seemed disposed to continue their sport, when their mother, assuring them that she could not use more birds than those already killed, asked if I did not think some means of snaring them might be contrived, as much powder and shot would be expended if they fired on at this rate.

Entirely agreeing with this view of the subject, I desired the lads to lay aside their guns for the present, and the younger ones readily applied themselves to making snares of the long threads drawn from the leaves of the karatas, in a simple way I taught them, while Fritz and Ernest gave me substantial assistance in the manufacture of the new sledge.

We were busily at work, when a tremendous disturbance among our fowls led us to suppose that a fox or wild cat had got into their midst.

The cocks crowed defiantly, the hens fluttered and cackled in a state of the wildest excitement. We hastened toward them, but Ernest remarking Master Knips slipping away, as though conscious of some misdemeanor, went to watch him, and presently caught him in the act of eating a new-laid egg, which he had carried off and hidden among the grass and roots. Ernest found several others. These were very welcome to my wife, for hitherto the hens had not presented us with any eggs. Hereafter she determined to imprison the monkey every morning until the eggs had been collected.

Soon after this, as Jack was setting the newly made snares among the branches, he discovered that a pair of our own pigeons were building in the tree. It was very desirable to increase our stock of these pretty birds, and I cautioned the boys against shooting near our tree while they had nests there, and also with regard to the snares, which were meant only to entrap the wild fig-eaters.

Although my sons were interested in setting the snares, they by no means approved of the new order to economize the ammunition. No doubt they had been discussing this hardship, for little Franz came to me with a brilliant proposal of his own.

"Papa," said he, "why should not we begin to plant some powder and shot immediately? It would be so much more useful than bare grain for the fowls."

His brothers burst into a roar of laughter, and I must confess I found it no easy matter to keep my countenance.

"Come, Ernest," said I; "now we have had our amusement, tell the little fellow what gunpowder really is."

"It is not seed at all, Franz," Ernest explained. "Gunpow-

"A huge porcupine! a most enormous porcupine!"
(Page 72)

der is made of charcoal, sulphur, and saltpeter, mixed cleverly together; so you see it cannot be sown like corn, any more than shot can be planted like peas and beans."

My carpentering meantime went on apace. In order to shape my sledge with ends properly turned up in front, I had chosen wood which had been part of the bow of the vessel, and was curved in the necessary way for my purpose. Two pieces, perfectly similar, formed the sides of my sleigh, or sledge, and I simply united these strongly by fixing short bars across them. Then, when the ropes of the donkey's harness were attached to the raised points in front, the equipage was complete and ready for use.

My attention had been for some time wholly engrossed by my work, and I only now observed that the mother and her little boys had been busily plucking above two dozen of the wild birds, and were preparing to roast them, spitted in a row on a long, narrow sword blade, belonging to one of our ship's officers.

It seemed somewhat wasteful to cook so many at once; but my wife explained that she was getting them ready for the butter-cask I was going to fetch for her on the new sledge, as I had advised her to preserve them half-cooked, and packed in butter.

Amused at her promptitude, I could do nothing less than promise to go for her cask directly after dinner. For her part, she resolved in our absence to have a grand wash of linen and other clothes, and she advised me to arrange regular baths for all the boys in future.

Early in the afternoon Ernest and I were ready to be off, equipped as usual. Fritz presented us each with a neat case of margay skin to hang at our girdles.

We harnessed both cow and ass to the sledge, and, accompanied by Juno, cheerfully took our departure, choosing the way by the sands, and reaching Tentholm without accident or adventure.

There unharnessing the animals, we began at once to load the sledge, not only with the butter cask, but with a powder chest, a barrel of cheese, and a variety of other articles—ball, shot, tools, and Turk's armor, which had been left behind on our last visit.

Our work had so closely engaged our attention, that when we were ready to leave it and go in search of a good bathing place, we discovered that our two animals had wandered quite out of sight, having crossed the bridge to reach the good pasture beyond the river.

I sent Ernest after them, and went alone to the extremity of the bay. It terminated in bold and precipitous cliffs, which extended into the deep water, and rose abruptly, so as to form an inaccessible wall of rock and crag. Swampy ground, overgrown with large canes, intervened between me and these cliffs. I cut a large bundle of the reeds, and returned to Ernest. It was some time before I found him, comfortably extended full length on the ground near the tent, and sleeping as sound as a top, while the cow and the ass, grazing at will, were again making for the bridge.

"Get up, Ernest, you lazy fellow!" exclaimed I, much annoyed; "why don't you mind your business? Look at the animals! They will be over the river again!"

"No fear of that, father," returned he, with the utmost composure. "I have taken a couple of boards off the bridge. They won't pass the gap."

I could not help laughing at the ingenious device by which the boy had spared himself all trouble; at the same time I observed that it is wrong to waste the precious moments in sleep when duty has to be performed. I then bid him go and collect some salt, which was wanted at home, while I went to bathe.

On coming back, much refreshed, I again missed Ernest, and began to wonder whether he was still gathering salt, or whether he had lain down somewhere to finish his nap, when I heard him loudly calling:

"Father, father, I've caught a fish! an immense fellow he is. I can scarcely hold him, he drags the line so!"

Hastening toward the spot, I saw the boy lying in the grass, on a point of land close to the mouth of the stream, and with all his might keeping hold of a rod. The line was strained to the utmost by the frantic efforts of a very large fish, which was attempting to free itself from the hook.

I quickly took the rod from him, and giving the fish more line, led him by degrees into shallow water. Ernest ran in with his hatchet and killed him.

It proved to be a salmon of full fifteen pounds weight, and I was delighted to think of taking such a valuable prize to the mother.

"This is capital, Ernest!" cried I; "you have cleared yourself for once of the charge of laziness! Let us now carry this splendid salmon to the sledge. I will clean and pack it for the journey, that it may arrive in good condition, while you go and take a bath in the sea."

All this being accomplished, we harnessed our beasts to the well-laden vehicle, and replacing the boards on the bridge, commenced the journey home.

We kept inland this time, and were skirting the borders of a grassy thicket, when Juno suddenly left us, and plunging into the bushes, with fierce barking hunted out, right in front of us, the most singular-looking creature I ever beheld. It was taking wonderful flying leaps, apparently in a sitting posture, and got over the ground at an astonishing rate. I attempted to shoot it as it passed, but missed. Ernest, who was behind me, observed its movements very coolly, and seeing that the dog was puzzled, and that the animal, having paused, was crouching among the grass, went cautiously nearer, fired at the spot he had marked, and shot it dead.

The extraordinary appearance of this creature surprised us very much. It was as large as a sheep, its head was shaped like that of a mouse; its skin also was of a mouse color, it had long ears like a hare, and a tail like a tiger's. The fore-paws resembled those of a squirrel, but they seemed only half-grown, while the hind legs were enormous, and so long that, when upright on them, the animal would look as if mounted on stilts.

For some time we stood silently wondering at the remarkable creature before us. I could not recollect to have seen or heard of any such.

"Well, father," said Ernest at last, "I should say this was about the queerest beast to be met with anywhere. I am glad I knocked it over. How they will all stare when I carry it home!"

"You have had a lucky day altogether, certainly," said I; "but I cannot think what this animal can be. Examine its teeth, and let us see to what class of mammalia it belongs. We may be led to guess at its name in that way."

"I see four sharp incisor teeth, father—two upper, and two under, as a squirrel has."

"Ah! then he is a rodent. What rodents can you remember, Ernest?"

"I do not know them all, but there are the mouse, the marmot, the squirrel, the hare, the beaver, the jerboa——"

"The jerboa!" I exclaimed, "the jerboa! now we shall have it. This is really very like a jerboa, only far larger. It must be a kangaroo, one of the class of animals which has a pouch or purse beneath the body, in which its young can take refuge. They were discovered in New Holland, by the great Captain Cook, and I congratulate you on being the first to obtain a specimen in New Switzerland!" I added, laughing, as I extemporized the name.

The kangaroo was added to the already heavy load on our sledge, and we proceeded slowly, arriving late at Falconhurst, but meeting with the usual bright welcome.

Very eager and inquisitive were the glances turned toward the sledge, for the load piled on it surpassed all expectation; we on our part staring in equal surprise at the extraordinary rig of the young folks who came to meet us.

One wore a long night-shirt, which, with a belt, was a convenient length in front, but trailed behind in orthodox ghost fashion.

Another had on a very wide pair of trousers, braced up so short that each little leg looked like the clapper in a bell.

The third, buttoned up in a pea-jacket which came down to his ankles, looked for all the world like a walking portmanteau.

Amid much joking and laughter, the mother explained that she had been washing all day, and while their clothes were drying, the boys amused themselves by dressing up in things they found while rummaging the sailor's chest, and had kept them on, that Ernest and I might see the masquerade. It certainly amused us, but made me regret that so little belonging to ourselves had been saved from the wreck, in consequence of which the children had scarcely a change of linen.

Turning now to our new acquisitions, we excited great interest by exhibiting each in turn; the large salmon, but more especially the kangaroo, surprised and delighted everyone.

Fritz alone wore a look expressive of dissatisfaction, and I saw that he was envious of his younger brother's success. Vexed that so noble a prize had fallen to Ernest's gun, instead of his own, he treated it rather slightingly; but I could see that he was struggling against his jealous feelings, and he, after a while, succeeded in recovering his good humor, and joined pleasantly in the conversation.

"What a famous day's sport you have had altogether!" said he, coming close up to me. "It will be my turn to go out with you next, will it not, father? Just about here there is nothing to shoot, and I have found it very dull."

"Still you have been doing your duty, my dear boy; you were entrusted with the care of the family, and a youth of manly character will not depend for happiness on mere excitement."

As the shades of night approached, we made haste to conclude the day's work, by preparing the kangaroo, part for immediate use, and part for salting. The animals were fed, and a plentiful allowance of salt made to them. Our own supper of broiled salmon and potatoes was dispatched with great appetite, and we retired, with thankful hearts, to sound and well-earned repose.

Chapter Five

NEXT morning, while the breakfast was getting ready, I attended to the beautiful skin of the kangaroo, which I was anxious to preserve entire; and afterward, when Fritz had prepared everything in readiness for our trip to the wreck, I called Ernest and Jack in order to give them some parting injunctions. They, however, had disappeared directly after breakfast, and their mother could only guess, that, as we required potatoes, they might have gone to fetch a supply. I desired her to reprove them, on their return, for starting away without leave; but, as it appeared they had taken Turk, I satisfied myself that no harm was likely to befall them, although it was not without reluctance that I left my dear wife alone with little Franz, cheering her with hopes of our speedy return with new treasures from the wreck.

Advancing steadily on our way, we crossed the bridge at Jackal River, when suddenly, to our no small astonishment, Jack and Ernest burst out of a hiding place where they had lain in wait for us, and were enchanted with the startling effect of their unexpected appearance upon their unsuspecting father and brother. It was evident that they fully believed they might now go with us to the wreck.

To this notion I at once put a decided stop, although I could not find it in my heart to scold the two merry rogues for their thoughtless frolic, more especially as I particularly wished to send back a message to my wife. I told them they must hurry home, so as not to leave their mother in suspense, although, as they were already so far, they might collect some salt. And I instructed them to explain that, as my work on board would take up a long time, she must try to bear with our absence for a night. This I had meant to say when we parted, but my courage had failed, knowing how much she would object to such a plan, and I had resolved to return in the evening.

On consideration, however, of the importance of constructing a raft, which was my intention in going, and finishing it without a second trip, I determined to remain on board for the night, as the boys had, unintentionally, given me the chance of sending a message to that effect.

"Good-by, boys, take care of yourselves! we're off," shouted Fritz, as I joined him in the tub-boat, and we shoved off.

The current carried us briskly out of the bay; we were very soon moored safely alongside the wreck, and scrambling up her shattered sides, stood on what remained of the deck, and began at once to lay our plans.

I wanted to make a raft fit to carry on shore a great variety of articles far too large and heavy for our present boat. A number of empty water casks seemed just what was required for a foundation; we closed them tightly, pushed them overboard, and arranging twelve of them side by side in rows of three, we firmly secured them together by means of spars, and then proceeded to lay a good substantial floor of planks, which was defended by a low bulwark. In this way we soon had a first-rate raft, exactly suited to our purpose.

It would have been impossible to return to land that same evening, for we were thoroughly fatigued by our labors, and had eaten only the light refreshment we had brought in our wallets, scarcely desisting a moment from our work.

Rejoicing that we were not expected home, we now made an excellent supper from the ship's provisions, and then rested for the night on spring mattresses, a perfect luxury to us, after our hard and narrow hammocks.

Next morning we actively set about loading the raft and boat: first carrying off the entire contents of our own cabins; and passing on to the captain's room, we removed the furniture, as well as the doors and window-frames, with their bolts, bars, and locks. We next took the officers' chests, and those belonging to the carpenter and gunsmith; the contents of these latter we had to remove in portions, as their weight was far beyond our strength.

One large chest was filled with an assortment of fancy goods, and reminded us of a jeweler's shop, so glittering was the display of gold and silver watches, snuff-boxes, buckles, studs, chains, rings, and all manner of trinkets; these, and a box of money, drew our attention for a time; but more useful to us at present was a case of common knives and forks, which I was glad to find, as more suited to us than the smart silver ones we had previously taken on shore. To my delight we found, most carefully packed, a number of young fruit trees: and we read on the tickets attached to them the names, so pleasant to European ears, of the apple, pear, chestnut, orange, almond, peach, apricot, plum, cherry, and vine.

The cargo, which had been destined for the supply of a distant colony, proved, in fact, a rich and almost inexhaustible treasure to us. Ironmongery, plumber's tools, lead, paint, grindstones, cart wheels, and all that was necessary for the work of a smith's forge, spades and plowshares, sacks of maize, peas, oats, and wheat, a hand-mill, and also the parts of a saw-mill so carefully numbered that, were we strong enough, it would be easy to put it up, had been stowed away.

So bewildered were we by the wealth around us that for some time we were at a loss as to what to remove to the raft. It would be impossible to take everything; yet the first storm would complete the destruction of the ship, and we should lose all we left behind. Selecting a number of the most useful articles, however, including of course the grain and the fruit trees, we gradually loaded our raft. Fishing lines, reels, cordage, and a couple of harpoons were put on board, as well as a mariner's compass.

Fritz, recollecting our encounter with the shark, placed the harpoons in readiness; and amused me by seeming to picture himself a whaler, flourishing his harpoon in most approved fashion.

Early in the afternoon, both our crafts were heavily laden, and we were ready to make for the shore. The voyage was begun with considerable anxiety, as, with the raft in tow, there was some danger of an accident.

But the sea being calm and the wind favorable, we found we could spread the sail, and our progress was very satisfactory.

Presently, Fritz asked me for the telescope, as he had observed something curious floating at a distance. Then handing it back, he begged me to examine the object; which I soon discovered to be a turtle asleep on the water, and of course unconscious of our approach.

"Do, father, steer toward it!" exclaimed he.

I accordingly did so, that he might have a nearer look at the creature. Little did I suspect what was to follow. The lad's back was turned to me, and the broad sail was between us, so that I could not perceive his actions; when, all of a sudden, I experienced a shock, and the thrill as of line running through a reel. Before I had time to call out, a second shock, and the sensation of the boat being rapidly drawn through the water, alarmed me.

"Fritz, what are you about?" cried I, "you are sending us to the bottom."

"I have him, hurrah! I have him safe!" shouted he, in eager excitement.

To my amazement, I perceived that he really had struck the tortoise with a harpoon; a rope was attached to it, and the creature was running away with us.

Lowering the sail and seizing my hatchet, I hastened forward, in order to cut the line, and cast adrift at once turtle and harpoon.

"Father! do wait!" pleaded the boy, "there is no danger

just yet. I promise to cut the line myself the instant it is necessary! Let us catch this turtle if we possibly can."

"My dear boy, the turtle will be a very dear bargain, if he upsets all our goods into the sea, even if he does not drown us too. For Heaven's sake, be careful! I will wait a few minutes, but the minute there is danger, cut the line."

As the turtle began to make for the open sea, I hoisted the sail again; and, finding the opposition too much for it, the creature again directed its course landward, drawing us rapidly after it. The part of the shore for which the turtle was making was considerably to the left of our usual landing place. The beach there shelved very gradually, and at some distance from land we grounded with a sharp shock, but fortunately without a capsize.

The turtle was evidently greatly exhausted, and no wonder, since it had been acting the part of a steam tug, and had been dragging, at full speed, a couple of heavily laden vessels. Its intention was to escape to land; but I leaped into the water, and wading up to it, dispatched it with my ax. Such was its tenacity of life, however, that it did not cease its struggles, until I had actually severed its head from its body.

As we were by no means far from Falconhurst, Fritz gave notice of our approach by firing off his gun, as well as shouting loudly in his glee; and, while we were yet engaged in securing our boats and getting the turtle on shore, the whole family appeared in the distance, hastening eagerly toward us; and our new prize, together with the well-laden boat and raft, excited the liveliest interest; my wife's chief pleasure, however, consisted in seeing us back, as our night's absence had disturbed her, and she was horrified by the description of our dangerous run in the wake of the fugitive turtle.

Being anxious to remove some of our goods before night, the boys ran off to fetch the sledge; while I, having no anchor, contrived to moor the boats by means of some of the heavy blocks of iron we had brought.

It required our united strength to get the turtle hoisted on to the sledge, its weight being prodigious; we found it, indeed, with the addition of the sapling fruit trees, quite a sufficient load.

We then made the best of our way home, chatting merrily about our various adventures. The first thing to be done on arriving was to obtain some of the turtle's flesh and cook it for supper. To my wife this appeared necessarily a work of time, as well as of difficulty; but I turned the beast on its back, and soon detached a portion of the meat from the breast with a hatchet, by breaking the lower shell: and I then directed that it should be cooked, with a little salt, shell and all.

"But let me first cut away this disgusting green fat," said my wife, with a little shudder. "See how it sticks all over the meat. No one could eat anything so nasty."

"Leave the fat, whatever you do!" exclaimed I. "Why, my dear, that is the very best part, and the delight of the epicure. If there be really too much, cut some off—it can be used as lard, and let the dogs make a supper of the refuse.

"And the handsome shell!" cried Fritz; "I should like to make a water-trough of that, to stand near the brook, and be kept always full of clear water. How useful it would be!"

"That is a capital idea," I replied, "and we may manage it easily, if we can find clay so as to make a firm foundation on which to place it."

"Oh, as to clay," said Jack, "I have a grand lump of clay there under that root."

"Well done, my lad! when did you find it?"

"He found a bed of clay near the river this morning," said his mother, "and came home in such a mess, I had regularly to scrape his clothes and wash him thoroughly!"

"Well, mother, I can only tell you I should never in all my days have found the clay, if I had not slipped and fallen among it."

"That I can well believe," returned his mother; "only, to hear your talk this morning, one would have thought your discovery of clay the result of very arduous search indeed."

"When you have ended the question of the clay and the turtle shell," said Ernest, "I should like to show you some roots I found to-day; they are getting rather dry now. They look something like radishes, although the plant itself was almost a bush; but I have not ventured to taste them, although our sow was devouring them at a great rate."

"In that you did wisely, my boy. Swine eat many things injurious to men. Let me see your roots. How did you discover them?"

"I was rambling in the wood this morning, and came upon the sow, very busy grubbing under a small bush, and eating something ravenously; so I drove her away, and I found a number of these roots, which I brought for you to see."

"Indeed, Ernest," I exclaimed, after taking the roots in my hand and considering them attentively, "I am inclined to believe that you have really made a brilliant discovery! If this proves to be, as I expect, the manioc root, we might lose every other eatable we possess, and yet not starve. In the West Indies, cakes called cassava bread are made from it; and, already having potatoes, we shall be very independent if we can succeed in preparing flour from these roots. Great care must be taken in the manufacture to express the juice, otherwise the flour may be injurious and even poisonous.

"If we can collect a sufficient quantity, we will attempt bread-making. I think I know how to set about it."

Finding there was still time to make another trip with the sledge, I went off with the elder boys, leaving Franz with his mother; and we all looked forward with satisfaction to the prospect of the princely supper they were to have ready for us, for our day's work had been none of the lightest.

"I have been thinking about my turtle, father," said Fritz, as we went along; "is not the shell very valuable? Surely beautiful combs, boxes, and a number of ornamental things are made of tortoise shell, and if so, it seems a pity to use it for a water trough."

"Your turtle, Fritz, is only fit for eating, its shell is worthless as regards ornament; whereas the species whose shell is prized so much is unfit for food. Tortoise shell is subjected to the action of the heat, the outer layer peels off, leaving a beautifully marked, semi-transparent surface, which is susceptible of a very high polish."

The sledge quickly received its second load from the raft. Chests, four cart-wheels, and the hand-mill were placed on it, with all manner of smaller articles, and we lost no time in returning to Falconhurst.

The mother welcomed us joyfully, for she said we had been

regularly overworked during the last two days. "However, now you are come home to rest," said she, "and you little think what refreshment awaits you here in the shade. Come and see my cellar!" and she smilingly exhibited a small cask, half sunk in the ground, and well sheltered with leaves and branches.

"Ah! you wonder where this came from," continued the mother; "well, I found it myself on the sands, to-day, while you were all absent; and fancying it was wine of some sort, I got it up here on purpose to be ready for you. The boys are most anxious to know what sort of wine it will prove to be."

As the simplest method of ascertaining this, I inserted a straw at the vent-hole, and presently announced, that in all my life I had never enjoyed a more delicious draught of Canary sack. The mother was immensely pleased to find that her exertions in my behalf had not been thrown away, and the boys pressed around me, armed with straws, and begging for a taste.

After so strongly expressing my own enjoyment of the wine, it seemed unreasonable to deny them this, and I let them come in turns, but was speedily obliged to call a halt; for the rogues got so eager and excited that I had to reprove them for their greediness, and warn them of the risk they ran of being intoxicated. In fact, I blamed myself for allowing them to have this strong wine as a beverage at all. They were wholly unaccustomed to it, and were, besides, fatigued and very hungry. Supper was more to the purpose; and, as the turtle proved delicious, it was heartily enjoyed, and gave us strength to haul the mattresses we had brought from the ship up into our sleeping rooms, so that very refreshing slumbers closed the day.

Early next morning I got up without rousing any of the others, intending to pay a visit to the beach; for I had my doubts about the safety of my vessels on the open shore. The dogs were delighted when I descended the ladder, and bounded to meet me; the cocks crowed and flapped their wings; two pretty kids gamboled around; all was life and energy; the ass alone seemed disinclined to begin the day, and as I especially required his services, this was unfortunate. I put his morning dreams to flight, however, and harnessed him to the sledge; the cow, as she had not been milked, enjoyed the privilege of further repose, and, with the rest of the family, I left her dozing.

My fears as to the safety of the boats were soon dispelled, for they were all right; and, being in haste to return, the load I collected from their freight was but a light one, and the donkey willingly trotted home with it, he, as well as I, being uncommonly ready for breakfast. Approaching the tree, not a sound was to be heard, not a soul was to be seen, although it was broad day; and great was my good wife's surprise, when, roused by the clatter and hullabaloo I made, she started up, and became aware of the late hour!

"What can have made us oversleep ourselves like this?" she exclaimed. "It must be the fault of those mattresses; they are delightful, but really too lulling; see, the children are sound asleep still."

With much stretching and many yawns, the boys at last came tumbling down from the tree, rubbing their eyes and seeming but half awake; Ernest last, as usual.

"Come, my boys," said I, "this will never do! Your beds were too luxurious last night, I see." In my own opinion, however, I felt there was something else to blame besides the comfortable mattresses, and I made a mental resolve that the captain's fine Canary should be dealt with very sparingly in future. "So now for prayers and breakfast," I continued, "and then off to work. I must have our cargo landed in time to get the boats off with the next tide."

By dint of downright hard work, we accomplished this, and I got on board with Fritz as soon as they were afloat; the rest turned homeward, but Jack lingered behind with such imploring looks, that I could not resist taking him with me.

My intention had been simply to take the vessels round to the habor in Safety Bay, but the calm sea and fine weather tempted me to make another trip to the wreck. It took up more time than I expected, so that, when on board, we could only make a further examination of the cargo, collect a few portable articles, and then avail ourselves of the sea-breeze, which would fail us later in the evening.

To Jack the pleasure of hunting about in the hold was novel and charming, and very soon a tremendous rattling and clattering heralded his approach with a wheel-barrow, in the highest spirits at his good fortune in having found such a capital thing in which to bring home potatoes.

He was followed by Fritz, whose news was still more important. He had found, carefully packed and enclosed within partitions, what appeared to be the separate parts of a pinnace, with rigging and fittings complete, even to a couple of small brass guns. This was a great discovery, and I hastened to see if the lad was right. Indeed he was, but my pleasure was qualified by a sense of the arduous task it would be to put such a craft together so as to be fit for sea. For the present we had barely time to get something to eat and hurry into the boat, where were collected our new acquisitions, namely, a copper boiler, iron plates, tobacco-graters, two grindstones, a small barrel of powder, and another of flints, two wheel-barrows, besides Jack's, which he kept under his own especial care.

As we drew near the shore, we were surprised to see a number of little figures ranged in a row along the water's edge, and apparently gazing fixedly at us. They seemed to wear dark coats and white waistcoats, and stood quite still with their arms dropping by their sides, only every now and then one would extend them gently, as though longing to embrace us.

"Ah! here at last come the pigmy inhabitants of the country to welcome us!" cried I, laughing.

"Oh, father!" exclaimed Jack, "I hope they are Lilliputians! I once read in a book about them, so there must be such people, you know, only these look rather too large."

"You must be content to give up the Lilliputians and accept penguins, my dear Jack," said I. "We have not before seen them in such numbers, but Ernest knocked one down, if you remember, soon after we landed. They are excellent swimmers, but helpless on land, as they can neither fly nor run."

We were gradually approaching the land as I spoke, and no sooner was the water shallow, than out sprang Jack from his tub, and wading ashore, took the unsuspecting birds by surprise, and with his stick laid half a dozen, right and left, either stunned or dead at his feet. The rest escaped into the water, dived, and disappeared.

As these penguins are disagreeable food, on account of their strong, oily taste, I was sorry Jack had attacked them; but going to examine them when we landed, some of the fallen arose from their swoon, and began solemnly to waddle away, upon which we caught them, and tying their feet together with long grass, laid them on the sand to wait until we were ready to start.

The three wheel-barrows then each received a load, the live penguins, seated gravely, were trundled along by Jack, and away we went at a great rate.

The unusual noise of our approach set the dogs barking furiously, but discovering us, they rushed forward with such forcible demonstrations of delight, that poor little Jack, who, as it was, could scarcely manage his barrow, was fairly upset, penguins and all. This was too much for his patience, and it was absurd to see how he started up and cuffed them soundly for their boisterous behavior.

This scene, and the examination of our burdens, caused great merriment: the tobacco-grater and iron plates evidently puzzling everybody.

I sent the boys to catch some of our geese and ducks, and bid them fasten a penguin to each by the leg, thinking that it was worth while to try to tame them.

My wife had exerted herself in our absence to provide a good store of potatoes, and also of manioc root. I admired her industry, and little Franz said, "Ah, father! I wonder what you will say when mother and I give you some Indian corn, and melons, and pumpkins, and cucumbers!"

"Now, you little chatterbox!" cried she, "you have let out my secret! I was to have the pleasure of surprising your father when my plants were growing up."

"Ah, the poor disappointed little mother!" said I. "Never mind! I am charmed to hear about it. Only do tell me, where did those seeds come from?"

"Out of my magic bag, of course!" replied she. "And each time I have gone for potatoes, I have sown seeds in the ground which was dug up to get them; and I have planted potatoes also."

"Well done, you wise little woman!" I exclaimed. "Why, you are a model of prudence and industry!"

"But," continued she, "I do not half like the appearance of those tobacco-graters you have brought. Is it possible you are going to make snuff? Do, pray, let us make sure of abundance of food for our mouths, before we think of our noses!"

"Make your mind easy, my wife," said I. "I have not the remotest intention of introducing the dirty, ridiculous habit of snuffing into your family! Please to treat my graters with respect, however, because they are to be the means of providing you with the first fresh bread you have seen this many a long day."

"What possible connection can there be between bread and tobacco-graters? I cannot imagine what you mean, and to talk of bread where there are no ovens is only tantalizing."

"Ah, you must not expect real loaves," said I. "But on these flat iron plates I can bake flat cakes or scones, which will be excellent bread; I mean to try at once what I can do with Ernest's roots. And first of all, I want you to make me a nice strong canvas bag."

This the mother willingly undertook to do, but she evidently had not much faith in my powers as a baker, and I saw her set on a good potful of potatoes before beginning to work, as though to make sure of a meal without depending on my bread.

Spreading a piece of sailcloth on the ground, I summoned my boys to set to work. Each took a grater and a supply of well-washed manioc root, and when all were seated round the cloth —"Once, twice, thrice! Off!" cried I, beginning to rub a root as hard as I could against the rough surface of my grater. My example was instantly followed by the whole party, amid bursts of merriment, as each remarked the funny attitude and odd gestures of his neighbors while vehemently rubbing, rasping, grating, and grinding down the roots allotted to him. No one was tempted by the look of the flour to stop and taste it, for in truth it looked much like wet sawdust.

"Cassava bread is highly esteemed in many parts of the New World, and I have even heard that some Europeans there prefer it to the wheaten bread of their own country. There are various species of manioc. One sort grows quickly, and its roots ripen in a very short time. Another kind is of somewhat slower growth. The roots of the third kind do not come to maturity for two years. The two first are poisonous, if eaten raw, yet they are preferred to the third, which is harmless, because they are so much more fruitful, and the flour produced is excellent, if the scrapings are carefully pressed."

"What is the good of pressing them, father?" inquired Ernest.

"It is in order to express the sap, which contains the poison. The dry pith is wholesome and nourishing. Still, I do not mean to taste my cakes, until I have tried their effect on our fowls and the ape."

By this time our supply of roots being reduced to damp powder, the canvas bag was filled with it, and tying it tightly up, I attempted to squeeze it, but soon found that mechanical aid was necessary in order to express the moisture. My arrangements for this purpose were as follows: A strong, straight beam was made flat on one side, smooth planks were laid across two of the lower roots of our tree; on these we placed the sack, above the sack another plank, and over that the long beam; one end was passed under a root near the sack, the other projected far forward. And to that we attached all the heaviest weights we could think of, such as an anvil, iron bars, and masses of lead. The consequent pressure on the bag was enormous, and the sap flowed from it to the ground.

"Will this stuff keep any time?" inquired my wife, who came to see how we were getting on. "Or must all this great bagful be used at once? In that case we shall have to spend the whole of to-morrow in baking cakes."

"Not at all," I replied; "once dry, the flour in barrels will keep fresh a long time. We shall use a great deal of this, however, as you shall see."

"Do you think we might begin now, father?" said Fritz. "There does not seem the least moisture remaining."

"Certainly," said I. "But I shall only make one cake to-day for an experiment; we must see how it agrees with Master Knips and the hens before we set up a bakehouse in regular style."

I took out a couple of handfuls of flour for this purpose, and with a stick loosened and stirred the remainder, which I intended should again be pressed. While an iron plate, placed over a good fire, was getting hot, I mixed the meal with water and a little salt, kneaded it well, and forming a thickish cake, laid it on the hot plate, when one side presently becoming a nice yellow-brown color, it was turned and was quickly baked.

It smelt so delicious that the boys quite envied the two hens and the monkey, who were selected as the subjects of this interesting experiment, and they silently watched them gobbling up the bits of cake I gave them, until Fritz turned to me, saying, "Suppose the cake is poisonous, what effect will it have on the creatures? Will they be stupefied, or will they suffer pain?"

"That depends upon the nature of the poison. Some cause violent pain, as colchicum, hellebore, and aconite. Others produce stupefaction and paralysis, as opium, hemlock, and prussic acid; while others again, as strychnine, are followed by violent convulsions, or, as belladonna, by delirium. The effects of course vary according to the quantity taken, and such remedies should be applied as will best counteract the effect of each poison: emetics in any case, to remove as much as possible of the noxious substance, combined with oils and mucilaginous drinks to soothe and protect the stomach in the case of irritants; stimulants, such as spirits, ammonia, or strong coffee to rouse from the stupor of the narcotics; and sedative drugs, which are perhaps in themselves poisons, to counteract the over stimulation of the nerves caused by the convulsant poisons. But now let us think no more of poisons; here is supper ready and we need not be afraid to eat roast penguin and potatoes."

No sooner said than done; we left the fowls picking up the least crumb they could find of the questionable food, and assembled to enjoy our evening meal. The potatoes were as usual, excellent, the penguin really not so bad as I expected, although fishy in taste and very tough.

Next morning everyone expressed the tenderest concern as to the health of Knips and the hens; and lively pleasure was in every countenance when Jack, who ran first to make the visit of inquiry, brought news of their perfect good health and spirits.

No time was now to be lost, and the bread-baking commenced in earnest. A large fire was kindled, the plates heated, the meal made into cakes, each of the boys busily preparing his own, and watching the baking most eagerly. Mistakes occurred, of course; some of the bread was burnt, some not done enough; but a pile of nice, tempting cakes was at length ready, and with plenty of good milk we breakfasted right royally, and in high spirits at our success.

Soon after, while feeding the poultry with the fragments of the repast, I observed that the captive penguins were quite at ease among them and as tame as the geese and ducks; their bonds were therefore loosed, and they were left as free as the other fowls.

Chapter Six

HAVING now discovered how to provide bread for my family, my thoughts began to revert to the wreck and all the valuables yet contained within it. Above all, I was bent on acquiring possession of the beautiful pinnace, and aware that our united efforts would be required to do the necessary work, I began to coax and persuade the mother to let me go in force with all her boys except Franz.

She very unwillingly gave her consent at last, but not until I had faithfully promised never to pass a night on board. I did so with reluctance, and we parted, neither feeling quite satisfied with the arrangement.

The boys were delighted to go in so large a party, and

merrily carried provision bags filled with cassava bread and potatoes.

Reaching Safety Bay without adventure we first paid a visit to the geese and ducks which inhabited the marsh there, and having fed them and seen they were thriving well, we buckled on each his cork belt, stepped into the tub-boat, and, with the raft in tow, steered straight for the wreck.

When he got on board, I desired the boys to collect whatever came first to hand, and load the raft to be ready for our return at night, and then we made a minute inspection of the pinnace.

I came to the conclusion that difficulties, well-nigh insuperable, lay between me and the safe possession of the beautiful little vessel. She lay in a most un-get-at-able position at the further end of the hold, stowed in so confined and narrow a space, that it was impossible to think of fitting the parts together there. At the same time these parts were so heavy, that removing them to a convenient place piece by piece was equally out of the question.

I sent the boys away to amuse themselves by rummaging out anything they liked to carry away, and sat down quietly to consider the matter.

As my eyes became used to the dim light which entered the compartment through a chink or crevice here and there, I perceived how carefully every part of the pinnace was arranged and marked with numbers, so that if only I could bestow sufficient time on the work, and contrive space in which to execute it, I might reasonably hope for success.

"Room! room to work in, boys! that's what we need in the first place!" I cried, as my sons came to see what plan I had devised, for so great was their reliance on me that they never doubted the pinnace was to be ours.

"Fetch axes, and let us break down the compartment and clear space all round."

To work we all went, yet evening drew near, and but little impression was made on the mass of woodwork around us. We had to acknowledge that an immense amount of labor and perseverance would be required before we could call ourselves the owners of the useful and elegant little craft, which lay within this vast hulk like a fossil shell embedded in a rock.

Preparations for returning to shore were hastily made, and we landed without much relish for the long walk to Falconhurst, when, to our great surprise and pleasure, we found the mother and little Franz at Tentholm awaiting us. She had resolved to take up her quarters there during the time we should be engaged on the wreck. "In that way you will live nearer your work, and I shall not quite lose sight of you!" said she, with a pleasant smile.

"You are a good, sensible, kind wife," I exclaimed, delighted with her plan, "and we shall work with the greater diligence, that you may return as soon as possible to your dear Falconhurst."

"Come and see what we have brought you, mother!" cried Fritz; "a good addition to your stores, is it not?" and he and his brothers exhibited two small casks of butter, three of flour, corn, rice, and many other articles welcome to our careful housewife.

Our days were now spent in hard work on board, first cutting and clearing an open space round the pinnace, and then putting the parts together. We started early and returned at night, bringing each time a valuable freight from the old vessel.

At length, with incredible labor, all was completed. The pinnace stood actually ready to be launched, but imprisoned within massive wooden walls which defied our strength.

It seemed exactly as though the graceful vessel had awakened from sleep, and was longing to spring into the free blue sea, and spread her wings to the breeze. I could not bear to think that our success so far should be followed by failure and disappointment. Yet no possible means of setting her free could I conceive, and I was almost in despair, when an idea occurred to me which, if I could carry it out, would effect her release without further labor or delay.

Without explaining my purpose, I got a large cast-iron mortar, filled it with gunpowder, secured a block of oak to the top, through which I pierced a hole for the insertion of the match, and this great petard I so placed, that when it exploded it should blow out the side of the vessel next which the pinnace lay. Then securing it with chains, that the recoil might do no damage, I told the boys I was going ashore earlier than usual, and calmly desired them to get into the boat. Then lighting a match I had prepared, and which would burn some time before reaching the powder, I hastened after them with a beating heart, and we made for the land.

We brought the raft close in shore and began to unload it; the other boat I did not haul up, but kept her ready to put off at a moment's notice; my anxiety was unobserved by anyone, as I listened with strained nerves for the expected sound. It came!—a flash! a mighty roar—a grand burst of smoke!

My wife and children, terror-stricken, turned their eyes toward the sea, whence the startling noise came, and then, in fear and wonder, looked at me for some explanation. "Perhaps," said the mother, as I did not speak, "perhaps you have left a light burning near some of the gunpowder, and an explosion has taken place."

"Not at all unlikely," replied I quietly; "we had a fire below when we were caulking the seams of the pinnace. I shall go off at once and see what has happened. Will anyone come?"

The boys needed no second invitation, but sprang into the boat, while I lingered to re-assure my wife by whispering a few words of explanation, and then joining them, we pulled for the wreck at a more rapid rate than we ever had done before.

No alteration had taken place in the side at which we usually boarded her, and we pulled round to the further side, where a marvelous sight awaited us. A huge rent appeared, the decks and bulwarks were torn open, the water was covered with floating wreckage—all seemed in ruins; and the compartment where the pinnace rested was fully revealed to view. There sat the little beauty, to all appearance uninjured; and the boys, whose attention was taken up with the melancholy scene of ruin and confusion around them, were astonished to hear me shout in enthusiastic delight: "Hurrah! she is ours! The lovely pinnace is won! we shall be able to launch her easily after all. Come, boys, let us see if she has suffered from the explosion which has set her free."

The boys gazed at me for a moment, and then guessing my secret, "You planned it yourself, you clever, cunning father! Oh, that machine we helped to make was on purpose to blow it up!" cried they; and eagerly they followed me into the shattered opening, where, to my intense satisfaction, I found everything as I could wish, and the captive in no way a sufferer from the violent measures I had adopted for her deliverance.

The boys were deeply interested in examining the effects of the explosion, and in the explanation I gave them of the principle and proper way to manage a petard.

It was evident that the launch could now be effected without much trouble; I had been careful to place rollers beneath the keel, so that by means of levers and pulleys we might, with our united strength, move her forward toward the water. A rope was attached by which to regulate the speed of the descent, and then, all hands putting their shoulders to the work, the pinnace began to slide from the stocks, and finally slipped gently and steadily into the water, where she floated as if conscious it was her native element; while we, wild with excitement, cheered and waved enthusiastically. We then only remained long enough to secure our prize carefully at the most sheltered point, and went back to Tentholm, where we accounted for the explosion; saying that having blown away one side of the ship, we should be able to obtain the rest of its contents with a very few more days' work.

These days were devoted to completing the rigging, the mounting of her two little brass guns, and all necessary arrangements about the pinnace. It was wonderful what martial ardor was awakened by the possession of a vessel armed with two real guns. The boys chattered incessantly about savages, fleets of canoes, attack, defense, and final annihilation of the invaders.

I assured them that, brilliant as their victories would doubtless be, we should have good cause to thank God if their fighting powers and new-born valor were never put to the test.

The pinnace was fully equipped and ready to sail, while yet no idea of the surprise we were preparing for her had dawned upon my wife, and I permitted the boys, who had kept the secret so well, to fire a salute when we entered the bay.

Casting off from the ship, and spreading the sail, our voyage began. The pinnace glided swiftly through the water. I stood at the helm, Ernest and Jack manned the guns, and Fritz gave the word of command, "Fire!" Bang! bang! rattled out a thrilling report, which echoed and re-echoed among the cliffs, followed by our shouts and hurrahs.

The mother and her little boy rushed hastily forward from near the tent, and we could plainly see their alarm and aston-ishment; but speedily recognizing us, they waved joyfully, and came quickly to the landing place to meet us.

By skillful management we brought the pinnace near a pro-jection of the bank, and Fritz assisted his mother to come on board, where, breathless with haste and excitement, she ex-claimed, "You dear, horrid, wonderful people, shall I scold you or praise you? You have frightened me out of my wits! To see a beautiful little ship come sailing in was startling enough, for I could not conceive who might be on board, but the report of your guns made me tremble with fear—and had I not recognized your voices directly after, I should have run away with Franz—Heaven knows where! But have you really done all this work yourselves?" she continued, when we had been forgiven for terrifying her with our vainglorious salute. "What a charming little yacht! I should not be afraid to sail in this myself."

After the pinnace had been shown off, and received the ad-miration she deserved, while our industry, skill, and persever-ance met with boundless praise: "Now," said my wife, "you must come with me, and see how little Franz and I have im-proved our time every day of your absence."

We all landed, and with great curiosity followed the mother up the river toward the cascade; where, to our astonishment, we found a garden neatly laid out in beds and walks; and she continued, "We don't frighten people by firing salutes in honor of our performances; although, by and by, I too shall want fire in a peaceable form. Look at my beds of lettuce and cabbages, my rows of beans and peas! Think what delicious dinners I shall be able to cook for you, and give me credit for my diligence."

"My dear wife!" I exclaimed, "this is beautiful! You have done wonders! Did you not find the work too hard?"

"The ground is light and easy to dig hereabouts," she re-plied. "I have planted potatoes, and cassava roots; there is space for sugar-canes, and the young fruit trees, and I shall want you to contrive to irrigate them, by leading water from the cascades in hollow bamboos. Up by the sheltering rocks

I mean to have pine-apples and melons; they will look splendid when they spread there. To shelter the beds of European vegetables from the heat of the sun, I have planted seeds of maize around them. The shadow of the tall plants will afford protection from the burning rays. Do you think that is a good plan?"

"I do, indeed; the whole arrangement is capital. Now, as sunset approaches, we must return to the tent for supper and rest, for both of which we are all quite ready."

The time passed in happy talk over our many new interests; everyone had the pleasant sensation which attends successful labor, as well as experiencing the joy of affording unexpected pleasure to others; and I especially pointed out to my sons how true, genuine happiness consists in that, rather than in mere self-gratification.

Next morning, my wife said: "If you can exist on shore long enough to visit Falconhurst, dear husband, I should like you to attend to the little fruit trees. I fear they have been too much neglected. I have watered them occasionally, and spread earth over the roots as they lay, but I could not manage to plant them."

"You have done far more than I could have expected, my wife," I replied, "and provided you do not ask me to give up the sea altogether, I most willingly agree to your request, and will go to Falconhurst as soon as the raft is unloaded, and everything safely arranged here."

Life on shore was an agreeable change for us all, and the boys went actively to work, so that the stores were quickly brought up to the tent, piled in order, and carefully covered with sailcloths, fastened down by pegs all round. The pinnace being provided with an anchor, was properly moored, and her elegant appearance quite altered the looks of our harbor, hitherto occupied only by the grotesque tub-boat, and flat, uninteresting raft.

Taking an ample supply of everything we should require at Falconhurst, we were soon comfortably re-established in that charming abode, its peaceful shade seeming more delightful than ever, after the heat and hard work we had lately undergone.

Several Sundays had passed during our stay at Tentholm, and the welcome Day of Rest now returned again, to be observed with heartfelt devotion and grateful praise.

I did not attempt too much in the form of preaching, as I could not have secured the attention of my hearers to any long-winded discourse, but they were interested in the Bible reading and simple instructions I drew from it, and their young voices joined sweetly in favorite hymns, which my wife sang from memory.

In the evening I desired the boys to let me see their dexterity in athletic exercises, such as running, leaping, wrestling, and climbing; telling them they must keep up the practice of these things, so as to grow strong, active men, powerful to repel and cope with danger, as well as agile and swift-footed to escape from it. No man can be really courageous and self-reliant without an inward consciousness of physical power and capability.

"I want to see my sons strong, both morally and physically," said I; "that means, little Franz," as the large blue eyes looked inquiringly up at me, "brave to do what is good and right, and to hate evil, and strong to work, hunt, and provide for themselves and others, and to fight if necessary."

On the following day, the boys seeming disposed to carry out my wishes by muscular exercise of all sorts, I encouraged them by saying I meant to prepare a curious new weapon for them, only they must promise not to neglect the practice of archery; as to their guns, I had no reason to fear they would be laid aside.

Taking a long cord, I attached a leaden bullet to each end and had instantly to answer a storm of questions as to what this could possibly be for.

"This is a miniature lasso," said I; "the Mexicans, Patagonians, and various tribes of South America, make use of this weapon in hunting, with marvelous dexterity, only, having no bullets, they fasten stones to their ropes, which are immensely longer than this. One end is swung round and round the mounted hunter's head, and then cast with skill and precision toward the animal he wishes to strike; immediately drawing it back, he can repeat the blow, and either kill or wound his prey. Frequently, however, the intention is to take the animal, wild horse, or buffalo, or whatever it may be, alive; and in that case, the lasso is thrown, while riding in hot pursuit, in such a way as to make the stone twist many times round the neck, body, or legs of the fugitive, arresting him even in full career."

"Oh, father, what a splendid contrivance! Will you try it now? There is the donkey, father! do catch the donkey."

Not at all certain of my powers, I declined to practice upon a live subject, but consented to make a trial of skill by aiming at the stump of a tree at no great distance.

My success surpassed my own expectations; the stump was entwined by the cord in such a way as to leave no doubt whatever as to the feasibility of the wonderful performances I described, and I was assailed by petitions from the boys, each anxious to possess a lasso of his own without a moment's delay.

As the manufacture was simple, their wishes were speedily gratified, and lasso practice became the order of the day.

Fritz, who was the most active and adroit, besides having, of course, the greatest muscular strength, soon became skilled in the art.

That night a change came over the weather, and early next morning I perceived that a gale of wind was getting up. From the height of our trees I could see that the surface of the sea was in violent agitation.

It was with no small satisfaction that I thought of our hard-won pinnace, safely moored in the harbor, and recollected that there was nothing to call us to the wreck for the next few days.

My attention was by no means monopolized by my sons and their amusements. The good mother had much to show me demanding my approval, advice, or assistance, as the case might be.

A good supply of wild pigeons and ortolans had been snared, partly cooked, and preserved in lard. Of these she showed me her small cask well filled.

Then the nests of various pairs of tame pigeons were exhibited, but her chief care was the unpromising condition of her dear little fruit trees, for, having been forgotten, they were so dry and withered, that unless planted without further delay, she feared we should lose them.

This needful work we set about, therefore, at once, proposing afterward an excursion to the Calabash Wood, in order to manufacture a large supply of vessels and utensils of all sorts and sizes.

Everyone was inclined for this expedition; consequently the planting of the orchard was carried on with surprising vigor, but was not completed until toward evening; and then all sorts of arrangements were made for an early start next day. The mother and Franz were to be of the party, and their equipment took some time, for we meant to make a grand family excursion, attended by our domestic pets and servants!

By sunrise we were all astir, and everything quickly made ready for a start.

The sledge, loaded with ammunition and baskets of provisions, and drawn by the donkey, was to be used for carrying home our gourd manufactures, as well as any other prize we might fall in with.

Turk, as usual, headed the procession, clad in his coat of mail.

Then came the boys with their guns and game bags. Their mother and I followed, and behind trotted Juno, not in very good spirits, poor dog! because Master Knips, who had no idea of being left alone, must needs ride on her back.

On this occasion I took two guns with me, one loaded with shot for game, another with ball for our defense against beasts of prey.

Flamingo Marsh was quickly crossed, and the magnificent country beyond lay extended in all its beauty and fertility before our eyes. It was new to my wife and two of the boys, and the lovely prospect enchanted them.

Here Fritz and Jack turned aside into the bush, where presently loud barking was followed by the quick report of a gun, and a large bird, which had risen from thicket, fell heavily to the ground before us. Far from resigning itself, however, to death or captivity, it sprang to its feet, and, unable to fly, rushed away with extraordinary speed, hotly pursued by the excited dog, while Fritz ran, panting, in the same direction, and Juno, eager to join the chase, sprang aside so suddenly that her rider was flung unceremoniously on the sand, as she

A grand family excursion. (Page 128)

darted to intercept the retreat of the active bird. This she cleverly accomplished, but its defense was maintained so fiercely, as it struck out with its powerful legs and sharp claws, that neither Fritz nor the dogs could master it.

I hastened to their assistance, and found Juno holding on nobly by the wing she had seized, while the bird, which proved to be a magnificent bustard, struggled and fought fiercely. Watching my opportunity, I threw a large handkerchief over it, and with difficulty succeeded in binding its legs and wings. It was borne in triumph to the rest of our party, who meantime had been reclining on the sand.

"What have you got?" "What has Fritz shot?" cried the boys, starting up at our approach. "A bustard! oh, that is splendid!"

"To be sure, it is the one we missed that day, don't you remember, mother? Ah, ha! old fellow, you are done for this time!" said Jack.

"I think this is a hen bustard; it is the mother bird," said Ernest.

"Ah, yes, poor thing!" exclaimed my wife, in a tone of concern; "it is most likely the same, and I know she had a brood of young birds, and now they will be left unprotected and miserable. Had we not better let her go?"

"Why, my dear, kind-hearted wife, that was weeks and weeks ago! Those little birds are all strong and big by this time, and I dare say Mrs. Bustard here has forgotten all about them. Besides, she is badly wounded, and we must try to cure the hurt. If we succeed, she will be a valuable addition to our poultry yard; if we cannot, you shall roast her for dinner."

Resuming our march, we next arrived at the Monkey Grove, which was the scene of the tragi-comic adventure by which Fritz became the guardian of the orphan ape.

While he amused us all by a lively and graphic description of the scene, Ernest was standing apart under a splendid cocoanut palm, gazing in fixed admiration at the grand height of the stem, and its beautiful, graceful crown of leaves. The cluster of nuts beneath these evidently added interest to the spectacle, for, drawing quietly near him, I heard a long-drawn sigh, and the words:

"It's awfully high! I wish one would fall down!"

Scarcely had he uttered these words, than, as if by magic, down plumped a huge nut at his feet.

The boy was quite startled, and sprang aside, looking timidly upward, when, to my surprise, down came another.

"Why, this is just like the fairy tale of the wishing cap!" said Ernest. "My wish is granted as soon as formed!"

"I suspect the fairy in this instance is more anxious to pelt us and drive us away than to bestow dainty gifts upon us," said I. "I think there is most likely a cross-grained old ape sitting up among those shadowy leaves and branches."

We examined the nuts, thinking they were perhaps old ones, and had fallen, in consequence, naturally, but they were not even quite ripe.

Anxious to discover what was in the tree, we all surrounded it, gaping and gazing upward with curious eyes.

"Hullo! I see him!" shouted Fritz presently. "Oh, a hideous creature! what can it be? flat, round, as big as a plate, and with a pair of horrid claws! Here he comes! He is going to creep down the tree!"

At this, little Franz slipped behind his mother, Ernest took a glance round to mark a place of retreat, Jack raised the butt-end of his gun, and every eye was fixed on the trunk of the tree, down which a large land-crab commenced a leisurely descent. As it approached within reach, Jack hit at it boldly, when it suddenly dropped the remaining distance, and opening its great claws, sidled after him with considerably rapidity, upon which he fairly turned tail and ran. We all burst into a roar of laughter, which soon made him face about, and then, to our infinite amusement, the little fellow prepared for a fresh onset; laying down all he was carrying, pulling off his jacket and spreading it wide out in both hands, he returned to the charge, suddenly threw his garment over the creature, wrapped it well round it, and then pummeled it with all the strength of his fists.

For a few minutes I could do nothing but laugh, but then running to him with my hatchet, I struck several sharp blows on his bundle, which we opened carefully, and found within the land-crab perfectly dead.

"Well, this is an ugly rascal!" cried Jack; "if he hadn't been

so hideous, I should not have dealt so severely with him. I wasn't a bit afraid. What is the creature's name?"

"This is a crab, a land-crab," said I, "of which there are many varieties, and this, I think, is called a cocoanut crab, or at least it deserves the name, for it is evidently very fond of eating these nuts, since it takes the trouble to climb the trees for them; the difficulty of getting at the kernel, too, is considerable. You showed no little presence of mind, Jack, when you thought of catching it in your jacket; in fact, it might have been more than a match for you otherwise, for some are most determined fighters, and are very swift, too. Now let us take it, as well as the nuts, to the sledge, and go on our way."

Progress became difficult, for we were constantly stopped in passing through the wood, by having to cut away the hanging boughs and creeping plants which interlaced them. Ernest was behind, and by-and-by called me back to see what proved to be an important discovery; from the several stalks of one of these creepers flowed clear, cold water, and I recognized the "liane rouge," which is known in America, and is so precious to the thirsty hunter or traveler. This is truly one of God's good gifts to man!

The boys were much delighted with this curious plant. "Only fancy, mother," said Ernest, as he showed it to her, "how cheering and refreshing to find this if one were lost and alone in a vast forest, wandering for days and days without being near a natural spring of water."

"But are you certain it is safe to drink this?" asked she.

I assured her it was so, and advised the boys to cut enough to quench the thirst of the whole party, including our animals. This they did, only finding it necessary, as with the sugar canes, to cut air holes above the joints.

After struggling onward for a short time, we emerged from the thickets into open ground, and saw the calabash trees in the distance. As we drew near, their curious appearance and singular fruit caused much surprise and also amusement, for we were speedily established among the trees, where, as I chose and cut down the gourds most likely to be useful, everyone engaged merrily in the work of cutting, carving, sawing, and scooping some manner of dish, bowl, cup, jar, or platter, according to his taste or ability.

We were to dine here, and after a time Fritz and Jack began to prepare a fireplace, their great ambition being to heat the stones red hot, and cook the crab in a hollow gourd. Their mother, therefore, left them to their own devices, and attended to the hungry animals, unharnessing the ass to graze, and giving cocoanut milk to the poor little monkey, who had been obliged to travel in a covered basket for some time, lest he should be lost in the woods. The wounded bustard had been completely forgotten, and from heat and thirst was suffering greatly until her friendly care revived it, and it was tied to a tree and allowed to move about, its fierce spirit greatly tamed by adversity.

The cooking operations came to a stand soon after the fire was lighted, for it appeared that we had no more water in the jars we had brought, so the boys proposed to go in search of a spring. I agreed to accompany them; Ernest also wished to join us, and as our intention was to examine merely the surrounding wood, I saw no objection to leaving their mother and Franz for a short time.

Very soon after our exploration began, Ernest, who was in front, turned with a face of terror, shouting, "A wild boar! an immense wild boar, father! Do come, quick!" And sure enough, I heard a loud snorting and puffing as some large animal passed hastily through the thick underwood beyond us. "After him lads, after him!" cried I, hurrying forward. "Call the dogs! stand ready to fire!" And we pressed through the bushes to the spot where Ernest had seen the creature. The ground was grubbed up, and some potatoes lay about, showing that we had disturbed him at his mid-day meal. Ernest and Jack were more disposed to gather the roots than to follow up the chase. Fritz and I alone went after the dogs, who eagerly pushed on, and by the sounds we heard had evidently attacked the boar at no great distance. Terrific barking, snarling, and grunting guided us to the scene of action, and we beheld our mastiffs one on each side of a large respectable-looking pig, holding on by the great ears, while the animal, on seeing us, appeared rather to beseech our interference than to propose to offer a desperate resistance.

In a moment the truth became apparent! The captive grunter was no fierce native of the forest, but our own runaway sow! Our excitement had been wound to so high a pitch that the discovery was quite a shock, and we felt half angry with the creature who had disappointed us; then the absurdity of the whole thing made us laugh heartily, and calling off the dogs, the old lady was released from her ignominious position. Our laughter resounding through the wood, brought Ernest and Jack from their potatoes, to see what was going on.

"Much use you two would have been suppose we had required help," cried Fritz, as they recognized their old friend.

"Ah, well, you see," returned Jack, "Ernest and I had a sort of a kind of presentiment that this was going to be the old sow. And just look at our fine potatoes!"

A good deal of joking on the subject ensued, but was interrupted by Ernest, who drew our attention to fruit resembling apples on the surrounding bushes, and on the grass beneath them.

The sow was making amends for the fright and pain she had endured by munching and crunching this fruit at a great rate. Fritz feared that it might be the poisonous manchineel, against which I once warned them, but on examining it, I was induced to pronounce a more favorable opinion, and we collected a quantity in hopes that, if the monkey approved of it as well as the old sow, we might be able to enjoy a feast ourselves.

All this time not a drop of water had we seen, and our own thirst increasing, we felt eager to procure some before returning to our resting-place.

Jack preceded us, and we made our way toward a high rock, which rose above the thickets, when he suddenly startled us by a loud cry of "A crocodile! father! father! A crocodile!"

"Nonsense, boy! A crocodile, of all things, in this dry, parched forest, where we can't get so much as a mouthful of water!"

On advancing to where Jack stood, I perceived that his mistake was not so very silly after all, for I beheld an iguana, one of the largest of the lizard species, and a truly formidable-looking fellow. I was glad to assure Jack that the strange creature he had found was perfectly harmless, and that its flesh being esteemed a delicacy, it would be a valuable prize to carry back with us.

In another moment Fritz would have fired, but arresting his

hand, "Your shot," I said, "would probably only wound the animal, and being extremely tenacious of life, it would certainly escape; we must gain possession of the sleeping beauty by a gentler method."

"You are not going to kiss it, are you, father?" asked Jack, with a grin.

I tried to rebuke him for his impertinence, but, failing, I commenced operations. I first attached a cord and running-noose to a stout stick, and holding a light switch in my other hand, I began to approach the creature with soft, slow steps, while the boys looked on with the utmost curiosity.

Presently I began very softly to whistle a sweet, yet very lively air, which I continued more and more distinctly as I drew near the lizard; until, awaking, it seemed to listen with pleasure—raising its head as though better to catch the sounds, or to discover whence they came.

When near enough, I began gently to stroke and tickle him with the wand, continuing to whistle the prettiest tunes I could think of; and the lizard gave signs of pleasurable contentment, stretching his limbs and moving his tail in token of enjoyment.

Suddenly, availing myself of a movement of his head, I cast the noose over it, drew the cord tight, and placing my foot on the body, I was about to kill it by piercing the nostril—almost the only vulnerable part of this singular reptile—when Jack received such a slap from its tail, which was furiously driving in all directions, as sent him rolling over like a ninepin. At the same time he opened his jaws, when the boys took fright at the row of sharp teeth, and thinking that the sooner he was dead the better, were for battering him with sticks; but I assuring them my method would kill him more quickly and without pain, thrust my rod into his nostril, on which the blood flowed and the lizard soon expired.

The boys seemed to think me as wonderful a person as a snake charmer, and the success of my stratagem, as well as of the means by which the lizard was slain, called forth great admiration, since they had never heard of the animal, nor of the method of capturing it so commonly practised in the West Indies.

Now came the question of how we were to carry this unwieldy burden. I had a great dislike to killing any creature and leaving it useless behind me; so, without more ado, I fairly took it on my back, and marched off with it.

As we came toward the Calabash Wood, we could hear the voices of the deserted mother and child calling us in anxious tones; for indeed our protracted absence alarmed them. We shouted joyously in reply, and our appearance, as we issued from the woods, afforded them welcome relief from their fears, although the dreadful creature on my back startled them not a little.

There was so much to tell, so much to be seen, that for a time hunger and thirst were forgotten; and no one thought even of the water we had vainly gone in search of, until Master Knips, having slyly possessed himself of some of our new-found apples, was discovered munching away and enjoying them amazingly—which instantly gave the boys a strong wish to eat some also; and as the bustard likewise pecked at them without hesitation, I felt sure there could be no danger; and on tasting them, I concluded it was the fruit of the guava, a West Indian plant, which we were delighted to have.

Although refreshing, this fruit rather sharpened than appeased our appetites, and we were glad to eat the provisions we had brought from home, without waiting to cook anything, as we had originally intended.

It was, in fact, high time to move homeward, and we thought it best not to encumber ourselves with the sledge and the greater part of its load, but to leave it until the next day. The ass was laden with the iguana and the bustard; and little Franz, tired as he was, looked in vain for a spare seat on its back.

Our road home lay through a majestic forest of oak trees, beneath which lay numberless acorns, some of which we gathered as we went along; and at length, before night closed in, we all reached Falconhurst in safety.

When supper was ready, we were thankful to recruit our exhausted strength by eating heartily of a piece of broiled iguana, with potatoes and roast acorns, which tasted like excellent chestnuts.

Chapter Seven

THE first thing to be done on the following day was to return to the Calabash Wood, to fetch the sledge with the dishes, bowls, and baskets we had made.

Fritz alone accompanied me. I desired the other boys to remain with their mother, intending to explore beyond the chain of rocky hills, and thinking a large party undesirable on the occasion.

Passing through the wood of evergreen oaks, we observed our sow feasting on the acorns, evidently not a whit the worse for the fright we had given her the previous day—in fact, she appeared more friendly disposed toward us than usual, possibly considering us as her deliverers from the jaws of the savage dogs.

Many birds tenanted this grove, and were undisturbed by our movements, until Fritz fired and shot a beautiful bluejay and a couple of parroquets, one a brilliant scarlet, the other green and gold.

Fritz was in the act of reloading his gun, when an unaccountable noise struck our ears, and put us instantly on the alert, because it appeared like the dull thumping sound of a muffled drum, and reminded us of the possible presence of savages.

With the greatest caution we drew nearer the sound, concealing ourselves among the low bushes and thick grass and creepers, until we reached an open glade; where, standing on an old prostrate log, was a beautiful bird, about the size of a cock, of a rich chestnut brown color, finely mottled with dark brown and gray. On the shoulders were curious tufts of velvety black feathers, glossed with green. He was ruffling his wings, erecting his tail and neck feathers, strutting and wheeling about in a most strange and stately fashion. After maneuvering for some time in this manner, greatly to the edification of a party of birds resembling him, but without any ruff, who, assembled round the stump, were enjoying his performances, he spread out his tail like a fan, stiffened his wings, and began to strike with them in short, rapid beats, faster and faster, until a rumbling sound like very distant thunder was produced, and the whirring wings enveloped him as in a cloud. This was the drumming noise which had alarmed us, increased, as I imagine, by the wing strokes falling at times on the decayed and hollow stump on which the curious pantomime was acted.

I was watching it with the utmost interest, when a shot from behind me was fired, and in a moment the play was at an end; my over-hasty son had changed the pretty comedy into a sad and needless tragedy. The enthusiastic drummer fell dead from his perch, and the crowd of admiring companions fled in dismay.

The cruel interruption of a scene so rare and remarkable annoyed me extremely, and I blamed Fritz for firing without my leave. I felt sure the bird was the ruffed grouse, and a very fine specimen. We placed it on the ass, which was patiently awaiting our return, and went on our way.

The sledge was quite safe where we had left it; it was early in the day, and I resolved to explore, as I had intended, the line of cliff and rocky hills, which, at more or less distance from the seashore, extended the whole length of coast known or visible to us.

I desired to discover an opening, if any existed, by which to penetrate the interior of the country, or to ascertain positively that we were walled in and isolated on this portion of the coast.

Leaving Calabash Wood behind us, we advanced over ground covered with manioc, potatoes, and many plants unknown to us; pleasant streamlets watered the fruitful soil, and the view on all sides was open and agreeable.

Some bushes attracted my notice, loaded with small white berries, of peculiar appearance like wax, and very sticky when plucked. I recognized in this a plant called by botanists *Myrica cerifera,* and with much pleasure explained to Fritz that, by melting and straining these berries, we might easily succeed in making candles, and afford very great satisfaction to the mother, who did not at all approve of having to lay her work aside and retire to rest the moment the sun set. The greenish wax to be obtained would be more brittle than beeswax, but it would burn very fairly, and diffuse an agreeable perfume. Having the ass with us, we lost no time in gathering berries enough to fill one of the large canvas bags he carried, and we then continued our route.

Very soon we met with another natural curiosity, the curious appearance of which surprised us much. This was the abode, under one roof, of a whole colony of birds, about the size of yellow hammers, but of plain brown plumage. The nests were built in a mass round the stem and among the branches of a tree standing alone, and a kind of roof formed of grass, straws, and fibers covered them all, and sheltered the community from rain and the heat of the sun. There were numbers of openings into the irregular sides of the group of dwellings, the nests resembling different apartments in a house common to all; twigs and small branches emerged here and there from the walls, and served as perches for the young birds, and resting-places and posts of observation for all. The general appearance of the establishment reminded us of a huge bath-sponge. The feathered inhabitants swarmed in and out by thousands, and we saw among them many beautiful little parrots, who seemed in many instances to contest possession of the nest with the lawful owners.

Fritz, being an expert climber and exceedingly anxious to examine the nests more closely, ascended the tree, hoping to obtain one or two young birds, if any were hatched. He put his hand into several holes, which were empty; but at last his intended theft and robbery met with repulse and chastisement he little expected; for, reaching far back into the nest, his finger was seized and sharply bitten by a very strong beak, so that with a cry he withdrew his hand, and shook it vigorously to lessen the pain. Recovering from the surprise, he again and more resolutely seized the unkind bird, and, despite its shrieks and screams, drew it from its retreat, crammed it into his pocket, buttoned up his coat, and slid quickly to the ground, pursued by numbers of the captive's relations, who darted from the other holes and flew round the robber, screeching and pecking at him in a rage.

Fritz's prize was not one of the real owners of the nests, which were those of the sociable grosbeak, but a very pretty small green parrot, with which he was greatly pleased, and which he at once determined to tame and teach to speak; for the present it was carefully remanded to prison in his pocket.

This curious colony of birds afforded us matter for conversation as we went on our way; their cheerful, sociable habits, and the instinct which prompted them to unite in labor for the common good, appearing most wonderful to us.

"Examples of the kind, however," said I, "are numerous, in various classes of animals. Beavers, for instance, build and live together in a very remarkable way. Among insects, bees, wasps, and ants are well known as social architects; in like manner, the coral insect works wonders beneath the ocean waves, by force of perseverance and united effort."

"I have often watched ants at work," said Fritz; "it is most amusing to see how they carry on the various works and duties of their commonwealth."

"Have you ever noticed how much trouble they take with the eggs?" inquired I, to see how far he understood the process; "carrying them about in the warmth of the sun until they are hatched?"

"Ah! that is rather the chrysalis of the antworm, or larva which is produced from an egg. I know they are called ants' eggs, but, strictly speaking, that is incorrect."

"You are perfectly right, my boy. Well, if you have taken so much interest in watching the little ants of your native country, how delighted and astonished you would be to see the wonders performed by the vast tribes of large ants in foreign lands.

"Some of these build heaps or nests, four or six feet high and proportionately broad, which are so strong and firm that they defy equally sunshine and rain. They are, within, divided into regular streets, galleries, vaults, and nurseries. So firmly are these mounds built, that with interior alterations, a deserted one might be used for a baking-oven.

"The ant, although respected since the days of King Solomon as a model of industry, is not in itself an attractive insect.

"It exudes a sticky moisture, its smell is unpleasant, and it destroys and devours whatever eatable comes in its way. Although, in our own country it does little harm, the large ants of foreign lands are most destructive and troublesome; it being very difficult to check their depredations. Fortunately they have enemies by whose exertions their numbers are kept down; birds, other insects, and even four-footed beasts prey upon them. Chief among the latter is the ant-bear, or tamanoir, of South America, a large creature six or seven feet in length, covered with long coarse hair, drooping like a heavy plume over the hind quarters. The head is wonderfully elongated and very narrow; it is destitute of teeth, and the tongue resembles somewhat a great red earth-worm. It has immensely strong curved claws, with which it tears and breaks down and scratches to pieces the hard walls of the ant-heaps; then, protruding its sticky tongue, it coils and twists it about among the terrified millions disturbed by its attack; they adhere to this horrible invader, and are drawn irresistibly backward into the hungry, toothless jaws awaiting them.

"The little ant-eater is not more than about twenty-one inches in length, has a shorter and more natural looking head, and fine silky fur. It usually lives in trees."

I was pleased to find my memory served me so well on this subject, as it interested my boy amazingly; and occupied us for a considerable time while we traveled onward.

Arriving presently at a grove of tall trees, with very strong, broad thick leaves, we paused to examine them; they bore a round, fig-like fruit, full of little seeds and of a sour, harsh taste.

Fritz saw some gummy resin exuding from cracks in the bark, and it reminded him of the boyish delight afforded by collecting gum from cherry-trees at home, so that he must needs stop to scrape off as much as he could. He rejoined me presently, attempting to soften what he had collected in his hands; but finding it would not work like gum, he was about to fling it away, when he suddenly found that he could stretch it and that it sprang back to its original size.

"Oh, father, only look! this gum is quite elastic! Can it possibly be india-rubber?"

"What!" cried I; "let me see it! a valuable discovery that would be, indeed; and I do believe you are perfectly right!"

"Why would it be so very valuable, father?" inquired Fritz. "I have only seen it used for rubbing out pencil marks."

"India-rubber," I replied, "or, more properly, caoutchouc, is a milky, resinous juice which flows from certain trees in considerable quantities when the stem is purposely tapped. These trees are indigenous to the South American countries of Brazil, Guiana, and Cayenne. The natives, who first obtained it, used to form bottles by smearing earthen flasks with repeated coatings of the gum when just fresh from the trees, and when hardened and sufficiently thick, they broke the mold, shook out the fragments, and hung the bottles in the smoke, when they became firmer and of a dark color. While moist, the savages were in the habit of drawing rude figures and lines on the resin by way of ornament; these marks you may have observed, for the bottles obtained from the natives by the Spaniards and Portugese have for years been brought to Europe, and cut into portions to be sold for use in drawing. Caoutchouc can be put to many uses, and I am delighted to have it here, as we shall,

I hope, be able to make it into different forms; first and foremost, I shall try to manufacture boots and shoes."

Soon after making this discovery, we reached the cocoanut wood, and saw the bay extending before us, and the great promontory we called Cape Disappointment, which hitherto had always bounded our excursions.

In passing through the wood, I remarked a smaller sort of palm, which, among its grand companions, I had not previously noticed. One of these had been broken by the wind, and I saw that the pith had a peculiar mealy appearance, and I felt convinced that this was the world-renowned sago-palm.

In the pith I saw some fat worms or maggots, and suddenly recollected that I had heard of them before as feeding on the sago, and that in the West Indies they are eaten as a delicacy.

I felt inclined to try what they tasted like; so at once kindling a fire, and placing some half-dozen, sprinkled with salt, on a little wooden spit, I set them to roast.

Very soon rich fat began to drop from them, and they smelt so temptingly good that all repugnance to the idea of eating worms vanished; and, putting one like a pat of butter on a baked potato, I boldly swallowed it and liked it so much that several others followed in the same way. Fritz also summoned courage to partake of this novel food, which was a savory addition to our dinner of baked potatoes.

Being once more ready to start, we found so dense a thicket in the direct route that we turned aside without attempting to penetrate it, and made our way toward the sugar brake near Cape Disappointment. This we could not pass without cutting a handsome bundle of sugar-canes, and the donkey carried that, in addition to the bag of wax berries.

In time we reached the sledge in Calabash Wood: the ass was unloaded, everything placed on the sledge, and our patient beast began calmly and readily to drag the burden he had hitherto borne on his back.

No further adventure befell us, and we arrived in the evening at Falconhurst, where our welcome was as warm as usual— all we had to tell listened to with the greatest interest, all we had to show most eagerly examined, the pretty green parroquet enchanting the boys most particularly.

An excellent supper was ready for us, and with thankful

hearts we enjoyed it together; then, ascending to our tree-
castle, and drawing up the ladder after us, we betook ourselves
to the repose well earned and greatly needed after this fatiguing day.

The idea of candle-making seemed to have taken the fancy
of all the boys; and next morning they woke, one after the
other, with the word candle on their lips. When they were
thoroughly roused they continued to talk candles; all break-
fast-time, candles were the subject of conversation; and after
breakfast they would hear of nothing else but setting to work
at once and making candles.

"So be it," said I; "let us become chandlers."

I spoke confidently, but to tell the truth, I had in my own
mind certain misgivings as to the result of our experiment.
In the first place, I knew that we lacked a very important ingredient—animal fat, which is necessary to make candles burn
for any length of time with brilliancy. Besides this, I rather
doubted how far my memory would recall the various operations necessary in the manufacture. Of all this, however, I said
nothing; and the boys, under my direction, were soon at work.
We first picked off the berries and threw them into a large
shallow iron vessel placed on the fire. The green, sweet-scented
wax was rapidly melted, rising to the surface of the juice
yielded by the berries. This we skimmed off and placed in a
separate pot by the fire, ready for use; repeating the operation
several times, until we had collected sufficient liquid wax for
our purpose. I then took the wicks my wife had prepared, and
dipped them one after the other into the wax, handing them
as I did so to Fritz, who hung them up on a bush to dry. The
coating they thus obtained was not very thick; but, by repeating the operation several times, they at length assumed very
fair proportions, and became real sturdy candles. Our wax
being at an end, we hung these in a cool, shady place to harden;
and that same night we sat up like civilized beings three whole
hours after sunset, and Falconhurst was for the first time brilliantly illuminated.

We were all delighted with the success of our experiment.

"You are indeed clever," said my wife; "I only wish that
with your ingenuity you would show me how to make butter.
Day after day I have the annoyance of seeing a large supply

of good cream go bad under my very eyes, simply because I have no use to which to put it. Invent a plan, please do."

"I think that perhaps I can help you," I replied, after a little consideration; "not that I can claim the honor of the invention of my plan; that is due to the Hottentots. I will see what I can do. Jack, bring me one of our gourd bottles."

I took the gourd, one of those I had previously prepared, with a small hole at one end and well hollowed out and cleaned; this I partially filled with cream and then corked up the hole tightly.

"Here boys," said I, "you can continue the operation, while I turn carpenter and make a cart to take the place of our sledge."

I gave them their directions, and then set about my own work. They fixed four posts in the ground, and to them fastened a square piece of sail-cloth by four cords attached to the corners. In this cradle they placed the gourd of cream, and each taking a side rolled it backward and forward continuously for half an hour.

"Now," I cried, looking up from my work, "open the gourd and take the contents to your mother, with my compliments."

They did so; and my good wife's eyes were delighted with the sight of a large lump of capital fresh butter.

With my son's assistance the cart was in time completed; a clumsy vehicle it was, but strong enough for any purpose to which we might put it, and, as it proved, of immense use to us in collecting the harvest.

We then turned our attention to our fruit-trees, which we had planted in a plot ready for transplanting. The walnut, cherry, and chestnut trees we arranged in parallel rows, so as to form a shady avenue from Falconhurst to Family-bridge; and between them we laid down a tolerable road, that we might have no difficulty in reaching Tentholm, be the weather bad as it might. We planted the vines round the arched roots of our great mangrove, and the rest of the trees in suitable spots; some near Falconhurst, and others away over Jackal River, to adorn Tentholm. Tentholm had been the subject of serious thoughts to me for some time past, and I now turned all my attention thither. It was not my ambition to make it beautiful, but to form of it a safe place of refuge in a case of emergency. My first care, therefore, was to plant a thick, prickly hedge capable of protecting us from any wild animal, and forming a tolerable obstacle to the attack of even savages, should they appear. Not satisfied with this, however, we fortified the bridge, and on a couple of hillocks mounted two guns which we brought from the wreck, and with whose angry mouths we might bark defiance at any enemy, man or beast.

Six weeks slipped away while we were thus busily occupied, six weeks of hard, yet pleasant, labor. We greeted each Sunday and its accompanying rest most gratefully, and on that day always, especially thanked God for our continued health and safety. I soon saw that this hard work was developing in the boys remarkable strength, and this I encouraged by making them practise running, leaping, climbing, and swimming; I also saw, however, that it was having a less satisfactory effect upon their clothes, which, though a short time before remarkably neat, were now, in spite of the busy mother's mending and patching, most untidy and disreputable. I determined, therefore, to pay another visit to the wreck, to replenish our wardrobe and to see how much longer the vessel was likely to hold together. Three of the boys and I went off in the pinnace. The old ship seemed in much the same condition as when we had left her; a few more planks had gone, but that was all.

"Come, boys," cried I, "not an article of the slightest value must be left on board; rummage her out to the very bottom of her hold."

They took me at my word: sailors' chests, bales of cloth and linen, a couple of small guns, ball and shot, tables, benches, window shutters, bolts and locks, barrels of pitch, all were soon in a heap on the deck. We loaded the pinnace and went on shore. We soon returned with our tub-boat in tow, and after a few more trips nothing was left on board.

"One more trip," said I to my wife, before we started again, "and there will be the end of the brave ship which carried us from Switzerland. I have left two barrels of gunpowder on board and mean to blow her up."

Before we lighted the fusee, I discovered a large copper cauldron which I thought I might save. I made fast to it a couple of empty casks, that when the ship went up it might

float. The barrels were placed, the train lighted, and we returned on shore.

The supper was laid outside the tent, at a spot from whence
we might obtain a good view of the wreck. Darkness came on.
Suddenly a vivid pillar of fire rose from the black waters, a
sullen roar boomed across the sea, and we knew that our good
old ship was no more.

We had planned the destruction of the vessel; we knew that
it was for the best; and yet that night we went to bed with a
feeling of sadness in our hearts, as though we had lost a dear
old friend.

Next morning all our sadness was dispelled, and it was with
pleasure that we saw the shore lined with a rich store of planks
and beams, the remnants of the wreck. I soon found, too, the
copper cauldron which was successfully floated by the casks;
this I got on shore, and hauling it up among the rocks, stored
under it the powder casks we had landed the day before. Collecting all these valuables gave us some little trouble, and
while we were thus engaged my wife brought us good news.
She had discovered that two ducks and a goose had each reared
a large family among the reeds by the river; and they presently
appeared waddling past us, apparently vastly well-pleased with
their performance. We greeted them joyfully.

"Hurrah!" cried Ernest, "we'll be able to afford duck and
green peas some day soon, and imagine we're once more civilized mortals."

The sight of these birds reminded me of our family at
Falconhurst, and I announced my intention of paying them a
visit.

Everyone was delighted and everyone would come with me.
As we approached Falconhurst I noticed that several young
trees in our avenue were considerably bent by the wind, and
this resolved me to make an expedition next day to cut bamboos for their support. As Fritz was the only one besides myself who had visited Cape Disappointment and the surrounding country, my wife and the younger boys begged hard to be
allowed to accompany me. I consented; and next morning we
started, bringing with us the cart, drawn by the cow and ass,
and laden with everything necessary for an expedition of several days—a tent, provisions, a large supply of ammunition,

and all sorts of implements and utensils; for I intended to make a great collection of fruits and the produce of different trees. It was a lovely morning, and passing gayly through the plantations of potatoes, manioc, and cassavas, we came to the nests of the sociable grosbeak, the sight of which charmed the children immensely.

We reached the wax trees, and there I called a halt, for I wished to gather a sack or two of the berries that we might renew our stock of candles. The berries were soon plucked; and I stored them away among the bushes, marking the spot that we might find them on our return.

"Now for the caoutchouc tree," said I; "now for the water-proof boots and leggings to keep your feet dry, Ernest." To the caoutchouc tree we directed our steps, and were soon busily engaged in stabbing the bark and placing vessels beneath to catch the sap. We again moved forward; and, crossing the palm wood, entered upon a delightful plain bounded on one side by an extensive field of waving sugar-cane, on the other by a thicket of bamboos and lovely palms, while in front stretched the shining sea, calm and noiseless.

"How beautiful!" exclaimed Jack, "let us pitch our tent here and stay here always instead of living at Falconhurst. It would be jolly."

"Very likely," replied I, "and so would be the attacks of wild beasts; imagine a great tiger lying in wait in the thicket yonder, and pouncing out on us at night. No, no, thank you, I much prefer our nest in the tree, or our impregnable position at Tentholm. We must make this our headquarters for the present, however; for, though perhaps dangerous, it is the most convenient spot we shall find. Call a halt and pitch the tent."

Our beasts were quickly unyoked, the tent arranged, a large fire lit, supper started, and we dispersed in various directions, some to cut bamboos, and some to collect sugar-cane. We then returned; and, as supper was still not ready and the boys were hungry, they decided to obtain some cocoanuts. This time, however, no assistance was to be had from either monkeys or land-crabs, and they gazed up with longing eyes at the fruit above them.

"We can climb," said Fritz, "up with you, boys."

Jack and he each rushed at one of the smooth, slippery trunks; right vigorously they struggled upward, but to no purpose; before they had accomplished one-quarter of the distance they found themselves slipping rapidly to the ground.

"Here, you young athletes," cried I, "I foresaw this difficulty, and have provided for it." So saying I held up buskins of shark's skin which I had previously prepared, and which I now bound on to their legs. Thus equipped they again attempted the ascent, and with a loop of rope passed round their body and the trunk of the tree, quickly reached the summit. My wife joined me, and together we watched the boys as they ascended tree after tree, throwing down the best fruit from each.

They then returned and jestingly begged Ernest to produce the result of his labor. The professor had been lying on the grass gazing at the palms; but, on this sarcastic remark, he sprang to his feet. "Willingly," he exclaimed, and seizing a pair of buskins he quickly donned them. "Give me a cocoanut shell," said he. I gave him one, and he put it in his pocket. He ran to a tree, and, with an agility which surprised us all, quickly reached the top. No sooner had he done so than Fritz and Jack burst into a roar of laughter. He had swarmed a tree which bore no nuts. Ernest apparently heard them; for, as it seemed in a fit of anger, he drew his knife and severed the leafy crest, which fell to the ground. I glanced up at him, surprised at such a display of temper. But a bright smile greeted me, and in a merry tone he shouted:

"Jack, pick that palm-cabbage up and take it to father; that is only half my contribution, and it is worth all your nuts put together."

He spoke truly; the cabbage palm is rare, and the tuft of leaves at its summit is greatly prized by the South Americans for its great delicacy and highly nutritive qualities.

"Bravo!" I cried, "you have retrieved your character; come down and receive the thanks of the company. What are you waiting up there for?"

"I am coming presently," he replied, "with the second half of my contribution; I hope it will be as fully appreciated as the first."

In a short time he slipped down the tree, and, advancing to

his mother, presented her with the nutshell he had taken up with him.

"Here," he said, "is a wine which the greatest connoisseur would prize. Taste it, mother."

The shell was filled with a clear, rosy liquor, bright and sparkling. My wife tasted it. "Excellent, excellent," she exclaimed. "Your very good health, my dear boy!"

We drank the rosy wine in turn, and Ernest received hearty thanks from all.

It was getting late, and while we were enjoying our supper before our tent, our donkey, who had been quietly browsing near us, suddenly set up a loud bray, and, without the least apparent cause, pricked up his ears, threw up his heels, and galloped off into the thicket of bamboos. We followed for a short distance, and I sent the dogs in chase, but they returned without our friend, and, as it was late, we were obliged to abandon the chase.

I was annoyed by this incident, and even alarmed; for not only had we lost the ass, but I knew not what had occasioned his sudden flight. I knew not whether he was aware, by instinct, of the approach of some fierce wild beast. I said nothing of this to my family, but, making up an unusually large fire, I bade them sleep with their arms by their sides, and we all lay down.

A bright morning awoke us early, and I rose and looked out, thinking that perhaps our poor donkey might have been attracted by the light of the fires, and have returned. Alas! not a sign of him was to be seen. As we could not afford to lose so valuable a beast, I determined to leave no attempt untried to regain him. We hurriedly breakfasted, and, as I required the dogs to assist me in the search, I left my elder sons to protect their mother, and bade Jack get ready for a day's march. This arrangement delighted him, and we quickly set out.

For an hour or more we trudged onward, directed by the print of the ass's hoofs. Sometimes we lost the track for a while, and then again discovered it as we reached softer soil. Finally this guide failed us altogether, for the donkey seemed to have joined in with a herd of some larger animals, with whose hoof-prints his had mingled. I now almost turned back in despair, but Jack urged me to continue the search; "For," said he, "if we once get upon a hill we shall see such a large herd, as this must be, at almost any distance. Do let us go on, father."

I consented, and we again pushed forward, through bushes, and over torrents, sometimes cutting our way with an ax, and sometimes plunging knee-deep through a swamp. We at length reached the border of a wide plain, and on it, in the distance, I could see a herd of animals browsing on the rich grass. It struck me that it might be the very herd to which our good donkey had joined himself; and, wishing to ascertain whether this was so, I resolved to make a detour through a bamboo marsh, and get as near as possible to the animals without disturbing them. The bamboos were huge, many of them over thirty feet in height; and, as we made our way through them, I remembered an account of the giant cane of South America, which is greatly prized by the Indians on account of its extreme usefulness; the reeds themselves make masts for their canoes, while each joint will form a cask or box. I was delighted, for I had little doubt that the bamboos we were among were of the same species. I explained this to Jack, and as we discussed the possibility of cutting one down and carrying a portion of it home, we reached the border of the marsh, and emerged upon the plain. There we suddenly found ourselves face to face with the herd which we sought—a herd of buffaloes. They looked up and stared at us inquisitively, but without moving. Jack would have fired, but I checked him. "Back to the thicket," I said, "and keep back the dogs!"

We began to retreat, but before we were again under cover the dogs joined us; and, in spite of our shouts and efforts to restrain them, they dashed forward and seized a buffalo calf. This was a signal to the whole herd to attack us. They bellowed loudly, pawed the ground, and tore it up with their horns, and then dashed madly toward us. We had not time to step behind a rock before the leader was upon us. So close was he that my gun was useless. I drew a pistol and fired. He fell dead at my feet. His fall checked the advance of the rest. They halted, snuffed the air, turned tail, and galloped off across the plain. They were gone, but the dogs still held gallantly to the calf. They dragged and tussled with him, but with their utmost efforts they could not bring him to the ground. How to assist them without shooting the poor beast

I knew not; and this I was unwilling to do, for I hoped that,
if we could not capture him alive, we might in time manage
to tame him, and use him as a beast of burden. Jack's clever
little head, however, suddenly devised a plan for their aid, and
with his usual promptitude, he at once put it into execution.
He unwound the lasso, which was coiled round his body, and,
as the young bull flung up his heels, he cast it and caught him
by his hind legs. The noose drew tight, and in a twinkling
the beast was upon the ground. We fastened the other end
of the cord round a stout bamboo, called off the dogs, and the
animal was at our mercy.

"Now we have got him," said Jack, as he looked at the poor
beast, lying panting on the ground, "what are we to do with
him?"

"I will show you," said I; "help me to fasten his fore-legs
together, and you shall see the next operation."

The bull, thus secured, could not move; and while Jack
held his head I drew my knife and pierced the cartilage of his
nose, and when the blood flowed less freely, passed a stout
cord through the hole. I felt some repugnance at thus pain-
ing the animal, but it was a case of necessity, and I could not
hesitate. We united the ends of the cord, freed the animal,
set him upon his legs, and, subdued and overawed, he followed
us without resistance. I now turned my attention to the dead
buffalo, but as I could not then skin it, I contented myself
with cutting off the most delicate parts, its tongue, and a
couple of steaks, and, packing them in salt in my wallet, abandoned the rest to the dogs. They fell upon it greedily, and
we retired under the shade to enjoy a meal after our hard
work. The dogs, however, were not to have undisputed possession of the carcase; vultures, crows, and other birds of prey,
with that marvelous instinct which always leads them to a
dead body, quickly filled the air, and, with discordant cries,
swooped down upon the buffalo. An amusing contest ensued;
the dogs again and again drove off the intruders, and they, as
often, returned re-enforced by others who swarmed to the spot.
Jack, with his usual impetuosity, wished to send a shot in
among the robber band, but I prevented him, for I knew
that the bird or two he might kill would be of no use to us,
while his shot would not drive away the rest, even had we

wished it. Both we and the dogs were at length satisfied, and as it was getting late, I determined to give up for the present the search for the ass, and to return to our camp. We again made our way through the bamboos, but before we left the thicket I cut down one of the smallest of the reeds, the largest of whose joints would form capital little barrels, while those near the tapering top would serve as molds for our next batch of candles.

The buffalo, with a dog on either side and the rope through his nose, was following us passively, and we presently induced him to submit to a package of our goods laid upon his back. We pushed rapidly forward, Jack eager to display our latest acquisition. As we repassed the rocky bed of a stream we had crossed in the morning, Juno dashed ahead, and was about to rush into a cleft between the rocks, when the appearance of a large jackal suddenly checked her further progress. Both dogs instantly flew at the animal, and though she fought desperately, quickly overpowered and throttled her. From the way the beast had shown fight, I concluded that her young must be close by, probably within the very cleft Juno was about to enter.

Directly Jack heard this, he wished to creep in and bring out the young jackals. I hesitated to allow him to do so, for I thought it possible that the male jackal might be still lying in wait within the cave. We peered into the darkness, and, after a while, Jack declared he could discern the little yellow jackals, and that he was quite sure the old one was not there. He then crept in, followed closely by the dogs, and presently emerged, bearing in his arms a handsome cub of a beautiful golden yellow and about the size of a small cat. He was the only one of the brood he had managed to save, for Turk and Juno, without pity for their youth or beauty, had worried all the rest. I did not much regret this, however, for I firmly believe that, had he saved them, Jack would have insisted upon bringing up the whole litter. As it was, I considered that one jackal was, with our young bull, quite sufficient an addition to our livestock.

During the halt we had made I had fastened the buffalo to a small tree, and as I was now again about to move on, I recognized it as the dwarf-palm, whose long, sharp leaves form an excellent barrier if it is planted as a hedge. I determined to return and get some young plants to strengthen our hedge at Tentholm. It was late before we reached our camp, where we found our family anxiously awaiting our return.

The sight of the new animals delighted the children immensely, and in their opinion amply compensated for the loss of our poor donkey. Jack had to answer a host of questions concerning their capture, and to give a minute account of the affray with the buffaloes. This he did, with graphic power certainly, but with so much boasting and self-glorification that I was obliged to check him, and give a plain and unvarnished account of the affair.

Suppertime arrived, and as we sat at that meal, for which Jack and I were heartily thankful, my wife and her party proceeded to give an account of their day's work.

Ernest had discovered a sago-palm, and had, after much labor, contrived to fell it. Franz and his mother had collected dry wood, of which a huge heap now stood before the tent, sufficient to keep up a fire all the rest of the time we should stay on the spot. Fritz had gone off shooting and had secured a good bag. While they had been thus variously employed, a troop of apes had visited the tent, and when they returned, they found the place ransacked and turned upside down. The provisions were eaten and gnawed, the potatoes thrown about, the milk drunk and spilt; every box had been peeped into, every pot and pan had been divested of its lid; the palisade round the hut had been partly destroyed, nothing had been left untouched. Industriously had the boys worked to repair the damage, and when we returned not a sign was to be seen of the disorder. No one would have guessed what had occurred from the delicious supper we were eating.

After matters had been again arranged, Fritz had gone down to the shore, and, among the rocks at Cape Disappointment, had discovered a young eaglet which Ernest declared to be a Malabar or Indian eagle; he was much pleased with his discovery, and I recommended him to bring the bird up and try to train it to hunt as a falcon.

"Look here, though, boys," said I, "you are now collecting a good many pets, and I am not going to have your mother troubled with the care of them all; each must look after his own, and if I find one neglected, whether beast or bird, I set it at liberty. Mark that and remember it!"

My wife looked greatly relieved at this announcement, and the boys promised to obey my directions. Before we retired for the night I prepared the buffalo meat I had brought. I lit a large fire of green wood, and in the smoke of this thoroughly dried both the tongue and steaks. We then properly secured all the animals, Jack took his little pet in his arms, and we lay down and were soon fast asleep.

At daybreak we were on foot, and began to prepare for a return to Falconhurst.

"You are not going to despise my sago, I hope," said Ernest; "you have no idea what a trouble it was to cut it down; and I have been thinking too, that, if we could but split the tree, we might make a couple of long useful troughs, which might, I think, be made to carry water from Jackal River to Tentholm. Is my plan worth consideration?"

"Indeed it is," I replied; "and at all events we must not abandon such a valuable prize as a sago palm. I would put off our departure for a day rather than leave it behind.

We went to the palm, and with the tools we had with us attempted to split the trunk. We first sawed off the upper end, and then with an ax and saw managed to insert a wedge. This accomplished, our task was less difficult, for with a heavy mallet we forced the wedge in further and further, until at length the trunk was split in twain. From one half of the trunk we then removed the pith, disengaging it, with difficulty, from the tough wood fibers; at each end, however, I left a portion of the pith untouched, thus forming a trough in which to work the sago.

"Now, boys," said I, when we had removed the pith from the other half of the trunk, "off with your coats and turn up your shirt-sleeves; I am going to teach you to knead."

They were all delighted, and even little Franz begged to be allowed to help. Ernest brought a couple of pitchers of water, and throwing it in amongst the pith, we set to work right heartily. As the dough was formed and properly kneaded, I handed it to the mother, who spread it out on a cloth in the sun to dry. This new occupation kept us busy until the evening, and when it was at length completed we loaded the cart with the sago, a store of cocoanuts, and our other possessions, that we might be ready to start early on the following morning. As the sun rose above the horizon, we packed up our tent and set forth, a goodly caravan. I thought it unfair to the cow to make her drag such a load as we now had alone, and determined if possible to make the young buffalo take the place of our lost donkey: after some persuasion he consented, and soon put his strength to the work and brought the cart along famously. As we had the trough slung under the cart we had to choose the clearest possible route, avoiding anything like a thicket; we, therefore, could not pass directly by the candleberry and caoutchouc trees, and I sent Ernest and Jack aside to visit the store we had made on our outward journey.

They had not long been gone when I was alarmed by a most terrible noise, accompanied by the furious barking of the dogs and shouts from Jack and Ernest. Thinking that the boys had been attacked by some wild beasts, I ran to their assistance. A most ludicrous scene awaited me when I reached the spot. They were dancing and shouting round and round a grassy glade, and I as nearly as possible followed their example, for in the center, surrounded by a promising litter, lay our old sow, whose squeals, previously so alarming, were now subsiding into comfortable grunts of recognition. I did not join my boys in their triumphal dance, but I was nevertheless very much pleased at the sight of the flourishing family, and immediately returned to the cart to obtain biscuits and potatoes for the benefit of the happy mother. Jack and Ernest meanwhile pushed further on and brought back the sack of candleberries and the caoutchouc, and as we could not then take the sow with us, we left her alone with her family and proceeded to Falconhurst.

The animals were delighted to see us back again, and received us with manifestations of joy, but looked askance at the new pets. The eagle especially came in for shy glances, and promised to be no favorite. Fritz, however, determined that his pet should at present do no harm, secured him by the leg to a root of a fig tree and uncovered his eyes. In a moment the aspect of the bird was changed; with his sight returned all his savage instincts, he flapped his wings, raised his head, darted to the full length of his chain, and before anyone could prevent him seized the unfortunate parrot, which stood near, and tore it to pieces. Fritz's anger rose at the sight, and he was about to put an end to the savage bird.

"Stop," said Ernest, "don't kill the poor creature, he is but following his natural instincts; give him to me, and I will tame him."

Fritz hesitated. "No, no," he said, "I don't want really to kill the bird, but I can't give him up; tell me how to tame him, and you shall have Master Knips.

"Very well," replied Ernest, "I will tell you my plan, and if it succeeds, I will accept Knips as a mark of your gratitude. Take a pipe and tobacco, and send the smoke all around his head, so that he must inhale it; by degrees he will become stupified, and his savage nature from that moment subdued."

Fritz was rather inclined to ridicule the plan, but, knowing that Ernest generally had a good reason for anything of the sort that he proposed, he consented to make the attempt. He soon seated himself beneath the bird, who still struggled furiously, and puffed cloud after cloud upward, and as each cloud circled round the eagle's head he became quieter and quieter, until he sat quite still, gazing stupidly at the young smoker.

"Capital!" cried Fritz, as he hooded the bird, "capital, Ernest; Knips is yours."

Chapter Eight

N EXT morning the boys and I started with the cart, laden with our bundles of bamboos, to attend to the avenue of fruit trees. The buffalo we left behind, for his services were not needed, and I wished the wound in his nostrils to become completely cicatrized before I again put him to work. We were not a moment too soon; many of the young trees, which before threatened to fall, had now fulfilled their promise, and were lying prostrate on the ground, others were bent, some few only remained erect. We raised the trees, and digging deeply at their roots, drove in stout bamboo props, to which we lashed them firmly with strong broad fibers.

"Papa," said Franz, as we were thus engaged, and he handed

me the fibers as I required them, "are these wild or tame trees?"

"Oh, these are wild trees, most ferocious trees," laughed Jack, "and we are tying them up lest they should run away, and in a little while we will untie them and they will trot about after us and give us fruit wherever we go. Oh, we will tame them; they shall have a ring through their noses like the buffalo!"

"That's not true," replied Franz gravely, "but there *are* wild and tame trees, the wild ones grow out in the woods like the crab-apples, and the tame ones in the garden like the pears and peaches at home. Which are these, papa?"

"They are not wild," I replied, "but grafted or cultivated, or, as you call them, tame trees. No European tree bears good fruit until it is grafted!" I saw a puzzled look come over the little boy's face as he heard this new word, and I hastened to explain it. "Grafting," I continued, "is the process of inserting a slip or twig of a tree into what is called an eye; that is, a knot or hole in the branch of another. This twig or slip then grows and produces, not such fruit as the original stock would have borne, but such as the tree from which it was taken would have produced. Thus, if we have a sour crab tree, and an apple tree bearing fine ribston pippins, we would take a slip of the latter, insert it in an eye of the former, and in a year or two the branch which would then grow would be laden with good apples."

"But," asked Ernest, "where did the slips of good fruit trees come from, if none grow without grafting?"

"From foreign countries," I replied. "It is only in the cold climate of our part of the world that they require this grafting; in many parts of the world, in more southern latitudes than ours, the most luscious fruit trees are indigenous to the soil, and flourish and bear sweet, wholesome fruit, without the slightest care or attention being bestowed upon them; while in England and Germany, and even in France, these same trees require the utmost exertion of horticultural skill to make them bring forth any fruit whatever. Thus, when the Romans invaded England they found there nothing in the way of fruit trees but the crab-apple, nut bushes, and bramble bushes, but by grafting on these, fine apples, filberts, and raspberries were produced, and it was the same in our own dear Switzerland—all our fruit trees were imported."

"Were cherries, father? May we not even call cherries Swiss? I always thought they grew nowhere else."

"I am afraid we cannot even claim cherries as our own, not even the name of them; they are called cherries from Cerasus, a state of Pontus, in Asia, whence they were brought to Europe by Lucullus, a Roman general, about seventy years before Christ. Hazelnuts also came from Pontus; walnuts, again, came originally from Persia. As for grapes, they are of the greatest antiquity. We hear, if you remember, of Noah cultivating vines, and they have been brought from one place to another until they now are to be found in most parts of the civilized world."

"Do you think all these trees will grow?" asked Fritz, as we crossed Jackal River and entered our plantation at Tentholm: "here are lemons, pomegranates, pistachio nuts, and mulberries."

"I have little doubt of it," I replied, "we are evidently within the tropics, where such trees as these are sure to flourish. These pines, now, come from France, Spain, and Italy; the olives from Armenia and Palestine; the figs originally from the island of Chios; the peaches and apricots from Persia; plums from Damascus in Syria, and the pears of all sorts from Greece. However, if our countries have not been blessed in the same way with fruit, we have been given wisdom and skill, which has enabled us to import and cultivate the trees of other lands."

We thus talked and worked until every tree that required the treatment was provided with a stout bamboo prop, and then, with appetites which a gourmand might well have envied, we returned to Falconhurst. I think the good mother was almost alarmed at the way we fell upon the corned beef and palm-cabbage she set before us, but at length these good things produced the desired effect, and one after another declared himself satisfied. As we sat reclining after our labor and digesting our dinner, we discussed the various projects we had in contemplation. "I wish," said my wife, "that you would invent some other plan for climbing to the nest above us; I think that the nest itself is perfect—I really wish for nothing better, but I should like to be able to get to it without scaling that dreadful ladder every time; could you not make a flight of steps to reach it?"

I carefully thought over the project, and turned over every plan for its accomplishment.

"It would be impossible, I am afraid," said I, "to make stairs outside, but within the trunk it might be done. More than once have I thought that this trunk might be hollow, or partly so, and if such be the case our task would be comparatively easy. Did you not tell me the other day that you noticed bees coming from a hole in the tree?"

"Oh, yes," said little Franz, "and I went to look at them and one flew right against my face and stung me, and I almost cried, but I didn't."

"Brave little boy," said I. "Well, now, if the trunk be sufficiently hollow to contain a swarm of bees, it may be, for all we can tell, hollow the greater part of its length, for like the willow in our own country it might draw all its nourishment through the bark, and in spite of its real unsoundness retain a flourishing appearance."

Master Jack, practical as usual, instantly sprang to his feet to put my conjecture to the proof. The rest followed his example, and they were all soon climbing about like squirrels, peeping into the hole, and tapping the wood to discover by sound how far down the cavity extended.

They forgot, in their eagerness, who were the tenants of this interesting trunk. They were soon reminded of it, however, for the bees, disturbed by this unusual noise, with an angry buzz burst out, and in an instant attacked the causers of the annoyance; they swarmed round them, stung them on the hands, face, and neck, settled in their hair, and pursued them as they ran to me for assistance. It was with difficulty that we got rid of the angry insects and were able to attend to the boys. Jack, who had been the first to reach the hole, had fared the worst, and was soon a most pitiable sight, his face swelled to an extraordinary degree, and it was only by the constant application of cold earth that the pain was alleviated. They were all eager to commence an organized attack upon the bees at once, but for an hour or more, by reason of their pain, they were unable to render me much assistance. In the

meantime I made my arrangements. I first took a large calabash gourd, for I intended to make a beehive, that, when we
had driven the insects from their present abode, we might
not lose them entirely. The lower half of the gourd I flattened,
I then cut an arched opening in the front for a doorway, made
a straw roof as a protection from the rain and heat, and the
little house was complete.

Nothing more, however, could then be done, for the irritated
bees were still angrily buzzing round the tree. I waited till
dark, and then, when all the bees had again returned to their
trunk, with Fritz's assistance, I carefully stopped up every
hole in the tree with wet clay, that the bees might not issue
forth next morning before we could begin operations. Very
early were we up and at work. I first took a hollow cane, and
inserted one end through the clay into the tree; down this
tube with pipe and tobacco I smoked most furiously.

The humming and buzzing that went on within was tremendous; the bees evidently could not understand what was
going to happen. I finished my first pipeful, and putting my
thumb over the end of the cane, I gave the pipe to Fritz to
refill. He did so and I again smoked. The buzzing was now
becoming less noisy, and was subsiding into a mere murmur.
By the time I had finished this second pipe all was still; the
bees were stupefied.

"Now then, Fritz," said I, "quick, with a hammer and chisel,
and stand here beside me."

He was up in a moment, and, together, we cut a small door
by the side of the hole; this door, however, we did not take
out, but we left it attached by one corner that it might be removed at a moment's notice; then giving the bees a final dose
of tobacco smoke, we opened it.

Carefully but rapidly we removed the insects, as they clung
in clusters to the sides of the tree, and placed them in the
hive prepared for their reception. As rapidly I then took every
atom of wax and honey from their storehouse, and put it in a
cask I had made ready for the purpose

The bees were now safely removed from the trunk, but I
could not tell whether, when they revived from their temporary stupor, they might not refuse to occupy the house with
which I had presented them, and insist on returning to their

old quarters. To prevent the possibility of this occurrence, I took a quantity of tobacco, and placing it upon a board nailed horizontally within the trunk, I lighted it and allowed it to burn slowly, that the fumes might fill the cavity. It was well I did, for, as the bees returned to consciousness, they left their pretty hive and buzzed away to the trunk of the tree. They seemed astonished at finding this uninhabitable, and an immense deal of noisy humming ensued. Round and round they flew, backward and forward between the gourd and tree, now settling here and now there, until, at length, after due consideration, they took possession of the hive and abandoned their former habitation to us, the invaders of their territory. By the evening they were quite quiet, and we ventured to open the cask in which we had stored our plunder. We first separated the honey from the honeycomb and poured it off into jars and pots; the rest we then took and threw into a vessel of water placed over a slow fire. It soon boiled and the entire mass became fluid. This we placed in a clean canvas bag, and subjected to a heavy pressure. The honey was thus soon forced out, and we stored it in a cask, and, though not perhaps quite equal to the former batch in quality, it was yet capital. The wax that remained in the bag I also carefully stored, for I knew it would be of great use to me in the manufacture of candles. Then after a hard day's work we turned in.

The internal architecture of the tree had now to be attended to, and early the following morning we prepared for the laborious task. A door had first to be made, so at the base of the trunk we cut away the bark and formed an opening just the size of the door we had brought from the captain's cabin, and which, hinges and all, was ready to be hung. The clearing of the rotten wood from the center of the trunk occupied us some time, but at length we had the satisfaction of seeing it entirely accomplished, and, as we stood below, we could look up the trunk, which was like a great smooth funnel, and see the sky above. It was now ready for the staircase, and first we erected in the center a stout sapling to form an axis round which to build the spiral stairs; in this we cut notches to receive the steps, and corresponding notches in the tree itself to support the outer ends. The steps themselves we formed carefully and neatly of planks from the wreck, and clenched them firmly in their places with stout nails. Upward and upward we built, cutting windows in the trunk as we required, to admit light and air, until we were flush with the top of the center pole. On this pole were erected another to reach the top of the tree, and securing it firmly, built in the same way round it until we at length reached the level of the floor of the nest above. To make the ascent of the stairs perfectly easy we ran a hand-rail on either side, one round the center pillar, and the other following the curve of the trunk.

This task occupied us a whole month, and by the end of that period, so accustomed had we become to having a definite piece of work before us that we began to consider what other great alteration we should undertake. We were, however, of course not neglecting the details of our colonial establishment. There were all the animals to be attended to; the goats and sheep had both presented us with additions to our flock, and these frisky youngsters had to be seen after; to prevent them straying to any great distance—for we had no wish to lose them—we tied round their necks little bells, which we had found on board the wreck, and which would assist us to track them. Juno, too, had a fine litter of puppies, but, in spite of the entreaties of the children, I could not consent to keep more than two, and the rest disappeared in that mysterious way in which puppies and kittens are wont to leave the earth. To console the mother, as he said, but also, I suspect, to save himself considerable trouble, Jack placed his little jackal beside the remaining puppies, and, to his joy, found it readily adopted. The other pets were also flourishing, and were being usefully trained. The buffalo, after giving us much trouble, had now become perfectly domesticated, and was a very useful beast of burden, besides being a capital steed for the boys. They guided him by a bar thrust through the hole in his nose, which was now perfectly healed, and this served the purpose just as a bit in the mouth of a horse. I began his education by securing round him a broad girth of buffalo hide and fastening to it various articles, to accustom him to carrying a burden. By degrees he permitted this to be done without making the slightest resistance, and soon carried the paniers, before borne by the ass, readily and willingly.

I then made Master Knips sit upon his back and hold the

reins I had prepared for him, that the animal might become accustomed to the feeling of a rider, and finally allowed Fritz himself to mount. The education of the eagle was not neglected. Fritz every day shot small birds for his food, and these he placed, sometimes between the wide-spreading horns of the buffalo or goat, and, sometimes upon the back of the great bustard, that he might become accustomed to pounce upon living prey. These lessons had their due effect, and the bird, having been taught to obey the voice and whistle of his master, he was soon allowed to bring down small birds upon the wing, when he stooped and struck his quarry in most sportsmanlike manner. We kept him well away from the poultry yard, lest his natural instincts should show themselves and he should put an untimely end to some of our feathered pets.

Neither was Master Knips allowed to remain idle, for Ernest, now that he was in his possession, wished to train him to be of some use. With Jack's help he made a little basket of rushes, which he so arranged with straps that it might be easily fitted on to the monkey's back. Thus equipped, he was taught to mount cocoanut palms and other lofty trees, and to bring down their fruit in the hamper.

Jack was not so successful in his educational attempts. Fangs, as he had christened his jackal, used his fangs, indeed, but only on his own account; nothing could persuade him that the animals he caught were not at once to be devoured, consequently poor Jack was never able to save from his jaws anything but the tattered skin of his prey. Not disheartened, however, he determined that Fangs could be trained, and that he would train him.

These, and such like employments, afforded us the rest and recreation we required while engaged in the laborious task of staircase building.

Among minor occupations, I applied myself to the improvement of our candles. Though the former batch had greatly delighted us at first, yet we were soon obliged to acknowledge that the light they gave was imperfect, and their appearance was unsightly; my wife, too, begged me to find some substitute for the threads of our cotton neckties, which I had previously used as wicks. To give the proper shape and smoothness to the candles, I determined to use the bamboo molds I had prepared. My first idea was to pour the wax in at the end of the mold, and then when the candles were cooled to slip them out; but I was soon convinced that this plan would not succeed. I therefore determined to divide the molds lengthways, and then having greased them well, we might pour the melted wax into the two halves bound tightly together, and so be able to take out the candles when cool without injuring them. The wicks were my next difficulty, and as the mother positively refused to allow us to devote our ties and handkerchiefs for the purpose, I took a piece of inflammable wood from a tree, a native of the Antilles, which I thought would serve our purpose; this I cut into long slips, and fixed in the centers of the molds. My wife, too, prepared some wicks from the fibers of the karata tree, which she declared would beat mine completely out of the field. We put them to the proof.

On a large fire we placed a pot, in which we prepared our wax mixture—half beeswax and half wax from the candleberries. The molds, carefully prepared—half with karata fiber, and half with wooden splint wicks—stood on their ends in a tub of cold water, ready to receive the wax. They were filled; the wax cooled; the candles taken out and subjected to the criticism of all hands. When night drew on, they were formally tested. The decision was unanimous: neither gave such a good light as those with the cotton wicks; but even my wife declared that the light from mine was far preferable to that emitted by hers, for the former, though rather flaring, burned brilliantly, while the latter gave out such a feeble and flickering flame that it was almost useless.

I then turned shoemaker, for I had promised myself a pair of waterproof boots, and now determined to make them.

Taking a pair of socks, I filled them with sand and then coated them over with a thin layer of clay to form a convenient mold; this was soon hardened in the sun, and was ready for use. Layer after layer of caoutchouc I brushed over it, allowing each layer to dry before the next was put on, until at length I considered that the shoes were of sufficient thickness. I dried them, broke out the clay, secured with nails a strip of buffalo hide to the soles, brushed that over with caoutchouc, and I had a pair of comfortable, durable, respectable-looking waterproof boots.

I was delighted; orders poured in from all sides, and soon everyone in the family was likewise provided for.

One objection to Falconhurst was the absence of any spring close by, so that the boys were obliged to bring water daily from the stream; and this involving no little trouble, it was proposed that we should carry the water by pipes from the stream to our present residence. A dam had to be thrown across the river some way up stream, that the water might be raised to a sufficient height to run to Falconhurst. From the reservoir thus made we led the water down by pipes into the turtle's shell, which we placed near our dwelling, and from which the superfluous water flowed off through the hole made in it by Fritz's harpoon. This was an immense convenience, and we formally inaugurated the trough by washing therein a whole sack of potatoes. Thus day after day brought its own work, and day after day saw that work completed. We had no time to be idle, or to lament our separation from our fellow creatures.

One morning, as we were completing our spiral staircase, and giving it such finish as we were capable of, we were suddenly alarmed by hearing a most terrific noise, the roaring or bellowing of a wild beast; so strange a sound was it, that I could not imagine by what animal it was uttered.

Jack thought it perhaps a lion, Fritz hazarded a gorilla, while Ernest gave it as his opinion, and I thought it possible that he was right, that it was a hyena.

"Whatever it is," said I, "we must prepare to receive it; up with you all to the nest while I secure the door."

Then arming the dogs with their collars, I sent them out to protect the animals below, closed the door, and joined my family. Every gun was loaded, every eye was upon the watch. The sound drew nearer, and then all was still; nothing was to be seen. I determined to descend and reconnoiter, and Fritz and I carefully crept down; with our guns at full cock we glided among the trees; noiselessly and quickly we pushed on further and further; suddenly, close by, we heard the terrific sound again. Fritz raised his gun, but almost as quickly again dropped it, and burst into a hearty fit of laughter. There was no mistaking those dulcet tones—he-haw, he-haw, he-haw—resounded through the forest, and our ass, braying his approach right merrily, appeared in sight. To our surprise, however, our friend was not alone: behind him trotted another animal, an ass no doubt, but slim and graceful as a horse. We watched their movements anxiously.

"Fritz," I whispered, "that is an onager. Creep back to Falconhurst and bring me a piece of cord—quietly now!"

While he was gone, I cut a bamboo and split it half-way down to form a pair of pincers, which I knew would be of use to me should I get near the animal. Fritz soon returned with the cord, and I was glad to observe also brought some oats and salt. We made one end of the cord fast to a tree, and at the other end made a running noose. Silently we watched the animals as they approached, quietly browsing; Fritz then arose, holding in one hand the noose and in the other some oats and salt. The ass, seeing his favorite food thus held out, advanced to take it; Fritz allowed him to do so, and he was soon munching contentedly. The stranger, on seeing Fritz, started back; but finding her companion show no signs of alarm, was reassured, and soon approached sniffing, and was about to take some of the tempting food. In a moment the noose left Fritz's adroit hand and fell round her neck; with a single bound she sprang backward the full length of the cord, the noose drew tight, and she fell to the earth half strangled. I at once ran up, loosened the rope, and replaced it by a halter; and placing the pincers upon her nose, secured her by two cords fastened between two trees, and then left her to recover herself.

Everyone hastened up to examine the beautiful animal as she rose to the ground and cast fiery glances around. She lashed out with her heels on every side; and, giving vent to angry snorts, struggled violently to get free. All her endeavors were vain: the cords were stout, and after a while she quieted down and stood exhausted and quivering. I then approached; she suffered me to lead her to the roots of our tree, which for the present formed our stables, and there I tied her up close to the donkey, who was likewise prevented from playing truant.

Next morning I found the onager after her night's rest as wild as ever, and as I looked at the handsome creature I almost despaired of ever taming her proud spirit. Every

expedient was tried, and at length, when the animal was
subdued by hunger, I thought I might venture to mount her;
and having given her the strongest curb and shackled her feet
I attempted to do so. She was an unruly as ever, and as a last
expedient I resolved to adopt a plan which, though cruel, was I
knew attended with wonderful success by the American Indians, by whom it is practiced. Watching a favorable opportunity, I sprang upon the onager's back, and seizing her long ear in
my teeth, in spite of her kicking and plunging, bit it through.
The result was marvelous, the animal ceased plunging, and,
quivering violently, stood stock still. From that moment we
were her masters, the children mounted her one after the
other, and she carried them obediently and quietly. Proud,
indeed, did I feel as I watched this animal, which naturalists
and travelers have declared to be beyond the power of man to
tame, guided hither and thither by my youngest son.

Additions to our poultry yard reminded me of the necessity
of providing some substantial shelter for our animals before
the rainy season came on; three broods of chickens had been
successfully hatched, and the little creatures, forty in all,
were my wife's pride and delight. We began by making a
roof over the vaulted roots of our tree, forming the framework of bamboo canes, which we laid close together and
bound tightly down; others we fixed below as supports. The
interstices were filled up with clay and moss; and coating the
whole over with a mixture of tar and lime-water, we obtained a firm balcony, and a capital roof impervious to the
severest fall of rain. I ran a light rail round the balcony to
give it a more ornamental appearance, and below divided the
buildings into several compartments. Stables, poultry yard,
hay and provision lofts, dairy, kitchen, larder, and dining-hall
were united under one roof.

Our winter quarters were now completed, and we had but
to store them with food. Day after day we worked, bringing in
provisions of every description.

As we were one evening returning from gathering potatoes, it struck me that we should take in a store of acorns; and
sending the two younger boys home with their mother and
the cart, I took a large canvas bag, and with Fritz and Ernest,
the former mounted on his onager, and the latter carrying

his little favorite, Knips, made a detour toward the Acorn Wood.

We reached the spot, tied Lightfoot to a neighboring tree, and began rapidly to fill the sack. As we were thus engaged, Knips sprang suddenly into a bush close by, from which, a moment afterward, issued such strange cries that Ernest followed to see what could be the matter.

"Come!" he shouted; "come and help me! I've got a couple of birds and their eggs. Quick! Ruffed grouse!"

We hurried to the spot. There was Ernest with a fluttering, screaming bird in either hand; while, with his foot, he was endeavoring to prevent his greedy little monkey from seizing the eggs. We quickly tied the legs of the bird, and removing the eggs from the nest, placed them in Ernest's hat; while he gathered some of the long, broad grass, with which the nest was woven, and which grew luxuriantly around, for Franz to play at sword-drill with. We then loaded the onager with the acorns, and moved homeward. The eggs I covered carefully with dry moss, that they might be kept warm, and as soon as possible I handed them over to my wife, who managed the mother so cleverly that she induced her to return to the eggs, and in a few days, to our great delight, we had fifteen beautiful little Canadian chicks.

Franz was greatly pleased with the "swords" his brother brought him; but having no small companion on whom to exercise his valor, he amused himself for a short time in hewing down imaginary foes, and then cut the reeds in slips, and plaited them to form a whip for Lightfoot. The leaves seemed so pliable and strong that I examined them to see to what further use they might be put. Their tissue was composed of long silky fibers. A sudden thought struck me—this must be New Zealand flax. I could not rest till I had announced this invaluable discovery to my wife. She was no less delighted than I was.

"Bring me the leaves!" she exclaimed "Oh, what a delightful discovery! No one shall now be clothed in rags; just make me a spindle, and you shall soon have shirts and stockings and trousers, all good homespun! Quick, Fritz, and bring your mother more leaves!"

We could not help smiling at her eager zeal; but Fritz and

Ernest sprang on their steeds, and soon the onager and buffalo were galloping home again, each laden with a great bundle of flax. The boys dismounted and deposited their offering at their mother's feet.

"Capital!" she exlaimed. "I shall now show you that I am not at all behindhand in ingenuity. This must be retted, carded, spun, and woven, and then with scissors, needle, and thread I will make you any article of clothing you choose."

We decided that Flamingo Marsh would be the best spot for the operation of steeping or "retting" the flax, and next morning we set out thither with the cart drawn by the ass, and laden with the bundles, between which sat Franz and Knips, while the rest of us followed with spades and hatchets. I described to my boys as we went along the process of retting, and explained to them how steeping the flax leaves destroys the useless membrane, while the strong fibers remain.

As we were employed in making beds for the flax and placing it in them, we observed several nests of the flamingo. These are most curiously and skillfully made of glutinous clay, so strong that they can neither be overturned nor washed away. They are formed in the shape of blunted cones, and placed point downward; at the upper and broader end is built a little platform to contain the eggs, on which the female bird sits, with her long legs in the water on either side, until the little birds are hatched and can take to the water. For a fortnight we left the flax to steep, and then taking it out and drying it thoroughly in the sun, stored it for future use at Falconhurst.

Daily did we load our cart with provisions to be brought to our winter quarters: manioc, potatoes, cocoanuts, sweet acorns, sugar-canes, were all collected and stored in abundance —for grumbling thunder, lowering skies, and sharp showers warned us that we had no time to lose. Our corn was sowed, our animals housed, our provisions stored, when down came the rain.

To continue in our nest we found impossible, and we were obliged to retreat to the trunk, where we carried such of our domestic furniture as might have been injured by the damp. Our dwelling was indeed crowded: the animals and provisions below, and our beds and household goods

around us, hemmed us in on every side; by dint of patience and better packing, we obtained sufficient room to work and lie down in; by degrees, too, we became accustomed to the continual noise of the animals and the smell of the stables. The smoke from the fire, which we were occasionally obliged to light, was not agreeable; but in time even that seemed to become more bearable.

To make more space, we turned such animals as we had captured, and who therefore might be imagined to know how to shift for themselves, outside during the daytime, bringing them under the arched roots only at night. To perform this duty Fritz and I used to sally forth every evening, and as regularly every evening did we return soaked to the skin. To obviate this, the mother, who feared these continual wettings might injure our health, contrived waterproofs: she brushed on several layers of caoutchouc over stout shirts, to which she attached hoods; she then fixed to these duck trousers, and thus prepared for each of us a complete waterproof suit, clad in which we might brave the severest rain.

In spite of our endeavors to keep ourselves busy, the time dragged heavily. Our mornings were occupied in tending the animals; the boys amused themselves with their pets, and assisted me in the manufacture of carding-combs and a spindle for the mother. The combs I made with nails, which I placed head downward on a sheet of tin about an inch wide; holding the nails in their proper positions I poured solder round their heads to fix them to the tin, which I then folded down on either side of them to keep them perfectly firm. In the evening, when our room was illuminated with wax candles, I wrote a journal of all the events which had occurred since our arrival in this foreign land; and, while the mother was busy with her needle and Ernest making sketches of birds, beasts, and flowers with which he had met during the past months, Fritz and Jack taught little Franz to read.

Week after week rolled by. Week after week saw us still close prisoners. Incessant rains battered down above us; constant gloom hung over the desolate scene.

Chapter Nine

THE winds at length were lulled, the sun shot his brilliant rays through the riven clouds, the rain ceased to fall— spring had come. No prisoners set at liberty could have felt more joy than we did as we stepped forth from our winter abode, refreshed our eyes with the pleasant verdure around us, and our ears with the merry songs of a thousand happy birds, and drank in the pure, balmy air of spring.

Our plantations were thriving vigorously. The seed we had sown was shooting through the moist earth. All nature was refreshed.

Our nest was our first care; filled with leaves and broken and torn by the wind, it looked indeed dilapidated. We worked hard, and in a few days it was again habitable. My wife begged that I would now start her with the flax, and as early as possible I built a drying-oven, and then prepared it for her use; I, also, after some trouble, manufactured a beetle-reel and spinning-wheel, and she and Franz were soon hard at work, the little boy reeling off the thread his mother spun.

I was anxious to visit Tentholm, for I feared that much of our precious stores might have suffered. Fritz and I made an excursion thither. The damage done to Falconhurst was as nothing compared to the scene that awaited us. The tent was blown to the ground, the canvas torn to rags, the provisions soaked, and two casks of powder utterly destroyed. We immediately spread such things as we hoped yet to preserve in the sun to dry. The pinnace was safe, but our faithful tub-boat was dashed in pieces, and the irreparable damage we had sustained made me resolve to contrive some safer and more stable winter-quarters before the arrival of the next rainy season. Fritz proposed that we should hollow out a cave in the rock, and though the difficulties such an undertaking would present appeared almost insurmountable, I yet determined to make the attempt; we might not, I thought, hew out a cavern of sufficient size to serve as a room, but we might at least make a cellar for the more valuable and perishable of our stores.

Some days afterward we left Falconhurst with the cart laden with a cargo of spades, hammers, chisels, pickaxes, and crowbars, and began our undertaking. On the smooth face of the perpendicular rock I drew out in chalk the size of the proposed entrance, and then, with minds bent on success, we battered away. Six days of hard and incessant toil made but little impression; I do not think that the hole would have been a satisfactory shelter for even Master Knips; but we still did not despair, and were presently rewarded by coming to softer and more yielding substance; our work progressed, and our minds were relieved.

On the tenth day, as our persevering blows were falling heavily, Jack, who was working diligently with a hammer and crowbar, shouted:

"Gone, father! Fritz, my bar has gone through the mountain!"

"Run round and get it," laughed Fritz; "perhaps it has dropped into Europe—you must not lose a good crowbar."

"But, really, it is through; it went right through the rock; I heard it crash down inside. Oh, do come and see!" he shouted excitedly.

We sprang to his side, and I thrust the handle of my hammer into the hole he spoke of; it met with no opposition, I could turn it in any direction I chose. Fritz handed me a long pole; I tried the depth with that. Nothing could I feel. A thin wall, then, was all that intervened between us and a great cavern.

With a shout of joy, the boys battered vigorously at the rock; piece by piece fell, and soon the hole was large enough for us to enter. I stepped near the aperture, and was about to make a further examination, when a sudden rush of poisonous air turned me giddy, and shouting to my sons to stand off, I leaned against the rock.

When I came to myself I explained to them the danger of approaching any cavern or other place where the air has for a long time been stagnant. "Unless air is incessantly renewed it becomes vitiated," I said, "and fatal to those who breathe it. The safest way of restoring it to its original state is to subject it to the action of fire, a few handfuls of blazing hay thrown into this hole may, if the place be small, sufficiently purify the air within to allow us to enter without danger." We tried the experiment. The flame was extinguished the instant it entered. Though bundles of blazing grass were thrown in, no difference was made.

I saw that we must apply some more efficacious remedy, and sent the boys for a chest of signal rockets we had brought from the wreck. We let fly some dozens of these fiery serpents, which went whizzing in, and disappeared at apparently a vast distance from us. Some flew like radiant meteors round, lighted up the mighty circumference and displayed, as by a magician's wand, a sparkling, glittering roof. They looked like avenging dragons driving a foul, malignant fiend out of a beauteous palace.

We waited for a little while after these experiments, and I then again threw in lighted hay. It burned clearly; the air was purified.

Fritz and I enlarged the opening, while Jack, springing on his buffalo, thundered away to Falconhurst to bear the great and astonishing news to his mother.

Great must have been the effect of Jack's eloquence on those at home, for the timbers of the bridge were soon again resounding under the swift but heavy tramp of his steed; and he was quickly followed by the rest of our party in the cart.

All were in the highest state of excitement. Jack had stowed in the cart all the candles he could find, and we now, lighting these, shouldered our arms and entered. I led the way, sounding the ground as I advanced with a long pole, that we might not fall unexpectedly into any great hole or chasm. Silently we marched—the mother, the boys, and even the dogs seeming overawed with the grandeur and beauty of the scene. We were in a grotto of diamonds—a vast cave of glittering crystal: the candles reflected on the walls a golden light, bright as the stars of heaven, while great crystal pillars rose from the floor like mighty trees, mingling their branches high above us and drooping in hundreds of stalactites, which sparkled and glittered with all the colors of the rainbow.

The floor of this magnificent palace was formed of hard, dry sand, so dry that I saw at once that we might safely take up our abode therein, without the slightest fear of danger from damp.

From the appearance of the brilliant crystals round about us I suspected their nature.

I tasted a piece. This was a cavern of rock salt. There was no doubt about it—here was an unlimited supply of the best and purest salt! But one thing detracted from my entire satisfaction and delight—large crystals lay scattered here and there, which, detached from the roof, had fallen to the ground; this, if apt to recur, would keep us in constant peril. I examined some of the masses and discovered that they had been all recently separated, and therefore concluded that the concussion of the air occasioned by the rockets had caused their fall. To satisfy ourselves, however, that there were no more pieces tottering above us, we discharged our guns from the entrance, and watched the effect. Nothing more fell—our magnificent abode was safe.

We returned to Falconhurst with minds full of wonder at

our new discovery, and plans for turning it to the best possible advantage.

Nothing was now talked of but the new house, how it should be arranged, how it should be fitted up. The safety and comfort of Falconhurst, which had at first seemed so great, now dwindled away in our opinion to nothing; it should be kept up, we decided, merely as a summer residence, while our cave should be formed into a winter house and impregnable castle. Our attention was now fully occupied with this new house. Light and air were to be admitted, so we hewed a row of windows in the rock, where we fitted the window cases we had brought from the officers' cabins. We brought the door, too, from Falconhurst, and fitted it in the aperture we had made. The opening in the trunk of the tree I determined to conceal with bark, as less likely to attract the notice of wild beasts or savages should they approach during our absence. The cave itself we divided into four parts: in front, a large compartment into which the door opened, subdivided into our sitting, eating, and sleeping apartments; the right-hand division containing our kitchen and workshop, and the left our stables; behind all this, in the dark recesses of the cave, was our storehouse and powder-magazine. Having already undergone one rainy season, we knew well its discomforts, and thought of many useful arrangements in the laying out of our dwelling. We did not intend to be again smoke-dried; we therefore contrived a properly built fire place and chimney; our stable arrangements, too, were better, and plenty of space was left in our workshop that we should not be hampered in even the most extensive operations.

Our frequent residence at Tentholm revealed to us several important advantages which we had not foreseen. Numbers of splendid turtles often came ashore to deposit their eggs in the sand, and their delicious flesh afforded us many a sumptuous meal. When more than one of these creatures appeared at a time, we used to cut off their retreat to the sea, and, turning them on their backs, fasten them to a stake driven in close by the water's edge, by a cord passed through a hole in their shell. We thus had fresh turtle continually within our reach; for the animals throve well thus secured, and appeared in as good condition, after having been kept thus for several weeks, as others when freshly caught. Lobsters, crabs, and mussels also abounded on the shore. But this was not all; an additional surprise awaited us.

As we were one morning approaching Tentholm, we were attracted by a most curious phenomenon. The waters out at sea appeared agitated by some unseen movement, and as they heaved and boiled, their surface, struck by the beams of the morning sun, seemed illuminated by flashes of fire. Over the water where this disturbance was taking place hovered hundreds of birds, screaming loudly, which ever and anon would dart downward, some plunging beneath the water, some skimming the surface. Then again they would rise and resume their harsh cries. The shining, sparkling mass then rolled onward, and approached in a direct line our bay, followed by the feathered flock above. We hurried down to the shore to further examine this strange sight.

I was convinced as we approached that it was a shoal or bank of herrings.

No sooner did I give utterance to my conjecture than I was assailed by a host of questions concerning this herring-bank, what it was, and what occasioned it.

"A herring-bank," I said, "is composed of an immense number of herrings swimming together. I can scarcely express to you the huge size of this living bank, which extends over a great area many fathoms deep. It is followed by numbers of great ravenous fish, who devour quantities of the herrings, while above hover birds, as you have just seen, ready to pounce down on stragglers near the top. To escape these enemies, the shoal makes for the nearest shore, and seeks safety in those shallows where the large fish cannot follow. But here it meets with a third great enemy. It may escape from the fish, and elude the vigilance of sharp-sighted birds, but from the ingenuity of man it can find no escape. In one year millions of these fish are caught, and yet the roes of only a small number would be sufficient to supply as many fish again."

Soon our fishery was in operation. Jack and Fritz stood in the water with baskets, and baled out the fish, as one bales water with a bucket, throwing them to us on the shore. As quickly as possible we cleaned them, and placed them in casks with salt, first a layer of salt, and then a layer of herrings, and so on, until we had ready many casks of pickled fish.

As the barrels were filled, we closed them carefully, and rolled them away to the cool vaults at the back of our cave.

Our good fortune, however, was not to end here. A day after the herring fishery was over, and the shoal had left our bay, a great number of seals appeared, attracted by the refuse of the herrings which we had thrown into the sea. Though I feared they would not be suitable for our table, we yet secured a score or two for the sake of their skins and fat. The skins we drew carefully off for harness and clothing, and the fat we boiled down for oil, which we put aside in casks for tanning, soap-making, and burning in lamps.

These occupations interfered for some time with our work at Rock House; but as soon as possible we again returned to our labor with renewed vigor.

I had noticed that the salt crystals had for their base a species of gypsum, which I knew might be made of great service to us in our building operations as plaster.

As an experiment, I broke off some pieces, and, after subjecting them to great heat, reduced them to powder. The plaster this formed with water was smooth and white, and as I had then no particular use to which I might put it, I plastered over some of the herring casks, that I might be perfectly certain that all air was excluded. The remainder of the casks I left as they were, for I presently intended to preserve their contents by smoking. To do this, the boys and I built a small hut of reeds and branches, and then we strung our herrings on lines across the roof. On the floor we lit a great fire of brushwood and moss, which threw out a dense smoke, curling in volumes round the fish, and they in a few days seemed perfectly cured.

About a month after the appearance of the herrings, we were favored by a visit from other shoals of fish. Jack espied them first, and called to us that a lot of young whales were off the coast. We ran down and discovered the bay apparently swarming with great sturgeon, salmon, and trout, all making for the mouth of Jackal River, that they might ascend it and deposit their spawn among the stones.

Jack was delighted at his discovery.

"Here are proper fish!" he exclaimed; "none of your paltry fry. How do you preserve these sorts of fish? Potted, salted, or smoked?"

"Not so fast," said I, "not so fast; tell me how they are to be caught, and I will tell you how they are to be cooked."

"Oh! I'll catch them fast enough," he replied, and darted off to Rock House.

While I was still puzzling my brains as to how I should set to work, he returned with his fishing apparatus in hand; a bow and arrow, and a ball of twine.

At the arrow-head he had fastened a barbed spike, and had secured the arrow to the end of the string. Armed with this weapon, he advanced to the river's edge.

His arrow flew from the bow, and, to my surprise, struck one of the largest fish in the side.

"Help, father, help!" he cried, as the great fish darted off, carrying arrow and all with it; "help! or he will pull me into the water."

I ran to his assistance, and together we struggled with the finny monster. He pulled tremendously, and lashed the water around him; but we held the cord fast, and he had no chance of escape. Weaker and weaker grew his struggles, and, at length, exhausted by his exertions and loss of blood, he allowed us to draw him ashore.

He was a noble prize, and Fritz and Ernest, who came up just as we completed his capture, were quite envious of Jack's success. Not to be behindhand, they eagerly rushed off for weapons themselves.

We were soon all in the water, Fritz with a harpoon, Ernest with a rod and line, and I myself, armed, like Neptune, with an iron trident, or more properly speaking, perhaps, a pitchfork. Soon the shore was strewn with a goodly number of the finest fish—monster after monster we drew to land. At length Fritz, after harpooning a great sturgeon full eight feet long, could not get the fish ashore; we all went to his assistance, but our united efforts were unavailing.

"The buffalo!" proposed my wife, and off went Jack for Storm. Storm was harnessed to the harpoon rope, and soon the monstrous fish lay panting on the sand.

We were in . . . a vast cave of glittering crystal. (Page 180)

We at length, when we had captured as many fish as we could possibly utilize, set about cleaning and preparing their flesh. Some we salted, some we dried like the herrings, some we treated like the tunny of the Mediterranean—we prepared them in oil. Of the roe of the sturgeon I decided to form caviare, the great Russian dish. I removed from it all the membranes by which it is surrounded, washed it in vinegar, salted it, pressed out all the moisture caused by the wet-absorbing properties of the salt, packed it in small barrels, and stowed it away in our storehouse.

I knew that of the sturgeon's bladder the best isinglass is made, so carefully collecting the air-bladders from all those we had killed, I washed them and hung them up to stiffen. The outer coat or membrane I then peeled off, cutting the remainder into strips, technically called staples. These staples I placed in an iron pot over the fire, and when they had been reduced to a proper consistency I strained off the glue through a clean cloth, and spread it out on a slab of stone in thin layers, letting them remain until they were dry. The substance I thus obtained was beautifully transparent, and promised to serve as an excellent substitute for glass in our window-frames.

Fortunately, in this beautiful climate little or no attention was necessary to the kitchen garden, the seeds sprang up and flourished without apparently the slightest regard for the time or season of the year. Peas, beans, wheat, barley, rye, and Indian corn seemed constantly ripe, while cucumbers, melons, and all sorts of other vegetables grew luxuriantly. The success of our garden at Tentholm encouraged me to hope that my experiment at Falconhurst had not failed, and one morning we started to visit the spot.

As we passed by the field from which the potatoes had been dug, we found it covered with barley, wheat, rye, and peas in profusion.

I turned to the mother in amazement.

"Where has this fine crop sprung from?" said I.

"From the earth," she replied laughing, "where Franz and I sowed the seed I brought from the wreck. The ground was ready tilled by you and the boys; all we had to do was to scatter the seed."

I was delighted at the sight, and it augured well, I thought, for the success of my maize plantation. We hurried to the field. The crop had indeed grown well, and what was more, appeared to be duly appreciated. A tremendous flock of feathered thieves rose as we approached. Among them Fritz espied a few ruffed grouse, and, quick as thought, unhooding his eagle, he started him off in chase, then sprung on his onager and followed at full gallop. His noble bird marked out the finest grouse, and, soaring high above it, stooped and bore his prey to the ground. Fritz was close at hand, and springing through the bushes he saved the bird from death, hooded the eagle's eyes, and returned triumphantly. Jack had not stood idle, for slipping his pet, Fangs, he had started him among some quails who remained upon the field, and to my surprise the jackal secured some dozen of the birds, bringing them faithfully to his master's feet.

We then turned our steps toward Falconhurst, where we were refreshed by a most delicious drink the mother prepared for us: the stems of the young Indian corn, crushed, strained, and mixed with water and the juice of the sugar-cane.

We then made preparations for an excursion the following day, for I wished to establish a sort of semi-civilized farm at some distance from Falconhurst, where we might place some of our animals, which had become too numerous with our limited means to supply them with food. In the large cart, to which we harnessed the buffalo, cow, and ass, we placed a dozen fowls, four young pigs, two couple of sheep, and as many goats, and a pair of hens and one cock grouse. Fritz led the way on his onager, and by a new track we forced a passage through the woods and tall grasses toward Cape Disappointment.

The difficult march was at length over, and we emerged from the forest upon a large plain covered with curious little bushes; the branches of these little shrubs and the ground about them were covered with pure white flakes.

"Snow! snow!" exclaimed Franz. "Oh, mother, come down from the cart and play snowballs. This is jolly; much better than the ugly rain."

I was not surprised at the boy's mistake, for indeed the flakes did look like snow; but before I could express my opinion, Fritz declared that the plant must be a kind of dwarf cotton tree. We approached nearer and found he was right—soft fine wool inclosed in pods, and still hanging on the bushes or lying on the ground, abounded in every direction. We had indeed discovered this valuable plant. The mother was charmed; and gathering a great quantity in three capacious bags, we resumed our journey.

Crossing the cotton field we ascended a pretty wooded hill. The view from the summit was glorious: luxuriant grass at our feet stretching down the hillside, dotted here and there with shady trees, among which gushed down a sparkling brook, while below lay the rich green forest, with the sea beyond.

What better situation could we hope to find for our new farm? Pasture, water, shade, and shelter, all were here.

We pitched our tent, built our fireplace, and leaving the mother to prepare our repast, Fritz and I selected a spot for the erection of our shed. We soon found a group of trees so situated that the trunks would serve as posts for our intended building. Thither we carried all our tools, and then, as the day was far advanced, enjoyed our supper, and lay down upon most comfortable beds, which the mother had prepared for us with the cotton.

The group of trees we had selected was exactly suited to our purpose, for it formed a regular rectilinear figure, the greatest side of which faced the sea. I cut deep mortices in the trunks about ten feet from the ground, and again ten feet higher up to form a second story. In these mortices I inserted beams, thus forming a framework for my building, and then, making a roof of laths, I overlaid it with bark, which I stripped from a neighboring tree, and fixed with acacia thorns, and which would effectually shoot off any amount of rain.

While clearing up the scraps of bark and other rubbish for fuel for our fire, I noticed a peculiar smell, and stooping down I picked up pieces of the bark, some of which, to my great surprise, I found was that of the terebinth tree, and the rest that of the American fir. The goats, too, made an important discovery among the same heap, for we found them busily rooting out pieces of cinnamon, a most delicious and aromatic spice.

"From the fir," said I to the boys, "we get turpentine and tar, and thus it is that the fir tree becomes such a valuable article of commerce. So we may look forward to preparing pitch for our yacht, with tar and oil, you know, and cart-grease, too, with tar and fat. I do not know that you will equally appreciate the terebinth tree; a gum issues from incisions in the bark which hardens in the sun, and becomes as transparent as amber; when burned it gives forth a most delicious perfume, and when dissolved in spirits of wine, forms a beautiful transparent varnish."

The completion of our new farmhouse occupied us several days; we wove strong lianas and other creepers together to form the walls to the height of about six feet; the rest, up to the roof, we formed merely of a lattice-work of laths to admit both air and light. Within we divided the house into three parts; one subdivided into stalls for the animals; a second fitted with perches for the birds, and a third, simply furnished with a rough table and benches, to serve as a sleeping apartment for ourselves, when we should find it necessary to pay the place a visit. In a short time the dwelling was most comfortably arranged, and as we daily filled the feeding troughs with the food the animals best liked, they showed no inclination to desert the spot we had chosen for them.

Yet, hard as we had worked, we found that the provisions we had brought with us would be exhausted before we could hope to be able to leave the farm. I therefore dispatched Jack and Fritz for fresh supplies.

During their absence, Ernest and I made a short excursion in the neighborhood, that we might know more exactly the character of the country near our farm.

Passing over a brook which flowed toward the wall of rocks, we reached a large marsh, and as we walked round it, I noticed with delight that it was covered with the rice plant growing wild in the greatest profusion. Here and there only were there any ripe plants, and from these rose a number of ruffed grouse, at which both Ernest and I let fly. Two fell, and Fangs, who was with us, brought them to our feet. As we advanced, Knips skipped from the back of his steed Juno and began to regale himself on some fruit, at a short distance off; we followed the little animal and found him devouring delicious strawberries. Having enjoyed the fruit ourselves, we filled the hamper Knips always carried, and secured the fruit from his pilfering paws with leaves fixed firmly down.

I then took a sample of the rice seeds to show the mother, and we continued our journey.

Presently we reached the borders of the pretty lake which we had seen beyond the swamp. The nearest aspect of its calm blue waters greatly charmed us, and still more so the sight of numbers of black swans, disporting themselves on the glassy surface, in which their stately forms and graceful movements were reflected as in a mirror. It was delightful to watch these splendid birds, old and young swimming together in the peaceful enjoyment of life, seeking their food, and pursuing one another playfully in the water.

I could not think of breaking in upon their happy, beautiful existence by firing among them, but our dog Juno was by no means so considerate; for all at once I heard a plunge, and saw her drag out of the water a most peculiar-looking creature, something like a small otter, but not above twenty-two inches in length, which she would have torn to pieces had we not hurried up and taken it from her.

This curious little animal was of a soft, dark brown color, the fur being of a lighter shade under the body; its feet were furnished with large claws, and also completely webbed, the head small, with deeply set eyes and ears, and terminating in a broad flat bill like that of a duck.

This singularity seemed to us so droll that we both laughed heartily, feeling at the same time much puzzled to know what sort of animal it could possibly be. For want of a better, we gave it the name of the "Beast with a Bill," and Ernest willingly undertook to carry it, that it might be stuffed and kept as a curiosity.

After this we returned to the farm, thinking our messengers might soon arrive, and sure enough, in about a quarter of an hour Fritz and Jack made their appearance at a brisk trot, and gave a circumstantial account of their mission.

I was pleased to see that they had fulfilled their orders intelligently, carrying out my intentions in the spirit and not blindly to the letter.

Next morning we quitted the farm (which we named Woodlands) after providing amply for the wants of the animals, sheep, goats, and poultry which we left there.

Shortly afterward, on entering a wood, we found it tenanted

by an enormous number of apes, who instantly assailed us with showers of fir-cones, uttering hideous and angry cries, and effectually checking our progress, until we put them to flight by a couple of shots, which not a little astonished their weak minds.

Fritz picked up some of their missiles, and, showing them to me, I recognized the cone of the stone-pine.

"By all means gather some of these cones, boys," said I; "you will find the kernel has a pleasant taste, like almonds, and from it we can, by pressing, obtain an excellent oil. Therefore I should like to carry some home with us."

A hill, which seemed to promise a good view from its summit, next attracted my notice, and, on climbing it, we were more than repaid for the exertion by the extensive and beautiful prospect which lay spread before our eyes. The situation altogether was so agreeable, that here also I resolved to make a settlement, to be visited occasionally, and, after resting awhile and talking the matter over, we set to work to build a cottage such as we had lately finished at Woodlands. Our experience there enabled us to proceed quickly with the work, and in a few days the rustic abode was completed, and received, by Ernest's choice, the grand name of Prospect Hill.

My chief object in undertaking this expedition had been to discover some tree from whose bark I could hope to make a useful light boat or canoe. Hitherto I had met with none at all fit for my purpose, but, not despairing of success, I began, when the cottage was built, to examine carefully the surrounding woods, and, after considerable trouble, came upon two magnificent, tall straight trees, the bark of which seemed something like that of the birch. Selecting one whose trunk was, to a great height, free from branches, we attached to one of the lower of the boughs the rope ladder we had with us, and Fritz, ascending it, cut the bark through in a circle; I did the same at the foot of the tree, and then, from between the circle we took a narrow perpendicular slip of bark entirely out, so that we could introduce the proper tools by which gradually to loosen and raise the main part, so as finally to separate it from the tree uninjured and entire. This we found possible, because the bark was moist and flexible. Great care and exertion was necessary, as the bark became detached, to support it, until the whole was ready to be let gently down upon the grass. This seemed a great achievement; but our work was by no means ended, nor could we venture to desist from it until, while the material was soft and pliable, we had formed it into the shape we desired for the canoe.

In order to do this, I cut a long triangular piece out of each end of the roll, and, placing the sloping parts one over the other, I drew the ends into a pointed form and secured them with pegs and glue.

This successful proceeding had, however, widened the boat, and made it too flat in the middle, so that it was necessary to put ropes round it, and tighten them until the proper shape was restored, before we could allow it to dry in the sun.

This being all I could do without a greater variety of tools, I determined to complete my work in a more convenient situation, and forthwith dispatched Fritz and Jack with orders to bring the sledge (which now ran on wheels taken from gun-carriages) that the canoe might be transported direct to the vicinity of the harbor at Tentholm.

During their absence I fortunately found some wood naturally curved, just suited for ribs to support and strengthen the sides of the boat.

When the two lads returned with the sledge, it was time to rest for the night; but with early dawn we were again busily at work.

The sledge was loaded with the new boat, and everything else we could pack into it, and we turned our steps homeward, finding the greatest difficulty, however, in getting our vehicle through the woods. We crossed the bamboo swamp, where I cut a fine mast for my boat, and came at length to a small opening or defile in the ridge of rocks, where a little torrent rushed from its source down into the larger stream beyond; here we determined to make a halt, in order to erect a great earth wall across the narrow gorge, which, being thickly planted with prickly pear, Indian fig, and every thorny bush we could find, would in time form an effectual barrier against the intrusion of wild beasts, the cliffs being, to the best of our belief, in every other part inaccessible. For our own convenience we retained a small winding-path through this barrier, concealing and defending it with piles of branches and thorns, and also we contrived a light drawbridge over the stream, so that we rendered the pass altogether a very strong position, should we ever have to act on the defensive.

This work occupied two days, and continuing on our way, we were glad to rest at Falconhurst before arriving (quite tired and worn out) at Tentholm.

It took some time to recruit our strength after this long and fatiguing expedition, and then we vigorously resumed the task of finishing the canoe. The arrangements, I flattered myself, were carried out in a manner quite worthy of a ship builder; a mast, sails, and paddles were fitted, but my final touch, although I prized it highly and considered it a grand and original idea, would no doubt have excited only ridicule and contempt had it been seen by a naval man. My contrivance was this: I had a couple of large air-tight bags made of the skins of the dog-fish, well tarred and pitched, inflated, and made fast on each side of the boat, just above the level of the water. These floats, however much she might be loaded, would effectually prevent either the sinking or capsizing of my craft.

I may as well relate in this place what I omitted at the time of its occurrence. During the rainy season our cow presented us with a bull-calf, and that there might never be any difficulty in managing him, I at a very early age pierced his nose and placed a short stick in it, to be exchanged for a ring when he was old enough. The question now came to be, who should be his master, and to what should we train him?

"Why not teach him," said Fritz, "to fight the wild animals, and defend us, like the fighting bulls of the Hottentots? That would be really useful!"

"I am sure I should much prefer a gentle bull to a fighting one!" exclaimed his mother; "but do you mean to say tame oxen can be taught to act rationally on the defensive?"

"I can but repeat what I have heard or read," replied I, "as regards the race of Hottentots who inhabit the south of Africa, among all sorts of wild and ferocious animals.

"The wealth of these people consists solely in their flocks and herds, and, for their protection, they train their bulls to act as guards.

"These courageous animals keep the rest from straying away, and when danger threatens, they give instant notice of it, drive the herd together in a mass, the calves and young cows being placed in the center; around them the bulls and strong oxen make a formidable circle with their horned heads turned to the front, offering determined resistance to the fiercest foe.

"These fighting bulls will even sometimes rush with dreadful bellowing to meet the enemy; and should it be a mighty lion or other strong and daring monster, sacrifice their own lives in defense of the herd.

"It is said that formerly, when Hottentot tribes made war on one another, it was not unusual to place a troop of these stout-hearted warriors in the van of the little army, when their heroism led to decisive victory on one side or the other.

"But," continued I, "although I can see you are all delighted with my description of these fine, warlike animals, I think we had better train this youngster to be a peaceable bull. Who is to have charge of him?"

Ernest thought it would be more amusing to train his monkey than a calf. Jack, with the buffalo and his hunting jackal, had quite enough on his hands. Fritz was content with the onager. Their mother was voted mistress of the old gray donkey. And I myself being superintendent-in-chief of the whole establishment of animals, there remained only little Franz to whose special care the calf could be committed.

"What say you, my boy—will you undertake to look after this little fellow?"

"Oh, yes, father!" he replied. "Once you told me about a strong man, I think his name was Milo, and he had a tiny calf, and he used to carry it about everywhere. It grew bigger and bigger, but still he carried it often, till at last he grew so strong that when it was quite a great big ox, he could lift it as easily as ever. And so, you see, if I take care of our wee calf and teach it to do what I like, perhaps when it grows big I shall still be able to manage it, and then—oh, papa—do you think I might ride upon it?"

I smiled at the child's simplicity, and his funny application of the story of Milo of Cortona.

"The calf shall be yours, my boy. Make him as tame as you can, and we will see about letting you mount him some day; but remember, he will be a great bull long before you are nearly a man. Now, what will you call him?"

"Shall I call him Grumble, father? Hear what a low muttering noise he makes!"

"Grumble will do famously."

"Grumble, Grumble. Oh, it beats your buffalo's name hollow, Jack!"

"Not a bit," said he; "why, you can't compare the two names. Fancy mother saying, 'Here comes Franz on Grumble, but Jack *riding on the Storm*.' Oh, it sounds sublime!"

We named the two puppies Bruno and Fawn, and so ended this important domestic business.

For two months we worked steadily at our salt-cave, in order to complete the necessary arrangement of partition walls, so as to put the rooms and stalls for the animals in comfortable order for the next long rainy season, during which time, when other work would be at a standstill, we could carry on many minor details for the improvement of the abode.

We leveled the floors first with clay; then spread gravel mixed with melted gypsum over that, producing a smooth, hard surface, which did very well for most of the apartments; but I was ambitious of having one or two carpets, and set about making a kind of felt in the following way:

I spread out a large piece of sailcloth, and covered it equally all over with a strong liquid, made of glue and isinglass, which saturated it thoroughly. On it we then laid wool and hair from the sheep and goats, which had been carefully cleaned and prepared, and rolled and beat it until it adhered tolerably smoothly to the cloth. Finally it became, when perfectly dry, a covering for the floor of our sitting room by no means to be despised.

One morning, just after these labors at the salt-cave were completed, happening to awake unusually early, I turned my thoughts, as I lay waiting for sunrise, to considering what length of time we had now passed on this coast, and discovered, to my surprise, that the very next day would be the anniversary of our escape from the wreck. My heart swelled with gratitude to the gracious God, who had then granted us deliverance, and ever since had loaded us with benefits; and I resolved to set to-morrow apart as a day of thanksgiving, in joyful celebration of the occasion.

My mind was full of indefinite plans when I rose, and the

day's work began as usual. I took care that everything should be cleaned, cleared, and set in order both outside and inside our dwelling; none, however, suspecting that there was any particular object in view. Other more private preparations I also made for the next day. At supper I made the coming event known to the assembled family.

"Good people, do you know that to-morrow is a very great and important day? We shall have to keep it in honor of our merciful escape to this land, and call it Thanksgiving-Day."

Everyone was surprised to hear that we had already been twelve months in the country—indeed, my wife believed I might be mistaken, until I showed her how I had calculated regularly ever since the 31st of January, on which day we were wrecked, by marking off in my almanac the Sundays as they arrived for the remaining eleven months of that year.

"Since then," I added, "I have counted thirty-one days. This is the 1st of February. We landed on the 2d, therefore to-morrow is the anniversary of the day of our escape. As my bookseller has not sent me an almanac for the present year, we must henceforth reckon for ourselves."

"Oh, that will be good fun for us," said Ernest. "We must have a long stick, like Robinson Crusoe, and cut a notch in it every day, and count them up every now and then, to see how the weeks and months and years go by."

"That is all very well, if you know for certain the number of days in each month, and in the year. What do you say, Ernest?"

"The year contains 365 days, 5 hours, 48 minutes, and 45 seconds," returned he promptly.

"Perfectly correct!" said I, smiling; "but you would get in a mess with those spare hours, minutes, and seconds in a year or two, wouldn't you?"

"Not at all! Every four years I would add them all together, make a day, stick it into February, and call that year leap year."

"Well done, Professor Ernest! We must elect you astronomer royal in this our kingdom, and let you superintend and regulate everything connected with the lapse of time, clocks and watches included."

Before they went to sleep, I could hear my boys whispering

among themselves, about "father's mysterious allusions" to next day's festival and rejoicings; but I offered no explanations, and went to sleep, little guessing that the rogues had laid a counter-plot, far more surprising than my simple plan for their diversion.

Nothing less than roar of artillery startled me from sleep at daybreak next morning. I sprang up and found my wife as much alarmed as I was by the noise, otherwise I should have been inclined to believe it fancy.

"Fritz! dress quickly and come with me!" cried I, turning to his hammock. Lo, it was empty! neither he nor Jack were to be seen.

Altogether bewildered, I was hastily dressing, when their voices were heard, and they rushed in shouting:

"Hurrah! didn't we rouse you with a right good thundering salute?"

But perceiving at a glance that we had been seriously alarmed, Fritz hastened to apologize for the thoughtless way in which they had sought to do honor to the Day of Thanksgiving, without considering that an unexpected cannon-shot would startle us unpleasantly from our slumbers.

We readily forgave the authors of our alarm, in consideration of the good intention which had prompted the deed, and, satisfied that the day had at least been duly inaugurated, we all went quietly to breakfast.

Afterward we sat together for a long time, enjoying the calm beauty of the morning, and talking of all that had taken place on the memorable days of the storm a year ago; for I desired that the awful events of that time should live in the remembrance of my children with a deepening sense of gratitude for our deliverance. Therefore I read aloud passages from my journal, as well as many beautiful verses from the Psalms, expressive of joyful praise and thanksgiving, so that even the youngest among us was impressed and solemnized at the recollections of escape from a terrible death, and also led to bless and praise the name of the Lord our Deliverer.

Dinner followed shortly after this happy service, and I then announced for the afternoon a "Grand Display of Athletic Sports," in which I and my wife were to be spectators and judges.

"Father, what a grand idea!"

"Oh, how jolly! Are we to run races?"

"And prizes! Will there be prizes, father?"

"The judges offer prizes for competition in every sort of manly exercise," replied I. "Shooting, running, riding, leaping, climbing, swimming; we will have an exhibition of your skill in all. Now for it!"

"Trumpeters! sound for the opening of the lists."

Uttering these last words in a stentorian voice and wildly waving my arms toward a shady spot, where the ducks and geese were quietly resting, had the absurd effect I intended.

Up they all started in a fright, gabbling and quacking loudly, to the infinite amusement of the children, who began to bustle about in eager preparations for the contest, and begging to know with what they were to begin.

"Let us have shooting first, and the rest when the heat of the day declines. Here is a mark I have got ready for you," said I, producing a board roughly shaped like a kangaroo, and of about the size of one. This target was admired, but Jack could not rest satisfied till he had added ears, and a long leather strap for a tail.

It was then fixed in the attitude most characteristic of the creature, and the distance for firing measured off. Each of the three competitors was to fire twice.

Fritz hit the kangaroo's head each time; Ernest hit the body once; and Jack, by a lucky chance, shot the ears clean away from the head, which feat raised a shout of laughter.

A second trial with pistols ensued, in which Fritz again came off victor.

Then desiring the competitors to load with small shot, I threw a little board as high as I possibly could up in the air, each in turn aiming at and endeavoring to hit it before it touched the ground.

In this I found to my surprise that the sedate Ernest succeeded quite as well as his more impetuous brother Fritz.

As for Jack, his flying board escaped wholly uninjured.

After this followed archery, which I liked to encourage, foreseeing that a time might come when ammunition would fail; and in this practice I saw with pleasure that my elder sons were really skillful, while even little Franz acquitted himself well.

A pause ensued, and then I started a running match.

Fritz, Ernest, and Jack were to run to Falconhurst, by the most direct path. The first to reach the tree was to bring me, in proof of his success, a penknife I had accidentally left on the table in my sleepingroom.

At a given signal, away went the racers in fine style. Fritz and Jack, putting forth all their powers, took the lead at once, running in advance of Ernest, who started at a good, steady pace, which I predicted he would be better able to maintain than such a furious rate as his brothers.

But long before we expected to see them back, a tremendous noise of galloping caused us to look with surprise toward the bridge, and Jack made his appearance, thundering along on his buffalo, with the onager and the donkey tearing after him riderless, and the whole party in the wildest spirits.

"Hullo!" cried I, "what sort of footrace do you call this, Master Jack?"

He shouted merrily as he dashed up to us; then flinging himself off and saluting us in a playful way:

"I very soon saw," said he, "that I hadn't a chance; so renouncing all idea of the prize, I caught Storm, and made him gallop home with me, to be in time to see the others come puffing in. Lightfoot and old Grizzle chose to join me—I never invited them!"

By and by the other boys arrived, Ernest holding up the knife in token of being the winner; and after hearing all particulars about the running, and that he had reached Falconhurst two minutes before Fritz, we proceeded to test the climbing powers of the youthful athletes.

In this exercise Jack performed wonders. He ascended with remarkable agility the highest palms whose stems he could clasp. And when he put on the shark-skin buskins, which enabled him to take firm hold of larger trees, he played antics like a squirrel or a monkey, peeping and grinning at us, at first on one side of the stem, and then on the other, in a most diverting way.

Fritz and Ernest climbed well, but could not come near the grace and skill of their active and lively young brother.

Riding followed, and marvelous feats were performed, Fritz and Jack proving themselves very equal in their management of their different steeds.

I thought the riding was over, when little Franz appeared from the stable in the cave, leading young Grumble, the bull-calf, with a neat saddle of kangaroo hide, and a bridle passed through his nose ring.

The child saluted us with a pretty little air of confidence, exclaiming:

"Now, most learned judges, prepare to see something quite new and wonderful! The great bull-tamer, Milo of Cortona, desires the honor of exhibiting before you."

Then taking a whip, and holding the end of a long cord, he made the animal, at the word of command, walk, trot, and gallop in a circle round him.

He afterward mounted, and showed off Grumble's somewhat awkward paces.

The sports were concluded by swimming matches, and the competitors found a plunge in salt water very refreshing after their varied exertions.

Fritz showed himself a master in the art. At home in the element, no moment betokened either exertion or weariness.

Ernest exhibited too much anxiety and effort, while Jack was far too violent and hasty, and soon became exhausted.

Franz gave token of future skill.

By this time, as it was getting late, we returned to our dwelling, the mother having preceded us in order to make arrangements for the ceremony of prize-giving.

We found her seated in great state, with the prizes set out by her side.

The boys marched in pretending to play various instruments in imitation of a band, and then all four, bowing respectfully, stood before her, like the victors in a tournament of old, awaiting the reward of valor from the Queen of Beauty, which she bestowed with a few words of praise and encouragement.

Fritz, to his immense delight, received, as the prize for shooting and swimming, a splendid double-barreled rifle, and a beautiful hunting-knife.

To Ernest, as winner of the running match, was given a handsome gold watch.

For climbing and riding, Jack had a pair of silver plated spurs, and a riding whip, both of which gave him extraordinary pleasure.

Franz received a pair of stirrups, and a driving whip made of rhinoceros hide, which we thought would be of use to him in the character of bull-trainer.

When the ceremony was supposed to be over, I advanced, and solemnly presented to my wife a lovely work-box, filled with every imaginable requirement for a lady's work-table, which she accepted with equal surprise and delight.

The whole entertainment afforded the boys such intense pleasure, and their spirits rose to such a pitch, that nothing would serve them but another salvo of artillery, in order to close with befitting dignity and honor so great a day. They gave me no peace till they had leave to squander some gunpowder, and then at last their excited feelings seeming relieved, we were able to sit down to supper; shortly afterward we joined in family worship and retired to rest.

Soon after the great festival of our grand Thanksgiving-Day I recollected that it was now the time when, the figs at Falconhurst being ripe, immense flocks of ortolans and wild pigeons were attracted thither, and as we had found those preserved last year of the greatest use among our stores of winter provisions, I would not miss the opportunity of renewing our stock; and therefore, laying aside the building work, we removed with all speed to our home in the tree, where sure enough we found the first detachment of the birds already busy with the fruit.

In order to spare ammunition, I resolved to concoct a strong sort of birdlime, of which I had read in some account of the Palm Islanders, who make it of fresh caouthouc mixed with oil, and of so good a quality that it has been known to catch even peacocks and turkeys.

Fritz and Jack were therefore dispatched to collect some fresh caoutchouc from the trees, and as this involved a good gallop on Storm and Lightfoot, they, nothing loath, set off.

They took a supply of calabashes, in which to bring the gum, and we found it high time to manufacture a fresh stock of these useful vessels. I was beginning to propose an expedition

to the Gourd-tree Wood, regretting the time it would take
to go such a distance, when my wife reminded me of her plantation near the potato field.

There to our joy we found that all the plants were flourishing, and crops of gourds and pumpkins, in all stages of ripeness, covered the ground.

Selecting a great number suited to our purpose, we hastened
home, and began the manufacture of basins, dishes, plates,
flasks, and spoons of all sorts and sizes, with even greater success than before.

When the riders returned with the caoutchouc, they brought
several novelties besides.

A crane, for example, shot by Fritz, and an animal which
they called a marmot, but which to me seemed much more like
a badger.

Aniseed, turpentine, and wax berries for candles, they had
also collected, and a curious root which they introduced by
the name of the monkey plant.

"And pray wherefore 'monkey plant,' may I ask?"

"Well, for this reason, father," answered Fritz: "we came
upon an open space in the forest near Woodlands, and perceived a troop of monkeys, apparently engaged, as Jack said,
in cultivating the soil! Being curious to make out what they
were at, we tied up the dogs, as well as Storm and Lightfoot,
and crept near enough to see that the apes were most industriously grubbing up and eating roots. This they did in a way
that nearly choked us with laughter, for when the root was
rather hard to pull up, and the leaves were torn off, they seized
it firmly in their teeth, and flung themselves fairly heels-over-
head in the most ludicrous fashion you ever saw, and up came
the root, unable to resist the leverage! Of course we wanted
to see what this dainty morsel was like, so we loosed the dogs,
and the apes cleared out double quick, leaving plenty of the
roots about. We tasted them, and thought them very nice.
Will you try one?"

The plant was quite new to me, but I imagined it might be
what is called in China "ginseng," and there prized and valued
beyond everything. The children being curious to hear more
about this ginseng, I continued:

"In China it is considered so strengthening and wholesome

that it is used as a sort of universal medicine, being supposed to prolong human life.

"The emperor alone has the right to permit it to be gathered, and guards are placed round land where it grows.

"Ginseng is to be found in Tartary, and has lately been discovered in Canada; it is cultivated in Pennsylvania, because the Americans introduce it secretly into China as smuggled merchandise."

Fritz then continued:

"After this we went on to Woodlands; but mercy on us! what a confusion the place was in! Everything smashed or torn, and covered with mud and dirt; the fowls terrified, the sheep and goats scattered, the contents of the rooms dashed about as if a whirlwind had swept through the house."

"What!" I exclaimed, while my wife looked horrified at the news, conjuring up in her imagination hordes of savages who would soon come and lay waste Falconhurst and Tentholm as well as Woodlands. "How can that have happened? Did you discover the authors of all this mischief!"

"Oh," said Jack, "it was easy to see that those dreadful monkeys had done it all. First they must have got into the yards and sheds, and hunted the fowls and creatures about; and then I dare say the cunning rascals put a little monkey in at some small opening, and bid him unfasten the shutters—you know what nimble fingers they have. Then of course the whole *posse* of them swarmed into our nice tidy cottage and skylarked with every single thing they could lay paws on, till perhaps they got hungry all at once, and bethought them of the 'ginseng,' as you call it, out in the woods yonder, where we found them so busy refreshing themselves, the mischievous villians!"

"While we were gazing at all this ruin in a sort of bewilderment," pursued Fritz, "we heard a sound of rushing wings and strange ringing cries, as of multitudes of birds passing high above us, and looking up we perceived them flying quickly in a wedge-shaped flock at a great height in the air. They began gradually to descend, taking the direction of the lake, and separated into a number of small detachments, which followed in a long, straight line, and at a slower rate, the movements of the leaders, who appeared to be examining the neighborhood. We could now see what large birds they must be, but dared not show ourselves or follow them, lest they should take alarm.

"Presently, and with one accord, they quickened their motion, just as if the band had begun to play a quick march after a slow one, and rapidly descended to earth in a variety of lively ways, and near enough for us to see that they must be cranes.

"Some alighted at once, while others hovered sportively over them. Many darted to the ground, and, just touching it, would soar again upward with a strong but somewhat heavy flight.

"After gamboling in this way for a time, the whole multitude, as though at the word of command, alighted on the rice fields, and began to feast on the fresh grain.

"We thought now was our time to get a shot at the cranes, and cautiously approached; but they were too cunning to let themselves be surprised, and we came unexpectedly upon their out-posts or sentinels, who instantly sprang into the air, uttering loud, trumpet-like cries, upon which the whole flock arose and followed them with a rush like a sudden squall of wind. We were quite startled, and it was useless to attempt a shot; but unwilling to miss the chance of securing at least one of the birds, I hastily unhooded my eagle, and threw him into the air.

"With a piercing cry he soared away high above them, then shot downward like an arrow, causing wild confusion among the cranes. The one which the eagle attacked sought to defend itself; a struggle followed, and they came together to the ground not far from where we stood.

"Hastening forward, to my grief I found the beautiful crane already dead. The eagle, luckily unhurt, was rewarded with a small pigeon from my gamebag.

"After this we went back to Woodlands, got some turpentine and a bag of rice—and set off for home."

Fritz's interesting story being ended, and supper ready, we made trial of the new roots, and found them very palatable, either boiled or stewed; the monkey plant, however, if it really proved to be the ginseng of the Chinese, would require to be used with caution, being of an aromatic and heating nature.

We resolved to transplant a supply of both roots to our kitchen garden.

Chapter Ten

O N the following morning we were early astir; and as soon as breakfast was over, we went regularly to work with the birdlime. The tough, adhesive mixture of caoutchouc, oil, and turpentine turned out well.

The boys brought rods, which I smeared over, and made them place among the upper branches, where the fruit was plentiful, and the birds most congregated.

The prodigious number of the pigeons, far beyond those of last year, reminded me that we had not then, as now, witnessed their arrival at their feeding-places, but had seen only the last body of the season, a mere party of stragglers, compared to the masses which now weighed down the branches of all the trees in the neighborhood.

The sweet acorns of the evergreen oaks were also patronized; large flocks were there congregated; and from the state of the ground under the trees it was evident that at night they roosted on the branches. Seeing this, I determined to make a raid upon them by torchlight, after the manner of the colonists in Virginia.

Meantime, the birdlime acted well: the pigeons alighting, stuck fast. The more they fluttered and struggled, the more completely were they bedaubed with the tenacious mixture, and at length, with piteous cries, fell to the ground, bearing the sticks with them. The birds were then removed, fresh lime spread, and the snare set again.

The boys quickly became able to carry on the work without my assistance; so, leaving it to them, I went to prepare torches, with pine wood and turpentine, for the night attack.

Jack presently brought a very pretty pigeon, unlike the rest, to show me, as he felt unwilling to kill it; and seeing that it must be one of our own European breed, which we wished to preserve until their numbers greatly increased, I took the trembling captive, and gently cleansed its feet and wings with oil and ashes from the stiff, sticky mess with which it was bedaubed, placing it then in a wicker cage, and telling Jack to bring me any others like it which were caught. This he did; and we secured several pairs, greatly to my satisfaction, as having necessarily let them go free when we landed, they had become quite wild and we derived no advantage from them: whereas now we would have a cot, and pigeon-pie whenever we liked.

When evening drew on, we set out for the wood of sweet acorns, provided merely with long bamboo canes, torches, and canvas sacks.

These weapons appeared very curious and insufficient to the children; but their use was speedily apparent; for darkness having come upon us almost before we reached the wood, I lighted the torches, and perceived, as I expected, that every branch was thickly laden with ortolans and wild pigeons, who were roosting there in amazing numbers.

Suddenly aroused by the glare of light, confusion prevailed

among the terrified birds, who fluttered helplessly through the branches, dazzled and bewildered, and many falling, even before we began to use the sticks, were picked up, and put in the bags. When we beat and struck the branches, it was as much as my wife and Franz could do to gather up the quantities of pigeons that soon lay on the ground. The sacks were speedily quite full. We turned homeward, and on reaching Falconhurst, put our booty in safety, and gladly withdrew to rest.

The following day was wholly occupied in plucking, boiling, roasting, and stewing, so that we could find time for nothing else; but next morning a great expedition to Woodlands was arranged, that measures might there be taken to prevent a repetition of the monkey invasion.

I hoped, could I but catch the mischievous rascals at their work of destruction, to inflict upon them such a chastisement as would effectually make them shun the neighborhood of our farm for the future.

My wife provided us with a good store of provisions, as we were likely to be absent several days, while she, with Franz and Turk, remained at home.

I took with me abundance of specially prepared birdlime, far stronger than that which we used for the pigeons; a number of short posts, plenty of string, and a supply of cocoanut shells and gourds.

The buffalo carried all these things, and one or two of the boys besides. I myself bestrode the ass, and in due time we arrived at a convenient spot in the forest, near Woodlands, well concealed by thick bushes and underwood, where we made a little encampment, pitching the small tent, and tethering the animals. The dogs, too, were tied up, lest they should roam about and betray our presence.

We found the cottage quite quiet and deserted; and I lost no time in preparing for the reception of visitors, hoping to be all ready for them and out of sight before they arrived.

We drove the stakes lightly into the ground, so as to form an irregular paling round the house, winding string in and out in all directions between them, thus making a kind of labyrinth, through which it would be impossible to pass without touching either the stakes or the cords.

Everything was plentifully besmeared with birdlime, and

basins of the mixture were set in all directions, strewn with rice, maize, and other dainties for bait.

Night came without any interruption to our proceedings; and all being then accomplished, we retired to rest beneath the shelter of our little tent.

Very early in the morning we heard a confused noise, such as we knew betokened the approach of a large number of apes. We armed ourselves with strong clubs and cudgels, and holding the dogs in leash, made our way silently behind the thickets, till, ourselves unseen, we could command a view of all that went on; and strange indeed was the scene which ensued!

The noise of rustling, cracking, and creaking among the branches, with horrid cries, and shrieks, and chattering, increased to a degree sufficient to make us perfectly giddy; and then out from the forest poured the whole disorderly rabble of monkeys, scrambling, springing, leaping from the trees, racing and tumbling across the grassy space toward the house; when, at once attracted by the novelties they saw, they made for the jars and bowls.

They seemed innumerable; but the confused, rapid way in which they swarmed hither and thither, made it difficult to judge accurately of their numbers. They dashed fearlessly through and over the palings in all directions, some rushing at the eatables, some scrambling on to the roof, where they commenced tugging at the wooden pegs, with a view to forcing the entrance.

Gradually, however, as they rambled over the place, all in turn became besmeared with our birdlime on head, paws, or back or breast. The wretched predicament of the apes increased every instant.

Some sat down, and with the most ludicrous gestures, tried to clean themselves. Others were hopelessly entangled in stakes and cordage, which they trailed about after them, looking the picture of bewildered despair.

Others, again, endeavored to help one another, and stuck fast together; the more they pulled, and tugged, and kicked, the worse became their plight.

Many had the gourds and cocoanut shells lumbering and clattering about with them, their paws having been caught when they sought to obtain the rice or fruit we had put for bait.

Everybody came to the dovecot. (Page 211)

Most ridiculous of all was the condition of one old fellow, who had found a calabash containing palm wine, and, eagerly drinking it, was immediately fitted with a mask, for the shell stuck to his forehead and whiskers, of course covering his eyes; and he blundered about, cutting the wildest capers in his efforts to get rid of the encumbrance.

Numbers took to flight; but, as we had spread birdlime on several of the trees around, many apes found themselves fixed to, or hanging from the branches, where they remained in woeful durance, struggling and shrieking horribly.

The panic being now general, I loosed the three dogs, whose impatience had been almost uncontrollable, and who now rushed to the attack of the unfortunate monkeys, as though burning with zeal to execute justice upon desperate criminals.

The place soon had the appearance of a ghastly battlefield; for we were obliged to do our part with the clubs and sticks, till the din of howling, yelling, barking, in every conceivable tone of rage and pain, gave place to an awful silence, and we looked with a shudder on the shocking spectacle around us.

At least forty apes lay mangled and dead, and the boys began to be quite sad and down-hearted, till I, fully sharing their feelings, hastened to turn their thoughts to active employment in removing and burying the slain, burning the stakes, cordage bowls, everything concerned in the execution of our deadly stratagem.

After that we betook ourselves to the task of restoring order to our dismantled cottage; and seeking for the scattered flock of sheep, goats, and poultry, we gradually collected them, hoping to settle them once more peacefully in their yards and sheds.

While thus engaged, we repeatedly heard a sound as of something heavy falling from a tree. On going to look, we found three splendid birds, caught on some of the limed sticks we had placed loose in the branches.

Two of these proved to be a variety of the blue Molucca pigeon; the third I assumed to be the Nicobar pigeon, having met with descriptions of its resplendent green, bronze, and steely blue plumage; and I was pleased to think of domesticating them, and establishing them as first tenants of a suitable dwelling near the cave.

"First tenants, father!" said Fritz; "do you expect to catch more like these?"

"Not exactly catch them; I mean to practise a secret art. Much can be done by magic, Fritz!"

Further explanation I declined to give.

In a few days Woodlands was once more set in order, and everything settled and comfortable, so that we returned without further adventure to Falconhurst, where we were joyfully welcomed.

Everyone agreed that we must go at once to Tentholm, to make the proposed pigeon-house in the rock. Several other things there also requiring our attention, we made arrangements for a prolonged stay.

My plan for the pigeon-house was to hollow out an ample space in the cliff, facing toward Jackal River, and close to our rocky home, fitting that up with partitions, perches, and nesting places; while a large wooden front was fitted on to the opening, with entrance-holes, slides or shutters, and a broad platform in front, where the birds could rest and walk about.

When, after the work of a few weeks, we thought it was fit for habitation, I set the other children to work at some distance from our cavern, and summoning Fritz:

"Now, my faithful assistant," said I, "it is time to conjure the new colonists to their settlement here. Yes," I continued, laughing at his puzzled look, "I mean to play a regular pigeon-dealer's trick. You must know such gentry are very ingenious, not only in keeping their own pigeons safe, but in adding to their numbers by attracting those of other people. All I want is some soft clay, aniseed, and salt, of which I will compound a mixture which our birds will like very much, and the smell of which will bring others to share it with them."

"I can easily get you those things, father."

"I shall want some oil of aniseed besides," said I, "to put on the pigeon-holes, so that the birds' feathers may touch it as they may pass in and out, and become scented with what will attract the wild pigeons. This I can obtain by pounding aniseed; therefore, bring me the mortar and some oil."

When this was strongly impregnated with the aromatic oil from the seeds (for I did not propose to distill it in regular style), I strained it through a cloth, pressing it strongly; the result answered my purpose, and the scent would certainly remain for some days.

All my preparations being completed, the pigeons were installed in their new residence, and the slides closed. The European birds were by this time quite friendly with the three beautiful strangers; and when the other boys came home, and scrambled up the ladder to peep in at a little pane of glass I had fixed in front, they saw them all contentedly picking up grain, and pecking at the "magic food," as Fritz called it, although he did not betray my secret arts to his brothers.

Early on the third morning, I aroused Fritz, and directed him to ascend the rope ladder, and arrange a cord on the sliding door of the dovecot, by which it could be opened or closed from below. Also he poured fresh aniseed oil all about the entrance, after which we returned, and awoke the rest of the family, telling them that if they liked to make haste, they might see me let the pigeons fly.

Everybody came to the dovecot, understanding that some ceremony was to attend the event, and I waved a wand with mock solemnity, while I muttered a seeming incantation, and then gave Fritz a sign to draw up the sliding panel.

Presently out popped the pretty heads of the captives, the soft eyes glanced about in all directions; they withdrew, they ventured forth again, they came timidly out on "the veranda," as little Franz expressed it; then, as though suddenly startled, the whole party took wing, with the shrill whizzing sound peculiar to the flight of pigeons, and circling above us as they rose higher and higher, finally darting quite out of sight.

While we were yet gazing after them, they reappeared, and settled quietly on the dovecot; but as we congratulated ourselves on a return which showed that they accepted this as a home, up sprang the three blue pigeons, the noble foreigners, for whom chiefly I had planned the house, and rising in circles high in air, winged their rapid way direct toward Falconhurst.

Their departure had such an air of determination and resolve about it, that I feared them lost to us forever.

Endeavoring to console ourselves by petting our four remaining birds, we could not forget this disappointment, and all day long the dovecot remained the center of attraction.

Nothing, however, was seen of the fugitives until about the

middle of the next day; when most of us were hard at work inside the cavern, Jack sprang in full of excitement, exclaiming:

"He is there! He is come! he really is!"

"Who? Who is there? What do you mean?"

"The blue pigeon, to be sure! Hurrah! Hurrah!"

"Oh, nonsense!" said Ernest. "You want to play us a trick."

"Why should it be 'nonsense'?" cried I. "I fully believe we shall see them all soon!"

Out ran everybody to the dovecot, and there, sure enough stood the pretty fellow, but not alone, for he was billing and cooing to a mate, a stranger of his own breed, apparently inviting her to enter his dwelling; for he popped in and out of the door, bowing, sidling, and cooing, in a most irresistible manner, until the shy little lady yielded to his blandishments, and tripped daintily in. "Now, let's shut the door."

"Pull the cord and close the panel!" shouted the boys, making a rush at the string.

"Stop!" cried I, "let the string alone! I won't have you frighten the little darlings. Besides, the others will be coming—would you shut the door in their faces?"

"Here they come! here they come!" exclaimed Fritz, whose keen eyes marked the birds afar, and to our delight the second blue pigeon arrived, likewise with a mate, whom, after a pretty little flirtation scene of real and assumed modesty on her part, he succeeded in leading home.

The third and handsomest of the new pigeons was the last in making his appearance. Perhaps he had greater difficulty than the others in finding a mate as distinguished in rank and beauty as himself.

However, we fully expected them, and the boys talked of the arrival of "Mr. and Mrs. Nicobar," as a matter of course.

Late in the day Franz and his mother went out to provide for supper, but the child returned directly, exclaiming that we must hasten to the dovecot to see something beautiful.

Accordingly a general rush was made out of the cave, and we saw with delight that the third stranger also had returned with a lovely bride, and encouraged by the presence of the first arrivals, they soon made themselves at home.

In a short time nest-building commenced, and among the

materials collected by the birds, I observed a long gray moss or lichen, and thought it might very possibly be the same which, in the West Indies, is gathered from the bark of old trees, where it grows, and hangs in great tuft-like beards, to be used instead of horse-hair for stuffing mattresses.

My wife no sooner heard if it than her active brain devised fifty plans for making it of use. Would we but collect enough, she would clean and sort it, and there would be no end to the bolsters, pillows, saddles, and cushions she would stuff with it.

For the discovery of nutmegs we had also to thank the pigeons, and they were carefully planted in our orchard.

For some time no event of particular note occurred, until at length Jack, as usual, got into a scrape, causing thereby no little excitement at home.

He went off early on one of his own particular private expeditions.

He was in the habit of doing this that he might surprise us with some new acquisition on his return.

This time, however, he came back in most wretched plight, covered with mud and green slime; a great bundle of Spanish canes was on his back, muddy and green like himself; he had lost a shoe, and altogether presented a ludicrous picture of misery, at which we could have laughed had he not seemed more ready to cry!

"My dear boy! what has happened to you? Where have you been?"

"Only in the swamp behind the powder magazine, father," replied he. "I went to get reeds for my wicker-work, because I wanted to weave some baskets and hen-coops, and I saw such beauties a little way off in the marsh, much finer than those close by the edge, that I tried to get at them.

"I jumped from one firm spot to another, till at last I slipped and sank over my ankles; I tried to get on toward the reeds, which were close by, but in I went deeper and deeper, till I was above the knees in thick soft mud, and there I stuck!"

"I screamed and shouted, but nobody came, and I can tell you I was in a regular fright.

"At last who should appear but my faithful Fangs! He knew my voice and came close up to me, right over the swamp, but all the poor beast could do was to help me to make a row; I wonder you did not hear us! The very rocks rang, but nothing came of it, so despair drove me to think of an expedient. I cut down all the reeds I could reach round and round me, and bound them together into this bundle, which made a firm place on which to lean, while I worked and kicked about to free my feet and legs, and after much struggling, I managed to get astride on the reeds.

"There I sat, supported above the mud and slime, while Fangs ran yelping backward and forward between me and the bank, seeming surprised I did not follow. Suddenly I thought of catching hold of his tail. He dragged and pulled, and I sprawled and crawled, and waded, sometimes on my reeds like a raft, sometimes lugging them along with me, till we luckily got back to terra firma. But I had a near squeak for it, I can tell you."

"A fortunate escape indeed, my boy!" cried I, "and I thank God for it. Fangs has really acted a heroic part as your deliverer, and you have shown great presence of mind. Now go with your mother, and get rid of the slimy traces of your disaster! You have brought me splendid canes, exactly what I want for a new scheme of mine."

The fact was, I meant to try to construct a loom for my wife, for I knew she understood weaving, so I chose two fine strong reeds, and splitting them carefully, bound them together again, that when dry they might be quite straight and equal, and fit for a frame. Smaller reeds were cut into pieces and sharpened, for the teeth of the comb. The boys did this for me without in the least knowing their use, and great fun they made of "father's monster toothpicks."

In time all the various parts of the loom were made ready, and put together, my wife knowing nothing of it, while to the incessant questions of the children, I replied mysteriously.

"Oh, it is an outlandish sort of musical instrument; mother will know how to play upon it."

And when the time came for presenting it, her joy was only equaled by the amusement and interest with which the children watched her movements while "playing the loom," as they always said.

About this time, a beautiful little foal, a son of the onager, was added to our stud, and as he promised to grow up strong and tractable, we soon saw how useful he would be. The name of Swift was given to him, and he was to be trained for my own riding.

The interior arrangements of the cavern being now well forward, I applied myself to contriving an aqueduct, that fresh water might be led close up to our cave, for it was a long way to go to fetch it from Jackal River, and especially inconvenient on washing days. As I wanted to do this before the rainy season began, I set about it at once.

Pipes of hollow bamboo answered the purpose well, and a large cask formed the reservoir. The supply was good, and the comfort of having it close at hand so great, that the mother declared she was as well pleased with our engineering as if we had made her a fountain and marble basin adorned with mermaids and dolphins.

Anticipating the setting in of the rains, I pressed forward all work connected with stores for the winter, and great was the ingathering of roots, fruits, and grains, potatoes, rice, guavas, sweet acorns, pine-cones; load after load arrived at the cavern, and the mother's active needle was in constant requisition, as the demand for more sacks and bags was incessant.

Casks and barrels of all sorts and sizes were pressed into the service, until at last the raft was knocked to pieces, and its tubs made to do duty in the storerooms.

The weather became very unsettled and stormy.

Heavy clouds gathered in the horizon, and passing storms of wind, with thunder, lightning, and torrents of rain swept over the face of nature from time to time.

The sea was in frequent commotion; heavy ground swells drove masses of water hissing and foaming against the cliffs. Everything heralded the approaching rains. All nature joined in sounding forth the solemn overture to the grandest work of the year.

It was now near the beginning of the month of June, and we had twelve weeks of bad weather before us.

We established some of the animals with ourselves at the salt cave. The cow, the ass, Lightfoot, Storm, and the dogs, were all necessary to us, while Knips, Fangs, and the eagle were sure to be a great amusement in the long evenings.

The boys would ride over to Falconhurst very often to see that all was in order there, and fetch anything required.

Much remained to be done in order to give the cave a comfortable appearance, which became more desirable now that we had to live indoors.

The darkness of the inner regions annoyed me, and I set myself to invent a remedy.

After some thought, I called in Jack's assistance, and we got a very tall, strong bamboo, which would reach right up to the vaulted roof. This we planted in the earthen floor, securing well by driving wedges in round it. Jack ascended this pole very cleverly, taking with him a hammer and chisel to enlarge a crevice in the roof so as to fix a pulley, by means of which, when he descended, I drew up a large ship's lantern, well supplied with oil, and as there were four wicks, it afforded a very fair amount of light.

Several days were spent in arranging the different rooms.

Ernest and Franz undertook the library, fixing shelves, and setting the books in order.

Jack and his mother took in hand the sitting room and kitchen, while Fritz and I, as better able for heavy work, arranged the workshops. The carpenter's bench, the turning lathe, and a large chest of tools were set in convenient places, and many tools and instruments hung on the walls.

An adjoining chamber was fitted up as a forge, with fireplace, bellows, and anvil, complete, all which we had found in the ship, packed together, and ready to set up.

When these great affairs were settled, we still found in all directions work to be done. Shelves, tables, benches, movable steps, cupboards, pegs, door handles, and bolts—there seemed no end to our requirements, and we often thought of the enormous amount of work necessary to maintain the comforts and conveniences of life which at home we had received as matters of course.

But in reality, the more there was to do the better; and I never ceased contriving fresh improvements, being fully aware of the importance of constant employment as a means of strengthening and maintaining the health of mind and body. This, indeed, with a consciousness of continual progress toward a desirable end, is found to constitute the main element of happiness.

Our rocky home was greatly improved by a wide porch which I made along the whole front of our rooms and entrances, by leveling the ground to form a terrace, and sheltering it with a veranda of bamboo, supported by pillars of the same.

Ernest and Franz were highly successful as librarians.

The books, when unpacked and arranged, proved to be a most valuable collection, capable of affording every sort of educational advantage.

Besides a variety of books of voyages, travels, divinity, and natural history (several containing fine colored illustrations), there were histories and scientific works, as well as standard fictions in several languages; also a good assortment of maps, charts, mathematical and astronomical instruments, and an excellent pair of globes.

I foresaw much interesting study on discovering that we possessed the grammars and dictionaries of a great many languages, a subject for which we all had a taste. With French we were well acquainted. Fritz and Ernest had begun to learn English at school, and made further progress during a visit to England. The mother, who had once been intimate with a Dutch family, could speak that language pretty well.

After a great deal of discussion, we agreed to study different languages, so that in the event of meeting with people of other nations, there should be at least one of the family able to communicate with them.

All determined to improve our knowledge of German and French.

The two elder boys were to study English and Dutch with their mother.

Ernest, already possessing considerable knowledge of Latin, wished to continue to study it, so as to be able to make use of the many works on natural history and medicine written in that language.

Jack announced that he meant to learn Spanish, "because it sounded so grand and imposing."

I myself was interested in the Malay language, knowing it

to be so widely spoken in the islands of the Eastern Seas, and thinking it as likely as any other to be useful to us.

Our family circle by and by represented Babel in miniature, for scraps and fragments of all these tongues kept buzzing about our ears from morning to night, each sporting his newly acquired word or sentence on every possible occasion, propounding idioms and peculiar expressions like riddles, to puzzle the rest.

In this way, the labor of learning was very considerably lightened, and everyone came to know a few words of each language.

Occasionally we amused ourselves by opening chests and packages hitherto untouched, and brought unexpected treasures to light—mirrors, wardrobes, a pair of console tables with polished marble tops, elegant writing tables and handsome chairs, clocks of various descriptions, a musical box, and a chronometer were found; and by degrees our abode was fitted up like a palace, so that sometimes we wondered at ourselves, and felt as though we were strutting about in borrowed plumes.

The children begged me to decide on a name for our salt-cave dwelling, and that of Rockburg was chosen unanimously.

The weeks of imprisonment passed so rapidly, that no one found the time hanging heavily on his hands.

Books occupied me so much that but little carpentering was done, yet I made a yoke for the oxen, a pair of cotton wool carders, and a spinning wheel for my wife.

As the rainy season drew to a close, the weather for awhile became wilder, and the storms fiercer than ever. Thunder roared, lightning blazed, torrents rushed toward the sea, which came in raging billows to meet them, lashed to fury by the tempests of wind which swept the surface of the deep.

The uproar of the elements came to an end at last.

Nature resumed her attitude of repose, her smiling aspect of peaceful beauty; and soon all traces of the ravages of floods and storms would disappear beneath the luxuriant vegetation of the tropics.

Gladly quitting the sheltering walls of Rockburg to roam once more in the open air, we crossed Jackal River, for a walk along the coast, and presently Fritz with his sharp eyes observed something on the small island near Flamingo Marsh, which was, he said, long and rounded, resembling a boat bottom upward.

Examining it with the telescope, I could form no other conjecture, and we resolved to make it the object of an excursion next day, being delighted to resume our old habit of starting in pursuit of adventure.

The boat was accordingly got in readiness; it required some repairs, and fresh pitching, and then we made for the point of interest, indulging in a variety of surmises as to what we should find.

It proved to be a huge, stranded whale.

The island being steep and rocky, it was necessary to be careful; but we found a landing-place on the further side. The boys hurried by the nearest way to the beach where lay the monster of the deep, while I clambered to the highest point of the islet, which commanded a view of the mainland, from Rockburg to Falconhurst.

On rejoining my sons, I found them only half-way to the great fish, and as I drew near they shouted in high glee:

"Oh! father, just look at the glorious shells and coral branches we are finding. How does it happen that there are such quantities?"

"Only consider how the recent storms have stirred the ocean to its depths! No doubt thousands of shell-fish have been detached from their rocks and dashed in all directions by the waves, which have thrown ashore even so huge a creature as the whale yonder."

"Yes; isn't he a frightful great brute!" cried Fritz. "Ever so much larger than he seemed from a distance. The worst of it is, one does not well see what use to make of the huge carcase."

"Why, make train oil, to be sure," said Ernest. "I can't says he's a beauty, though, and it is much pleasanter to gather these lovely shells, than to cut up blubber."

"Well, let us amuse ourselves with them for the present," said I, "but in the afternoon, when the sea is calmer, we will return with the necessary implements, and see if we can turn the stranded whale to good account."

We were soon ready to return to the boat, but Ernest had

a fancy for remaining alone on the island till we came back, and asked my permission to do so, that he might experience, for an hour or two, the sensations of Robinson Crusoe.

To this, however, I would not consent, assuring him that our fate, as a solitary family, gave him quite sufficient idea of shipwreck on an uninhabited island, and that his lively imagination must supply the rest.

The boys found it hard work to row back, and began to beg of me to exert my wonderful inventive powers in contriving some kind of rowing machine.

"You lazy fellows!" returned I; "give me the great clockwork out of a church tower, perhaps I might be able to relieve your labors."

"Oh, father!" cried Fritz, "don't you know there are iron wheels in the clockwork of the large kitchen-jacks? I'm sure mother would give them up, and you could make something out of them, could you not?"

"By the time I have manufactured a rowing-machine out of a roasting-jack, I think your arms will be pretty well inured to the use of your oars! However, I am far from despising the hint, my dear Fritz."

"Is coral of any use?" demanded Jack suddenly.

"In former times it was pounded and used by chemists; but it is now chiefly used for various ornaments, and made into beads for necklaces, etc. As such, it is greatly prized by savages, and were we to fall in with natives, we might very possibly find a store of coral useful in bartering with them.

"For the present, we will arrange these treasures of the deep in our library, and make them the beginning of a Museum of Natural History, which will afford us equal pleasure and instruction."

"One might almost say that coral belongs at once to the animal, vegetable, and mineral kingdoms," remarked Fritz; "it is hard like stone, it has stems and branches like a shrub, and I believe tiny insects inhabit the cells, do they not, father?"

"You are right, Fritz; coral consists of the calcareous cells of minute animals, so built up as to form a tree-like structure.

"The coral fishery gives employment to many men in the Persian Gulf, the Mediterranean Sea, and other places. The instrument commonly used consists of two heavy beams of wood, secured together at right angles, and loaded with stones. Hemp and netting are attached to the under side of the beams, to the middle of which is fastened one end of a strong rope, by which the apparatus is let down from a boat, and guided to the spots where the coral is most abundant.

"The branches of the coral become entangled in the hemp and network; they are broken off from the rock, and are drawn to the surface of the water.

"Left undisturbed, these coral insects, laboring incessantly, raise foundations, on which, in course of time, fertile islands appear, clothed with verdure, and inhabited by man."

"Why, father, here we are at the landing place!" exclaimed Jack. "It has seemed quite easy to pull since you began to tell us such interesting things."

"Very interesting, indeed; but did you notice that the wind had changed, Jack?" remarked Ernest as he shipped his oar.

The animated recital of our adventures, the sight of the lovely shells and corals, and the proposed work for the afternoon, inspired the mother and Franz with a great wish to accompany us.

To this I gladly consented, only stipulating that we should go provided with food, water, and a compass. "For," said I, "the sea has only just ceased from its raging, and being at the best of times of uncertain and capricious nature, we may chance to be detained on the island, or forced to land at a considerable distance from home."

Dinner was quickly dispatched, and preparations set on foot.

The more oil we could obtain the better, for a great deal was used in the large lantern which burnt day and night in the recesses of the cave; therefore, all available casks and barrels were pressed into the service; many, of course, once full of pickled herrings, potted pigeons, and other winter stores, were now empty, and we took a goodly fleet of these in tow.

Knives, hatchets, and the boy's climbing buskins, were put on board, and we set forth, the labor of the oar being greater than ever, now that our freight was so much increased.

The sea being calm, and the tide suiting better, we found it easy to land close to the whale; my first care was to place the boat, as well as the casks, in perfect security, after which we proceeded to a close inspection of our prize.

Its enormous size quite startled my wife and her little boy; the length being from sixty to sixty-five feet, and the girth between thirty and forty, while the weight could not have been less than 50,000 pounds.

The color was a uniform velvety black, and the enormous head about one-third of the length of the entire bulk, the eyes quite small, not much larger than those of an ox, and the ears almost undiscernible.

The jaw opened very far back, and was nearly sixteen feet in length, the most curious part of its structure being the re- markable substance known as whalebone, masses of which appeared all along the jaws, solid at the base, and splitting into a sort of fringe at the extremity. This arrangement is for the purpose of aiding the whale in procuring its food, and separating it from the water.

The tongue was remarkably large, soft, and full of oil; the opening of the throat wonderfully small, scarcely two inches in diameter.

"Why, what can the monster eat?" exclaimed Fritz; "he never can swallow a proper mouthful down this little gullet!"

"The mode of feeding adopted by the whale is so curious," I replied, "that I must explain it to you before we begin work.

"This animal (for I should tell you that a whale is not a fish; he possesses no gills, he breathes atmospheric air, and would be drowned if too long detained below the surface of the water) ; this animal, then, frequents those parts of the ocean best supplied with the various creatures on which he feeds. Shrimps, small fish, lobsters, various molluscs, and me- dusæ form his diet. Driving with open mouth through the congregated shoals of these little creatures, the whale engulfs them by millions in his enormous jaws, and continues his destructive course until he has sufficiently charged his mouth with prey.

"Closing his jaws and forcing out, through the interstices of the whalebone, the water which he has taken together with his prey, he retains the captured animals, and swallows them at his leisure.

"The nostrils, or blow-holes, are placed, you see, on the upper part of the head, in order that the whale may rise to breathe, and repose on the surface of the sea, showing very little of his huge carcase.

"The breathings are called 'spoutings,' because a column of mixed vapor and water is thrown from the blow-holes, sometimes to a height of twenty feet.

"And now, boys, fasten on your buskins, and let me see if you can face the work of climbing this slippery mountain of flesh, and cutting it up."

Fritz and Jack stripped, and went to work directly, scrambling over the back to the head, where they assisted me to cut away the lips, so as to reach the whale bone, a large quantity of which was detached and carried to the boat.

Ernest labored manfully at the creature's side, cutting out slabs of blubber, while his mother and Franz helped us as well as they could to put it in casks.

Presently we had a multitude of unbidden guests.

The air was filled by the shrill screams and hoarse croaks and cries of numbers of birds of prey, they flew around us in ever narrowing circles and becoming bolder as their voracity was excited by the near view of the tempting prey, they alighted close to us, snatching morsels greedily from under the very strokes of our knives and hatchets.

Our work was seriously interrupted by these feathered marauders, who, after all, were no greater robbers than we ourselves. We kept them off as well as we could by blows from our tools, and several were killed, my wife taking possession of them immediately for the sake of the feathers.

It was nearly time to leave the island, but first I stripped off a long piece of the skin, to be used for traces, harness, and other leather-work. It was about three-quarters of an inch thick, and very soft and oily—but I knew it would shrink and be tough and durable.

I also took a part of the gums in which the roots of the baleen or whalebone were still embedded, having read that this is considered quite a delicacy, as well as the skin, which, when properly dressed and cut in little cubes, like black dice, has been compared, by enthusiastic and probably very hungry travelers, to cocoanut and cream-cheese.

The boys thought the tongue might prove equally palatable, but I valued it only on account of the large quantity of oil it contained.

With a heavy freight we put to sea, and made what haste we could to reach home, and cleanse our persons from the unpleasant traces of the disgusting work in which we had spent the day.

Next morning we started at dawn.

My wife and Franz were left behind, for our proposed work was even more horrible than that of the preceding day; they could not assist, and had no inclination to witness it.

It was my intention to open the carcase completely, and, penetrating the interior, to obtain various portions of the intestines, thinking that it would be possible to convert the larger ones into vessels fit for holding the oil. This time we laid aside our clothes and wore only strong canvas trousers when we commenced operations, which were vigorously carried on during the whole of the day; then, satisfied that we could do so with a clear conscience, we abandoned the remains to the birds of prey, and, with a full cargo, set sail for land.

On the way, it appeared to strike the boys (who had made not the slightest objection to the singularly unpleasant task I had set them), as very strange that I should wish to possess what they had been working so hard to procure for me.

"What can have made you wish to bring away that brute's entrails, father? Are they of any use?"

"There are countries," I replied, "where no wood grows of which to make barrels, and no hemp for thread, string, and cordage. Necessity, the mother of all the more valuable inventions, has taught the inhabitants of those countries, Greenlanders, Esquimaux, and others, to think of substitutes, and they use the intestines of the whale for one purpose, the sinews and nerves for the other."

We were right glad to land, and get rid, for the present, of our unpleasant materials, the further preparation of which was work in store for the following day.

A refreshing bath, clean clothes, and supper, cheered us all up, and we slept in peace.

Chapter Eleven

"Now for the finishing up of this dirty job," cried I, merrily, as we all woke up next morning at daybreak. And after the regular work was done, we commenced operations by raising a stand or rough scaffold on which the tubs full of blubber were placed and heavily pressed, so that the purest and finest oil overflowed into vessels underneath.

The blubber was afterward boiled in a cauldron over a fire kindled at some distance from our abode, and by skimming and straining through a coarse cloth, we succeeded in obtaining a large supply of excellent train-oil, which in casks, and bags made of the intestines, was safely stowed away in the "cellar," as the children called our roughest storeroom. This day's work was far from agreeable, and the dreadful smell oppressed us all, more especially my poor wife, who, nevertheless, endured it with her accustomed good temper. Although she very urgently recommended that the new island should be the headquarters for another colony, where, said she, "any animals we leave would be safe from apes and other plunderers, and where you would find it so very convenient to boil whale-blubber, strain train-oil and the like."

This proposal met with hearty approval, especially from the boys, who were always charmed with any new plan; and they were eager to act upon it at once, but when I reminded them of the putrifying carcase which lay there, they confessed it would be better to allow wind and storms, birds and insects to do their work in purging the atmosphere, and reducing the whale to a skeleton before we revisited the island.

The idea of a rowing-machine kept recurring to my brain. I determined to attempt to make one.

I took an iron bar, which when laid across the middle of the boat projected about a foot each way. I provided this bar in the middle with ribbed machinery, and at each end with a sort of nave, in which, as in a cart wheel, four flat spokes, or paddles, were fixed obliquely. These were intended to do the rowers' part.

Then the jack was arranged to act upon the machinery in the middle of the iron cross-bar, in such a way that one of its strong cogwheels bit firmly into the ribs, so that, when it was wound up, it caused the bar to revolve rapidly, of course turning with it the paddles fixed at either end, which consequently struck the water so as to propel the boat.

Although this contrivance left much to be desired in the way of improvement, still when Fritz and I wound up the machinery, and went off on a trial trip across the bay, we splashed along at such a famous rate, that the shores rang with the cheers and clapping of the whole family, delighted to behold what they considered my brilliant success.

Everyone wanted to go on board, and take a cruise, but as it was getting late, I could not consent. A trip next day, however, was promised to Cape Disappointment and the little settlement of Prospect Hill.

This proposal satisfied everybody. The evening was spent

in preparing the dresses, arms, and food which would be required, and we retired early to rest.

Intending to be out all day, the house was left in good order, and we departed on our expedition, provided, among other things, with spades and mattocks, for I wished to get young cocoanut trees and shrubs of different kinds, that, on our way back, we might land on Whale Island, and begin our plantation there.

We directed our course toward the opposite side of the bay. The sea was smooth, my rowing machine performed its work easily, and, leaving Safety Bay and Shark Island behind us, we enjoyed at our ease the panorama of all the coast scenery.

Landing near Prospect Hill, we moored the boat, and walked through the woods to our little farm, obtaining some fresh cocoanuts, as well as young plants, on the way.

Before coming in sight of the cottage at the farm, we heard the cocks crow, and I experienced a sudden rush of emotion as the sound recalled, in a degree painfully vivid, the recollection of many a ride and walk at home, when we would be greeted by just such familiar sounds as we approached some kind friend's house. Here, but for the unconscious animals, utter solitude and silence prevailed, and I with my dear family, whose visit would have been hailed with delight in so many homes, advanced unnoticed to this lonely cottage. So long had been our absence that our arrival created a perfect panic. The original animals had forgotten us, and to their progeny, lambs, kids, and chickens, who had never seen the face of man, we seemed an army of fierce foes.

The boys found it impossible to milk the goats, until, by the use of the lasso, they captured them one after the other, bound their legs, then giving them salt to lick, they soon obtained a supply of excellent milk, which was poured from the cocoanut shells they used into calabash flasks, so that we could take with us what was not required at dinner.

The fowls were enticed by handfuls of grain and rice, and my wife caught as many as she wished for.

We were by this time very ready for dinner, and the cold provisions we had with us were set forth, the chief dish consisting of the piece of whale's tongue, which, by the boys' desire, had been cooked with a special view to this entertainment.

But woeful was the disappointment when the tongue was tasted! One after another, with dismal face, pronounced it "horrid stuff," begged for some pickled herring to take away the taste of train-oil, and willingly bestowed on Fangs the cherished dainty.

Fortunately there was a sufficient supply of other eatables, and the fresh, delicious cocoanuts and goat's milk put everyone in good humor again.

While the mother packed everything up, Fritz and I got some sugar-cane shoots which I wished to plant, and then we returned to the shore and again embarked.

Before returning to Whale Island, I felt a strong wish to round Cape Disappointment and survey the coast immediately beyond, but the promontory maintained the character of its name, and we found that a long sandbank, as well as hidden reefs and rocks, ran out a great way into the sea.

Fritz espying breakers ahead, we put about at once, and aided by a light breeze, directed our course toward Whale Island.

On landing, I began at once to plant the saplings we had brought. The boys assisted me for a while, but wearied somewhat of the occupation, and one after another went off in search of shells and coral, leaving their mother and me to finish the work.

Presently Jack came back, shouting loudly:

"Father! Mother! do come and look. There is an enormous skeleton lying here; the skeleton of some fearful great beast— a mammoth, I should think."

"Why, Jack!" returned I, laughing, "have you forgot our old acquaintance, the whale? What else could it be?"

"Oh, no, father, it is not the whale. This thing has not fish bones, but real good, honest, huge beast bones. I don't know what can have become of the whale—floated out to sea, most likely. This mammoth is ever so much bigger. Come and see!"

As I was about to follow the boy, a voice from another direction suddenly cried:

"Father! father! a great enormous turtle! Please make haste. It is waddling back to the sea as hard as it can go, and we can't stop it."

This appeal being more pressing, as well as more important

than Jack's, I snatched up an oar and hastened to their assistance.

Sure enough, a large turtle was scrambling quickly toward the water, and was within a few paces of it, although Ernest was valiantly holding on by one if its hind legs.

I sprang down the bank, and making use of the oar as a lever, we succeeded with some difficulty in turning the creature on its back.

It was a huge specimen, fully eight feet long, and being now quite helpless, we left it sprawling, and went to inspect Jack's mammoth skeleton, which, of course, proved to be neither more nor less than that of the whale. I convinced him of the fact by pointing out the marks of our feet on the ground, and the broken jaws where we had hacked out the whalebone.

"What can have made you take up that fancy about a mammoth, my boy?"

"Ernest put it into my head, father. He said there seemed to be the skeleton of an antediluvian monster there, so I ran to look closer, and I never thought of the whale, when I saw no fish bones. I suppose Ernest was joking."

"Whales are generally considered as fishes by those little acquainted with the animal kingdom, but they belong to the class of mammals, which comprises man, the monkey tribes, the bats, the dogs and cats, all hoofed animals, whales and their allies, with other animals, the last on the list being the sloth.

"The name by which they are distinguished is derived from the Latin word 'mamma,' a breast, and is given to them because all the species belonging to this class are furnished with a set of organs called the mammary glands, secreting the liquid known as milk, by which the young are nourished.

"The bones of the whale differ from those of animals, simply in being of a hollow construction, and filled with air so as to render the carcase more buoyant. The bones of birds are also hollow, for the same reason, and in all this we see conspicuously the wisdom and goodness of the great Creator."

"What a marvelous structure it is, father!" said Fritz. "What a ponderous mass of bones! Can we not make use of any of them?"

"Nothing strikes me at this moment; we will leave them to bleach here yet awhile, and perhaps, by sawing them up afterward, make a few chairs, or a reading desk for the museum. But now it is time to return home. Bring the boat round to where the turtle awaits his fate; we must settle how to deal with him."

It was soon decided that he must swim. I fastened the empty water-cask to a long line, one end of which was made fast to the bow of the boat, the other carefully passed round the neck and fore-paws of the creature, who was then lifted, so as to let him regain his feet, when he instantly made for the water, plunged in, the cask floated after him, and prevented his sinking. We were all on board in a moment; and the worthy fellow, after vainly attempting to dive, set himself diligently to swim right forward, towing us comfortably after him. I was ready to cut the line on the least appearance of danger, and kept him on the course for Safety Bay by striking the water with a boat-hook, right or left, according as the turtle was disposed to turn too much one way or the other.

The boys were delighted with the fun, and compared me to Neptune in his car, drawn by dolphins, and accompanied by Amphitrite and attendant Tritons.

We landed safely at the usual place, near Rockburg, and the turtle was condemned and executed soon afterward; the shell, which was quite eight feet long, and three broad, was, when cleaned and prepared, to form a trough for the water supply at the cave, and the meat was carefully salted, and stored up for many a good and savory meal.

It had been my intention to bring a piece of land under cultivation before the next rainy season, to be sown with different sorts of grain; but many unforeseen circumstances had intervened to hinder this, and our animals, unaccustomed to the yoke, were not available for the plow.

I therefore gave up the idea for the present, and applied myself, with Ernest's assistance, to completing the loom, which, although the workmanship was clumsy, I succeeded in making quite fit for use. I had fortunately in my younger days spent many hours in the workshops of weavers and other artisans, and therefore I understood more than might have been expected of their various crafts.

Paste or size was required to smear over the threads; but we could not spare flour for such a purpose, and I used isinglass, which kept the warp moist perfectly well, and spared us the necessity of setting up the loom in a damp uncomfortable place, which has often to be done to prevent the over-drying of the web.

Of this isinglass I also made thin plates, to be used as window-panes; they were at least as transparent as horn, and when fixed deep in the rock, and beyond the reach of rain, did good service in admitting light.

Success encouraging me to persevere, I next began harness-making; the spoils of the chase having furnished us with plenty of leather, with which I covered light frames of wood, using the hairy moss or lichen for stuffing, and ere long the animals were equipped with saddles, stirrups, bridles, yokes, and collars, to the very great satisfaction of their youthful riders and drivers.

This occupation was followed by a great deal of work connected with the annual return of the herring shoals, which now took place; to them succeeding, as on former occasions, shoals of other fish, and many seals. More than ever aware of the value of all these, we did not fail to make good use of our opportunities, and captured large numbers.

The boys were getting anxious for another shooting expedition; but before undertaking that, I wished to do some basket-making, as sacks were beginning to fail us, and there was constant demand for baskets in which to carry and keep our roots and fruits. Our first attempts were clumsy enough; but, as usual, perseverance was rewarded, and we produced a good supply of all sorts and sizes. One very large basket I furnished with openings through which to pass a strong stick, so that it might, when heavily laden, be carried by two persons.

No sooner did the children see the force of this idea, than they got a bamboo, and popping little Franz into the basket, carried him about in triumph.

This amusement suggested a fresh notion to Fritz. "Oh, father," cried he, "don't you think we might make something like this for mother, and carry her much more comfortably than jolting along in the cart?"

The boys shouted with glee at the proposal, and though

their mother thought the plan feasible enough, she confessed that she did not much like the thoughts of sitting in the middle of a basket, and just looking out now and then over the rim.

However, I assured her it should be a well-shaped, comfortable sedan-chair, or litter; and the next question was how it should be carried, since the boys could not play the part of Indian palanquin-bearers, either with safety to their mother, or with any pleasure to themselves.

"The bull and the buffalo!" cried Jack. "Why not use them for it? Let's go and try them now!"

Off ran the boys, and in a short time the basket was securely hung between Storm and Grumble. Fritz and Jack sprang into their saddles, and Ernest very gingerly deposited himself in the "cradle," as Franz called it; they set forth at a most sober pace, the animals, who were perfectly docile, appearing only a little surprised at the new arrangement.

"Oh, it is so pleasant, mother, it is a delightful motion," cried Ernest, as they passed us; "it swings and rocks really soothingly. Quicker, Fritz! go quicker!" and the trot pleasing him equally well, the pace gradually quickened, till the animals were going along at a rate which shook and jolted the basket about most fearfully. Ernest called and screamed in vain for a halt. His brothers thought it capital fun to "shake up" the "professor," and made the circuit of the level ground near Rockburg, finally pulling up in front of us, like performers stopping to receive the applause of spectators.

It was impossible to keep from laughing, the scene was so ridiculous, but Ernest was very angry with his brothers, his reproaches provoked high words in reply, and a quarrel was imminent, but I interfered, and showed them how easily a joke, carried too far, would lead to disputes and bad feeling, urging them to avoid on all occasions any breach of the good-fellowship and brotherly love which was the mainstay of our strength and happiness.

Good humor was soon restored, Ernest himself helped to unharness the beasts, and got some handfuls of salt and barley to reward their exertions; saying that they must have some more palanquin-practice another day.

I was seated with my wife and Fritz beneath the shade of the veranda, engaged in wicker-work, and chatting pleasantly, when suddenly Fritz got up, advanced a step or two, gazing fixedly along the avenue which led from Jackal River, then he exclaimed:

"I see something so strange in the distance, father! What in the world can it be? First it seems to be drawn in coils on the ground like a cable, then uprises as it were a little mast, then that sinks, and the coils move along again. It is coming toward the bridge."

My wife took alarm at this description, and calling the other boys, retreated into the cave, where I desired them to close up the entrances, and keep watch with firearms at the upper windows. These were openings we had made in the rock at some elevation, reached within by steps, and a kind of gallery which passed along the front of the rooms.

Fritz remained by me while I examined the object through my spyglass.

"It is, as I feared, an enormous serpent!" cried I; "it advances directly this way, and we shall be placed in the greatest possible danger, for it will cross the bridge to a certainty."

"May we not attack it, father?" exclaimed the brave boy.

"Only with the greatest caution," returned I; "it is far too formidable, and too tenacious of life, for us rashly to attempt its destruction. Thank God, we are at Rockburg, where we can keep in safe retreat, while we watch for an opportunity to destroy this frightful enemy. Go up to your mother now, and assist in preparing the firearms; I will join you directly, but I must further observe the monster's movements."

Fritz left me unwillingly, while I continued to watch the serpent, which was of gigantic size, and already much too near the bridge to admit of the possibility of removing that means of access to our dwelling. I recollected, too, how easily it would pass through the walls. The reptile advanced with writhing and undulatory movements, from time to time rearing its head to the height of fifteen or twenty feet, and slowly turning it about, as though on the lookout for prey.

As it crossed the bridge, with a slow, suspicious motion, I withdrew, and hastily rejoined my little party, which was preparing to garrison our fortress in warlike array, but with considerable trepidation, which my presence served in a measure to allay.

We placed ourselves at the upper openings, after strongly barricading everything below, and, ourselves unseen, awaited with beating hearts the further advance of the foe, which speedily became visible to us.

Its movements appeared to become uncertain, as though puzzled by the trace of human habitation; it turned in different directions, coiling and uncoiling, and frequently rearing its head, but keeping about the middle of the space in front of the cave, when suddenly, as though unable to resist doing so, one after another the boys fired, and even their mother discharged her gun. The shots took not the slightest effect beyond startling the monster, whose movements were accelerated. Fritz and I also fired with steadier aim, but with the same want of success, for the monster, passing on with a gliding motion, entered the reedy marsh to the left, and entirely disappeared.

A wonderful weight seemed lifted from our hearts, while all eagerly discussed the vast length and awful though magnificent appearance of the serpent. I had recognized it as the boa constrictor. It was a vast specimen, upward of thirty feet in length.

I explained to the children that its name in South America is Boaguacu; the first syllable of that word, with the Latin addition, which indicates that it kills its prey by pressure, or "constriction," gives the name by which it is commonly known.

The near neighborhood of this terrific reptile occasioned me the utmost anxiety; and I desired that no one should leave the house on any pretense whatever, without my express permission.

During three whole days we were kept in suspense and fear, not daring to stir above a few hundred steps from the door, although during all that time the enemy showed no sign of his presence.

In fact, we might have been induced to think the boa had passed across the swamp, and found his way by some cleft or chasm through the walls of cliffs beyond, had not the restless behavior of our geese and ducks given proof that he still lurked in the thicket of reeds which they were accustomed to make their nightly resting place.

They swam anxiously about, and with much clapping of wings and disturbed cackling showed their uneasiness; finally taking wing they crossed the harbor, and took up their quarters on Shark Island.

My embarrassment increased, as time passed on. I could not venture to attack with insufficient force a monstrous and formidable serpent concealed in dense thickets amidst dangerous swamps; yet it was dreadful to live in a state of blockade, cut off from all the important duties in which we were engaged, and shut up with our animals in the unnatural light of the cave, enduring constant anxiety and perturbation.

Out of this painful state we were at last delivered by none other than our good old simple-hearted donkey; not, however, by the exercise of a praiseworthy quality, such as the vigilance of the time-honored geese of the Capitol, but by sheer stupidity.

Our situation was rendered the more critical from having no great stock of provisions, or fodder for the animals; and the hay failing us on the evening of the third day, I determined to set them at liberty by sending them, under the guidance of Fritz, across the river at the ford.

He was to ride Lightfoot, and they were to be fastened together until safely over.

Next morning we began to prepare for this by tying them in a line, and while so engaged my wife opened the door, when old Grizzle, who was fresh and frolicsome after the long rest and regular feeding, suddenly broke away from the halter, cut some awkward capers, then bolting out, careered at full gallop straight for the marsh.

In vain we called him by name. Fritz would even have rushed after him, had not I held him back. In another moment the ass was close to the thicket, and with the cold shudder of horror, we beheld the snake rear itself from its lair, the fiery eyes glanced around, the dark, deadly jaws opened widely, the forked tongue darted greedily forth—poor Grizzle's fate was sealed.

Becoming aware on a sudden of his danger, he stopped short, spread out all four legs, and set up the most piteous and discordant bray that ever wrung echo from rocks.

Swift and straight as a fencer's thrust, the destroyer was

upon him, wound round him, entangled, enfolded, compressed him, all the while cunningly avoiding the convulsive kicks of the agonized animal.

A cry of horror arose from the spectators of this miserable tragedy.

"Shoot him, father! oh, shoot him—do save poor Grizzle!"

"My children, it is impossible!" cried I. "Our old friend is lost to us for ever! I have hopes, however, that when gorged with his prey we may be able to attack the snake with some chance of success."

"But the horrible wretch is never going to swallow him all at once, father?" cried Jack. "That will be too shocking!"

"Snakes have no grinders, but only fangs, therefore they cannot chew their food, and must swallow it whole. But although the idea is startling, it is not really more shocking than the rending, tearing, and shedding of blood which occurs when the lions and tigers seize their prey."

"But," said Franz, "how can the snake separate the flesh from the bones without teeth? And is this kind of snake poisonous?"

"No, dear child," said I, "only fearfully strong and ferocious. And it has no need to tear the flesh from the bones. It swallows them, skin, hair, and all, and digests everything in its stomach."

"It seems utterly impossible that the broad ribs, the strong legs, hoofs, and all, should go down that throat," exclaimed Fritz.

"Only see," I replied, "how the monster deals with his victim; closer and more tightly he curls his crushing folds, the bones give way, he is kneading him into a shapeless mass. He will soon begin to gorge his prey, and slowly but surely it will disappear down that distended maw!"

The mother, with little Franz, found the scene all too horrible, and hastened into the cave, trembling and distressed.

To the rest of us there seemed a fearful fascination in the dreadful sight, and we could not move from the spot. I expected that the boa, before swallowing his prey, would cover it with saliva, to aid in the operation, although it struck me that its very slender forked tongue was about the worst possible implement for such a purpose.

It was evident to us, however, that this popular idea was erroneous.

The act of lubricating the mass must have taken place during the process of swallowing; certainly nothing was applied beforehand.

This wonderful performance lasted from seven in the morning until noon. When the awkward morsel was entirely swallowed, the serpent lay stiff, distorted, and apparently insensible along the edge of the marsh.

I felt that now or never was the moment for attack!

Calling on my sons to maintain their courage and presence of mind, I left our retreat with a feeling of joyous emotion quite new to me, and approached with rapid steps and leveled gun the outstretched form of the serpent. Fritz followed me closely.

Jack, somewhat timidly, came several paces behind; while Ernest, after a little hesitation, remained where he was.

The monster's body was stiff and motionless, which made its rolling and fiery eyes, and the slow, spasmodic undulations of its tail more fearful by contrast.

We fired together, and both balls entered the skull; the light of the eye was extinguished, and the only movement was in the further extremity of the body, which rolled, writhed, coiled, and lashed from side to side.

Advancing closer, we fired our pistols directly into its head, a convulsive quiver ran through the mighty frame, and the boa constrictor lay dead.

As we raised a cry of victory, Jack, desirous of a share in the glory of conquest, ran close to the creature, firing his pistol into its side, when he was sent sprawling over and over by a movement of its tail, excited to a last galvanic effort by the shot.

Being in no way hurt, he speedily recovered his feet, and declared he had given it its quietus.

"I hope the terrible noise you made just now was the signal of victory," said my wife, drawing near, with the utmost circumspection, and holding Franz tightly by the hand. "I was half afraid to come, I assure you."

"See this dreadful creature dead at our feet; and let us thank God that we have been able to destroy such an enemy."

"What's to be done with him now?" asked Jack.

"Let us get him stuffed," said Fritz, "and set him up in the museum among our shells and corals."

"Did anybody ever think of eating serpents?" inquired Franz.

"Of course not!" said his mother. "Why, child, serpents are poisonous—it would be very dangerous."

"Excuse me, my dear wife," said I. "First of all, the boa is not poisonous; and then, besides that, the flesh of even poisonous snakes can be eaten without danger; as, for instance, the rattlesnake, from which can be made a strong and nourishing soup, tasting very like good chicken broth—of course, the cook must be told to throw away the head, containing the deadly fangs.

"It is remarkable that pigs do not fear poisonous snakes, but can kill and eat them without injury. An instance of this occurs to my memory. A vessel on Lake Superior, in North America, was wrecked on a small island abounding in rattlesnakes, and for that reason uninhabited.

"The vessel had a cargo of live pigs. The crew escaped to the mainland in a boat, but the pigs had to be left for sometime, till the owner could return to fetch them, but with the small hope of finding many left alive.

"To his surprise, the animals were not only alive, but remarkably fat and flourishing, while not a single rattlesnake remained on the island. The pigs had clearly eaten the serpents."

"But might not some other cause have been assigned for their disappearance?" asked Ernest. "Suppose, for example, that a great flight of secretary birds had arrived, they might have cleared the island of rattlesnakes."

"Oh, what is a secretary bird?" interrupted Franz. "I thought a secretary meant a man who wrote letters?"

"So it does, Franz, and the bird Ernest spoke of has curious long feathers projecting from either side of its head, something like pens stuck behind a man's ear; hence its name.

"It is perfectly true that it lives on snakes, lizards, toads, and frogs, but, Ernest, I cannot give up my pigs; for, in the first place, the secretary bird is an inhabitant of Southern Africa, and is never seen in North America, neither does it ever fly in a flock; still, so ravenous is its appetite, that, no doubt, even one or two, had they by some miracle found themselves on Lake Superior, would have been able to give a very good account of the deadly reptiles, and at least shared in the glory of their extermination."

My wife having gone to prepare dinner, we continued talking as we rested in the shade of some rocks, near the serpent, for a considerable time. The open air was welcome to us after our long imprisonment: and we were, besides, desirous to drive off any birds of prey who might be attracted to the carcase, which we wished to preserve entire.

My boys questioned me closely on the subject of serpents in general; and I described to them the action of the poison fangs; how they folded back on the sides of the upper jaw; and how the poison-secreting glands and reservoir are found at the back and sides of the head, giving to the venomous serpents that peculiar width of head which is so unfailing a characteristic.

"The fangs are hollow," said I, "and when the creature bites, the pressure forces down a tiny drop of the liquid poison, which enters the wound, and, through the veins, quickly spreads over the entire system. Sometimes, if taken in time, cures are effected, but in most cases the bite of a serpent is followed by speedy death."

The children were much interested in my account of the snake-charmers of India, how they fearlessly handle the most deadly of the serpent tribe, the Cobra di Capello—or hooded cobra—cause them to move in time to musical sounds from a small pipe, twine the reptile about their arms and bare necks, and then, to prove that the poison fangs have not been removed, make them bite a fowl, which soon dies from the effects.

"How is it possible to extract the fangs, father!" asked Ernest.

"No instrument is required," replied I; "I have read the account written by a gentleman in India, who saw a snake-charmer catch a large cobra in the jungle, and for the purpose of removing the fangs, hold up a cloth at which the irritated snake flew, and the fangs being caught in it, the man seized the reptile by the throat, extracted them, and then squeezed out the poison, a clear oily substance, upon a leaf."

"What does the rattle of the rattlesnake look like? and how does it sound?"

"At the tip of the tail are a number of curious, loose, horny structures formed of the same substance as the scales. A very good idea of the structure of the rattle may be formed by slipping a number of thimbles loosely into each other.

"The rattlesnake lies coiled with its head flat, and the tip of its tail elevated; when alarmed or irritated it gives a quivering movement to the tail which causes the joints of the rattle to shake against each other with a peculiar sound not easily described; all animals, even horses newly brought from Europe, tremble at this noise, and try to escape."

"What is the best thing to be done for the bite of a serpent?" inquired Fritz.

"Remedies are very various, very uncertain, and differ with the species inflicting the bite.

"Suction, ammonia, oil, the use of the knife, application of fresh mold, lunar caustic, leaves of certain plants, all these and more are mentioned. There is a creeping plant, called *Aristolochia indica*, the leaves of which have in repeated instances done wonders for fearful bites. It is found in many parts of the world, but most plentifully in the hotter regions.

"A mode of cure adopted by the natives of India, Ceylon, and parts of Africa, is by the application of a remarkable object called snake-stone. These are described as flattish, something like half an almond with squared ends, rather light, bearing a very high polish, and of an intense jetty black.

"On being bitten by a cobra, the sufferer applies one of these 'stones' to each puncture, where they adhere strongly for a time, five or six minutes being about the average. They seem to absorb the blood as it flows from the wound, and at last fall off, when the danger is considered to be over.

"But now we must leave this fertile subject of discussion, and I can only say I sincerely trust we may never have cause to resume it from the appearance of another serpent here of any sort, size, or description.

"Come, Ernest, can you not give us an epitaph for our unfortunate friend the donkey?

"We must afford him more honorable sepulture than he enjoys at present, when we proceed, as we speedily must, to disembowel his murderer."

Ernest took the matter quite seriously, and planting his elbows on his knees, he bent his thoughtful brow in his hands, and remained wrapt in poetic meditation for about two minutes

"I have it!" cried he; "but perhaps you will all laugh at me?"

"No, no, don't be shy, old fellow; spit it out!" and thus encouraged by his brother, Ernest, with the blush of a modest author, began:

> *"Beneath this stone poor Grizzle's bones are laid,*
> *A faithful ass he was, and loved by all.*
> *At length, his master's voice he disobeyed,*
> *And thereby came his melancholy fall.*
> *A monstrous serpent, springing from the grass,*
> *Seized, crushed, and swallowed him before our eyes.*
> *But we, though yet we mourn our honest ass,*
> *Are grateful; for he thereby saved the lives*
> *Of all the human beings on this shore—*
> *A father, mother, and their children four."*

"Hurrah for the epitaph! Well done, Ernest!" resounded on all sides, and taking out a large red pencil I used for marking wood, the lines were forthwith inscribed on a great flat stone, being, as I told the boy, the very best poetry that had ever been written on our coast.

We then had dinner, and afterward went to work with the serpent.

The first operation was to recover the mangled remains of the ass, which being effected, he was buried in the soft marshy ground close by, and the hole filled up with fragments of rock.

Then we yoked Storm and Grumble to the serpent, and dragged it to a convenient distance from Rockburg, where the process of skinning, stuffing, and sewing up again afforded occupation of the deepest interest to the boys for several days.

We took great pains to coil it round a pole in the museum, arranging the head with the jaws wide open, so as to look as alarming as possible, and contriving to make eyes and tongue sufficiently well to represent nature; in fact, our dogs never passed the monster without growling, and must have wondered at our taste in keeping such a pet.

Over the entrance leading to the museum and library were inscribed these words:

NO ADMITTANCE FOR ASSES.

The double meaning of this sentence pleased us all immensely.

Chapter Twelve

T HE greatest danger to which we had yet been exposed was now over, but there remained much anxiety in my mind lest another serpent might, unseen by us, have entered the swamp, or might appear, as this had done, from the country beyond Falconhurst.

I projected then two excursions, the first to make a thorough examination of the thicket and morass; the next right away to the Gap, through which alone the arch-enemy could have entered our territory.

On summoning my sons to accompany me to the marsh, I found neither Ernest nor Jack very eager to do so, the latter vowing he had the cold shivers each time he thought how his ribs might have been smashed by the last flap of the snake's tail; but I did not yield to their reluctance, and we finally set about crossing the marsh by placing planks and wicker hurdles on the ground, and changing their places as we advanced.

Nothing was discovered beyond tracks in the reeds and the creature's lair; where the rushes, grass, and bog-plants were beaten down.

Emerging beyond the thicket we found ourselves on firm ground, near the precipitous wall of rock, and perceived a clear sparkling brook flowing from an opening, which proved to be a cave or grotto of considerable size.

The vaulted roof was covered with stalactites, while many formed stately pillars, which seemed as though supporting the roof. The floor was strewn with fine snow-white earth, with a smooth soapy feeling, which I felt convinced was fuller's earth.

"Well, this is a pleasant discovery!" said I. "This is as good as soap for washing, and will save me the trouble of turning soap-boiler."

Perceiving that the streamlet flowed from an opening of some width in the inner rock, Fritz passed through, in order to trace it to its source, presently shouting to me that the opening widened very much, and begging me to follow him.

I did so, leaving the other boys in the outer cave, and fired a pistol-shot—the reverberating echoes of which testified to the great extent of the place; and lighting the bit of candle I always carried with me, we advanced, the light burning clear and steadily, though shedding a very feeble light in so vast a space.

Suddenly Fritz exclaimed:

"I verily believe this is a second cave of salt! See how the walls glance! and how the light is reflected from the roof!"

"These cannot be salt crystals," said I; "the water which flows over them leaves no track, and tastes quite sweet. I am rather inclined to believe that we have penetrated into a cave of rock crystal!"

"Oh, how splendid! Then we have discovered a great treasure!"

"Certainly, if we could make any use of it; otherwise, in our situation, it is about as valuable as the lump of gold found by good old Robinson Crusoe."

"Anyhow, I will break off a piece for a specimen. See, here is a fine bit, only rather dull, and not transparent; what a pity! I must knock off another."

"You must go more carefully to work, or it will look as dull as the first. You destroyed its true form, which is that of a pyramid, with six sides or faces."

We remained some time in this interesting grotto, but our light burnt low after we had examined it in different directions; and Fritz having secured a large lump, which exhibited several crystals in perfection, we quitted the place, Fritz discharging a farewell shot for the sake of hearing the grand echoes.

On reaching the open air we saw poor Jack sobbing bitterly, but as soon as we appeared he ran joyfully toward us, and threw himself into my arms.

"My child, what is the matter?" I cried anxiously.

"Oh, I thought you were lost! I heard a noise twice, as if the rocks had shattered down; and I thought you and Fritz were crushed in the ruins! It was horrible! How glad I am to see you!"

I comforted the child, and explained the noises he had heard, inquiring why he was alone?

"Ernest is over there among the reeds: I daresay he did not hear the shots."

I found Ernest busily engaged in weaving a basket in which to catch fish; he had devised it ingeniously, with a funnel-shaped entrance; through which the fish passing would not easily find their way out, but would remain swimming about in the wide part of the apparatus.

"I shot a young serpent while you were away, father," said he. "It lies there covered with rushes; it is nearly four feet long, and as thick as my arm."

"A serpent!" cried I, hurrying toward it in alarm, and fearing there must be a brood of them in the swamp after all.

"A fine large eel, you mean, my boy. This will provide an excellent supper for us to-night. I am glad you had the courage to kill it, instead of taking to your heels and fleeing from the supposed serpent."

"Well, I thought it would be so horrid to be pursued and caught that I preferred facing it; my shot took effect, but it was very difficult to kill the creature outright, it moved about although its head was smashed."

"The tenacity of life possessed by eels is very remarkable," I said. "I have heard that the best mode of killing them is to grasp them by the neck and slap their tails smartly against a stone or post."

We made our way back more easily by keeping close to the cliffs, where the ground was firmer, and found the mother washing clothes at the fountain. She rejoiced greatly at our safe return, and was much pleased with the supply of fuller's earth, as she said there was now very little soap left. The eel was cooked for supper, and during the evening a full account was given of our passage through the swamp, and discovery of the rock-crystal cavern.

It was most important to ascertain whether any serpent lurked among the woods of our little territory between the cliffs and the sea. Preparations were set on foot for the second and greater undertaking of a search throughout the country beyond the river, as far as the Gap. I wished all the family to go on the expedition, a decision which gave universal satisfaction.

Intending to be engaged in this search for several weeks, we took the small tent and a store of all sorts of necessary provisions, as well as firearms, tools, cooking utensils, and torches.

All these things were packed on the cart, which was drawn by Storm and Grumble. Jack and Franz mounted them, and acted at once the part of riders and drivers. My wife sat comfortably in the cart, Fritz rode in advance, while Ernest and I walked; we were protected in flank by the dogs and Fangs, the tame jackal.

Directing our course toward Woodlands, we saw many traces of the serpent's approach to Rockburg. In some places, where the soil was loose, the trail, like a broad furrow, was very evident indeed.

At Falconhurst we made a halt, and were, as usual, welcomed by the poultry, as well as by the sheep and goats.

We then passed on to Woodlands, where we arrived at nightfall. All was peaceful and in good order; no track of the boa in that direction; no sign of visits from mischievous apes; the little farm and its inhabitants looked most flourishing.

Next day was passed in making a survey of the immediate neighborhood, at the same time collecting a quantity of cotton, which was wanted for new pillows and cushions. In the afternoon Franz was my companion, carrying a small gun entrusted to him for the first time.

We took Floss and Bruno with us, and went slowly along the left bank of the lake, winding our way among reedy thickets, which frequently turned us aside a considerable distance from the water. The dogs hunted about in all directions, and raised duck, snipe, and heron. These usually flew directly across the lake so that Franz got no chance of a shot. He began to get rather impatient, and proposed firing at the black swans we saw sailing gracefully on the glassy surface of the lake.

Just then a harsh booming sound struck our ears. I paused in wonder as to whence the noise proceeded, while Franz exclaimed, "Oh, father, can that be Swift, our young onager?"

"It cannot possibly be Swift," said I; adding, after listening attentively a minute or two, "I am inclined to think it must be the cry of a bittern, a fine handsome bird of the nature of a heron."

"Oh! may I shoot it, father? But I wonder how a bird can make that roaring noise! One would think it was an ox, it is more like lowing than braying."

"The noise creatures make depends more on the construction of the windpipe, its relation to the lungs and the strength of the muscles which force out the breath, than on their size. As, for example, how loud is the song of the nightingale and the little canary bird? Some people say that the bittern booms with his long bill partly thrust into the boggy ground, which increases the hollow muffled sound of its very peculiar cry."

Franz was very anxious that the first trophy of his gun should be so rare a bird as the bittern; the dogs were sent into the wood, and we waited some distance apart, in readiness to fire.

All at once there was a great rustling in the thicket, Franz fired, and I heard his happy voice calling out:

"I've hit him! I've hit him!"

"What have you hit?" shouted I in return.

"A wild pig," said he; "but bigger than Fritz's."

"Aha! I see you remember the agouti! Perhaps it is not a

hog at all but one of our little pigs from the farm. What will the old sow say to you, Franz?"

I soon joined my boy, and found him in transports of joy over an animal certainly very much like a pig, although its snout was broad and blunt. It was covered with bristles, had no tail, and in color was a yellowish gray.

Examining it carefully, and noticing its web feet and its curious teeth, I decided that it must be a capybara, a water-loving animal of South America, and Franz was overjoyed to find that he had shot "a new creature," as he said. It was diffi-cult to carry it home, but he very sensibly proposed that we should open and clean the carcase, which would make it lighter —and then putting it in a game bag, he carried it till quite tired out; he then asked if I thought Bruno would let him strap it on his back. We found the dog willing to bear the burden, and reached Woodlands soon afterward.

There we were surprised to see Ernest surrounded by a number of large rats which lay dead on the ground.

"Where can all these have come from?" exclaimed I. "Have you and your mother been rat-hunting instead of gathering rice as you intended?"

"We came upon these creatures quite unexpectedly," he re-plied, "while in the rice swamp. Knips, who was with us, sprang away to a kind of long-shaped mound among the reeds, and pounced upon something, which tried to escape into a hole. He chattered and gnashed his teeth, and the creature hissed and squeaked, and running up I found he had got a big rat by the tail; he would not let go, and the rat could not turn in the narrow entrance to bite him, but I soon pulled it out and killed it with my stick.

"The mound was a curious looking erection, so I broke it open with some difficulty, and in doing this dislodged quite a dozen of the creatures. Some I killed, but many plunged into the water and escaped.

"On examining their dwelling I found it a vaulted tunnel made of clay and mud, and thickly lined with sedges, rushes, and water-lily leaves.

"There were other mounds or lodges close by, and seeking an entrance to one I stretched my game bag across it, and then hammered on the roof till a whole lot of rats sprang out, several right into the bag. I hit away right and left, but began to repent of my audacity when I found the whole community swarming about in the wildest excitement, some escaping, but many stopping in bewilderment, while others actually at tacked me.

"It was anything but pleasant, I assure you, and I began to think of Bishop Hatto in the Mouse Tower on the Rhine. Knips liked it as little as I did, and skipped about desperately to get out of their way, though he now and then seized a rat by the neck in his teeth.

"Just as I began to shout for help, Juno came dashing through the reeds and water, and made quick work with the enemy, all flying from her attack.

"My mother had great difficulty in forcing her way through the marsh to the scene of action, but reached me at last; and we collected all the slain to show you, and for the sake of their skins."

This account excited my curiosity, and I went to examine the place Ernest described: where I found, to my surprise, an arrangement much like a beaver dam, though on a small scale, and less complete.

"You have discovered a colony of beaver rats," said I to Ernest, "so called from their resemblance in skill and manner of life to that wonderful creature.

"Muskrat, musquash, and ondatra are other names given to them. They have, you see, webbed feet and flattened tails, and we shall find that they carry two small glands containing the scented substance called musk. The sooner we strip off the skins the better; they will be useful for making caps."

We went back to the house, and met Fritz and Jack just returned from their excursion, reporting that no trace of serpents, great or small, had been met with.

Jack carried in his hat about a dozen eggs; and Fritz had shot a couple of heath fowls, a cock and hen.

We sat down to supper, Franz eager to partake of his capybara. Even he himself made a face at the peculiar flavor of the meat.

"It is the musk which you taste," said I; and I described to them the various animals in which this strange liquid is found; the musk deer, musk ox, crocodile, muskrat of India (also called soudeli, which taints a corked bottle of wine, if it only runs across it), concluding with an account of the civet, called also civet-cat.

"The civet," said I, "is a handsome black and white animal, and the perfume obtained from it was formerly considered a valuable medicine; in the present day it is used chiefly as a scent. This odoriferous substance is secreted, *i. e.,* formed, in a double glandular pouch near the tail, and the Dutch keep the creature in captivity, so that it shall afford them a continuous supply.

"The method of removing the civet perfume is ingenious. The animal is very quick and elastic in its movements, and having sharp teeth it is not pleasant to handle. So it is put into a long, narrow cage in which it cannot turn round, a horn spoon is then introduced, and the perfume, a thick, oily stuff something like butter, is coolly scraped from the pouch, the plundered civet being then released from strait durance, until the supply is re-formed."

Presently Jack ran for his game bag, producing some fruit which he had forgotten. Several pale green apples, quite new to us, excited general attention.

"Why, what are those? Are they good?" I asked.

"I hope so, for we sadly want something to take away the taste of Franz's beast," said Jack: "but Fritz and I were afraid of eating some awful poison or other, like the manchineel, so we brought them for the inspection of the learned Master Knips."

I took one and cut it in two, remarking that it contained a circle of seeds or pips, instead of the stone of the manchineel. At that moment Knips slyly came behind me, and snatching up one half, began to munch it with the liveliest satisfaction, an example which the boys were so eager to follow that a general scramble ensued, and I had some trouble in securing a couple of the apples for myself and their mother.

I imagined this to be the cinnamon apple of the Antilles.

Everyone seeming wearied by the fatigues of the day, our mattresses and pillows were arranged, and the inmates of Woodlands betook themselves to repose.

With early light we commenced the next day's journey, directing our course to a point between the sugar-brake and the

Gap, where we had once made a sort of arbor of the branches of trees; as this remained in pretty good condition, we spread a sailcloth over the top of it, instead of pitching the tent, and made it very comfortable quarters for the short time I proposed to stay there.

Our object being to search the neighborhood for traces of the boa constrictor, or any of his kindred, Fritz, Jack, and Franz went with me to the sugar-cane brake, and satisfied ourselves that our enemy had not been there. It was long since we had enjoyed the fresh juice of these canes, and we were refreshing ourselves therewith, when a loud barking of dogs, and loud rustling and rattling through the thicket of canes, disturbed our pleasant occupation, and, as we could see nothing a yard off where we stood, I hurried to the open ground, and with guns in readiness we awaited what was coming.

In a few minutes a herd of creatures like little pigs issued from the thicket, and made off in single file at a brisk trot; they were of a uniform gray color, and showed short sharp tusks.

My trusty double-barrel speedily laid low two of the fugitives; the others continued to follow the leader in line, scarcely turning aside to pass the dead bodies of their comrades, and maintaining the same steady pace, although Fritz and Jack also fired and killed several.

I felt certain that these were peccaries, and recollected that an odoriferous gland in the back must be removed immediately, otherwise the meat will become tainted, and quite unfit to eat. This operation, with the help of my boys, I accordingly performed at once.

Presently, hearing shots in the direction of the hut where we had left Ernest and his mother, I sent Jack to their assistance, desiring him to fetch the cart, that the booty might be conveyed to our encampment, employing the time of his absence in opening and cleaning the animals, thus reducing their weight.

Ernest came back with Jack and the cart, and told us that the procession of peccaries had passed near the hut, and that he, with Juno's help, had secured three of them.

I was glad to hear this, as I had determined to cure a good supply of hams, and we made haste to load the cart; the boys adorned it with flowers and green boughs, and with songs of triumph which made the woods ring they conveyed the valuable supply of game to the hut, where their mother anxiously waited for us.

After dinner we set to work upon our pigs, singeing and scalding off the bristles; I cut out the hams, divided the flitches, bestowed considerable portions of the carcase on the dogs, and diligently cleansed and salted the meat, while the boys prepared a shed, where it was to be hung to be cured in the smoke of fires of green wood.

This unexpected business of course detained us in the place for some time. On the second day, when the smoking shed was ready, the boys were anxious to cook the smallest porker in the Otaheitian fashion. For this purpose they dug a hole, in which they burned a quantity of dry grass, sticks, and weeds, heating stones, which were placed round the sides of the pit.

While the younger boys made ready the oven, Fritz singed and washed his peccary, stuffing it with potatoes, onions, and herbs, and a good sprinkling of salt and pepper.

He then sewed up the opening, and enveloped the pig in large leaves to guard it from the ashes and dust of its cooking-place.

The fire no longer blazed, but the embers and stones were glowing hot; the pig was carefully placed in the hole, covered over with hot ashes, and the hole with earth, so that it looked like a big mole heap.

Dinner was looked forward to with curiosity, as well as appetite; my wife, as usual, distrusting our experiments, was not sanguine of success, and made ready some plain food as a *pis aller*.

She was well pleased with the curing-hut, which was roomy enough to hang all our hams and bacon. On a wide hearth in the middle we kindled a large fire, which was kept constantly smoldering by heaping it with damp grass and green wood. The hut being closed in above, the smoke filled it, and penetrated the meat thoroughly; this process it had to undergo for several days.

In a few hours Fritz gave notice that he was going to open his oven.

Great excitement prevailed as he removed the earth, turf,

and stones, and a delicious appetizing odor arose from the opening. It was the smell of roast pork, certainly, but with a flavor of spices which surprised me, until I thought of the leaves in which the food had been wrapped up.

The peccary was carefully raised, and when a few cinders were picked off, it looked a remarkably well-cooked dish. Fritz was highly complimented on his success, even by his mother.

The scented leaves were, I thought, those of a tree which I knew to be found in Madagascar, called by the natives ravensara, or "good leaf." It is said to combine the scent of the nutmeg, clove, and cinnamon. The fruit is a species of nut, possessing the scent of the leaves in a more delicate degree, and from it an oil or essence is distilled, which is highly valued in native cookery.

During the process of curing our large supply of hams and bacon, which occupied several days, we roamed about the neighborhood in all directions, finding no trace of the serpent, but making many valuable acquisitions, among which were some gigantic bamboos, from fifty to sixty feet in length and of proportionate thickness. These, when cut across near the joints, formed capital casks, tubs, and pots; while the long sharp thorns, which begirt the stem at intervals, were as strong and useful as iron nails.

One day we made an excursion to the farm at Prospect Hill, and were grievously provoked to find that the vagabond apes had been there, and wrought terrible mischief, as before at Woodlands.

The animals and poultry were scattered, and everything in the cottage so torn and dirtied, that it was vain to think of setting things right that day. We therefore very unwillingly left the disorder as we found it, purposing to devote time to the work afterward.

When all was in readiness for the prosecution of our journey, we closed and barricaded the hut, in which, for the present, we left the store of bacon; and arranging our march in the usual patriarchal style, we took our way to the Gap, the thorough defense of which defile was the main object we had in view.

Our last halting-place being much enclosed by shrubs, bamboos, and brushwood, we had during our stay opened a path through the cane thicket in the direction we were about to travel; this we now found of the greatest assistance, and the loaded cart passed on without impediment.

The ground was open and tolerably level beyond, so that in a few hours we arrived at the extreme limit of our coast territory.

We halted on the outskirts of a little wood, behind which, to the right, rose the precipitous and frowning cliffs of the mountain gorge, while to the left flowed the torrent, leaving between it and the rocks the narrow pass we called the Gap, and passing onward to mingle its water with the sea.

The wood afforded us pleasant shelter, and standing high, and within gunshot of the mouth of the rocky pass, I resolved to make it our camping place. We therefore unpacked the cart, and made our usual arrangements for safety and comfort, not forgetting to examine the wood itself, so as to ascertain whether it harbored any dangerous animals.

Nothing worse than wild cats was discovered. We disturbed several of these creatures in their pursuit of birds and small game, but they fled at our approach.

By the time dinner was ready we felt much fatigued, and some hours of unusually sultry and oppressive heat compelled us to rest until toward evening, when returning coolness revived our strength. We pitched the tent, and then occupied ourselves with preparations for the next day, when it was my intention to penetrate the country beyond the defile, and make a longer excursion across the Savannah than had yet been undertaken.

All was ready for a start at an early hour; my brave wife consented to remain in camp with Franz as her companion, while the three elder boys, and all the dogs, except Juno, went with me.

We expected to find it somewhat difficult to make our way through the narrowest part of the pass, which had been so strongly barricaded and planted with thorny shrubs, but found on the contrary that the fences and walls were broken down and disarranged. It was thus very evident that the great snake, as well as the herd of peccaries, had made an entrance here.

This barricade was the first check that had been placed by

hand of man upon the wild free will of nature in this lonely place.

With one consent storms, floods, torrents, and the wild beasts of the forest, had set themselves to destroy it.

We resolved to make the defenses doubly strong, being convinced that the position was capable of being barricaded and fortified so as to resist the invaders we dreaded.

The prospect which opened before us on emerging from the rocky pass was wide and varied. Swelling hills and verdant wooded vales were seen on one hand, while a great plain stretched before us, extending from the banks of the river toward a chain of lofty mountains, whose summits were rendered indistinct in the haze of the distance.

We crossed the stream, which we named East River, filling our flasks with water, and it was well we did so, for in continuing our journey, we found the soil become more arid and parched than we had expected; in fact we soon appeared surrounded by a desert.

The boys were astonished at the altered appearance of the country, part of which had been explored when we met with the buffaloes. I reminded them of the difference of the season; that the expedition had been made directly after the rains, when vegetation had clothed with transient beauty this region, which, possessing no source of moisture itself, had become scathed and bare during the blazing heat of summer.

Our march proceeded slowly, and many were the uncomplimentary remarks made on the "new country."

It was "Arabia Petrea," groaned one. "Desert of Sahara," sighed another. "Fit abode for demons," muttered a third. "Subterranean volcanic fires are raging beneath our feet."

"Patience, my good fellows!" cried I; "you are too easily discouraged. Look beyond the toilsome way to those grand mountains, whose spurs are already stretching forward to meet us. Who knows what pleasant surprises await us amid their steep declivities? I, for my part, expect to find water, fresh grass, trees, and a lovely resting-place."

We were all glad to repose beneath the shade of the first over-hanging rock we came to, although, by pressing further upward, we might have attained to a pleasanter spot.

Looking back toward the Gap, we marked the strange contrast of the smiling country bordering the river, and the dreary, monotonous plain we had traversed.

After gazing on the distant scene, we produced our store of provisions, and were busily engaged, when Knips (our constant companion) suddenly began to snuff and smell about in a very ridiculous way; finally, with a shriek which we knew was expressive of pleasure, he set off at full speed, followed by all the dogs, up a sort of glen behind us.

We left them to their own devices, being far too pleasantly engaged with our refreshments to care much what fancy the little rogue had got in his head.

When hunger was somewhat appeased, Fritz once more cast his eyes over the expanse of plain before us, and after looking fixedly for a moment, exclaimed:

"Is it possible that I see a party of horsemen riding at full gallop toward us! Can they be wild Arabs of the desert?"

"Arabs, my boy! certainly not; but take the spyglass and make them out exactly. We shall have to be on our guard, whatever they are!"

"I cannot see distinctly enough to be sure," said he presently, "and imagination supplies the deficiency of sight in most strange fashion. I could fancy them wild cattle, loaded carts, wandering haycocks, in fact almost anything I like."

The spyglass passed from hand to hand; Jack and Ernest agreed in thinking the moving objects were men on horseback; but when it came to my turn to look, I at once pronounced them to be very large ostriches.

"This is fortunate, indeed!" I exclaimed; "we must try to secure one of these magnificent birds; the feathers alone are worth having."

"A live ostrich, father! that would be splendid. Why, we might ride upon him!"

As the ostriches approached, we began to consider in what way we should attempt a capture. I sent Fritz and Jack to recall the dogs, and placed myself with Ernest behind some shrubs which would conceal us from the birds as they came onward.

The boys did not rejoin us for some little time; they found Knips and the dogs at a pool of water formed by a small mountain stream, which the monkey's instinct had detected; his sudden departure was thus accounted for, and they availed themselves right gladly of his discovery, filling their flasks, and hastily bathing before their return.

The ostriches continued to come in our direction, varying their pace as though in sport, springing, trotting, galloping, and chasing each other round and round, so that their approach was by no means rapid.

I could now perceive that of the five birds one only was a male, the white plumes of the wings and tail contrasting finely with the deep glossy black of the neck and body.

The color of the females being ashen brown, the effect of their white plumes was not so handsome.

"I do not believe we shall have a chance with these birds," said I, "except by sending Fritz's eagle in pursuit; and for that we must bide our time, and let them come as near as possible."

"In what way, then, are ostriches caught by the natives of the African deserts?" inquired Fritz.

"Sometimes by chase on horseback; but their speed is so very great, that even that must be conducted by stratagem.

"When these birds are pursued, they will run for hours in a wide circle; the hunter gallops after them, but describes a much smaller circle, and can therefore maintain the pace for a longer time, waiting to make the attack until the bird is fatigued.

"Among the Bushmen, the hunter sometimes envelopes himself in the skin of an ostrich, his legs doing duty for those of the bird, and his arm managing the head and neck so as to imitate the movements of the bird when feeding. The enterprising hunter is thus enabled to get among a flock of ostriches, and to shoot them with arrows one after another.

"When aware of an enemy they defend themselves desperately, using their powerful legs as weapons, always kicking forward, and inflicting dreadful injuries on dogs, and even on men, if attacked without due precaution. But let us take up our positions, and keep perfectly still, for the ostriches are at hand!"

We held the dogs concealed as much as possible; the stately birds suddenly perceiving us, paused, hesitated, and appeared uneasy. Yet as no movement was made, they drew a few steps nearer, with outstretched necks, examining curiously the unwonted spectacle before them.

The dogs became impatient, struggled from our grasp, and furiously rushed toward our astonished visitors. In an instant they turned and fled with the speed of the wind; their feet seemed not to touch the ground, their wings aiding the marvelously rapid progress.

In a few moments they would have been beyond our reach, but as they turned to fly the eagle was unhooded. Singling out the male bird the falcon made his fatal swoop, and piercing the skull, the magnificent creature was laid low. Before we could reach the spot the dogs had joined the bird of prey, and were fiercely tearing the flesh and bedabbling the splendid plumes with gore.

This sight grieved us.

"What a pity we could not capture this glorious bird alive!" exclaimed Fritz, as we took its beautiful feathers; "it must, I am sure, have stood more than six feet high, and two of us might have mounted him at once!"

"In the vast sandy deserts where nothing grows, what can flocks of these birds find to live upon?" inquired Ernest.

"That would indeed be hard to say, if the deserts were utterly barren and unfruitful," returned I; "but over these sandy wastes a beneficent Providence scatters plants of wild melons, which absorb and retain every drop of moisture, and which quench the thirst as well as satisfy the hunger of the ostriches and other inhabitants of the wilds. These melons, however, do not constitute his entire diet; he feeds freely on grasses, dates, and hard grain, when he can obtain them."

"Does the ostrich utter any cry?"

"The voice of the ostrich is a deep, hollow, rumbling sound, so much resembling the roar of the lion as to be occasionally mistaken for it. But what does Jack mean by waving his cap and beckoning in that excited fashion? What has the boy found, I wonder!"

He ran a little way toward us, shouting:

"Eggs, father! Ostriches' eggs! a huge nest full—do come quick!"

We all hastened to the spot, and in a slight hollow of the

ground beheld more than twenty eggs, as large as an infant's head.

The idea of carrying more than two away with us was pre-posterous, although the boys, forgetting what the weight would be, seriously contemplated clearing the nest.

They were satisfied when a kind of landmark had been set up, so that if we returned we might easily find the nest.

As each egg weighed about three pounds, the boys soon found the burden considerable, even when tied into a hand-kerchief and carried like a basket. To relieve them, I cut a strong elastic heath stick, and suspending an egg in its sling at each end, laid the bent stick over Jack's shoulder, and like a Dutch dairy-maid with her milk pails, he stepped merrily along without inconvenience.

We presently reached a marshy place, surrounding a little pool evidently fed by the stream which Knips had discovered. The soft ground was trodden and marked by the footsteps of many different sorts of animals; we saw tracks of buffaloes, antelopes, onagas or quaggas, but no trace whatever of any kind of serpent; hitherto our journey in search of monster reptiles had been signalized by very satisfactory failure.

By this brook we sat down to rest and take some food; Fangs presently disappeared, and Jack calling to his pet discovered him gnawing at something which he had dug from the marsh. Taking it for a root of some sort, Jack brought it for my in-spection. I dipped it in water to clear off the mud, and to my surprise found a queer little living creature, no bigger than half an apple, in my hand. It was a small tortoise.

"A tortoise, I declare!" cried Fritz. "What a long way from the sea. How came it here, I wonder?"

"Perhaps there has been a tortoise-shower," remarked Ernest. "One reads of frog-showers in the time of the ancient Romans."

"Hullo, Professor! you're out for once," said I. "This is nothing but a mud-tortoise, which lives in wet, marshy ground and fresh water. They are useful in gardens; for although they like a few lettuce leaves now and then, they will destroy num-bers of snails, grubs, and worms."

Resuming our journey, we arrived at a charming valley,

verdant, fruitful, and shaded by clumps of graceful trees. It afforded us the greatest delight and refreshment to pass along this cool and lovely vale, which we agreed to call Glen Verdant.

In the distance we could see herds of antelopes or buffaloes feeding; but as our dogs continually ranged a long way ahead of us, they were quickly startled, and vanished up one or other of the narrow gorges which opened out of the valley.

Following the imperceptible windings of the vale, we were surprised, on quitting it for the more open ground, to find ourselves in a country we were already acquainted with, and not far from the Jackal Cave, as we called the place where Fangs had been captured in cubhood.

On recognizing the spot, Ernest, who was in advance with one of the dogs, hastened toward it. We lost sight of him for a few minutes, and then arose a cry of terror, violent barking, and deep, surly growls.

As we rushed forward, Ernest met us, looking white as ashes, and calling out:

"A bear, a bear, father! He is coming after me!"

The boy clung to me in mortal fear. I felt his whole frame quivering.

"Courage, my son!" cried I, disengaging myself from his grasp; "we must prepare for instant defense!"

The dogs dashed forward to join the fray, whatever it was; and not long were we in doubt. To my no small consternation, an enormous bear made his appearance, quickly followed by another.

With leveled guns, my brave Fritz and I advanced slowly to meet them. Jack was also ready to fire, but the shock had so unnerved Ernest that he fairly took to his heels. We fired together, one at each bear; but though hit, the monsters were unfortunately only wounded. We found it most difficult to take aim, as the dogs beset them on all sides. However, they were much disabled, one having the lower jaw broken, and the other, with a bullet in his shoulder, was effectually lamed. The dogs, perceiving their advantage, pressed more closely round their foes, who yet defended themselves furiously, with frightful yells of pain and rage. Such was the confusion and perpetual movement of the struggle, that I dared not fire

again, seeing that even slightly wounding one of our gallant hounds would instantly place him in the power of the raging bears.

Watching our opportunity, we suddenly advanced with loaded pistols to within a very few paces of the animals, and firing, both fell dead, one shot through the head, the other, in the act of rearing to spring on Fritz, received his charge in its heart.

"Thank Heaven!" cried I, as with dull groans the brutes sank to the ground. "We have escaped the greatest peril we have yet encountered!"

The dogs continued to tear and worry the fallen foe, as though unwilling to trust the appearance of death. With feelings somewhat akin, I drew my hunting-knife, and made assurance doubly sure.

Seeing all safe, Jack raised a shout of victory, that poor Ernest might gain courage to approach the scene of conflict, which at last he did, and joined us in examining the dangerous animals, as they lay motionless before us.

Every point was full of interest, their wounds, their sharp teeth, their mighty claws, the extraordinary strength of neck and shoulder, all were remarked and commented on, and observing that the shaded brown hair was tipped with glossy white, I thought that these might be the silver bears mentioned in Captain Clarke's journey to the northwest coasts of America.

"Well, my lads," said I, "if we have failed to catch sight of serpents, we have at least made good riddance of some other bad rubbish! These fellows would one day have worked us woe, or I am much mistaken. What's to be done next?"

"Why, skin them, to be sure," said Fritz. "We shall have a couple of splendid bearskin rugs."

As this process would take time and evening drew on, we dragged the huge carcases into their den, to await our return, concealing them with boughs of trees and fencing the entrance as well as we could. The ostrich eggs we also left behind us, hidden in a sandy hole.

By sunset we reached the tent, and joyfully rejoined the mother and Franz, right glad to find a hearty meal prepared for us, as well as a large heap of brushwood for the watch-fire.

When a full account of our adventures had been given, with

a minute and special description of the bear fight, the mother related what she had done during our absence. She and Franz had made their way through the wood up to the rocks behind it, and discovered a bed of pure white clay, which it seemed to her might be used for making porcelain. Then she had contrived a drinking trough for the cattle out of a split bamboo.

She had arranged a hearth in a sheltered place by building up large stones, cemented with the white clay; and, finally, she had cut a quantity of canes and brought them, on the cart, to be in readiness for the building we had in hand.

I praised the thoughtful diligence which had effected so much that was of real and definite use. In order to try the clay, I put some balls of it in the fire now kindled, to burn during the night, and we then betook ourselves to rest under shelter of our tent.

I awoke at dawn and aroused my little party. My first idea was to examine the clay balls, which I found baked hard and finely glazed, but too much melted down by the heat—a fault which, seeing the excellent quality of the clay, I knew it would be well worth while to remedy.

After breakfast, and our accustomed devotions, we harnessed the cart, and took the way to the bears' den. Fritz headed the party, and, coming in sight of the entrance to the cave, called out softly:

"Make haste and you will see a whole crowd of wild turkeys, who seem to have come to attend the funeral obsequies of their respected friend and neighbor, Bruin, here. But there appears to be a jealous watcher who is unwilling to admit the visitors to the bed of state!"

The Watcher, as Fritz called him, was an immensely large bird, with a sort of comb on his head, and a loose, fleshy skin hanging from beneath the beak. Part of the neck was bare, wrinkled, and purplish-red, while around it, resting on the shoulders, was a downy collar of soft, white feathers. The plumage was grayish-brown, marked here and there with white patches; the feet appeared to be armed with strong claws. This great bird guarded the entrance to the cave, occasionally retiring into it himself for a few minutes; but as soon as the other birds came pressing in after him, he hurried out again, and they were forced to retire.

We stopped to observe this curious scene, and were startled suddenly by a mighty rush of wings in the air above us. We looked up; at the same moment Fritz fired, and an enormous bird fell heavily head foremost on the rocks, by which its neck was broken, while blood flowed from a wound in the breast.

We had been holding back the dogs, but they, with Fritz, now rushed toward the cave, the birds rising around them and departing with heavy, ungainly flight, leaving only Fritz's prize, and one of the other birds killed by the large one in its fall.

With the utmost caution I entered the cave, and rejoiced to find that the tongue and eyes only of the bears had been devoured; a little later and we should have had the handsome skins pecked and torn to rags, and all chance of steaks and bears' paws gone.

On measuring the wings of the large bird from tip to tip, I found the length exceeded eleven feet, and concluded it to be a condor; it was evidently the mate of the "Watcher," as Fritz called the first we saw.

To work we now went on the bears, and no slight affair we found it to skin and cut them up, but by dint of perseverance, we at last succeeded in our object.

Determining to smoke the meat on the spot, we cut magnificent hams, and took off the rest of the meat in slices after the manner of the buccaneers in the West Indies, preserving the paws entire to be cooked as a delicacy, and obtaining from the two bears together a prodigious supply of lard, which my wife gladly undertook to melt and prepare for keeping.

The bones and offal we drew to some distance with the help of our cattle, and made the birds of the air most welcome to feast upon it. This, with the assistance of all sorts of insects, they did so effectually that before we left the place the skulls were picked perfectly clean, the sun had dried them, and they were ready for us to carry off to our museum.

The skins had to be very carefully scraped, washed, salted, cleansed with ashes, and dried; which occupied fully two days.

I was lamenting our distance from the rascusara tree, the leaves of which had flavored our roast peccary so nicely, when

I observed among the brushwood which the boys had brought from the thickets around us, a climbing plant, whose leaves had a very strong smell; the stem resembled a vine, and the fruit grew in clusters like currants. Some were red, and some of a green color, which I supposed to denote various degrees of ripeness. They were hard, and the outer skin was quite thin.

I recognized in this the pepper plant, a discovery particularly agreeable at this moment.

The boys soon gathered a large supply; the red berries were soaked in salt and water for several days, then washed and rubbed, and finally, becoming perfectly white, were dried in the sun. The treatment of the green berries was simple; they were merely exposed to the sun's heat for a day or two, and then stored: in this way we obtained enough, both of black and white pepper, to last us a very long time.

I took also a number of young plants, that we might have pepper growing at Rockburg and our various settlements. Some roots of another plant were also taken, which, from the pods, appeared to be a kind of bean.

We were glad of this occupation during the tedious business of smoking the bears' meat, and availed ourselves of the leisure time by also preparing for stuffing the condor and the turkey buzzard, urubu or black vulture—for I could not determine to which species the smaller bird belonged.

The four boys at length became so weary of inaction, that I determined to let them make an excursion alone on the Savannah. Three of them received this permission with eager delight, but Ernest said he would prefer to remain with us; to which, as the expedition was to be entirely one of pleasure, I could make no objection.

Little Franz, on the other hand, whom I would willingly have kept with us, was wild to go with his brothers, and I was obliged to consent, as I had made the proposal open to all, and could not draw back.

In the highest spirits they ran to bring their steeds (as we were fain to call the cattle they rode) from their pasturage at a short distance. Speedily were they saddled, bridled, and mounted—the three lads were ready to be off.

It was my wish that our sons should cultivate a habit of bold independence, for well I knew that it might be the will of God to deprive them easily of their parents; when, without an enterprising spirit of self reliance, their position would be truly miserable.

My gallant Fritz possessed this desirable quality in no small degree, and to him I committed the care of his young brothers, charging them to look up to and obey him as their leader.

They were well armed, well mounted, had a couple of good dogs; and, with a hearty "God speed and bless you, my boys!" I let them depart.

We, who remained behind, passed the day in a variety of useful occupations.

The bears' meat, which was being cured in a smoking shed such as that we set up for the peccary hams, required a good deal of attention from my wife. Ernest had a fancy for making ornamental cups from the ostrich eggs, while I investigated the interior of the cave.

I found the inner wall to consist of a kind of talc, mingled with threads of asbestos, and also indications of mica. Examining further, I detached a large block, and found to my joy that I could split it into clear transparent sheets, which would serve admirably for window panes.

My wife saw this substitute for glass with unfeigned satisfaction, declaring that although she would not complain, yet the want of glass for windows had been a downright trouble to her.

Chapter Thirteen

As evening approached, the bears' paws, which were stewing for supper, sent forth savory odors; and we sat talking round the fire, while listening anxiously for sounds heralding the return of our young explorers.

At last the tramp and beat of hoofs struck our ears; the little troop appeared, crossing the open ground before us at a sharp trot, and a shrill ringing cheer greeted us as we rose and went to meet them.

They sprang from their saddles, the animals were set at liberty to refresh themselves, and the riders eagerly came to exhibit their acquisitions and give an account of themselves.

Funny figures they cut! Franz and Jack had each a young

kid slung on his back, so that the four legs, tied together, stuck out under their chins.

Fritz's game bag looked remarkably queer—round lumps, sharp points, and an occasional movement seemed to indicate a living creature or creatures within.

"Hurrah! for the chase, father!" cried Jack. "Nothing like real hunting after all. And just to see how Storm and Grumble go along over a grassy plain! It is perfectly splendid! We soon tired out the little antelopes, and were able to catch them."

"Yes, father," said Franz; "and Fritz has two Angora rabbits in his bag, and we wanted to bring you some honey. Only think! such a clever bird—a cuckoo, showed us where it was!"

"My brothers forget the chief thing," said Fritz. "We have driven a little herd of antelopes right through the Gap into our territory; and there they are, all ready for us to hunt when we like—or to catch and tame!"

"Well done!" cried I; "here is indeed a list of achievements. But to your mother and me, the chief thing of all, is God's goodness in bringing you safe back to us. Now, let us hear the whole story, that we may have a definite idea of your performances."

"We had a splendid ride," said Fritz, "down Glen Verdant, and away to the defile through our Rocky Barrier, and the morning was so cool and fresh that our steeds galloped along, nearly the whole way, at the top of their speed. When we had passed through the Gap we moderated our furious pace and kept our eyes open on the lookout for game; we then trotted slowly to the top of a grassy hill, from whose summit we saw two herds of animals, whether antelopes, goats, or gazelles, we did not know, grazing by the side of the stream below us. We were about to gallop down and try to get a shot at them, when it struck me that it would be wiser to try and drive the whole herd through the Gap into our own domain, where they would be shut up, as it were, in a park, free and yet within reach. Down the hill we rode as hard as we could go, formed in a semi-circle behind the larger herd—magnificent antelopes—and, aided by the dogs, with shouts and cries drove them along the stream toward the Gap; as we came near the opening they appeared inclined to halt and turn, like sheep about to be driven into the butcher's yard; and it was all we could do to prevent them from bolting past us; but, at length, one made a rush at the opening and, the rest following, they were soon all on the other side of the frontier, and inhabitants of New Switzerland."

"Capital," I said, "capital, my boy! But I don't see what is to make them remain inhabitants of our domain, or to prevent them from returning through the Gap whenever they feel inclined."

"Stop, father," he replied, "you interrupt me too soon; we thought of that possibility, too, and provided against it. We stretched a long line right across the defile and strung on it feathers and rags and all sorts of other things, which danced and fluttered in the wind, and looked so strange that I am perfectly certain that the herd will never attempt to pass it; in fact, Levaillant, from whom I learned the trick, says, in his *Voyage au Cap de Bonne Espérance,* that the Hottentots make use of the method for penning in the antelopes they have caught in the chase."

"Well done," said I, "I am glad to see that you remember what you have read. The antelopes are welcome to New Switzerland, but, my boy," I added, "I cannot say the same for the rabbits you have there; they increase so rapidly that if you establish a colony of the little wretches your next difficulty will be to get rid of them."

"True," he replied, "but my idea was to place them upon Whale Island, where they would find abundant food, and at the same time in no way trouble us. May I not establish a warren there? It would be so useful. Do you know, my eagle caught these pretty little fellows for me? I saw a number of them running about and so unhooded him, and in a few minutes he brought me three—one dead, with whose body I rewarded him, and these two here, unhurt."

"Now, father," said Jack, interrupting him, "do listen to me and hear my story, or else Fritz will begin upon my adventures and tire you out with his rigmarole descriptions."

"Certainly, Jack," I said, "I am quite ready to listen to you. First and foremostly, how did you bring down those beautiful little animals you have there?"

"Oh, we galloped them down. The dogs sniffed about in

The return of our young explorers. (Page 270)

the grass while Fritz was away after the rabbits, out popped those little fawns, and away they went bounding and skipping, at the rate of thirty miles an hour, with Storm, Grumble, and the dogs at their heels. In about a quarter of an hour we had left the dogs behind and were close upon our prey. Down went the little creatures in the grass, and, overcome with terror and fatigue, were at our mercy. So we shouted to Fritz, and——"

"My dear boy," said I, "according to your statement, Fritz must have been seven miles and a half off."

"Oh, well, father, perhaps we did not ride for quite a quarter of an hour, and, of course, I can't say exactly how fast we were going; and then, you see, the fawns did not run in a straight line; at any rate Fritz heard us, and he and Franz and I leashed the legs of the pretty creatures, and then we mounted again, and presently saw a wretch of a cuckoo, who led us ever so far out of our course by cuckoo-ing and making faces at us, and then hopping away. Franz declared it must be an enchanted princess, and so I thought I would rid it of its spell; but Fritz stopped me shooting it, and said it was a 'Honey Indicator,' and that it was leading us probably to a bees' byke, so we spared its life, and presently, sure enough, it stopped close by a bees' nest in a hollow tree. This was capital, we thought, and, as we were in a great hurry to taste the honey, I threw in a lot of lighted lucifer matches, but somehow it did not kill the bees at all, but only made them awfully angry, and they flew out in a body and stung me all over. I rushed to Storm and sprang on his back, but, though I galloped away for dear life, it was an age before I got rid of the little wretches, and now my face is in a perfect fever. I think I will get mother to bathe it for me;" and off rushed the noisy boy, leaving Fritz and me to see to the fawns and examine the rabbits. With these latter I determined to do as Fritz proposed, namely, to colonize Whale Island with them. I was all the more willing to do this because I had been considering the advisability of establishing on that island a fortress to which we might retreat in any extreme danger, and where we should be very thankful, in case of such a retreat, to possess means of obtaining a constant supply of animal food.

Having ministered to the wants of the antelopes, I tried to interest the boys in my discovery of the block of talc, but just then their mother summoned us to dinner.

The principal dish in this meal consisted of the bears' paws —most savory smelling delicacies, so tempting that their close resemblance to human hands, and even the roguish "Fee-fo-fum" from Jack, did not prevent a single member of the family from enjoying them most heartily.

Supper over, we lit our watch-fire, retired to our tent, and slept soundly.

We had been working very diligently; the bears' meat was smoked, the fat melted down and stored, and a large supply of bamboos collected. But I wished to make yet another excursion, and at early dawn I aroused the boys.

Fritz mounted the mule, I rode Lightfoot, Jack and Franz took their usual steeds, and, with the two dogs, we galloped off—first to visit the euphorbia to collect the gum, and then to discover whether the ostrich had deserted her eggs in the sand.

Ernest watched us depart without the slightest look or sigh of regret, and returned to the tent to assist his mother and study his books.

Our steeds carried us down the Green Valley at a rapid rate, and we followed the direction we had pursued on our former expedition. We soon reached Turtle Marsh, and then, filling our water-flasks, we arrived at the rising ground where Fritz discovered the mounted Arabs.

As Jack and Franz wanted a gallop, I allowed them to press forward, while Fritz and I visited the euphorbia trees. A quantity of the red gum had exuded from the incisions I had made, and as this had coagulated in the sun, I rolled it into little balls and stored it in a bamboo jar I had brought with me for the purpose.

As we rode after the boys, who were some way ahead, Fritz remarked:

"Did you not tell me that the juice of that tree was poisonous, father; why have you collected such a quantity?"

"I did indeed say so," I replied; "it is a most deadly poison. The inhabitants of the Cape of Good Hope use it to poison the springs where wild animals assemble to quench their thirst; and they thus slaughter an immense number of the creatures for the sake of their hides. I intend, however, to use it to destroy the apes should they again commit depredations, and also in preparing the skins of animals to protect them from the attacks of insects."

The two boys were still at some distance from us, when suddenly four magnificent ostriches rose from the sand where they had been sitting.

Jack and Franz perceived them, and, with a great shout, drove them toward us. In front ran a splendid male bird, his feathers of shining black, and his great tail plume waving behind. Three females of an ashen gray color followed him. They approached us with incredible swiftness, and were within gunshot before they perceived us. Fritz had had the forethought to bind up the beak of his eagle so that, should he bring down an ostrich, he might be unable to injure it.

He now threw up the falcon which, towering upward, swooped down upon the head of the foremost bird, and so confused and alarmed him, that he could not defend himself nor continue his flight. So greatly was his speed checked that Jack overtook him, and hurling his lasso, enfolded his wings and legs in its deadly coils and brought him to the ground. The other ostriches were almost out of sight, so leaving them to their own devices, we leaped from our steeds and attempted to approach the captured bird. He struggled fearfully, and kicked with such violence, right and left, that I almost despaired of getting him home alive.

It occurred to me, however, that if we could cover his eyes, his fury might be subdued. I instantly acted upon this idea, and flung over his head my coat and hunting-bag, which effectually shut out the light.

No sooner had I done this than his struggles ceased, and we were able to approach. We first secured round his body a broad strip of sealskin, on each side of which I fastened a stout piece of cord, that I might be able to lead him easily. Then, fastening another cord in a loop round his legs that he might be prevented from breaking into a gallop, we released him from the coils of the lasso.

"Do you know," said I to the boys, "how the natives of India secure a newly captured elephant?"

"Oh, yes!" said Fritz; "they fasten him between two tame elephants. We'll do that to this fine fellow, and tame him double quick."

"The only difficulty will be," remarked Jack, "that we have no tame ostriches. However, I daresay Storm and Grumble will have no objection to perform their part, and it will puzzle even this great monster to run away with them."

So we at once began operations. Storm and Grumble were led up on either side of the recumbent ostrich, and the cords secured to their girths. Jack and Franz, each armed with a stout whip, mounted their respective steeds, the wrappers were removed from the bird's eyes, and we stood by to watch what would next occur.

For some moments after the return of his sight he lay perfectly still, then he arose with a bound and, not aware of the cords which hampered him, attempted to dash forward. The thongs were stout, and he was brought to his knees. A fruitless struggled ensued, and then at length, seeming to accommodate himself to circumstances, he set off at a sharp trot, his guards making the air re-echo with their merry shouts. These cries stimulated the ostrich to yet further exertions, but he was at length brought to a stand by the determined refusal of his four-footed companions to continue such a race across loose sand.

The boys having enjoyed the long run, I told them to walk with the prisoner slowly home, while Fritz and I returned to examine the ostrich's nest. The eggs were quite warm, and I was certain that the mother had quite recently left the nest; leaving about half, I packed the rest of the eggs in a large bag I had brought for the purpose, and slung it carefully on the saddle before me. We soon caught up our advance guard, and without other notable incident reached our tent.

Astonishment and dismay were depicted on the face of the mother as we approached.

"My dear husband," she exclaimed, "do you think our provisions so abundant that you must scour the deserts to find some great beast to assist us to devour them? You must discover an iron mine next, for iron is what ostriches chiefly live on, is it not? Oh, I do wish you would be content with the menagerie you have already collected, instead of bringing in a specimen of every beast you come across. And this is such a useless monster!"

"Useless! mother," exclaimed Jack; "you would not say so had you seen him run; why, he will be the fleetest courser in our stables. I am going to make a saddle and bridle for him, and in future he shall be my only steed. Then as for his appetite, father declares it is most delicate, he only wants a little fruit and grass, and a few stones and tenpenny nails to help his digestion."

The way in which Jack assumed the proprietorship of our new prize seemed to strike his brothers as rather cool, and there was instantly a cry raised on the subject.

"Very well," said Jack, "let us each take possession of the part of the ostrich we captured. Your bird, Fritz, seized the head, keep that; father shall have the body, I'll have the legs, and Franz a couple of feathers from the tail."

"Come, come," said I, "I think that Jack has a very good right to the ostrich, seeing that he brought it to the ground, and if he succeeds in taming it and converting it into a saddle horse it shall be his. From this time, therefore, he is responsible for its training."

The day was now too far advanced to allow us to think of setting out for Rockburg, so we fastened up the ostrich between two trees, and devoted the remainder of the evening to making preparations for our departure.

At early dawn our picturesque caravan was moving homeward. The ostrich continued so refractory that we were obliged to make him again march between Storm and Grumble, and as these gallant steeds were thus employed, the cow was harnessed to the cart, laden with our treasures. Room was left in the cart for the mother, Jack and Franz mounted Storm and Grumble, I rode Lightfoot, and Fritz brought up the rear on Swift.

At the mouth of the Gap we called a halt, and replaced the cord the boys had strung with ostrich feathers by a stout palisade of bamboos. I also took the opportunity of collecting a store of pipeclay, as I intended during the winter months, which were close at hand, to try my hand at china making.

When we reached the sugar-cane grove, we again stopped to collect the peccary hams we had left to be smoked; and my wife begged me to gather some seeds of an aromatic plant which grew in the neighborhood, and which had the scent of vanilla. I obtained a good supply, and we moved forward toward Woodlands, where we intended to rest for the night, after our long and fatiguing march.

Our tent was pitched, and on our beds of cotton we slept soundly.

Next morning early we examined our farmyard, which appeared in a most prosperous and flourishing condition. The sight of all these domestic animals made us long even more than ever for our home at Rockburg, and we determined to hasten thither with all possible speed.

The number of our pigs, goats, and poultry had greatly increased since we had last visited our colony; and some of these, two fine broods of chickens especially, my wife wished to take back with her.

We found that the herd of antelopes, which Fritz and Jack had driven through the Gap, had taken up their abode in the neighborhood, and several times we saw the beautiful animals browsing among the trees.

While at the farm, we repaired both the animals' stalls and our dwelling room, that the former might be more secure against the attacks of wild beasts, and the latter fitted for our accommodation when we should visit the spot.

Everything at length being satisfactorily arranged, we again retired to rest, and early next morning completed our journey to Rockburg.

By midday we were once more settled at home. Windows and doors were thrown open to admit fresh air; the animals established in their stalls; and the cart's miscellaneous cargo discharged and arranged.

As much time as I could spare, I devoted to the ostrich, whom we fastened, for the present, between two bamboo posts in front of our dwelling.

I then turned my attention to the eggs we had brought, and which I determined to hatch, if possible, by artificial heat. For this purpose I arranged a stove, which I maintained at a uniform temperature, and on it I placed the eggs, carefully wrapped in cotton wool.

Next morning Fritz and I went off in the boat, first to Whale Island, there to establish our colonists, the Angora rabbits, and then to Shark Island, where we placed the dainty little antelopes. Having made them happy with their liberty and abundance of food, we returned as quickly as possible to cure the bearskins, and add the provisions we had brought to the stores lying in our cellar.

As we returned, we caught up Jack, making his way in great glee toward Rockburg. He was carrying, in a basket, an immense eel, which he and Ernest had secured.

Ernest had set, on the previous night, a couple of lines; one had been dragged away, but on the other they found this splendid fellow.

It proved delicious. Half was prepared for dinner, and the other half salted and stowed away.

We now, for a short time, again turned our attention to our duties about the house.

Thinking that the veranda would be greatly improved by some creepers, I sowed, round the foot of each bamboo pillar, vanilla and pepper-seed, as well as that of other creeping plants, which would not only give the house a pleasanter aspect, but also afford us shade during the summer months.

I constructed a couple of hencoops too, for the hens and their little chicks which we had brought from Woodlands, for I knew that if I left them unprotected, the inquisitive dispositions of Knips and Fangs might induce them to make anatomical experiments which would be detrimental to the welfare of the youngsters.

Ernest's rat skins were voted a nuisance within doors, and were tied together and hung up outside; so powerful was the odor they emitted, that even then Jack would pretend to faint every time he passed near them.

The museum received its additions: the condor and vulture were placed there, to be stuffed when we should find time during the rainy season. The mica and asbestos, too, were brought in for the present, not to lie there idle, but to wait until I could use them as I intended, for china and lamp-wicks.

Having occupied two days in this way, we turned our attention to other duties: the cultivation of a wheat, barley, and maize field, the management of the ostrich's eggs, and the taming of the captives.

As agriculture was, though the least to our taste, the most important of these several duties, we set about it first. The animals drew the plow, but the digging and hoeing taxed our powers of endurance to the utmost.

We worked two hours in the morning and two in the evening. Fully did we realize the words of Scripture: "In the sweat of thy face shalt thou eat bread."

In the interval we devoted our attention to the ostrich. But our efforts on behalf of his education seemed all in vain. He appeared as untameable as ever. I determined, therefore, to adopt the plan which had subdued the refractory eagle.

The effect of the tobacco fumes almost alarmed me. The ostrich sank to the ground and lay motionless. Slowly, at length, he arose, and paced up and down between the bamboo posts.

He was subdued, but to my dismay resolutely refused all food. I feared he would die; for three days he pined, growing weaker and weaker each day.

"Food he must have!" said I to my wife; "food he must have!" The mother determined to attempt an experiment. She prepared balls of maize flour, mixed with butter. One of these she placed within the bird's beak. He swallowed it, and stretched out his long neck, looking inquiringly for a second mouthful. A second, third, and fourth ball followed the first. His appetite returned, and his strength came again.

All the wild nature of the bird had gone, and I saw with delight that we might begin his education as soon as we chose. Rice, guavas, maize, and corn he ate readily—*washing it down*, as Jack expressed it, with small pebbles, to the great surprise of Franz, to whom I explained that the ostrich was merely following the instinct common to all birds; that he required these pebbles to digest his food, just as smaller birds require gravel.

After a month of careful training, our captive would trot, gallop, obey the sound of our voice, feed from our hand; and, in fact, showed himself perfectly docile. Now our ingenuity was taxed to the utmost. How were we to saddle and bridle

a bird? First, for a bit for his beak. Vague ideas passed through my mind, but every one I was obliged to reject. A plan at length occurred to me. I recollected the effect of light and its absence upon the ostrich, how his movements were checked by sudden darkness, and how, with the light, power returned to his limbs.

I immediately constructed a leathern hood, to reach from the neck to the beak, cutting holes in it for the eyes and ears.

Over the eyeholes I contrived square flaps or blinkers, which were so arranged with whalebone springs that they closed tightly of themselves. The reins were connected with these blinkers, so that the flaps might be raised or allowed to close at the rider's pleasure.

When both blinkers were open, the ostrich would gallop straight ahead; close his right eye and he turned to the left, close his left and he turned to the right, shut both and he stood stock still.

I was justly proud of my contrivance, but, before I could really test its utility, I was obliged to make a saddle. After several failures, I succeeded in manufacturing one to my liking, and in properly securing it; it was something like an old-fashioned trooper's saddle, peaked before and behind—for my great fear was lest the boys should fall. This curious-looking contrivance I placed upon the shoulders as near the neck as possible, and secured it with strong girths round the wings and across the breast, to avoid all possibility of the saddle slipping down the bird's sloping back.

I soon saw that my plan would succeed, though skill and considerable practice was necessary in the use of my patent bridle. It was difficult to remember that to check the courser's speed it was necessary to slacken rein, and that the tighter the reins were drawn, the faster he would fly. We at length, however, all learned to manage Master Hurricane, and the distance between Rockburg and Falconhurst was traversed in an almost incredibly short space of time. The marvelous speed of the bird again revived the dispute as to the ownership, and I was obliged to interfere.

"Jack shall retain the ostrich," said I, "for it is most suited to him; he is a lighter weight than either of you his elder brothers, and Franz is not yet strong enough to manage such a fleet courser. But he is so far to be considered common property, that all may practice on him occasionally; and, in a case of necessity, anyone may mount him."

Our field work was by this time over. The land had been plowed and sown with wheat, barley, and maize. On the other side of Jackal River we had planted potatoes and cassava roots, and all sorts of other seeds had been carefully sown.

We had not neglected the ostrich's eggs, and one day Fritz introduced me with great glee to three little ostriches. But alas, the little creatures were not destined to enjoy life long. One died almost as soon as it was hatched, and the others, after tottering about on their stilt-like legs for a few days, followed its example.

I now found time to turn my attention to the bears' skins, which required preparation before they would be fit for use as leather. They had been salted and dried, and now required tanning. I had no tan, however. This was unfortunate; but not to be deterred from my purpose, I determined to use a mixture of honey and water in its place.

The experiment proved successful. When the skins were dried they remained flexible and free from smell, while the fur was soft and glossy.

This was not the only result of the experiment, for the honey-water which I boiled appeared so clear and tempting, that it struck me that I might prepare from it an excellent drink. I put by some of the liquid before making use of it as tan, and reboiled it with nutmeg and cinnamon. The preparation, which much resembled English mead, was pronounced delicious, and the mother begged me to brew a large supply. As our cellar was now well stocked with provisions for the winter, and our other preparations were completed, I was able to turn my attention to details of lesser importance. The boys had been clamoring for hats, and as my success in so many trades had surprised me, I agreed to turn hatter for the nonce. With the rat skins and a solution of india rubber, I produced a kind of felt, which I dyed a brilliant red with cochineal, and stretching this on a wooden block I had prepared, I passed over it a hot iron, to smooth the nap, and by next morning had the satisfaction of presenting to my wife a neat little red Swiss cap, to be lined and finished by her for one of the boys. The mother admired the production immensely, and lining it with silk, added yet more to its gay appearance by adorning it with ribbons and ostrich feathers, and finally placed it upon the head of little Franz.

So delighted was everyone with the hat, that all were eager to be similarly provided, and begged me to manufacture more. I readily agreed to do so, as soon as they should furnish me with the necessary materials, and advised them to make half a dozen rat traps, that they might secure the water rats with which the stream abounded, and whose rich glossy fur would serve admirably for felt.

Every fifth animal that they brought me I told them should be mine, that I might obtain material for a hat for myself and their mother.

The boys at once agreed to this arrangement, and began the manufacture of the traps, which were all so made that they should kill the rats at once, for I could not bear the idea of animals being tortured or imprisoned.

While they were thus engaged I applied myself to the manufacture of porcelain. I first cleaned the pipeclay and talc from all foreign substances, and made them ready to be beaten down with water into a soft mass, and then prepared my molds of gypsum plaster. These preparations were at length made, and the molds received a thin layer of the porcelain material. When this was partly baked, I sprinkled over it a powder of colored glass beads which I had crushed, and which looked very pretty in patterns upon the transparent porcelain.

Some of my china vessels cracked with the heat of the stove, some were very ill-shaped; but, after many failures, I succeeded in producing a set of white cups and saucers, a cream-jug, a sugar-basin, and half a dozen small plates.

I must allow that my china was far from perfect; the shape of some of the vessels was faulty, and none were really transparent; nevertheless, the general appearance gave great satisfaction, and when the plates were filled with rosy and golden fruit resting on green leaves, and fragrant tea filled the cups, it greatly added to the appearance of the table.

Chapter Fourteen

SCARCELY had I completed my pottery, when great black clouds and terrific storms heralded the approach of another winter. The rainy season having set in, we were compelled to give up our daily excursions.

Even in the spacious house which we now occupied, and with our varied and interesting employments, we yet found the time dragging heavily. The spirits of all were depressed, and even occasional rapid rides, during a partial cessation of the rain, failed permanently to arouse them. Fritz, as well as I, had perceived this, and he said to me:

"Why, father, should we not make a canoe, something swifter and more manageable than those vessels we as yet possess? I often long for a light skiff, in which I might skim over the surface of the water."

The idea delighted all hands, but the mother, who was never happy when we were on the sea, declared that our chances of drowning were, with the pinnace and canoe, already sufficiently great, and that there was not the slightest necessity for our adding to these chances by constructing another craft which would tempt us out upon the perfidious element. My wife's fears were, however, speedily allayed, for I assured her that the boat I intended to construct should be no flimsy cockle-shell, but as safe and stout a craft as ever floated upon the sea. The Greenlander's cajack I intended to be my model, and I resolved not only to occupy the children, but also to produce a strong and serviceable canoe—a masterpiece of art.

The boys were interested, and the boat-building was soon in operation. We constructed the skeleton of whalebone, using split bamboo canes to strengthen the sides and also to form the deck, which extended the whole length of the boat, leaving merely a square hole in which the occupant of the canoe might sit.

The work engrossed our attention most entirely, and by the time it was complete the rain had passed away and the glorious sun again shone brightly forth.

Our front door was just wide enough to admit of the egress of our boat, and we completed her construction in the open air. We quickly cased the sides and deck with sealskin, making all the seams thoroughly watertight with caoutchouc.

The cajack was indeed a curious looking craft, yet so light that she might be lifted easily with one hand, and when at length we launched her she bounded upon the water like an india rubber ball. Fritz was unanimously voted her rightful owner, but before his mother would hear of his entering the frail-looking skiff she declared that she must contrive a swimming dress, that "should his boat receive a puncture from a sharp rock or the dorsal fin of a fish and collapse, he might yet have a chance of saving his life."

Though I did not consider the cajack quite the soap bubble the mother imagined it, I yet willingly agreed to assist her in the construction of the dress.

The garment we produced was most curious in appearance, and I must own that I doubted its efficiency. It was like a double waistcoat, made of linen prepared with a solution of india rubber, the seams being likewise coated with caoutchouc, and the whole rendered perfectly airtight. We so arranged it that one little hole was left, by means of which air could be forced into the space between the outer covering and the lining, and the dress inflated.

Meanwhile I perceived with pleasure the rapid vegetation the climate was producing. The seeds we had scattered had germinated, and were now promising magnificent crops. The veranda, too, was looking pleasant with its gay and sweet-scented creepers, which were already aspiring to the summit of the pillars. The air was full of birds, the earth seemed teeming with life.

The dress was at length completed, and Fritz one fine afternoon offered publicly to prove it. We all assembled on the beach, the boy gravely donned and inflated the garment, and, amid roars of laughter from his brothers, entered the water. Quickly and easily he paddled himself across the bay toward Shark Island, whither we followed in one of our boats.

The experiment was most successful, and Ernest, Jack, and Franz, in spite of their laughter at their brother's garment, begged their mother to make for each of them a similar dress.

While on the island we paid a visit to the colonists whom we had established there the previous autumn. All were well; we could perceive by the footprints that the antelopes had discovered and made use of the shelter we had erected for them, and feeling that we could do nothing more we scattered handfuls of maize and salt, and strolled across to the other side of the island. The shore was covered with lovely shells, many of which, with beautiful pieces of delicate coral, the boys collected for their museum; strewn by the edge of the water too lay a great quantity of seaweed of various colors, and as the mother declared that much of it was of use, the boys assisted her to collect it and store it in the boat. As we pulled back to the land I was surprised to see that my wife chose from among the seaweed a number of curious leaves with edges notched like a saw. When we reached home she carefully washed these and dried them in the oven. There was evidently something mysterious about this preparation, and my curiosity at length prompted me to make an attempt to discover the secret.

"Are these leaves to form a substitute for tobacco?" said I; "do you so long for its refreshing smell?"

My wife smiled, for her dislike to tobacco was well known, and she answered in the same jocular tone:

"Do you not think that a mattress stuffed with these leaves would be very cool in summer?"

The twinkle in her eyes showed me that my curiosity must still remain unsatisfied, but it nevertheless became greater than ever.

The boys and I had one day made a long and fatiguing expedition, and, tired out, we flung ourselves down in the veranda. As we lay there resting, we heard the mother's voice.

"Could any of you enjoy a little jelly?"

She presently appeared, bearing a porcelain dish laden with most lovely transparent jelly. Cut with a spoon and laid before us it quivered and glittered in the light.

"Ambrosia!" exclaimed Fritz, tasting it. It was indeed delicious, and, still marveling from whence the mother could have obtained a dish so rare, we disposed of all that she had set before us.

"Aha," laughed the mother, "is not this an excellent substitute for tobacco, far more refreshing than the nasty weed itself? Behold the product of my mysterious seaweed."

"My dear wife," exclaimed I, "this dish is indeed a masterpiece of culinary art, but where had you met with it? What put it into your head?"

"While staying with my Dutch friends at the Cape," replied she, "I often saw it, and at once recognized the leaves on Shark Island. Once knowing the secret, the preparation of the dish is extremely simple; the leaves are soaked in water, fresh every day, for a week, and then boiled for a few hours with orange juice, citron, and sugar."

We were all delighted with the delicacy, and thanked the mother for it most heartily, the boys declaring that they must at once go off again to the island to collect as many of the leaves as they could find. I agreed to accompany them, for I wished to examine the plantations we had made there.

All were flourishing, the palms and mangroves had shot up in a most marvelous manner, and many of the seeds which I had cast at random among the cliffs in the rocks had germinated, and promised to clothe the nakedness of the frowning bowlders.

Away up among the rocks, too, we discovered a bright sparkling spring of delicious water, at which, from the footprints around, we saw that the antelopes must have refreshed themselves.

Finding everything so satisfactory, we were naturally anxious to discover how our colony and plantations on Whale Island had fared. It was evident at a glance that the rabbits had increased; the young and tender shoots of the trees bore the marks of many greedy, mischievous little teeth. The cocoanut palms alone had they spared.

Such depredations as these could not be allowed, and with the help of the boys I erected round each stem a hedge of prickly thorn, and then prepared again to embark; before we did so, however, I noticed that some of the seaweed had also been gnawed by the rabbits, and wondering what it could have been to tempt them, I collected some of it to examine more fully at home.

The skeleton of the whale, too, attracted our attention, for, picked clean by the birds and bleached by the sun and rain, the bones had been purified to a most perfect whiteness. Thinking that the joints of the vertebræ might be made of use, I separated some ten or twelve, and rolled them down to the boat, and then returned to the shore, towing them after us.

A scheme now occupied my mind for the construction of a crushing machine, which would prove of the greatest service to us. I knew that to make such a machine of stone was far beyond my power, but it had struck me that the vertebræ of the whale might serve my purpose.

I determined next morning to look out a tree from which I might cut the blocks of wood that I should require to raise my crushers.

My expedition was destined to be a solitary one, for when I went to the stables for a horse, I discovered that the boys had gone off by themselves with their guns and traps, and had left to me a choice between the bull and buffalo.

With Storm, therefore, I was fain to be content. I crossed the bridge, but as I reached the cassava field I noticed to my great annoyance that it had been overrun and laid waste by some mischievous animals. I examined the footprints, and seeing that they greatly resembled those of pigs, determined to follow the trail, and see who these invaders of our territory would prove to be. The track led me on for some way until I almost lost sight of it near our old potato field. For some time I hunted backward and forward without seeing a sign of the animals; at length a loud barking from Floss and Bruno, who were with me, announced that they had been discovered.

The whole family of our old sow, and she herself, were standing at bay, showing their teeth and grunting so savagely, that the dogs feared to approach them.

I raised my gun and fired twice among the herd; two of the pigs fell, and the rest fled, followed by the dogs. I picked up the pigs, and calling back the pursuers, continued my way through the forest.

A tree suited to my purpose was soon found; I marked it and returned home.

Ernest, who had remained at home, assisted me to flay the young porkers, and I handed them over to the mother to prepare for supper; by which time I hoped the other lads would have returned.

Late in the evening we heard the sounds of trampling hoofs, and presently Jack appeared, thundering along upon his two-legged steed, followed in the distance by Fritz and Franz. These latter carried upon their cruppers game bags, the contents of which were speedily displayed; four birds, a kangaroo, twenty muskrats, a monkey, two hares, and half a dozen beaver rats, were laid before me. Besides these, Fritz threw down, without a word of explanation, a bundle of thistles.

The boys seemed almost wild with excitement at the success of their expedition, and presently Jack exclaimed:

"Oh, father, you can't think what grand fun hunting on an ostrich is; we flew along like the wind; sometimes I could scarcely breathe, we were going at such a rate, and was obliged to shut my eyes because of the terrific rush of air; really, father, you must make me a mask with glass eyes to ride with, or I shall be blinded one of these fine days."

"Indeed!" replied I, "I must do no such thing."

"Why not?" asked he, with a look of amazement upon his face.

"For two reasons; firstly, because I do not consider that I

must do anything that you demand; and, secondly, because I think that you are very capable of doing it yourself. However, I must congratulate you upon your abundant supply of game; you must have indeed worked hard. Yet I wish that you would let me know when you intend starting on such a long expedition as this; you forget that though you yourselves know that you are quite safe, and that all is going on well, yet that we at home are kept in a constant state of anxiety. Now, off with you, and look to your animals, and then you may find supper ready."

Presently the boys returned, and we prepared for a most appetizing meal which the mother set before us.

While we were discussing the roast pig, and washing it down with fragrant mead, Fritz described the day's expedition.

They had set their traps near Woodlands, and had there captured the muskrats, attracting them with small carrots, while with other traps, baited with fish and earthworms, they had caught several beaver rats, and a duck-billed platypus. Hunting and fishing had occupied the rest of the day, and it was with immense pride that Jack displayed the kangaroo which he had run down with his swift courser. Contributions to the garden had not been forgotten, and Fritz handed over to his mother several cuttings from cinnamon and sweet-apple trees. Finally, when all the other treasures had been displayed, Fritz begged me to examine his thistles which he had gathered, thinking, he said, that it was a plant used in the manufacture of wool. He was perfectly right, for I recognized it at once as the "fuller's teazle," a plant whose sharp little thorns, which cover the stem and leaves, are used to raise the nap of cloth.

We resolved to be up betimes the following morning, that we might attend to the preparation of the booty, and as I now noticed that the boys were all becoming extremely drowsy, I closed the day with evening devotions.

The number of the creatures we killed rendered the removal of their skins a matter of no little time and trouble. It was not an agreeable task at any time, and when I saw the array of animals the boys had brought me to flay, I determined to construct a machine which would considerably lessen the labor. Among the ship's stores, in the surgeon's chest, I discovered a large syringe. This, with a few alterations, would serve my purpose admirably. Within the tube I first fitted a couple

of valves, and then, perforating the stopper, I had in my possession a powerful air pump.

The boys stared at me in blank amazement when, armed
with this instrument, I took up the kangaroo, and declared
myself ready to commence operations.

"Skin a kangaroo with a squirt?" said they, and a roar of
laughter followed the remark.

I made no reply to the jests which followed, but silently
hung the kangaroo by its hind legs to the branch of a tree. I
then made a small incision in the skin, and inserting the
mouth of the syringe forced air with all my might between the
skin and the body of the animal. By degrees the hide of the
kangaroo distended, altering the shape of the creature entirely.

Still I worked on, forcing in yet more air until it had become
a mere shapeless mass, and I soon found that the skin was almost entirely separated from the carcase. A bold cut down the
belly, and a few touches here and there where the ligatures
still bound the hide to the body, and the animal was flayed.

"What a splendid plan?" cried the boys; "but why should
it do it?"

"For a most simple and natural reason," I replied; "do you
not know that the skin of an animal is attached to its flesh
merely by slender and delicate fibers, and that between these
exist thousands of little bladders or air chambers; by forcing
air into these bladders the fibers are stretched, and at length,
elastic as they are, cracked. The skin has now nothing to unite
it to the body, and, consequently, may be drawn off with perfect ease. This scientific fact has been known for many years;
the Greenlanders make constant use of it; when they have
killed a seal or walrus, they distend the skin that they may tow
the animal more easily ashore, and then remove its hide at a
moment's notice."

The remaining animals were subjected to the same treatment, and, to my great joy, in a couple of days the skins were
all off, and being prepared for use.

I now summoned the boys to assist me in procuring blocks
of wood for my crushing machine, and the following day we
set forth with saws, ropes, axes, and other tools. We soon
reached the tree I had selected for my purpose, and I began by
sending Fritz and Jack up into the tree with axes to cut off
the larger of the high branches that, when the tree fell, it

might not injure its neighbors. They then descended, and Fritz and I attacked the stem. As the easiest and most speedy method we used a saw, such a one as is employed by sawyers in a saw-pit, and Fritz taking one end and I the other, the tree was soon cut half through. We then adjusted ropes that we might guide its fall, and again began to cut. It was laborious work, but when I considered that the cut was sufficiently deep we took the ropes and pulled with our united strength. The trunk cracked, swayed, tottered, and fell with a crash.

The boughs were speedily lopped off, and the trunk sawed into blocks four feet long.

To cut down and divide this tree had taken us a couple of days, and on the third we carted home four large and two small blocks, and with the vertebræ joints of the whale I, in a very short time, completed my machine.

While engaged on this undertaking I had paid little attention to our fields of grain, and, accordingly, great was my surprise when one evening the fowls returned, showing most evident indifference to their evening meal, and with their crops perfectly full. It suddenly struck me that these birds had come from the direction of our cornfield. I hurried off to see what damage they had done, and then found to my great joy that the grain was perfectly ripe.

The amount of work before us startled my wife. This unexpected harvest, which added reaping and threshing to the fishing, salting, and pickling already on hand, quite troubled her.

"Only think," said she, "of my beloved potatoes and manioc roots! What is to become of them, I should like to know? It is time to take them up, and how to manage it, with all this press of work, I can't see."

"Don't be down-hearted, wife," said I; "there is no immediate hurry about the manioc, and digging potatoes in this fine, light soil is easy work compared to what it is in Switzerland, while as to planting more, that will not be necessary if we leave the younger plants in the ground. The harvest we must conduct after the Italian fashion, which, although anything but economical, will save time and trouble, and as we are to have two crops in the year, we need not be too particular."

Without further delay, I commenced leveling a large space

of firm, clayey ground to act as a threshing floor: it was well sprinkled with water, rolled, beaten, and stamped; as the sun dried the moisture it was watered anew, and the treatment continued until it became as flat, hard, and smooth as threshing floor need be.

Our largest wicker basket was then slung between Storm and Grumble; we armed ourselves with reaping hooks, and went forth to gather in the corn in the simplest and most expeditious manner imaginable.

I told my reapers not to concern themselves about the length of the straw, but to grasp the corn where it was convenient to them, without stooping; each was to wind a stalk around his own handful, and throw it into the basket; in this way great labor was saved. The plan pleased the boys immensely, and in a short time the basket had been filled many times, and the field displayed a quantity of tall, headless stubble, which perfectly horrified the mother, so extravagant and untidy did she consider our work.

"This is dreadful!" cried she; "you have left numbers of ears growing on short stalks, and look at that splendid straw completely wasted! I don't approve of your Italian fashion at all."

"It is not a bad plan, I can assure you, wife, and the Italians do not waste the straw by not cutting it with the grain; having more arable than pasture land, they use this high stubble for their cattle, letting them feed in it, and eat what grain is left; afterward, allowing the grass to grow up among it, they mow all together for winter fodder. And now for threshing, also in Italian fashion. We shall find it spares our arms and backs as much in that as in reaping."

The little sheaves were laid in a large circle on the floor, the boys mounted Storm, Grumble, Lightfoot, and Hurry, starting off at a brisk trot, with many a merry jest, and round they went, trampling and stamping out the grain, while dust and chaff flew in clouds about them.

My wife and I were incessantly occupied with hayforks, by means of which we shook up and moved the sheaves over which the threshers rode, so as to throw them in the track.

From time to time the animals took mouthfuls of the tempting food they were beating out; we thought they well deserved it, and called to mind the command given to the Jews, "Thou shall not muzzle the ox that treadeth out the corn."

After threshing, we proceeded to winnowing; by simply throwing the threshed corn with shovels high in the air when the land or sea-breeze blew strong, the chaff and refuse was carried away by the wind and the grain fell to the ground.

During these operations our poultry paid the threshing-floor many visits, testifying a lively interest in the success of our labors, and gobbling up the grain at such a rate that my wife was obliged to keep them at a reasonable distance; but I would not have them altogether stinted in the midst of our plenty. I said, "Let them enjoy themselves; what we lose in grain, we gain in flesh. I anticipate delicious chicken-pie, roast goose, and boiled turkey!"

When our harvest stores were housed, we found that we had reaped sixty, eighty, even a hundred fold what had been sown. Our garner was truly filled with all manner of store.

Expecting a second harvest, we were constrained to prepare the field for sowing again, and immediately therefore commenced mowing down the stubble. While engaged in this, flocks of quails and partridges came to glean among the scattered ears. We did not secure any great number, but resolved to be prepared for them next season, and by spreading nets, to catch them in large quantities.

My wife was satisfied when she saw the straw carried home and stacked; our crop of maize, which of course had not been threshed like the other corn, afforded soft leaves which were used for stuffing mattresses, while the stalks, when burnt, left ashes so rich in alkali as to be especially useful.

I changed the crops sown on the ground to rye, barley, and oats, and hoped they would ripen before the rainy season.

The shoals of herring made their appearance just as we finished our agricultural operations. This year we pickled only two barrels of them; but we were not so merciful toward the seals, which arrived on the coast directly afterward. We hunted them vigorously, requiring their skins for many purposes, more especially for the completion of the cajack. On the little deck of that tiny vessel I had made a kind of magazine, in which to store pistols, ammunition, water, and provisions, and this I meant to cover with sealskin, so as to be quite watertight. A couple of harpoons furnished with seal bladders were to be suspended alongside.

Chapter Fifteen

At last came the day when Fritz was to make his trial trip with the cajack. Completely equipped in swimming costume—trousers, jacket, and cap—it was most ludicrous to see him cower down in the canoe and puff and blow till he began to swell like the frog in the fable.

All trace of his original figure was speedily lost, and shouts of laughter greeted his comical appearance. Even his mother could not resist a smile, although the dress was her invention.

I got the other boat out, that my wife might see we were ready to go to his assistance the moment it became necessary.

The cajack was launched from a convenient shelving point, and floated lightly on the sea-green ocean mirror. Fritz with his paddles then began to practise all manner of evolutions: darting along with arrowy swiftness, wheeling to the right, then to the left; and at last, flinging himself quite on his side, while his mother uttered a shriek of terror, he showed that the tiny craft would neither capsize nor sink. Then, recovering his balance, he sped securely on his further way.

Encouraged by our shouts of approbation, he now boldly ventured into the strong current of Jackal River, and was rapidly carried out to sea.

This being more than I had bargained for, I lost no time in giving chase in the boat, with Ernest and Jack; my wife urging us to greater speed, and declaring that some accident could not fail to happen to "that horrid soap-bubble."

We soon arrived outside the bay, at the rocks where formerly lay the wreck, and gazed in all directions for signs of the runaway.

After a time we saw, at a considerable distance, a faint puff of smoke, followed by the crack of a pistol. Upon this we fired a signal shot, which was presently answered by another, and, steering in the direction of the sound, we soon heard the boy's cheery halloo; the cajack darted from behind a point of land, and we quickly joined company.

"Come to this rocky beach," cried Fritz, "I have something to show you."

With blank amazement we beheld a fine, well-grown young walrus, harpooned and quite dead.

"Did you kill this creature, my dear Fritz?" I exclaimed, looking round in some anxiety, and half expecting to see a naked savage come to claim the prize.

"To be sure, father! don't you see my harpoon? Why do you doubt it?"

"Well, I scarcely know," replied I, laughing; "but success so speedy, so unexpected, and so appropriate, to an amateur Greenlander, took me by surprise. I congratulate you, my boy! But I must tell you that you have alarmed us by making this long trip. You should not have gone out of the bay. I left your mother in grievous trouble."

"Indeed, father, I had no idea of passing out of sight, but once in the current, I was carried along, and could not help myself. Then I came on a herd of walruses, and I did so long to make a prize of one that I forgot everything else, and made chase after them when beyond the influence of the current, until I got near enough to harpoon this fine fellow. He swam more slowly, and I struck him a second time; then he sought refuge among these rocks, and expired. I landed, and scrambled to where he lay, but I took care to give him the contents of my pistol before going close up, having a salutary recollection of the big serpent's parting fling at you, Jack."

"You ran a very great risk," said I. "The walrus is an inoffensive creature; but when attacked and wounded, it often becomes furious, and, turning upon its pursuer, can destroy, with its long tusks, a strongly built whale boat. However, thank God for your safety! I value that above a thousand such creatures. Now, what's to be done with him? He must be quite fourteen feet long, although not full grown."

"I am very glad you followed me, father," said Fritz; "but our united strength will not remove this prodigious weight from among these rocks; only do let me carry away the head, with these grand, snow-white tusks! I should so like to fasten it on the prow of the cajack, and name it the *Sea-horse.*"

"We must certainly carry away the beautiful ivory tusks," said I; "but make haste; the air feels so excessively close and sultry, I think a storm is brewing."

"But the head! the head! we must have the whole head," cried Jack; "just think how splendid it will look on the cajack!"

"And how splendid it will smell too, when it begins to putrefy," added Ernest; "what a treat for the steersman?"

"Oh, we will prepare for that," said Fritz; "it shall be soaked and cleaned, and dried until it is as hard as a wooden model; it shall not offend your delicate nose in the least, Ernest!"

"I supposed the walrus to be an animal peculiar to the Arctic regions," remarked Ernest.

"And so it is," I replied; "though they may occasionally be seen elsewhere; these may have wandered from the Antarctic seas. I know that on the eastern coast of Africa is found a smaller species of walrus called the dugong; it has long incisor teeth, but not tusks; and certainly resembles a seal, rather than a walrus."

While thus speaking, we were actively engaged in the decapitation of the walrus, and in cutting off long strips of its skin. This took some time, as we had not the proper implements, and Fritz remarked that in future the cajack must be provided with a hunting-knife and a hatchet; adding that he should like to have a small compass in a box, with a glass top, fixed in front of the hole where the steersman sits. I saw the necessity of this, and I promised it should be done.

Our work being accomplished, we were ready to go, and I proposed to take Fritz and the canoe on board our boat, so that we might all arrive together; but I yielded to his earnest wish to return alone as he came; he longed to act as our avant-courier, and announce our approach to his mother; so he was soon skimming away over the surface of the water, while we followed at a slower rate.

Black clouds meanwhile gathered thick and fast around us, and a tremendous storm came on. Fritz was out of sight, and beyond our reach.

We buckled on the swimming belts and firmly lashed ourselves to the boat, so that we might not be washed overboard by the towering seas which broke over it.

The horizon was shrouded in darkness, fearful gusts of wind lashed the ocean into foam, rain descended in torrents, while livid lightning glared athwart the gloom. Both my boys faced the danger nobly; and my feelings of alarm were mingled with hope on finding how well the boat behaved.

The tempest swept on its way, and the sky began to clear as suddenly as it had been overcast; yet the stormy waves continued for a long time to threaten our frail bark with destruction, in spite of its buoyancy and steadiness.

Yet I never lost hope for ourselves—all my fears were for Fritz; in fact I gave him up for lost, and my whole agonized heart arose in prayer for strength to say, "Thy will be done!"

At last we rounded the point, and once more entering Safety Bay, quickly drew near the little harbor.

What was our surprise—our overwhelming delight—when there we saw the mother with Fritz, as well as her little boy, on their knees in prayer so earnest for our deliverance, that our approach was unperceived, until with cries of joy we attracted their notice. Then indeed ensued a happy meeting, and we gave thanks together for the mercy which had spared our lives.

Returning joyfully to Rockburg, we changed our drenched garments for warm, dry clothes; and, seated at a comfortable meal, considered and described at our ease the perils of the storm.

Afterward, the head of the walrus was conveyed to our workshop; where it underwent such a skillful and thorough process of cleaning, embalming, and drying, that ere long it was actually fixed on the prow of the cajack, and a most imposing appearance it presented!

The strips of hide, when well-tanned and prepared, made valuable leather.

Much damage had been done by the late storm. The heavy rain had flooded all the streams, and injured crops which should have been housed before the regular rainy season.

The bridge over Jackal River was partly broken down, and the water tanks and pipes all needed repair. So our time was much occupied in restoring things to order.

On going to work one day, near the cascade, we found a great number of dark red berries scattered on the ground; they were about the size of ordinary hazel nuts, with small leafy coronets at the tip.

The boys thought them so inviting, that they tasted them at once, but angry exclamations and much spitting and spluttering followed the experiment; even Knips rejected them, and they would have been cast aside with contempt, had not the smell induced me to examine them. I decided that this was the fruit of the clove.

Some plants were immediately set in the nursery garden, and my wife was pleased to have this excellent spice wherewith to flavor her boiled rice and other dishes, in lieu of pepper—a very welcome variety to everyone.

Having a good supply of clay, brought from the bed near Falconhurst, I proposed to use it for making aqueducts; and, observing how much the recent rain had promoted the growth of our young corn, I determined to irrigate the fields with the drainage from our crushing mill.

The fishing season was again successful. Large takes of

salmon, sturgeon, and herring rewarded our annual exertions, and our storeroom again assumed a well-stocked appearance. Much as I wished that we could obtain a constant supply of these fish fresh, I was obliged to reject the naïve proposal from Jack, that we should tether a shoal of salmon by the gills to the bottom of the bay as we had secured the turtles.

Many quiet uneventful days passed by, and I perceived that the boys, wearied by the routine of farm work at Rockburg, were longing for a cruise in the yacht or an expedition into the woods, which would refresh both mind and body.

"Father," said Fritz at length, "we want a quantity of hurdles, and have scarcely any more bamboos of which to make them. Had we not better get a supply from Woodlands? And you said, too, the other day, that you wished you had some more of the fine clay: we might visit the Gap at the same time."

I had really no objection to propose; and it was shortly afterward settled that Fritz, Jack, and Franz should start together; and that Ernest, who had no great desire to accompany his brothers, should remain with his mother and me, and assist in the construction of a sugar mill, the erection of which I had long contemplated.

Before they started, Fritz begged some bear's meat from the mother, to make pemmican.

"And what may pemmican be?" she asked.

"It is food carried by the fur-traders of North America on their long journeys through the wild country they traverse; and consists of bear or deer's flesh, first cooked and then pounded or ground to powder. It is very portable, and nourishing."

His mother consented "to humor him," as she said, although without much faith in the value of the preparation; and in the course of two days a stock of pemmican, sufficient for a Polar expedition, was fabricated by our enthusiastic son.

They were ready to start, when I observed Jack quietly slip a basket, containing several pigeons, under the packages in the cart.

"Oh, oh!" thought I, "the little fellow has his doubts about that pemmican, and thinks a tough old pigeon would be preferable."

The weather was exquisite; and, with exhortations to prudence and caution from both me and their mother, the three lads started in the very highest spirits. Storm and Grumble, as usual, drew the cart, and were ridden by Fritz and Franz; while Hurry carried Jack swiftly across the bridge in advance of them; followed by Floss and Bruno, barking at his heels.

The sugar mill occupied us for several days, and was made so much like our other mills that I need not now describe it.

On the evening of the first day, as we sat resting in the porch at Rockburg, we naturally talked of the absentees, wondering and guessing what they might be about.

Ernest looked rather mysterious, and hinted that he might have news of them next morning.

Just then a bird alighted on the dovecot, and entered. I could not see, in the failing light, whether it was one of our own pigeons or an intruder. Ernest started up, and said he would see that all was right.

In a few minutes he returned with a scrap of paper in his hand.

"News, father! The very latest news by pigeon post, mother!"

"Well done, boys! what a capital idea!" said I, and taking the note I read:

"Dearest Parents and Ernest:

"A brute of a hyena has killed a ram and two lambs. The dogs seized it. Franz shot it. It is dead and skinned. The pemmican isn't worth much, but we are all right. Love to all.

"Fritz.

"WOODLANDS, 15TH INSTANT."

"A true hunter's letter!" laughed I; "but what exciting news. When does the next post come in, Ernest?"

"To-night, I hope," said he, while his mother sighed, and doubted the value of such glimpses into the scenes of danger through which her sons were passing, declaring she would much rather wait and hear all about it when she had them safe home again.

Thus the winged letter-carriers kept us informed from day to day of the outline of adventures which were afterward more fully described.

On approaching the farm at Woodlands, the boys were

startled by hearing, as they thought, human laughter, repeated again and again; while, to their astonishment, the oxen testified the greatest uneasiness, the dogs growled and drew close to their masters, and the ostrich fairly bolted with Jack into the rice swamp.

The laughter continued, and the beasts became unmanageable.

"Something is very far wrong!" cried Fritz. "I cannot leave the animals; but while I unharness them, do you, Franz, take the dogs, and advance cautiously to see what is the matter."

Without a moment's hesitation, Franz made his way among the bushes with his gun, closely followed by the dogs; until, through an opening in the thicket, he could see, at a distance of about forty paces, an enormous hyena, in the most wonderful state of excitement; dancing round a lamb just killed, and uttering, from time to time, the ghastly hysterical laughter which had pealed through the forest.

The beast kept running backward and forward, rising on its hind legs, and then rapidly whirling round and round, nodding its head, and going through most frantic and ludicrous antics.

Franz kept his presence of mind very well; for he watched till, calming down, the hyena began with horrid growls to tear its prey; and then, firing steadily both barrels, he broke its foreleg, and wounded it in the breast.

Meanwhile Fritz, having unyoked the oxen and secured them to trees, hurried to his brother's assistance. The dogs and the dying hyena were by this time engaged in mortal strife; but the latter, although it severely wounded both Floss and Bruno, speedily succumbed, and was dead when the boys reached the spot. They raised a shout of triumph, which guided Jack to the scene of action; and their first care was for the dogs, whose wounds they dressed before minutely examining the hyena. It was as large as a wild boar; long stiff bristles formed a mane on its neck, its color was gray marked with black, the teeth and jaws were of extraordinary strength, the thighs muscular and sinewy, the claws remarkably strong and sharp altogether. But for his wounds he would certainly have been more than a match for the dogs.

After unloading the cart at the farm, the boys returned for

" 'Welcome, fair stranger!' " (Page 345)

the carcase of the tiger-wolf, as it is sometimes called, and occupied themselves in skinning it during the remainder of the day, when, after dispatching the carrier-pigeon to Rockburg, they retired to rest on their bearskin rugs, to dream of adventures past and future.

The following day they devised no less a scheme than to survey the shores of Wood Lake, and place marks wherever the surrounding marsh was practicable, and might be crossed either to reach the water or leave it.

Fritz in the cajack, and the boys on shore, carefully examined the ground together; and when they found firm footing to the water's edge, the spot was indicated by planting a tall bamboo, bearing on high a bundle of reeds and branches.

They succeeded in capturing three young black swans, after considerable resistance from the old ones. They were afterward brought to Rockburg, and detained as ornaments to Safety Bay.

Presently a beautiful heron thrust his long neck from among the reeds, to ascertain what all the noise on the lake was about. Before he could satisfy his curiosity, Fritz unhooded his eagle, and though vainly he flapped and struggled, his legs and wings were gently but firmly bound, and he had to own himself vanquished, and submit to the inspection of his delighted captors.

It was their turn to be alarmed next, for a large powerful animal came puffing, with a curious whistling sound, through the dense thicket of reeds, passing close by and sorely discomposing them by its sudden appearance. It was out of sight immediately, before they could summon the dogs, and from their description it must have been a tapir, the color dark brown, and in form resembling a young rhinoceros, but with no horn on the nose, and the upper lip prolonged into a trunk something like that of an elephant on a smaller scale. It is a gentle creature, but when attacked becomes a fierce opponent, and can wound dogs dangerously with its powerful teeth.

The tapir can swim and dive with perfect ease, and abounds in the densely wooded swamps and rivers of tropical America.

Fritz in his cajack followed for a time the direction in which the tapir proceeded, but saw no more of it.

Meanwhile the other two boys returned to the farm by the

rice fields, and there fell in with a flock of cranes, five or six of which they caught alive, among them two demoiselles or Numidian cranes. These birds they shot at with arrows arranged in a skillful and original way, with loops of cord dipped in birdlime attached to them, so that it often happened that the bird aimed at was entangled and brought down uninjured.

The young hunters seemed to have lived very comfortably on peccary ham, cassava bread and fruit, and plenty of baked potatoes and milk.

One trial of the pemmican was sufficient, and it was handed over to the dogs. Fritz, however, determined again to attempt the manufacture, knowing its value when properly prepared.

After collecting a supply of rice and cotton, they took their way to Prospect Hill; "and," said Fritz, as he afterward vividly described the dreadful scene there enacted, "when we entered the pine wood, we found it in possession of troops of monkeys, who resolved to make our passage through it as disagreeable as possible, for they howled and chattered at us like demons, pelting us as hard as they could with pine cones.

"They became so unbearable, that at last we fired a few shot right and left among them; several bit the dust, the rest fled, and we continued our way in peace to Prospect Hill, but only to discover the havoc the wretches had made there.

"Would you believe it, father? The pleasant cottage had been over-run and ruined by apes just as Woodland last summer! The most dreadful dirt and disorder met our eyes wherever we turned, and we had hard work to make the place fit for human habitation; and even then we preferred the tent. I felt quite at a loss how to guard the farm for the future; but seeing a bottle of the poisonous gum of the euphorbia in the tool chest, I devised a plan for the destruction of the apes which succeeded beyond my expectations.

"I mixed poison with milk, bruised millet, and anything I thought the monkeys would eat, and put it in cocoanut shells, which I hung about in the trees, high enough to be out of reach of our own animals. The evening was calm and lovely; the sea murmured in the distance, and the rising moon shed a beauty over the landscape which we seemed never before to have so admired and enjoyed. The summer night closed around us in all its solemn stillness, and our deepest feelings were touched; when suddenly the spell was broken by an outburst of the most hideous and discordant noises. As by one consent, every beast of the forest seemed to arise from its den, and utter its wild nocturnal cry. Snorting, snarling, and shrieking filled the wood beneath us.

"From the hills echoed the mournful howl of jackals, answered by Fangs in the yard, who was backed up by the barking and yelping of his friends Floss and Bruno. Far away beyond the rocky fastnesses of the Gap, sounded unearthly, hollow snortings and neighings, reminding one of the strange cry of the hippopotamus; above these, occasional deep majestic roaring made our hearts quail with the conviction that we heard the voices of lions and elephants.

"Overawed and silent, we retired to rest, hoping to forget in sleep the terrors of the midnight forest, but ere long the most fearful cries in the adjoining woods gave notice that the apes were beginning to suffer from the poisoned repast prepared for them.

"As our dogs could not remain silent amid the uproar and din, we had not a wink of sleep until the morning. It was late, therefore, when we rose, and looked on the awful spectacle presented by the multitude of dead monkeys and baboons thickly strewn under the trees round the farm. I shall not tell you how many there were. I can only say, I wished I had not found the poison, and we made all haste to clear away the dead bodies, and the dangerous food, burying some deep in the earth, and, carrying the rest to the shore, we pitched them over the rocks into the sea. That day we traveled on to the Gap."

The same evening that the boys reached the rocky pass, a messenger pigeon arrived at Rockburg, bearing a note which concluded in the following words:

"The barricade at the Gap is broken down. Everything laid waste as far as the sugar-brake, where the hut is knocked to pieces, and the fields trampled over by huge footmarks. Come to us, father—we are safe, but feel we are no match for this unknown danger."

I lost not an instant, but saddled Swift, late as it was, in order to ride to the assistance of our boys, desiring Ernest to prepare the small cart, and follow me with his mother at day-

break, bringing everything we should require for camping out
for some days.

The bright moonlight favored my journey, and my arrival
at the Gap surprised and delighted the boys, who did not expect me till the next day. Early on the following morning I
inspected the footprints and ravages of the great unknown.
The cane-brake had, without doubt, been visited by an elephant. That great animal alone could have left such traces and
committed such fearful ravages. Thick posts in the barricade
were snapped across like reeds; the trees in the vicinity, where
we planned to build a cool summer-house, were stripped of
leaves and branches to a great height, but the worst mischief
was done among the young sugar-cane plants, which were all
either devoured or trampled down and destroyed.

It seemed to me that not one elephant, but a troop must
have invaded our grounds. The tracks were very numerous,
and the footprints of various sizes; but, to my satisfaction, I
saw that they could be traced not only from the Gap, but back
to it in evidently equal numbers.

We did not, therefore, suppose that the mighty animals remained hidden in the woods of our territory; but concluded
that, after this freebooting incursion, they had withdrawn to
their native wilds, where, by greatly increasing the strength of
our ramparts, we hoped henceforth to oblige them to remain.

In what manner to effect this we laid many plans, during
the night of my arrival, when, sitting by an enormous watch-
fire, I chatted with my boys, and heard details of their numerous adventures, so interesting for them to relate, and for me
to hear, that everyone was more disposed to act sentinel than
retire to sleep.

The mother and Ernest arrived next day, and she rejoiced
to find all well, making light of trodden fields and trampled
sugar-canes, since her sons were sound in life and limb.

A systematic scheme of defense was now elaborated, and
the erection of the barricade occupied us for at least a month,
as it was to be a firm and durable building, proof against all
invasion. As our little tent was unsuited to a long residence
of this sort, I adopted Fritz's idea of a Kamschatchan dwelling,
and, to his great delight, forthwith carried it out.

Instead of planting four posts, on which to place a platform, we chose four trees of equal size, which, in a very suitable place, grew exactly in a square, twelve or fourteen feet apart. Between these, at about twenty feet from the ground, we laid a flooring of beams and bamboo, smoothly and strongly planked. From this rose, on all four sides, walls of cane; the frame of the roof was covered so effectually by large pieces of bark that no rain could penetrate.

The staircase to this tree-cottage was simply a broad plank with bars nailed across it for steps. The flooring projected like a balcony in front of the entrance door, and underneath, on the ground, we fitted up sheds for cattle and fowls.

Various ornaments in Chinese or Japanese style were added to the roof and eaves, and a most convenient, cool, and picturesque cottage, overhung and adorned by the graceful foliage of the trees, was the result of our ingenuity.

I was pleased to find that the various birds taken by the boys during this excursion seemed likely to thrive; they were the first inmates of the new sheds, and even the black swans and cranes soon become tame and sociable.

Constantly roaming through the woods, the children often made new discoveries.

Fritz brought one day, after an excursion to the opposite side of the stream beyond the Gap, a cluster of bananas, and also of cacao beans, from which chocolate is made.

The banana, although valuable and nourishing food for the natives of the tropical countries where it grows, is not generally liked by Europeans, and probably this variety was even inferior to many others, for we found the fruit much like rotten pears, and almost uneatable.

The cacao seeds tasted exceedingly bitter, and it seemed wonderful that by preparation they should produce anything so delicious as chocolate.

My wife, who now fancied no manufacture beyond my skill, begged for plants, seeds, or cuttings to propagate in her nursery garden, already fancying herself in the enjoyment of chocolate for breakfast, and I promised to make a cacao plantation near home.

"Let me have bananas also," said she, "for we may acquire a taste for that celebrated fruit, and, at all events, I am sure I can make it into an excellent preserve."

The day before our return to Rockburg, Fritz went again to the inland region beyond the river to obtain a large supply of young banana plants, and the cacao fruit. He took the cajack, and a bundle of reeds to float behind him as a raft to carry the fruit, plants, and anything else he might wish to bring back.

In the evening he made his appearance, coming swiftly down stream. His brothers rushed to meet him, each eager to see and help to land his cargo.

Ernest and Fritz were quickly running up the bank, with arms full of plants, branches, and fruits, when Fritz handed to Jack a dripping wet bag which he had brought along partly under water. A curious pattering noise proceeded from this bag, but they kept the contents a secret for the present, Jack running with it behind a bush before peeping in, and I could just hear him exclaim:

"Hullo! I say, what monsters they are. It's enough to make a fellow's flesh creep to look at them!"

With that he hastily shut up the bag, and put it away safely out of sight in water.

Securing the cajack, Fritz sprang toward us, his handsome face radiant with pleasure, as he exhibited a beautiful water-fowl.

Its plumage was rich purple, changing on the back to dark green; the legs, feet, and a mark above the bill, bright red. This lovely bird I concluded to be the sultan cock described by Buffon, and as it was gentle, we gladly received it among our domestic pets.

Fritz gave a stirring account of his exploring trip, having made his way far up the river, between fertile plains and majestic forests of lofty trees, where the cries of vast numbers of birds, parrots, peacocks, guinea fowls, and hundreds unknown to him, quite bewildered, and made him feel giddy.

"It was in the Buffalo Swamp," continued he, "that I saw the splendid birds you call sultan cocks, and I set my heart on catching one alive, which, as they seemed to have little fear of my approach, I managed by means of a wire snare. Farther on I saw a grove of mimosa trees, among which huge dark masses were moving in a deliberate way. Guess what they were!"

"Savages?" asked Franz timidly.

"Black bears, I bet!" cried Jack.

"Your words suggest to my mind the manner and appearance of elephants," said Ernest.

"Right you are, Professor!" exclaimed Fritz gaily, the words producing quite a sensation on the whole attentive family. "From fifteen to twenty elephants were feeding peacefully on the leafy boughs, tearing down branches with their trunks and shoving them into their mouths with one jerk, or bathing in the deep waters of the marsh for refreshment in the great heat. You cannot imagine the wild grandeur of the scene! The river being very broad, I felt safe from wild animals, and more than once saw splendid jaguars crouched on the banks, their glossy skin glancing in the sunlight.

"While considering if it would be simply foolhardy to try a shot at one of these creatures, I was suddenly convinced that discretion is the better part of valor, and urging my canoe into the center current, made a rapid retreat down the river. For just before me, in the calm deep water of a sheltered bay where I was quietly floating, there arose a violent boiling, bubbling commotion, and for an instant I thought a hot spring was going to burst forth—instead of that, uprose the hideous head and gaping jaws of a hippopotamus, who, with a hoarse, terrific snort, seemed about to attack me. I can tell you I did not wait to see the rest of him! a glimpse of his enormous mouth and its array of white gleaming tusks was quite enough. 'Right about face!' said I to myself, and shot down the stream like an arrow, never pausing till a bend in the river brought me within sight of the Gap, where I once more felt safe, and joyfully made my way back to you all."

This narrative was of thrilling interest to us, proving the existence of tribes of the most formidable animals beyond the rocky barrier which defended, in so providential a manner, the small and fertile territory on which our lot was cast.

During the absence of the adventurer we had been busily engaged in making preparations for our departure—and everything was packed up and ready by the morning after his return.

After some hesitation I yielded to his great wish, which was to return by sea in his cajack round Cape Disappointment, and so meet us at Rockburg.

He was much interested in examining the outlines of the

coast and the rugged precipices of the Cape. These were ten-anted by vast flocks of sea fowl and birds of prey; while many varieties of shrubs and plants, hitherto unknown to us, grew in the clefts and crevices of the rocks, some of them diffusing a strong aromatic odor. Among the specimens he brought I recognized the caper plant, and, with still greater pleasure, a shrub which was, I felt sure, the tea-plant of China—it bore very pretty white flowers, and the leaves resembled myrtle.

Our land journey was effected without accident or adven-ture of any kind.

Jack, mounted as usual on Hurry, the ostrich, carried the mysterious wet bag very carefully slung at his side, and when near home started off at a prodigious rate in advance of us.

He let fall the drawbridge, and we saw no more of him until, on reaching Rockburg, he appeared leisurely returning from the swamp, where apparently he had gone to deposit his "moist secret," as Franz called it.

We were all glad to take up our quarters once more in our large and convenient dwelling, and my first business was to provide for the great number of birds we now had on our hands, by establishing them in suitable localities, it being im-possible to maintain them all in the poultry yard. Some were, therefore, taken to the islands; and the black swans, the heron, the graceful demoiselle cranes, and our latest acquisition, the splendid sultan cock, soon became perfectly at home in the swamp, greatly adding to the interest of the neighborhood of Safety Bay.

The old bustards were the tamest of all our feathered pets, and never more so than at meal times. They were unfailing in their attendance when we dined or supped in the open air.

Toward evening, as we sat in the veranda listening to Fritz's account of his trip round the Cape, an extraordinary hollow, roaring noise sounded from the swamp not unlike the angry bellowing of a bull.

The dogs barked, and the family rose in excitement; but I remarked a look of quiet humor in Fritz's eye, as he stood leaning against one of the veranda pillars, watching Jack, who, in some confusion, started off toward the marsh.

"Come back, you silly boy!" cried his mother; "the child

has not so much as a pistol, and is rushing off alone to face he knows not what!"

"Perhaps," said I, looking at Fritz, "this is not a case requiring the use of firearms. It may be only the booming of a bittern which we hear."

"You need not be uneasy, mother," said Fritz; "Jack knows what he is about; only this charming serenade took him by surprise, and I fancy he will have to exhibit his treasures before they reach perfection. Yes, here he comes!"

Lugging his "moist secret" along with him, Jack, flushed and breathless, came up to us, exclaiming:

"They were to grow as big as rabbits before you saw them! Such a shame! I never thought they would kick up a row like that. Now for it!"—and he turned out the bag. "This is 'Grace,' and this is 'Beauty.' "

Two immense frogs rolled clumsily on the ground, and recovering their feet, sat squat before us, swelling and puffing with a ludicrous air of insulted dignity, while peals of laughter greeted them on all sides.

"Ladies and Gentlemen, these are two very handsome young specimens of the famous African bullfrog," said Jack, pretending to be offended at the mingled disgust and amusement occasioned by their appearance; "they are but half-grown, and I hoped to maintain them in seclusion until they reached full size, when I would have introduced them with proper *éclat*. But since their talent for music has brought them precociously into public notice, I must beg for your kind and indulgent patronage, and—leave to take them back to the swamp!"

Great clapping of hands followed Jack's speech.

"Grace" and "Beauty" were examined, and commented on with much interest, and voted decidedly handsome "in their way."

Their general color was greenish brown, mottled and spotted with reddish brown and yellow; the sides green and black; the under part yellow, mottled with orange. The eyes were positively beautiful, of a rich chestnut hue, covered with golden white dots, which shone with a metallic luster. The skin of the body was puckered into longitudinal folds.

By general consent they were remanded to the swamp.

Shortly after our return to Rockburg, my wife drew my attention to the somewhat neglected state of our dear old summer residence at Falconhurst, begging me to devote some time to its restoration and embellishment.

This I most willingly undertook, and we removed thither, as soon as the boys had completed the arrangement of the artificial salt-lick to their satisfaction.

At Falconhurst things were quickly in good order, and we made a great improvement by completing the broad terrace supported on the arching roots of the trees—it was better floored—and rustic pillars and trelliswork sustained a bark roof which afforded a pleasant shade.

After this was done, I was compelled to consent to a plan long cherished by Fritz, who wished to construct a watch-tower and mount a gun on Shark Island. After great exertion, both mental and bodily, this piece of military engineering was completed; and a flagstaff erected, on which the guard at this outpost could run up a white flag to signal the approach of anything harmless from the sea, while a red flag would be shown on the least appearance of danger.

To celebrate the completion of this great work, which occupied us during two months, we hoisted the white flag, and fired a salute of six guns.

Chapter Sixteen

"WE spend our years as a tale that is told," said King David.

These words recurred to me again and again as I reviewed ten years, of which the story lay chronicled in the pages of my journal.

Year followed year; chapter succeeded chapter; steadily, imperceptibly, time was passing away.

The shade of sadness cast on my mind by retrospect of this kind was dispelled by thoughts full of gratitude to God, for the welfare and happiness of my beloved family during so long a period. I had cause especially to rejoice in seeing our sons

advance to manhood, strengthened by early training for lives
of usefulness and activity wherever their lot might fall.

And my great wish is, that young people who read this
record of our lives and adventures should learn from it how
admirably suited is the peaceful, industrious, and pious life of
a cheerful, united family, to the formation of strong, pure, and
manly character.

None take a better place in the great national family, none
are happier or more beloved than those who go forth from
such homes to fulfil new duties, and to gather fresh interests
around them.

Having given a detailed account of several years' residence
in New Switzerland, as we liked to call our dominion, it is
needless for me to continue what would exhaust the patience
of the most long-suffering, by repeating monotonous narratives
of exploring parties and hunting expeditions, wearisome descriptions of awkward inventions and clumsy machines, with
an endless record of discoveries, more fit for the pages of an
encyclopedia than a book of family history.

Yet before winding up with the concluding events, I may
mention some interesting facts illustrative of our exact position at the time these took place.

Rockburg and Falconhurst continued to be our winter and
summer headquarters, and improvements were added which
made them more and more convenient, as well as attractive in
appearance.

The fountains, trellised verandas, and plantations round
Rockburg, completely changed the character of the residence
which, on account of the heat and want of vegetation, had in
former days been so distasteful to my wife. Flowering creepers
overhung the balconies and pillars; while shrubs and trees,
both native and European, grew luxuriantly in groves of our
planting.

In the distance, Shark Island, now clothed with graceful
palms, guarded the entrance to Safety Bay, the battery and
flagstaff prominently visible on its crested rock.

The swamp, cleared and drained, was now a considerable
lake, with just marsh and reeds enough beyond it to form
good cover for the waterfowl whose favorite retreat it was.

On its blue waters sailed stately black swans, snow-white geese, and richly colored ducks; while out and in among the water plants and rushes would appear at intervals glimpses of the brilliant sultan, marsh-fowl, crimson flamingoes, soft, blue-gray, demoiselle cranes, and crested heron, all associating in harmony, and with no fear of us, their masters.

The giant frogs, Grace and Beauty, delighted Jack by actually attaining in time to the size of small rabbits; and, perfectly knowing their very appropriate names, would waddle out of the marsh at his call, to eat a grasshopper or dainty fly.

Beneath the spreading trees, and through the aromatic shrubberies, old Hurry, the ostrich, was usually to be seen marching about, with grave and dignified pace, as though monarch of all he surveyed. Every variety of beautiful pigeon nested in the rocks and dovecots, their soft cooing and glossy plumage making them favorite household pets.

By the bridge alone could Rockburg be approached; for higher up the river, where, near the cascade, it was fordable, a dense and impenetrable thicket of orange and lemon trees, Indian figs, prickly pears, and all manner of thorn-bearing shrubs, planted by us, now formed a complete barrier.

The rabbit warren on Shark Island kept us well supplied with food, as well as soft and useful fur; and, as the antelopes did not thrive on Whale Island, they also were placed among the shady groves with the rabbits, and their own island devoted to such work as candle-making, tanning, wool-cleaning, and any other needful but offensive operations.

The farm at Woodlands flourished, and our flocks and herds supplied us with mutton, beef, and veal, while my wife's dairy was almost more than she could manage.

My boys retained their old love for giving names to the animals. They had a beautiful creamy-white cow called Blanche, and a bull with such a tremendous voice, that he received the name of Stentor. Two fleet young onagers were named Arrow and Dart; and Jack had a descendant of his old favorite Fangs, the jackal, which he chose to call Coco, asserting that no word could be distinguished at a distance without the letter "o" in it, giving illustrations of his theory till our ears were almost deafened.

Excellent health had been enjoyed by us all during these ten years, though my wife occasionally suffered from slight attacks of fever, and the boys sometimes met with little accidents.

They were all fine, handsome fellows; Fritz, now twenty-four, was of moderate height, uncommonly strong, active, muscular, and high-spirited.

Ernest, two years younger, was tall and slight; in disposition, mild, calm, and studious; his early faults of indolence and selfishness were almost entirely overcome. He possessed refined tastes and great intellectual power.

Jack, at twenty, strongly resembled Fritz, being about his height, though more lightly built, and remarkable rather for active grace and agility than for muscular strength.

Franz, a lively youth of seventeen, had some of the qualities of each of his brothers; he possessed wit and shrewdness, but not the arch drollery of Jack.

All were honorable, God-fearing young men, dutiful and affectionate to their mother and myself, and warmly attached to each other.

Although so many years had elapsed in total seclusion, it continued to be my strong impression that we should one day be restored to the society of our fellow-men.

But time, which was bringing our sons to manhood, was also carrying their parents onward to old age; and anxious, gloomy thoughts relating to their future, should they be left indeed alone, sometimes oppressed my heart.

On such occasions, I would not communicate the sense of depression to my family, but, turning in prayer to the Almighty Father, laid my trouble before Him, with never-failing renewal of strength and hope.

My elder sons often made expeditions of which we knew nothing until their return after many hours; when any uneasiness I might have felt was dissipated by their joyous appearance, and reproof always died away on my lips.

Fritz had been absent one whole day from Rockburg, and not until evening did we remark that his cajack was gone, and that he must be out at sea.

Anxious to see him return before nightfall, I went off to

Shark Island with Ernest and Jack, in order to look out for him from the watch tower there, at the same time hoisting our signal flag and loading the gun.

Long we gazed across the expanse of ocean glittering in the level beams of the setting sun, and finally discerned a small black speck in the distance which, by the telescope, was proved to be the returning wanderer.

I remarked that his skiff sailed at a slower rate than usual toward the shore. The cannon was fired to let him know that his approach was observed, and then we joyfully hurried back to receive him at the harbor.

It was easy to see, as he drew near, what had delayed his progress. The cajack towed a large sack, besides being heavily laden.

"Welcome, Fritz!" I cried. "Welcome back, wherever you come from, and whatever you bring. You seem to have quite a cargo there!"

"Yes, and my trip has led to discoveries as well as booty," answered he; "interesting discoveries which will tempt us again in the same direction. Come, boys, let's carry up the things, and while I rest I will relate my adventures."

As soon as possible all assembled around him.

"I think my absence without leave deserves reproach instead of this warm reception, father, and I must apologize for it," he began. "But ever since I possessed the cajack it has been my ambition to make a voyage of discovery along the coast, which we have never explored beyond the point at which I killed the walrus.

"In order to be ready to start without delay when a convenient opportunity offered, I made preparations beforehand, such as provisioning my skiff, fixing the compass in front of my seat, arranging conveniently rifle, harpoon, ax, boat-hook, and fishing net. I also resolved to take with me Pounce, my eagle, and this I always will do in future.

"This morning dawned magnificently; the calm sea, the gentle breeze, all drew me irresistibly to the fulfillment of my purpose.

"I left the harbor unperceived, the current quickly bore me out to sea, and I rounded the point to the left, passing just

over the spot where, beneath the waves, lie the guns, cannon
balls, ironwork, and all that was indestructible about our good
old wreck. And would you believe it? Through the glassy,
clear water, undisturbed by a ripple, I actually saw many
such things strewn of the flat rocky bottom.

"Pursuing my way, I passed among rugged cliffs and rocks
which jutted out from the shore, or rose in rugged masses
from the water. Myriads of sea fowl inhabited the most inaccessible of these, while on the lower ridges, seals, sea bears,
and walruses were to be seen, some basking lazily in the sun,
some plunging into the water, or emerging awkwardly from
it, hoisting their unwieldy bodies up the rocks by means of
their tusks.

"I must confess to feeling anything but comfortable while
going through the places held in possession by these monsters
of the deep, and used every effort to pass quickly and unnoticed. Yet it was more than an hour and a half before I
got clear of the rocks, cliffs, and shoals to which they re-
sorted, and neared a high and precipitous cape, running far
out to sea. Right opposite to me, in the side of this rocky
wall, was a magnificent archway, forming, as it first appeared
to me, a lofty entrance to an immense vaulted cavern. I
passed beneath this noble portal and examined the interior.
It was tenanted by numbers of a small species of swallow,
scarcely larger than a wren, and the walls were covered by
thousands of their nests. They were rudely built, and their
peculiarity was that each rested on a kind of platform, something like a spoon without the handle. I detached a number,
and found that they had a curious appearance, seemingly
made of something fibrous and gelatinous, and more like a set
of sponges, corals, or fungi, than nests of birds. I have brought
them home in my fishing net."

"If we had commercial dealings with the Chinese," said I,
"your discovery would be of value; these are doubtless edible
birds' nests. The bird is called the esculent swallow, and the
trade in this strange article of diet is a very large one. The
nests are of different value, but those which are quite new,
and nearly white, are held in such esteem that they are worth
their weight in silver.

"There are tremendous caverns in Java and other places

where, at great risk, these nests are procured; the annual weight obtained being upward of fifty thousand pounds, and the value more than £200,000.

◄"When placed in water and well soaked, they soften and swell, and are made into soup of very strengthening and restorative quality.

"I think you might try your hand on these, mother, just for curiosity's sake."

"I can't say I fancy the look of the queer things," said she, "but I don't mind trying if they will turn to jelly; though boiling birds' nests is cookery quite out of my line."

"Oh, do, mother; let us taste birds' nests as soon as you can, though the idea makes me fancy my mouth full of feathers!" laughed Jack.

"It is really a most curious formation," said Fritz. "From whence are the swallows supposed to get this kind of gelatine?"

"It has never been exactly ascertained," I replied, "whether the birds discover or produce this curious substance. But whatever may be its basis, it is clear that a very large portion of it is furnished by certain glands, which pour out a viscid secretion."

"After laying in my store of nests," continued Fritz, "I pursued my way through this vaulted cave or corridor; which, presently turning, opened into a very lonely bay, so calm and lake-like, that, although of considerable size, I concluded at once it must be nearly land locked. Its shores, beyond the rocky boundary through which I penetrated, extended in a fertile plain toward what seemed the mouth of a river, beyond which lay rough, and probably marshy, ground, and a dense forest of cedars, which closed the view.

"The water beneath me was clear as crystal; and, gazing into its depths and shallows, I perceived beds of shell-fish, like large oysters, attached to the rocks and to each other by tufts of hairy filaments.

" 'If these are oysters,' thought I, 'they must be better worth eating, as far as size goes, than our little friends in Safety Bay,' and thereupon I hooked up several clusters with my boat-hook, and landing soon after on the beach, I flung them on the sand, resolving to fetch another load, and then tow them after me in the fishing-net.

"The hot sun disagreed with their constitution, I suppose; for when I came back the shells were all gaping wide open; so I began to examine them, thinking that after all they were probably much less delicate than the small oysters we have learnt to like so much.

"Somehow, when a thing is to be 'examined,' one generally needs a knife. The blade met with resistance here and there in the creature's body; and still closer 'examination' produced from it several pearly balls like peas, of different sizes. Do you think they can be pearls? I have a number here in a box."

"Oh, show them to us, Fritz!" cried the boys. "What pretty shining things! and how delicately rounded, and how softly they gleam!"

"You have discovered treasure, indeed!" I exclaimed; "why these are most beautiful pearls! Valueless, certainly, under present circumstances; but they may prove a source of wealth, should we ever again come into contact with the civilized world. We must visit your pearl-oyster beds at the earliest opportunity."

"After resting for some time, and refreshing myself with food," pursued Fritz, "I resumed my survey of the coast, my progress somewhat impeded by the bag of shell-fish, which I drew after me; but I proceeded without accident past the mouth of the stream to the further side of the bay, which was there inclosed by a point corresponding to that through which I had entered; and between these headlands I found a line of reefs and sandbanks, with but a single channel leading out to the open sea; from which, therefore, Pearl Bay, as I named it, lies completely sheltered.

"The tide was setting strongly in shore, so that I could not then attempt a passage through it, but examined the crags of the headland, thinking I might perchance discover a second vaulted archway. I saw nothing remarkable, however, but thousands of sea fowl of every sort and kind, from the gull and sea swallow to the mighty albatross.

"My approach was evidently regarded as an invasion and trespass; for they regularly beset me, screaming and wheeling over my head, till, out of all patience, I stood up, and hit furiously about me with the boat-hook; when, rather to my surprise, one blow struck an albatross with such force, that he fell stunned into the water.

"I now once more attempted to cross the reef by the narrow channel, and happily succeeding, found myself in the open sea, and speeding homeward, joyfully saw our flag flying, and heard the welcome salute you fired."

Here ended the narrative; but next morning Fritz drew me aside, and confided to me a most remarkable sequel, in these words:

"There was something very extraordinary about that albatross, father. I allowed you to suppose that I left it as it fell, but in reality I raised it to the deck of the canoe, and then perceived a piece of rag wound round one of its legs. This I removed, and, to my utter astonishment, saw English words written on it, which I plainly made to be: 'Save an unfortunate Englishwoman from the smoking rock!'

"This little sentence sent a thrill through every nerve: my brain seemed to whirl. I doubted the evidence of my senses.

" 'Is this reality, or delusion?' thought I. 'Can it be true, that a fellow-creature breathes with us the air of this lonely region?'

"I felt stupified for some minutes: the bird began to show signs of life, which recalled me to myself; and, quickly deciding what must be done, I tore a strip from my handkerchief, on which I traced the words—'Do not despair! Help is near!'

"This I carefully bound round one leg, replacing the rag on the other, and then applied myself to the complete restoration of the bird. It gradually revived; and after drinking a little, surprised me by suddenly rising on the wing, faltering a moment in its flight, and then rapidly disappearing from my view in a westerly direction.

"Now, father, one thought occupies me continually: will my note ever reach this Englishwoman? Shall I be able to find, and to save her?"

I listened to this account with feelings of the liveliest interest and astonishment.

"My dear son," said I, "you have done wisely in confiding to me alone your most exciting discovery. Unless we know more, we must not unsettle the others by speaking of it; for it appears to me quite possible that these words were penned

long ago on some distant shore, where, by this time, the unhappy stranger may have perished miserably. By the 'smoking
rock' must be meant a volcano. There are none here."

Fritz was not disposed to look at the case from this gloomy
point of view; did not think the rag so very old; believed
smoke might rise from a rock which was not volcanic; and
evidently cherished the hope that he might be able to respond
effectually to this touching appeal.

I was in reality as anxious as himself on the subject, but
judged it prudent to abate rather than excite hopes of success
which might be doomed to bitter disappointment.

After earnest consultation on the subject, we decided that
Fritz should go in search of the writer of the message, but
not until he had so altered the canoe as to fit it for carrying
two persons, as well as provisions sufficient to admit of his
absence for a considerable time. Impatient as he was, he could
not but see the wisdom of this delay.

We returned to the house, and saw the boys busily opening
the oysters, which they had had no time to do the previous
night, and greatly excited as ever and anon a pearl was found.

"May we not establish a pearl fishery at once, father?"
shouted they. "We might build a hut on the shore of the bay,
and set about it regularly."

An excursion to Pearl Bay was now the event to which all
thoughts turned, and for which preparations on a grand scale
were made. It was to form, as it were, the basis of the more
important voyage Fritz had in view, and to which, unsuspected
by the rest, he could devote all his attention.

I took an opportunity, one day, when all were present, to
remark in a serious tone:

"I have been considering, dear wife, that our eldest son is
now of an age to be dependent on himself. I shall, therefore,
henceforth leave him at liberty to act in all respects according
to his own judgment; and, especially in the matter of voyages
or excursions, he must not be hampered by the fear of alarming us should he choose to remain absent longer than we
expect. I have such entire confidence in his prudence, and at
the same time in his affection for us, that I am certain he will
never needlessly cause us anxiety."

Fritz looked gratefully toward me as I spoke; and his mother ratified my words, embracing him affectionately, and saying, with emotion, "God bless and preserve thee, my boy!"

It took some time to make several raking or scraping machines, which I invented for the purpose of detaching and lifting the oysters from their native rocks; but that gave Fritz leisure to change the fittings of his canoe, so as to have a spare seat in it.

His brothers naturally concluded he meant to take one of them as shipmate on board, and he allowed the mistake to continue. They occupied themselves in making various articles they expected to be of use, and bore the delay with tolerable patience.

At last came the day, when, taking leave of the mother and Franz, we went on board the yacht, accompanied by some of the dogs; while Jack, proudly occupying the new seat beside Fritz in the canoe, shared with him the honor of leading the way in the character of pilots.

We passed safely through the rocks and shoals near Walrus Island into an expanse of calm water, sheltered by jutting cliffs, where the sea glanced like a mirror, and for the first time we observed the fairy-like shells of the paper-nautilus sailing lightly over the dazzling surface.

It was impossible to see these lovely seafarers without wishing to obtain specimens; and the canoe accordingly gave chase, presently securing half a dozen, which were handed to us in the yacht to be carefully preserved for the museum, and the place was ever after called Nautilus Creek.

Further on we rounded a short promontory, flat, with an abrupt rock at the extremity, to which we gave the name of Cape Pug-Nose; and then, at some distance, appeared the grand cliffs of a headland running far out to sea.

This I supposed we should have to weather, but my pilots made no change in our course, and, following the canoe, we soon came in sight of the majestic archway which offered us a short passage to Pearl Bay.

The wonderfully architectural appearance of the pillars, arches, and pinnacles, surrounding and surmounting this noble entrance, struck me with admiration, resembling parts of a fine Gothic cathedral, and inducing me to propose for it the name, Cape Minster.

A perfect cloud of little swallows darted from the cavernous entrance on our approach, divided into flocks, soared, wheeled, flew right and left, and finally returned in a body as swiftly as they came, to the sides of the long dark tunnel, which were festooned with their nests.

We detached a number of these as we passed, taking care to leave those containing eggs of young. The best were at a considerable height, but the broken and shelving rocks afforded, in some places, footing for such daring and active climbers as Fritz and Jack, and they quickly obtained as many as we could possibly require.

Our progress was much assisted by the tide, which, like a current, bore us onward along the nave of this natural cathedral; aisles, transepts, screens, and side-chapels appearing between the columns and arches which in the "dim religious light" were revealed to our wondering eyes.

On emerging into the dazzling sunshine, we found ourselves floating in the calm expanse of Pearl Bay; but it was some minutes before we could look around on the bright and lovely scene.

Fritz had not over-rated its beauty, and the romantic islets which studded its waters seemed to give the effect of a pleasant smile to features already perfect.

We cruised about for some time, surveying the coast with its fertile meadows, shady groves, gently swelling hills, and murmuring brooks, seeking a convenient landing place in the vicinity of the shallows where lay the oyster-beds.

This we found, close to a sparkling streamlet; and, as the day was fast declining, we made speedy arrangements for burning a watch-fire; after which we partook of a hasty supper, and leaving the dogs, with Coco, the jackal, to sleep on shore, we returned on board the yacht for the night, anchoring within gunshot of the land.

The coast being quite strange to us, I knew not what wild beasts might frequent it; but, though I did not fear that any would approach us by swimming, yet I was glad to have with us our lively little ape, Mercury (the successor of our old favorite, Knips, long since gathered to his fathers), for he occupied at night a cosy berth on deck, and was certain to give vociferous notice should anything alarming occur.

Fritz moored the cajack alongside, and came on board. The night passed in peace, although for a time we were disturbed by the yelping of jackals, with whom Coco persisted in keeping up a noisy conversation.

We awoke at daybreak, and after breakfasting *à la fourchette,* we repaired in haste with nets, scrapers, and all other requisites, to the oyster-beds, where we worked with such diligence and success that in the course of two days we had an immense pile of shells built up like a stack on the beach, and left to decay.

I collected a quantity of sea-weed to spread over them, which was afterward burnt to make alkali, when we returned to secure our harvest of pearls.

Every evening we went out shooting in the neighborhood, and kept ourselves supplied with game of one sort or another. The last day of our fishery we started earlier, intending to make a longer excursion into the woods.

Ernest set off first with Floss; Jack and Coco strolling after them. Fritz and I were still employed in taking on board the last load of our tools, when we suddenly heard a shot, a loud cry of pain or fear, and then another shot.

At the first alarm, the other two dogs rushed away from us toward the spot, and Fritz, who had just called Pounce from his perch, to accompany us in the ramble, let him fly, and seizing his rifle darted off in the same direction.

Before I could reach the scene of action, more shots were heard, and then a shout of victory; after which appeared through the stems of the trees the disconsolate figure of Jack, hobbling along like a cripple, supported on each side by his brothers.

When they came near me they stopped; and poor Jack moaning and groaning, began to feel himself all over, as if to search for broken bones, crying out:

"I'm pounded like a half-crushed pepper-corn!"

On examination I found some severe bruises.

"Who or what has been pommeling the boy?" I exclaimed; "one would think he had been beaten."

"It was a huge wild boar," said Ernest, "with fierce eyes, monstrous tusks, and a snout as broad as my hand."

We took Jack down to the yacht, bathed his bruises, gave

him a cooling drink, and he soon fell fast asleep in his berth, where I left him and returned to the shore.

"Now, Ernest," said I, "enlighten me on the subject of this adventure! What you and the boar did, is quite a mystery to me."

"Floss and I were going quietly along," replied he, "when suddenly there was a rustling and snorting close by, and a great boar broke through the bushes, making for the outskirts of the wood. Floss gave chase directly, and the boar turned to bay. Then up came Jack with Coco, and the gallant little jackal attacked the monster in the rear. In another moment, however, he was sent sprawling upon his back, and this so provoked his master that he fired a hasty ill-directed shot. The brute's notice and fury at once turned upon Jack, who prudently took to his heels, when I attempted to check the career of the boar by a shot, which, however, only slightly wounded it. Jack stumbled and fell over the root of a tree, just as the animal came up with him. 'Help! murder,' shouted he; and if the other dogs had not then arrived, and all together tackled the boar, I fear it would have been a case of murder indeed! as it was, the poor fellow got mauled and trampled upon dreadfully.

"As I was waiting for an opportunity to fire without any risk of hitting Jack, Pounce rushed through the air and darted upon the beast, and Fritz came up quickly and shot it dead with a pistol.

"While we were helping Jack along, and passing a place where the boar had been grubbing, I noticed some such curious knotty roots or tubercles, that I brought away specimens. Are they worth anything, do you think? They have a strong smell."

"If I may trust my nose," said I, "you have brought something by no means to be despised. Yes!" I continued, putting them to my lips, "these are very fine truffles! Taste them, Fritz."

"Indeed, they are excellent," said he; "very different from the tough, leathery things I remember in Europe; these are tender and well flavored."

"Because they are fresh," said I. "You have before tasted those only which have been brought from a distance. They are found in different parts of Europe, buried at a depth of ten or twelve inches in the soil of oak or beech woods. A small dog is employed to hunt for them, who perceives their musky odor in a singularly acute way, and at once scratches at the spot where they lie."

"Have the truffles no leaves or stalks," inquired Fritz, "by which they might be found without the help of the dog?"

"They have nothing of the sort," I replied; "they are discovered simply by scent, and are considered to belong to the tribe of Fungi."

By this time it was late; we took supper, made up the watchfire, and withdrew to our yacht, where we slept peacefully.

Early next morning we proceeded to visit the field of battle. The wild boar, which I had not before seen, proved to be much larger and more formidable in appearance than I had imagined, and Jack's escape seemed to me perfectly marvelous.

The boys took it as a matter of course that we were to cut out hams and flitches; and we therefore did so, though I warned them that they need not expect much pleasure in eating bacon from a tough old African boar like this. We conveyed the mighty hams to the beach, each on a sledge of plaited boughs and twigs, and drawn by one of the dogs. The monstrous head traveled in the same way, and we collected a large number of truffles before quitting the forest.

As soon as the dogs were released, they rushed back to the scene of operations in the wood, comprehending that they were now free to feast on what remained there.

There was so much to be done in consequence of this affair that Fritz, who had hoped to set out on his solitary expedition that day, deferred it until the next; and was, therefore, fortunately with us, when late in the evening we desisted from our labors, and, having supped, were preparing to retire to rest.

All at once a deep, fearful sound echoed through the neighboring woods. It made our blood curdle in our veins. We listened with straining ears, hoping it would not be repeated. With a shudder we heard the dread voice roar again, yet nearer to us, and an answer peal from the distance.

"We must find out who are the performers in this concert!" exclaimed Fritz, springing to his feet and snatching up his rifle. "Make the fire blaze; get on board the yacht, and have all the guns in readiness. I am off to reconnoiter in the canoe."

We mechanically obeyed his rapid orders, while the bold youth disappeared in the darkness; and, after heaping fuel on the fire, we went on board and armed ourselves with cutlasses, besides loading all the guns, waiting in readiness either to land again or to quit the coast.

We presently saw the whole pack of our dogs, as well as Coco, the jackal, and the little ape, Mercury (who had been tempted by the truffles to stay with them in the woods), come galloping at full speed up to the fire.

Mercury was evidently excessively discomposed at finding us gone; he gnashed his teeth, and chattered, as though in fear, looking hopelessly at the water, through which he could not venture.

The dogs planted themselves by the fire, gazing fixedly landward, with ears erect, and occasionally uttering a barking challenge, or a suppressed howl.

Meantime, the horrid roarings approached nearer, and I concluded that a couple of leopards or panthers had been attracted by the scent of the boar's carcase.

But not long after I had expressed this opinion, we beheld a large, powerful animal spring from the underwood, and, with a bound, and muttered roar, approach the fire. In a moment I recognized the unmistakable outlines of the form of a lion, though in size he far surpassed any I had ever seen exhibited in Europe.

The dogs slunk behind the fire, and the lion seated himself almost like a cat on his hind legs, glaring alternately at them, and at the great boar hams which hung near, with doubtless a mixed feeling of irritation and appetite, which was testified by the restless movement of his tail.

He then arose, and commenced walking up and down with slow and measured pace, occasionally uttering short, angry roars, quite unlike the prolonged, full tones we had heard at first.

At times he went to drink at the brook, always returning with such haste, that I fully expected to see him spring.

Gradually his manner became more and more threatening;

he turned toward us, crouched, and with his body at full stretch, waved his tail, and glared so furiously, that I was in doubt whether to fire, or retreat, when through the darkness rang the sharp crack of a rifle.

"That is Fritz!" exclaimed everyone; while, with a fearful roar, the lion sprang to his feet, stood stock still, tottered, sank on his knees, rolled over, and lay motionless on the sand.

"We are saved!" I cried; "that was a masterly shot. The lion is struck to the heart; he will never stir again. Stay on board, boys. I must join my brave Fritz."

In a few moments I landed; the dogs met me with evident tokens of pleasure, but kept whining uneasily, and looking toward the deep darkness of the woods whence the lion had come.

This behavior made me cautious; and, seeing nothing of Fritz, I lingered by the boat, when suddenly a lioness bounded from the shadow of the trees, into the light diffused by the fire.

At sight of the blazing faggots she paused, as though startled; passed with uncertain step round the outskirts of the illuminated circle; and uttered roarings, which were evidently calls to her mate, whose dead body she presently discovered.

Finding him motionless, her manner betokened the greatest concern; she touched him with her fore-paws, smelt round him, and licked his bleeding wounds. Then, raising her head, she gnashed her teeth, and gave forth the most lamentable and dreadful sound I ever heard; a mingled roar and howl, which was like the expression of grief, rage, and a vow to be revenged, all in one.

Crack! Another shot: the creature's right fore-paw was lamed; and the dogs, seeing me raise my gun, suddenly gathered courage, and ran forward just as I fired. My shot also wounded the lioness, but not mortally, and the most terrific combat ensued.

It was impossible to fire again, for fear of wounding the dogs. The scene was fearful beyond description. Black night surrounded us; the fitful blaze of the fire shed a strange, unnatural light on the prostrate body of the huge dead lion, and on the wounded lioness, who fought desperately against the attack of the four gallant dogs; while the cries, roars, and groans of anguish and fury uttered by all the animals were enough to try the stoutest nerves.

Old Juno, staunch to the last, was foremost in the fray. After a time, I saw her change her plan of attack, and spring at the throat of the lioness; who, in an instant, raised her left paw, and at one blow the cruel claws had laid open the body of the dog, and destroyed the life of the true and faithful companion of so many years.

Just then Fritz appeared. The lioness was much weakened, and we ventured to go near enough to fire with safety to ourselves; and finally I dispatched her by plunging a hunting-knife deep in her breast.

Ernest and Jack were summoned from the yacht to witness the completed victory; and I regretted having left them on board, when I saw how greatly the noise and tumult had alarmed them, unable, as they were, to ascertain what was going on.

They hastened toward us in great agitation, and their joy on seeing us safe was only equaled by the grief they felt on learning the death of Juno.

The night was now far advanced; the fire burnt low; but we piled on more wood, and, by the renewed light, drew poor Juno from between the paws of the lioness; and by the brook-side, washed and bound up the torn body, wrapping it carefully in canvas, and carrying it with us on board the yacht, that it might be buried at Rockburg, whither on the following day it was our purpose to return.

Wearied and sorrowful, but full of thankfulness for our personal safety, we at length lay down to sleep, having brought all the dogs on board.

Next morning, before quitting Pearl Bay, we once more landed, that we might possess ourselves of the magnificent skins of the lion and lioness, whose visit, fatal to themselves, had caused such a commotion during the night.

In about a couple of hours we returned to the yacht, leaving the flayed carcases to the tender mercies of the birds of prey sure to be attracted to them.

"Homeward bound," sang out the boys, as they cheerily weighed anchor, and prepared to stand out to sea. I could see, though he did not complain, that poor Jack had not recovered from the boar's rough treatment, and moved very stiffly.

"You must pilot us through the channel in the reef this time, Fritz," said I; adding, in a lower tone, "and then is it to be 'farewell,' my son?"

"Yes, dear father—*Au revoir!*" returned he, brightly, with a glance full of meaning, while he threw into his canoe a cushion and a fur cloak.

"Thanks, Fritz! but I'm going to honor them with the care of my battered bones in the yacht here. You are awfully considerate though, old fellow," remarked Jack, not for a moment doubting that his brother expected him to return, as he came, beside him in the cajack.

Fritz laughed, and commended his decision. Then springing into his skiff, he led the way toward the open sea.

We followed, carefully, and soon passed the reef; after which the boys were very busy with the sails, putting the vessel on the homeward course, when, waving his hand to me, Fritz turned in the opposite direction, and quickly vanished behind the point, which I afterward named Cape Farewell.

When missed by his brothers, I said he had a fancy to explore more of the coast, and if he found it interesting he might, instead of only a few hours, remain absent for two or three days.

Toward evening, we sailed into Safety Bay.

Chapter Seventeen

THE mother and Franz, though somewhat startled by the unexpected absence of Fritz, were delighted to see us return
safely, and listened with eager interest to our adventures.
My wife shuddered, and scarcely suppressed an involuntary
scream as she heard of our desperate encounter with the lion
and his mate. Jack's danger and providential escape, too,
made her tremble; and so pale did he still look, that she could
scarcely believe he was uninjured.

Tears came into Franz's eyes when he heard of the sad
death of poor old Juno; and he inquired most tenderly
whether her remains had been brought back, that they might

be interred near the house which had been her home for so many years.

Next day he saw her buried carefully; and Ernest, at his request, produced an epitaph, which was inscribed upon a slab of stone above her grave.

J U N O ,

A servant true lies here;

A faithful friend,

A Dog,

To all most dear;

Who met her end

Fighting right bravely in her master's cause.

The flesh of the wild boar and the truffles were handed over to the mother, who received them with delight, promising us therefrom many a savory dish. She would fain have had the boar's head too; but my word was pledged to Ernest that it should adorn his museum, and, though my lips watered to taste it baked in Hottentot fashion, I would not break my promise.

This splendid head, therefore, together with the lions' skins, we carried to the tannery on Whale Island, where they were cleaned and dressed.

Five days passed, but Fritz still remained absent. I could not conceal my anxiety, and at length determined to follow him. All were delighted at the proposal, and even the mother, when she heard that we were to sail in the pinnace, agreed to accompany us.

The boat was stored, and on a bright morning, with a favorable breeze, we five, with the dogs, stepped aboard, and ran for Cape Minster.

Our beautiful little yacht bounded over the water gaily, and the bright sunshine and delicious sea breeze put us all in the highest spirits. The entrance of the archway was in sight, and thither I was directing the boat's course. Suddenly, right ahead, I saw a dark and shadowy mass just below the surface of the water. "A sunken rock!" I thought to myself, "and yet it is strange that I never before noticed it." I put down the helm in a moment, but a catastrophe seemed inevitable.

We surged ahead! A slight shock, and all was over! The danger was passed!

I glanced astern, to look again at the dangerous spot; but the rock was gone, and, where but a moment before I had distinctly seen its great green shadow, I could now see nothing. Before we had recovered from our amazement, a shout from Jack surprised me.

"There is another," he exclaimed, "to starboard, father!"

Sure enough, there lay, apparently, another sunken rock.

"The rock is moving!" shouted Franz; and a great black body emerged from the sea, while from the upper extremity rushed a column of water, which, with a mighty noise, rose upward, and then fell like rain all around. The mystery was explained; for, as the great beast emerged yet further from the water, I recognized, from its enormous size and great length of head, the cachalot whale.

The monster was apparently enraged at the way we had scratched his back; for, retreating to a short distance, he evidently meditated a rush upon us.

Fearful stories occurred to me of the savage temper of this whale, how he has been known to destroy boat after boat, and even ships, and with a feeling of desperation I sprang to one of the guns. Jack leaped to the other, and almost simultaneously we fired. Both shots apparently took effect; for the whale, after lashing the water violently for a few seconds, plunged beneath its surface, and disappeared. We kept a sharp lookout for him, for I was unwilling to lose such a valuable prize, and, reloading, stood toward the shore, in which direction he was apparently making. Presently we again sighted him in shallow water, lashing fearfully with his tail, and dyeing the waves around him with blood. Approaching the infuriate animal as nearly as I dared, we again fired.

The struggles of the whale seemed for a few moments to become even yet more frantic, and then, with a quiver from head to tail, he lay motionless—dead!

The boys were about to raise the cry of victory, but checked the shout upon their very lips; for darting behind a rock they espied a canoe paddled by a tall and muscular savage, who now stood up in his skiff and appeared to be examining us attentively. Seeing that we were standing toward him, the swarthy native seized his paddle and again darted behind a rock. An awful thought now took possession of me. There must be a tribe of blacks lurking on these shores, and Fritz must have fallen into their hands. We, however, I determined, should not be easily taken; and our guns were loaded and run out.

Presently a dusky face appeared, peeping at us from a lofty rock; it vanished, and we saw another peeping at us from lower down. Then, again, the skiff put out as though to make a further reconnoiter. All, even Jack, looked anxious, and glanced at me for orders.

"Hoist a white flag," said I, "and hand me the speaking-trumpet."

I seized the instrument and uttered such peaceable words in the Malay language as I could recall; neither the flag nor my words seemed to produce any effect, and the savage was about to return to the shore.

Jack hereupon lost patience, and in his turn took up the trumpet.

"Come here, you black son of a gun," he exclaimed. "Come on board and make friends, or we'll blow you and your——"

"Stop! stop! you foolish boy," I said; "you will but alarm the man, with your wild words and gestures."

"No! but, see," he cried, "he is paddling toward us!"

And sure enough the canoe was rapidly approaching.

Presently a cry from Franz alarmed me. "Look! look!" he shrieked, "the villain is in Fritz's cajack. I can see the walrus' head."

Ernest alone remained unmoved. He took the speaking-trumpet:

"Fritz, ahoy!" he shouted; "welcome, old fellow!"

The words were scarcely out of his mouth when I, too, recognized the well-known face beneath its dusky disguise.

In another minute the brave boy was on board, and in spite of his blackened face was kissed and welcomed heartily. He was now assailed with a storm of questions from all sides: "Where had he been?" "What had kept him so long, and why had he turned blackamoor?"

"The last question," replied he, with a smile, "is the only one I will now answer; the others shall be explained when I give a full account of my adventures. Hearing guns fired, my mind was instantly filled with ideas of Malay pirates, for I never dreamed that you could be here in the yacht, so I disguised myself as you now see me, and came forth to reconnoiter. When you addressed me in Malay you only added to my terror, for it left not a doubt in my mind that you were pirates."

Having in our turn described to him our adventure with the cachalot whale, I asked him if he knew of a suitable spot for the anchorage of the yacht.

"Certainly," he replied, casting toward me a glance full of meaning; "I can lead you to an island where there is a splendid anchorage, and which is itself well worth seeing, for it contains all sorts of strange things." And after removing the stains from his skin, and turning himself once more into a civilized being, he again sprang into his canoe and piloted us to a picturesque little island in the bay.

Now that there could be no doubt as to the success of Fritz's expedition, I no longer hesitated to give to my wife an account of his project, and to prepare her mind for the surprise which awaited her. She was greatly startled, as I expected, and seemed almost overcome with emotion at the idea of seeing a human being, and that being one of her own sex.

"But why," she asked, "did you not tell me of this at first? Why wait until the last moment with such joyful news?"

"I was unwilling," I replied, "to raise hopes which might never be realized: but now, thank Heaven, he has succeeded, and there is no need for concealment."

The boys could not at all understand the evident air of mystery and suppressed excitement which neither their mother, Fritz, nor I could entirely conceal. They cast glances of the greatest curiosity toward the island, and as soon as the sails were furled and the anchor dropped, they sprang eagerly ashore. In a body we followed Fritz, maintaining perfect silence. Presently we emerged from the thicket through which we were passing, and saw before us a hut of sheltering boughs, at the entrance of which burned a cheerful fire.

Into this leafy bower Fritz dived, leaving his brothers with-

out, mute with astonishment. In another moment he emerged, leading by the hand a slight, handsome youth, by his dress apparently a young English naval officer. The pair advanced to meet us; and Fritz, with a countenance radiant with joy, briefly introduced his companion as Edward Montrose.

"And," he continued, looking at his mother and me, "will you not welcome him as a friend and a brother to our family circle?"

"That will we, indeed!" I exclaimed, advancing and holding out my hands to the fair young stranger. "Our wild life may have roughened our looks and manners, but it has not hardened our hearts, I trust."

The mother, too, embraced the seeming youth most heartily. The lads, and even the dogs, were not behind hand in testifying their gratification at the appearance of their new friend—the former delighted at the idea of a fresh companion, and the latter won by her sweet voice and appearance.

From the expression made use of by Fritz I perceived that the girl wished her sex to remain unrevealed to the rest of the party until the mother could obtain for her a costume more suited to her real character.

The young men then ran down to the yacht to bring up what was necessary for supper, as well as to make preparations for a camp in which we might spend the night. This done, the mother hastened to set before us a substantial meal, while the boys, anxious to make their new acquaintance feel at home among them, were doing their best to amuse her. She herself, after the first feeling of strangeness had worn off, entered fully into all their fun; and by the time they sat down to supper was laughing and chattering as gaily as anyone of the rest. She admired the various dishes, tasted our mead, and, without alluding once to her previous life, kept up a lively conversation.

The mere fact of meeting with any human being after so many years of isolation was in itself sufficient to raise the boys to the greatest state of excitement; but that this being should be one so handsome, so gay, so perfectly charming, seemed completely to have turned their heads; and when I gave the sign for breaking up of the feast, and their new friend was

about to be led to the night quarters which had been prepared
for her on board the yacht, the health of Edward Montrose
was proposed, and drunk in fragrant mead, amid the cheers
and acclamations of all hands.

When she was gone, and silence had been restored, Jack
exclaimed:

"Now, then, Fritz, if you please, just tell me where you came
across this jolly fellow. Did you take your mysterious voyage
in search of him, or did you meet him by chance? Out with
your adventures, while we sit comfortably round the fire."

So saying, Jack cast more wood upon the blazing pile, and
throwing himself down in his usual, careless fashion, prepared
to listen attentively.

Fritz, after a few moments' hesitation, began:

"Perhaps you remember," said he, "how, when I returned
from my expedition in the cajack the other day, I struck down
an albatross. None but my father at the time knew, however,
what became of the wounded bird, or even thought more about
it. Yet it was that albatross who brought me notice of the shipwrecked stranger and he, too, I determined should carry back
a message, to cheer and encourage the sender.

"I first, as you know, prepared my cajack to carry two persons; and then, with a heart full of hope and trust, left you
and the yacht, and, with Pounce seated before me, made for
the open sea. For several hours I paddled steadily on, till, the
wind freshening, I thought it advisable to keep in nearer
shore; that, should a regular storm arise, I might find some
sheltered bay in which to weather it.

"It was well I did so; for, scarcely had I reached a quiet cove
which promised to afford me the protection I desired than the
sea appeared one mass of foam: great surging waves arose; and
even in the comparative calm of the bay I felt that I was in
some danger.

"I passed the night in my cajack; and next morning, after
a frugal meal of pemmican, and a draught of water from
my flask, once more ventured forth. The wind had subsided,
and the sea was tolerably smooth; and, keeping my eyes busily
employed in seeking in every direction to detect, if possible,
the slightest trace of smoke, or other sign of human life, I
paddled on till noon.

"The aspect of the coast now began to change: the shores were sandy, while further inland lay dense forests, from whose gloomy depths I could ever and anon hear the fierce roar of beasts of prey, the yell of apes, the fiendish laugh of the hyena, or the despairing death cry of a hapless deer. Seldom have I experienced a greater feeling of solitude than while listening to these strange sounds, and knowing that I, in this frail canoe, was the only human being near. Giving myself up to contemplation, I rested my paddle, and allowed my cajack to drift slowly on.

"As I neared the shore, I noticed a large number of stranger looking birds, who would sometimes flutter round me, and then dart back again to the border of the forest, where they were feeding on what appeared to be the pepper plant; they seized the berries in their great, ponderous beaks, threw them up into the air, and then dexterously caught them in their fall. Their beaks were really something extraordinary: they looked as though they must give their owners a perpetual headache, from their immense weight. The only thing that relieved the extreme ugliness of these great appendages was their gorgeous color, which was only rivaled by the gay hue of the plumage. I wished now that I had brought home a specimen; but at the time I was so much amused by watching the grotesque antics of the birds that I did not think of obtaining one. When I left the spot, I settled in my own mind that they were toucans: was I right, Ernest?"

The Professor, unwilling to interrupt the narrative, merely gave an oracular nod, and Fritz continued:

"For some hours after this I paddled quickly on, sometimes passing the mouth of a stream, sometimes that of a broad river. Had I been merely on an exploring expedition, I should have been tempted, doubtless, to cruise a little way up one of these pathways into the forest; but now such an idea did not enter my head. On, on, on, I felt I must go, until I should reach the goal of my voyage.

"The shades of night at length drew on, and, finding a sheltered cove, I moored my cajack, and stepped on shore. You may imagine how pleasant it was to stretch my legs, after sitting for so long in the cramped position which my cajack enforces. It would not do, however, to sleep on shore; so after preparing and enjoying my supper, I returned on board, and there spent the night.

"Next morning Pounce and I again landed for breakfast. I lit my fire, and hung before it a plump young parrot to roast. As I was so doing, I heard a slight rustle among the long grass behind me. I glanced round, and there, with glaring eyes and his great tail swaying to and fro, I saw an immense tiger.

"In another moment his spring would have been made. I should have been no more, and our young guest would have been doomed to, God only knows how many, years of frightful solitude!

"My gun was lying by my side. Before I could have stooped to pick it up, the monster would have seized me.

"Pounce saw and comprehended my danger: the heroic bird darted upon my enemy, and so blinded him with his flapping wings, and the fierce blows of his beak, that his spring was checked, and I had time to recover my self-possession. I seized my gun, and fired; and the brute, pierced to the heart, gave one spring, and then rolled over at my feet.

"My enemy was dead; but beside him, alas! lay poor Pounce, crushed and lifeless. One blow of the great beast's paw had struck him down, never to rise again!"

Fritz's voice shook as he came to this point; and, after remaining silent for a moment or two, he continued hurriedly:

"With a sad and desolate feeling at my heart, I buried the faithful bird where he had met his death; and then, unable longer to continue near the spot, I returned to my cajack, and leaving the great tiger lying where he fell, paddled hastily away.

"My thoughts were gloomy. I felt as though, now that my companion was gone, I could no longer continue the voyage. The albatross, I thought, may have flown for hundreds of miles before it reached me. This stranger may be on different shores from these entirely; every stroke of my paddle may be carrying me further from the blazing signal: who knows?

"This feeling of discouragement was not, however, to be of long duration; for in a moment more a sight presented itself, which banished all my doubts and fears, and raised me to the highest pitch of excitement.

"A high point of land lay before me. I rounded it, and beyond found a calm and pleasant bay, from whose curved and thickly wooded shores ran out a reef of rocks. From the point of this reef rose a column of smoke, steadily and clearly curling upward in the calm air. I could scarcely believe my senses, but stopped, gazing at it as though I were in a dream; then, with throbbing pulse and giddy brain, I seized my paddle, and strained every nerve to reach it.

"A few strokes seemed to carry me across the bay, and, securing my canoe, I leaped upon the rock, on which the beacon was blazing, but not a sign of a human being could I see. I was about to shout, for as the fire had evidently been recently piled up, I knew the stranger could not be far off; but, before I could do so, I saw a slight figure passing along the chain of rocks toward the spot on which I stood. You may all imagine my sensations.

"I advanced a few paces; and then mastering my emotion as best I could, I said in English:

" 'Welcome, fair stranger! God, in his mercy, has heard your call, and has sent me to your aid!'

"Miss Montrose came quickly forward——"

"Who? What?" shouted the boys, interrupting the narrative; "who came forward?" and amid a general hubbub, Ernest, rising and advancing to his brother, said in his quiet way:

"I did not like to make any remark till you actually let out the secret, Fritz, but we need no longer pretend not to see through the disguise of Edward Montrose."

Fritz, though much disconcerted by the discovery of the secret, recovered his self-possession; and, after bearing with perfect equanimity the jokes with which his brothers assailed him, joined in three cheers for their new sister, and when the confusion and laughter which ensued had subsided, continued his story:

"Miss Montrose grasped my hands warmly, and guessing from my pronunciation, I am afraid, that I was not in the habit of speaking English every day of my life, said in French:

" 'Long, long, have I waited since the bird returned with your message. Thank God, you have come at last!'

"Then, with tears of joy and gratitude, she led me to the shore, where she had built a hut and a safe sleeping-place, like

Falconhurst on a small scale, among the branches of a tree.
I was delighted with all she showed me, for indeed her hut and
its fittings evinced no ordinary skill and ingenuity. Round
the walls hung bows, arrows, lances, and bird-snares; while on
her work-table, in boxes and cases, carved skillfully with a
knife, were fish-hooks of mother-of-pearl, needles made from
fish-bones, and bodkins from the beaks of birds, fishing-lines
of all sorts, and knives and other tools. These latter she told
me were, with a chest of wearing apparel, almost the only
things washed ashore after the wreck, when three years ago
she was cast alone upon this desolate coast. I marveled more
and more at the wonderful way in which this girl had surmounted obstacles, the quarter of which would completely
have appalled the generality of her sex. The hut itself was a
marvel of skill; stout posts had been driven into the ground,
with cross pieces of bamboo, to form a framework; the walls
had been woven with reeds, the roof thatched with palm-
leaves, and the whole plastered smoothly with clay, an open
space being left in the center of the roof for a chimney to
carry off the smoke of the fire.

"As we entered, a cormorant, with a cry of anger, flew from
under the table toward me, and was about to attack me fiercely.
Miss Montrose called it off, and she then told me she had captured and tamed the bird soon after first landing, and since
that time had contrived to train it to assist her in every conceivable way; it now not only was a pleasant companion, but
brought her food of every description, fish, flesh and fowl, for
whether it dived into the waters, according to its natural habit,
struck down birds upon the wing, or seized rabbits and other
small animals upon the land, it laid all its booty at her feet.

"Before darkness closed in, all the curiosities and ingenious
contrivances of the place had been displayed—the kitchen
stove, cooking utensils, skin bottles, shell plates and spoons,
the fishing raft and numberless other things—and then, sitting
down with my fair hostess to a most appetizing meal, she gave
me a short account of her life:

"Jenny Montrose was the daughter of a British officer, who
had served for many years in India, where she herself was
born. At the early age of three years she lost her mother.

"After the death of his wife, all the colonel's love and care were centered upon his only child; under his eye she was instructed in all the accomplishments suited to her sex; and from him she imbibed an ardent love of field sports. By the time she was seventeen, she was as much at home upon her horse in the field as in her father's drawing room. Colonel Montrose now received orders to return home with his regiment, and as for certain reasons he did not wish her to accompany him in the ship with the troops, he obtained a passage for her on board a vessel which was about to sail at the same time.

"The separation was extremely painful to both the old soldier and his daughter, but there was no alternative. They parted, and Miss Montrose sailed in the *Dorcas* for England. A week after she had left Calcutta, a storm arose and drove the vessel far out of her course; more bad weather ensued; and at length, leaks having been sprung in all directions, the crew were obliged to take to the boats. Jenny obtained a place in one of the largest of these. After enduring the perils of the sea for many days, land was sighted; and, the other boats having disappeared, an attempt was made to land. The boat was capsized, and Miss Montrose alone reached the shore. For a long time she lay upon the sand almost inanimate; but, reviving sufficiently to move, she at length obtained some shellfish, and by degrees recovered her strength. From that time forth until I appeared she never set eyes upon a human being. To attract any passing vessel, and obtain assistance, however, she kept a beacon continually blazing at the end of the reef; and, with the same purpose in view, attached missives to the feet of any birds she could take alive in her snares. The albatross, she told me, she had kept for some time, and partially tamed; but, as it was in the habit of making long excursions on its own account, she conceived the idea of sending it also with a message, that, should it by chance be seen and taken alive, it might return with an answer.

"Our supper was over, and, at length, both wearied out with the anxieties and excitement of the day, we retired to rest, she to her leafy bower, and I to sleep in the hut below.

"Next morning, having packed her belongings in the cajack, we both went on board; and bidding adieu to her well-known bay she took her seat before me, and I made for home.

"We should have reached Rockburg this evening had not an accident occurred to our skiff and compelled us to put in at this island. The boat was scarcely repaired when I heard your first shots. I instantly disguised myself; and, never doubting that Malay pirates were near, came forth to reconnoiter. Glad, indeed, I was to find my fears ungrounded."

All had listened attentively to Fritz's story, but now a dreadful yawn from Franz, followed by others from Jack, Ernest, and Fritz, and a great desire on my own part to follow their example, warned me that it was time to dismiss the party for the night. Fritz retired to his cajack, the boys and I to the deck of the yacht, and the remainder of the night passed quietly away.

Next morning, as we assembled for breakfast, I took the opportunity of begging Miss Montrose no longer to attempt to continue her disguise, but to allow us to address her in her real character.

Jenny smiled; for she had noticed, as the young men met her when she came from the cabin, a great alteration in their manner, and had at once seen that her secret was guessed.

"After all," she said, "I need not be ashamed of this attire; it has been my only costume for the last three years, and in any other I should have been unable to manage all the work which during that time has been necessary."

Our pleasant meal over, I prepared to start for home, but Fritz reminded me of the cachalot, and although he confessed he should not care to repeat the operation of cutting up a whale, he thought it would be a pity to lose such a chance of obtaining a supply of spermaceti.

I fully agreed with him; and embarking, we quickly reached the sandbank on which the monster lay. No sooner did we come near, than the dogs leaped ashore, and before we could follow, rushed round to the other side of the great beast; snarling, growling, and howling ensued, and when we reached the spot we found a terrific combat going on. A troop of wolves were disputing fiercely with the dogs their right to the prey. Our appearance, however, quickly settled the matter; two of the brutes already lay dead, and those that now escaped our guns galloped off. Among the pack were a few jackals, and no sooner did Coco catch sight of these, his relations, than, suddenly attracted by his instinct, he left his master's side, and in spite of our shouts and cries, joined them, and disappeared into the forest.

As it would have been useless and dangerous to attempt to follow the deserter into the woods, we left him alone, trusting that he would return before we again embarked. Fritz then climbed up the mountain of flesh, and with his hatchet quickly laid open the huge skull; Jack and Franz joined him—Ernest having remained on the island, where we had left the mother and Jenny—and with buckets assisted him to bail out the spermaceti. The few vessels we possessed were soon full, and having stored them in the yacht, we once more embarked and arrived at the little island shortly before the dinner hour.

A capital meal had been prepared for us, and, when we had made ourselves presentable, we sat down to it, and related our adventures. The account of Coco's desertion was received with exclamations of surprise and sorrow. "Yet," said Jenny, after a time, "I do not think you should despair of his recovery, for animals in their native state seldom care to allow those that have been once domesticated to consort with them. My poor albatross, even though he was never thoroughly tamed, and certainly did finally desert me, yet used to return at intervals; and I am pretty sure that were you, Jack, to search the wood early to-morrow morning, you would find your pet only too willing to come back to civilized life; or, if you like, I will go myself and find him, for I should immensely like to have a paddle in the cajack all by myself."

Jack was delighted at the former suggestion, and though he would not listen for a moment to Jenny's request to be allowed to go alone, he agreed, if she cared for the fun of an early cruise, to accompany her in the canoe next morning, and to return to the yacht in time to start for Rockburg.

At sunrise they were off, armed with "bait" in the shape of meat and biscuit, and a muzzle and chain which Jack had manufactured in the evening to punish the runagate for his offenses, should they catch him. Arrived at the sandbank, they landed; and, after entering the forest and shouting "Coco, Coco!" till the woods rang again, they presently espied the truant, slouching disconsolately toward them, looking very miserable and heartily ashamed of himself.

With torn ears, and coat ruffled and dirty, he sneaked up. There was no need to use the bait to entice him; and when the poor beast thus came, unhappy and begging forgiveness, Jack had not the heart to degrade him further with the muzzle and chain. He had evidently attempted to join his wild brethren, and by them had been scouted, worried, and hustled, as no true jackal; and, as Jenny had foretold, was now only too glad to return to bondage and to comfort.

Poor Coco had recovered his spirits slightly by the time the yacht was reached; and, after a hearty meal, again took his place among the dogs, whom I had little doubt he would never again desert.

All was now bustle and activity; and breakfast over, we went aboard the yacht. Fritz and Jack stepped into the canoe; and we soon left Fair Isle and Pearl Bay far behind.

The morning was delightful. The sea, excepting for the slight ripple raised by the gentle breeze wafting us homeward, was perfectly calm. Slowly and contentedly we glided on through the wonders of the splendid archway, threaded our passage among the rocks and shoals, and passed out to the open sea. So slowly did we make our way, that the occupants of the cajack announced that they could not wait for us when they had once piloted us out from among the shoals and reefs, and plied their paddles to such good purpose that they were soon out of sight. Nautilus Bay and Cape Pug-Nose were in due time passed, however, and Shark Island hove in sight. With great astonishment Jenny gazed at our watch tower, with its guard-house, the fierce-looking guns, and the waving flag upon the heights. We landed, that she might visit the fortification; when we displayed all our arrangements with great pride. When they and the herd of lovely gazelles had been sufficiently admired, we again embarked, and steered toward Deliverance Bay. On reaching the entrance, a grand salute of twelve shots welcomed us and our fair guest to Rockburg. Not pleased with the even number, however, Ernest insisted upon replying with thirteen guns, an odd number being, he declared, absolutely necessary for form's sake.

As we neared the quay, Fritz and Jack stood ready to receive us, and with true politeness handed their mother and Jenny ashore. They turned and led the way to the house through the gardens, orchards, and shrubberies which lay on the rising ground that sloped gently upward to our dwelling.

Jenny's surprise was changed to wonder as she neared the villa itself—its broad, shady balcony, its fountains sparkling in the sun, the dovecots, the pigeons wheeling above, and the bright, fresh creepers twined round the columns, delighted her. She could scarcely believe that she was still far from any civilized nation, and that she was among a family wrecked like herself upon a lonely coast.

My amazement, however, fully equaled that of my little daughter when, beneath the shade of the veranda, I saw a table laid out with a delicious luncheon. All our china, silver, and glass had been called into requisition, and was arranged upon the spotless damask cloth.

Wine sparkled in the decanters, splendid pine-apples, oranges, guavas, apples, and pears resting on cool green leaves, lay heaped in pyramids upon the porcelain dishes. A haunch of venison, cold fowl, ham, and tongues occupied the ends and sides of the table, while in the center rose a vase of gay flowers, surrounded by bowls of milk and great jugs of mead. It was, indeed, a perfect feast, and the heartiness of the welcome brought tears of joy into the lovely eyes of the fair girl in whose honor it had been devised.

All were soon ready to sit down; and Jenny, looking prettier than ever in the dress for which she had exchanged her sailor's suit, took the place of honor between the mother and me. Ernest and Franz also seated themselves; but nothing would induce Fritz and Jack to follow their example. They considered themselves our entertainers, and waited upon us most attentively, carving the joints, filling our glasses, and changing the plates; for, as Jack declared to Miss Montrose, the servants had all run away in our absence, and, for the next day or two, perhaps we should be obliged to wait upon ourselves.

When the banquet was over, and the waiters had satisfied their appetites, they joined their brothers, and with them displayed all the wonders of Rockburg to their new sister. To the house, cave, stables, gardens, fields and boathouses, to one after the other did they lead her.

Not a corner would they have left unnoticed, had not the mother, fearing they would tire the poor girl out, come to the rescue, and led her back to the house.

On the following day, after an early breakfast, we started, while it was yet cool, for Falconhurst; and as I knew that repairs and arrangements for the coming winter would be necessary, and would detain us for several days, we took with us a supply of tools, as well as baskets of provisions, and other things essential to our comfort.

The whole of our stud, excepting the ostrich, were in their paddocks near the tree; but Jack, saying that his mother and Jenny really must not walk the whole way, to the great amusement of the latter, leaped on Hurry, and fled away in front of us. Before we had accomplished one quarter of the distance, we heard the thundering tread of many feet galloping down the avenue, and presently espied our motley troop of steeds being driven furiously toward us. Storm, Lightfoot, Swift, Grumble, Stentor, Arrow and Dart were there, with Jack, on his fleet two-legged courser, at their heels. At his saddle-bow hung a cluster of saddles and bridles, the bits all jangling and clanking, adding to the din and confusion, and urging on the excited animals, who thoroughly entered into the fun, and with tails in the air, ears back, and heels ever and anon thrown playfully out, seemed about to overwhelm us.

We stepped aside to shelter ourselves behind the trees from the furious onset; but a shout from Fritz brought the whole herd to a sudden halt, and Jack spurred toward us.

"Which of the cattle shall we saddle for you, Jenny?" he shouted; "they're all as gentle as lambs, and as active as cats. Everyone has been ridden by mother; and knows what a side-saddle means, so you can't go wrong."

To his great delight, Jenny quickly showed her appreciation of the merits of the steeds by picking out Dart, the fleetest and most spirited in the whole stud.

The ostrich was then relieved of his unusual burden, the animals were speedily equipped, and Lightfoot bearing the baskets and hampers, the whole party mounted and trotted forward. Jenny was delighted with her palfry, and henceforward he was reserved for her special use.

The work at Falconhurst, as I had expected, occupied us

for some time, and it was a week before we could again return to Rockburg. Yet the time passed pleasantly; for though the young men were busy from morning to night, the presence of their new companion, her lively spirits and gay conversation, kept them in constant good humor.

When the repairs were all finished, we remained yet a day or two longer, that we might make excursions in various directions to bring in poultry from Woodlands, stores of acorns for the pigs, and grass, willows, and canes, to be manufactured during the winter into mats, baskets, hurdles, and hencoops.

Many a shower wetted us through during these days, and we had scarcely time to hurry back to Rockburg and house our cattle and possessions before the annual deluge began.

Never before had this dreary season seemed so short and pleasant; with Jenny among us, the usual feeling of weariness and discontent never appeared; the English language was quickly acquired by all hands, Fritz, in particular, speaking it so well that Jenny declared she could scarcely believe he was not an Englishman. She herself already spoke French, and therefore easily learned our native language and spoke it fluently before we were released from our captivity.

Chapter Eighteen

Many wondrous tales were told or read in turn by the boys and Jenny during the long evenings as we sat drawing, weaving, and plaiting in our cozy study. In fact this winter was a truly happy time, and when at length the rain ceased and the bright sun again smiled upon the face of nature, we could scarcely believe, as we stepped forth and once more felt the balmy breath of spring, that, for so many weeks, we had been prisoners within our rocky walls.

All was once more activity and life; the duties in field, garden, and orchard called forth the energy of the lads, while their mother and sister found abundant occupation in the poultry yard and house.

Our various settlements and stations required attention. Falconhurst, Woodlands, Prospect Hill, Shark and Whale Islands were in turn visited and set in order. The duty of attending to the island battery fell to Jack and Franz.

They had been busy all day repairing the flagstaff, rehoisting the flag, and cleaning and putting into working order the two guns.

Evening was drawing on and our day's work over; the rest of us were strolling up and down upon the beach, enjoying the cool sea breeze. They loaded and ran out their guns, and paddling off with an empty tub in the cajack, placed it out at sea as a mark for practice. They returned and fired, and the barrel flew in pieces, and then, with a shout of triumph, they cleaned the guns and ran them in.

Scarcely had they done so when, as though in answer to their shots, came the sound of three guns booming across the water from the westward.

We stopped, speechless. Was it fancy? Had we really heard guns from a strange ship? Or had the boys again fired? No! there were the lads leaping into their canoe and paddling in hot haste toward us. They, too, had heard the sound.

A tumult of feelings rushed over us—anxiety, joy, hope, doubt, each in turn took possession of our minds. Was it a European vessel close upon our shores, and were we about to be linked once more to civilized life? Or did those sounds proceed from a Malay pirate, who would rob and murder us! What was to be the result of meeting with our fellow beings; were they to be friends who would help us, enemies who would attack us, or would they prove unfortunate creatures in need of our assistance? Who could tell?

Before we could express these thoughts in words the cajack had touched the shore, and Jack and Franz were among us.

"Did you hear them? Did you hear them?" they gasped. "What shall we do? Where shall we go?"

"O Fritz," continued my youngest son, "it must be a European ship. We shall find her. We shall see our Fatherland once more," and in an emotion of joy he grasped his brother's hands.

Till then I knew not what a craving for civilized life had been aroused in the two young men by the appearance of their European sister.

All eyes were turned toward me. What would I advise?

"At present," I said, "we can do nothing, for night is drawing on. We must make what preparations we can, and pray for guidance."

In the greatest excitement we returned to the house, all talking eagerly, and till late no one could be persuaded to retire to rest.

Few slept that night. The boys and I took it in turn to keep watch from the veranda, lest more signals might be fired, or a hostile visit might be paid us. But about midnight the wind began to rise, and before we reassembled to discuss our plans a fearful storm was raging; so terrific was the sea that I knew no boat could live, and had a broadside been fired at the entrance of the bay we should not have heard it through the howling of the blast. For two days and two nights the hurricane continued, but on the third day the sun again appeared, and, the wind lulling, the sea went rapidly down. Full of anxiety, I readily complied with the boys' desire to put off to Shark Island and discharge the guns; for who could tell what had been the result of the gale; perhaps the vessel had been driven upon the rocky shore, or, fearing such a fate, she had left the coast and weathered the storm out at sea; if so, she might never return.

With these thoughts I accompanied Jack and Franz to the fort. One—two—we fired the guns and waited.

For some minutes there was no reply, and then an answering report rolled in the distance. There was no longer room for doubt; the strangers were still in the vicinity, and were aware of our presence. We waved the flag as a signal to those on shore that all was well, and quickly returned. We found the whole family in a state of the greatest excitement, and I felt it necessary to calm them down as much as possible, for neither could I answer the questions with which I was besieged, nor could I conceal the fact that the visit of the vessel might not prove so advantageous as they expected.

Fritz and I at once prepared to make a reconnoissance; we armed ourselves with our guns, pistols, and cutlasses, took a spyglass, seated ourselves in the cajack, and with a parting entreaty from the mother to be cautious, paddled out of the bay and round the high cliffs on our left. For nearly an hour we advanced in the direction from which the reports of the guns seemed to proceed. Nothing could we see, however, but the frowning rocks and cliffs, and the waves beating restlessly at their base. Cape Pug-Nose was reached, and we began to round the bluff old point. In a moment all our doubts were dispelled, and joy and gratitude to the Great Giver of all good filled our hearts. There, in the little sheltered cove beyond the cape, her sails furled, and anchor dropped, lay a brig of war with the English colors at her masthead.

With the glass I could discern figures upon the deck, and upon the shore beyond several tents pitched under the shelter of the trees, and the smoke of fires rising among them. As I handed the glass to Fritz, I felt a sudden misgiving. "What," said I to myself, "can this English vessel be doing thus far from the usual track of ships?" and I called to mind tales of mutinous crews who have risen against their officers, have chosen some such sheltered retreat as this; have disguised the vessel, and then sailed forth to rob and plunder upon the high seas.

Fritz then exclaimed: "I can see the captain, father; he is speaking to one of the officers, and I can see his face quite well; he is English, I am certain he is English, and the flag speaks the truth!" and he put the glass again in my hand that I might see for myself.

Still keeping under the shelter of the cliff, I carefully surveyed the vessel. There was no doubt that Fritz was right, and my fears were once more dispelled; all was neatness and regularity on board; the spotless decks, the burnished steel and brass, and the air of perfect order which pervaded both ship and camp, betokened that authority and discipline there reigned. For some minutes longer we continued our examination of the scene, and then, satisfied by the appearance of the camp on shore that there was no chance of the brig quitting the coast for several days, we resolved to return without betraying our presence, for I was unwilling to appear before these strangers until we could do so in better form, and in a manner more in accordance with our actual resources.

We again landed at Rockburg, where our family awaited our arrival in eager expectation, and as fully as possible we told them of all we had seen. They thoroughly approved of our caution, and even Jenny, whose hopes had been excited to the highest pitch by our description of the English vessel, and who longed to meet her countrymen once more, agreed to postpone the visit until the following day, when, having put our yacht into good order, we might pay our respects to the captain, not as poor shipwrecked creatures begging assistance, but as lords and masters of the land, seeking to know for what purpose strangers were visiting the coast.

The rest of the day was occupied in making our preparations. Our dainty little craft was made to look her very best; her decks were scrubbed, her brass guns burnished, all lumber removed and put ashore, and the flag of England hoisted to her peak. The mother overhauled our wardrobes, and the neatest uniforms were put ready for the boys and me, for though neither my wife nor Jenny had ever dreamed of appearing otherwise than they would have done had they been at home among civilized people in Europe, yet we, accustomed daily to rough and often even dirty work, had adopted just that costume which best suited our comfort and inclination. We should indeed have surprised the smart man-o'-war's men, had we appeared in our great, shapeless, wide-brimmed hats, our linen coats and trousers, our broad leathern belts and hairy buskins; so we next day readily donned the more becoming costumes.

At the break of that eventful morn, when we were destined once more to set our eyes upon our fellow-men, and to hear news of the outer world, from which for so many years we had been exiled, we assembled in our little breakfast room. The meal was eaten hurriedly and almost in silence, for our hearts were too full, and our minds too busily occupied, to allow of any outward display of excitement. Fritz and Jack then slipped quietly out, and presently returned from the garden with baskets of the choicest fruits in fresh and fragrant profusion, and with these, as presents for the strangers, we went on board our yacht.

The anchor was weighed, the sails set, and with the canoe in tow the little vessel, as though partaking of our hopes and joyous expectation, bounded merrily over the waters of Safety Bay, gave a wide berth to the Reef, against whose frowning rocks the sea still lashed itself to foam, and kept away for the cove, where the English ship unconsciously awaited us. The Pugnosed Cape was reached, and, to the surprise and utter amazement of the strangers, we rounded the point and brought up within hail. Every eye on board and on shore was turned toward us, every glass was produced and fixed upon our motions; for of all the strange sights which the gallant crew may have looked for, such an anomaly as a pleasure yacht, manned by such a party as ours, and cruising upon this strange and inhospitable shore, was the furthest from their thoughts.

Fritz and I stepped into our boat and pulled for the brig. In another minute we were upon her deck. The captain, with the simple frankness of a British seaman, welcomed us cordially, and having led us into his cabin, begged us to explain to what good fortune he owed a visit from residents upon a coast generally deemed uninhabited, or the abode of the fiercest savages.

I gave him an outline of the history of the wreck, and of our sojourn upon these shores, and spoke to him, too, of Miss Montrose, and of the providential way in which we had been the means of rescuing her from her lonely position.

"Then," said the gallant officer, rising and grasping Fritz by the hand, "let me heartily thank you in my own name, and in that of Colonel Montrose; for it was the hope of finding some trace of that brave girl that led me to these shores. The disappearance of the *Dorcas* has been a terrible blow to the colonel, and yet, though for three years no word of her or of any of those who sailed in her has reached England, he has never entirely abandoned all hope of again hearing of his daughter. I knew this, and a few weeks ago, when I was about to leave Sydney for the Cape, I found three men who declared themselves survivors of the *Dorcas* and said that their boat, of four which left the wreck, was the only one which, to their knowledge, reached land in safety. From them I learned all particulars, and applying for permission to cruise in these latitudes, I sailed in hopes of finding further traces of the unfortunate crew. My efforts have been rewarded by unlooked-for success."

Fritz replied most modestly to the praises which he received, and then the captain begged to be introduced to my wife and Miss Montrose.

"And," he continued, "if it be not contrary to your rules of discipline for the whole ship's company to be absent at once, I will now send a boat for the remainder of your party."

One of the officers was accordingly dispatched to the yacht with a polite message, and the mother, Jenny, and the boys were presently on board.

Our kind host greeted them most warmly, and he and his officers vied with one another in doing us honor. They proved, indeed, most pleasant entertainers, and the time passed rapidly away. At luncheon the captain told us that there had sailed with him from Sydney an invalid gentleman, Mr. Wolston, his wife, and two daughters; but that, though the sea voyage had been recommended on account of his health, yet it had not done Mr. Wolston so much good as had been anticipated, and he had suffered so greatly from the effects of the storm, which had driven the *Unicorn* into the bay for repairs, that he had been eager to rest for a short time on land.

We were anxious to meet the family, and in the afternoon it was decided that we should pay them a visit. Tents had been pitched for their accommodation under the shady trees, and when we landed we found Mr. Wolston seated by one of them, enjoying the cool sea breeze. He and his family were delighted to see us, and so much did we enjoy their society, that evening found us still upon the shore. It was too late then to return to Rockburg, and the captain kindly offered tents for the accommodation of those who could not find room in the yacht. The boys spent the night on land.

That night I had a long and serious consultation with my wife, as to whether or not we really had any well grounded reason for wishing to return to Europe. It would be childish to undertake a voyage thither simply because an opportunity offered for doing so.

Neither knew to what decision the feelings of the other inclined; each was afraid of expressing what might run counter to those feelings; but gradually it began to appear that neither entertained any strong wish to leave the peaceful island; and finally we discovered that the real wish which lay at the bottom of both our hearts was to adopt New Switzerland as thenceforward our home.

What can be more delightful than to find harmony of opinion in those we love, when a great and momentous decision has to be taken?

My dear wife assured me that she desired nothing more earnestly than to spend the rest of her days in a place to which she had become so much attached, provided I, and at least two of her sons, also wished to remain.

From the other two she would willingly part, if they chose to return to Europe, with the understanding that they must endeavor to send out emigrants of a good class to join us, and form a prosperous colony, adding that she thought the island ought to continue to bear the name of our native country, even if inhabited in future time by colonists from England, as well as from Switzerland.

I heartily approved of this excellent idea, and we agreed to mention it, while consulting with Captain Littlestone on the subject of placing the island under the protection of Great Britain.

Then came the question as to which of our sons were best suited to remain with us, and which to go away.

This point we left undecided, thinking that in the course of a few days they would probably make a choice of their own accord, which they did, even sooner than we anticipated.

After breakfast, it was proposed that Captain Littlestone should bring his ship round to Safety Bay, that we might receive a visit from him and his party, at Rockburg—where we invited the invalid, Mr. Wolston, and his family, in hopes that his health might benefit by a comfortable residence on shore.

No sooner was this plan adopted, than Fritz and Jack hurried off in the canoe to prepare for their reception, being followed in more leisurely style by the brig and our yacht.

But what words can express the amazement of our guests, when, rounding the Rocky Cape at the entrance, Safety Bay, the beautiful domain of Rockburg lay before them.

Still greater was their astonishment, as a salute of eleven guns boomed from the battery on Shark Island, where the royal standard of England was displayed and floated majestically on the morning breeze.

A glow of surprise and pleasure beamed on every countenance, and poor Wolston's spirits appeared to revive with the very idea of peace and happiness to be enjoyed in such a home.

He was carried on shore with the utmost care and tenderness, and comfortably established in my room, a camp-bed for Mrs. Wolston being added to the furniture there, that she might be able conveniently to attend on her husband.

Meantime the scene at the harbor and all round Rockburg was of the liveliest description; merriment and excitement prevailed in all directions, as the beauties and wonders of our residence were explored, so that a summons to dinner scarcely attracted notice.

However, as a visit to Falconhurst was projected, the company was at length induced to be seated, and to partake of our good cheer, but the spirit of restlessness soon returned, and the young people kept roaming about through our hitherto quiet lawns, avenues, and shrubberies, until I was ready to believe their number three times what it actually was.

Toward evening the universal excitement began to abate, and the party assembled for supper with tolerable composure.

Mr. Wolston was able to join us, as the rest he had enjoyed, and the pleasure inspired by the hope of a residence among us, seemed to have given him new life. This wish he now distinctly expressed in his own name, and in that of his wife; inquiring what our intentions were, and proposing, if agreeable to us, that they, with their eldest daughter, whose health, like his own, was delicate, should make a long stay on the island, while the younger daughter went for the present to her brother at the Cape of Good Hope.

In the event of his ultimately deciding to settle altogether among us, Mr. Wolston would propose that his son should leave the Cape, and join our colony.

With sincere satisfaction I welcomed this proposal, saying that it was my wish and that of my wife to remain for the rest of our days in New Switzerland.

"Hurrah for New Switzerland!"

"New Switzerland forever!" shouted the whole company enthusiastically, as they raised their glasses, and made them touch with a musical ring, which so expressively denotes a joyful unanimity of sentiment.

"Prosperity to New Switzerland: long may she flourish," echoed on all sides.

"Long life and happiness to those who make New Switzerland their home!" added Ernest, to my great surprise, leaning forward as he spoke, to ring his glass with mine, his mother's, and Mr. Wolston's.

"Won't somebody wish long life and prosperity to those who go away?" inquired Jenny, with a pretty, arch look. "Much as I long to return to England and my father, my inclination will waver if all the cheers are for New Switzerland!"

"Three cheers for England and Colonel Montrose," cried Fritz; "success and happiness to us who return to Europe!" and while the vaulted roofs rang with the cheering elicited by this toast, a glance from Jenny showed him how much she thanked him for appreciating her wish, to return to her father, notwithstanding her attachment to our family.

"Well," said I, when silence was restored, "since Fritz resolves to go to England, he must undertake for me the duty of bringing happiness to a mourning father by restoring to him this dear daughter, whom I have been ready to regard as my own, by right of her cast on the shores of my island.

"Ernest chooses to remain with me. His mother and I rejoice heartily in this decision, and promise him all the highest scientific appointments in our power to bestow.

"And now what is Jack's choice? The only talent I can say he possesses is that of a comic actor, and to shine on the stage he must needs go to Europe."

"Jack is not going to Europe, however," was his reply. "He means to stay here, and when Fritz is gone he will be the best rider and the best shot in New Switzerland, which is the summit of his ambition.

"The fact is," he continued, laughing, "I rather stand in awe of their European schools, and should expect to find myself caught and clapped into one if I ventured too near them."

"A good school is exactly what I want," said Franz. "Among a number of students there is some emulation and enthusiasm, and I shall have a chance of rising in the world."

"Fritz will probably return here some day; but it might be well for one member of the family to go home with the intention of remaining there altogether, and as I am the youngest I could more easily than the rest adapt myself to a different life. My father, however, will decide for me."

"You may go, my dear son," I replied; "and God bless all

our plans and resolutions. The whole earth is the Lord's, and where, as in His sight, you lead good and useful lives, there is your home.

"And now that I know your wishes, the only question is whether Captain Littlestone will kindly enable you to carry them out?"

All eyes were fixed eagerly upon him, and after a moment's pause the gallant officer spoke as follows:

"I think my way in this matter is perfectly clear, and I consider that I have been providentially guided to be the means of once more placing this family in communication with their friends and with the civilized world.

"My orders were to search for a shipwrecked crew.

"Survivors from two wrecks have been discovered.

"Three passengers express a wish to leave my ship here, instead of at the Cape, while, at the same time, I am requested to give to three persons a passage to England.

"Could anything suit better? I am most willing to undertake the charge of those who may be committed to my care.

"Every circumstance has been wonderfully ordered and linked together by Divine Providence, and if England gains a prosperous and happy colony, it will prove a fitting clasp to this fortunate chain of events. Three cheers for New Switzerland!"

Deep emotion stirred every heart as the party separated for the night. Many felt that they were suddenly standing on the threshold of a new life, while, for myself, a weight was rolled from my heart, and I thanked God that a difficulty was solved which, for years, had oppressed me with anxiety.

After this nothing was thought of but making preparations for the departure of the dear ones bound for England. Captain Littlestone allowed as much time as he could spare; but it was necessarily short, so that incessant movement and industry pervaded the settlement for several days.

Everything was provided and packed up that could in any way add to our children's comfort on the voyage, or benefit them after their arrival in England, and a large share of my possessions in pearls, corals, furs, spices, and other valuables would enable them to take a good position in the world of commerce.

I committed to their care private papers, money, and jewels which I knew to have been the personal property of the captain of our ill-fated ship, desiring them to hand them over, if possible, to his heirs. A short account of the wreck, with the names of the crew, a list of which I had found, was given to Captain Littlestone.

Fritz, having previously made known to me, what indeed was very evident, the attachment between himself and Jenny, I advised him to mention it to Colonel Montrose as soon as possible after being introduced to him, and ask for his sanction to their engagement. I, on my part, gladly bestowed mine, as did his mother, who loved the sweet girl dearly, and heartily grieved to part with her.

On the evening before our separation, I gave to Fritz the journal in which, ever since the shipwreck, I had chronicled the events of our life, desiring that the story might be printed and published.

"It was written, as you well know," said I, "for the instruction and amusement of my children, but it is very possible that it may be useful to other young people, more especially to boys.

"Children are, on the whole, very much alike everywhere, and you four lads fairly represent multitudes, who are growing up in all directions. It will make me happy to think that my simple narrative may lead some of these to observe how blessed are the results of patient continuance in well-doing, what benefits arise from the thoughtful application of knowledge and science, and how good and pleasant a thing it is when brethren dwell together in unity, under the eye of parental love."

.   .   .   .

Night has closed around me.

For the last time my united family slumbers beneath my care.

To-morrow this closing chapter of my journal will pass into the hands of my eldest son.

From afar I greet thee, Europe!

I greet thee, dear old Switzerland!

Like thee, may New Switzerland flourish and prosper—good, happy, and free!

The Swiss Family Robinson

illustrated by Jeanne Edwards, is one of the series of

RAINBOW   CLASSICS

Edited under the supervision of May Lamberton Becker

Typesetting by Westcott and Thomson, Inc.

Binding pattern by Leo Manso

Typography by Peter Oldenburg